MINK!

MINK!

Peter Chippindale

SIMON & SCHUSTER

LONDON · SYDNEY · NEW YORK · TOKYO · SINGAPORE · TORONTO

First published in Great Britain by Simon & Schuster Ltd, 1995

The right of Peter Chippindale to be identified as author of this
work has been asserted in accordance with sections 77 and 78 of the
Copyright, Designs and Patents Act 1988.

Simon & Schuster Ltd
West Garden Place
Kendal Street
London W2 2AQ

Simon & Schuster of Australia Pty Ltd
Sydney

A CIP catalogue record for this book is available from the British
Library

ISBN 0-671-71916-5

Typeset in Goudy Modern 13/14pt by
Palimpsest Book Production Limited, Polmont, Stirlingshire
Printed and bound in Great Britain by
Butler & Tanner Ltd, Frome & London

For my daughter,
Lucy Dorothy Jane

Author's Note and Acknowledgements

'Old Wood' is a figment of my imagination, based on particular fond memories of the Yorkshire Dales, Cumbria and the valley of the River Camel in North Cornwall.

I would like to thank the many people who have helped with this book, one way or another, and specifically my wife, Susie, for her inspiration, along with my friends Roger Mitchell, John 'Chalkie' Backland and Ray Bowler, for being such an inseparable part of the Cornish landscape where it was written.

I would also like to record my appreciation to my agents, Carole Blake and Julian Friedmann, for their help and encouragement and all the staff at Simon and Schuster for their hard work.

Most of all, however, I am indebted to Nick Webb for his unwavering faith in this project from the outset.

St. Mabyn
North Cornwall

Contents

PART III

PART IV

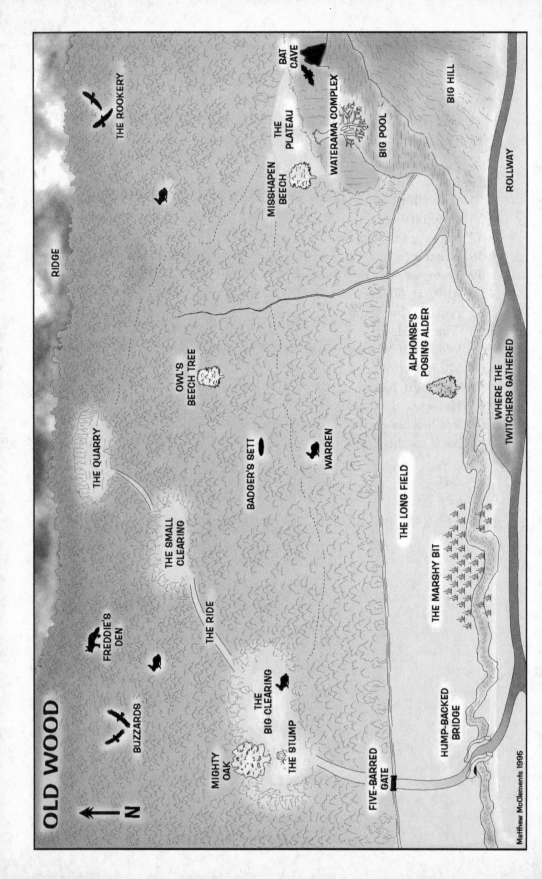

OLD WOOD

N

RIDGE

THE ROOKERY

BAT CAVE

THE PLATEAU

WATERAMA COMPLEX

BIG POOL

BIG HILL

MISSHAPEN BEECH

THE QUARRY

OWL'S BEECH TREE

BADGER'S SETT

WARREN

ALPHONSE'S POSING ALDER

BUZZARDS

FREDDIE'S DEN

THE SMALL CLEARING

THE RIDE

MIGHTY OAK

THE BIG CLEARING

THE STUMP

THE LONG FIELD

THE MARSHY BIT

WHERE THE TWITCHERS GATHERED

ROLLWAY

FIVE-BARRED GATE

HUMP-BACKED BRIDGE

Matthew McClements 1995

Prologue

'Out! Out! Out! We're getting out!'

Full-moon madness had gripped the mink colony. The cages were erupting.

'Out! Out! Out! We're getting out!' whooping gangs yelled as they careered wildly round the communal exercise area.

They weren't, of course. They all knew that. The cages the Keeper held them in were so strong, and the wire so stout, no-one had ever escaped. But for the moment, as the great round disc edged over the rooflight, they could at least pretend. And did they need to! It had been a filthy day inside the shed, even by their degraded standards. Everyone's nerves were in shreds – especially the Elders'. The older mink who controlled cage life had already had to read the riot act after a bloody and vicious fight broke out amongst a group of pregnant females. In an equally ugly scene, a gang of bullyboys had nearly beaten their squealing victim to death, while a string of minor incidents wound everyone up even further.

It was always the same, to some degree. The cages were a pressure cooker. No matter how much individual mink tried to get on with each other – and with their aggressive nature plenty didn't – the tensions and rivalries between them would build and build, until the atmosphere was snapping and crackling with tension. A real sense of menace would permeate the air as the suppressed mayhem threatened to boil over – which it would have done except for full-moon madness. This event was organised by the Elders as a safety valve for that complex mass of emotions and yearnings which they referred to officially as 'bad thoughts' and at all other times taught everyone rigidly to suppress. But on full-moon nights, in contrast, the mink were actively encouraged to let rip. The Elders knew full well how working off pent-up frustrations helped to make life in their cramped environment halfway tolerable again.

As the first pallid moonbeam reached down into the shed, the Elders were even joining in themselves, throwing their normal inhibitions to the wind as they ran to join the demented mob. They had nothing to be alarmed about. By morning moon madness would have passed like a dream. Under the more benign influence of the sun they would be back in control, their subjects freshly resigned to knuckling under to their regime.

Right now, though, madness reigned. They, and their charges, could run amok.

The males rushed to form the traditional conga as the moon began to sail across the grubby glass of the rooflight, bathing the cages in its cold blue light.

'Out! Out! Out! We're getting out!'

Snaking brown bodies swayed deliriously across the exercise area, while fierce pointed faces were thrust upwards to drink in the illuminating rays.

The chanting changed to cheers as the first male followed ritual by breaking away and hurling himself against the wire.

'Go! Go! Go for it!' the conga screamed as he staggered back, dazed.

The males set up a rhythmic stamping as the next male rolled into a ball and whacked into the mesh with the small of his back. One by one the rest followed, until the length of netting was shuddering and trembling from the succession of impacts, while the shed walls echoed with pings and twangs as females worried at individual strands.

'Out! Out! Out! We're getting out!' bold individuals shrieked, hanging from the roof wires as they urged their fellows on to fresh excesses.

Someone overturned a food tray and began kicking it against

the back of their cage with a tinny clatter, while the conga reformed for another triumphal parade.

Whack! The first male smashed into the wire.

Whack! Whack! Whack! The others followed.

Suddenly an unexpected cry cut through the bedlam: 'Look at that!'

One by one the mink stopped in their tracks and the shed fell silent as they stared up through the rooflight in awe. The moon, so round a moment ago, was shrinking. A shadow was creeping across its face, gradually blacking it out, even though there wasn't a cloud in the sky. A frisson of fear ran through them all as they watched it slowly reducing itself to a thin crescent, until it disappeared completely.

They were just turning towards each other in panic when they heard the first shrill noise from the segregation cage where the Keeper had placed Sheba.

Instantly their attention switched.

'The bitch is having them at last,' they hissed, rushing across to the wire.

They had all hated Sheba, even before the Keeper separated her from the main cages. She was the odd one out, brought in from another colony when she was just a little cub after illness had killed the rest of her family, rendering her an orphan. That alone had been enough to make her automatically suspect. The Elders' regime taught everyone to be suspicious of anything, or anyone, new. Then, as she grew up, Sheba had made things worse for herself by declaring she was not interested in joining the female circle – or the 'harridans', as the males sneeringly dubbed them. It had therefore been bad enough when the Keeper had selected her for the segregation cage and brought in the big blue stud mink from outside to mate with her. But the antagonism had risen to even greater heights as the others saw the special treatment he was giving her. Most tantalising and galling of all had been her individual food. The sight and smell of him carrying plump silvery fish down the aisle had sent everyone into paroxysms of slavering envy.

'Choke, you fat bitch, choke!' the females had hissed, beaming waves of venom at her. 'Die, Sheba, die!'

Now they strained and peered to see how many kits she was going to produce. All the females either were pregnant or had already given birth in what was the climax of their otherwise dull cage life. Normally this was dominated by the males, who regarded themselves as the superior sex and reinforced that claim through the simple expedient of being bigger, heavier and stronger. But the process of reproduction temporarily elevated the females to higher status. The greatest kudos of all would attach to the one producing the largest litter and above all else they were determined that was not going to be Sheba.

'She's had the first,' they hissed to each other.

'How many do you reckon altogether?'

'I think four.'

'Five.'

'How about seven?'

'Not Sheba. She could never manage the magic seven.'

They waited a bit longer. Yet there was still only that one high mew.

'She must have some more, surely?' they began asking each other, looking puzzled. 'One's not possible, surely? We always have at least three.'

'Remember Mekow!'

The legendary Mekow, whom the Elders constantly reminded them about, had had ten.

'Look at me. I've already had four,' came a boastful cry.

'I've had six,' another reminded them triumphantly. 'And I'm not a stuck-up bitch like her — I'm just an ordinary mink.'

They waited some more until finally, when nothing else had happened, they could no longer contain themselves.

'Can you believe it?' they shouted, dancing round each other in triumph. 'She's only had one!'

'Sheba! Sheba! She's a one-kit wonder!' someone shouted.

The chant was quickly taken up.

'Sheba! Sheba! She's a one-kit wonder!'

Just then the moon started to come back — gradually, as it had disappeared — triggering off a new burst of speculation. None of them had ever seen anything like it, both males and females rushed to agree. But why had the moon thing happened just as

Sheba's lone kit was emerging? Surely the two events couldn't be linked? The moon held the power. How could Sheba, of all of them, possibly have influenced it?

'Maybe it was to show she was producing next to nothing,' someone shouted.

There was nervous laughter.

'Or to hide her shame,' cried another female.

'Seriously though, what was it?' came a chorus of worried voices.

They clustered anxiously round the Elders' spokesmale, Gabbla.

'What was it?' He smiled benignly at them, seeming not the slightest bit concerned. 'On behalf of the Elders I can officially inform you that it was only a rogue cloud. This temporarily obscured the moon as it passed over, even though the sky was otherwise clear. You all saw it, surely? You know clouds have often done the same in the past. No doubt they will continue to in the future. That is all it was — a rogue cloud. You may now all disperse.'

The mink drifted back towards the wire, relieved that the lone birth had now been officially robbed of any special significance.

'A rogue cloud, eh?' they spat viciously to each other. 'Typical Sheba — always doing something to try and upset us.'

'Sheba! Sheba! She's a one-kit wonder,' the spiteful chant began again.

From the beginning of her pregnancy Sheba had been thrillingly aware that she was carrying a special litter. Even if she had been in the regular cages, though, she wouldn't have told anyone — not even the few members of her underground intellectuals' group. As for the rest, she never told them anything. They were such abject slaves to the Elders' doctrine she regarded them as mere ciphers.

But although Sheba thought of herself as strong, she had still found coping with the females' sheer vindictiveness hard at the beginning. The males had been almost as bad. They had their own axe to grind. Sizing up the females before she was removed, they had all agreed that Sheba, with her big eyes, rich coat and perfect bottom, was by far the most sexy. There had been massive squabbling between her multiple suitors, followed by bitter disappointment when the Keeper rejected them all in favour of the stud from outside.

'Never mind him, you old shagbag, cop a load of this,' they had jeered, making crude gestures of copulation and exposing their erect penises to her. 'Get one of these inside you, you bitch – then you'll know what a proper shafting feels like!'

Yet, thanks to her outside mate, Solomon, Sheba had not only endured this but positively blossomed. She had been expecting him to be some thick stud, all balls and no brain. On that front he had turned out as strong, handsome and good in the hay as she could have wished for. She had found his distinctive blue coat, so different from their uniform chocolate brown, a tremendous turn-on. But it was after she had allowed him to penetrate her deliciously and repeatedly that he had electrified her even more. To her huge delight she had discovered he was a real gentlemale – intelligent, caring and, most important of all, hugely knowledgeable.

And it was his knowledge that had changed her life for ever.

'In my job I spend a lot of my life moving about,' he had explained. 'So I've been to countless colonies and seen all sorts of different systems. If there's anything you want to know about yours, you just have to ask.

'Only be certain that you're sure first, Sheba. There are times when it's best not to know and I don't want to upset your life too much.'

She had smiled appreciatively at him, understanding the caring nature of the thought. But did she want to know? She wanted to know absolutely everything!

Until then Sheba had been the leading light of the intellectuals' group, a small and furtive occasional gathering which endlessly questioned the central mystery of their lives – why did the Keeper hold them in the cages and then take away their eldest generation just when it was in its prime? The Elders' doctrine decreed that it was because he loved them. He was their special friend, the official legend ran. And if they were good, as their reward he took them off to the Happy Land, where they lived comfortably ever after.

The rest of the mink, brainwashed, meekly accepted this, while the tiny intellectuals' group was united by scepticism. Yet, despite all its efforts, it had always failed to come up with a credible alternative.

But now Solomon was here, offering to give the answer.

'Are we mink really wild creatures, born to be free?' was her first question.

'Yes.'

'So why does our Keeper hold us in these cages?' she went on greedily.

'The answer is staring you in the face, my pretty one,' he smiled back. 'Look at me – what do you see?'

She regarded him fondly, thinking how handsome he was with his blue coat.

'A lovely, gorgeous, wonderful mate!' she smiled back, puzzled about what he was driving at.

'What else apart from that?'

He teased and teased her until finally he told her, making the connection that solved the mystery for ever. And while he stressed he could never prove his answer, it made such sense that Sheba accepted it without further question. As the iniquity of the Elders' system sank in, she knew life would never be the same again. Now that she had her own alternative, at last she could reject the stultifying doctrine by which they ruled.

But Solomon then went on to impart something even more shattering. Not only was the Elders' teaching now blown out of the water, but they all had a real hope of getting out of the shed for ever, back to the wild where they belonged. Freedom was no longer an unattainable, nebulous concept, as the intellectuals' group had always believed. Now it was a tangible reality, that they could work towards. Most thrillingly of all, she personally was paving the way by the very process of being pregnant.

When her time came, like the others she was initially awed by the shrinking moon but soon overtaken by the more urgent throes of giving birth. She sobbed with joy as she saw the first-born was a male. He appeared healthy and normal, except for a strong touch of his father's blue, which gave him a distinctive coat.

Satisfied, she lay back, panting, as she gathered her strength to push out the next kit. Would it be another male, she wondered? But instead, as she waited and waited, she only felt a dull ache growing inside her. She began to experience a melancholy greater than anything she ever had known. She might not have thought it possible, but she was having to face the dreadful truth. There weren't any more to come!

She started to weep, feeling how badly she had failed. As aware of the importance of numbers as everybody else she had been secretly hoping for the magic seven. The paltry consolation of understanding at last why she had put on so little weight, despite her special diet, was no real comfort.

She tried to shut out the derisive chanting from the regular cages as she nursed the wet little body with fierce affection, noticing meanwhile that the moon was now shining down as brightly as before. After all her expectations, why had this happened to her? What had she done wrong? Then, as the other mink got bored and returned to their rampaging, her spirits began to lift. With a dawning sense of wonder, she was slowly appreciating what it must mean. Before Solomon was taken away they had agreed she must choose the colony's first leader — the one she would then groom to smash the Elders' conspiracy and lead everyone to freedom — from the several kits she could expect.

Yet now there was nothing to do. The choice had been made for her.

'You must be the one, for you are the only one,' she whispered as the little snout sucked contentedly at the teat it had selected from the many on offer. 'I shall call you Mega. For one day, my brave son, that is what you will be!'

PART I

I

The Pits

Mega shut his nostrils and reversed his rear over the latrine pit. What were they all doing in this place? he thought with disgust as one of his back feet slipped and he nearly lost his balance. The wood he was standing on was not only coated with a slimy mixture of urine and spraint, but so rotten it had soaked it up like a sponge to exude a sour stench that clung to your fur. It never really went away, even after the Keeper had just cleaned them out. On occasions – and today was one of them – it was so strong it made your eyes water.

With renewed abhorrence he felt the wetness seeping up his pads. He looked down and saw the slime forcing its horrible gluey consistency over the web between his toes. Lifting one foot in automatic repulsion, he lurched and nearly slipped again. He shuddered, recalling the incident in the early days when a gang of bullies had nearly thrown him bodily in. He had been hanging over the edge, screaming in terror as he stared upside down at the sea of filth, when his mother had rushed across and rescued him. Even then she had not been in time to stop them dunking the top of his head, and for days afterwards he had been unable to rid himself of the conviction that the foul mixture was still visibly there, making him a public, and odorous, laughing stock.

That had been the low point in his life so far. Now, as a bouncing young adolescent, he had established such a position in the generational hierarchy that he was respectfully left alone. But he still hated the latrines more than anything. It wasn't just that the conditions were so vile. What allowance was made for the natural male instinct to mark out territory? Why couldn't all they just do it where they wanted, and in some sort of privacy? He already knew the answer, of course. Specifically, the Elders decreed it was for reasons of hygiene, which was hard to argue with. Yet it was also part of the overriding stress they laid on individual mink not 'privatising' their lives, as they put it. Like the Keeper, they made no attempt to encourage anyone to be spontaneous and natural — to be themselves. Rather they seemed determined to suppress them all, regimenting their existence by organising and controlling as many aspects of it as they could. Each mink became a unit, rather than an individual, whose sole purpose was to be processed through the system.

The same applied to their food — the reason Mega was now resigning himself to crouching over the latrine for some time. Their regular feeding times were supposedly the high spot of their day. Every morning and evening the Keeper would open the shed door to excited chittering, which would mount in volume as he went to the back of the shed and poured the soft stuff into their trays. Yet after he had put the trays into the cages everyone still had to wait, slobbering with frustration, their stomachs rumbling, while the Elders leisurely took their fill. The bloated Chief, Massam, was invariably the last to finish. Giving his customary loud belch, he would painstakingly wipe the grease from his mouth before he finally lumbered off, farting loudly. Only then would Gabbla, the Elders' spokesmale, give the signal for them all to rush forward, pushing and shoving each other out of the way in their haste to gorge themselves.

Recently, though, the Keeper had changed their diet. The Elders had claimed their new food was yet another of his caring gestures, with Gabbla giving out an official statement about its increased nutrient value. Mega had wolfed it down out of necessity rather than pleasure, finding it as bland and uninspiring as its predecessor. Now he was terminally constipated like everyone else, yet his belly was so swollen and aching he had to force something out of it somehow. He screwed up his face and concentrated on trying to breathe through his mouth as he arched his back and strained away. It wasn't just the latrine, he thought, despondently looking round for any diversion that would take his mind off what he was doing. The whole shed, and everything in it, was the pits.

It was a basic enough set-up to start with, as he remembered Sheba telling him when she had first given him the tour. She had shown him how the system was raised off the floor, at the same height as the Keeper's middle. Individual cages ran in two parallel rows overlooking the aisles he used to get to the back of the shed where he kept their supplies and various bits of equipment. It had been in the far corner there, his mother had pointed out through the wire, that Mega had been born. Unenthusiastically, she had gone on to demonstrate how each cage was separated from the next by a thin wooden partition. The Keeper could unbolt the front wire, but the only exits for the mink were through the doorways at the back leading out on to the communal exercise area. This facility was another key Elders' point in emphasising the kindness of their Keeper, and even Sheba had grudgingly admitted the oblong space was large enough to run about without feeling too cramped. That was, she had warned, if there weren't too many other mink about. Youngsters were continuously sent flying by rowdy older mink charging madly around, either heedless of whether they were in the way or deliberately knocking them over. But, with wire at either end and above, the exercise area at least had an open feeling, although that was poor consolation when everything was further enclosed within the stifling confines of the shed itself. The only sight of the outdoors was through the dirt-streaked rooflight, which meant they lived mostly in a gloomy half-light – apart from the times the Keeper did his click thing to create lights brighter than the sun.

The various activities laid on by the Elders brought little more cheer, either to her or to him. Sheba had explained the different organised games and shown him the grooming sessions and the keep-fit class huffing and puffing away. Some mink got excited by these, she said, while at the same time confessing she herself found them dull beyond belief. No matter how often the Elders emphasised the importance of group participation, she couldn't take to organised activity.

'Maybe it'll be better for you, Mega,' she had told him hopefully, although he could tell she was doubting it. 'Most of the games – like the tag competitions and the structured rough and tumbles – are males' stuff. You might enjoy them.

'That's it, really, my dear,' she had concluded, before adding brightly: 'There is one other thing, Mega. If you look hard enough at the patterns on the walls, you can sometimes see faces.'

What use was that? he had thought at the time. Since then, of course, he had changed his mind as he searched for anything to break up the uniformity and give his imagination something to work on. It was the same with the floor. He now knew every bump and gradation of it by heart.

As he now looked round, it struck him again how drab and shabby everything was. There was no colour, no life – nothing to uplift the spirit or bring joy. However much the Elders impressed on them that their Keeper loved them, he could see nothing that backed that statement up. The place felt rundown, as if it was tired and worn out. From the rust-streaked wire, to the rime of dirt and dust that clung to every surface, there was nothing you could feel pride in, nothing that made you want to be there. Apart from the general grubbiness, in heavily used places the dirt was so thick you could scratch a groove in it with your claw, while even the air itself smelt old and stale. No wonder, with such a rank and fetid atmosphere, they spent a lot of time in a semi-torpor – when they weren't squabbling amongst themselves.

But another factor had quickly intervened as he grew out of being a kit. He had soon found he and Sheba were different from the other mink. She seemed to be a good mother to him and he loved her dearly, yet they lived together in a curious isolation. Then he had noticed how they were both shunned by the others, when they were not being actively hostile. Meanwhile, in contrast to the hugger-mugger existence in the other family cages, he had no-one to share growing up with.

He had begun pestering her with resentful questions.

'Mummy, why can't I have brothers and sisters like the other kits?' he would ask again and again.

'It's not that you can't, my dear. It's just that you don't,' she would always reply gently.

'Why not?'

'Because you're different, my son.'

'Why, Mummy?'

'You just are.'

'But do I have to be, Mummy? Why can't I be like the others?'

'Everyone is born with a role in life, my son,' she would repeat. 'Yours is to be different. You must accept that and learn to be glad about it.'

'Is that why I don't have a daddy either?'

'You do, my dear. It's just that he's just not here.'

'Where is he then?'

And so it had gone on, with her endlessly repeating the same answer: 'You must wait, Mega. All will be revealed in the fullness of time.'

'Is that when I'll see dad?' he would ask sadly.

'No, my dear,' she always had to tell him, equally sadly. 'Whatever happens I'm afraid neither of us can expect to see Solomon ever again.'

Only once had she given him a glimpse of what the 'the fullness of time' might have in store for him.

'What's my dad like?' he had asked as usual.

'Your father was very special. You can't imagine how special – he changed my life.' She had given her standard reply. 'But he wasn't as special as you, my darling,' she had unexpectedly added. 'You see, your destiny is not to just change my life, but to change everybody's.'

'What do you mean, Mum?' Mega had asked sharply, fixing her with his deep black eyes. 'Tell me!'

But she wouldn't. And no matter how much he had badgered

her since, she had reverted to the 'all in the fullness of time' answer with which she always stalled him.

Mega broke off from his reverie as he heard footsteps approaching. If it was an Elder, contrary to the general lack-of-privacy principle they espoused, he would have to vacate the area until they had finished their business. Then he relaxed as he saw it was only Mata from the cage next door. Yet, his concentration broken, he now had to admit defeat. He was plainly not going to get a result, no matter how long he crouched there.

He rose up, squelched a few paces forward out of the slime and greeted her. Mata was friendly and actually talked to him, although he always kept his distance, studiously avoiding going into her family cage. Something about her, and her life, made him wary. Her father, Mugger, was notoriously cruel and violent, and Mega and Sheba would sit together in shame and silence as screams and thuds of heavy blows came through the partition. One day, unable to stand it any longer, Sheba had swallowed her pride and appealed to the Elders to step in. But, she had told him sadly afterwards, they had ignored her. Although domestic violence was endemic within the colony, as a matter of policy the Elders left individuals to sort matters out for themselves and never intervened. It had been the same when he was being bullied. It was Sheba who had helped him to learn how to stand up for himself and earn the respect he was now accorded.

'How long have you been here?' Mata asked, wrinkling up her black nose in automatic disgust.

'Too long,' Mega replied, smiling.

'Any time's too long,' she replied sharply. 'Not just here, but in the whole place.'

Mega, although silently agreeing with her, said nothing. Sheba had counselled him against drawing attention to himself by joining the huddled subversive conversations the other youngsters occasionally indulged in.

'They're what's known as "bad thoughts",' his mother had explained. 'We all have them. The Elders will explain them fully when they indoctrinate you, along with the rest of your generation. In the meantime, Mega, I want you to concentrate on enjoying yourself. Try to forget all about them – or at the very least keep them to yourself.'

Mega had since thought with considerable bitterness how easy that was when most of the others wouldn't even talk to him.

'It's time we all got out,' Mata went on, almost as if he wasn't there. 'Speaking for myself, I don't think I can stand it much longer. Have you seen the one going stir-crazy? She's really bad today.'

Mega had. Young though he was, he had been there long enough to watch this older mink's neurosis grow – the outward signs of the nervous tic, the involuntary spasm, the far-off look, the repetitive pacing up and down the edge of the wire. Mega had felt for the afflicted, seeing how the other mink, recognising the symptoms, were giving her a wide berth, thereby increasing her anxiety and making her even worse.

'We youngsters will all get like that one day,' Mata went on despondently. 'And sooner than we might think. You know we're to be indoctrinated shortly?'

'Yes,' Mega replied briefly.

How could he not? All the cubs were horribly aware of the forthcoming event, after which the Elders would officially classify them as young adults, rather than children. Until recently it had seemed ages off. But now it was suddenly rushing towards them, and they all knew how it would change their lives. As their parents were impressing on them, with adulthood would come responsibility. No longer cubs, they would have no excuse for not toeing the official line.

'Well, what are you going to do about it?' Mata demanded.

Mega was surprised. What could he do about it?

'Nothing,' he replied, as neutrally as he could. 'Sheba says I have to go. She says none of us has any choice.'

'She's right there,' Mata admitted. 'I have to as well. But I'm not just going to swallow it. Inside my head I'll be resisting it with all my might. There are a few other females who think the same. We're not like the males. We've got minds of our own and, what's more, we're determined to keep them.'

'Oh, are you?' Mega replied non-committally.

But underneath he was irritated. Mata was always running down males in general.

'Tell me,' he asked, for the first time voicing the thought that had often occurred to him, 'if all us males are so awful, why are you about the only mink who talks to me?'

'You must know the answer to that, Mega,' she smiled. 'You're not like the others — you're different. We may not have seen it, but we all know about the moon business. Do you believe the Elders' rogue cloud explanation?'

'I'm not sure,' Mega replied carefully.

Although he had asked Sheba about it many times, she always remained studiously vague.

'I don't know, Mega. I was too busy having you,' she normally fudged the answer.

'Have you forgotten, Mega — I was born at precisely the same time?' Mata now demanded. 'That means we're both different. Can't you see it — we're a pair?'

Were they? Mega thought. Surely that had to be a joint decision? This was all getting far too heavy for his liking.

Suddenly he didn't want to see her any more for the moment.

'Well, we've certainly got one thing in common,' he joked, watching her reverse gingerly into the slime area, a nauseated expression on her face. 'I hope you have more luck than I did.'

'It's not funny, Mega,' she snapped angrily. 'It's horrible, it's degrading and it's filthy — like everything in this place. You know as well as I do that we weren't born to lead our lives like this.

'Now leave me to it, will you?'

'I'm sorry, Mata,' he apologised, thinking how right she was. There was no point in pretending cage existence was anything other than all those things — and more.

He padded back across the exercise area, wet footprints marking his passage, stomach as swollen and aching as before. Suddenly he was terminally depressed. He still loved Sheba and had implicit faith in what she said, yet her promises about the fullness of time when all would be revealed had an increasingly hollow ring. With their indoctrination looming so close, first he was going into the brainwashing process alongside everyone else.

2

Rabbiting On

It was so comfy and dry inside the burrow that if it hadn't been for the crucial importance of his task Burdock wouldn't have gone up top. On days like this he and his fellow rabbits usually tolerated pangs of hunger in the night rather than emerging for their normal early-evening feed. However, as leader of the delegation to Owl he had no choice, even though the weather had worsened since morning. The cutting east wind had now increased to a gale that was penetrating right down here, sending piercing draughts surging along the runs. Little patters of falling earth had been indicating how much the roots of the oak were flexing to compensate for the swaying of the massive trunk they supported, while the temperature had dropped so sharply everyone had temporarily gone into huddle mode. All in all — at least for rabbits — it was an entirely filthy day.

He gave Dandelion a reluctant nudge. She woke with a start and stared at him uncomprehendingly for a moment before breaking into a loving smile.

'Time for me to go,' he mouthed, smiling back. 'But not for you — you've got to stay behind today. It's much too nasty out there for my beautiful mate.'

She gave him a grateful grin and he crept off to round up the others, finding them no more inclined to go out than he was. The little group looked distinctly surly as he addressed it.

'Comrades, this will be our seventeenth consecutive visit to Owl's nest in our delegation's ongoing attempts to recruit him. As you will be aware, the weather outside is somewhat inclement. However, we must not let that deflect us from our task. It hardly needs me, as your team leader, to remind you of our fundamental importance in determining the future of the Concerned Woodland Guardians by upholding the principles of reason and friendship to all creatures that we hold most dear.'

As they kept their eyes fixed on the sandy floor the lack of response didn't altogether surprise him. So often in Concerned Woodland Guardian affairs, the initial enthusiasm for a project quickly faded as the practicalities became apparent.

'Team leader, whilst being equally concerned that we succeed in our declared objective, is it absolutely imperative we go this afternoon?'

Burdock stared balefully at the speaker. If anyone was going to try to get out of it, it had to be 'Grumbling Groundsel', who was frequently to be overheard moaning to the others. It might not be right to pass critical judgement on others, but none the less Groundsel was acknowledged within the warren to be 'a shade on the lethargic side'. In other words, thought Burdock, bone bloody idle.

'May I be so bold as to put it that a break in our visitations might be to our advantage?' the morose rabbit was now continuing. 'Meanwhile it would give each of us, who we must surely agree have already demonstrated our unfaltering commitment, the opportunity for a well-earned rest. Not, I hasten to add, that I am putting forward any such proposal unilaterally. May I suggest, however, that a vote might be advantageous?'

'Thank you, comrade,' Burdock replied, relieved the revolt had taken a form he could so easily deal with. 'However I must remind you that, under our duly constituted procedures, what you are putting forward is a policy-determination proposal. As this involves a fundamental reappraisal of our basic strategy, it requires a formal meeting, with all due notice. Is it the case therefore that you wish to schedule one for the near future?'

Groundsel looked round. The others' eyes remained fixed on the floor.

'No, no, team leader!' he laughed woodenly. 'I just thought it might be helpful, and hopefully in the best interests of all, to raise it as a mere suggestion. Of course, if you think not . . .'

His voice tailed away and he too dropped his eyes.

Burdock allowed the silence to drag on.

'Fellow delegation members, as I take it we are all in agreement, shall we now proceed?' he said, leading the way into the tunnel without waiting for a reply.

He shivered as he neared the exit and heard the wind thrashing the leafless branches. It was going to be bitter out there and Groundsel was right in saying that they should not have to go. Normally, as the long nights drew in, the affairs of the Concerned Woodland Guardians would have been winding down, in parallel with activity in the wood as a whole. Confined to their burrows, rabbits would be whiling away their time sleeping, telling stories and, above all, planning the next moves in their unceasing campaign to improve the quality of life in the wood. But this natural timetable had been wrecked by the militant youngsters who were still causing so much trouble. Throughout the spring and summer they had racked the regular meetings with arguments and dissension, until matters had reached such a crisis that Burdock and his supporters had seen they must act immediately.

After setting up a secret working party to tackle the problem, Burdock, as long as he lived, would never forget the horror that had greeted his blunt opening proposition: 'Comrades, to regain control at our meetings we need an extremely firm creature on our side. I therefore propose we recruit one.'

'That would mean bringing in a predator, though, wouldn't it?' Cowslip, wearing her normal silly grin, had inquired. This young doe, with her long narrow face, had pushed herself to the forefront of the youngsters through a mixture of her large size and vociferous advocacy of both feminism and the Worms' Liberation Front.

As she spoke the others had smiled at the very idea.

'Precisely,' Burdock had replied. 'And I also have a particular one in mind.'

That had wiped the smiles off their faces.

'Bringing in a predator — a filthy hunter and slaughterer of the innocent!' Cowslip had screamed. 'You know that would violate every principle we CWGs stand for. Why, we can't even consider it!'

Burdock had sat, unmoved, until the clamour had subsided somewhat and someone had the presence of mind to inquire above the din: 'Who are you thinking of?'

'Ollie the owl,' he had replied, and the uproar had started again.

He had then used every weapon in his considerable political armoury to talk them round by repeatedly defying them to come up with an alternative.

'You agree that what you are proposing involves abandoning our fundamental principles?'

Cowslip had been banging on at him again.

'Temporarily.'

'That it's the kind of short-term expediency we utterly oppose?'

'If you put it that way.'

'And that, above all, it's a sell-out?'

'Maybe.'

'Well, really, that's just not good enough! I'm not saying that I have a better proposal. But that's not the point . . .'

It had taken many meetings, and much lobbying behind the scenes, before he had finally turned their mood. His core supporters, who recognised something had to be done — no matter how unpalatable — had remained loyal. He had then wheeled in his main weapon, his great-grandfather, the Venerable Buck, with whom he had cleared the proposal beforehand. Although now unbelievably decrepit, this ancient buck still commanded huge respect. When he had briefly appeared before the working party wheezingly to declare his support, the opposition had finally crumbled and sanctioned the present delegation, with its declared objective of enticing Owl.

'I myself will be holding true to my principles by with-drawing my co-operation and not taking part,' Cowslip had then announced, her long face nodding angrily up and down.

Burdock, secretly thankful for this unexpected piece of good fortune, had just beamed at her.

As he hopped about outside, the wind cutting through his fur to the bone, Burdock at least had the consolation that no-one would be hanging about today. On more benign afternoons the others had tended to stop to admire the scenery and chat to their friends. Burdock had a lingering sympathy with them. All CWGs went out of their way to enjoy, and comment at length upon, the beauty of Old Wood and its outlying fields, and until recently there had been much to wonder at. A long lull had unexpectedly taken the place of the gales that normally swept away the summer. Despite the ceasing of the rising sap the leaves had clung to the trees, and a pair of sharp frosts had then ushered in a glorious kaleidoscope of lemon yellow, straw yellow, chrome, orange, red, vermilion, crimson lake, magenta, purple, russet, indigo, raw sienna, burnt ochre, umber — the rabbits had quite exhausted their colour vocabularies in trying to outdo each other as they verbally analysed the glorious palette laid before them.

Although the sun's power had waned as it dropped lower in the sky, the wood had basked in a succession of balmy mild days. Heavy dews had clung to the grass, highlighting delicate spiders' webs that artistically minded rabbits had enthused over. A smell of decay had permeated the air and in the damp steamy atmosphere fungi had flourished, bringing a heavy crop of delicious field mushrooms. The blackberries had turned soft and bitter as the trees began to give up their fruits. Acorns and hazel and beech nuts had showered down, alongside sycamore spinners and ash keys, while everywhere it became red berries' time. Brilliant holly, as shiny as that tree's spiky evergreen leaves, had outshone the deeper rowan fruit hanging in plump round bunches. In the undergrowth, russet dogrose hips had clashed with orange honeysuckle, whilst red twining bryony glistened amongst grey patches of old males' beard. Matt, heart-shaped spindleberries, the softest of pinks and the favourite of romantics, had set off the purple hawthorn that cloaked the hedgerows like a mist, while interspersed in their similarly spiky branches had hung fat sloes, adding an almost black tinge to the birds' droppings.

It had been so warm and gentle the wood had become almost indolent. Those part-time residents, the migratory birds, had flocked without their normal urgency, lingering unusually late before they left the wood to its hard-core inhabitants. Bank voles had blundered through the slowly withering vegetation, gnawing the pointed ends of acorns to release the tasty kernel inside, while squirrels got almost bored with gathering their stores and hiding them from prying eyes. Hedgehogs and dormice had postponed plans to hibernate. As they paused for reflection and quiet contemplation, the rabbits and their friends had all agreed – there had never been a more lush and succulent passing away of the summer. If that was not a contradiction in terms, they hastened to add. Meanwhile, between chattering, they feasted richly on the grass, which was continuing to grow as though the Big Cold was never going to arrive.

At this time all rabbits normally enjoyed playing 'catch a falling leaf', which was more than just a game. The object was to catch a leaf before it touched the ground, which then had special significance in symbolising the end of the season. They would take their precious catches down to their underground chambers, keeping them as reminders, until fresh leaves unfurled in the spring. But so few had wafted down in the light breezes that practically nobody, Burdock included, had caught one before, with a roar, the gales had come sweeping down the valley as if making up for lost time. As the Big Cold arrived with a vengeance the trees had been stripped bare almost overnight.

It had been much like that ever since and, as the delegation hopped off in a straggling line, there was nothing for it to admire. The howling wind seemed to have a vindictive life of its own, tearing viciously into drifts of crunchy leaves and throwing them into their faces in stinging clouds. This unaccustomed battering made the rabbits even more nervous than usual. Being off their home territory anyhow contradicted their natural instincts, as was shown by their being so ill-designed for travelling any distance. With no real way of progress between a fast run and a gentle hop, the delegation habitually progressed in a series of quick dashes from one clump of cover to the next. It was hardly stately, as Burdock was cringingly aware, but it was the only way to achieve the required result.

After crossing the open space of the Ride without mishap, the rabbits came within sight of the stream that ran down the middle of the wood. It was so swollen and piled with choking debris that Burdock was working out where they could possibly cross without getting their feet wet, when he heard a sudden commotion behind him. He looked round to see that Clover had stopped so abruptly Ragwort had bumped into her, sending them both sprawling. Burdock instantly presumed that it wasn't Clover's fault. Ragwort shouldn't be there as, although pleasant enough, he was also officially recognised as being mentally disadvantaged. Burdock had only included him when Cowslip, after withdrawing, had come back to insist the delegation include a tangible demonstration of CWG commitment to aiding the more unfortunate. Having rammed that through, she had then lobbied further for the inclusion of the three-legged Toadflax, who could hardly hop. She would represent both disabled and female factions in one, Cowslip had explained, meanwhile studiously ignoring Toadflax's personal inclination that she would much rather stay at home. To Toadflax's enormous gratitude, tucked up in the burrow as she now was, after a hard fight Burdock had won that one.

Ragwort now painstakingly disentangled himself, thereby allowing Clover to sit bolt upright, her normally floppy ears quiveringly erect. Knowing she was gifted with supersharp hearing, Burdock twitched his up as well. But he had still not picked up anything unusual above the roaring in the trees when a sudden gust rocked him, blotting out all other sound. He cursed. Today was proving quite impossible – as the other delegation members were obviously agreeing. Flattened to the ground, eyes screwed up against the wind, they looked totally fed up.

Groundsel squinted venomously at him as he hopped back to Clover.

'Can you hear something, or what?' he yelled.

'No, no! I'm not listening to what I can hear,' she shouted back, highly agitated. 'It's what I can't hear that I'm listening to.'

Burdock quickly worked his way through the various convolutions of this statement. No matter how much the education committee stressed the importance of clear expression in demonstrating rabbits' superior intelligence and reasoning power, there were still problems.

He was just deciding whether to ask, 'What are you not hearing?' or, 'What are you not listening to?' when he got the answer for himself. The drone of a human volver passing along the rollway, which he had previously registered as background noise, had now ceased entirely.

'What I can't now hear sounded like the volver that brings the human with the yellow dog,' Clover informed him.

Burdock cursed again. If she was right, they would have to abandon the expedition and return to base. And, the way matters were so delicately poised, that could be the quickest route to disaster.

3

Skylarks

'May I sit next to you, Mega?' Mata asked, plonking herself down without waiting for a reply.

Mega nodded in happy agreement. In one way he had come to the indoctrination eagerly, not for the message he and the rest of his generation were to be given, but as his first opportunity to be part of a group. He might have had to accept being different, as Sheba insisted, but that didn't mean part of him didn't dearly want to be like the rest. Now here he was, mixed in with everyone else, and he had already been beaming round at his fellows, who for once seemed friendly enough. And, on a public occasion like this, to have such an attractive female as Mata coming and openly sitting beside him! He had never felt so proud.

As he heard his fellow males sniggering he turned his head from side to side, largely causing them to stop. The attempts by the family gangs to bully him had gone away since he began sorting out their members on a one-to-one basis. Now other youngsters deferred to him — not that he pushed it with them. But it was so useful to have that power when you needed it. He felt very much at home

as they settled themselves down and Mata smiled charm-
ingly at him.

The Elders could have formally indoctrinated the young
mink much earlier. Their policy, however, was to wait until
the youngsters were on the verge of adulthood. Parents were
relied on to mould the required frame of mind. The formal
indoctrination was merely to institutionalise what they had
already drummed into their youngsters. Sheba, in contrast, had
taken the middle way, not going as far as openly criticising the
Elders and their rules, but not endorsing them either. Rather,
she had seemed determined to remain neutral.

'Just keep an open mind and observe, Mega. It's for you to
make your own decisions about what's right and wrong. Best
of all, forget all about the Elders for the moment. Concentrate
on enjoying yourself while you can wait for—'

'The fullness of time,' he had interrupted and they had burst
out laughing, both able to share the joke now he was relaxing
more about his 'being different' status.

However Sheba had been emphatic about how her son should
conduct himself outwardly.

'Different you may be, Mega, but don't act differently for the
sake of it. Remember the rules: keep your eyes down when you
pass an Elder, always walk to their left, and never speak unless
you're spoken to.'

Mega had dutifully followed her advice, and as a result had
had no meaningful direct communication with any of them.
They had simply ignored him, as did the rest of the older
mink except for Ramses, a member of the middle of the three
generations. This imposing male seemed to go out of his way to
be friendly – not just to Mega but to all the young mink – and
as a result was enormously popular. As Sheba had recommended,
though, Mega had watched the Elders carefully, seeing how
they curried favour with the Keeper. Whenever he came into
the shed they rushed to greet him, smarming up to him while
he prepared their food or cleaned them out, and he responded
to their sycophancy by talking to them fondly and sometimes
giving them little titbits. Clearly, they were his favourites.

Mega then slowly became aware how carefully the Elders

had arranged cage life to give them the best of everything – the largest cages in the most prime locations, uninterrupted passage in the exercise area, privacy in the latrines and, above all, first place at the feeding trays. No mink ever went really hungry, but the Elders had still grown conspicuously sleek and fat. Massam practically waddled, while even the more active Gabbla had such a fatty face that his eyes looked tiny and deep-set, in contrast to a normal mink's bold stare. Mega never felt scared of them, as some of his fellow youngsters did, or the rest of their particular generation. These mink, naturally inferior in their own pecking order, grovelled and abased themselves in a way that he found quite sickening. He had further taken his mother's advice by not treating the Elders, or their doctrine, as a major part of his life. Now he was to have no choice. Like him, all the youngsters had been as naughty as they liked that morning, knowing that their licence was about to be officially withdrawn.

As Gabbla walked over and called them to attention, Mega shuffled closer to Mata, who smiled in a way that made his head spin.

Gabbla cleared his throat.

'As you know, our Keeper is a human,' he said in his rich, deep voice. 'Extraordinary creatures, aren't they?'

His pupils nodded dutifully.

'They're so huge that we must treat them with respect, mustn't we?'

The pupils nodded again. They knew full well how size, coupled with strength, was the determining factor in cage life.

'And what about the way they walk?'

Mega joined in the laughter. Amid much hilarity and falling about, many of the youngsters had tried to get about using only their back legs. But it both looked and felt so funny they had soon given it up.

'And they don't have only one coat like us, do they?' Gabbla reminded them. 'They have interchangeable ones, which they can put on and take off at will.'

He was right. In the heat of the summer, now thankfully over, the Keeper had switched to a lightweight coat, while they sweltered. Interchangeable coats were really clever, they had all decided.

'Humans are indeed very clever,' Gabbla went on, as if reading their minds. 'That's why it is they, and not us, who have created this world that we live in! It was they who built this strong shed and our fine cages and there is no end to what they can do – such as turning night into day whenever it suits them.'

The youngsters nodded back vigorously. This trick by their Keeper had never ceased to amaze them.

'But the humans' power is good for us mink,' Gabbla smiled reassuringly. 'For, you see, they love us – none more than our Keeper. He is our very special friend. For who gives us our lovely food?'

'Our Keeper,' the pupils chorused back, not without a little hesitation. The memory of the constipation episode, since rectified, still lingered.

'That's right – not forgetting our water. And one day, if we are good, he takes each of us to the Happy Land, where we live comfortably ever after.'

Gabbla regarded them benevolently.

'Now, let's suppose for a moment that our Keeper is not our friend. Let's pretend he's our enemy.'

He frowned at the very thought.

'If that was the case he would hardly keep us in these nice cages, would he?' he went on, the fat round his eyes creasing as he smiled again. 'What could be in it for him? I don't think he'd want to eat us? We're a bit too tough for that, aren't we?'

The pupils laughed.

'No, obviously he would kill us. Yet think instead of all the hard work he does – including dirty jobs like removing your spraint.'

There was a titter. 'Spraint' was a rude word.

Gabbla paused and ran his eyes along the shining young faces staring up at him so expectantly.

'Now, let's get on to the next subject. You young cubs' primary duty is to continue the line.'

There were stifled giggles. Some of the youngsters were already interested in sex, although they had got little further than exhaustively examining their own, and each other's, parts.

'By copulating?' came a brave voice amid bursts of suppressed glee. 'Copulating' was a dirty word. Mega, grinning along with the others, glanced at Mata, but was puzzled to see her looking grim-faced. He did like her, but why did she have to be so serious about everything, he wondered. He had little taste for the crude and rude jokes which the other youngsters constantly swopped, but that didn't mean you couldn't enjoy yourself from time to time!

'You'll be coming to that bit later,' Gabbla admonished them with a stony glare, only to provoke more open laughter. 'Coming' was to do with 'copulating', and therefore dirty by association.

'That's enough,' Gabbla said sharply. 'Now listen to me. To continue our species you must forever stay in the cages. And this is where your bad thoughts come in. You've all been having them, haven't you? I know. And not just on moon madness nights either. Admit it — you've all been thinking about how to escape.'

As the pupils shot guilty sideways glances at each other, Mega looked at Mata again. But she just stared woodenly ahead.

'When you are young you think as a child, you speak as a child and you understand as a child,' Gabbla went on sternly. 'But now it is time for you to grow up. The outside world may seem attractive to you. You may well be tempted by it. But let me tell you — there is nothing out there for you!'

Gabbla's voice had become terrible and he was now thumping the floor with his front paw.

'You must all understand that if one of you ever puts a paw outside these cages the sky will fall in! That is the wisdom that has been passed down to your Elders through the generations. That is the sacred knowledge with which they have been entrusted. And if the sky falls in it means all mink everywhere will be wiped out. Mink will become extinct!

'I cannot say this too strongly or too often — from now on you must never think, speak, or even dream bad thoughts. The fact is that there never can be a different life for you on the outside, whatever you may think. For what will happen if even one of you tries to escape?'

'The sky will fall in,' came a few cries from swots.

'It will indeed!' Gabbla screamed at the top of his voice, thumping the floor again. 'And that will be due to the mink who has retained his bad thoughts! He will bear personal responsibility for killing us all! It will be entirely his fault!

'For what will happen?'

'The sky will fall in!'

This time they were all chanting, Mega and Mata included.

'Correct,' said Gabbla, relaxing slightly. 'Never, ever, forget that.'

After Gabbla had dismissed them, Mega strolled proudly round the exercise area beside Mata. Like the others, they were quiet as they digested their indoctrination. No-one dared mention bad thoughts any more.

'Did you notice that when Gabbla talked about a mink escaping he always said "he", not "she"?' Mata asked suddenly.

'No,' replied Mega, who had not.

'That's typical, isn't it? Well why do you think he did it?'

'Maybe he just forgot the females?' Mega replied, frowning. Mata's preoccupation seemed such a sideshow, compared to the totality Gabbla had been impressing on them.

'Forgot!' Mata exclaimed scornfully. 'He didn't forget. He's just like all males – including you. You think the only purpose of females is to breed, don't you? Well you just wait. Things are about to change round here. In the future we females intend to have our rightful say.'

Mega noticed that one or two other youngsters were now looking at them curiously.

'But Gabbla didn't say the sky falling in thing would just happen to the males,' he protested. 'He said we'd all die – and that means the females as well.'

'True,' Mata conceded. 'But then why are all the Elders males anyway?'

Mega could see more of their fellows turning round. He tried to laugh Mata's remark off, feeling uncomfortable at the attention she was drawing to herself.

'You're not suggesting it's all a male conspiracy again, are you?'

'Aren't I?' Mata replied, looking sour. 'You can hardly hold us females responsible for the way things are, can you? They'd be very different if we were in charge. My father would be for it, for a start.'

Mega could sense the ugly mood that had developed round them. Why was Mata going on like this when so many others were listening? He had been enjoying feeling at one with them, but now he could feel the alienation coming back as they bracketed him with this stroppy female. What did Mata think she was gaining by being so openly provocative just after the law had been laid down to them all? It was as if she was trying to pick an argument for the sake of it. Yet at the same time he couldn't help admitting to himself that her audacity made her even more attractive. With her shining bright eyes and determined expression, she was so alive compared to the others.

All the same he needed to get away from her overwhelming physical presence. Gabbla had already given him enough to think about without her female stuff muddling things up.

'If the females were in charge some of them might learn to keep their mouths shut,' he said crushingly, turning away to go to his own cage.

4

The Yellow Peril

Burdock had thought their luck might run out soon. Only the other day Dandelion had remarked how fortunate it was that previous expeditions had not fallen foul of the human and his yellow dog, although they weren't something to grumble about too much. All the creatures of Old Wood were aware of their incredible good fortune in having only this one human come on to their territory when the stories from all around painted a nightmare picture of how elsewhere they were taking over more and more space. According to the interminable discussions at Concerned Woodland Guardian meetings, the humans had elevated themselves to being the species every other form of life had to revolve round. Many sub-committees had been set up and resolutions passed, all deeply regretting this and none doing the slightest thing to stop it.

Burdock peered through the branches in exasperation. Because the hillside fell away he could see much of the rollway and he had no reason to doubt Clover's extraordinary ability to distinguish between the notes of different volvers. What he really needed, though, was an aerial view. So where were the blasted dunnocks? They were the birds most keen on attending meetings, although personally Burdock found them deeply disappointing. He could never stop thinking how dreary they were and wishing they had more spark. Not, of course, that he said so openly. That would not be politically correct, and he had to keep his nose clean in that department if he was not to alienate his potential supporters. But the dunnocks' most infuriating aspect, which nobody denied, was that they were never there when you needed them — as was proving the case right now.

Burdock sighed with relief as he saw a grey squirrel scampering adroitly through the swaying branches towards the halted delegation. Squirrels might not attend meetings as often as dunnocks, but at least you could rely on them.

'It's the yellow dog,' the squirrel shouted down in confir- mation. 'And it's coming this way!'

Burdock now saw the dunnocks rise in a cloud further down the hill. Nearer a pair of wood pigeons started up, the wind amplifying the clatter of their wings as they made off through the trees. A violent gust carried across the sound of deep barking and Burdock estimated the human and his dog were making their way up the Ride, sending a shockwave ahead of them. The delegation could look for a hiding place, but they were a long way from the nearest burrow. Or else they could risk staying out in the open. The dog's human did not seem dangerous. Certainly he never carried a bang-bang, that fearsome and unnatural instrument of death that the rabbits' friends, the pheasants, lived in such dread of. The yellow dog itself was huge and superficially threatening, yet seemed fundamentally harmless, almost as if it just wanted to play. But the problem was that its human encouraged it to run about in such an irrational and unpredictable way it was impossible to know where to go to avoid it.

He would have to call the expedition off, he decided. His job now was to organise getting the delegation to beat an orderly retreat. Setting off smartly, he succeeded in holding everyone together until they got back to the Ride. Then, as they crossed the broad expanse of open grass, the yellow dog spotted them and with a loud woof came bounding towards them, urged on by shouts from its human. Burdock's control went as the delegation members, led by a suddenly speedy Groundsel, abandoned their joint responsibility and scattered in panic.

Burdock refused to join the mad rush. His heart might be pounding as much as the others but he had a point to prove. Suspecting that rabbits were capable of being a lot braver than they were often made out to be, he welcomed opportunities like this to put his theory to the test. It wasn't that he was interested in raw courage. Anyone could have that. He wanted to establish that the way forward for rabbits was through the application of reason — in this case that the scatter-brained dog would be unable to follow his scent — and therefore there was no cause for alarm.

Deliberately, he began hopping as steadily but as unhurriedly as he could through the undergrowth. The wind was still roaring, its sound amplified now that the muffling leaves had been blown off the trees, but he caught snatches of the tinkling calls of a pair of bright goldfinches as he concentrated on following the well-worn path. All the time he was steeling himself not to look back as he heard clumsy crashes behind him. The dog was still on his tail, that was for sure. But was it getting closer, or was he allowing his imagination to get the better of him? His imagination, he decided, nevertheless cutting off the path and pushing his way through a mound of scratchy brambles to make his pursuer's task more difficult. As he came out the other side he heard yelps of pain and smiled to himself. Reason did prevail!

He rejoined the path, concentrating all his attention on the fallen sycamore trunk that bisected it in the distance. Was his imagination taking over again, or could he hear heavy breathing and pounding feet behind him? He focused more desperately on the trunk. The noises were getting louder, yet he must not look back. He broke into a run, stretching his legs to their fullest extent. The noises were getting closer still. There was now no doubt — the dog was gaining on him. Theory was being overtaken by practice. Or was it? Suddenly he found he had stopped and turned to face his enemy. There it was, ears flying back, chops slavering, huge feet eating up the ground. But, without knowing why, he was now finding himself running full-tilt, not away from it, but towards it. He was grimacing, baring his teeth and, to his further astonishment, letting out a fearsome growl. And the dog had responded! It had first braked, then hesitated, then turned. Now he was chasing it. He was pounding along in the wake of flying feet and gaining every moment!

He was also getting right out of here, he thought, doing a skidding turn. Quit while you're ahead — there must only be so far you could reasonably push your luck.

Arriving safely back at the warren without further incident he ostentatiously stayed outside to take his evening feed. A few dunnocks cheeped feebly about, occasionally sent reeling by a violent gust, and he smiled at them politely. Everything might have gone against the delegation today, but there was no point in slagging everyone off. He must still provide leadership. Strategically placing himself close to a hole, just in case he had to make a bolt for it, he crouched alone and nibbled on the short grass. Did the dreadful dog and its human have any idea what disruption they caused, and to so many different creatures, by their uncaring and inconsiderate actions? Probably not. Only Concerned Woodland Guardians were unselfish enough to think of others, rather than merely gratifying their own desires.

There was still no sign of the dog as he retreated gratefully into the calm of the burrow, his head ringing from the cruel buffeting of the wind.

'You're freezing!' Dandelion exclaimed. 'Where have you been? The others all got back ages ago. Here, let me warm you up.'

She snuggled close.

'It is indeed most unfortunate there was such an unwarranted human intrusion today,' she said as he pushed gratefully up against her toasty fur. 'Groundsel has been telling the others that if his proposal had only been accepted they could all have had the day off without it making any difference — never mind everyone getting such a fright. What cheek, eh? As if he could have foreseen the yellow dog!

'But there is a bright side, dear. As the human and his dog do not come to the wood that often, it must be highly unlikely they will visit again during the short period in which I am certain we will achieve our objective.'

As she smiled cheerfully at him Burdock smiled fondly back, his shivering subsiding. Dandelion might be a trifle naive about the realities of politics, but few rabbits – especially those as involved in it as he was – could claim to have a more supportive partner. He didn't say anything about the experiment in reason he had conducted with the yellow dog. It would only worry her and anyhow it wasn't something he intended to repeat. Once was enough!

But although he said nothing about that either, he had less faith in Dandelion's analysis. When he had set up the delegation his strategy had been to turn up at Owl's tree every afternoon without fail, which was why he had given Groundsel's proposal such short shrift. The key to success had to lie in appearing so regularly that Owl's curiosity, which he was counting on, would become engaged, and until today's aborted mission he had been convinced he was on the verge of a breakthrough. Now the disruption of the regular pattern could have broken the hypnotic spell he had been trying to weave, meaning they would be back at square one.

On his way back in Burdock had peeped into the Venerable Buck's bedchamber and seen his great-grandfather asleep, as he was so often these days. There had been no point in waking him to inform him of such a serious potential setback. The delegation would go again tomorrow, regardless.

'We must all hope for the best, my dear,' Dandelion suddenly interrupted his gloomy chain of thought.

She sympathised with the way her beloved mate tried so hard to make things work for everyone, but she did wish he could relax more and trust in events to take their correct course. He shouldn't worry so much. The stress was bad for his health.

'Try and get a good sleep, my love, rather than staying up all night fretting,' she said, nuzzling her cheek against his.

Then she closed her eyes and was instantly fast asleep.

Oh for such simple faith! Burdock thought, staring into the darkness.

5

Custard Pie

Massam looked even more gloomy than usual as he and Gabbla sat in the exercise area watching Mega demolish yet another challenger.

'I'm afraid he's turned into an accomplished scrapper,' the Chief sighed as the young mink delivered a devastating chopping blow to the back of his opponent's neck. 'You can see why, can't you, Gabbla? It's not his size, is it? Or his stockiness. It's that uncanny ability he has of foreseeing the next move.'

Even as he spoke Mega executed a flawless double feint, which he then followed through with a perfect body slam.

'He can certainly look after himself,' Gabbla agreed reluctantly.

The Elders had been keeping a careful eye on Mega as the youngsters reached the last stage of establishing their generational hierarchy. None of them had liked what they saw.

'We've got to do something, Gabbla,' Massam went on peevishly. 'He's rising right to the top, you know. Of course he still can't join a gang — all the parents are still obeying our instructions and telling their children not to have anything to

do with him. Except for Atara of course – but then we marked
her card a long time ago. Anyhow, we've got Mugger to knock
some sense into her at last. Her daughter seems interested in
Mega, though, which is another thing I don't like. She's a rum
one as well.

'But the real point is, Gabbla, nothing's stopped him yet, has
it?'

'I'm afraid not, Chief.'

As the Elders' spokesmale Gabbla prided himself on being the
one who was most in touch with the general mood of the colony.
He understood even better than his Chief how Mega was making
his mark.

'He is a male,' he reminded him patiently. 'And you know
how it is. The hierarchy's a natural process. We can't just
interfere with it willy-nilly.'

'I don't see why not. We manage to interfere with enough
other natural processes already,' Massam replied crossly. 'I'm
telling you, Gabbla, we've got to do something.'

Gabbla suppressed his irritation. It wasn't that simple. He
might have been made the spokesmale for the Elders' Council
because he was clever at talking. But that didn't mean Massam
could always expect him to come up with some magic solution
when there plainly wasn't one.

'Have you noticed how Mega doesn't throw his weight
about?' Massam was now continuing, more cantankerously than
ever. 'He confines his advantage to the ritualised challenges,
while I've seen him doing something even more unusual that
I find particularly worrying.

'The other day I was watching the others bully Psycho – that
nasty runt who spies for us – when Mega stepped in and rescued
him. I don't know whether it was by design, or whether his
mother had told him to – we all know what Sheba's like. He's
made a few other kind gestures like that already and I can see
the result – he's gathering his acolytes. Psycho's quite hooked
on him.'

Gabbla sighed. Like his Chief, he was suspicious of Mega's
association with this weedy cub. On the face of it he seemed the
one of his generation Mega had the least in common with. The

runt of the litter, unloved and rejected by his parents, he was universally despised and remained stuck firmly at the bottom of the hierarchy. Yet Gabbla, as well as Massam, had seen him and Mega going round as a pair, the physical disparity making them look quite comical. Their link, he had realised, was that they were both outsiders. Whether Massam had grasped that Gabbla was not so sure, but he wasn't going to bring trouble on his own head by mentioning it.

'And there's another thing — what are we doing about Maxi?' his chief inquired, moving on to the next grumble.

Gabbla sighed again. Maxi, who was at the opposite end of the hierarchy spectrum from Psycho, was another problem Massam had dumped on his plate.

'Maxi may be thick, Gabbla, but he's very strong,' his Chief continued. 'He should have challenged Mega by now. But he looks up to him so much I now don't think he's ever going to.

'I'm telling you, Gabbla, I don't like the way things are going. The whole idea from the beginning was to ensure Mega remained a complete outsider like his mother.'

'None of us likes the way it's going, Chief,' Gabbla replied, trying to keep his annoyance out of his voice. 'But we decided we could handle him, and I see no reason to change our minds. Remember, I've now indoctrinated him along with all the others. Don't worry — he'll soon come to heel.'

Massam was looking dubious when they heard a rousing cheer. They looked across to see Mega standing quietly over his opponent, who was on his back, legs spread open in submission posture. Maxi was gazing on adoringly, while beside him Psycho grinned with delight.

'Another one down, Gabbla, I'm afraid.'

Why do you have to be so morose about everything, you miserable old sod? Gabbla was thinking, when he saw the young mink turn their attention to the shed door. The Keeper had left it open today, as he occasionally did to give them some welcome fresh air, and there had been plenty of it. Ragged clouds were still scudding across the rooflight, while the shed walls continued to shudder and creak as the gale slammed against them. The exhilarating blasts of cold air that were whipping down the exercise area, stirring the dust up into whirling eddies, had already woken the colony out of its normal torpor. The mink had been in a wild mood all afternoon.

'Custard's come to see us,' they were now shouting excitedly.

Gabbla suddenly perked up. The labrador bitch belonging to the Keeper was an essential plank in his indoctrination programme, but to his continual annoyance had been unaccountably missing of late.

'Here's your opportunity to impress young Mega still further, Gabbla,' Massam grunted.

'Indeed, Chief,' he grovellingly agreed. 'And if you'll now excuse me, I'll be off to make the most of it!'

Relieved to get away, Gabbla bustled importantly towards the growing crowd near the shed door.

'Don't mess it up now, will you?' he heard Massam call after him.

'I won't,' he shouted back, resisting the temptation to ask his Chief why he always had to stab him in the back just as he was leaving.

He increased speed. He didn't want any of the young mink starting a dialogue.

'Only I am allowed to converse with Custard because of the special relationship between us,' he had already instructed them in preparation. 'As you listen to us talking, you will come to understand the depth of our Keeper's commitment to the welfare, not just of ourselves, but of all other animals.

'More importantly, our Keeper takes Custard on regular visits to the Happy Land you will all go to one day if you are good. She will describe to you exactly how wonderful it is.'

Mega pressed himself against the wire, Mata squashed against him, and together they gazed spellbound at the animal in front of them. Custard had made the odd visit in the past, but they had been too young to appreciate her fully.

'Isn't she gigantic, Mega?' Mata breathed, running her eyes up and down the creamy rotund body, while the dog sat panting with her huge pink tongue lolling out. 'And doesn't she smell funny?'

'She stinks,' Mega replied, thinking how she differed from mink – if not from the latrine pit. He could see she was plastered in caked mud. And, if he was not mistaken, something even worse.

'She's covered in spraint, Mata,' he whispered wonderingly. 'Look – it's all over her.'

Mata was even more taken aback. Custard was a female.

'How absolutely disgusting,' she replied, appalled. 'She's not like Pussles, is she?'

Pussles the cat was the only other creature who regularly visited the shed. But they didn't speak to her either. Gabbla, castigating her as a greasy feline and the mink's sworn enemy, had given the youngsters strict instructions to ignore her. When they first saw her fierce face and sharp teeth, both Mega and Mata had been initially puzzled by his directive. Superficially, at least, she looked a bit like them, although, unlike their uniform colour, her coat was an apparently random mixture of black and orange.

Then Pussles had launched into her standard routine and they had begun to understand what Gabbla meant.

'How are you, my dears? Still here, eh?' she had asked as she paraded haughtily around, looking at them contemptuously with her slanting green eyes. 'Nothing changes does it? Let me remind you again why. It's because you're inferior, especially to myself, being a cat.

'So superior am I, as I have informed you before many times, that your Keeper credits me with special powers. He believes, for example, that I have nine lives. I have even heard tell that his ancestors once used to worship mine. Certainly, you know how he, and even more his mate, dote on me, ensuring that I live off the cream of the land. My every wish, as you are aware, is their command.

'But you, on the other paw, are such a rough and scummy lot that he keeps you in these revolting cages, where he has correctly estimated you quite rightly belong.

'So let me summarise it for you with my own little joke.

Your trouble is that, unlike us cats — and especially myself — you are not purrfect.'

She had then departed with a dismissive flick of her black and orange striped tail.

Mega and Mata had both felt their anger rising at these outrageous slurs, but contained themselves when they saw the Elders frowning and shaking their heads to indicate they must not rise to the bait. Afterwards an official game of tag had been hurriedly organised to enable everyone to work off their feelings.

But Gabbla had told all the young mink that Custard was different and they stepped back expectantly to make space for him as he rushed up.

'Hello, Custard. Nice to see you,' he hailed the dog cheerily. 'And how is Master today?'

'Very well, thank you,' Custard replied politely.

'Custard, do you love your Master?'

'I do. And my Mistress as well. They're so good to me. They really know how to look after us creatures, don't they?'

'They do indeed,' Gabbla agreed, nodding emphatically to the enthralled throng round him. 'By "Master" Custard means our Keeper,' he stage-whispered for the benefit of the more dense. From bitter experience Gabbla always worked on the premise that you could never spell things out enough.

Custard looked on expectantly. She was somewhat in awe of the mink, whom she found alternately fascinating and repelling. Yet she was naturally gregarious and had only the superior Pussles to talk to otherwise, while sneaking into their shed had an additional thrill as she suspected it was naughty. But she had had few opportunities lately. First Mistress had taken her on a long holiday, then Master had been so busy that he had largely confined her to the house. It had only been that afternoon that he had finally taken her to their special place of the wonderful wood, despite the roaring gale.

But when they returned he had banned her from the house because she had been rolling. She had been lying disconsolately in the porch, wondering when she would ever be let in, when the bell thing had sounded and Master had rushed off with Mistress in the volver. Left to wander around in the yard, Custard had found the mink shed door open.

As she now looked at the eager questing faces in front of her, she was reminded again of how much they looked like Pussles. They were so much more friendly though, especially the fat one who always talked to her. He seemed as delighted as ever to see her.

Gazing at him with dewy eyes, she wagged her tail.

'Has Master been doing anything exciting recently, Custard?' he asked.

'Funny you should say that,' she replied enthusiastically. 'In fact I've just returned from the wonderful wood – which is why I'm so muddy!'

What a stupid and revolting animal she was, Gabbla thought, as he saw her wearing her dishevelment as if it was a trophy. But it was still an unexpected break for him. He'd show Massam what he could do.

'Do you mean the Happy Land?' he inquired in simulated wonder.

Custard wagged her tail and nodded her head in eager confirmation. The mink who asked the questions always called the wood that and she never disagreed. After all, it was such a happy place for her!

'What a lucky dog you are, Custard. Tell me, is the Happy Land still as wonderful as ever?'

'Absolutely.'

Custard had discovered the Happy Land – or rather the wonderful wood – was a special place the first time Master had taken her there. Although he had shushed her as they arrived, she had been unable to stop herself barking in her uncontrollable excitement. Immediately she had found herself shoved back into the volver and Master had rolled off at high speed. It was only then she'd realised that they weren't supposed to be there and ever since thrilled to their joint conspiracy.

'Tell us about the Happy Land, Custard.'

The mink who asked the questions never seemed to tire of hearing the details, while she in turn never tired of repeating them.

'It's a big wood that goes right down a hillside — so big I've still not found the edge. There are thickets and bushes and grassy patches and trees in all directions as far as you can see. Some of them are absolutely gigantic, especially the one that stands on its own right in the middle.'

'The creatures, Custard?'

'There are lots and lots of them. All sort of birds — pheasants, pigeons, rooks, magpies, chaffinches, jackdaws, robins — even a scary owl that I've heard hooting once or twice. Then on the ground there are millions of little animals like mice, shrews, voles, rats — they're rather horrid actually — then bigger things like weasels and hedgehogs and foxes and badgers — they're a bit big, even for me. Oh, and there are loads and loads of rabbits. I like them best of all. You should see the number of holes I explore. Today, when I was going up the big wide path, I came across a whole collection of them and chased one so far through the bushes that I got lost.'

The labrador's soft eyes had gone bright with the recollection.

'Did you catch it, Custard?'

'Well not quite, now you come to mention it,' Custard said hurriedly, reluctantly reminded of how at one stage it had actually been chasing her. What had turned it so aggressive? she had been wondering ever since. 'But I did get quite close,' she went on, fudging the truth. 'And, do you know, it had the biggest bum I've ever seen.'

'Well done, Custard! You are a brave dog,' Gabbla said approvingly, while speculating inwardly on how she could be so pathetic and still live.

'The river,' he prompted, moving her on to the next item in the litany.

'That's where Master takes me at the end to get clean,' Custard explained dutifully. 'But today I'm afraid I was rather naughty and rolled in some cow stuff afterwards.'

'So we can tell,' Gabbla said drily.

The youngsters all giggled as he turned towards them and ostentatiously held his nose in his paw, his little eyes sparkling, while Custard gave a sloppy grin.

'The river,' Gabbla repeated firmly, wiping the grin off her face immediately.

'Oh, sorry,' she apologised. 'Well, it's so wide and deep that in places I can't touch the bottom. There was lots of water today, all brown, and I had to swim my very best to retrieve my sticks. Master's very good at throwing sticks, you know. He never chooses ones that sink or are too long. But they're not too short either. And always the right weight—'

Gabbla recognised the signs of a long Custard loop.

'What about the fish?' he interrupted.

'There are loads of fish. I've seen them jumping and some are as long as my leg. There are ducks as well, which I made fly off today. And a heron. I saw that too.'

'So all's well in the Happy Land, is it, Custard?'

'Better than ever, really.'

'We're all very glad to hear that, aren't we?'

The mink who asked the questions had now turned to his fellows and was nodding emphatically.

'It really is an absolutely fabulous place, everyone,' Custard added unprompted. 'And it's all thanks to Master. He's so good to me, you know.'

'I couldn't have put it better myself, Custard,' the mink smiled back. 'And, talking of Master, hadn't you better run along before he finds you here?'

'I suppose I should really,' Custard said uncertainly, suddenly thinking that the wind was so loud she might not hear the volver roll up. Then she'd be in real trouble.

'Goodbye,' she said, deciding. 'See you again soon.'

'Bye-bye, Custard,' the mink chorused as she padded cheerfully out to return to the porch. She hoped Master would not be long. It was fun to share her adventures but the mink shed was very bare and uncomfortable. She needed one of Master's roaring log fires.

Gabbla turned to the others.

'There, you've heard it for yourselves straight from the dog's mouth. The Happy Land is just as fabulous as we always told you. Isn't Custard lucky to be sharing the love of our kind and caring Keeper?' he smiled, fixing his eyes specifically on Mega.

But for the first time his normal authoritative gaze wavered and then finally dropped as Mega's black eyes bored back into his own.

While the others soon dispersed, chittering excitedly, Mega and Mata both sat staring at the damp patch Custard had left on the floor. They stayed silent for a long time, savouring the warmth of their contact, and lost in their own thoughts.

'Well, Mega, what do you think of the Happy Land then?' Mata asked eventually.

'It sounds like a different world, doesn't it, Mata?' he replied non-committally, trying to hide how much he was bubbling inside. It was impossible to imagine, yet there was obviously so much to explore, so much to experience, so much space to go wild in. As Custard babbled on, he had been feeling within him a deep longing to be there.

'It is, Mega,' Mata said simply. 'But have you thought how odd it is that only Gabbla is allowed to talk to Custard?'

Mega, as so often with her, was now unsure where the conversation was heading.

He took refuge in ribbing her about her feminist tendencies.

'You mean someone else should talk to her to make it female to female?' he asked lightly.

'Not necessarily!' Mata replied sharply. 'But a female would at least ask the right questions, instead of encouraging her go on and on about how wonderful it all is.'

'Don't you believe her, then?'

'I'm not saying the wood doesn't exist,' Mata replied, staring boldly at him. 'Custard's as thick as spraint. She doesn't have the wit to invent it and for her it's probably as wonderful as she says. But I'd like to ask her, if it is the Happy Land as we're told, then how come it isn't full of mink? She never mentioned them, which is very peculiar, isn't it?'

'It is,' Mega said slowly. He had not thought about that. But Mata was correct – by all rights the wood should be overrun by them.

They looked into each other's eyes for a long time.

'You know something, Mega?' Mata remarked finally, in a

matter-of-fact manner. 'I don't think I believe a word of this Happy Land stuff the Elders peddle to us. And neither, I know, do you.'

Their eyes locked and Mega sensed how she was challenging him. He had never had that from a female before and wasn't at all sure what to make of it. Mata always acted more like a male in the way she first took the lead and then was so upfront and direct.

He continued to stare at her, waiting for her to look away, as all other mink did in the end. But she only opened her eyes wider, glaring so forcibly that eventually he felt compelled to speak.

'Maybe I don't, Mata,' he replied slowly. 'But even so, the question is: what are we going to do about it?'

Mata continued to stare at him.

'I don't know, Mega,' she replied, shrugging her shoulders. 'But we're going to do something.'

6

Bottoming Out

Owl had programmed himself to wake early. He gave a quiet stretch, glanced surreptitiously at Ula and tiptoed towards the light, across the debris in the bottom of the nest. The rabbits hadn't come yesterday, leaving him feeling vaguely cheated and realising he missed them. The reason, he presumed, was that their lives, along with so many others' in the wood, had been thrown into temporary chaos by the visit of the human and his yellow dog.

Owl himself, woken by the din, had been unable to get back to sleep, even though he knew that he was perfectly safe high up in his nest. Giving up trying, he had sat listening to the crashings in the undergrowth and mindless barking, Ula's constant moans increasing his irritation. At one stage he had even heard the panting breath of the idiot animal careering wildly about below them. Eventually he had caught the sound of the human's volver rolling away and sat waiting for the rabbits until he had finally gone out to ride the stormy night. But there was no reason they should not be back today. The gale had been so intense it had already blown itself out.

'You're not talking to those bloody bunnies again,' a cutting voice stopped him in his tracks.

'Pellets!' he whispered to himself.

He had been certain Ula was asleep. But when he swivelled his head round there she was, feathers fluffed up.

'How many times do I have to tell you I'm not having you talking to those nibblers right outside our nest? They're not real creatures, they're pathetic veggies. And you're just as pathetic taking any notice of them.'

Owl hopped out on to the branch, trying to ignore her. The site for their nest, chosen in the heady days when love – or, as he now saw it, lust – had been all-consuming, was high off the ground in the bole of a magnificent beech. Its entrance was small, making it safe and dry in all weathers, while the branch he was now on provided a natural perch. Their home was the one thing they still agreed they had done well together. Some of Owl's fondest memories were of them combining passion with practicality, vying with each other to bring back the softest materials for their bed and then tumbling into it to test them out one by one. The resulting nest had been one to be proud of, at least until neglect reduced it to its present slummy state.

Automatically, he swept the panorama in front of him. The beech was situated near the middle of the wood, not far from the stream, and through the leafless canopy he could see the hillside falling away to the Long Field. Beyond, the river winked in the weak sunlight before reflecting more strongly off a shiny volver making its way along the rollway. More flashes marked where human activity was taking place in a field on the other side of the valley, the rooks wheeling and turning as they followed the plough.

Owl's feelings were always mixed whenever he gazed at the chequered pattern the humans had painted on the landscape. Once, before they had reorganised it for their own benefit, he supposed it must have looked very different – possibly entirely like Old Wood, according to his friend Boris Badger, whose species had a long, and as far as Owl knew justifiable, grumble about the way it had been persecuted ever since. But at the same time he, Owl and Freddie Fox, who met occasionally to swap notes under the loose label of the Dead Vole Society, acknowledged that it was so long ago it was irrelevant. Boris had even grudgingly said the humans seemed less vindictive lately, at least towards badgers. Owl didn't know about that. What he did know was that he would have given anything for just one night when their multiple marks were eradicated and he could see a world without them – which was why the human with the yellow dog was such a nuisance. Owl didn't think he owned the wood, but he bitterly resented these incursions into what was otherwise a sanctuary for them all. Freddie, naturally, disagreed. He saw the humans as there to give creatures opportunities, such as his beloved chickenhouse raves.

'And the hunt, of course,' Owl would always say, trying to provoke him.

But Freddie was too relaxed to be wound up so easily.

'Win one, lose one,' he would shrug in reply. 'I didn't make it as it is, Ollie. I just live in it.'

None of them, of course, knew who or what had made it as it was, as Ula always crossly reminded him whenever he tried to discuss it with her.

'Why don't you stick to being an owl, Ollie, and stop this constant wondering about everything? You'll never come up with any answers – especially not from Boris or Freddie.'

Owl had soon concluded, somewhat justifiably, that she was simply jealous of his friends. Ula, he had found, was a bird with the narrowest of horizons. It was primarily because he had found life with her increasingly intolerable that he had turned his attention outwards towards the wood as a whole. Which was why, he presumed, the Concerned Woodland Guardian rabbits had been coming to see him. And why he, in turn, was interested in talking to them . . .

He snapped out of his reverie and turned his attention to immediately below him. To his great satisfaction, he saw the rabbits were back, white tails bobbing as they waved from the cover of the holly thicket into which they always tucked themselves.

'Cooee! Cooee, mighty Owl!' they called.

The rabbits were always nervous at first, as they had reason to be: they were on Owl and Ula's preferred food list. But if Owl was honest – and honesty was a quality he prided himself on – he could only really cope with young or old ones. When out hunting he looked for something more mouse or vole-sized, especially vole-sized. Voles always had been, and always would be, his favourite food.

The rabbits had now been coming to his beech for more than half a moon. They had appeared unexpectedly one day, for no particular reason he had since been able to fathom. Owl could easily have frightened them off, but as they called when he was only pottering around, waiting for nightfall, he had tolerated their presence. At first he had taken little notice of them. But when their visitations had settled down to a regular pattern he had become intrigued. Something interesting must be going on for them to show such uncharacteristic courage, when normally they avoided him like myxomatosis.

Burdock, the big one with the distinctive white blaze on his forehead, now hopped forward and waved a front paw in greeting.

'Hello, esteemed comrade,' he shouted up. 'How goes it this evening – and a very nice evening too, if I may say so?'

'Fine,' Owl hooted back. 'Better than yesterday, eh?'

'Indeed, comrade. I must apologise for being unable to make our normal pilgrimage to see you. It was due to a combination of such inclement weather and the unfortunate presence in the wood of the human and his yellow dog, which I trust did not overly interrupt your sleep pattern.

'As you know, we Concerned Woodland Guardians, on behalf of all creatures, deeply regret this rude invasion and you will doubtless be glad to hear we are planning a protest meeting.'

Owl sat silent, as fascinated as ever by the convoluted way in which Burdock spoke. How many words did you need to make a point? Not for nothing were the rabbits known throughout the wood as 'the chattering creatures'. Yet, as so often, Burdock's verbose statement had somehow ended hanging in the air and Owl was now not all sure how to reply.

'Still dying for me to come and see you?' he hooted as a holding measure.

'Yes indeed, mighty Owl.'

'How do you know you wouldn't die if I did?'

He had tried this joke before and been pleased with how it had made the rabbits even more nervous.

'Very funny, Ollie. Isn't he a humorist, comrades? Most droll. But we still want him to come, don't we?'

Burdock's question triggered the pleading chorus: 'Please come and see us, mighty Owl! Please come and see us, mighty Owl!'

It was the same request they had been making every day.

'Why not come over for a chat?' Burdock had kept asking. 'Nothing too formal, I assure you, no agenda to worry about or anything so structured. More a wide-ranging discussion, during which we can hopefully fill you in about our meetings and oblige by answering any points you might care to raise.

'Then we could chew over an idea of ours, which I'm sure you'll find of great interest. You see, not to put too fine a point upon it, Ollie, we need you. And, after all, what harm can it do?'

'What harm indeed?' his pretty doe, Dandelion, would add, fluttering her soft eyelashes as she peered round the prickly leaves. 'I'm sure we all agree we're reasonable creatures, don't we?'

Owl, who was not sure what a reasonable creature was, would nod.

Then Burdock would start flattering him.

'The fact of the matter, mighty Owl, is that you're so wise, so forceful, so much a creature born to lead,' he would say, eliciting further praise from his fellows.

'Yes, mighty Owl, such authority.'

'Such overwhelming gravitas.'

'Such bottom. Hasn't he got a huge amount of bottom, comrades?'

'Indeed he has,' they would affirm, restarting their chant. 'Please come and see us, mighty Owl! Please come and see us, mighty Owl!'

Owl didn't know what gravitas was. And as for bottom! He always flexed the smoothly tapered rear he was so proud of whenever they mentioned that. In contrast to rabbits' gigantic bums, bottom was the last thing he had. It was the way they were designed, he supposed. Those powerful back legs were all they had to save their furry skins. But that didn't stop them looking eminently kickable – especially the monster one belonging to Burdock, whom he had nicknamed 'Big Arse' as a result.

Burdock was just starting his flattery when his voice was drowned out as Ula emerged.

'I'm telling you to get rid of them now!' she screeched directly into Owl's ear, making him wince with pain. 'How dare you show us up yet again outside our own home? Have you forgotten we're top predators with a position to maintain in this wood?'

As Owl swivelled his head she thrust her face hard up against his, her black orbs blazing. Why did she allow herself to get so worked up? he thought, not for the first time. She was absolutely beside herself.

'We're not lowly herbivores who nibble bloody grass, we're owls!' she continued her diatribe. 'We're supposed to eat rabbits, not chatter to them. You're making us the laughing stock of the wood.'

Owl was overwhelmed by a rush of anger.

'Why do you spend your whole time bothering about what everybody else thinks?' he yelled back. 'Haven't you got a mind of your own?'

'Yes, I bloody well have! And its not full of stupid rabbit thoughts like what passes for yours,' she screeched harshly. 'The way you're going you might as well become one. Then you could join their Concerned Woodland Guardians, or whatever pellets they call their stupid group. It makes me ashamed, thinking I'm mated to a pillock like you!'

Owl stretched his wings. 'Pillock' was the worst insult. He had never forgotten the time Ula had openly called him that in front of a group of their fellow predators and he had seen how they sniggered. He had suspected ever since that they still called him it behind his back.

'Why don't you fly off and never come back?' Ula added gratuitously.

'I might just do that, you old ratbag,' he hooted, swooping off the branch.

'And what about the nest repairs you promised to do?' He heard her parting sally as he zoomed downwards, seeing out of the corner of his eye the rabbits watching forlornly as they continued to mouth their pleading chorus.

Ignoring them, he tilted and gave two hard beats of his wings to propel him through the treetops. Then he was out into the open sky, greeting the glorious rosy flush that heralded the oncoming night.

Gone! That was the beauty of being a bird. When it all became too much you were just gone.

7

Killjoys

It was the Elders' bad luck that the two birds got into the system the day after Custard's visit. Rushing out of his cage, Mega saw them beating themselves frantically against the wire at the far end of the exercise area. A shower of brown feathers was drifting down and as he ran to join his fellow juveniles he caught one and waved it about. The others waved ones back, temporarily forgetting their differences with him in their joint exhilaration. Birds had occasionally flown into the shed before, but never inside their wire.

The babble of speculation round him was presuming that they had somehow squeezed through to get to the food trays. Various youngsters were pointing upwards, trying to identify where they had managed it. But this detail didn't interest Mega. Instead the birds' flapping and squawking distress was awakening something from his remote past, something so utterly basic he felt it must have been handed down by his ancestors. His mind suddenly filled with the vision of a line of them stretching back until they were lost in the fog of time. The feeling wasn't like full-moon madness. That was a mania dictated by the Elders. This was atavistic, coming from within, and as such should have been within his control – except that it was doing precisely the opposite, sending him out of control by triggering such an urgent desire that his mind was filled by just one thought.

'Kill!' he found himself screaming at the top of his voice

All around him the shout went up: 'Kill! Kill! Kill!'

Suddenly a howling juvenile mob was dancing up and down underneath the birds, whose frenzy increased as they too recognised the inevitability of what was about to happen. Dazed by the blows they were inflicting on themselves, they now started slipping downwards. A fresh roar went up from the mob, while individuals scrambled over each other to lunge at them. This caused the birds to summon fresh reserves of strength and beat their way back up to the roof netting. But they soon slid down again, only escaping to stay up for a shorter period. The pattern was set.

Mega struggled to keep his feet as his fellows snapped and snarled in a jumble of frustrated bloodlust. Like them, he could see that the birds were nearing the point of exhaustion. He must get away from the others! He must have one for himself! He broke out of the sea of writhing bodies and found the Elders hanging back, the older mink slavishly following their lead. As he dodged past Massam's huge bulk he nearly collided with Gabbla, who stared open-mouthed after him as he rushed to the far side of the exercise area. Obeying some instinct, he pushed his rump hard against the wire. He would give himself a launching pad to provide greater velocity, just as he did when playing. Trembling almost uncontrollably, he watched the smaller and weaker bird slip down until he knew the timing was right. Then he sprang.

As he hurtled across the floor, out of the corner of his eye he saw another mink streaking by his side. It was Mata. She must have had the same idea. But there was no time for them to communicate. Lips drawn back, mouths open in silent screams, in unison they catapulted themselves on to the backs and heads of their fellows. Using them as springboards, they leapt upwards to smash simultaneously into their victim. The momentum sent them tumbling to the floor, each with their teeth clamped on to a wing. Behind them they heard a roar as the other bird slipped for a final time and was dragged down by the mob.

Alone to one side, Mega and Mata spat at each other, suddenly the bitterest of enemies as each tried to wrest the prey away for themselves. Then their eyes locked and they both froze as something indefinable passed between them. An instant later they had both plunged themselves back in, no longer enemies, but now working together as partners. Mega bit down on the bird's throat and almost gagged with a delight purer than he had ever known as he felt a hot spurting between his teeth. Red blood – and now red meat, he exulted as they both started tearing at the flesh, ripping off the wings and slitting in half the still-twitching body!

As they crouched opposite each other and set about stuffing themselves, he could see the glitter in Mata's eyes. He spat out a mouthful of choking feathers and grinned at her. She grinned back even more madly, showing the red stains on her teeth. Some bond was being forged between them, Mega realised, and for a terrible moment he had a feeling that he was to be first subjugated and then enslaved. He shook his head briskly as he put it to the back of his mind. Mata might be some female – and maybe the only one for him – but she was just a female all the same.

Suddenly the shed resounded with a chorus of warning hisses. Their Keeper was coming! A communal guilt seized everyone and they abandoned the mangled remains, scurrying into their individual cages just as the Keeper entered the doorway. He walked silently down the aisle and they peeped out, watching as he opened the wire door at the back of the exercise area and reached in to sweep away the remaining bits of the birds' corpses. Then, ignoring their food trays, he mutely delivered his verdict by closing the shed door and leaving them without sustenance for the night.

Once certain he was not returning, the mink crept out and all eyes turned to Massam's cage, where the Elders were going into huddled conference. But although they hung about, it finally broke up without any statement. A few older mink trailed after Gabbla as he returned to his cage, but stopped when he turned and gave them an annoyed shake of his head. They drifted off, whispering uneasily. Not just the youngsters', but their own instincts had been aroused by the birds and they had had to check themselves so as not to join in. Now their leaders were letting them down, they grumbled to each other. It was Gabbla's job to reassure them by providing an explanation, just as he had with the rogue cloud.

Meanwhile the youngsters, although outwardly sheepish, were ecstatic under the surface. They had already had some experience of wildlife. For a start there were the rats, who ignored the mink as they quartered the floor, scavenging for anything they could find. Other small creatures occasionally also ran about, thrilling them with the scamper of their tiny feet. More directly, flying and crawling insects came into the exercise area and they found themselves naturally chasing these, to pounce and then crunch them up with their sharp teeth. But there had never been anything as exciting as the birds. They had opened up a whole new dimension.

Gabbla's indoctrination temporarily forgotten, the youngsters began surreptitiously confiding individual 'bad thoughts' to each other.

'Gabbla was right. We've all been having them.'

'I have, all the time. And after that I can't wait to get out.'

'Me too. That's what it must be like on the outside all the time.'

'Yeh — killing birds whenever you feel like it.'

They'd all been chafing at the restrictions of cage life, they confessed to each other. There was the weather alone — the roaring winds; the sighing breezes; the rain which pitter-pattered, drummed and sometimes lashed on the shed roof; the blinding sunlight which from time to time came through the rooflight in golden shafts, holding glittering particles of dust in suspended animation; the deep twilight and beckoning darkness that urged them into its cold and mysterious embrace. Then there were the glorious smells which wafted in, redolent and reeking of excitement and adventure; the tantalising views through the rooflight and occasionally the open shed door; the constant sounds — growling volvers, human voices and the noises of so many other living creatures, twitterings, lowings, hootings, squeakings – a thousand mysteries just waiting to be explored. Until this moment those sounds had all been part of a world closed off to them, a world they could never experience, and in a way had meant nothing. But now they had been blooded. Now they were killers. How could cage life ever measure up after that?

But their exhilaration was short-lived.

'It's working,' Gabbla reported smugly back to Massam, the fat round his eyes creasing with satisfaction. It had been his idea not to issue a statement after the meeting. 'Wait for them to hang themselves,' he had advised his Chief confidently. 'I haven't indoctrinated them for nothing.'

Now, as he had predicted, gloom was creeping into the subversive conversations. Massam's smile broadened as he waddled furtively around, picking up odd snatches.

'The whole point is that we'll never get out.'

'There's no way.'

'Never will be – that's the trouble.'

'And Gabbla said that even if there was the sky would fall in.'

'We don't know that,' came one brave voice.

But it was alone.

'No, no, we mustn't ever try,' came anxious cries.

'Because no sky means no birds anyhow.'

'Or anything else.'

'And that includes no us.'

Observing them looking at each in despair, Massam returned to his cage smiling.

'Well done, Gabbla,' he congratulated him. 'We seem to have scotched that one for the moment. But we're not out of the wood yet. Think of something else, will you?'

'Yes, Chief,' Gabbla replied, smiling in turn at his Chief's unconscious play on words. For a moment he thought of pointing it out. Then he promptly buried the idea. Massam had never been a great one for humour, conscious or unconscious. Instead he narrowed his eyes and scowled as Massam turned his back. No matter what he came up with, it seemed his Chief would never be satisfied. Yet for once Gabbla had a funny feeling his habitual pessimism might be justified. They weren't out of the wood yet – or, rather, into it by convincing the youngsters about the Happy Land story.

He stared through the wire for a long time as he pondered his decision. Then he made his mind up. It had never happened before, as far as he was aware, but he would put the youngsters through the indoctrination process a second time.

There was no harm in making doubly sure, and meanwhile doing something would keep Massam off his back.

8

Rooked

It took two long sweeps of Old Wood before Owl's seething rage subsided. But whatever he shouted at Ula, and she back, it was just talk. Even if she did call him a pillock, they were mated for life, locked into a partnership neither could ever break. At the very least their relationship should be supportive. It could even be wonderful, as Owl fondly remembered it at the very beginning. But too many layers of acrimony had buried that since, and these days and nights neither could tolerate the other's company. The tragedy, they both knew, was in being unable to break the spiral. It was as if they were in a dumping air current, neither willing or able to search out the rising thermal they needed to send them soaring back to the heights. The rabbit row was only the latest in a succession of disputes. But, somehow encompassing all the differences between them, it had mushroomed to become the most bitter and long-standing yet.

'You're more interested in rabbits than in me,' Ula had remarked dolefully the previous evening and Owl had dragged things down further by not denying it.

Now, out in the great wide open, he could forget all that. The sky gave him not only freedom but the overview – the capacity to look down on Old Wood, his familiar home and his whole world. The sight of it always made his heart lift, for it was the one he loved and lived for more than any other. Why couldn't Ula share his enthusiasm? he thought. Why couldn't she see further than the end of her own beak and join him in wondering at the myriad marvels all around them?

Then, his jangling nerves soothed by the silence below him, he began to relax. Nothing appeared to be moving below. He listened, but it was one of those moments when the wood was so quiet you would think nobody lived there. Soon, though, it would erupt with so many pursuits and gurgling death throes that you seemed to hear nothing but chomping jaws and beaks. It all depended on your attitude: you saw the wood either as a haven of beauty and tranquillity, or as a place of continuous and violent death.

Ula's opinion was forthright.

'This wood exists for killers, especially top predators like us. We're the only ones who count. The others are just here to be eaten.'

She was right in that there was always a lot of eating going on, Owl mused. He gave a series of short pushes with his stubby wings and launched on a long, noiseless glide. Especially at night, the leaf litter became a hive of foraging creatures, each with the objective of finding a meal, while at the same time avoiding becoming one. He recalled Ula once stating so vividly how all they were doing was prolonging the inevitable.

'I'm fed up with all this rabbit stuff about what a wonderful wood we live in!' she had screeched, losing her temper. 'It's not wonderful – it's extremely nasty! Can't you see, you pillock, that there are a thousand ways to die, most of them horrible? If you don't depart prematurely – if you aren't hunted, chased, swooped on, lured, trapped, buried alive, crushed, stamped on, smashed against a rock, dropped from a great height – if you're not gobbled up, crunched up, slurped up, swallowed wholesale, pecked to death, sucked dry – if you don't get your brains bashed in, your throat ripped out, if you aren't torn to pieces, if parasites don't destroy your guts, insects methodically dissect you, if you don't get diseased, if you don't starve, if you don't drown or die of thirst, if you aren't fried by heat, frozen by cold or blown away by the wind – that is, if you actually expire naturally, it's always the same. Even dead you're food for all manner of scavengers from crows to beetles, until your corpse teems with maggots and you finally go to the worms!

'Don't give me any pellets about a haven of beauty and tranquillity! Only Concerned Guardian veggies think that. And what do they know about the wood? Come to think of it, what do they know about anything?

'Why mess your life up with manky herbivores, Ollie?' she had concluded somewhat sadly. 'Why not enjoy being a proper predator?'

Owl had been impressed. It was the longest speech he had ever heard her make and she had never been so lucid since. He had also understood what she was getting at. The rabbits, who lived in vast numbers in the wood and the outlying fields, had been responsible for the formation of the Concerned Woodland Guardians. Under this umbrella they had gathered a disparate collection of grazers, nibblers, and plant and seed-eaters, along with various omnivores, who they constantly prevailed upon to stay on the herbivore side of the fence. No-one doubted they were well-meaning and hugely sincere, but Ula had a point when she asked where that got you in life? All the rabbits were actually known to do was hold meetings. Ula's 'proper predator' remark had still stung, though. Owl was a proper predator! He killed with as much ruthless efficiency and necessary lack of compassion as she did. After all, you couldn't start feeling sorry for your food. But in his eyes that didn't stop him being interested in rabbits as well.

Giving another push with his wings, he looked down on the darkening wood. The storm had blown away the haze of damp to leave the air bracing and crystal-sharp. The spreads of the bare branches, interspersed with patches of grass in the clearings, were assuming that deep shade of grey which was one of his all-time favourites. By now, calmed down, he was back to feeling sorry for Ula. Whatever she said about tranquillity, couldn't she see the beauty? It was his love affair with the wood, and all the natural elements that made it up, that gave Owl his reason for living. He'd never lose it, whatever Ula-style trials afflicted him.

Having worked it out of his system, he slowed as he reached the end of the Ridge beat and with a deft flick of his wings turned for the reverse fly. The rosy glow in the sky was deepening to purple, and he could feel the chill permeating the air. While he was sleeping he had unconsciously felt the warmth of the sun. But the wood was still in the grip of the Big Cold and with the gale blown out tonight the sky would be clear. Bright stars and a big moon would illuminate the hard frost, that would gradually coat the ground in glittering white. The wood would be utterly still and even more beautiful. He was looking forward to it.

Approaching him now was the untidy rook convoy, returning from its normal hard day of drudgery. The highly sociable rooks were considered a steady element in the wood. Despite their raucous ways they were methodical workers, rising early to set off as a flock for the outlying fields, where they stayed all day searching for the grubs, leatherjackets and worms they required for their daily food intake.

As Owl hoped, Raka peeled off.

'Hi, Ollie,' she cried cheerfully. 'How's the rabbit business?'

Owl didn't reply, but she wasn't deterred.

'Don't tell me – Ula's been on at you again,' she cawed. 'You can't really blame her, Ollie. Why don't you drop the silly buggers? Never mind you – don't you realise that you're only getting her more and more wound up?'

'Why should I, Raka?' Owl flared back. He knew that while the rook and he regarded themselves as friends, she and Ula still chatted. There were times when he wondered whose side she was on.

'You're as bad as she is,' he said as they flew along side by side. 'It's not a female's job to dictate who a male can and can't talk to.'

'Maybe, Ollie. But what other predator talks to rabbits? What other carnivore, even?'

Like Owl, Raka ate living creatures. But she wasn't strictly speaking a predator. You could hardly classify the juicy, but moronic, worms she dug out of the fields as proper prey that required serious hunting.

'They've invited us rooks to the meetings a thousand times,' she went on. 'But how many of have ever gone? None, that's the answer. The dunnocks are the only birds who are really keen. And who wants to be like a dunnock?'

Owl's feathers bristled. Any suggestion of being called a dunnock was almost as bad as a pillock. He held these dreary little hedge sparrows in deep contempt for their timidity and the way they flew around the wood in drab flocks, before creeping diffidently about on the ground searching out their miserable diet. Yet they had found their *métier* in being what he regarded as the rabbits' stooges. As a result they had now assumed a hugely exaggerated sense of their own importance, which made them more annoying. Yet Owl still felt an irrational need to defend rabbits, if not dunnocks.

'There are lots of other birds who go along, Raka — wrens, goldfinches, skylarks, all kinds of tits—'

'Exactly,' Raka interjected coarsely.

'—and earth carnivores as well,' Owl carried on, ignoring the crude interruption. 'Mole's always there, and he eats nothing but worms. The frogs and toads are regulars, the eels slither along sometimes, the rats have attended. Then there are the shrews. Now, they're fierce carnivores!'

'Yes, but they're not serious creatures, Ollie,' Raka interrupted. 'Not like you and Ula, or the weasels and stoats, or Freddie or Boris — or the buzzards.'

'The buzzards don't go to anything,' Owl said grumpily. Had Raka forgotten he had inadvertently rescued her from almost certain death at the talons of one? he thought. He had been concentrating so hard on dropping on a vole he had failed to spot the pair locked in mortal struggle nearby. His unexpected appearance had so startled the buzzard that it had momentarily released its hold and Raka had wriggled free. It was when she had come to thank him later that he had discovered she was no ordinary rook.

'I was a brancher, shoved out when the nest got overcrowded,' she explained. 'My parents still fed me, but in the end I lost my hold and fell to the ground. I survived by feeding on the corpses of other branchers and was lucky enough not to be picked off by a predator before I could manage to fly.

'I'm the only brancher known to have survived and I seem to have been lucky ever since – like you rescuing me just now. I feel so fortunate to be here, I've got a different outlook from other rooks. I'm interested in everything, if you know what I mean.'

'I know exactly what you mean,' Owl had replied excitedly. He had been cultivating Freddie and Boris to widen his horizons. But a fellow bird he could talk to would be even better. He had confided in Raka about his mating troubles and found her sympathetic, as well as useful in pointing out the female point of view. Although he had long since given up on that front they had stayed friends – until this evening, when he was thinking they were in serious danger of falling out.

'Raka, I thought we had agreed we were both curious about everything?' he said. 'Well, if the rabbits keep coming to see me they must have got hold of something. Don't you want me to find out what it is?'

'No,' Raka cawed. 'They're just chatterers, Ollie, they've got nothing to say. But why don't you go ahead and see them anyhow to get them out of your system? I'm as sick of hearing about them as Ula. You know what, Ollie? They're turning you into a bore!'

She swerved as Owl veered towards her, trying to peck at her wing.

'A bore now, am I?' he shouted. 'Well, there's nothing more boring than your humdrum life, Raka. At least rabbits think, instead of spending their whole time working like you. So I will go and see them, as you suggest. And when I do find out something you'll be the last to hear about it.'

Raka already knew she had gone too far. But she no longer cared. It was time Owl was told.

'Ula told me the real reason you listen to them. It's because they tell you how wonderful you are. You're not just a bore, Ollie, you're a vain bore to boot.'

Owl lunged again with his beak, but despite her black bulk she was surprisingly quick and easily evaded him.

'Enjoy your meeting,' she taunted, dropping down towards the clump of elms that housed the rookery. 'Hope they give you some nice grass to eat.'

Beating his wings hard, Owl made off towards the outlying fields. A vain bore, was he? Well, in that case he'd get up especially early tomorrow to make the rabbit meet. Raka was right. At least that would end it – one way or the other.

9

Hot Spurts

Mega ran and crouched over the latrine pit, feeling terminal disgust at the watery stuff splashing out of his bowels. The Keeper had changed their food once again, and now they all had the runs. The pit area was crammed with miserable figures, huddling forlornly. A youngster who had earlier lost control in the exercise area had been torn off such a terrible strip none of them were daring to move in case they were caught short in a similar manner.

Shutting them out of his consciousness, Mega stayed where he was and gave in to the thoughts rushing through his head. He had made a point of staying away from Mata in the aftermath of the bird incident, feeling strangely shy after that seminal moment when they had been tearing at the still-living bird. What had passed between them had been so deep he needed time to let it sink in. It wasn't just Mata. His whole world had been turned upside down by a combination of the bird incident, Custard's visit and Gabbla's indoctrination. He still found the latter oddly unconvincing, even though all the youngsters had unexpectedly been put through it a second time. There was no logic in his mind that he could point to, just a burning feeling that he and

Mata were right. The Elders' tame version of cage life simply didn't ring true. When Sheba had told him to forget them and get on with enjoying himself, he now realised, he had done just that. He had been determined to remain cheerful and outgoing, despite the way he was treated by the older mink and the ban they put on his fellows associating with him. What point was there in doing otherwise?

The early bullying days were long gone, and he had forgiven and forgotten. Sheba had given him a grounding in how to fight, but in what he regarded as a somewhat female way – through out-thinking his opponents and anticipating their moves, then using their own weight against them. Meanwhile, like his other fellows, he had revelled in exploring his rapidly developing physical power. As he entered the serious business of establishing his place in the generational hierarchy, he had been happily resigned to taking up whatever position events had cast for him. Of course he had fought to win – who would do otherwise? But on occasions he had wondered whether Sheba was pushing him too hard with the 'being different' business and what was coming 'in the fullness of time'. Was it her ambition that was driving him, so she could live out her own life vicariously? He would love her no less if that was the case, but above all he wanted to be himself and do what was right for him.

Then, as he had won one ritualised challenge after another, he had begun to realise that he was destined for the top, whatever his mother's desires or wishes. The knowledge had introduced a feeling of satisfaction, but not in a crowing way. Power, he soon saw from watching those below him who nevertheless lorded it over their inferiors, could be an ugly thing. If abused, he felt, it was demeaning – look at the Elders and the way everyone was expected to kow-tow to them. He approved more of those who recognised it implicitly and did not continuously flaunt it. On a few occasions he had even allowed his emotions to dictate his moving in, unasked, to aid some unfortunate who was being victimised. It wasn't something he did every day, but it gave him a satisfaction he could never gain from the crude manifestations of brute strength that were all so many of his fellows seemed capable of.

But what was he to do now, poised on the cusp as he was? Not on the cusp of the latrine, he thought wryly to himself, but the cusp of his life. It was the bird incident that had finished everything previous by filling him with such a rush of new feelings. The chaos, the confusion, the flapping, the squawking – those had fast receded, just like moon madness. But what had stayed imprinted on his mind was the moment he had sunk his teeth into that jerking body and felt the hot blood spurting to hit the roof of his mouth. In his mind's eye he could still see Mata grinning madly at him with her red staining her white bib. She must have felt it too and, like him, known it was much more real than anything they had yet experienced. It had felt the essence of being a mink.

So was he to block out these new feelings, try to forget them as the Elders demanded? So far he had lived his own life, yet overshadowing it had always been Sheba's 'fullness of time when all would be revealed'. Whatever she was going to impart, he knew instinctively that afterwards his life would never be the same. His own way would be submerged by being put on a particular track, whether he liked it or not. He would have to bow to something outside himself, surrender his identity, in a way sacrifice himself by losing control. Yet the birds had already caused him to do that. He could never suppress the glimpse of a different life they had given him. Reluctant though he might be to end his innocence, he had to know. And if his life then changed irrevocably – along with everybody else's, as Sheba had once let slip – he must accept that.

Anyhow he owed it to himself, not just to the rest, he thought, looking round. What was the alternative? Staying as they were in this filthy spraint-hole? Staying cowed, suppressed, held back? Waiting for feeding time, playing structured rough and tumble, trying, in desperation, to imagine faces on the wall? Crouching here, as he was now, enduring the latest ignominy their so-called 'caring' human Keeper had inflicted on them? The stench! He winced as the mink crammed next to him suddenly erupted and he felt the watery splashes spattering vilely on to his own coat.

Never had so many let go so much in so short a time. It was so bad the Elders had even had temporarily to suspend their privacy rule, with Massam suffering the double humiliation of crouching there alongside his subjects, farting and leaking most odorously of all. Anything had to be better than this, no matter how much they might suffer for it one day, Mega thought conclusively.

Yet the decision led irrevocably to something more painful, which was causing him considerable anguish. Until now he had prided himself on being utterly truthful, as Sheba had always instructed him. Some other young mink, he knew, told lies. But, his mother had warned him, if he tried deceiving others. he would just end up deceiving himself. So what was he to do, when all his instincts told him he should not mention to Sheba that it had been Mata, not himself, who had first raised doubts about the Elders and their teaching? He would have − if not to lie − at least to deceive her by default, which was the last thing he wanted to do. For where would he stop? Would he even be able to stop? Would he end up deceiving himself? Maybe, yet to gain the knowledge it was he who had to move, not she. By simply asking in a deceptive way he would already have surrendered control, putting himself on the new track. It was not for him to say where it would lead.

Suddenly there was angry chittering, followed by screams. He whipped round as fast as he dared to in the slippery slime to see a fight had broken out between two females on the far side of the pit. As they grappled with each other, they teetered on the edge. Then, slowly and irrevocably, they toppled, locked together, into the sea of spraint. There was a deep plop, followed by frantic splashing as they thrashed about, while the scummy surface heaved and lurched in parallel with his own stomach. This had to be the end! Even Massam was looking appalled as he stood as helpless alongside all the others. They all knew the two females could get themselves out all right. But who could ever forget the shame, the horror, the sheer degradation of seeing them there, coughing and spluttering, eyes screwed tight shut, while they scrabbled desperately for the edge? These were his fellows and this was their life − unless he did something.

No longer caring whether he was caught short, he ran to find Sheba.

Sheba, noticing how preoccupied her son was, had carefully given him space.

Now, as he backed her up against the wall of the cage, she could sense his new determination.

'Sheba, there's something I must ask you,' he demanded without more ado. 'If the wood that Custard goes to really is the Happy Land, how come she didn't tell us it was full of mink?'

'A very good question, Mega,' she replied, thrilled to the core. This was what she had been waiting for. 'You know the fullness of time I always promised you, Mega, when all would be revealed? Well, that always had to be decided by you, not me. But now it has arrived. So, first, tell me what you already know.'

'I don't know anything, Mum,' Mega protested. 'All I've been thinking is that maybe there isn't a Happy Land after all?'

'So why do the Elders teach us there is, Mega?'

She was not being hard on him, merely feeling her way. How much had he already unravelled for himself?

'It's not fair to ask me that,' her son replied, sounding even more aggrieved. 'It's nothing I can explain. It's just that the whole thing doesn't feel right. The sky falling in thing either. How can we ever know whether that's true? But it was when the birds got in that I really felt different — as though something was being lifted off me — as if I was truly living for the first time.'

He looked at her appealingly.

'Do you know what I mean, Mum?' he asked anxiously.

She smiled happily at him.

'Precisely, Mega. I had that feeling when I was with your father. And it's him you have to thank for what I'm about to reveal to you.

'Come with me.'

He followed her to the little hidey-hole he already knew about behind the end cage but which they had never been to together before.

It was empty.

'Your father, Solomon, had been around, Mega,' she said, settling down and allowing the memories to flood back. 'He had put together a lot of things, which he then passed on to me. And, contrary to the Elders' teaching, what he informed me was that most humans – including our Keeper – are not our friends, but our enemies.'

'What about the Happy Land, Sheba?' Mega asked, frowning.

'There is no Happy Land.'

He looked at her questioningly. This wasn't his mother speaking. It was someone else.

'Why didn't you tell me this before?' he asked in a voice with a new edge of authority.

'You didn't raise it, Mega,' she said rather weakly, while still looking fondly at him.

'I did, but you told me to just go and enjoy myself,' he protested.

Sheba felt a wave of love sweep over her.

'That's true, my son. And wasn't I right to do so?'

'You were, Mum,' he replied, smiling. 'And I'm grateful to you. I got a lot out of it, you know that. Now, though, I feel as though there's something new coming. I don't know what it is, and I'm not altogether sure whether I welcome it. But, if you say so, I'm prepared to accept it.'

Sheba felt as though her heart would burst. Solomon's strength and clear-headedness were running through him as if they were the blood in his veins!

'May I please ask you something else, Mum?' he said politely

She nodded.

'Anything, Mega.'

'At our indoctrination Gabbla asked why the Keeper would look after us if he was our enemy? What could be in it for him? he said. He'd hardly want to eat us. If he was our enemy he'd kill us. Is that right, Mum?'

'Nobody, myself included, could answer that until I met your father.' She replied. 'Your father teased and teased me when I asked him, until in the end he had to tell me: "He does kill us. He kills us for our coats," he said.

'"The Keeper can't eat our coats," I replied – I'm not always that quick on the uptake, Mega.'

She smiled at him lovingly.

Despite the shock of what she had said, he smiled back.

'"He doesn't want to eat them, silly," Solomon then told me. "He wants them for other humans to put on to keep warm."

'Do you see, Mega?'

Mega saw instantly. The humans' clever interchangeable coats! With no fur of their own, what could keep a human warmer than thick mink?

'There is a problem, Mega,' Sheba hurried to warn him. 'Solomon told me it was only theory, a story which did the rounds. He could never prove it. But I believed it instantly, I've never known why.'

'So do I,' Mega replied without further thought.

A lot of things were suddenly going on in his head.

'Then your father asked me: "Does your eldest generation get taken away by your Keeper?,"' Sheba continued. '"Yes," I said. "The Elders say he's taking them to the Happy Land."

'"They might even believe that themselves, though I doubt it," your father replied. "You can never tell, though. Other colonies have the same sort of groups – prefects, seniors, rulers. Different names, same thing.

'"But even if your Elders don't believe in your Happy Land, they'll never say so, and I'll tell you why. What if the mink here had to face the fact that they were really going to be culled? Think about it. With no prospect of escape, they'd be living in misery waiting for the day, wouldn't they? Far happier, surely, to be looking forward to something – like the Happy Land?

'"As for your Elders themselves, of course, meanwhile it keeps them on top."'

Now Mega was struggling. Mata's doubts about the Happy Land had gone no further than scepticism. But Sheba had an entire alternative answer.

She sat waiting for him to raise the next point.

'So there's nothing wrong with bad thoughts?' he asked finally.

'Nothing at all, Mega,' she said, smiling. 'Far from being bad thoughts, my son, they are correct thoughts, true mink thoughts.'

'But what about what Solomon said? Gabbla told us we've no chance of escape, and we haven't, have we?'

Sheba recalled the wave of depression which had always hit the intellectuals' group as it set off round this same old circle.

'That was the real news your father brought, my son,' she said gently. 'One day we are to be freed!'

Mega stared silently back at her. His mind should be racing with this flood of astonishing information. But instead a deep relaxation was suffusing his whole body. Starting somewhere in the small of his back, it was spreading right through him, bringing an inner calmness he had never felt before. Even as his mother spoke he realised he had always known it unconsciously. And as he did so consciously, his whole life was slipping into place.

'I'll try to remember your father's precise words, Mega. I know it's important to you,' Sheba continued, feeling how the balance of power had already transferred. '"Funny things are happening these days," he said. "It started when I arrived at a farm to do my stud duties and found a riot going on. The night before some humans had broken into the shed and cut open half the cages. They would have opened them all, but there was a noise outside and they panicked and ran off.

'"I've heard of so many similar incidents on the grapevine since that I've now no doubt that there are some humans on our side — not in the way your Elders would have you believe, but as true friends, dedicated to freeing us."

'"Why?"' I asked.

'You see, Mega, it was all very well his confirming the Keeper was our enemy. I'd always suspected that was the case. But that the truth was somewhere in between — that there were humans both for and against us — was something I'd never even considered. The trouble was that your father couldn't really explain it, or not in a way that made any sense to me. All he could say was that humans are complicated creatures, who don't always see eye to eye.

'What had confirmed it for him more than anything had been seeing how furious the Keeper was later about the liberators. Your father was convinced he would have killed them if he'd had the chance. And they must have been frightened of him, otherwise they wouldn't have run off as they did.

'"As I see it, the problem now is with us mink," your father then told me. "When our new human friends free colonies they're not prepared. They just can't cope. In this case a few got away by accident, but the rest simply milled about and were soon recaptured. Some didn't step outside their cages, others stopped at the shed door. A few even came back because it was feeding time!"

'Your father laughed about that, Mega.'

Then she stopped as she saw him staring at her intently with his piercing black eyes. He already knows, she thought with a gasp, he already knows!

She hurried to end her story.

'This is what Solomon told me, Mega: "What every colony now needs is a strong leader. Not a committee like your Elders, but someone to convince them freedom really is coming and then spearhead a successful breakout."

'My dear son, as you may have guessed, that mink is you. That is why you were an only one. That is why you have always been different. That is why you always will be. For that is your destiny – to lead the way.'

Mega did know it. He had always known it, he realised. It was his place in the hierarchy. Not just the physical hierarchy – it went way beyond that. How far he did not know, but whatever, it made no difference. He must accept it.

Her heart in her mouth, Sheba watched him frown with concentration. It was no good his just taking it in intellectually, she thought anxiously. He had to feel it.

Then, to her great joy, he got up and began striding imperiously up and down the little hidden patch.

'Mother, this oppression can go on no longer,' he pronounced.

Sheba was transfixed. She had never seen her son like this before, so commanding, so in control, so utterly sure he was right.

As he wheeled round and came close, black eyes blazing, she felt the extent of his power.

'I accept all that you say, Sheba. I accept that I, Mega, am the chosen one. I accept that I, Mega, shall end the domination of our Elders and our human enemy. I accept too that I, Mega, will then lead the way to freedom.'

Sheba was crying with gratitude and relief as she hugged him. He was accepting the mantle.

'I accept it too, my dear son. I always have. And my only hope is that you will not have to wait too long. For the one thing I cannot tell you is when our human rescuers will open the cages. But, sooner or later, liberation day will come.'

As she held him her thoughts flicked back to the strangeness of the blacked-out moon he had been born under. It was only as it was lifted from her shoulders that she could feel the weight she had been carrying ever since. Had she, therefore, as much as he, been a chosen one? she wondered. Had she too been predestined – cast in the role of enabler to empower him? It was something she would never know. But now her task was over. She could rest content.

Mega looked at her lovingly, then rubbed his nose gently against hers. It was one of the fondest gestures between them and made her heart melt. How could she explain the love that a mother felt for her son – the pride, the sense of achievement, yet the pain of having to let go?

'Together, dear mother, we shall be free,' he said gravely.

Yet she only burst into deep sobs, it was so bittersweet.

For all that her son had listened so intently, and might have understood so clearly, there was one thing he had not yet grasped.

10

Mighty Millipede

The delegation was out in the open, crossing the Ride, when Owl came swooping over the treetops. As everyone stopped dead, Groundsel let out a whimper, while Burdock, out in the lead, felt a mixture of elation and terror. Going to his beech to talk to Owl from the safety of the undergrowth was one thing. But experiencing this huge bird blotting out the sky, curved wings outstretched and cruel talons dangling, was quite another!

'Attention all rabbits, your time is up,' Owl hooted, pleased with his dramatic entrance. He waited for them to laugh. Then, when they remained petrified, he saw he might have overdone it and flew over to settle on a low elder branch inside the trees. As the rabbits slowly came back to life, Burdock hopped nervously across, meanwhile doing some quick calculations. He had always presumed the meeting with Owl would take place near his nest. But after Ula's vociferous objections he was not altogether surprised their target had chosen this neutral ground. The point to be seized was that he had come at all.

'I said it'd turn out all right,' Dandelion whispered delightedly. With the more benign weather she had insisted on coming along and seemed not the least startled by the sudden apparition. But as Burdock introduced the others they all looked deeply unhappy, with Groundsel staring uncomprehendingly, as if he was in terminal shock.

'As you know, mighty Owl, I am Burdock, and this is Groundsel, Campion, Bryony, Bluebell, Vetch, Meadowsweet – and of course my doe, Dandelion.'

'I believe we've met,' Owl said, playing along with the social niceties now he was entirely committed. His attempt to creep away had been foiled by Ula, who had once again stopped him in his tracks as he tiptoed across the nest.

'You're sneaking off to see those bloody rabbits, aren't you?'

That didn't follow, as they both knew. Owl had always been the earlier riser, welcoming what he called his 'quiet time' to gather his thoughts before Ula roused herself. He also habitually left the nest before her, so as to see the wood in daylight, when it was so different from the shadowy black and white half-tones of night. Ula, contending there was no point in owls being out at a time which was so much poorer for hunting, always waited until later. It was just another of the differences between them.

But Owl still saw no point in pretence.

'What if I am?' he inquired sharply in return. 'It's none of your business.'

'It's both our businesses, actually,' she screeched back, instantly incandescent. 'When word gets out it'll be me who has to suffer the shame of everyone saying you've gone mad. But you don't care how much you embarrass me, do you?'

'So good riddance, pillock! At least those bloody bunnies won't be coming here any more.'

Owl, seeing that nothing would be gained by opening his beak, had flown off silently. Ula was wrong. He wasn't going to see the rabbits just to spite her. But at the same time he was not quite clear why he was. It was like hunting – he was searching for something he would only know when he found it. But as he flew the short distance to the Ride, Raka's 'vain bore' remark floated into his mind and suddenly he was very determined the rabbits be made to come up with something.

'We're absolutely delighted to see you, mighty Owl, aren't we, comrades?' Burdock now enthused.

'Indeed we are,' the rest chorused back dutifully, while sounding so worried that they were entirely unconvincing. Owl mischievously flexed a talon and saw Groundsel nearly keel over. Burdock himself was nervous enough. He found it easier to stand his ground, though, because he had always thought he had an element of predator in his make-up. Not actual killing, of course – he would never stoop as low as that – but in having a certain attitude. Why, he had demonstrated it just yesterday with the yellow dog. He had also identified one predator quality as being able to seize opportunities ruthlessly, which was something he was certain he shared. His size might have helped him rise to top of the warren hierarchy, but more crucial had been the way he had wasted no time in turning events to his advantage – as he was about to do now.

The problem with that afternoon's delegation, as Groundsel had already complained at length, was that it clashed with the extraordinary meeting scheduled to discuss the yellow dog invasion. But now Burdock could see how he could put the two elements together. There was an element of risk, certainly. But then chancing his leg was another predator characteristic he had awarded himself.

Making a snap decision, he scrapped his original plan to lead Owl immediately to meet his great-grandfather, the Venerable Buck.

'Mighty Owl, there are many things for us to discuss,' he explained instead. 'But, right now, we're about to hold an extraordinary meeting to discuss the human and his yellow dog. Why not come along? Not that we're telling you to, of course. We'd never presume to do that, would we, comrades?'

The others shook their heads in emphatic denial.

'It would be a wonderful chance for you to see what this is all about,' Burdock said, leaning closer and dropping his voice to a conspiratorial whisper. 'Best of all, you could be in the background, so no-one knew you were there.

'Let me get rid of the others.'

Owl gave him the nod.

'Comrades, Owl in his great wisdom has kindly consented to release you in order that you may attend our all-important meeting,' Burdock then announced to the quivering delegation. 'Would you therefore like to leave now?'

He hardly needed to ask. Led by Groundsel, who had instantly come out of his trance, the delegation scampered off with such indecent haste that Burdock had to wince.

'I hope you don't think they're being rude,' he apologised as the last white rump hurtled out of sight. 'It's just that they can't help feeling slightly apprehensive, being so far from their burrows and in your powerful presence.'

Dandelion, who was the only other rabbit who had stayed, now smiled benignly at him as she belatedly picked up the meeting thread.

'You could be there, seeing but not being seen, just like it must be when you're hunting,' she beamed cheerfully.

Owl took quick stock. His hearing was acute enough for what they were proposing. And Dandelion was right: it would be a good halfway house to see what he was letting himself in for. He also liked the idea of being undercover.

'OK. Let's go,' he said, not thinking about it any more.

Burdock smiled blissfully. Owl had already passed his first test by being obviously curious and interested. But on top of that to give such a demonstration of being a creature who could make his mind up without messing. Wait until the young militants got a blast of this secret weapon!

Abandoning normal convoluted Concerned Guardianspeak, he risked a joke.

'The meeting's in the Big Clearing as usual. See you — or not see you — there.'

To his disappointment Owl failed to smile back.

Owl chose a convenient cleft in one of the oaks that flanked the Big Clearing. With his silent flight it had been easy to slip noiselessly through the trees without triggering any alarm calls, and he was confident his arrival had not been observed. Half-hidden behind the trunk, he could now see and hear, but not be seen, as Dandelion had suggested.

Although he had heard a lot about CWG meetings, Owl had never actually seen one. Until he met Freddie and Boris and the rabbits had started calling on him, they had been an irrelevance in his life, while his two friends' comments had been scathing.

'Unbelievably dull,' Boris had harumphed. 'The tossers just sit around and chatter, chatter, chatter — procedures, points of order, amendments, objections — on and on until finally they pass some motion — and motion sums up the crap it always is. Then they go back to their burrows thinking they've changed the wood.'

'The pits, I'm afraid, Ollie,' Freddie had added in his more lackadaisical fashion. 'I wouldn't bother if I was you. You shouldn't either, Boris. You'll burst a blood-vessel one day.'

Seeing the badger spluttering with indignation, Owl was inclined to agree. But Boris's problem, as he freely admitted, was that he had become a CWG addict.

'I hate myself for it, Ollie. I wish I'd never heard of the tossers. But they're like having tics — so irritating you can't stop thinking about them. There's always some bloody drama getting me hooked.'

As Boris had previously explained, CWG meetings were always held at the foot of Mighty Oak, the huge old tree standing in the middle of the Big Clearing. This in turn lay at the end of the Ride, the broad avenue running down through the mossy five-barred gate into the Long Field. Not just CWGs, but everyone considered Mighty Oak to be by far the most imposing tree in the wood. Its magnificence didn't spring from being the most beautiful or delicate. Its bole was lumpen and misshapen and its limbs gnarled and twisted, with ugly gaps where branches had snapped under the battering it received in its comparatively isolated position. From his hiding place Owl could see a new raw wound, where another had been broken off by the recent gale. Yet Mighty Oak had been there for so long that its immense sturdiness and gigantic size gave it immense power. For as long as anyone could remember it had been regarded as the wood's symbol.

Peering round its trunk, Owl saw a rabbit now mounting the

remnant of another oak, which had been felled by the humans in the long-distant past and was known as the Stump. This, Freddie had informed him, was sacrosanct in the meetings culture.

'Once a speaker is on it nobody is allowed to interrupt them. And you should hear the result, Ollie! It's bad. Seriously bad!'

'On and on and bloody on,' Boris had spluttered.

As the rabbit on the Stump confirmed this in a monotonous drone, Owl looked around. The meeting was a curious collection. There were rabbits and other mild animals like voles and mice, along with various timid birds including, he saw with a sudden stab of hatred, droves of dunnocks. Oddly enough, though, there were also huge numbers of insects, which he had not expected. What were they doing there?

He soon discovered, as the meeting suddenly erupted in a forest of waving feelers and mandibles.

'What about the worms?' a young doe with a long face shouted angrily. 'Worms' Lib rules, OK?'

A mass of wet wriggling bodies reared up beside her.

'And spiders! Spider Support says end this web of discrimination now!'

As dozens of multiples of eight legs waved in vigorous agreement Owl saw Burdock spring to his feet.

'I must insist you observe due protocol!' Big Arse shouted. 'Please take heed of the fact that your comrade is on the Stump!'

But the militant chorus just kept on swelling.

'Centipede Concern asks: why not centipedes?'

Thousands of legs waved angrily.

'Make way for Mighty Millipede!'

Millions of legs rippled in protest.

Owl felt almost sorry for the way Burdock was being humiliated. The meeting, now out of control, had broken up into a series of furious arguments between different insect factions. As the rabbit on the Stump gave up the unequal struggle and hopped off, Burdock personally mounted it to yell that the meeting was over. But his audience, continuing the noisy disputes, ignored him until they gradually began to drift away, the rabbits towing their charges behind them. As the last pair, still noisily disputing the relative merits of Care for Caterpillars and Leatherjackets Live!, disappeared into the distance Burdock and Dandelion hopped over.

'You see the problem?' Big Arse called up.

Owl's head was splitting. He had been told the meeting was about the human and his yellow dog, not this lowlife nonsense!

'Problem?' he hooted back. 'I see nothing but problems!'

'That's the difficulty we're facing, Ollie. Next I want you to meet my great-grandfather, the Venerable Buck, who has a proposition to put to you. How about tomorrow?'

Owl's worst fears were being realised. But now he had no choice. He was in it up to his neck.

'It had better be an improvement on this shambles,' he replied, glaring down.

'It will be,' Burdock promised curtly. 'By the big burrow, just before sundown.'

'By the big burrow.'

'Mighty Owl, please don't worry about what you've seen today,' Dandelion added softly. 'We guarantee the Venerable Buck will make everything clear to you.'

'He'd better,' Owl replied, staring at the pair of rabbits ominously. So far everything was as clear as fog.

II

Takeaway

Sheba waited a whole day before telling Mega as gently as she could.

'My dear, there is something of great sadness that you must know: I myself am to be taken. I don't know when, but I feel it is coming. And as you know know, it won't be to the Happy Land. We may have only a short time together, so we must use it to prepare you to the utmost.'

'What rubbish you talk sometimes, mother!' Mega exclaimed, aghast. 'The human liberators will have come before then. And even if they haven't I'll save you — you just watch me!'

'You're a wonderful boy, Mega,' she smiled. 'I know you'll do your best. But there are some things we all must accept, my chosen one. You mustn't feel sad or worried about me. My part has been played.'

Mega was shocked by her fatalism. Even if she was right, how could she resign herself so easily?

'You can't just stand by and let it happen, mother. I'll help you. We'll fight. Together we shall overcome, I promise you. Better still, I'll inform everyone — then we'll start a revolution and you'll be saved.'

'No,' Sheba replied firmly, whilst still feeling a surge of pride as she looked at him. Born nine moons ago, he had grown into a magnificent specimen, now in the pride of his youth. His coat had bushed out and its blue tinge lightened, rather than darkening like the brown of his fellows, making him even more distinctive. Physically he was undoubtedly ready. Mentally, though, Sheba was not so sure. She was worried about his self-confident naivety, allied to that youthful male pride.

'You mustn't tell anyone under any circumstances,' she stressed. 'And that includes Mata. I presume she knows nothing about this?'

She gazed at him searchingly, receiving a steady stare in reply.

'Mega, I'm not asking you whether anything's going on, but I want you to keep her out of this. I'm not going to say anything against her, but she's got a strong will, while you've got a job to do.

'You must understand that Solomon's knowledge is for us, and us alone. Now, let's concentrate on how we proceed . . .'

Mega didn't say anything. He had been thinking of telling Mata the latest development, but was now grateful he hadn't succumbed to the temptation. He still felt guilty about deceiving his mother about her in the first place. He was also beginning to understand that he might not yet be ready. The initial surge of power he had felt as Sheba had enabled him was undiminished. But the practical problems were different and he was suddenly not sure what he was supposed to do. It wasn't just that he loved Sheba, he admitted to himself. He still needed her guiding paw.

'I'm sorry if I've done anything to upset you, mum,' he replied dutifully. 'But remember – I'll still save you. I've got to. Freedom wouldn't be the same without you.'

Sheba smiled at him lovingly. Mega might now be enabled, but he was still such a good boy.

But, when the event did arrive, as Sheba had predicted Mega was powerless. The Keeper came into the shed with a group of humans in the middle of the day, when all the mink were dozy and many asleep. The humans looked purposeful as they split up to go to different cages. Sheba was strangely calm as one came towards them.

'It is the time,' was all she said as a bedlam of squealing and chittering broke out all around. Mega watched a struggling mink being pulled out of a cage along the line before his view was blotted out by the human undoing their lock.

'No!' he screamed. 'They will not take you!'

When the front of their cage opened he sank his teeth into the great human hand that reached in for her. But instead of a hot spurt he found the flesh shielded by some hard material that he could not bite through. As he hung on with all his might he was blinded by tears of rage and frustration. Then an unseen hand seized him by the scruff of his neck and hurled him to the back of the cage with such force that he momentarily blacked out. By the time he regained his feet the cage door had banged shut.

Distraught, he hurled himself at the netting to see Sheba being pushed into a sack.

'Mother!' he cried.

'Be ready, my son! Be ready!' He heard her muffled voice. 'The liberators will come!'

Then the heaving sack was carried away.

With his different background Mega felt more grown-up emotionally than his fellows. Apart from Mata, they often seemed childish, while his mother treated him as an equal. By the time she disappeared he felt able to stand on his own four paws and think and act for himself. He still felt as passionate a bond to her, but it was as an adult, rather than a youth, that he mourned her. And although his grief was terrible, it was brief. Instead of collapsing under its weight, his anger hardened into cold determination, while thanks to Sheba's stoicism he did not feel a sense of failure at not preventing her removal. Not just she but Massam, Gabbla, Atara, Mugger and all the other mink of her generation had been taken as well, and with hindsight he could see there was nothing he, or any other mink, could have done.

'The old must always go, my son,' he remembered her saying. 'How else can we make way for the new?'

While he protested feebly that it was unnecessary, she had then given him a strategy and plan to follow.

'You must tell no-one,' she had instructed, filling him in about how the intellectuals' group had got nowhere. 'Then make your first statement boldly, openly and in front of everybody. The time to do that will be at the ceremony to swear in the new Council of Elders. Your task is to sow the seeds of revolution before they settle in, then wait for your true followers to manifest themselves.'

This grand meeting, she had further explained, would be familiar to the mink who had formerly been the middle generation and would now be the top. They had attended one before. But for Mega and his fellow youngsters it would be a first.

'I had no parents I knew of to lose but I can still remember how shocked everyone was,' she explained. 'They were looking to the ceremony to set their minds at rest about the Happy Land.

'But its real purpose, Mega, is to formalise the fresh faces taking over the institutional positions. As the choice is determined by natural hierarchy, I can tell you the new Chief will be Ramses. For all his outward pleasantness, don't underestimate him.'

So that was why the older mink had seemed so friendly, not just to him but all the youngsters, Mega thought. It was another insight into something he was becoming increasingly aware of – how ulterior motives often lay behind the seemingly innocent actions of adults.

'His friendliness is a front,' Sheba confirmed. 'Underneath he's shrewder and tougher than any of them. Yet he won't be expecting a dispute for a moment – providing you've kept quiet. A challenge is unheard of. But if there is to be one it has to be then. It'll be too late afterwards. The die will have been cast, the continuing authority established.'

Mega bore her words in mind as he took up a position at the back of the crowd as far away from Mata as possible. She had already tried to approach him several times in the confusion that had followed the taking of the older mink. Instead he ended up next to Maxi, who smiled deferentially.

The excited babble quietened to a hush as the Elders-To-Be solemnly filed out of Massam's former cage and processed to the end of the exercise area nearest the shed door.

'My fellow mink, it is impossible to grasp the good fortune of our brethren who have been transported to the Happy Land,' Ramses began in his avuncular style. 'You have already had a glimpse of its many wonders from our friend Custard. Please join with me in observing a brief silence during which we think of them, gambolling in their new home without a care.'

As the Elders-To-Be smugly closed their eyes, Mega took a swift peek round and saw the rest of the audience dutifully following suit.

'Did you see them?' Ramses asked, opening his eyes and smiling beatifically. 'I know I did. And what a splendid sight it was! Yes, our brethren have gone before us.

'Now, I can understand that the way the lucky ones were taken away may have looked a bit alarming. It was a bit rough, wasn't it? But we mustn't blame the Keeper for that. How is he, friend though he is, to know we understand and are quite relaxed about it? Not just relaxed, but willing. When it's our turn we'll all be eager to go, won't we? Speaking for myself, I just can't wait.'

Ramses broke off and stiffened as he imagined he heard a distinct snort of disbelief. But when there was only silence he moved on to read the standard banns.

'If any mink present has any questions, or any objection, as to why we here before you should not take over the mantle of the Elders, to keep order and harmony in our great colony, let them speak now, or forever remain silent.'

'I demand to know where my mother has gone!' came a loud cry from the back.

There was a flurry among the Elders-To-Be. They knew that voice.

'Why, you know very well, young Mega. She has gone to the Happy Land with all the others,' Ramses chuckled in attempted mollification. 'That's why we're all here — to rejoice that she, like them, has been so favoured by our wonderful Keeper.'

The other Elders-To-Be nodded in confirmation.

'No, she has not! She has been murdered! And not just my mother! They were all taken to be murdered!'

The audience stirred uneasily.

'Shut up, you young whippersnapper!' an older mink near Mega hissed.

'What do you mean, murdered, you little copulator?'

'Stop causing trouble!'

All the burning resentment of the older mink surfaced as they united against him. It was bad enough even daring to speak. The banns were such a pure formality no-one had ever said a word before. How dare he try to wreck the ceremony like this! Where was his respect for his Elders and betters — never mind their human benefactor?

'Our Keeper is our friend!' came a shout.

Before he first spoke Mega had been so nervous he had been worried Maxi might see his front paws shaking. But now, with his adrenalin pumping, he felt only elation.

'Our Keeper is not our friend, he is our enemy!' he shouted. 'He knows we are wild animals, born to be free. That is why he keeps us in cages, to stop us escaping. Then he takes us away to murder us for our coats. That's what we're here for — to provide interchangeable coats for humans to wear.'

'How dare you!' came more cries.

Ramses and the Elders-To-Be remained silent, allowing the meeting do their work for them. Meanwhile, as the others went on spitting their hatred, Mega was not surprised by the reaction. Sheba had forewarned him.

'It's not just the new Elders who will subscribe to the doctrine,' she had explained. 'The others of their generation are equally locked in by their past. You mustn't blame them. The most ignorant and stupid have swallowed everything and are lost. The brighter ones have more doubts, but they're the ones who won't want to know most of all. You'll be throwing up questions they can't answer, and they'll hate you for it. The only free thinkers will be among your fellow youngsters

– and then only if Gabbla and their parents haven't crushed their spirit.'

Remembering her words, Mega knew better than to push it any further at this stage, and remained silent. Meanwhile, to his gratifcation, Maxi stayed by him, joining him in bushing up his fur and growling loudly as they both defied anyone to have a go. But nobody did and eventually some semblance of order was established before the new Elders were hurriedly sworn in.

Ignoring the boos and hisses, Mega left feeling quietly content, Maxi padding wordlessly beside him. He had achieved what he had planned with Sheba. The new Elders might be official, but at the very moment they had expected to establish their absolute authority everything had been put into reverse. All the unanswered questions were back on the agenda and the shed was buzzing with anger and resentment. He might not be able to prove his case any more than the Elders could theirs. But he was harking back to the bird incident, going in deeper to dig out the mink's true selves – the original bad thoughts the regime was designed to suppress. He had set the ball rolling that would sweep him to power.

But he had no sooner just gone back inside his cage after nodding silent thanks to Maxi than Psycho came bursting in.

'The Elders wish to see you privately,' he squeaked nervously.

12

Bucking the Trend

When Owl flew into the Small Clearing a group of rabbits was waiting by the big burrow. He forgot their names even as Burdock introduced them. Rabbits were all much of a muchness to him, although he did note in passing that they were all called after plants – something which made Boris apopleptic.

'Typical!' he would shout. 'You call yourself after a piece of vegetation, simper over it, and then what do you do – you bloody eat it!'

'Which is why none's called Deadly Nightshade,' Freddie had grinned.

'Or Hemlock,' Owl had added, pleased to be in the swing.

Cow Parsley, Nipplewort, Bindweed and the other plant names were now extremely polite.

'We're so sorry, but due to our principles all we can offer by way of refreshment is nuts or berries,' they smiled. 'Why not try a beech nut, or an acorn? They're both very popular, especially with our friends the squirrels. Or a crab-apple, maybe? You might find the pleasantly dry tang appealing.'

Owl, declining equally politely, then listened as they resumed the eulogy to his wisdom, his gravitas, his bottom, his forceful-ness, his authority . . .

'You're so powerful,' they murmured, overcoming their nerves to touch his feathers shyly, while all the time gazing at him as adoringly as his mother had. 'So strong . . .'

Owl didn't believe all of it. Personally, he sometimes thought he was as dim as the gloom he liked to hunt in. But it was such a virtuoso performance, even by their standards, that he could not help feeling flattered. It was nice to be wanted for a change, even if it was only by rabbits.

Then Burdock abruptly broke in to announce: 'Ollie, be ready to meet the Venerable Buck.'

Before this creature had been mentioned Owl had assumed Big Arse was the head rabbit – inasmuch as they had a head at all. Compared to the others he appeared authoritarian. Apart from his prominent rear end, he stood out visually through the unusual white blaze on his forehead and, coming to wheedle Owl, had always hopped ahead of his fellows, while doing most of the talking. All in all he seemed more dominant – if any rabbit could be said to be dominant. Yet now, out of a nearby hole, came a rabbit whom Owl had never come across before and could see immediately was very, very old. Owl, with three sets of seasons behind him, was in the prime of his life, as were Ula, Raka and Freddie and Boris. In the way the wood worked, that was the main factor giving them their strength and power. Owl had once explained to Raka his fascination with how hard life was at each end of the age spectrum.

'It's funny, isn't it? In your childhood you're at your most vulnerable. Then as you get old you go backwards by weakening again. It's just the same for us top predators. Whatever else Old Wood may be, it's certainly not a retirement home, is it?'

'Indeed it isn't,' Raka had agreed. 'But you don't know how lucky you are, Ollie. For us rooks, and plenty of others, life here is just work, work and more work. And all the time, unlike you, we're in danger of being preyed upon. Take rabbits for example – you've seen to it personally many survive for less than a season. As for voles . . .'

Owl's father had told him much the same.

'You've really nothing to fear, my son, except maybe getting mobbed occasionally. And the humans, of course. They're the real enemy of us all. Stay away from them at all costs. Otherwise concentrate on enjoying your life — and never forget how fortunate you are.'

Yet the rabbit now hobbling towards him had somehow survived all this to become the most ancient creature Owl had seen in his life. The Venerable Buck's face was wizened, his whiskers quite white and the rest of his fur thin and grey. Underneath, his body was a mere bag of bones and as he extended a thin paw in greeting his movements were so slow and deliberate that it was clear his joints had virtually seized up. He was probably in great pain, Owl thought, noticing that beside him there was a ravishing young doe who seemed to be some sort of a nurse.

As the other rabbits gathered round in a reverential circle Owl proffered a talon, which was taken.

'Delighted to make your acquaintance, and first I must thank you for taking the trouble to come here this afternoon. It is most gracious of you. Most gracious . . .'

The Venerable Buck's voice was soft and slow, unlike those of the other chattering rabbits, who had now gone uncharacteristically quiet. Owl, not knowing what to say, remained equally silent. He might have had a multitude of praise showered on him, but no-one had ever called him gracious before. Wait until he told Ula! That was, he had a sudden bitter afterthought, if she had any idea what the word meant.

'Forgive any personal difficulty I may have in talking to you,' the ancient rabbit went on. 'You see, as a vegetarian I am a firm believer in non-violence, while you have it as a way of life.'

He glanced at Owl sharply.

'I have no doubt that, as a predator, with the best will in the world you dismiss us Concerned Woodland Guardians as tosspots.'

Owl started. How could any rabbit possibly know that? The Venerable Buck hadn't got it quite right — Boris called them 'tossers', not 'tosspots'. But Owl wasn't going to raise such a minor quibble. Boris should be here, he suddenly thought. He was so determinedly anti-CWG he had become totally blinkered, but this was in a different league to the meetings staff.

'It's easy enough to criticise us,' the old rabbit went on. 'There are many things about our way of life which can undoubtedly be derided. But the aspect distinguishing us and setting us apart is that we care. We care passionately, even though the wood is in many ways a cruel and painful place, a place, you might say, of continuous violent death, rather than beauty and tranquillity.'

Owl suppressed a surge of excitement. This was precisely his argument with Ula.

'As you will know,' the Venerable Buck continued, fixing him with a rheumy eye, 'there are many here who preach that might is right. They are the killers, who believe that they rule. But it is they who are wrong, not us. It is they who cannot bring themselves to acknowledge that we are all equal, and that each and every one of us has the same right to be here.'

The old rabbit looked up at the sky. Owl, bemused, joined him in gazing at the ruddy flush of another glorious sunset and both became temporarily lost in their individual thoughts. Owl already had an uncomfortable feeling that this old sage's perspective on life was a great deal wiser than his own, despite Burdock and his cronies' talk of gravitas and bottom. But what could he mean by saying everyone was equal? How could they be when Owl was a top predator, while the wood was full of lowlife, from maggots to earwigs? And voles, of course.

'How can a vole possibly be my equal?' he blurted out. 'Why, I eat one every night for breakfast.'

As the Venerable Buck smiled thinly, for the first time Owl felt the different dimension to woodland life he had been unconsciously seeking. He waited on tenterhooks for the answer, but to his disappointment the Venerable Buck did not take up the challenge.

'So beautiful, isn't it?' he remarked instead, returning his gaze to the sunset, now a deep crimson spreading into the eggshell blue. The wind had dropped to nothing and everything was very still. Nearby birds poured out their glorious evensong. 'I appreciate it more each day, you know. Alas, my eyes are fast failing me and I do not know how many more I will see.'

Owl took refuge in murmuring sympathy. A strange hypnotic quality about the old rabbit was forcing him to listen. He looked across to Burdock, sitting in the reverential ring, and received a nod of encouragement. 'Stay with it,' Big Arse seemed to be indicating.

'You wonder how we can all be equal, do you?' the old rabbit said, regarding him sympathetically. 'You imagine you are superior to your breakfast? My friend, you have so much to learn. But first you must unlearn . . .'

Owl squirmed. How could he feel so belittled by a bloody rabbit? It was a good job Boris hadn't come after all. He would have burst that bloodvessel by now.

'Let us move on to something more simple,' the Venerable Buck announced in a firm voice. 'It concerns our meetings, which I already know you and your friends consider to be utter pellets.'

Owl jumped. Pellets was an owl word. He had been given another unsettling glimpse of the incisiveness lying behind that grizzled facade.

'I have to agree that at this precise moment our meetings are extremely pelletty,' the Venerable Buck continued in a friendly fashion. 'Not to mention droppings-like. I believe you have some awareness of our problems?'

Owl nodded, hoping he would not have to explain what he had witnessed from his hidden vantage point behind the trunk. But the Venerable Buck spared him by breaking off to give a wheezing cough.

'The sad truth is that some of our young brethren have lost their way,' he went on, catching his breath while the nurse-doe passed a soothing paw along his brow. 'Some, no doubt, are acting with the best of intentions. But others, I fear, are more mischievous. Despite my belief in non-violence, I'm afraid that we have reached the point at which extreme firmness is required to sort matters out. Unfortunately, as you can see, I myself am too decrepit. In the old days, perhaps . . .'

He gave a self-deprecating chuckle, and as he looked deep into Owl's huge orbs both knew they were signalling mutual respect.

'You, however, are different, which is why I am issuing a direct appeal to you to take charge of the meetings by becoming our Permanent Executive Chaircreature and exercising the authority inherent in that office. This is a practical job, which will be of great service, not just to us but to the whole woodland community.'

The Venerable Buck's voice was now brisk and Owl saw how strong he must have been in his prime.

'If you do accept you will never be aware of the full ramifications of what you do. I also have no doubt that on occasions you will find your tolerance stretched to its limits. For, how can I put it, some of our brethren are easier to deal with than others.' He smiled thinly again. 'But, my friend, whatever tribulations you may have to put up with, I must implore you to exercise patience. For under the present confusion lie great principles and fundamental truths such as, for example, the importance of being equal.

'I will outline these to you on another occasion.'

The Venerable Buck gave a bigger smile, giving Owl a glimpse of teeth worn down to their stumps.

'All of us in the wood must never lose sight of these truths,' he added, suddenly looking grave. 'Particularly now when great change is about to overwhelm us. I can tell you no more, but I smell a great trouble coming – a trouble that will afflict us all equally, putting our principles to their severest test and questioning our essential truths as never before . . .'

The old rabbit faltered, and when he resumed his voice was so faint Owl had to bend to catch it.

'My friend,' he whispered, 'suffice it to say that of all the creatures in the wood, you are my choice. Could you therefore promise me you will accept? It would be such a great comfort . . .'

His eyes glazed and he stopped speaking.

As the nurse-doe struggled to support him Owl could see he would say little more, which would be no bad thing. Owl was suffering information overload. Great trouble coming? Him the choice? What was this?

Yet, without knowing why, or what he was letting himself in for, he had found himself whispering back: 'I accept.'

He looked across to Burdock, who smirked with satisfaction, whilst the Venerable Buck managed to refocus and gave him a look of such gratitude Owl knew he could never forget it.

'I was certain I could count on you,' he gasped. 'It is most gracious of you, most gracious. My great-grandson, Burdock, will now explain the details.

'Meanwhile, farewell – until we meet again.'

With a last effort he held out a paw and shook Owl by the talon before retreating, supported by the ravishing nurse-doe. As Owl watched his withered bottom shakily disappear, he couldn't help thinking that meeting again sounded optimistic.

Then Burdock was by his side.

'Impressive, isn't he, my great-grandfather? I told you he'd make it all clear for you. Now, this is what I've planned for us to do.'

'Stop right there,' Owl said sharply, the Venerable Buck's hypnotic spell already shattered. 'Before we go any further I demand to know more of what this is about.'

'Good idea, Ollie,' Burdock agreed with alacrity. 'Let's have another meeting, this time just me and you together, eh?'

Owl groaned inwardly. Another meeting! But what choice did he have? He had been warned often enough – meetings were what rabbits were all about.

13

Join Us

Mega was still on ground he had charted with Sheba as he walked across the exercise area to attend the Elders' private hearing. She had predicted accurately that this would be their next move, while warning him not to be overcome by his emotions. Right now, though, he felt this particular piece of counselling had been unnecessary. The worst hurdle had been the public ceremony. But even as he had opened his mouth an unexpected detachment had come over him, almost as if he was outside his own body, watching it perform actions over which he had no control. The feeling was still with him as he entered Massam's former cage.

He found the Elders sitting in a tight crescent, Ramses in the middle, and took up position in front of them, nodding politely as he noticed how they had done their best to give him space in the cramped area.

'Welcome, young fellow,' Ramses began in a friendly fashion. 'We just want to have a little chat about the extraordinary things you were saying. You must tell us where you got them from. You see, being so young, you might not appreciate the upset you have caused. But you do realise, don't you, that you were defiling your Elders as well as your Keeper through what you said? Do you really believe we would we stand idly by and allow your former leader, the great Massam, to be murdered? Or Gabbla, after he had worked so indefatigably on behalf of us all? Who do you think we are?'

He shook his distinguished head sorrowfully from side to side.

'The fact of the matter, young mink, is that the Keeper took your mother to the Happy Land, as he will take us all one day. For that is the reward he gives us.'

Mega let the familiar words wash over him. That was how the doctrine worked — the endless repetition, like the drip, drip, drip of water on stone, gradually wearing away minds and wills until they were reshaped to its formula. But he was beyond that now. He had a certainty so deeply ingrained he could never be reprogrammed. He might not yet be physically free, but he had achieved freedom of mind.

'We all have a great deal of respect for your mother,' Ramses was continuing as the other Elders nodded in agreement. 'But she's always had a very fanciful imagination. How can I put it politely — she gets a bit muddled about things. She had a thing called the intelleectuals' group, do you know that? It would meet to talk about freedom and swap tall stories. The old Elders tolerated it as a harmless talking-shop. But has it ever occurred to you that your mother might just have been passing on these stories?'

He smiled sympathetically.

'I'm sure they were jolly good stories — nobody ever accused your mother of being stupid. But I do have to inform you that they were stories just the same.'

Mega crouched defensively. Sheba had told him that as far as she knew the intellectuals' group had never been sussed, and this was therefore his first indication that she had not known everything. But, remembering her preparation, he remained silent.

'They will come to you with honeyed tongues, with blan-dishments, with threats,' she had warned him. 'They will try to blacken my name, put you in fear, put you in doubt. They will make you promises — power, position, privilege. But hold fast, my son, and do not weaken. For you know the truth. And, like all truth, it will prevail.'

Mega's previous emotional detachment was also vanishing, to be replaced by a growing anger that was fortifying him. He hadn't expected to be patronised like this. Just because he was young Ramses was treating him like a little cub and not even taking him seriously. The Elders must think they could deal with him easily behind the scenes.

Mega's instinct was correct. After being caught on the hop by his outburst, the new Elders were now confident they could scotch this adolescent revolt. All youngsters had original bad thoughts, but they grew out of them. Despite Mega's funny colour and undoubted nerve and talent, in the end he was just another young mink. The system would iron him out, just as it had other dissidents in the past.

'Why not settle for the quiet life like everyone else, Mega?' Ramses asked gently. 'Apart from your duty there's an awful lot to be said for it. Let me remind you, young fellow, what our Keeper provides — comfortable cages, shelter from all weathers, good food, a capacious exercise area. We're cleaned out regularly. If we fall ill we're attended to. What more could a mink possibly ask?

'Why not join us, young Mega? Because, you see, there's something special that I'm prepared to inform you of. It's highly irregular at such an early stage, but in the circumstances we have decided it would be best if you knew — you, Mega, have been earmarked as one of your generation destined to become an Elder. I can't make any promises, but you could even become Chief!

'Of course this is highly confidential and must remain a secret between us,' he smiled conspiratorially. 'But now you can see your future position in the colony is assured, why risk throwing it away?'

When Mega still remained silent, Ramses hardened the edge. The Elders had all agreed beforehand that if they couldn't bend him, they'd break him.

'Where's your proof about this coats business?' Ramses

demanded in a loud and threatening voice. 'You don't have any, do you? You and your mother made it all up.'

Ramses had hit on the weak link that Sheba had warned him about.

'Getting it out in the open at the swearing-in ceremony will allow everyone to make up their own minds,' she had explained. 'But because you can never prove it, you'll always be open to ridicule and doubt.'

'You're just out to cause trouble for the sake of it,' Ramses hammered on. 'You're not clever, you know. Any of us could do this sort of thing if we wanted to. It's highly irresponsible and just shows how immature you are. So grow up and take it back!'

When Mega continued to crouch in silent defiance, Ramses tried a new approach.

'Look, even if you're right about the coats — and I'm not saying for a moment that you are — what are we supposed to do, escape?'

'Yes,' Mega replied, speaking for the first time.

Ramses burst into laughter alongside the others. Now this youngster really was being silly!

'How precisely?' he inquired, as his fellow Elders pitched in.

'Eating our way through the wire?'

'Turning ourselves into humans?'

'Becoming birds and flying away?'

'We only have to wait for our human liberators to open the cages,' Mega interrupted.

That shook them.

'What human liberators?' Ramses asked, incredulous, his alarm bells now ringing. Did this stroppy young mink really know something after all?

Along with the other Elders he then listened in astonishment as Mega went through Solomon's information. None of them had appreciated the full extent of the alternative doctrine Sheba had instilled in him, and it was such an appalling mixture of heresy and hope they did not know how to react. If escape was now a real possibility even they might start thinking about it themselves — Happy Land or no Happy Land!

The questioning got fiercer as they demanded more and more detail. But when Mega could offer no proof — just like the coats business — they gave up. It was all so naive. Liberators! Escape! The whole point and central core of the doctrine was that there was absolutely no possibility of escape.

They smiled at each other as they relaxed.

'I'm afraid there are no liberators, young Mega,' Ramses said, shaking his head sorrowfully again. 'I'm sure we'd all love to believe there were, but it's just another of your mother's stories. So grow up, accept it's not so bad in here and that personally you are a very privileged young mink indeed. Be happy with what you've got, eh?'

When it was obvious Mega still wasn't budging, they only had to confer briefly.

'The Council has come to its decision,' Ramses announced, his voice silky with the full authority of his office. 'As you have refuted the doctrine in public, this matter must be resolved in public. We Elders therefore challenge you to a debate. We will argue our case and you yours. The colony as a whole will then decide, with both parties bound by its judgement. You have the right to refuse. But if you do we will announce the fact, thereby discrediting you anyway.

'Meanwhile, you are dismissed.'

PART II

14

Digging the Dirt

Owl was in no mood for messing about as he flew to his head-to-head with Burdock. He had demanded the old quarry up by the Ridge as the venue, reckoning it secluded enough for it to be unlikely they would be disturbed. The last thing he needed was Ula or Raka, or worse still Freddie or Boris, witnessing him asking a rabbit how things worked. Since he had plunged into the CWG morass he had been avoiding his old friends, while Ula, continuing to nag about the much-needed nest repairs, had disdainfully informed him she did not wish to hear a single word. Owl had been thankful for that. The Venerable Buck had somehow lifted a veil, making him feel he was on the verge of something entirely new, but nothing he could yet explain, least of all defend.

Finding Big Arse had not yet arrived, he settled on a convenient rock. The quarry was a reminder of a past invasion by the hated humans, who had crudely hacked out the stone and transported it down the Ride, leaving an ugly horseshoe depression. Misshapen lumps, like the one he was perched on, still lay about at random where they had been carelessly abandoned, while the quarry floor was speckled with sharp slivers. The soil was so thin only a few weedy silver birch had established themselves and the whole place had a desolate air. Most creatures avoided it. Something about it spooked them, especially on moonlit nights, when the depression leered like a sinister, malevolent face while the tree trunks round it glowed eerily white. It had never bothered Owl, though. Shadows were his hunting ground. But it had occurred to him that it might unsettle Burdock and in the current circumstances Owl felt he could use any advantage he could get.

'Hello, mighty Owl,' Burdock cried, panting up. 'Sorry to be a trifle late, but there were problems with the Code of Woodland Practice I'm putting the final touches to. The meeting dragged on rather, I'm afraid. Have you been waiting overlong?'

'Long enough,' Owl replied.'And it would also help if you spoke a language I understood. There's no such thing in my world as "overlong". I've been waiting, and that's enough.'

'I must apologise,' Burdock replied contritely. 'Most rabbits have a different attitude and like things put in a round-about way. However, I will now do my utmost to be pre-cise.'

'Good. So tell me, precisely, what this is all about,' Owl instructed.

He soon wished he hadn't bothered. The only thing he was grateful for was having only one rabbit to focus on. He wasn't sure yet whether he liked Big Arse, but he was at least confirming the first impression that he was a shrewd operator. The rabbit was supposed to be strapped by the group ethic binding all CWGs, yet he had marginalised the others and made himself the only line of communication. But what he was explaining – and not at all precisely – was so madly convoluted Owl's head ached.

'The problem at the meetings, Ollie, is that we've found a fatal flaw in the voting system. Meetings have always been entirely open, with decisions made on the principle of one creature, one vote. This worked very well when they were restricted to creatures like us rabbits, with the intellectual capacity to cast a meaningful vote.

'Unfortunately the new breed of militant youngsters has

turned that system upside down,' Burdock added sadly, looking down at the ground.

Owl was now getting on to familiar ground. These must be what Freddie and Boris called the 'Lapine Loonies', the earnest young rabbits who had roped in various forms of lowlife. Nobody had ever counted the number of different species and sub-species in Old Wood, but there were so many thousand it would have taken for ever. Nothing would be gained by it anyway, as nobody in their right mind had ever considered the lowlife worth talking to. The vast majority of its members were so uninteresting, if not plain weird, and possessed so few brain cells there would be virtually no communication to be had.

'The nonsenses!' Boris had snorted in disgust at the last gathering of the Dead Vole Society. 'Superslug, Frogs for Freedom, Liberated Leaf Cutters, Black Beetle Power, Grasshoppers Are Go! – I was making a list until I couldn't be bothered any more.'

He broke off to scratch vigorously.

'My fleas have been really uppity lately,' he complained.

'That must be Free the Flea at work,' Freddie grinned. 'Probably a splinter group from Free the Louse.'

Owl delved into Boris's fur and pecked a few out.

'I'll free you little bastards all right,' Boris announced, lowering his imposing muzzle and snuffling them all up.

When they had finished laughing Raka chipped in with complex news of Carrion Concern, a rival to Mighty Maggot, which in turn was linked to Bluebottles Are Best, all of which were now enmeshed in a fierce dispute with Dung Beetle Fightback.

'Have you ever heard such droppings?' she asked. The rook colony might have its malcontents, but at least it kept its affairs strictly to rooks.

'All in all the young militants have succeeded in stirring up a hornet's nest,' Burdock now said resignedly. 'In one case literally – High Time for Hornets! is the latest buzz.'

'I saw all this pellets,' Owl interrupted.

He sounded so impatient that Burdock sighed. Trying to

explain it all, away from the steaming hothouse of warren politics, made it sound mad even to him. Being here was much more the edge he enjoyed and other CWGs seemed determined to avoid. How deeply thrilling it was being on his own – in the spooky quarry of all places – with a predator who could swoop on him at any moment. Not quite on his own. Although Owl didn't know it, Dandelion had insisted on coming along as back-up and was out there, poised to rush to the rescue. But there would be little she could do if things went wrong. The least he could expect was a severe mauling. Not that Burdock considered himself in any real danger. He wasn't in the business of putting himself at undue risk.

He did, however, desperately want to impress Owl.

'The young militants are trying to create a "Rainbow Alliance", on the grounds it encompasses creatures of so many colours,' he explained. 'When the voting system was established no-one ever foresaw militants like these bringing their charges along en masse and giving themselves thousands of votes. With outfits like Ant Rule, en masse is exactly that, I can tell you.

'The debates fly straight over their heads, of course – which isn't difficult when you're at their level. But the militants still insist on that fundamental pillar of our democracy, "one creature, one vote".'

Owl would have liked to interrupt to ask what 'democracy' was, but did not want to appear ignorant in front of this know-it-all rabbit. He would ask the Venerable Buck later – if he was still with them.

'Fortunately, what's saved us more venerable Concerned Guardians so far is that the different factions keep falling out,' Burdock continued earnestly. 'But it's nearly as bad because we've been shoved aside, while the meetings have become the focus of all the power struggles.'

Owl shifted on his talons.

'Let me tell you the latest drama – it might amuse you,' Burdock smiled in a superior fashion, changing tack. 'It's about hosts and their parasites. The hosts insist that, as they are totally dependent on them, their parasites must vote the same way as they do. Not so, Parasite Power is now saying. Parasites are individual creatures in their own right and therefore entitled to vote as they wish. And that's causing a real problem, as they usually outnumber their host by hundreds to one.'

He chuckled.

'Funny eh? And now the young militants are hitting an even greater problem through bracketing forms of life which have no concept of being individuals. They don't even know what "me" is — never mind "me having a vote". All in all, it's a can of worms. Of course, you could never say that at a meeeting.' Burdock sighed deeply. 'Worms' Lib would jump straight down your throat.'

Owl hadn't found Parasite Power amusing, but he did raise a smile at the last remark. At least Burdock attempted humour, even if he failed. But there was still no point in pretending Owl could make head nor tail of any of this.

'I thought every creature was equal?' he asked, trying to sound authoritative. 'So what's wrong with each one having a vote?'

Burdock glanced at him so sharply Owl saw he must have put his talon on something.

'Equality is one thing,' the rabbit replied, speaking as though Owl had uttered some vile heresy. 'But in the real wood some creatures, in practice, have to be more equal than others — democracy notwithstanding.'

Burdock broke off as he saw Owl's huge orbs roll. 'Democracy' had tipped him over the edge. Having no time for insects himself, he had been trying to grasp the daymare Burdock was describing by imagining the ones in his nest all telling him what to do at once. The prospect didn't bear thinking about. Then he recalled another thing Boris had said: 'The whole point, Ollie, is that none of the resolutions or motions is designed to come to anything. Just passing them is the object of the whole exercise. Can you see that it's nothing but talk?'

Owl couldn't at the time. Yet he now thought Boris's remark might help him to cut through the fog.

'What difference does it make, when it's all nothing but talk?' he asked.

Burdock promptly glared at him so keenly Owl suddenly glimpsed a whole abyss of subtext that had not yet been explored. It was getting like talking to the Venerable Buck. There was always another layer waiting to be peeled away.

'Why not forget all this and just tell me what you want me to do?' he pleaded, trying to steer on to more familiar ground.

Burdock quickly readjusted his sights. What he had so far told Owl merely scratched the surface of the complex web of CWG politics. If only he could interest him in the multiple nuances and subtleties, it would come alive for him. But as a rabbit he was still feeling his way with predator-talk and maybe Owl was right that they should move on. Predators believed that action spoke louder than words. Anyhow they were here to plan action. Owl could pick up the rest of the background later.

'At the next meeting I will install you as Permanent Executive Chaircreature,' he replied briskly. 'You will then use extreme firmness to end the present situation. What I am going to do is table a "fur or feather" voting qualification. If passed, this will allow only those possessing either to vote, meaning the lowlife will be ruled out.

'I don't want you thinking I'm being elitist,' he added quickly. 'I have to admit the qualification is somewhat arbitrary – for example disqualifying anomalies like the frogs and toads, whom I consider invaluable for their input on behalf of FARF – that's Fish and Allied Riverside Folk, if you didn't know.'

Owl didn't know what 'elitist' was either. FARF was easier. It was just another stupid CWG organisation – like Bugs and Germs For Freedom.

'I wonder what the tossers from BUGGEROFF are up to today?' Boris would ask, harumphing to himself. 'Probably having a meeting with Thrushes and Warblers All Together, I should think!'

'We did consider including creatures which looked flabby on the surface but possessed internal skeletons,' Burdock was still rabbiting on. 'That would have given the frogs and toads a vote. But you can imagine how many fears were expressed that it would open up other determining factors, such as carapaces or shells. Sadly, we had to abandon it.'

Owl watched Burdock's mouth working away, while his eyes shone bright with enthusiasm for his subject matter. He clearly wasn't stupid, but how could any creature in its right mind get excited about the main madness, never mind the trivial detail lying behind it?

'But the really clever part is how we're going to get the motion passed. And that's where you come in,' Burdock was now saying, rubbing his front paws together with such smug glee that Owl squirmed.

But he began to cheer up as Burdock laid out the details of his plan of action. Owl might be baffled about 'equal or more equal' and 'democracy notwithstanding', but one thing was clear — predator power had been awarded the starring role in forthcoming events.

15

Latter-day Lateral

'They've got you, haven't they?'

Mega jumped. Mata had sneaked up on him as he was deeply immersed in thinking almost that − not that the Elders had got him exactly, but they had certainly boxed him in. And he could see no immediate way out. Sheba had failed to anticipate this development.

'You might as well tell me it all. I'm going to find out anyhow,' she added softly.

Mega knew he could not go on avoiding her for ever. She was right as well. Not just she, but everyone, was going to find out soon. The Elders had lost no time in informing the colony of the forthcoming public debate and the cages were buzzing with anticipation. He could see the result already written in the older mink's faces.

If he took Sheba's word though, Mata was manifesting herself as a follower − but with the additional complication that he had deceived his mother over her. Now he wished he had not done so but instead had sought Sheba's opinion. He found Mata the most disturbing, and in some ways the most frightening, mink in the colony. How could he feel so incredibly wary of her, yet so irresistibly drawn to her, both at once?

'You're planning to get us out, aren't you?'

Mega jumped.

'What makes you say that?'

'You would hardly be challenging the Elders otherwise,' Mata smiled. 'You would have crossed over to their side.'

Her voice was soft, but definite.

'I'm with you, Mega, you know that,' she smiled almost lovingly. 'We're always going to be together, come what may. We're a pair. Remember the bird?'

It was etched only too clearly on his memory – as was the feeling he had had that she was going first to subjugate and then to enslave him. His fur tingled as a shiver ran up and down his spine.

'I can only help you, Mega, if you tell me the full story – now.'

Without further thought he led her to the hidey-hole. How had she known that he had reached the stage when he had to confide in somebody, whatever his misgivings?

'It's clever,' Mata mused. 'There's no way you'll win. The older mink won't even be listening and whatever you may say, the Elders will fire back with the sky-falling-in thing. You can't test that by talking about it. Somebody's got to do it. And who's ever going to agree to that?'

Mega listened carefully. Mata had already astonished him by listening calmly as he explained about Solomon, the human liberators and, to a certain extent, his position as the 'chosen' leader – although he had not laid too much stress on that. He had expected her to be beside herself with excitement, yet, asking no questions, she had gone straight into this analysis. She wasn't speaking as a follower, though. She had already assumed equal status.

'They're clever, these males, you've got to give them that,' she added, as if talking to herself. 'But not as clever as a male with the right female by his side. It's time they realised they've shut us out for too long.'

Despite his inbuilt male prejudice, Mega silently agreed. Living with his mother had made him aware how influential the female side of the colony was, however much the arrogant males might think they ran the show.

'But I will admit that it's a particular male – rather than a female – we need to get on board right now,' Mata announced.

'What do you mean?' Mega asked, suddenly on his guard. 'I decide that sort of thing.'

'Do you?' Mata replied, looking fierce. 'And why is that?'

'Because I am the chosen one.'

'The only chosen one?' she asked quizzically. 'Didn't you hear me? We're always going to be together, come what may.'

Before Mega could reply she had shot out of the hidey-hole and was streaking across the exercise area. It was the middle of the day and only a few mink were mooching despondently about. None, as far as he could see, was an Elder, which fitted. They were almost certainly closeted in Ramses' cage, preparing for the showdown. None the less, as he watched Mata ostentatiously dance back out of one of the cages, Mega still thought she was taking an enormous risk – until he saw the method in her apparent madness. She was zig-zagging to disguise her direction, while the few mink who had previously been glancing curiously at her were losing interest, thinking she was just playing a game.

But now Mega was overtaken by fresh alarm. Mata was bringing Psycho with her.

His mind flashed back to the time his mother had singled out the runt as a special companion when they were young cubs.

'Why must I play with that little creep?' he had asked, aggrieved. 'Nobody likes him. He's horrible.'

'I know you don't think he's your sort, Mega,' Sheba had replied patiently. 'But play with him and look after him a bit, just the same. One day, I promise you, you'll find it was worthwhile.'

Mega had grudgingly bowed to parental will. Although he still didn't like him, he had found Psycho, with his sharp brain and even sharper turn of phrase, an entertaining companion on occasions, while in turn he had been pathetically grateful. But then the rumours had started. Psycho had always been notorious for the way he shamelessly sucked up to the Elders and tried to squirm his way into their favour. Word had gone round that in addition he was sneaking on his fellow youngsters and telling tales. There had been no direct evidence, but the mere suspicion had been enough for everyone to stop bullying him and instead make him a virtual outcast. Mega, now with a valid excuse for disobeying his mother, had thankfully joined the boycott.

Didn't Mata know any of this? he now asked himself as she wove across the exercise area, the little runt scrabbling in her wake, before they dived together into the hidey-hole.

'What do you think you're doing?' he hissed.

But Mata just hissed back at him to be quiet as she peeked round the end of the cage to see if they had been followed. Psycho, visibly trembling, just smiled weakly.

'Right, Mega,' Mata announced, drawing her head back. 'Tell him where we are.'

For a second Mega thought of walking out. Mata was no longer even speaking as an equal. She was taking over.

'You do know he's a spy for the Elders, don't you?' he asked her, curling his lip at the quivering figure.

'No, I'm not, honestly,' Psycho interjected in his high-pitched voice. 'I only made everyone think I was to stop them bullying me. I'm with you, Mega. Ask Mata — she believes me.'

'Shut up, you runt,' Mega instructed.

'Well?' he demanded of Mata.

'He's telling the truth, Mega. He is with me. I wouldn't have brought him here otherwise.'

'Told you so,' Psycho squeaked triumphantly, quailing as Mega aimed a cuff at his head.

'That's enough,' Mata said sharply. 'What you've got to accept, Mega, and accept right now, is that you've got to look to the edges for your support. That's how all revolutions start — with the disaffected, the personally twisted, the ones with the biggest grudges. The mainstream only comes on board later, when it's safe.

'You've got a problem and I think Psycho can solve it. I don't care if you don't like him. I don't like him. Nobody likes him. But we need him, and that's the plain fact of the matter.'

Mega looked at her in astonishment. Not only was she lecturing him, but she was discussing Psycho as if he was an inanimate object like a block of wood, a mere tool to be picked up and used. Mega didn't know whether he liked that or not. Psycho might be a nasty mink, but he was a mink just the same, and Mega's chosen destiny was to lead all mink, good and bad.

'Shall I tell you the real truth, Mega?' Mata went on, looking at the little runt with contempt. 'It's not pleasant, I'm afraid.

'Whatever Psycho may say, he did spy for the Elders. But now he's defected because he reckons he stands a better chance with us.'

As Psycho's eyes slid sideways in fear and guilt, Mega suppressed a desire to shudder. The thing he had always most disliked about him was those eyes. They were lighter than the universal jet black of other mink and lacked the same button brightness. Instead they had a curious metallic sheen and went opaque when they caught the light, which made it impossible to see what was going on in his mind. There were those other dislikeable features as well – the bony head, the highly pointed muzzle, the prominent teeth that stuck out when he smiled, as he was doing now in his ingratiating way.

'I've come to help you, Mega, honest,' he pleaded, hopping up and down. 'You see, I've got an idea for you which I know will work. Give me a chance.'

'How much does he know?' Mega asked, ignoring him.

'Not a lot,' Mata replied coolly. 'But enough for him to be the one who approached me.'

'Is that so?' Mega asked before demanding of him: 'What is it then?'

Psycho's eyes flashed.

'Bollocks!' he squeaked, following through with his peculiar habit of cackling for no apparent reason.

Mega shuddered and looked at Mata in outrage. Bollocks? What sort of spraint was that?

'What I mean is bollocks at the meeting, Mega,' Psycho went

on, cackling even more wildly and doing a little jig. 'You see, what you do is let the Elders state their case. Then, when it's your turn, you stand up and say: "Bollocks!" Can you see how clever it is?'

'No,' Mega replied, incredulous.

He liked words and 'bollocks' was undoubtedly the cheekiest in the colony's vocabulary. But where did that get them? Mata must be out of her head risking association with this rubbish!

'Then you switch to "bollo",' Psycho added. 'That's better still.'

'Why is it better?' Mega asked, this time genuinely puzzled.

'Because it's even more catchy,' Psycho cackled.

'Don't wind me up, you little bastard,' Mega growled, now not only angry, but deeply disappointed. This was no answer to anything.

'Hear him out!'

Mata's voice was like a whiplash. Instinctively he obeyed.

'Get on with it, Psycho,' she instructed.

'You know how I've always specialised in lateral thinking, Mega?' Psycho said, suddenly looking nervous. 'Remember, when we were cubs, my explaining how I thought sideways, instead of up and down in lines like other mink?'

Mega groaned inwardly. He had tried and tried to wrap his head round it at the time. Eventually he had given up after confiding in Sheba, who had told him flatly not to bother.

'That's why I want you to be friendly with him,' she had explained. 'It's very clever stuff, Mega, but it's not for you. Your job, as I keep telling you, is to be yourself. Leave it to him.'

Gratefully, Mega had done so ever since.

'Let's look laterally at your problem, Mega,' Psycho continued. 'Tell me, are your fellow mink intellectuals? Are they deep thinkers? Do they essentially preoccupy themselves with serious matters?'

Mega knew the answer to all those questions. On the contrary, the other youngsters were always larking around turning everything into a joke – or 'a good laugh', as they called it.

'They're just a load of cheerful yobs, aren't they?' Psycho

went on, without waiting for a reply. 'Let's face it, their only interests are food, fun and mindless violence – although they don't get much of that in here.

'Look at the life they lead, Mega,' he urged. 'It's so dull and serious it grinds them down to nothing. Although they may not know it, this place is boring the fur off them. They only stay quiet because no-one's ever encouraged them to do otherwise – apart from full-moon nights.'

Mega had now calmed down and was listening. He knew already that Psycho had been compensated for his physical deficiencies by being equipped with a razor-sharp mind, lashes of native cunning and an extraordinary inbuilt deviousness. On top of these he also had his natural snoopiness and previous access to both sides of the fence through his shameful interface with the Elders. All in all, he was probably better equipped than anyone to take the temperature of the community.

'So where does "bollo" fit in, then?' he asked reluctantly.

'We've all heard talk of rebellion, Mega,' Psycho replied eagerly. 'But it's never come to anything because it's always been furtive, resentful and negative. But what if we were to make revolution fun? What if we were to turn it into entertainment? Then the minions would be with us, wouldn't they?

'As things stand, Mega, you're going to lose the debate paws down. But if you were to say "bollo", rather than going on and on like the Elders, you'd turn the whole thing from being a heavy number into just the kind of fun they enjoy.'

'But bollo's not a real answer,' Mega protested. 'It's just stupid crap.'

'Of course it's crap,' replied Psycho, cackling insanely and doing a little jig of excitement. 'But it's not stupid crap, Mega – that's the point. Because it's not a real answer the colony's looking for. You know what the minions like more than anything else . . . ?'

'A good laugh,' Mega mouthed soundlessly to himself.

Maybe Psycho was on to something after all.

16

Hiss Off

Owl was looking forward to his first appearance as Executive Chaircreature when he took up station on a low branch of Mighty Oak. After much deliberation he had decided to use his frightening aggression display to impose the 'extreme firmness' that the Venerable Buck had specified. This consisted of glaring with his huge orbs, while fluffing up his feathers and hissing loudly. Out in the wood it paralysed small creatures with fear.

Burdock's introduction went smoothly, with the Rainbow Alliance rabbits joining in the polite applause. They had turned up in force, along with seething masses of the various lowlife they represented, presuming Owl would continue to enforce the current voting system in their favour. But the meeting had not been in progress long before, despite his best intentions, Owl let himself down. He had sat through some gibberish from Kingcup, a young rabbit representing an idiocy called Aphid Alert, when a female vole ran on to the Stump. Thinking beforehand, Owl had decided the dunnocks were likely to annoy him most. But he had not counted on the long diatribe against his species now launched on behalf of Voles Against

Violence. His annoyance level started rising in parallel with the vociferous slagging off.

'. . . vicious, spiteful, vindictive, malignant, mercilous, brutal, sadistic, callous, bloodthirsty, ruthless, hard-hearted, devoid of all creature feeling, single-mindedly dedicated to our destruction . . .'

It was so outrageous — as well as untrue — that Owl's temper snapped. Without warning he swooped off his perch, hurtled down on the Stump and seized the shrill speaker in his talons. Throwing her in the air, he opened his beak wide and as she tumbled back to earth caught her and swallowed her in one gulp. As her screams were abruptly cut off the meeting froze in aghast silence. The filthy predator had proved true to type! He had violated the overall rule which held the meetings together. 'No creature,' Rule One laid down, 'shall eat any other creature while a meeting is in progress.' Protocol now demanded he be purged. But there was a problem: as Permanent Executive Chaircreature, he also had to determine what was to happen next. All eyes turned on Burdock who, with his close interface with the predator, was most personally responsible.

Meanwhile Owl stood on the Stump feeling rather foolish. He was proud of having caught the vole so neatly, but also had a suspicion that it was not quite the kind of 'extreme firmness' the Venerable Buck would approve of. Having blown it by crossing the line, he was presumably about to be given his flying orders. Yet, without a word, Burdock had flicked his paw, signalling him to go back to his perch and call the next speaker.

Owl responded by zooming upwards and waving a female dunnock on to the Stump, from where she began piping away on behalf of Centipede Concern, while thousands of legs waved in mechanical approval.

As the dunnock's reedy voice floated across the meeting both he and Burdock avoided catching the eyes of the stunned Rainbow Alliance rabbits, who had raised a forest of protesting paws. Instead the young militants had to sit fuming as the dunnock piped on about the deliberations of the working party set up to decide which of their hundred legs centipedes should officially use to vote. This was another piece of nonsense Burdock had drawn Owl's attention to. It had started with accusations by Superslug that centipedes were using all their legs to increase their voting power massively. That had led to a sub-committee to establish a suitable voting method for the slugs themselves, as they were 'electorally disadvantaged' by having no legs at all. Owl had commented that slugs had no brains either, but been ticked off by Burdock, who said that was not 'a politically correct' remark. Owl had added this to 'democracy', 'elitist' and 'notwithstanding' as another future mystery to be solved.

'Our recommendation,' the dunnock now piped, 'is that slugs compress themselves into blocks to indicate "against" (or "no"), and fully elongate themselves to show "for" (or "yes"). While I am on this subject, the sub-committee looking into snails proposes they stick up one horn for "against" (or "no"), and two for "for" (or "yes"). Remaining in their shells will be deemed an abstention.

'Meanwhile, I am sure you will all be delighted to hear that we have now widened our remit from the vexing question of centipedes' legs to the even more multitudinous problem of millipedes.'

As the dunnock stood down to polite applause there was a stampede for the Stump by Rainbow Alliance rabbits. But Owl then raised his talon, stopping them in their tracks, while Burdock quickly quoted an obscure rule that he claimed ruled debate of the vole incident out of order. All eyes turned to the Permanent Executive Chaircreature. When he opened his orbs, hissed faintly and nodded in support of Burdock, the opposition crumbled. It was only then that Owl grasped how staggeringly successful his unintended vole gesture had been. As the meeting got back under way, he began to experiment, finding his merest gesture now froze them all. Finally he got bored and began absent-mindedly scratching his underwing, only to belatedly realise that his grooming was rendering the entire gathering catatonic.

But even Owl's brooding presence was insufficient to quell the storm of protest when Burdock sprang the fur and feather motion. The frogs and toads, now promised a clandestine side deal afterwards, stifled their croaks. The Lapine Loonies, however, orchestrated a mass demonstration and Owl watched in amazement as a mass of feelers, horns, mandibles, legs, wings and claws waved in opposition. For the first time the Alliance had achieved its objective of uniting its various factions. Ladybirds temporarily shelved their feud over the merits of two, seven or ten spots, slugs and snails forgot new voting methods in favour of glistening trails of outrage, while ant columns marched furiously up and down and worms writhed menacingly.

Burdock, wasting no time on a speech, simply ignored all this and moved the motion directly to the vote. Owl waited for the renewed opposition to peak before producing his full glaring, feather-fluffing and hissing anger display, at which the entire meeting went rigid. All, that was, except for Burdock and his supporters. Forewarned, they were braced and ready. Earlier in the day, as part of the Burdock masterplan, they had secretly gathered for Owl to demonstrate his display over and over again, gradually teaching them to overcome their paralysis. Now, as he called for votes in favour, they were the only ones able to move. They stuck up their paws before Owl, continuing to display, immediately called for votes against. In what he thought a neat final touch he added a short, but terrifying, screech. When not a leg, feeler, mandible or claw stirred, he announced the votes against as nil and smoothly rounded the operation off by declaring the motion carried and the meeting closed.

The protests erupted, but it was too late. Those without fur or feathers, equal though their militant representatives might claim them to be, had been banned from the decision-making process for ever.

Owl remained modestly perched on his branch afterwards while he received the congratulations of numerous adoring rabbits. He was pleased with the way he and Burdock had carried it off. Boris – and Raka and Ula – had underestimated the CWGs. In their own devious way Burdock and his supporters could be just as ruthless as any predator. And, as they were now telling him so rapturously, it had been he, Owl, who had made it all happen.

'Magnificent, Ollie,' Burdock enthused, flushed with victory. 'You must see the Venerable Buck again. I know he'll be absolutely delighted.'

17

Singalongabollo

Mega had not finished with Psycho, despite feeling that he might have a point with bollo. He found something ghastly in the runt's familiarity and the way he was acting as though he and Mega were the oldest friends in the world.

'Why are you coming over to my side?' he demanded, thinking how apt Psycho's nickname of 'ratfink' was. With his rodent-like face and thin fur, all he was missing was the scaly tail. 'And what's all this "we" business? There is no "we" here. It's "I" – because I'm the leader. And why should I believe that a creep like you would get out of your comfy bed with the Elders?'

As he spoke he glared at Mata, defying her to intervene.

But she kept quiet, while Psycho, seeming not the slightest offended, replied frankly: 'It's simple enough, Mega. There's no place for me here as things stand. Some Elders help me a bit, but not a lot. Remember the time you rescued me?'

Mega did. And he had to admit that what Psycho was saying was true. The Elders' Council might shape the colony's overall mindset, but it left each mink to fight their corner as best they could.

'It's not my fault I was born like this, Mega,' Psycho went on in a self-pitying whine. 'You wouldn't know, of course, being so strong. But have you ever thought what it's like at the bottom of the pile – the bullying, the cruelty, the jokes, the way you're despised, how, whatever you do, you just can't win?

'You can change things for me, though, Mega. Once I've proved how useful I am to you and you've taken control, you can give me power. And that's what I want. When it comes down to it, you know, we're just like each other – outsiders chasing the same thing.'

Mega felt his fur bristling and saw the ghost of a smile cross Mata's lips. She knew how mightily he would object to the runt bracketing them together. Yet if Mega said anything the little bastard would only come up with some even more clever remark. That was Psycho's trouble – he was too sharp, as he was now demonstrating by loading in the beloved ingredient he called 'spin'.

'I'm not sure how much you really know, Mega. I'm not asking either, although actually I know a fair amount myself. But, as your spindoctor, here comes the spin! With bollo it doesn't matter whether your killing-for-coats thing is right or wrong. I don't have to believe in it – and nor does anyone else. Because all we're setting out to do, remember, is give the minions a good laugh.

'Just listen to this . . .'

He started to sing softly: 'Bollo! Bollo! Bollo! It's all a load of bollo! Bollo! Bollo! Bollo! It's all a load of bollo!

'One thing's for sure,' he added with an eerie cackle. 'That isn't is a load of bollo. Because I absolutely guarantee you, Mega, now you've heard it you won't be able to get it out of your head.'

'Never mind my head, you get yourself out – and now,' Mega hissed disgustedly. He had never heard anything so low-grade.

Psycho looked across at Mata, received a confirmatory nod and scuttled off so hurriedly he didn't even stop to say goodbye.

'How dare you bring him in without asking me?' Mega asked, turning on her furiously.

'At least he's honest in admitting he's only in it for himself,' she fired back. 'And what difference does it make, as long as he's right?'

All the difference in the world, Mega thought bitterly. He was the chosen one, with a fervent and deep-rooted belief in the righteousness of his cause. Mata shouldn't devalue his noble objectives by suggesting he ally himself with such a blatant cynic. Psycho's mind was as twisted as his body. What did he know about beliefs, principles, a mission? He was like all those without power – not even aware there was more to it than merely having it for its own sake.

'What about the way the little bastard calls everyone "the minions"?' he demanded. 'It's immensely degrading and it just shows he has no respect. The worst thing is that he's wrong. It isn't the others' fault that they're so cowed. Once I strip away their passivity they'll emerge as themselves – proud, fierce, independent, like all true mink.'

'It's you who are wrong, Mega, not him,' Mata replied heatedly. 'Whatever we may be like underneath, the way we're living does make minions of us all, especially us females. We haven't got power within the cages, never mind outside. At the end of the day we're no better than Psycho says – obsequious and servile dependants on the system.'

'But what about him saying they're all yobs?' Mega protested. 'They're not yobs, they're mink.'

'But Psycho's right that they're not heavy thinkers, isn't he, Mega?' she came back at him remorselessly. 'And I'm not saying the females are any different either. They like simple pleasures and enjoying themselves, just as much as the males. It's only natural.'

By now Mega was intensely irritated. Mata seemed determined to contradict every point he raised. Yet he also realised that he had never really thought seriously about how to get others on his side. When Sheba had enabled him, the way forward had seemed clear. He had felt a great rush of warmth at the honour of being the one who had been chosen to rescue his fellows. But exactly how was a different matter. He had been so preoccupied by his guilt about deceiving his mother that he had never really thought about having to degrade himself. He shouldn't be messing about with low-grade stuff like 'bollo', surely? He was appealing to higher, not baser, instincts. Wasn't Psycho's way forward a wrong turn from the start? Did he have to sacrifice ideals for expediency?

He shook his head, trying to clear it. He had had quite enough of this for the moment.

'The one thing that's not natural for any mink is to switch sides, as Psycho claims to be doing,' he pronounced in the best parting sally he could manage.

He stomped angrily out of the hidey-hole, not caring if his departure was observed, yet still could not prevent Mata having the last word.

'But that's what we want everyone to do,' she shouted angrily after him.

Although Mega didn't say anything to Mata, as he chewed over Psycho's analysis he came to agree with it more and more. Another aspect, which he also hid from her, gave him even more food for thought. The runt's different angle had caused the first flicker of criticism he had ever felt about Sheba. Had his mother not seen that humour might be his most effective weapon? Probably not, he had to admit to himself. For all that he had loved her so dearly, she had been as intensely serious as any Elder. The idea of making the revolt 'a good laugh' would have horrified her. He was feeling strangely disloyal to her memory as his own gut instinct warmed towards 'bollo'. It was so directly and powerfully appealing he could now see how it could work. He couldn't stop grinning as he thought how devastatingly accurate Psycho was. The Elders' teaching was a load of bollo – there really was nothing else to say about it! And if he liked bollo so much – despite his reservations about the runt – the other youngsters were almost certain to love it. It cut through so much crap, which was what he was here to do. So was Mata right? Was that his role, not trying to impose high and mighty ideals on his fellows, but accepting them as they were, faults and all? The most important question, of course, was the one that neither he, Mata, nor anyone else could answer. Whose side was Psycho on? Was he really giving

Mega the key, or just setting him up on behalf of the Elders to be publicly rubbished?

The real clincher, however, as Psycho had so accurately predicted, was the ridiculously catchy bollo song. It had got so far inside his head he found it impossible to stop singing it, however hard he tried.

On the morning of the public debate, with no alternative in sight, he finally made up his mind. He would go for it. After all, he had nothing to lose.

'Bollo! Bollo! Bollo!' he sang softly to himself in preparation. 'It's all a load of bollo!'

Mega half-listened as, at great length, Ramses trotted out the official doctrine. The young pretender was concentrating his attention on the younger mink in the audience. They were playing about, obviously bored stiff, while their parents frowned and gave them occasional clouts. But even the disapproval seemed half-hearted and many of the older ones were openly yawning. So far lateral Psychothink was proving correct.

Everyone's concentration then snapped back as Ramses finally drew to a close: '. . . this young mink has been arrogant enough to challenge the sacred doctrine that is the cornerstone of our society. So be it. That is his prerogative. Equally though, he must justify himself. We therefore call on him to make his formal rebuttal of our teaching.'

Feeling all eyes on him, Mega rose and walked slowly up to the front. He turned to face his audience and took a deep breath.

'Bollocks!' he said.

Then he sat down.

There were gasps from the Elders and the older mink.

'Could you say that again?' Ramses asked, unable to believe his ears. The Council had spent a great deal of time preparing for the closely argued reply it had been expecting. What was this ridiculous riposte?

Mega stood up again.

'Bollocks!' he repeated as requested.

'Is that all you've got to say?' Ramses asked in a stran-gled voice.

'Yes. Your doctrine is absolute bollocks. There's no other way to describe it.'

Now he had grabbed the meeting's attention. The older mink were looking scandalised. But the first giggles were already coming from members of his generation, who were perking up enormously at the prospect of some fun to liven up the heavy stuff.

'Silence!' Ramses commanded.

'Sssssh!' parents added, rounding crossly on their young.

'I wish to change my previous statement,' Mega suddenly announced. 'Your doctrine isn't bollocks – it's bollo. Complete and utter bollo.'

The Elders looked confused. There were more titters as they broke off to confer. The giggling grew louder, until eventually Ramses emerged from the huddle.

'By the authority vested in us as the Ruling Council,' he addressed Mega, 'we order you either to answer rationally or to be silent.'

Recognising that matters had now become deadly serious, the gathering suddenly went quiet. Meanwhile, despite his outward calm, Mega's heart was pounding. This was moment that would decide it either for or against him!

'Bollo! Bollo! Bollo!' he sang in a cheeky cheerful voice. 'It's all a load of bollo!'

Loud giggles began spreading through the meeting like an infection.

'Bollo! Bollo! Bollo!' Mega sang more loudly in a sudden rush of elation.

It was working. The youngsters, no longer trying to hide their chortling, were openly digging each other in the ribs.

'Silence, all of you!' Ramses bellowed at the top of his voice. 'This is a serious meeting, not a playground!'

Mega saw the youngsters looking slightly chastened. Yet the giggling was continuing.

'Bollo! Bollo! Bollo!' he sang again, this time watching some bold members of the audience mouth the words.

'I said silence, you insubordinate toerags!' Ramses bellowed at them all.

'And I said bollo!' Mega shouted back defiantly. 'Altogether now — Bollo! Bollo! Bollo!'

'Bollo! Bollo! Bollo!' came a gruff, unmusical shout from the back.

It was Maxi.

The other youngsters looked round, grinning more widely as they gained new confidence from this first audience participation. What a good laugh, eh? they chortled. They'd never known Mega was such a joker. Old Ramses looked as though he was going to burst. What a wind-up. It was brilliant!

'Bollo! Bollo! Bollo!' sang Mega.

'Bollo! Bollo! Bollo!' they began singing back happily. 'It's all a load of bollo!'

'As you persist in this childish mindlessness you leave us no choice!' Ramses yelled above the din. 'These proceedings will be abandoned for the moment! You'll be hearing more about this later!'

But the bollo song was out and it was too late to put the lid on it. As the youngsters drifted away, still singing, Ramses and the other Elders had a sinking feeling. They had always stamped on anything that they felt might drive a generational rift through the colony. Yet the inane bollo song left them feeling powerless. Their system was designed to deal with intellecutal questioning. Being so serious themselves, they had no effective weapon with which to counter such a puerile form of revolt. Seething with suppressed fury, they responded by making a fatal error. Shortly after the meeting had been abandoned the mink were called together and informed that the bollo song was henceforth banned by Council decree. In addition all mink were never to allow even the word 'bollo' itself to cross their lips.

But then, to their further dismay, the Elders soon found that the solid ground they had previously been on — the doctrine, the sky-falling-in thing, the continuation of the species, the Keeper being their friend — all had been cut away as the youngsters charged off on the new minor sideshow.

Creeping up on the huddled little groups, the Elders caught snatches of the whispered conversations.

'Why shouldn't we sing it if we want to?' the youngsters were asking each other indignantly.

'Or say bollo if we feel like it?'

'What sort of crime is that?'

'The Elders' ban is a load of bollo, that's what I say!'

As the subversion became more open the spying Elders, to their further seething rage, overheard themselves being described as 'old bollobrains'. Meanwhile sing-song snatches of 'Bollo! Bollo! Bollo!' drifted round the exercise area, with some impertinent youngsters openly but silently mouthing the forbidden word in front of them.

Mega himself kept a low profile as the dissent grew. It was nothing to do with him any more. The younger generation was unilaterally deciding for itself that it wasn't going to give up a good laugh just because of stuffy old farts. More and more youngsters were coming up to him, pleading that he take the bollo ban up on their behalf. Meanwhile the Elders, monitoring the subversion, could see that it was only a matter of time before he made his next move. Their emergency meeting to head off the forthcoming crisis was a stormy affair. They had trapped themselves in a vicious circle, they had to admit. The more high-handed their efforts to stamp out the bollo virus, the more they isolated themselves as old spoilsports. Even they themselves, they further confessed to each other, were becoming contaminated. They couldn't even get the bollo song out of their own heads. Yet, they all agreed, they had laid down their marker and they could not go back.

They discussed Ramses' proposal at length. It would up the stakes, they all agreed, taking them on to much more dangerous ground. But it had always been successful in the past and anyhow, what else could they do? They had to make a pre-emptive strike, they concluded after much agonising. There was no other way.

'We'll freeze him out,' Ramses declared confidently. 'You watch — he'll come round.'

The news was announced to a hushed gathering: 'By command of the Council, from henceforth Mega is declared ostracised. He is now officially a non-creature, never to speak, or to be spoken to, until he has recanted in public.'

Ostracised! the mink whispered to each other in awed dread. That punishment had never been beaten by anybody.

18

Dead Loss

O wl had been responsible for instigating the Dead Vole
Society as an informal forum for generally chewing the
fat about woodland affairs. In complete antithesis to the rigidly
structured meetings of the CWGs, it was organised in the way
meat-eaters liked – which was hardly at all. There were no
rules or formal membership, apart from it being limited to
carnivores and omnivores. And although theoretically open to
females, in practice it had become an all-male club. In line with
this loose approach its irregular gatherings consisted of anyone
who bothered to turn up. But as these were usually held on
the spur of the moment they tended to be sparsely attended.
More often than not there were only the three core members
of Ollie, Freddie and Boris. Other serious predators, like the
weasels and stoats, used to drop in from time to time, along
with the occasional kestrel and sparrow-hawk. But when the
increasing addiction made CWG affairs virtually the sole topic
of conversation they lost interest. Like Ula, their line was that
the only purpose of veggies was to serve as prey.

'Look at how rabbits become hypnotised in your sights,' a
weasel once pointed out with unusual perspicacity. 'They could

run away, but they just freeze and sit there to fulfil their destiny as passive victims. They know their job in life is to be meals on legs.'

Owl, deeply struck by this thought, had tried to get the weasel to take it further. But he had dismissed it as being too obvious to be worth discussing any more.

Orwella the otter dropped in occasionally, filling them in on the latest doings of the amphibious and riverside CWGs. There was a strong contingent there, led by a clutch of coots and enthusiastically subscribed to by bank voles in particular. But the otter lived so far downstream she was not really part of the community, while the highly serious aerial predators in the wood, the pair of buzzards inhabiting the top corner by the Ridge, stayed even more distant, maintaining what they considered correct predator attitude by shunning all social contact.

Owl, bursting with news of his rabbit adventures, was confident his friends would be amazed when he called the Society together after the triumphant fur and feather meeting. There was so much to share – Burdock, the meeting, the vole episode (which Boris might even have observed), but above all the Venerable Buck's prophecy of doom. At first he was encouraged by his audience's reaction as he excitedly started going into detail. But a pair of weasels soon walked out, while Boris shifted into 'don't want to know' mode and Freddie appeared increasingly disinterested. For, unknown to Owl, while he had been taking his step forward into CWGland, his old friends had been taking one back. Boris had indeed crept up to the meeting, but after observing Owl sitting so pompously on his branch had left in disgust, missing the vole incident. When he bumped into Freddie afterwards, they had agreed Ollie was becoming insufferable. Neither now wanted to hear his long-winded version of it all.

'The tossers have become too silly, Ollie,' Boris rudely interrupted. 'I can't be bothered with them any more. Your joining hasn't helped. Neither of us has ever wanted to get any closer than watching from a distance.'

Seeing Owl looking crestfallen, he added: 'I'm sorry, Ollie, but I've got a lot on at home. You've no idea how complicated family life can get.'

Although Boris usually prided himself on calling a sett a sett, for once he was holding back his private opinion that Owl was becoming obsessed and had invented domestic difficulties to let his old friend down lightly. He had discussed it beforehand with Freddie as a friend who went back a long way. Before establishing his own den, Freddie had once even shared Boris's sett. As earth creatures, they had agreed, they had more in common with each other than with their winged friend, with his aerial perspective. They also had a strong bond in centring their lives round their loving families, which they regarded as private and did not bring into their relationship with Ollie, or anyone else. But it did give them the same strong base and relaxed attitude – although Boris was more vulnerable. He could be easily upset by anything that changed his routine and if he was ever roused his anger could be fearful.

They both liked Owl and still regarded him as their friend, they had agreed, while recognising he did not share their approach to life. Trying to be sympathetic, they had decided his problem might be Ula, whom they avoided whenever possible. None the less they could see her point. If they had to criticise their friend it would be for being far too serious and allowing himself to get too wound up. And there was another element in his make-up which they felt was very pertinent to the current situation.

'You seem to have really enjoyed being in charge, Ollie,' Freddie now gently ribbed him.

'Not that much,' Owl protested. 'I'm not just in this for myself, you know. There's the whole wood to consider. Because I've been given some very important news, which everyone needs to know. Something very serious is about to happen. Big trouble is coming.'

'Says who?' asked Boris.

Owl chronicled the Venerable Buck's prophecy of doom.

'Very CWG, Ollie,' Boris interjected. 'Don't you know that rabbits are always expecting terrible things to happen? I've never seen this geezer you're talking about, but he sounds like any old tosser.'

'Freddie, how many times have they predicted some problem's

going to mean the end of the wood as we know it.' He shook his great stripey head angrily. 'That it's the greatest crisis we've ever faced? That if something isn't done immediately there'll be disaster?'

'Quite a few, to put it mildly,' Freddie nodded in support.

'And what always happens to their end of the wood scenario?' Boris further demanded. 'Bugger all happens, Ollie, that's what. It just goes away, then they start banging on about some new one. Big trouble coming now, is it, eh? Well, that's what you get for talking to some geriatric grandad with half his marbles missing.'

It was a long speech for Boris and made Owl sigh. He had not been expecting such scathing sarcasm. The badger was right – the CWGs were always predicting doom of some sort. But this time, Owl was utterly convinced, it was different. How could he explain to his sceptical friends that he felt the Venerable Buck was on a different plane, in touch with elements they were only dimly aware of?

'What do you think?' he appealed to Freddie despairingly.

But he already expected little response; Freddie was so renowned for his laid-back approach. For all that many creatures regarded him as slinky and cunning, Ollie still warmed to him. He could be absolutely charming, especially when his gorgeous red fur was glowing and he was looking his best. But although Owl admired Freddie's intelligence, he knew he wasn't in the business of getting involved in anything. For him the main attraction of the Dead Vole Society was keeping up to date. Freddie might be the best-informed creature in the wood, but he only achieved that distinction by keeping his distance. He was the supreme opportunist, always sniffing round for the best scenario for himself, while keeping all his options open. Owl always felt he couldn't trust him further than he could throw him which, considering his size, would be no distance at all.

'I can hear it now, Ollie,' the fox replied, yawning. 'What are they always saying, Boris? "On the one paw this could be the end of the wood as we know it . . ."'

'But then on the other paw . . .,' Boris weighed in, wringing his powerful front diggers in mock anxiety. 'You'd better start practising, Ollie. "On the one talon . . ."'

'But what if the Venerable Buck's right?' Owl broke in. 'Can't you accept that I know somehow that this isn't a joke?'

'I haven't picked up anything myself,' Boris replied dismissively. 'Maybe it's just too deep for me, old chap,' he added, still trying to be kind. 'We badgers are only simple folk, after all.'

That wasn't true, Owl knew well. Boris's senses were acute enough and normally he prided himself on missing little.

'This Venerable Buck character will only mean big trouble for rabbits, even if he's right,' Freddie remarked. 'Myxomatosis, I shouldn't wonder. If it's anything else I'll eat my brush.'

'We don't want to spoil things, Ollie,' Boris said gently. 'But as you've so involved it might be best if we gave up meeting for a while.'

'I agree,' Freddie chipped in. 'Come back when you've got it out of your system, Ollie.'

'You mean we're not even going to meet any more?' Owl asked, appalled. 'Are we falling out so badly?'

'Looks like it, I'm afraid, Ollie,' Freddie replied levelly. 'Sorry and all that, but that's the way it is.'

Owl got an even shorter reception elsewhere.

'Permanent Executive Boastcreature, more like,' Raka snapped. 'You're not interested in rabbits, Ollie, or the wood. You're just on an ego trip. And as far as I'm concerned you're wel-come to it.'

'All I want to know is when you're going to mend that corner of the nest,' Ula contributed. 'This rabbit business has to stop.'

'Well it's not going to,' Owl replied defiantly.

He couldn't just expunge the deep impression the Venerable Buck had made on his thinking. If nobody else wanted to know, it only made it more urgent that he dig deeper himself. After all, flattery or no flattery, ego trip or no ego trip, he was the only creature in the wood possessing wisdom, gravitas, bottom and now, as Permanent Executive Chaircreature, real power.

19

Maximum

'We have to take it up another notch, Mega,' Mata said urgently. 'You may not be losing, but you're not winning either. It's a stalemate — which suits the Elders fine. They know that the longer this goes on, the more chance the whole thing will just peter out.'

Mega, ostracised and isolated, had been ignoring her visual signals for days. But, sensing he needed to speak to her, he had reluctantly agreed to meet. Back surreptitiously in the hidey-hole, she was now badgering him as he had expected. On a personal level, as he had just told her, he preferred to leave things as they were. He had been deriving fierce delight from seeing the Elders' dismay as he failed to crumble under the ostracisation pressure. With all the mink used to such a high degree of social interaction, it was supposed to be the ultimate punishment. All spoken contact with the victim was forbidden, while they in turn were not allowed to speak. Previously this had always been a devastatingly effective sanction. Sooner or later the shame and isolation became intolerable and the victim broke. They then had to make a humiliating repentance in front of the entire colony, before the Elders formally forgave them and welcomed them back into the fold.

By now, though, Mega was confident he could keep up his isolation indefinitely. It was partly because he was used to being the outsider, but he was also buoyed up by smouldering rage at the Elders' cowardice. How dare they ban all contact with him! He'd show them!

Sheba had also helped by preparing him. 'When the crunch comes,' she had predicted, 'it'll be the only way they know to shut you up.'

Being back on ground they had covered together had renewed Mega's sense of loss, while his isolation gave him an opportunity to reflect on how well her departure had been timed. He hated having to think of his mother like this, but he could now see that to be truly himself he had needed to be free of her. Since she was taken he had been unconsciously parting from her thinking, and with hindsight the way she had fired him with Solomon's knowledge seemed impossibly idealistic. Yet at the same time coming to terms with her naivety had made him even more fond of her.

'When you're ostracised you'll have already got the killing-for-coats business out into the open,' she had explained. 'The Elders simply won't be able to deal with it. You see, your strength, Mega, won't just be in being the messenger. You'll be carrying the truth – and like all truth it will prevail!'

It hadn't worked out like that. Psycho's bollo business had skewed things. But that had been Mega's decision, not Sheba's, and he was certain it had been the correct one. Once he began thinking for himself, it hadn't taken him long to comprehend that revolution wasn't a matter of simply telling the truth. Nor was it an exact science, with set rules. You couldn't plan in advance, as Mata was quite rightly underlining. As things stood – contrary to what Sheba had predicted – it was the Elders who had left him with it all to do.

Mata gazed at him sympathetically as he frowned with concentration. She knew what was going through his mind. Admiring the way he was beating his ostracisation on a day-by-day basis, she had decided to risk this clandestine conversation only after closely observing the colony's mindset. She had thought of openly speaking to Mega. But although direct action like that appealed to her, she could see it would be pointless. She would just be ostracised as well. She had also been nursing a slight hope – which Psycho had pooh-poohed – that the youngsters themselves, especially the females, would defy the ban by talking to Mega en masse. His support had increased, if anything, with the females now giggling over how romantic his outlaw status made him. Meanwhile young males had been sidling silently up to him to indicate solidarity and support. But Mata now recognised it was too much to expect them to go any further.

Psycho meanwhile, blinded by his success, had collapsed into hopeless self-congratulation.

'The Elders should hold a debate for or against the bollo song,' he had suggested in a silly, light-hearted way. 'It's so popular that they'd be bound to lose. Then we'd take over. How about that?'

'Do you really think they're stupid enough to risk that?' she had reprimanded him sharply. 'Anyhow, the youngsters may like bollo, but you can't expect them to put themselves on the line for it.'

'You never know your luck,' Psycho had replied, momentarily deflated. But he had soon perked up again. 'It did work brilliantly at the meeting though, didn't it? What a good scam, eh? I bet Mega's delighted.'

'Good for a lightweight,' Mata had replied crushingly. 'And as I've decided to talk to him, I'll ask him what he thinks – which leads me to your next job. Obviously I don't want to be seen with him, so you're going to arrange a diversion.'

'Any idea how, Mata?' he had asked, still grinning in a silly way.

'By picking a fight, pretending to be within an inch of your life, then keeping it going as long as you can,' she had rapped out.

Psycho had swallowed hard.

'You can choose your own opponent. Or else plenty of my female warriors will be happy to take on the job.'

'Don't worry – I'll choose,' Psycho had replied hastily.

Mega now listened with satisfaction to the shrill squeals of pain coming from the other end of the exercise area.

'I told my warriors to weigh in on his side,' Mata grinned. 'But we can't count on him lasting very long so let's get this sorted out quickly. I need your go-ahead to make the next move. In return all I ask is that you stay in sight of as many mink as possible – especially older ones.'

'I'm going to need an alibi, am I?' Mega accused her. 'What exactly for?'

'I'm not going to tell you,' she replied firmly. 'It's vital that you don't know. Just remember, I don't have to risk seeing you like this. In your current situation I can do anything I like.'

That was true, Mega thought. It had been nagging at the back of his mind that his isolation increased the power of his two subordinates. Unlike him, they were free to associate with whomever they wished. Yet he still felt Mata was raising a broader question that he had to resolve.

'Which of us is on top, then?' he asked, deliberately choosing a crude masculine jibe.

He added a lascivious leer, hoping to spark a reaction.

'Neither of us is on top – or underneath either,' Mata replied scathingly. 'We're equals. And what we're talking about is infinitely more serious than just copulating.'

It was the first time sex had been mentioned between them, even obliquely, and Mega was disappointed by her matter-of-fact dismissal of the subject. He was still trying to pin down what exactly it was about Mata that attracted him so strongly. Sex presumably had to come into it somewhere.

On the salient point, however, she was correct. On this occasion he did have no choice.

'So, are you going to give me the go-ahead?' she demanded.

'Yes, Mata,' he replied reluctantly. 'But only on condition that you keep the ratfink out of whatever it is that you're planning.'

Simultaneously they both realised the background squeals were diminishing in volume.

'Agreed,' Mata grinned wickedly. 'Anyway, he won't be fit for much after that!'

Mega burst out laughing. For the moment, at least, he and Mata were still buddies.

Maxi was feeling frustrated as he began his exercise routine. Even after all this time, he still didn't know what to make of the bollo song, which irritated him enormously. He liked to work things out by first making a list in his head of all that he knew. Then he lined up the various facts and marched them in correct military fashion. Each item of knowledge was a step, and each step took him relentlessly towards the logical conclusion he was seeking. But the bollo song had subverted this painstaking process by wheeling his thoughts on to precisely the kind of ground they found most difficult to cover.

He launched into front-leg press-ups, trying to think it through once more. When Mega had first introduced bollo, he had supported him loyally. But he had still had to use his peremptory barking laugh afterwards to cover his lack of comprehension. Maxi had always found any kind of humour difficult, making him the butt of sarcastic remarks and practical jokes ever since he could remember. It had been all right when he had been beside Mega at the swearing-in ceremony. Then his hero had been bravely standing up to state his beliefs. It had been really heavy and Maxi had revelled in his unofficial role of protector. Even then, though, he had not been quite sure what Mega was on about. It had never occurred to him really to question the Elders' official teaching before. Not that he had swallowed it wholesale, of course.

He switched to back-leg press-ups as he continued his sequence of thinking. Why had Mega switched to the stupid bollo song at the public debate? If he had something serious to say, why hadn't he repeated it? Instead he had descended to asinine nonsense. Was he seriously taking on the Elders, or what?

Then, when the ostracisation was put into force, Mega had pushed him away. Eager to please, he had complied. But he had still felt rejected — a feeling compounded when word reached him that the whole bollo business was a Psycho 'scam'. What had he done wrong that Mega should prefer that horrible runt to him? When, for some unknown reason, the little bugger had deliberately picked a fight yesterday it had been a positive pleasure to join in beating him up until – equally unaccountably – he had been rescued by such a snarling gang of females that even Maxi had taken a step backwards.

He wheeled out to start his circuit training. His plan today was forty laps, which he already knew would be more than any other mink in the system. He settled into a steady jog, yet again trying to marshal his jumbled thoughts into a logical line. What did excite him was the way the bollo song had energised the young mink. It had brought them together, which chimed with his own instinct about how suppressed they all were. Mink, Maxi firmly believed, needed more action than dull cage life could possibly provide. Yet now everything was an hold. Mega wouldn't get very far by simply enduring his punishment so stoically. If only he'd do something that would provide the spark – the aggro needed to get things going again. All in all, Maxi had to conclude, his leader had lost his way.

Coming into the long straight, he broke into a bounding sprint, catching up with Mata, who was also plugging round the circuit. As he drew abreast of her she speeded up. He piled on more pace, trying to lose her, but she stayed with him as they tore round the corner.

Grudgingly, he slowed and they jogged along side by side.

'I've got a message from Mega,' she then unexpectedly hissed out of the corner of her mouth.

Maxi's stride broke as he jumped with shock. Mata shouldn't be talking to him like that out in the open. Security must be paramount. Then he saw how shrewd she was. None of the other mink out jogging were Elders. To Maxi's eternal contempt they never took any exercise, which was one of the main reasons they were so disgustingly overweight. In Maxi's book any mink worth their meat kept themselves fit – cage or no cage. One of the things which drew him to Mata, when he didn't usually bother much with females, was the way she kept herself so trim. He looked across and ran his eyes down her body, thinking how attractively lithe and supple she was. She smiled back so invitingly he had to accelerate hard to cover his embarrassment.

As he slowed again she caught up with him. There were no other mink within earshot.

'Mega wants you to eliminate Ramses,' she whispered without moving her lips.

Maxi stumbled again with shock.

'You mean get rid of him?' he hissed back, astonished.

'Yes.'

'How?'

'By killing him, you fool. Any way you want. Just don't botch it – and don't get caught either.'

'Then what?'

'Then nothing. There'll be nothing to do. You'll already have triggered the revolution.'

He would have done as well, Maxi goggled in instant realisation. Now there was the prospect of action, his thoughts were back on line. There was plenty of violence in the cages, with serious wounding on occasions. But it always stopped short of murder. The Elders stressed that was utterly forbidden and all the mink, no matter how fierce their individual feuds, always concurred. They too instinctively recognised that it would cross the line drawn by their Keeper, and fear of his retribution, rather than the Elders', was the most powerful motivator of all. Not that death was entirely unknown inside the cages – a female had once sickened so suddenly she had died before the Keeper could remove her. They had all been to wonder at the body, finding it unsettling and disturbing. Murder – causing death to happen, not just observing it – was something else. But did Maxi like it? He loved it! It would be more than just the spark he had been looking to his leader for. It would be an absolute bombshell!

'Talk about aggro, eh,' he whispered wonderingly.

'Indeed, Maxi,' Mata smiled endearingly. 'You know what Mega's really like underneath.'

Maxi wasn't at all sure that he did. But he still felt enormously cheered. Here was his confirmation that the bollo song had been a temporary aberration, as he had hoped. Mega had found the way again. Furthermore, he was calling on Maxi to be his instrument.

He suddenly had an alarming thought.

'What's Psycho got to do with this?'

'Nothing,' Mata frowned. 'Do you think Mega's stupid?'

'Of course not,' Maxi replied hastily. Yet he still wanted to hear the message directly from his leader's lips, rather than having it passed on by, of all things, a female.

'You're absolutely sure Mega wants me to do it?' he hissed anxiously.

'Absolutely.'

'Can I ask him myself?'

'You know you're not allowed to speak to him under any circumstances,' Mata snapped back.

Recognising an order, Maxi carried on jogging silently.

'Above all, Mega told me, your job is to keep him right out of it,' Mata added gently but firmly. 'That's why he chose you, Maxi, don't you understand? He knows how reliable you are. Like me, he trusts you to just go away and get on with it. We're all counting on you, Maxi. You won't let us down, will you?'

She darted ahead, giving him an eyeful of her pert bottom, before peeling off and leaving him to complete his forty laps alone. To get his mind completely clear he added another ten for good measure until, by the time he puffed to a standstill, he had resolved everything.

Seeking out Mata, he gave her a meaningful confirmatory nod. Then, risking both security and her displeasure, he did the same to Mega. That he did not receive one back from either of them did not surprise him. It was obviously all part of the plan.

20

Passing the Buck

Owl was determined to start his next conversation with the Venerable Buck on his own terms. Even after Boris and Freddie had poured such withering scorn on the 'big trouble' prediction, he had still not changed his mind. Yet he knew that some power about the Venerable Buck had put him under the ancient rabbit's spell. How a rabbit could exercise it, and where it came from, he didn't know. But he had to recognise it was there and now he had to get things straight. If there really was nothing in it, as his friends insisted, he could still pull out.

Owl had got Big Arse to set the meeting up as before – in the Small Clearing during the late afternoon. But this time, he had insisted, it had to be strictly one to one. Burdock, who had seemed most displeased, had extracted the concession that the nurse-doe could attend, but otherwise Owl had remained adamant. Eventually Owl had hoisted the rabbit with his own petard by pointing out the terms were precisely what Burdock himself had wanted for their own meeting together.

When Owl flew in it was grey, dank and clammily cold, as it had been for a couple of days. There were the odd signs of new life – stubby catkins lengthening, a few wild daffodils pushing up through the leaf-litter, little groups of bright snowdrops nodding against the dun background as harbingers of better weather to come. But right now there was no point in pretending it was anything but plain miserable. Owl had even considered whether he should come at all. He felt slightly guilty about dragging the Venerable Buck out in conditions which could only worsen his multiple aches and pains.

As he feathered his wings to land on a convenient log, to his extreme annoyance he spotted Burdock lurking furtively behind a dripping holly bush. Bloody Big Arse had obviously positioned himself to try to earwig on the conversation. But there was no point in making an issue of it at this stage, so Owl shut him out of his mind as the Venerable Buck emerged from the warren and shuffled across the wet grass. He was practically draped round the nurse-doe and looked even more crumpled than ever. If he deteriorated any further, Owl thought to himself, he would need a litter, never mind a nurse.

'Horrible, isn't it?' he hailed him, nodding up at the glowering sky.

'Just another part of the cycle,' the old rabbit smiled gently as the nurse-doe painstakingly deposited him on the wet grass. 'It behoves us all to live through the bad, does it not? For how else can we fully appreciate the good?'

Owl could already feel himself submerging under the power of the uncanny spell. He himself said exactly that to the migratory birds when they enthused about the beauty of Old Wood. Not in those precise words – the VB had a knack of encapsulating key thoughts better than he could – but making the same point. Or at least Owl thought it was the same point. The trouble with all the VB stuff was that it slid around so much in his mind he found it harder to grasp than a talonful of wet guts.

'I feel the same,' he replied excitedly. 'It's all part of what I call the wood's rich pattern.'

'Indeed, indeed,' the Venerable Buck enthused with a friendly smile. 'You will recall my saying last time that I would explain how we are all equal? It sounds to me as if you may be further down the path than I'd expected. Perhaps it won't be so difficult for you to understand after all.'

Owl had never felt less far down a path in his life. Anyway, flightpaths were different from stumbling about on the ground.

'Forgive me, I was forgetting — you fly, don't you?' Owl jumped. The old rabbit was reading his mind again. 'You must tell me what it's like some time. I've always been curious to know more.'

Feeling himself being sucked in, Owl desperately tried to cling to what he had come for.

'You know the big trouble that's coming — is it myxomatosis?' he blurted out.

'You've been talking to your predator friends, haven't you?' the Venerable Buck smiled, seeming not the least perturbed. 'No, it's not that, although I almost wish that it was. Not that I would ever wish such a terrible curse on my fellows — I don't expect to be here myself, you see.

'No, unfortunately the big trouble I smell coming — and I smell it more stongly every day — could mean the end of the wood as we know it. Not just for us rabbits either, but for everyone, including your good self.'

Aided by the scorned 'end of the wood as we know it' phrase, Owl recovered some of his equilibrium.

'You rabbits are always making gloomy predictions,' he misquoted Boris.

'Just crying wolf, you think?' the old sage said ruminatively as he nodded slowly, the loose skin creasing on his sagging neck. 'You may well have a point there. Some of our brethren can be a little — how shall I put it? — hasty.' He smiled wistfully. 'I'll admit that they have raised a few false alarms in the past. But is it not true that in the end, sooner or later, the wolf does come?'

Owl felt stumped. He'd never thought of it like that. If only the Venerable Buck had been at his side when Freddie and Boris were taking him apart.

'My friend, it is most gracious of you to come and visit me again,' the old rabbit suddenly said, briskly seizing the reins of the conversation. 'My great-grandson, Burdock, has informed me of your recent meeting triumph. I am so pleased, not just for him and yourself, but for all of us. Burdock is a good buck and he means well.

'I do fear, however, that he has a tendency to become over-excited about meetings. They are such a minor matter compared to the totality of what we are here for and it's only too easy to become over-involved in them and lose sight of the bigger picture. You, no doubt, will prove invaluable in assisting him to put them into a more accurate perspective.'

Owl noticed the Venerable Buck seemed to have deliberately raised his voice. He twisted his head round to scrutinise the bush Burdock had concealed himself behind and saw what looked distinctly like an ear poking up. It was twitching violently. You sly old bugger, he thought, looking back at the Venerable Buck in renewed admiration. Is there anything you don't know?

He played along by raising his own voice.

'I have made a start with him, but I'm afraid that there's a long way to go,' he said, nodding conspiratorially. 'But then he is only a youth.' Burdock was probably as old as him, he thought as he spoke. 'We all must make allowances, mustn't we? Doubtless he will acquire more wisdom as we go along.'

He swivelled round again. The ear was now vibrating like a leaf in a gale.

'I call him Big Arse, by the way,' he added casually. 'Nothing personal, of course.'

'Physically correct, maybe. But not, I'm afraid, politically correct,' the Venerable Buck smiled. 'These days even I must be careful how I phrase things,' he added, dropping his voice to its normal soft whisper. 'As a predator, of course, you do not feel yourself so bound, which could lead to some interesting repercussions in the future . . .'

He chuckled to himself, while Owl looked blank. 'Politically correct' had suddenly caused him to drop off the map.

'Then there's my great-grandson's Woodland Code and Bill of Creatures' Rights which consume so much of his energy,' the VB continued, raising his voice again. 'While I applaud his efforts, I can't help wondering sometimes precisely whose benefit they are for.'

The VB's voice then became so soft Owl had to lean forward on his log to catch what he was saying.

'His mother spoilt him, you know,' he whispered. 'Gave him everything he asked for. He had so many leaves and sticks to play with no-one knew where to put them all. Yet he always demanded more. Then, with his size and his cleverness, he soon found he could get his own way, not just with her, but with everyone. That's when he got involved with the meetings. But there's still a good creature in there somewhere, I assure you — one of the best.'

Owl couldn't help twisting round again to glance at the bush. The ear was still visibly vibrating.

'Enough of him,' the Venerable Buck said, reverting to his normal tone. 'I'm afraid that in this weather I can't stay out all evening.'

Owl looked at the pretty nurse-doe, who rolled her liquid eyes as if to say he was completely mad to be outside in the first place.

'Let me fill in some background for you as quickly as I can. It isn't that easy to grasp, I'm afraid. Even many rabbits don't fully understand it. And as for your sceptical friends who think us mere tosspots . . .'

Owl jumped again, reminded of how much the VB knew.

He made a feeble attempt at denial.

'No, no,' the Venerable Buck said mildly, raising a self-deprecating paw. 'They are entitled to their viewpoint. I myself have been known to beat the meat, although, unfortunately, mostly when I was younger. This damp weather does nothing for the old tackle, does it, my dear?' he added, smiling at the ravishing nurse-doe.

As she fluttered her long eyelashes and giggled, Owl suddenly wondered how far the full nature of her caring service extended. Probably further than Ula's restricted repertoire and timetable, he thought with new respect for the old rabbit.

'Spring is not yet sprung, yet we are long past the season of mellow fruitfulness,' the Venerable Buck remarked enigmatically, gazing at the curtain of drizzle billowing across the clearing. 'Only the mist remains, I'm afraid. No sunset for any of us tonight. Yet, even so, it has its own beauty. Above all, a certain air of mystery, don't you think?'

Owl did. He often had thoughts like that, but had never found anyone to share them. Imagine discussing the mystery of mist with Boris!

'But I am circling,' the old rabbit said, pulling himself up short and looking directly at Owl with a strangely piercing stare. 'All I ask is that you now listen and, having done so, do your best never to forget . . .'

Then he went through his thesis, breaking off several times to have his brow wiped sympathetically by the ravishing nurse-doe. Owl struggled to keep up as words like 'interdependence', 'Gaia' and 'symbiotic relationships' sprinkled the dissertation. Meanwhile the old rabbit illustrated various points by drawing shaky lines in the mud with a stick held in his arthritic paw. These, he explained, demonstrated the manifold connections between different forms of life.

'Can you see, my friend, how they form a chain binding us all inexorably together?'

By now all Owl could see was a network intricate enough to make any self-respecting spider jealous. But as the stick sketched in yet more detail he slowly began to gather what he was being asked to believe. All the creatures living in the wood, as well as the surrounding fields – in fact everywhere in the world – were somehow interlinked.

'It's all to do with keeping the balance,' the ancient rabbit stressed. 'And to maintain that we all have an equal part to play. Which is why we are all equal. For who is to say that one is more important than another, or plays a greater part in the determination of events? The butterfly's wing, my dear friend. Have you ever considered the consequences that can flow from one stroke of a butterfly's wing . . . ?'

As the Venerable Buck's voice trailed away, Owl had a sudden thought. This stuff was taking away his very identity. A stroke of a butterfly's wing, indeed! What could the consequences of that be, compared to a stroke of a powerful owl's wing? There would be plenty of voles prepared to vouch for that – except that of course they were no longer present to do so. Was this all a load of pellets, then? he wondered yet again. But the old rabbit's power was still there. And even if it was pellets, it was enormously intriguing pellets. He just needed to wrap his head round it a bit more. This food-chain business was beginning to make some sense at last. Now, how did it go? The plants were eaten by the herbivores, the carnivores then ate them — with the omnivores meanwhile eating both — right up to the top of the tree, which was where he was. And the trees themselves started as seedlings and grew to maturity, only to die and rot down to provide succour for their successors springing up from their seeds to replace them. All the time the heat of the sun sucked up moisture, which then formed clouds and fell as rain to create rivers — like the one at the bottom of the wood. This then ran to the Big Water which the migratory birds talked about. There the moisture was sucked up again, only for the wind to blow it on to the land, where it fell as rain once more. The mixture of rain and sun caused the plants to grow, they were eaten by the herbivores, who in turn were eaten by the carnivores, with the omnivores meanwhile eating both . . .

'Everyone, and everything, is playing their part in making up the revolving whole,' the Venerable Buck was now emphasing, shivering while he painfully drew a thick line round the entire spidery network.

The nurse-doe shook her head and stared at Owl accusingly.

'Everything, and everyone, is going round and round the same wheel. Can you see, my friend, how it is all circles? Dust to dust . . .'

More like mud to mud, Owl thought. He would have liked to have asked some questions, but did not dare do so in case he interrupted the fragile flow.

'I fear I may not have made things clear enough for you,' the Venerable Buck said reflectively. 'It is such a long story . . .'

It is indeed, thought Owl. He couldn't remember ever hearing a longer one.

'Let me try and summarise it for you, my friend. This wood is a community, a community composed of millions of different forms of life. Together they form a stable balance. It has always been like that, and always should be. But the big trouble I feel coming will be as a mighty wind, putting our balance in mortal danger. I can tell you no more than this – it will be an invasion, the like of which none of us has ever experienced, which will sweep all before it with a rapacity as yet unknown.

'My friend, I need your strongest reassurances. I am too old and will no longer be here. It will be on my great-grandson, Burdock, that the burden will fall. Without you by his side, all we that Concerned Guardians stand for will be blown away, as if we were mere leaves in the wind that is coming.

'So tell me that you will help us hold fast to that which is good. Promise me you will be our strength, my dear, dear friend.'

The Venerable Buck's body was suddenly racked by a jerking spasm and his head lolled sideways.

'Promise me!' he wheezed urgently as the nurse-doe struggled to hold him upright. 'Promise me! For you are a creature of honour and once having given your pledge, I know I can trust you never to break it.'

Owl felt a stab of pity as he studied the ancient wreck. The Venerable Buck looked as though he was dying in front of him and suddenly Owl wanted very much for him not to go. He glanced upwards to see the curtain of mist had momentarily lifted, revealing the dripping trees on the far side of the clearing as clearly as if they were next to them. It felt like a portent of what was happening in his mind. He had arrived with his head full of doubts sown by Freddie and Boris and had yet to grasp the full detail of the Venerable Buck's explanation of how the wood worked. Yet he didn't need to. Instinctively, he knew, he accepted it all. He had always been in love with the totality of the wood, he realised. Now he had a clearer idea of where he fitted in, every aspect of his life already felt different.

And the Venerable Buck's last remark wasn't mere flattery, as he suspected deep inside that Burdock's eulogies were. Was Big Arse still there, by the way? he wondered. Even more so – two pricked-up ears were now plainly visible behind the dripping holly bush. Owl prided himself on being a creature of honour, and, as such, commitment was something he fully understood. Now he felt irresistibly impelled to make one – not just for the sake of the rabbits but, with his new perspective, for everyone in the wood.

'I promise you that I will be not just Burdock's, but the whole wood's, strength,' he announced slowly and gravely.

'I knew it,' the Venerable Buck whispered back, smiling with relief. 'For I already know you understand all that I explained to you. Now I am certain you will be with us, I can rest in peace.

'So, farewell, my dear friend, farewell . . .'

As the nurse-doe carted the old sage off, Owl's head reeled with the enormity of what he had let himself in for. He sat, dazed, until a sudden thought occurred to him. He stamped his talon on the log in exasperation. He had been so transfixed by the old rabbit's hypnotic spell that he had quite forgotten to ask the meaning of 'democracy' – never mind 'elitist', 'notwithstanding' or the baffling 'politically correct'.

But it was too late now. Ignoring the still-earwigging Burdock, he took off into the mist.

21

Mice or Mink?

The death of Ramses was discovered at dawn, when a regular
Elders' meeting had been scheduled inside his cage. The first
to arrive found his Chief lying quietly on his side in the corner
and, thinking he must be still asleep, was loth to rouse him.
Then, with a sudden chill, he noticed the pool of sticky red.
He crept gingerly forward, saw the yawning gap where the
throat had been and let out a blood-curdling cry of horror.
The other Elders, rushing in, quickly concluded the wound was
so enormous the blood must have rushed out of their leader in
seconds. He couldn't have stood a chance. Could it have been
a mink, therefore, or something else? But they had no time to
investigate any further before the shed door opened and the
Keeper entered to give them their morning feed. Fearful of
being held to be involved, they fled back to their own cages.

The Keeper obviously sensed something was wrong the instant
he did his click thing and illuminated the shed in bright light.
Dropping the buckets he was carrying, he ran down the aisle
looking into the cages until he reached Ramses', where he
stopped short. He looked warily inside, before undoing the
lock, slowly opening the door and pulling out the limp corpse.

Reverently he carried it out of the shed door. Then, looking even paler than usual, he used some tools to seal off the back of Ramses' cage before brusquely tipping their food into the trays. Finally he walked along, carefully checking the lock on every cage, before he left after fiddling for a long time with the lock on the shed door.

The mink re-emerged into the exercise area to find the Elders milling about in confusion. Assassination was so unimaginable they had never thought of making any security arrangements, let alone nominating a successor in case anything happened. Disorientated, they responded by hastily withdrawing into closed conference, where their initial bitterness was aimed at Psycho. He had been their insurance — their double-agent playing both ends against the middle. Why hadn't he warned them? But the one thing they were sure of was that he himself hadn't done it. Never mind his cowardly temperament, how could such a weak and scrawny individual inflict so terrible an injury on their all-powerful Chief? No, the immediate and obvious suspect had to be Mega. But two Elders then totally unexpectedly gave him a cast-iron alibi. He had never been out of their sight, they explained, even spending the whole of the previous night lying in full view outside their cage. It had been so unusual they had been about to report it at the meeting.

Seeing instantly how it fitted in, the Elders turned their attention to the next suspect, Mata. But it was hard to believe a female could possess both the temerity and the strength to carry out such a foul deed. Maxi was the only other suspect, but they had no information he had been directly recruited. They were left with Mega being indirectly responsible, and even then they did not know how. He was supposed to be ostracised, after all. Nor, with his alibi, was there anything they could do officially to touch him, while they now had to face the stomach-churning fact that he had an assassin in his camp. As they remarked apprehensively to each other, it was one thing laying down the law because it suited you. But it was quite another when you stood a high chance of being murdered for doing so.

*   *   *

Mega had put two and two together instantly, although until then murder had not been on his map. Sheba had never mentioned it, and he was still bound by her thinking. When Mata had asked him to provide an alibi he had decided to let events take their course. Now it had happened he felt curiously emotionless. His instinct told him it would work to his benefit, yet somehow it sullied Sheba's memory. First the bollo song, then murder, was not how she — nor he — had imagined it. It had needed another female to go straight for the jugular — literally.

He tracked Mata down to her cage.

'Why?' he demanded, shrugging off his ostracision as no longer relevant.

'We had to go one step further. Mega. It's the only way to win when everything's stacked against you.'

'Was it you, then?'

'What do you think?' she smiled.

Mega sensed she had delegated it. But he was also certain she had obeyed his instructions to keep Psycho out.

'Maxi?'

Mata smiled archly.

Another recruit, then, and not an unexpected one. He had Maxi unofficially on board already. But he was still very welcome in this dizzying female-led event — straightforward male muscle with, hopefully, no questions asked.

'Why didn't you clear it with me first?' he demanded.

'I did, in principle,' she smiled fondly at him. 'Can't you see that I had to keep your nose clean, Mega? You knew it as well. I watched how carefully you provided your alibi. The Elders already know it wasn't you, and soon everyone else will. You're the leader, Mega, not the hatchet-mink, and you have to be seen as such.'

Mega stared at her suspiciously.

'So Maxi takes the drop?'

'It's what he's for.'

'Does he know?'

Mata smiled enigmatically.

'He won't mind. He's proud of it,' she said confidently.

'You still shouldn't have brought him in without asking me,' Mega repeated weakly. 'And you should have cleared the specific action as well.'

'Would you have said no then?' Mata asked, smiling so disconcertingly that he just looked at her before leaving without a further word. How could she possibly see through him so easily?

He marched across the exercise area to Maxi.

'Welcome,' he called, giving him a comradely smile which had no pretence.

'A satisfactory job, my leader?' Maxi inquired anxiously.

'Admirable, Maxi!' he said, putting all the enthusiasm he could muster into his voice. 'Absolutely admirable! I will be amply rewarding you in due course. You couldn't have done better if I'd instructed you myself.'

Mega thought he detected a sudden flicker in Maxi's eyes. But then they settled back to that deep devotion which always reminded him of Custard talking about Master. Maxi was almost wagging his tail.

'You are most kind, my leader. I am now here to serve in any way you wish.'

'You can start by sticking with me,' Mega replied, watching how Maxi's eyes narrowed as Psycho came skittering up and broke into the conversation.

'You've got to address the minions now, Mega,' he squeaked, tugging at his leader's front leg. 'The Elders will be out soon. Everyone's waiting for a lead. There's no time to lose.'

Mega looked round to see all the mink staring at him. After the massive shockwave of the murder everyone was now having to cope with the new confusing event of his ignoring his ostracision. Several looked quite scared. He suddenly thought how sinister their little group, now joined by Mata, must appear – like some dark gang up to no good. Suddenly he felt unsure. This was not how he and Sheba had foreseen the backdrop to his first speech.

'What should I say, Mata?'

She shrugged indifferently.

'I've organised my bit. You're the leader, so organise yours.'

Mega cursed himself for falling into the trap. He hadn't meant to ask her. It had just slipped out, as if he had been addressing his mother. But however hard Mata's answer had been, he had to recognise she was right. This was his show, even if he was no longer in sole control and currently reacting to an event that had been nothing to do with him. It felt uncomfortable being so dependent upon his subordinates. Yet, if he was prepared to ask Mata, he could also try Psycho. At least he'd do his best.

Psycho, as ignorant as everyone else beforehand, had been briefly, but deeply, shocked. He was delighted to see the back of that old fart Ramses and, now it had happened, did not object *per se*. But the assassination had brought home to him how fast things were moving. He had gulped as the message had sunk in that this was no longer just a jolly bollo game. But he had quickly recovered as he saw his way forward. With an assassin in Mega's camp, there was no longer a fence for him to straddle. All he needed was confirmation of one thing. He looked at Maxi, who glared back coldly with what Psycho now imagined were killer's eyes. When Mega gave an affirmative nod, Psycho could not suppress a shudder, which deepened as Maxi gave an evil smile.

He rushed to take refuge in his own contribution.

'This is what we do, Mega,' he rattled off without hesitation. 'First we get the bollo song going. Then we move on to rubbish the Elders and finish up by giving the minions a blast of the freedom number. They've been terrified by Ramses. So what we must make clear is that it wasn't you. The line we're putting across is that you're the hard guy, but they've got to see you can be the nice guy as well. Let's lighten it up wherever we can, shall we?'

Mega became increasingly annoyed as Psycho yattered away. This was supposed to be his speech. He didn't want a cynic feeding him his lines – especially the bit that Psycho was now outlining about putting forward an Elders–Keeper conspiracy.

'Nice bit of spin, eh?' he was cackling. 'Two and two makes five.'

Yet, even though he might be both embroidering and

simplifying, what Psycho said was oddly compelling. Maxi looked dubious, while Mata's expression was blank, but it was all making sense to Mega. He and Psycho might be wildly dissimilar, but he did recognise they shared the same gut instinct. Furthermore, they both trusted that instinct absolutely.

'Round them up,' he instructed Maxi curtly, noticing how his hatchet-mink's look of devotion had now considerably diminished, while Psycho's smile had graduated to a particularly revolting smugness.

Maxi had little difficulty in getting everyone to gather at the end of the exercise area.

'If I were you I'd ignore the ostracision and go,' he whispered to each mink, implying something dreadful might happen if they didn't. Nobody thought to question what it might be. Even without any official verdict from the Elders, the shocked community was taking it for granted that Ramses had been Mega's work — one way or another. Maxi meanwhile made a point of leaving the Elders undisturbed in their meeting, while they in turn ducked the issue by not inviting themselves.

Psycho had suggested the line-up. He was on Mega's right, Mata on his left, while behind stood Maxi. The Mega–Mata tie-up was already known, while Psycho was also publicly part of the mix through being unable to stop claiming credit for the bollo song. The new element was Maxi. His coming out was to be the public declaration of who had killed Ramses.

'It'll be like the Elders' swearing-in, Mega,' Psycho had explained. 'If anybody's going to stand up against you they'll have to do it then. Otherwise you'll be in charge as surely as they were.'

It was also Psycho who kicked the meeting off. For once he looked as nervous as his audience.

'May I present myself, Mata, your new leader Mega, and Maxi — through whom Ramses has sent his apologies for being unable to be present,' he announced, giving his eerie cackle.

Maxi went ramrod stiff and there was a silence as the subtext filtered through. But nobody said anything. They just continued to look stunned.

Mega let a long pause elapse before waving Psycho to one side and giving everyone a friendly grin.

'Well, my fellow mink, how do you propose we now proceed?' he asked, mimicking Ramses' avuncular tones. 'I'm afraid we have a slight communication problem to deal with, you see. I'm not allowed to speak, you're not allowed to listen, and we're all banned from saying a certain word. So, shall I stand here in silence? Or do you all propose to cover your ears?'

His grin widened as he reverted to his normal voice.

'Come on, my mink. Let's state loud and clear what we think of this rubbish. What do I hear?'

'Bollo! Bollo! Bollo!' came a few hesitant voices.

Psycho mentally filed their owners for future reference. These were the mink they were looking for.

'Again!'

This time there were more.

'Again!'

As the bollo build-up continued, various members of the audience began to realise how much they were enjoying themselves. Bollo might be moronic, even for them, but who cared when it was so enormously rude and infectious? They were in a different world from Ramses' patronising chats and the dry pronouncements of the Elders.

'What do you think of the Elders' ban, then?' Mega thundered.

'Bollo! Bollo! Bollo!' the happy reply came back. 'It's all a load of bollo!'

'And what about the Elders themselves?'

Drunk with their chanting, they sang back automatically: 'Bollo! Bollo! Bollo! They're all a load of bollo!'

There was a sudden gasp as half of them took in what they had just said. Some immediately looked guilty. Psycho filed their faces as well. They were the ones to watch.

'The Elders are indeed a load of bollo,' Mega shouted. 'And they're now also history — as they richly deserve to be.'

His brow clouded over while the audience, recalling the late Ramses, went deathly quiet.

'Now, my mink, I have a grave matter to report to you,'

Mega continued in a terrible voice. 'For I have uncovered yet another dark and dreadful secret. I have already told you how the Keeper kills us for our coats. Now I can reveal that the sky-falling-in thing is a load of bollo as well.

'It's a myth, my mink, a myth dreamed up between the Elders and our Keeper. For that is the most terrible thing. There has been a conspiracy. The Elders have been in league with the Keeper. That is why they wanted you to be so nice to him. That is why they discouraged insubordination and made you so meek and mild. And that is why they always got the best of everything in return.'

He looked round, lip curled.

'Yet where are they now, these mink who claim to rule? In their Happy Land?' He mimicked Ramses again. 'Shall we observe a brief silence during which we think of them, gambolling in their new home without a care?'

As he briefly closed his eyes, the vision of the audience remained imprinted on his mind. He felt a sudden exuberance. It was all working!. Once again humour was the key. You had to admire Psycho's ideas.

'Did you see them?' he asked, opening his eyes and smiling as beatifically as Ramses once had. 'I didn't,' he snarled. 'Because that's another myth, my mink, another cornerstone of the foul conspiracy. There is no Happy Land. Instead your Elders are in there, skulking like the traitors they are!'

He indicated the cage where the meeting was still continuing.

'Why aren't they out here standing up for themselves?' he shouted, pointing an accusing paw. 'What are they afraid of?'

Psycho let out a muffled snort. That was rich, with Ramses still warm. But although Mata shot a warning glance, the irony seemed lost on his leader.

'I'll tell you what they're afraid of,' he yelled. 'They're afraid of us, and they're afraid of the truth. And so they should be. It's time to smash their conspiracy and break their tyranny. For what are we — mice or mink?'

'We are mink, Mega!' the reply thundered back.

'That is right. We are mink. And soon we shall be on the

outside, treading where no other mink has trod. For I, Mega, am here to summon your human liberators. I, Mega, am here to break you out of your cages. I, Mega, am here to restore you to the wild. Show me, my brave mink – who is for me?'

As Psycho commented acidly afterwards, they didn't all raise their paws at once. But in the end they all did.

22

Economical with the Truth

Despite his promise to the Venerable Buck, Owl felt he had had quite enough of normal rabbits for the moment. Yet, while he made a determined effort to ignore Burdock and his cronies, the thoughts the ancient sage had implanted in his head would not go away. He had landed in limbo, he realised – fallen out with his old friends, but incapable of being at one with the Concerned Guardians. And after enjoying the company of his fellow creatures so much he was finding his isolation hard to bear.

'Not interested,' was Raka's curt reply to the Venerable Buck's latest revelations. Freddie and Boris went a stage further by looking through him, as if he wasn't there. Ula, meanwhile, remained in a terminal sulk about the lack of nest repairs, which Owl now perversely set his heart against, pretending they were a matter of principle. Yet a couple of bright and sunny days, in which the air had felt almost warm, had made him aware of what was coming. Regardless of whether they were talking, he and Ula would soon be surrendering to the irresistible drive of their mating impulses. Like it or not, as lifelong mates they were irredeemably locked together.

But simply shrugging off the Concerned Guardians turned out to be harder than it looked. Owl soon become acutely conscious of how impossible it was for him to remain inconspicuous with his high aerial profile. He was now such a hero all kind of birds and ground creatures whom he normally spurned continuously waved at him in rapturous greeting. The despised dunnocks, in particular, treated him with such ghastly familiarity that it made him feel quite ill.

In the end Burdock anyhow torpedoed him by seizing the initiative and taking the decision out of his talons. When the rabbit reverted to coming to the beech to call Owl out, the explosions of wrath from Ula were so violent he caved in and agreed to another meeting at the Quarry.

This one, he was determined, was going to be short and to the point.

'The only rabbit I'm interested in talking to is the Venerable Buck,' he informed Burdock flatly as soon as he arrived.

'Unfortunately, Ollie that is not possible at present,' Big Arse sighed, shaking his head mournfully. 'My great-grandfather is still with us but not sufficiently *compos mentis* for any meaningful dialogue to take place.'

'Truth to say, he is fading fast,' Dandelion, who had come along unasked, added softly.

Owl stared at both of them suspiciously, realising with a jolt how much he had put himself in Burdock's paws. Having only this one rabbit as his line of communication meant there was no way of authenticating anything he said. Dandelion was useless as a cross-check. Her sole purpose in life, Owl thought with a tinge of bitterness against Ula, appeared to be to echo her mate's pronouncements slavishly. Not that Owl had any reason to doubt what they were both telling him. When he had last seen him, the Venerable Buck had virtually signed himself off by promoting his great-grandson into his place. Incidentally, Owl wondered, how much of their last conversation had Burdock managed to pick up? The Big Arse bit, he hoped.

'Never mind him — let me give you the good news,' Burdock suddenly grinned triumphantly. 'Thanks to you, Ollie, we have succeeded beyond my wildest dreams. The young militants have now dissolved into a furious argument about whose fault it was that they were so outmanoeuvred. By the way – I'm sure you'll be fascinated to know – I finally shafted them by giving insects the non-voting role of "observers". By now most of the lowlife has been dumped. Anyhow it's so short-lived all the insects are already being replaced by offspring who know nothing about what's happened.' Burdock gave a little laugh, revealing his prominent buck teeth. 'You won't recall More for Mayflies, of course,' he said, chuckling heartily. 'That was ages ago. But it was some performance, I can tell you. You see, they once turned up at a meeting in an enormous cloud and voted a motion through by sheer weight of numbers. But because their natural lifespan is only one day they were all dead by nightfall, so of course they couldn't attend the next meeting and their motion was overturned.

'Anyhow, all that's over now. We more sensible creatures, with – how can I put it? – higher IQs, are back in charge.'

Owl saw the chance to spear Burdock on his own logic.

'You won't need me any more then,' he said, nodding his head to emphasise the strength of his point.

'On the contrary,' Dandelion exclaimed, looked horrified. 'Rather, we need you even more than ever.'

'Indeed, Ollie,' Burdock cut across her. 'We can't manage without you. When we tried a meeting recently without you as Executive Chaircreature, it was absolute chaos. You see, we may be free of the insects, but now we're getting down to the really tendentious business – passing my Woodland Code, duly incorporating my Bill of Creatures' Rights. And we're absolutely reliant on you to help pilot them through.'

Burdock's voice had thrilled with pride as he pronounced the two grandiose titles, while Owl's heart sank. Boris had banged on about these twin horrors, quite apart from the Venerable Buck's disparaging reference to them. According to Boris, they had caused rows and arguments almost as great as the ones provoked by the young militants. As far as Owl could determine, through the haze cloaking previous CWG history in his mind, they might even have been responsible for the militancy in the first place.

'They're designed to set rules by which we're then all supposed to live,' Boris had explained scathingly. 'As if rabbits had the right to tell us what to do! As for their content – they're the worst hot air I've ever come across. And with the Guardians that's saying something.'

It was indeed, Owl had thought as Boris expanded further. Both Code and Bill, supposedly enshrining the rights and duties of every creature within the wood, had apparently been an interminable time in the making. As a result they had grown into glorious dissertations, containing many, many long words, all of which sounded tremendously imposing. In reality, though, their tortuous creation had spawned such an incomprehensible muddle of clauses, sub-clauses, riders, amendments and footnotes that all you could say in their favour was that they were well-meaning.

'Which, as we well know, gets you worse than nowhere,' Boris had concluded, angrily snuffling up a former member of Black Beetle Power.

Recalling this, Owl now turned to Burdock. 'Thank you, but I've decided I've had enough,' he said politely. 'After all, I've done the job you asked me to.'

'But what about your pledge to the Venerable Buck?' Burdock exclaimed, aghast.

'And your gravitas and bottom, Ollie,' Dandelion chipped in.

'Indeed, Ollie,' Burdock said urgently, launching into a convoluted and lengthy speech.

Owl switched him off. He had figured out gravitas by now. It was a meetings thing, to do with appearing to have a grave nature and looking important and serious. 'Bottom' was appearing to be weighted down, so you were heavy and stable and matters revolved round you. That was what meetings seemed to be about – putting on a convincing-looking show, even if there was nothing behind it. In fact the less there was behind it, the better the show must be. It was always the most timorous and pathetic rabbits, with nothing meaningful to contribute, who were the keenest to add a bleating 'Hear, hear!' to the current nonsense under discussion. But whatever the naive Dandelion might think, both he and Burdock knew neither gravitas nor bottom was the point. Owl had simply filled a power vacuum to become the boss. And, awful though the meetings were, he had to admit he enjoyed being the boss, especially now his CWG involvement had made him a pariah amongst his fellow predators.

Eventually, worn down by Burdock's torrent of words, he held out his wings in dramatic mock surrender.

'That's enough,' he said wearily. 'OK, you win. I'll stay. But only on two conditions – I get to see the Venerable Buck, and I bow out for good after your Code and Bill have been passed.'

'It's a deal,' Burdock replied instantly, suddenly becoming brisk and businesslike 'The first thing we need you for is to chair our initial pre-meeting. See you in the Small Clearing, tomorrow at sunset. OK?'

He bounded off at such high speed, towing Dandelion behind him, that Owl had no time to reply. As he looked round the deserted Quarry, he felt that somehow he had been taken for a ride.

Meanwhile Burdock was well satisfied as he ran quickly down the hillside. He was warming to the predator side of his character, which he was now certain he possessed in no small measure. Owl might not realise it, but he had been hooked. And having got him this far, Burdock was determined never to let him go.

Dandelion, struggling to keep up, was looking aghast.

'Why didn't you tell him any more about the Venerable Buck?' she gasped.

'Because he didn't ask,' Burdock snapped back.

Why was she so unable to grasp the realities of political manoeuvring? The chances of his great-grandfather coming out of his coma might be nil, but meanwhile he was admirably serving his purpose simply by continuing to exist.

'But that's not honest, Burdie,' Dandelion exclaimed, shocked.

'And it's not dishonest either,' Burdock replied sharply, accelerating away before he lost his temper with her. 'It's just being economical with the truth.'

23

Officially Dead

Locked in their meeting, the Elders listened gloomily to the shouts and cheers outside. Power was sliding away by the moment yet they felt lost, both individually and as a group. The shock of Ramses' murder had frozen them in inaction. It had come so out of nowhere they still found it hard to take it in, let alone respond to it, while without him in the chair they were effectively rudderless.

Their total inability to grasp the nettle was graphically indicated when the first period of silence, called in their late Chief's memory, was followed by an even grimmer one greeting the request for nominations as his successor. Then, when they heard the unmistakable strains of the banned bollo song, they knew how surely their fate was being sealed. They looked at each other aghast, the silence lengthening as they listened to Mega's speech.

Then came the endless justifications. What could they do against such a rabble-rouser? they asked each other helplessly. They couldn't inspire that kind of wild enthusiasm. Such fanaticism wasn't their style. And despite their official positions, they started confessing to each other, they hadn't been able to prevent feeling strange stirrings inside themselves at his words. None of them had mentioned it before, but what Mega had said when they hauled him in privately had been insidiously working away in their minds. It was easy enough having faith in what they preached so long as no-one was challenging it. But after the seeds of doubt had been sown so effectively it was a different matter. To their ultimate horror, they confessed, they still couldn't stop humming the infuriatingly catchy bollo song. You couldn't help it, could you? they tried to reassure each other. Yet therein lay the rub. Bollo was so base they could never have used it themselves. It was just vulgar populist nonsense with no thought or logic behind it. That wasn't how they did things — and it was too late to start now. There were subsidiary factors as well, especially the unfortunate timing of the birds incident that had negated so much of the youngsters' indoctrination. All in all, they concluded, it wasn't their fault the old order was finished.

They had also been struggling to hold back positive feelings about Mega himself, they further admitted. He had remained so loyal and faithful to his mother and coped in such a dignified manner with being ostracised. There was an awful lot to be said for him, even if he had become the ultimate thorn in their side. That he was now dazzling the colony with his message or his personal charisma — or both — was hardly surprising. And that was the central irony, they remarked ruefully. The way things had been going, Ramses' murder had probably been unnecessary. It only went to demonstrate the lack of political judgement on Mega's side.

Yet the murderer in his camp was still on the loose. If they attempted to defend their doctrine they would each be set to go the same way as their Chief. The maze of justifications and excuses was put behind them as the meeting focused on the main point. The doctrine could be temporarily ditched. Their most urgent responsibility now was to come up with something that would save their own necks. Briskly they assembled their strategy. Their only hope was total capitulation, followed by throwing themselves on the new leader's mercy. If that saved them, they'd find a way to fight back in the future.

Through force of habit it was put to the vote, but it proved a mere formality. Agreement was unanimous.

Mega was relaxing in his cage when Psycho came in and delivered the message that the Elders were requesting a private meeting. He smiled broadly, thinking what a great personal pleasure this was going to be. First, though, he would let them stew.

'Inform them, Psycho, that I am currently having a meeting with myself,' he replied airily. 'I will grant them an audience when I have finished.'

Psycho scurried off, immensely relieved at the delay. Although taking the credit for most of what Mega had said to the minions, he had been quite awed by his leader's messianic fervour. Going to see him immediately afterwards, he had found him still on a high.

'I'm going to show those bastard Elders, Psycho,' he had announced. 'I'll never forget that private meeting I had with them. You know, the copulators wouldn't even take me seriously. Well, now it's their turn and Maxi wants a Ramses done on the lot. He says it's the only way we'll get rid of them. He's even volunteered for the job himself. He says he enjoyed doing in Ramses even more than he'd expected.'

Psycho's alarm level had shot up. The stupid murdering wooden-head!

'No, no, Mega, we mustn't,' he had gabbled. 'Ramses was a one-off. We need the minions to be truly on our side, not just paying lip-service because they're terrified. We mustn't gain the reputation of being wholesale executioners. Anyhow, what'll the Keeper do if he finds dead bodies all over the place? He won't let that pass. Then we'll all be up spraint creek.

'I promise you, Mega, the Elders have crumbled. Be merciful, my leader. Let the minions see that you're magnanimous Mega, not murderous Mega. That way they'll follow you.'

Mega had smiled back so peculiarly Psycho had stopped short.

'There's nothing wrong with what I'm saying, is there, Mega?' he had asked uncertainly. 'You do agree with it, don't you?'

'Nothing at all, Psycho,' his leader had reassured him. 'Don't worry, I'll think about it. Not a lot of spin though, eh?'

A huge smile now spread across Mega's face. He'd give the little runt something to think about! He wasn't going to tell him, but Psycho's special pleading had already largely succeeded – particularly about the reaction of the Keeper. Maxi almost certainly hadn't thought that one through. Mega himself hadn't even sanctioned the first murder and was still not sure if he would ever have instigated it himself. He was a long way from Sheba by now, in every way. He had succeeded in the first stage thanks not to her but to his new advisers, who played a rougher game. He would go along with it, though. He needed to. With the Elders on their way out, his focus was already moving on to the next stage of overcoming the human enemy. Dealing with the Elders shouldn't be a personal matter – it was a job to be done.

But it was a new thought, which had come to him from nowhere, that was causing him such inward delight. He'd show his spin-doctor what spin was all about! Wait until Psycho heard his announcement to the young mink!

When the Elders crowded into his cage Mega could see immediately how correct Psycho was. Had they crumbled! They were looking abject and sorrowful and were craven in their apologies. It wasn't their fault as individuals, they fell over each other in their haste to explain. They'd only been following the system. Now they'd seen the light they realised how wrong they'd been all these generations. They'd do anything to make amends. They'd repent. If they were pardoned they promised never to revolt. They'd help in every way they could. All their vast political experience was available to him . . .

'Thanks, but no thanks,' Mega interrupted, going straight to their terms of surrender.

'You will all make public confessions.'

'Yes,' they replied eagerly.

'After that you'll all be ostracised.'

'We agree.'

They had worked out that would be coming.

Mega stared at them contemptuously, thinking how they would lick his balls if he put that on the agenda. But as they dropped their eyes, he knew something much worse was on their minds. Would any of them have the guts to raise it? He let the silence drag on, yet soon found he wasn't getting as much out of it as he had expected. The Elders were no longer daunting, they were just pathetic. It seemed impossible they could have ruled for so long. Meanwhile, their recantation was probably just a ploy.

Suddenly he felt immensely bored by them.

'Right, you lot, this is how it is,' he announced briskly. 'The bottom line is that you're not going to be killed, at least not now. But if one of you ever takes a step out of line, you all will be.'

He swept a sneering gaze across their frightened faces.

'Think of it as like your sky-falling-in bollo. Except that the line you mustn't cross isn't as easy to see as a cage front. It's more a question of attitude. I'm sure you're astute enough to work it out, and for all your sakes you better had. It only needs one of you to go wrong and you're all for the chop. You are therefore each placed firmly in the paws of your fellows.'

If that didn't sow dissension in their ranks nothing ever would, he thought, watching them glancing apprehensively at each other.

'Meanwhile I'm having the colony assembled. You can make your confessions now, before you hold another meeting and change your minds.'

He walked out without another word, leaving the job of supervising their humiliation to Mata, as she had earlier requested. Maxi, swallowing his disappointment, extracted what comfort he could from barking furiously at them as they lined up in the exercise area. Heads hung low, they separately and together mumbled their repentances while Mata lashed them for a catalogue of crimes, many specifically against females. All the time the youngsters jeered, hooted and endlessly sang the bollo song.

Mega reappeared at the end to deliver the final ignominy

before they began their new life as non-creatures, never to speak, or to be spoken to, again.

'For your information your Council of Elders is not to be formally abolished,' he announced to the exhausted group. 'Instead it has simply ceased to exist. From this moment on, you may be present physically, but officially you're dead. And that, you'll find out, is as final as anything that happened to Ramses.'

The young mink broke into a storm of applause. Many of them had found really dead, as in Ramses, exhilarating but scary. Still in shock, they were finding it hard to adjust. Would any of them be safe, now they had a leader who was prepared to kill? Officially dead, though, they could understand. It sounded much more like a good laugh — especially as it gave them such wonderful victims to torment.

'Goodbye, Elders, goodbye,' they sang ecstatically, 'Goodbye, Elders, goodbye.'

Mega waited until they had built up momentum.

'Silence!' he then shouted, bringing them up short. 'There is one more matter, my mink. I have already told you I am to summon our human liberators. But have any of you thought where we're going to go when we get out?'

There was no reply. The mere idea of freedom was so all-consuming, this aspect had not yet got on to any of their maps — not even his subordinates', Mega thought, judging from their blank looks. Except maybe Psycho, who now was shaking his pointed head in furious denial, as if imploring him not to say anything more. Mega ignored him. Whatever Psycho might be signalling, as his own idea had matured in his mind it had got better and better. It was so immensely satisfying in the way it turned the tables on their former rulers.

He stared at the hangdog Elders in front of him.

'I expect you're now looking to your beloved Keeper to save you, eh?' he asked, smiling cruelly. 'By taking you to the Happy Land, perhaps?'

He turned to his rapt audience.

'Well, if this horrible lot did ever get there, they'd have a problem,' he thundered. 'Because they'd find we'd got there first. Yes, my mink, that's where I am taking you. Not to the Happy Land as such — that was always a myth. But the place the Elders pretended was the Happy Land does exist — Custard's wonderful wood. And it's there that I shall lead you, to Custard's wood, now your Promised Land!'

24

The Good Old Days

O wl's deeper involvement with the CWGs got off on the wrong foot. At the first of a series of 'informal introductory getting-to-know-you sessions', his head was sent into such a spin he had to go for a long fly afterwards to clear it. His horror increased as he began comprehending how few of the intricacies of CWG affairs he and his predator friends had grasped. He had blithely assumed all he was letting himself in for was the main meetings, but underneath were now revealed dizzying strata of sub-meetings, discussion groups, workshops, ideas sessions, think tanks, revolving seminars and open-access briefings.

That was just the official side. Running in parallel was a network of unofficial meetings, starting with pre-meetings, at which rival factions worked out their strategies, and running through to post-meetings to analyse what had gone wrong. (Things going wrong seemed to be a natural CWG expectation, which later gave gloomy satisfaction when it happened.) Meanwhile a whole new collection of minor meetings, both official and unofficial, were set up at every main meeting. Even keeping track of them – never mind attending them – was soon quite beyond him.

The way meetings ran was just as confusing. Topics were discussed and decisions made, with everyone very keen and enthusiastic. Afterwards, though, they seemed to float away in a curious way which he could never put his talon on. In the end none was ever implemented. Even worse, at the next meeting discussions would backtrack beyond them, taking everyone back onto old ground. Rabbits, he quickly decided, worked rather like they ate — by nibbling. Presumably the idea of sinking their teeth into anything meaty and juicy was beyond them. All in all, as a creature who liked to know where he was, Owl found it immensely unsettling. The Venerable Buck's spell, which had temporarily convinced him some sense lay behind the rabbit way, was broken. But it was too late. By now he was immersed up to his wingtips.

Instead Owl found himself becoming increasingly preoccupied with the very title 'Concerned Woodland Guardians'. It was so typically vague and woolly that somehow it summed up all his feelings. 'Woodland' was straightforward enough — although there was a whole sub-argument about including the surrounding fields which he didn't dare think about. But 'Concerned' was more problematic. How did it translate into anything which made sense? Concern for what? Or for whom? Surely you couldn't be concerned about everything and everyone in general? So what, specifically, were CWGs concerned about? Nothing that he could see. And what did 'concerned' mean, anyhow, apart from expressing being troubled and anxious? And where did that get you? It was the same with 'Guardians'. What exactly did these veggies claim to be guardians of? Or was it whom? And if so, had they asked those involved beforehand? Or were they doing it without so much as a by your leave? How were they then exercising their guardianship in any practical way? What exactly was a guardian, anyway?

His head reeling, Owl tried several times to tackle Burdock to get some answers. But Big Arse was now entirely obsessed with his many and varied meetings, while continuously fobbing off any attempts to meet the Venerable Buck again on account of his fragile health.

Eventually, getting fed up, Owl tried pursuing the 'Concerned' and 'Guardian' angles by asking various rabbits for what they then defined as 'clarification'. But when he received only meaningless platitudes in return, he decided to try to run these particular hares to earth by talking to Marcus Mole.

Owl had mixed feelings as he tracked him down by following the pattern of molehills he and his fellows made in the open parts of the wood. But he was still irresistibly drawn by a combination of the way Marcus talked — which seemed a little like the Venerable Buck — and how he pointed up what Owl regarded as a central CWG hypocrisy. They included in their ranks creatures who ate low forms of life in addition to vegetation, but Marcus went one stage further by eating nothing but worms. In Owl's eyes that made him strictly a carnivore, yet his recruitment had still been hailed as a triumph by the CWG working party set up to entice omnivores to the meetings. Burdock had already proudly announced that they would be targetting hedgehogs the moment they woke from hibernation.

Spotting a line of molehills, Owl swooped down and took up station on the grass where he estimated the next one would appear. He had been almost too accurate, he thought proudly to himself as the ground beneath him suddenly heaved and Marcus's head popped up from the middle of a pile of soft earth.

'What do you want?' he asked irritably, nose twitching. 'Can't you see I'm busy?'

He reached down and popped a worm.

Marcus's other fascination was his insane metabolic rate, which meant he required constant sustenance. Apparently he had keeled over at his first meeting before it had even finished going through the minutes of the previous one. After that, in the face of furious opposition from Cowslip on behalf of Worms' Lib, he had wangled medical dispensation and was now the only creature allowed to eat while they were in progress.

Looking down on him, Owl could see what appealed to CWGs — those squat shovel paws, that velvety fur with a nap that ran both ways and was so short it looked almost like shiny black skin, those sweet little pink bits, the watery blinking eyes — as he had heard rabbits constantly repeating, Marcus was somehow so earthy!

'I've come to ask you precisely what "Concerned" and "Guardian" mean,' Owl said. 'None of the rabbits I've talked to seems to have any idea.'

Feeling the familiar surge of energy imparted by the worm hit, Marcus promptly launched into one of what the rabbits referred to as his 'explanations'.

'It's hard to describe exactly, but since I've been a CWG I've seen the light and become deeply concerned about others apart from myself,' he gabbled. 'That's meant putting myself into a guardianship role *vis-à-vis* my fellow creatures by taking an interest in their welfare and having feelings about them, which is what it's all about if you smell what I mean.'

'But that's all words,' Owl protested. 'It doesn't translate into anything real.'

'Aha!' Marcus exclaimed, pink nose twitching triumphantly. 'You mean communication, don't you? And quite rightly, too. For there you have it. Communication, you smell, is what it's all about. If we can't communicate, how can we possibly be concerned?'

Owl felt the fog descend.

'But you're not concerned about worms,' he said with sudden inspiration.

'Absolutely I am,' Marcus replied indignantly, while simultaneously popping another. 'Contrary to what you say, my attitude to them has changed completely. My concern for them is now paramount.'

'You still eat them, though,' Owl protested feebly.

'Ah yes, I agree that I do. But I now eat them as a fully fledged CWG and therefore in a concerned way. And that, as I'm sure you'll understand, is the whole point. Now, if you'll excuse me, I must be off to see how many more have fallen into my tunnels.'

Owl, bemused, watched silently as he vanished into the soft earth with a flurry of paws. Is Ula right? he wondered briefly. Am I in fact going mad? Then he suddenly recalled Freddie's frequent remark on the subject of the CWGs: 'Ah, 'tis a muddle,' he would say, tapping the side of his face knowingly with his front paw. 'Tis nothing but a muddle!'

Simultaneously he recalled the Venerable Buck's warning about his tolerance being tested to its limits. He would help himself by taking a leaf out of Freddie's book. If he recognised he was living in muddleland, then it would all make sense – or at least less nonsense, if that wasn't nonsensical in itself. For in muddleland, naturally, everything was a muddle.

The decision cheered Owl up. But unfortunately (a word he found rabbits particularly fond of) it did nothing to improve matters. For he now found everyday affairs dominating his life. Even simple arrangements, like where and when to meet, seemed mysteriously hard to make and were then continuously revised, or even broken. When they did finally take place, much time would then be wasted on detailed and agonised explanations as to why it was no-one's fault, with various outside factors, from the weather to accident and illness, being wheeled in as standard, and apparently quite acceptable, excuses.

Beginning to appreciate Boris's remark that the CWGs had no control over their lives, Owl decided to experiment. He arrived spectacularly late at one pre-meeting and proffered what seemed to him the limpest of excuses – that he had been searching for materials for the nest-rebuilding project. (In reality Ula, amid much acrimony, had now taken this on herself.)

To his mixed astonishment and disgust this was deemed perfectly valid.

'It's so hard to get hold of anything you need these days,' a rabbit called Corn Cockle sympathised.

'Isn't it just!' a dull specimen named Dead Nettle chimed in. 'Remember the good old days, when you just had to hop outside your burrow for a tasty snack, rather than running for ages as you do now?'

'Those were the days,' the others lamented, shaking their heads in what seemed genuine sorrow. 'Honestly, the wood's so crowded now that you can hardly move.'

Owl groaned out loud. Even if that were true, whose fault was it more than the rabbits', with their insane breeding rate?

'It's so busy isn't it? Nobody's got any time any more, have they?'

'Everything was so much better then, including the weather.'

'Too right! You used to know where you were. Nowadays it's nothing but change, change, change all the time. You can't plan anything, can you?'

'You don't know whether it's going to rain or shine from one moment to the next.'

'Or whether it'll be too hot or too cold.'

They all looked at each other, sighing deeply.

'Those were the days,' they repeated.

Just then Honeysuckle, the last rabbit needed to make up the quorum, panted up breathlessly. She was, in CWG talk, 'well-formed', which in Owl's eyes translated as plain fat.

'I'm so sorry, comrades,' she gasped, ample chest heaving, fleshy jowls wobbling. 'Please do accept my deepest apologies. You see, I was just trundling off when I realised I had to tell my mate something important I'd quite forgotten about. Then when I got back to the burrow one of the children started being sick – they'd eaten something they shouldn't, of course, as usual. How many times do you have to tell them before they get it into their heads? Anyhow they all began crying and of course after I'd settled them all down then I had to clean it up – and it wasn't a pretty sight, I can tell you. The smell! And, typically, she'd done it right in the middle of the main chamber. Not her fault, I suppose, but then she shouldn't have eaten what she did in the first place.

'Well, by then there'd been so much going on that I'd got into a quite a muddle and was thinking we were all supposed to be meeting at the Big Clearing. Of course when I got there nobody was around to ask because you were all here. So after a bit I thought I'd try coming here just in case and of course here you all are.

'Anyhow,' she concluded brightly, 'all's well that ends well, eh? But I don't mind telling you that all in all I've had quite enough for one day.'

'Poor Honeysuckle!' the others cried, sounding quite alarmed.

'You mustn't upset yourself so.'

'We don't mind.'

'We all appreciate how hard it is being a mother these days.'

'So many pressures.'

'So much hustle and bustle.'

'So many things to remember.'

'Not like the good old days, eh?'

'Everything was so much simpler then.'

'A golden era.'

'It'll never never come again, you know. I remember my grandfather telling me . . .'

Owl rolled his eyes skywards and switched them off. Why couldn't the dratted creatures live in the present? he thought irritably, gazing at the scudding clouds for comfort as the meeting degenerated into a dreary catalogue of moans about the way the whole wood was going downhill. Mind you, he thought, cheering up, if this sort of nonsense was the rabbits' present, it was hardly surprising they preferred to hark back to the past.

In the end he sat there for what felt like half a day. Because when a meeting did finally start it only raised the next problem of when was it going to end. This, too, appeared to be beyond anyone's control, until Owl studied Burdock at work and began to understand the art of getting a decision in your favour. The trick was to sit things out to the bitter end – or at least until your opponents' numbers were sufficiently diminished for you to be confident your side would win, at which point you moved smartly to the vote.

Hadn't any of them anything better to do? he asked himself as he sat through the interminable grind of mind-numbing minutiae. Apparently not, he was just thinking, when another Freddie remark popped into his head and brought everything into dreadful focus.

'If you were a rabbit, Ollie, could you think of anything more important to you than sitting in a meeting?'

25

Onwards and Upwards

From day one of the take-over Psycho impressed on Mega how vital it was they stay on good terms with the Keeper.

'He may be reclassified as our enemy, but until we're liberated he still controls our world,' he emphasised. 'To keep the minions in line we should play him down while you, more specifically, issue the direct order: "Don't upset him".'

Even though it went against the grain of the new freedom thinking, Mega had accepted the shrewdness of this advice. Yet, as he sat waiting for the approaching footsteps that would mean their evening feed, he was thinking that he might as well not have bothered. It wasn't anyone's particular fault that the honeymoon of the glorious revolution had been so short-lived. At first the cages had bubbled as their previously bored inhabitants breathed the heady air of freedom — or at least the promise of it. Glad of anything to spice up their dull life, at last the youngsters had something to talk and dream about. Everyday life was so much more fun with hope for the future.

At the same time, dutifully responding to Mega's directive, they had done nothing directly hostile towards the Keeper. But it had made little difference. There was Ramses' abrupt demise to start with. Then the new atmosphere had bred such natural insubordination they could see he realised something radical had happened. The biggest change of all was in his favourites, the former Elders. Cowed and silent, they no longer rushed to greet him, while all his efforts to encourage their previous sycophantic behaviour had no effect.

Matters had then spiralled as he reacted in kind by running things down even more. The exercise area was increasingly shut off, they weren't cleaned out at all, and their food was just slung roughly through the wire. The latrine pit was simply unspeakable, as well as overflowing. In the latest development the Keeper had started missing some of their regular mealtimes altogether. Bloody Psycho! Mega thought. Why had no-one seen the central contradiction in his argument? For, they were all now saying, if the Keeper was really their enemy, planning to kill them for their coats, why should they be nice to him, especially when he was treating them like spraint?

Looking out over the exercise area Mega saw another thing which must be riling the Keeper, and was certainly proving a growing source of tension inside the cages. Free of the Elders' yoke, the youngsters had reinforced Psycho's 'cheerful yobs' remark by forming a new hooligan element. Male and female juveniles now hung around in dishevelled gangs, always scrapping and mucking about. Their unkemptness and seemingly permanent state of grubbiness and untidyness was horrifying their parents. Meanwhile the youngsters insisted that it was all part of a new 'designer' look, which they said they had put together with great care and pride. Maxi, a stickler for neatness, had urged a crackdown but Mata had backed Mega in allowing the youth cult to continue. He liked the way his followers were changing to establish their identity and become more their true selves.

But that morning, in the regular progress report he insisted on delivering, Maxi had sounded a new warning note Mega had since been chewing over. His military adviser had begun well. From the moment his proposal for the serial killing of the Elders was rejected he had carried out his orders to the letter, not arguing once. The murder of Ramses had caused the jokes about him to dry up instantly. With sudden new confidence he had launched himself into living, breathing and sleeping his self-appointed task of moulding the rank and file into a force to be reckoned with. At first he had delivered a string of positive reports about the response of the increasingly organised ranks to his training programmes for the outside world. But then his tone had gradually changed and he had begun complaining the youngsters were becoming more and more insubordinate. His current assessment was his most gloomy to date.

'On the subject of security, my leader,' he had said plaintively, smoothing his whiskers as was his habit in moments of stress, 'may I raise the point that the ranks don't seem to listen to me any more? Until now it's mainly been cheek, but I fear it won't be long before we have a real mutiny on our paws. Unless we do something the lid's going to blow.'

'Have you forgotten your job is to sit on it?' Mega had snapped back. It was the first time he had spoken so sharply to Maxi and indicated that the pressure was getting to him as well. He didn't appreciate the way his military adviser dumped everything on his plate.

Maxi wasn't wrong, though. The bored and angry youngsters were now scuffling amongst themselves as they realised the Keeper wasn't going to feed them that night. Mega could see the anger and frustration oozing from Maxi's every pore as he charged round, vainly trying to break them up.

All in all, it was time he had a chat with Psycho.

'Don't get me wrong Mega – your freedom pitch was always the key to overthrowing the Elders,' Psycho said apprehensively. He had been expecting this meeting, and not looking forward to it. 'My bollo song was important, of course, and Ramses. What swung the balance though was that we had something new to offer. Freedom's so brilliant, isn't it? For if it never comes – or is never going to – who cares? Promises are only made to be broken, aren't they? And in the meantime we rule. But my advice now is that it's a bit played out. We must give the minions something else to focus their energy on.'

Like Maxi, Psycho had been transformed since the take-over.

As pathetically grateful as he had promised to be, he revelled in creeping around, monitoring the suspicions and grumbles, compounded by jealousies forming a constant series of cross-currents in the ranks. He was no longer a powerless runt as no minion could ever be sure whether he was eavesdropping on their conversation. Even Mega's supporters went silent when they spotted him, fearing that a chance remark could be misinterpreted. Yet there was always some argument going on that enabled him to worm his way into both sides and assiduously milk them for information, which he then passed on to his leader or filed in the personal dossiers he was proudly building up.

But Psycho too, had recently become more and more negative.

'Maxi's right, I'm afraid,' he went on nervously, knowing his news wasn't going to go down well. 'Of course most of the older mink still don't like you, but that's nothing new. What is new though is that they're becoming more openly rebellious. I can't confirm anything at this stage, but it may be that a plot's being hatched round the old Elders.'

Mega frowned. Maxi would be interested in that. He was always complaining about the way the ostracised figures drifted silently around. They were too visible, he kept saying. What an unlikely pair of allies he and Psycho made, especially bearing in mind Mega's conversation with Maxi shortly after recruiting him.

'You don't think I should be associating with the little creep, do you?' Mega had asked bluntly.

'Well, if you put it like that, boss, no I don't,' Maxi had replied, seeming embarrassed by such straight talking. 'He's not one of us, if you know what I mean.'

Mega had known precisely what he meant.

'Maybe, Maxi, but we need the runt because he's so clever. One of your main jobs, though, is my security, so you're going to make sure he doesn't stab me in the back.'

'Don't you worry about that, boss,' Maxi had grinned back, happy now he had been given something to do.

'Our generation's still with us though, isn't it?' Mega now asked Psycho.

'More bad news, I'm afraid, Mega,' his spin-doctor replied with growing trepidation. 'You see, that's where we've really got trouble. They're saying this dump has gone downhill so fast they all want out now. It's not looking good, Mega.'

Psycho screwed up his courage.

'They're always asking why haven't we gone to Custard's wood yet. You know what they're like, Mega — they want it all and they want it now. I keep reminding them that you never gave any timetable for liberation day, but it's like Maxi says — they just don't listen. You'll remember I thought it a bad idea even to mention the wood? Apart from anything else, they're now asking when Custard's coming to see us? As the sharper ones keep pointing out, we can hardly go to her wood when we don't know where it is.'

Psycho knew he was touching on a sore point. Custard's non-appearance was another of the rumbling worries in the background.

'In a way you can't blame them, Mega,' he went on, adding a dose of flattery to sweeten the pill. 'They believe your every word. Your speeches are so powerful and uplifting they get all their juices going.'

Seeing his leader frowning even more heavily, he tried to lighten the tone.

'It's a good job they aren't really getting out, isn't it, Mega?' he said with a knowing smile. 'In the real world this lot wouldn't know their arse from their kneecap. You know all the fuss about missed meals? Well, I heard one explaining in all seriousness that freedom would mean the Keeper serving our food when we ordered it, not just when he chose. That's not minion talk, is it, Mega? It's moron talk. They're just making it up as they go along.'

'Mind you,' he added with a sly cackle, 'I suppose we're in the business of doing that ourselves.'

Psycho gazed pensively through the wire at the wooden cladding of the shed. Loud yelling, fuelled by empty stomachs, was coming from the end of the exercise area,.

'By the way, Mega,' he said, by way of an afterthought, 'I've got a new line for you to slip in before we junk the whole thing: "Freedom is a way of thought!" Good, isn't it? Seems to say it all, but it's just more of the same old bollo. Or how about "Freedom is what you make it"?'

Until now, as he babbled away, Psycho had failed to note that Mega was remaining curiously silent. Too late, he now heeded the warning sign.

'I'm not knocking it, Mega,' he said quickly. 'Freedom's a good scam — the best. But we all know, don't we? These liberators — these humans who are supposed to open the cages — they aren't really coming, are they? Providing, of course, they even exist.'

He shook his head in simulated wondering admiration, only to see his leader's body stiffen and his eyes go incandescent. Before Psycho knew what was happening, he was pinned to the ground, flat on his back with his throat exposed and a fearsome pair of eyes boring into his opaque ones.

'Don't ever say anything like that again if you value your life, you rat,' Mega breathed slowly.

He glared down for what seemed an eternity before finally releasing him with a rough shove.

Psycho rose shakily to his feet, for once knowing better than to try to talk his way out of it. He tried to hide his trembling as his leader asked, 'What do you suggest then?'

'I just don't know, Mega,' he confessed lamely. 'Maybe there is no answer.'

He quivered even more as Mega continued to stare stonily at him.

'We could have a rethink about the Elders,' he suggested timorously. 'How how about setting up some sort of court? We could try them for crimes, find them guilty and then execute them?' A little of his old self came back. 'The minions would love it, Mega, and it'd provide a brilliant diversion. Just think — I could be the prosecutor, you could be the judge and Maxi could carry out the sentences.'

He shrank as Mega turned on him contemptuously.

'It was you, you stunted fool, who pointed out that harming

the Elders would just cause the Keeper to come down on us even harder. And that's the last thing we need right now.'

'Maybe, Mega,' Psycho replied, licking his thin lips nervously. 'But that's my point, really. The way the Keeper is, would it really make a difference any more?'

Mega's temper snapped.

'Get out of my sight!' he shouted. 'I won't have any more of this defeatist talk.'

Psycho crept away, shaken to the core. As he understood it, the object of the exercise was to seize power and then hang on to it at all costs — which was where freedom fitted in. But wasn't Mega aware that freedom was just like bollo? It was revolution as entertainment. Yet, incredibly, his leader appeared truly to believe in it. Well, he supposed, as he ruefully nursed his bruised ribs, presumably someone had to.

Limping back to his cage, he saw Maxi staring rudely at him. There was another convert he was going to have to watch, he thought bitterly. Of course for Maxi, with his bone-headed devotion and innate stupidity, not to believe in freedom would be astonishing. He was not so sure about Mata. Whenever he broached the subject she always turned the conversation. He had anyhow been wary of her ever since the manufactured fight to cover her conversation with Mega. No, what he needed was another mink who thought as realistically as he did. But with the chances of one appearing as likely as their liberators, he would have to soldier on on his own. Unless, of course, he crossed the tracks again and rejoined the Elders. The thought had been increasingly occurring to him. It would be dangerous, but if the Mega show was beginning to run out of steam, it might be his safest bet in the end.

'You're worried, aren't you?' Mata said as she walked into Mega's cage unannounced, interrupting his gloomy chain of thought. 'There's no need to be, you know.'

She sounded so sympathetic Mega suddenly felt an urgent need to unburden himself to her. He hadn't really had a chance to talk to her lately, she had been so busy training up her female 'warriors', as she insisted on calling them. Much to Maxi's annoyance, she had largely hived these off from his control while Mega, watching her parading them up and down the exercise area, smiled in admiration at the way she was inculcating them with such fierce pride.

'I've no regrets, if that's what you mean,' he blurted out, realising as he spoke how defensive he sounded.

'You've been thinking about Sheba, haven't you?' Mata inquired gently. 'I think about my mother as well, you know. We owe it to both of them not to lose faith.'

Mata wasn't quite right, Mega thought. Things had been so busy lately he had been thinking about Sheba less and less. But tomorrow would be the night of the full moon. He would celebrate the anniversary of his birth, as he always did, by taking time out to remember her, meanwhile dredging the past for any clues he might have missed. It wasn't that his faith had been shaken in any way. He was still certain he was the chosen one and that the liberating humans were coming. But the timing was now a serious problem. Maybe there would be another sign, another blackened moon — anything to confirm his destiny and give not just him, but everyone, something to believe in. As part of the new liberated attitude in the cages, structured moon madness had been abolished. But Maxi and his muscle-mink lieutenants were still going onto red alert, while at Psycho's suggestion Mega was to help defuse potential trouble by addressing the colony beforehand. What he was going to say was a different matter.

'I feel it's all going wrong somehow, Mata,' he confessed, grateful for the opportunity to unburden himself. Psycho and Maxi might have their uses, but he never felt able to confide in them deeply. Something about Mata, in stark contrast, actively encouraged him. There was a sureness about her, a stillness in her centre, which he found immensely calming.

'Sheba never told me it would be like this,' he went on quietly. 'Look at us — hiding away plotting our diplomatic decisions to keep things quiet. We're as bad as the Elders. And with creeps like Psycho on board you could say we're worse. What's happened to the spark, the spontaneity?

'I've never told anyone this before, Mata, but I remember one of the Elders saying privately to me after the bollo meeting: "It's easy enough to set a ball rolling. But you mark my words, young fellow, the trouble comes when you try to stop it." It didn't make much sense to me at the time, but now I understand it only too clearly.'

'Stability was the Elders' trump card, Mega,' Mata reminded him soothingly. 'Anyhow Psycho and Maxi are exaggerating. It's the males who want it all and want it now. There's not so much trouble with my female warriors. They're more realistic.'

'Male or female, they're still right to think they've been waiting long enough,' Mega replied morosely.

'What's long enough?' Mata asked sharply, her bright eyes boring into his. 'Who are you to decide that? You may see yourself as the ordained leader, but that doesn't mean you control everything. It was our choice to upset everything by forcing change. You saw how the Elders caved in. They had no real belief − they were only interested in power. But we have our mission, which means we have to keep going onwards and upwards. If you want something enough, Mega, you make it happen.'

Mega looked at her gratefully. He needed to be reminded of these basics. It was so easy to lose your way and he wished he shared the clarity of her vision. Her words comforted him just as Sheba's had when he was a cub, and he now felt foolish for allowing himself to be so assailed by doubt.

'It's that simple, is it, Mata − onwards and upwards?' he grinned wryly.

'You know we don't have any choice, Mega,' she smiled fondly. 'We can't go back. You mustn't fret. At the moment we're in the lull before the storm. Nothing happens, then everything happens at once. We'll get a break soon, I promise you.'

Mega smiled back affectionately, appreciating the way she had used the pun to lighten the message.

'Well, Mata,' he sighed. 'We certainly could use one. I'm getting worn out by all this.'

26

The Eyes Have It

Owl arrived at the Small Clearing in a foul mood. Ula's rebuilding project had rendered the nest virtually uninhabitable, yet when he had unwisely complained about the disruption she had rounded on him with such a string of invective that eventually he had had to fly off. As a result he was a little early, yet all the more determined to have it out with Burdock before the scheduled pre-meeting started.

Instead he flew into the middle of a leaf-litter sub-committee, to be told Big Arse's whereabouts were unknown, while various meetings were running so late no-one knew when to expect him.

Owl grimaced. He had made the appointment a couple of days previously but not seen any need to confirm it. An arrangement, as far as he was concerned, was an arrangement – except, he now thought bitterly, in CWGland.

'Please stay, however, mighty Owl,' the committee implored him. 'Why not sit in our discussion as an observer? I'm sure you'll find it of great interest.'

'I doubt it,' Owl replied grimly, considering leaving. But that would be more trouble than it was worth. He had expected to

be here until sundown anyway, and it was now too late to start
thinking of anything else.

'Why does nothing work round here?' he asked irritably.

The assorted collection of rabbits, surrounded by various voles
and mice, stared at him blankly.

'Everything seems to be working to us,' one replied, puzzled.
'Nothing's perfect of course, which is why we're all here, trying
to make things better. But as we understand it, it all works.
Perhaps there is some problem, of which we are unaware?'

'Forget it,' Owl replied wearily, settling down to listen as
requested. He brightened up as he thought that he might learn
something to his advantage. Instead, what followed shook him
to the very core.

The current motion, he slowly gathered, was about too much
activity at night. This had led to various complaints about their
sleep patterns being interrupted from day creatures, including
of course the dunnocks. Night creatures were now mounting a
vigorous defence, based round the fact that they had no choice
but to scurry about.

'It's the eyes,' a woodmouse insisted to vigorous nods of
agreement. 'We can never relax because of the eyes.'

Owl was intrigued. One of the features of living in Old Wood
that he took for granted was there being eyes everywhere. A
myriad other creatures were always present – camouflaged,
undercover, out in the open. You always felt, quite rightly, that
someone was looking at you, even if you couldn't see anything to
confirm it. Eyes were the normal backdrop.

But as the woodmouse chattered volubly away Owl found
himself listening to a description of somewhere he hardly
recognised. Instead of Old Wood being a friendly place – for
him almost a playground – the mouse was painting a picture
of a daymare of the real, and imagined, eyes of those out to get
you. This catalogue of dreaded foes, naturally enough, included
him. Seen through bright mouse eyes, Old Wood was a fearful
place where you had to spend your life permanently on the *qui
vive* in trembling anticipation of an imminent attack. You were
paranoid, your enemies – real or imagined – everywhere. As a
result you spent most of your time hiding. Normal activities, like

eating, were fraught with danger because they exposed you to risk. In short, your entire lifestyle was built round defensive thinking, with mere survival on a day-by-day basis counted as the ultimate success story.

Owl tried to imagine having the same attitude himself, but it was so far removed from his personal experience he gave up. Nobody – real or imagined – was out to get him, after all. Surely no creature could live like that all the time, he thought, dazedly shaking his head. He certainly couldn't – his nerves would be in shreds. What was he doing, associating with creatures holding such a fundamentally fearful attitude? Even Ula didn't take such a negative view of everyone else.

It was a relief to see Burdock bustle into the clearing, Dandelion by his side as always.

'We must get on with the meeting straight away, Ollie,' he said brusquely, neglecting any form of greeting. 'There's so little time and so much to get through.'

Owl bristled. Burdock's meetings preoccupation was making him feel some sort of minion, rather than the boss he was supposed to be.

'Not until I see the Venerable Buck,' he said flatly

As he spoke he noticed Dandelion suddenly looking shifty.

'I presume he's still with us?' he asked, his suspicions suddenly aroused.

'Not exactly, I'm afraid,' Burdock replied slowly, staring venomously at Dandelion.

'What do you mean, "not exactly"?'

There was a long pause.

'Well, Ollie, I'm sorry to have to inform you that my great-grandfather has in fact passed on,' Burdock finally confessed, looking down at the ground.

'Passed on?' Owl inquired.

'Died,' Burdock explained.

'When?'

There was a long pause

'Actually, a few days ago,' Burdock finally muttered, studiously avoiding Owl's gaze. There was another long pause. 'We were going to tell you eventually, of course. But we thought it would be nicer not to just yet. The news was bound to upset you.'

'Did you go along with this?' Owl demanded of the trembling Dandelion.

'I hope we haven't done wrong, but Burdie did persuade me it was the best course in the circumstances, Ollie,' she replied lamely. 'It's been a tremendous strain for him, as you can imagine. You've no idea how difficult it has been for him to carry on as normal. Why, the poor dear's been so affected he's had to attend grief counselling sessions, haven't you, Burdie?'

Big Arse nodded mournfully.

'I see,' Owl said, not sure how much he did actually see. They were quite right in thinking he would be upset and of course he was sad for the old rabbit. But Burdock, seeing how much Owl disliked daily CWG life, must have known the promise of meeting the ancient sage again was the mainstay keeping him involved. Without the Venerable Buck to give the bigger picture, CWGs had to be infinitely less appealing.

'Please don't give up on us now, Ollie. We're nearly there,' Burdock pleaded, looking suitably contrite.

'Please, please stay with us,' Dandelion echoed. 'You mustn't be too hard on Burdie – he was only thinking of the common good.'

Was he indeed? Owl thought, staring at the abject figure. What had the now late Venerable Buck said – 'There's a good creature in there somewhere, one of the best'? Maybe, but it was sometimes hard to see. Yet, if Owl had been taken for a deliberate ride, in many ways he'd prefer not to know. Meanwhile Burdock was right – the Code and Bill meeting was now on the agenda. They were nearly there.

'All right, I'll believe you just this once,' he said reluctantly, thinking as he spoke that, even if he wasn't going mad, contact with CWGs was at least making him soft in the head. 'I'll tell you one thing though – your great-grandfather was worth ten of you any day.'

'That's not fair, Ollie,' Dandelion burst out, shocked. 'None of us is perfect. It's quite wrong of you to be so judgemental. Burdie is doing his best.'

'No doubt,' Owl replied drily. 'But for whom, precisely?'

27

The Bendy Bit

Mega sprang alert as the cheerful figure of Custard padded into the shed. Although the labrador didn't know it, her arrival had never been so keenly anticipated, especially as while they had been waiting for her Psycho had introduced what had proved to be an unproductive and frustrating spin. Seeking to play up his commitment to the enterprise, he had suggested they approach Pussles as well.

'I reckon she's worth a try, Mega,' he urged brightly. 'She isn't thick like Custard. You never know what she might come up with. May I interrogate her?' he pleaded, opaque eyes flickering.

'All right,' Mega grudgingly agreed, thinking he'd rather not be interrogated by Psycho himself. 'Handle her carefully though. She's not on our side.'

Pussles was obviously suspicious on her next visit to the shed. For once she did not launch into her standard homily about feline superiority, but just paraded about inquisitively.

'Well, my dears, something has been going on in your tiny little world, hasn't it?' she asked knowingly.

'This and that,' Psycho smiled back in unconvincing rat-mode.

'Actually, Pussles, we're getting rather bored with this place,' he went on loftily. 'We're thinking it's time we left. The trouble is that we're not quite sure of the best place to go. I was just thinking that, as a creature of the world, you'd be bound to have some good ideas.'

He gave a nervous cackle to signal it was all really a joke.

Pussles, however, was not amused.

'Don't you realise you're never going to get out?' she asked, slanting emerald eyes widening in disbelief. 'Unlike us cats, you creatures are not deemed fit to exist in the real world. You're simply too uncouth.'

'But just out of interest?' Psycho persevered, trying to shut out the sinking feeling that he was on a losing streak.

'Why not go and live on the manure heap then?' Pussles spat at him. 'It's where all turds rightfully belong.'

Seeing his spin-doctor so wound up, Mega stepped in and signalled with a shake of his head for him to stop there.

'Now I think of it,' Pussles added, sniffing in the general direction of the heaving and overflowing latrine pit, 'you'd be cleaner there than you are in here.'

Mega had never had to work so hard to contain himself. As if the state of the latrine pit was their fault! Her human was to blame, not them. Then he saw the coldness in her eyes. She was a real predator, ice-cool, calculating, remorseless. But more than that, one who enjoyed playing with her victims first. No honour – not like a red-blooded mink.

'Leave it, Psycho,' he hissed. 'And the rest of you.'

Fortunately Pussles stalked out without another word, since when, after he had given Psycho the bollocking of his life, they had been waiting for Custard.

Mega ordered Maxi to hold back the excited young mink while he and Mata went forward to greet the labrador. After Psycho's fiasco, Mata had insisted that she be the one asking the questions.

'Female to female, I suppose?' Mega had sneered gently.

'Maybe, Mega,' she had replied, shooting him a level glance. 'But there's more to it than that. Just because you're the leader, it doesn't mean that you can do everything yourself

– or do everything best either. Do you want Psycho on the job? Maxi?'

Mega had given in.

Now he hung back, listening to her play the gender card.

'Hello, Custard,' she greeted the labrador with a warm smile. 'It's so nice to have a bitch to talk to. We females must stick together, mustn't we?'

'I suppose so,' Custard replied uncertainly.

She had been expecting changes in the shed after the kerfuffle when the older mink were taken away. But it had happened before and she was used to getting new ones to talk to. None the less something she couldn't put her paw on was making her nervous. And after the larger audiences she had been used to it was disappointing to have only two mink at the wire. Why were the others being restrained? Judging by their cries of greeting, they wanted to come closer. On the other paw, though, this particular female mink was being very friendly.

Custard wagged her tail uncertainly.

'I want you to listen carefully to this question, Custard,' the female mink continued, 'are there any mink living in your wonderful wood – what the other mink used to call the Happy Land?'

'Of course there aren't,' Custard replied, surprised.

'Quite sure, Custard?'

'Absolutely certain. With all the chasing I do I'd be bound to have found them by now.'

What an extraordinary question to ask, she was thinking. She'd never stopped to consider it before, but her wood might not be quite as wonderful if it had mink loose in it. She preferred them safely penned behind their wire.

'No fibbing. I'd tell you if there were, honest,' she added.

'I'm sure you would, Custard,' the female mink replied reassuringly. She dropped her voice to a conspiratorial whisper. 'Now tell me – strictly between us girls – how do you get to your wonderful wood?'

Mega could see that Mata had drawn Custard in. She would talk, although how far that would get them all was a very different matter. For the bitch was now embarrassedly scratching her ear.

'I'm not so sure I actually know,' she finally confessed, looking shame-faced. 'The wood's so special I don't go that often. Anyhow, I get there in the volver — Master's a very good driver and his volver's very safe, you know — so I don't take any notice of the route. It's not for me to decide where I'm going. My job is to just sit there and enjoy the ride. Oh, and not bark too much, of course.'

She smiled soppily, while Mata wondered at the extent of her pathetic dependence on her human. Didn't she do anything for herself?

'There's another problem as well,' Custard added unexpectedly. 'I've got a special place in the volver, with my own blanket! But because it's in the back I look out of the rear window. So I only see where I've come from and not where I'm going, if you see what I mean.'

You've just summed up your whole life, Mega thought grimly. He gritted his teeth as the labrador blinked and broke off to scratch herself again. How could Mata have such patience? If he had his way he'd throttle the truth out of her.

'Custard, you're such a clever dog you must be able to remember some of the way,' she was now saying encouragingly.

'I'll try,' the labrador replied, brightening up at this human-like praise. 'Master turns left out of the farm gate, right when he comes to another rollway . . .' Deep furrows creased her forehead. 'Then he goes round the bendy bit — that's where he shouts at volvers which are coming the other way — then right again and over a hill. Then he stops, opens the tailgate, and out I jump.'

She wagged her tail anxiously.

'There's a little bit more, Custard, isn't there?'

Mata's voice was as smooth as silk, but with an edge that Custard recognised as a command.

'Silly old me,' she added quickly. 'Then we walk across the hump-backed bridge, go up the track through the field, and into the wood through the five-barred gate. I don't know any more. No fibbing!'

Mata looked across to Mega, who nodded.

'Thank you, Custard,' she signed her off. 'I told you we

females would get along. Maybe we'll come and play with you in your wonderful wood one day,' she added wickedly.

'That'd be fun,' Custard replied hesitantly before padding dutifully out.

The leadership conference in Mega's cage was brief.

'Well, Maxi?' Mega asked after Mata had relayed the labrador's instructions.

'It'll have to do, my leader,' Maxi said, looking dubious. 'Although I'm not at all sure about entrusting ourselves to a dog. And I must say that Custard's visit proved highly alarming from a security point of view. It was all I could do to hold the ranks back. I can't give you any guarantees about tonight, I'm afraid.'

Mega smiled at Mata, sitting alongside him, and they all listened to the triumphant whooping and chanting from the exercise area backing up his military adviser's statement. After the Keeper had failed to feed them, the previous night had been a rough one and the mink had been fired up by the imminent prospect of the full moon even before Custard's visit.

But from Mega's point of view the long-awaited arrival of the labrador had taken a load off his mind. He was facing the future with renewed optimism. At last they knew the way.

'You worry too much, Maxi,' he dismissed him peremptorily. 'What about you, Psycho? Or have you got cold feet as well?'

'I must say, Mega, I have to agree with Maxi,' the runt replied, looking worried. 'Please, please, Mega, try to calm them down when you speak to them tonight.'

'You're scared, aren't you?' Mega asked in astonishment.

'Not exactly, Mega,' Psycho replied unconvincingly, his opaque eyes for once betraying his feelings. 'Let's just say I'm a shade on the apprehensive side.'

'Well you'd better stop being,' Mega said shortly. 'We're all in this as much as each other.'

'Yes, Mega,' Psycho replied humbly.

As soon as darkness fell Mega stepped up to the end of the exercise area and looked through the rooflight. It was a crystal-clear night and the first stars were already shining incredibly brightly, while the temperature had dropped sharply. Everything held out the promise of a perfect full moon. The Keeper had just belatedly appeared to give them their evening feed and the mink had been more bold and stroppy than ever. Picking up on their ugly mood, he had only dished out half-rations, provoking even more angry snarling and chittering, to which he had responded by slamming the shed door violently as he went out. The overflowing latrine pit, its noxious contents seeping outwards in an ever-widening circle of slime, remained unattended to. It was a new low point in their relationship.

Meanwhile Mega had been feeling wild moon stirrings within himself. He wasn't going to listen to scared little Psycho any more. He was going onwards and upwards, to energise the mink even further with his vision of the future.

'My mink, we have taken a further step towards the Promised Land,' he cried to the assembled throng. 'Custard has not only shown us the way, but confirmed that it is a land flowing with prey and victims. Awaiting you there, my mink, is the reality of killing in the wild. You'll bite into the necks of living creatures. You'll hear the shrieks of pain and shock. The warm flesh will wriggle as you search out the jugular. Then you'll sink your teeth in until the blood fountains out, thick and red.

'Thick and red, my beauties, thick and red. For that's the hot spurt. That's what we mink were made for. Blood, my boys, blood! You'll lick it, you'll gorge yourselves on it, you'll smear it all over yourselves, you'll bathe in it as it showers upwards. For once we are out nothing and no-one will hold us back. We will be ourselves. And that'll mean we'll have hot spurts – not just once, but time and time and time again. There are no limits in the free world, my mink, no limits.'

He looked over the sea of faces, feeling a huge and surging wave of affection overwhelm him.

'Bollo to chomping through our dull fodder here in the cages!' he grinned. 'Bollo to mechanically processing our basic fuel! We're going to have hot spurts. We're going to smash skulls to suck out the brains. We're going to kill whatever we like, whenever we like. Because that's what we mink were born for. Then we'll have the sweetness, my brave ones. Then we'll have the essence. For what is life without hot spurts but mere existence?'

'Give us, give us hot spurts,' his audience chanted ecstatically.

'I promise you, hot spurts are coming,' Mega yelled.

'But when?' came a cry came from the back.

There was a terrible silence. For the first time they saw their leader thrown as he struggled to reply. Beside him Maxi had gone stiff with fury. No-one was allowed to ask Mega questions like that.

'Say something, Mega,' Psycho hissed.

Mega recalled his spin-doctor's final desperate pleading: 'Please, please, Mega, don't talk about the timing. Don't commit us to anything. Otherwise we're on an even greater hiding to nothing.'

Mega watched his beady eyes now flickering about, trying to identify the culprit who had had the temerity to pose the question. A huge upsurge of hatred came over him. Who was running the show, him or that poisoned dwarf?

'Let me answer with the tidings of great joy I was about to bring you,' he shouted, thowing all caution to the wind. 'Our liberators will be here shortly. Liberation day is not long off. That is my pledge and promise to you all – freedom is coming.'

Even though he was in full view of everyone, Psycho sank his head into his paws and let out an audible groan. Now Mega had really stuffed them! For the minions were already breaking into their new anthem, derived from the original bollo song.

'Here we go! Here we go! Here we go!' they were sing-ing, swaying triumphantly from side to side. 'Here we go! Here we go! Here we go!'

'Here we go indeed!' Mega yelled. 'And very soon, I promise you, very, very soon!'

He broke off as he realised the mink had suddenly gone silent and were staring open-mouthed behind him. Whipping round along with the other leaders, he saw the shed door standing open. There was their Keeper. But what was really causing everyone's jaws to drop was that he was carrying a small cage.

In it were two mink they had never seen before.

28

Nicely Does It

Whatever he might have said to Burdock at the time, Owl's attitude to the CWGs had changed as the news of the Venerable Buck's demise sank in. With the old rabbit dead, he could no longer see any reason for having anything to do with them. Furthermore, suspecting Burdock had deliberately been hiding the knowledge, Owl decided to punish him even more by withdrawing without any notice. Big Arse could stew in his own juice.

Or Owl thought he could. But he soon found it was not that easy. Like Boris, he had become addicted and spent so much time wondering what was happening in the crucial run-up to the Woodland Code that in the end he decided he had to find out for himself.

Flying home one dawn, he spotted the hapless Honeysuckle trundling in her wobbly fashion across the Big Clearing. Silently swooping down behind her, he cruelly hurtled over the top of her head and turned in a sudden flurry of his broad wings.

'Hi there!' he cried cheerfully, dropping like a stone to land just in front of her.

'Oh,' she gasped, heaving backwards as she clutched at her

heart. 'You gave me such a fright! I thought the sky had fallen in!'

'No such luck,' Owl grinned. 'Now listen to me: tell Burdock I want him to meet me up at the Quarry – now!'

'I'll do my best to find him,' Honeysuckle gasped. 'But I'm not terribly sure I'll be able to, he's so awfully busy. And then I've just had such a terrible night with the children. First I couldn't get them off, then one of them insisted on playing with me and before I knew what was happening they were all at it. You've no idea how exhausting they can be at that age, I can tell you. They've got so much energy and one of them's hyper anyhow.

'You wouldn't believe what it was like – just one thing after another, until in the end I didn't get a wink of sleep. I've quite forgotten all the things I was meaning to do today! You see, for ages I've been going to—'

'Aaaaaaaaagh!'

Owl had mustered his most stentorian screech and Honey-suckle had gone rigid.

'All you are going to do now,' he commanded, pronouncing each word slowly and deliberately, as if addressing a mentally deficient inhabitant of the leaf-litter, 'is find Burdock and tell him to meet me at the Quarry – now!'

'Yes, mighty Owl,' Honeysuckle muttered humbly, meekly trundling off without any further argument.

Owl, watching her from behind, briefly considered whether her bum was even larger than Big Arse's. Then he dismissed the thought as irrelevant and went for a leisurely fly down the valley and back. After judging he had allowed Burdock enough time, he made for the Quarry.

Only Dandelion was present.

'I'm most frightfully sorry, Ollie,' she apologised. 'But Burdie can't be be here yet.'

'Don't tell me,' Owl interrupted. 'He's tied up in a meeting.'

'How did you know?' Dandelon asked, looking puzzled.

'Never mind,' Owl replied wearily.

Until now, he realised, he had never really talked to Dandelion. When she was with Burdock she always deferred to him and let him take the lead. But now, as Owl allowed her to make polite conversation to fill in the time, he noticed her edging round to the subject of his being a predator.

'I can't stop thinking how unfortunate it is that you have to kill to eat,' she confessed, looking at him pityingly. 'Don't you think it's such a shame, both for you and for us?'

'I can't help it if I have to eat flesh to live,' Owl screeched. 'You're not suggesting I try to exist on grass or plants, are you? What are you trying to do, murder me?'

While he posed the question as a half-joke, he was entirely serious. He had never thought being a carnivore was unfortunate, or a shame. Dandelion's remark was typical of the way CWGs poked their noses into other creatures' businesses, almost as though they were determined to try and prevent them being themselves.

'Of course I'm not trying to murder you,' she protested, sounding flustered. 'You mustn't make jokes like that. Nothing could be further from my mind, especially after all you've done for us, and I'm sure I speak here for all Concerned Guardians.

'Please don't misunderstand me – I do appreciate that it's not your fault you have to survive by feeding on others in this unfortunate way. I was, however, about to suggest that you could apply your mind to alleviating some of the distress you cause through your predatory activities.'

Recovering her composure, she fluttered her long eyelashes and looked at him winsomely.

'We had a meeting recently to discuss how we could best help you . . .'

'We predators have got other things to do besides hunt, you know,' Owl interrupted, now totally fed up. Wasn't this seemingly harmless doe aware that she only had this opportunity to attack him gratuitously because her own partner was late?

'We don't go round killing just for fun, or out of some sort of vindictiveness,' he added, feeling he had not driven the point entirely home.

Mind you, he thought as he spoke, you could enjoy hunting. There was a thrill attached, and a satisfaction, as well as the enormous sense of power. But it was still work, and for lesser predators than him often hazardous work at that. Plenty died on the job and you always ran a risk, no matter how superior your weaponry or apparently feeble your victim. You could land awkwardly, crash into something, choke on your prey, pick up a disease – there were a dozen ways any predator could go wrong. Hunting was no doddle either. It wasn't like preying on plants and grass, which stayed in the same place, stoically growing into meals for you to consume at your leisure. Predator food was always moving about, doing its utmost to escape your clutches. And it could be enormously difficult to find, especially in the depths of the now ending Big Cold, or the time that was coming when you had owlets to feed as well as yourself.

Equally there were times you just didn't feel like it. You might be under the weather – and you were certainly out in all weathers, not just when you were in the mood and conditions were favourable. It might not be Raka-style work, ploughing away all day, but it was work just the same. And as far as Owl was concerned, any sensible creature regarded work as a four-letter word and avoided it as much as possible.

One of the migratory birds had once told him that there were creatures in the hot countries called lions, who got their females to do the hunting. All the males had to do was look after their harem and give the odd roar from time to time. Owl had felt jealous. Rather than endlessly quartering the wood and outlying fields for his sustenance, he would much prefer just to give the occasional screech, then go for a good fly simply to admire the view and feel the wind in his feathers. He winced as he recalled Ula's scorn when he had mentioned the male lion business. In her opinion it should be the other way round, she had snapped.

But how could he explain any of this to Dandelion, a harmless doe who shared much the same perspective on life as the woodmouse he had talked to? Then he remembered a different tale he had been told by a migratory bird – had it been a swallow? He had been intending to bring it up in his next conversation with the Venerable Buck, but now there wasn't to be one he might as well try it out on Dandelion. At least it would fill in the time and stop her talking.

'Let me tell you a story,' he said, and saw her soft eyes light up with pleasure. 'It's about an animal called

an elephant, which lives in the hot lands and is gigantic.'

'And is also, if I may be allowed to point it out, vegetarian,'
Dandelion interrupted.

'And is vegetarian,' Owl agreed, refusing to be deflected.
'One day this elephant is walking along, when he comes to
some floodwaters which have trapped a vicious insect called a
scorpion.'

'Excuse me,' Dandelion interrupted again. 'Why is this story
about a male elephant? It may have escaped your attention, but
we're at present having a drive against gender discrimination
and sexual stereotyping.'

Owl stopped and considered for a moment before grinning to
himself. Dandelion did not yet know it, but changing the sex
of the creatures in the story would be a pleasure.

'This female elephant,' he went on with heavy emphasis,
'sees that the water is rising and the scorpion, who is also
female, is going to drown. She therefore stops and offers her
a lift to safety.

'The scorpion clambers on her back and the female elephant
carries her to dry land. When they get there the female scorpion
stings the female elephant, which falls over and begins to die.

'"Why did you do that?" she asks.

'The scorpion shrugs.

'"That's what I do," she says.

'And that's what I do, you see, Dandelion. I eat voles.'

The doe sat back on her haunches and regarded him
quizzically. There was a long pause while she frowned with
concentration.

'I'm afraid I don't quite see the point,' she replied eventually.

Neither did he exactly, Owl had thought as he stopped to
ponder it for the first time. Maybe he should have told the
story to the Venerable Buck after all. But he was certain it
was somehow on his side, as Dandelion now seemed to confirm
by switching to a new tack.

'Ollie, have you ever considered not what you do, but the way
you do it?' she asked. 'Something else we Concerned Guardians

sincerely believe in is being nice to other creatures. We're all capable of it and we believe it immeasurably improves the quality of life in the wood – like having good manners and being polite, other virtues we are keen to encourage. Above all else we want Old Wood to be a nicer place. I wonder if you've ever thought how you could contribute by being nicer to those ill-fated victims of yours?'

'Nicer?' Owl inquired, now genuinely puzzled.

He wasn't consciously nasty to voles. He just ate them. He felt himself being dragged back on to the confusing ground covered by Marcus Mole. Maybe Dandelion's slant would make it more explicable?

As her brow furrowed again, Owl thought how innocent she looked. She was almost sweet, with a sort of cheerful hopelessness he couldn't help finding endearing. He could see the attraction for her more hard-headed mate. But did she talk some pellets! She must be good in the bedchamber for Burdock to put up with it. Owl burst out laughing as his mind conjured up a rear view of Big Arse pumping away on the job.

'I don't see what's so amusing,' Dandelion said huffily. 'It would be polite at least to share the joke.'

'Just put it down to predator bad taste,' Owl replied.

As Dandelion backed off a couple of paces, looking uncertain, he took the opportunity to sweep the horizon for any sign of Burdock. There was none.

'Explain how I can I be nice, then,' he said, accepting he was trapped.

'How about, possibly, when you are about to kill someone, apologising to them beforehand?' Dandelion suggested, looking at him brightly. 'You could start by introducing yourself, and then do it politely, without leaving any mess behind.'

The thought sent her veering off down a fresh track.

'Have you ever considered how upsetting the debris that you predators leave behind is for us vegetarians? If you made less mess it would help another project which we're very keen on at the moment. You see, we not only want to make Old Wood a nicer place, but want it to look nicer too. In our view some areas of the leaf-litter have become particularly untidy, so we're in the process of organising some voluntary work teams to clean them up. Why don't you join one? Your aid would be invaluable, as well as being much appreciated, and the unaccustomed exercise would be terribly good for you.'

'Will Burdock be there as well?' Owl asked with a sudden flash of intuition.

'Naturally Burdie would love to be,' Dandelion replied primly. 'But I'm afraid that he simply can't spare the time. His Woodland Code is so close to being put to the vote that unfortunately he's far too busy with all the meetings that are needed.'

'I thought as much,' Owl replied, satisfied he had at last scored a direct hit.

He looked up at the darkening sky. Never mind Burdock and bloody meetings, his prime hunting time of dusk was rapidly slipping away. He was feeling extraordinarily peckish as well. Why should he wait any longer, especially as Dandelion had handed him his opportunity on a plate?

'Well, I'm too busy catching voles,' he announced, taking off without any further farewell.

'Well really,' he heard Dandelion's voice float up after him. 'There's no need to be so rude.'

He looked down on the human-made scar of the Quarry, watching her forlornly gazing around for her mate. But even from Owl's aerial vantage point the chief rabbit was not yet in sight.

'Poor old Burdie must be stuck in one of his grief-counselling sessions,' he taunted down cruelly, before striking out and winging it to the far side of the valley.

It was a good job, in retrospect, the chief rabbit hadn't turned up. If Dandelion hadn't taught him he'd had enough of CWGs, nothing ever would.

29

Critical Paths

All the mink, including Mega, remained frozen in their guilty tableau as the Keeper advanced into the shed. He had never interrupted them like this before and, if he sensed what had been going on, it could only lead to even greater hostility. But Mega could tell straight away it was not just at their end that things were abnormal. The Keeper had not done his click thing to cause the bright lights to appear, but was illuminating his way with a light like a moonbeam carried in his paw. All the time he was glancing over his shoulder, as if fearing something behind him. He was as jumpy as they were, Mega realised.

He looked across at Mata and his heart leapt as she mouthed: 'Onwards and upwards.' This could be what they were looking for. The two mink the Keeper was carrying could be refugees from a colony hit by the human liberators.

The Keeper had now reached the isolation cage where Mega had been born. At first it seemed that he was going to put the pair of new mink inside. But then another human hurried into the shed and started a heated argument. Mega watched, fascinated, as the Keeper deferred to him. As if he was no longer master in his own shed, he bowed to the other's will, picked up some tools and went to Ramses' old cage. All the time protesting in a loud whisper, he removed the boarding, opened the wire door and reluctantly released the two new mink. After he had locked it carefully the two humans then carried out a minute inspection of the lock on every cage before finally shutting the shed door. Maxi glared at everyone to stay quiet as they all listened to the lengthy testing of the main lock.

Finally the footsteps receded.

Mata was the first to react. She rushed across and placed herself at the cage entrance, preventing both the new mink from getting out and mob from getting in. Mega strolled over, trying to look casual while silently thanking her for her quick reactions. Inside he was as bursting with excitement as everyone else, yet he also recognised this unexpected turn of events was making him uneasy. He was getting more and more like an Elder, he thought with dismay, trying to shrug the feeling off. As Mata said, he should be welcoming change, not worrying about it. But he wanted so much for the new arrivals to be the sign he needed, in some ways he didn't want to confront the truth. Rather than helping him, it might just introduce more complications.

The jostling crowd parted to let him through and he peered inside to see the two new mink looking brightly at him

'Do come in,' one greeted him cheerfully, ushering him forward with a welcoming front paw. 'Please allow us to introduce ourselves – I'm MI, and this is my twin brother and amanuensis, M2. And can I tell you how delighted we are to make your acquaintance? Because we already know we're going to get on fine, don't we, 2?'

'Absolutely, I – I can see a very productive interface developing.'

'Could be the start of something big, eh 2?'

'Massively global, I'd say, I.'

They beamed at him enthusiastically.

'Whoever, and whatever, you are, just be quiet,' Mega instructed, trying to hide his astonishment.

He ducked back outside and saw that Maxi and his muscle-minks had belatedly taken over the job of holding back the buzzing crowd. Brusquely he nodded Mata and Psycho to one side.

'I don't know what's going on, but they're weird,' he informed them briefly. 'I want you to help me interrogate them before we let the others near.'

'The minions won't be happy about that, Mega,' Psycho piped up worriedly. 'They want to meet them now.'

'Well they can lump it,' Mega snapped back. 'When will they understand they can't have everything they want?'

'Never,' Psycho mouthed to himself. Rather, when would Mega understand the sort of material he had to work with? Never as well, he supposed, raising his eyes to the shed roof.

'Did you say something, Psycho?' Mega snapped suspiciously.

'No, Mega. Just thinking,' he replied quickly.

'Well don't,' Mega snapped again. Despite his efforts to stay cool he sounded as jumpy as everyone else. What had put this jangling into the atmosphere?

'Keep them all back, Maxi,' he ordered, ignoring the resulting chorus of boos as he, Mata and Psycho dived back inside the cage.

'Hi guys,' came the cheerful greeting. 'It looks as though we've got a real get-together at last! And as you're obviously in charge of corporate affairs here, I can't tell you how sincerely we appreciate your interest in our presence.

'Now, let me get the ball rolling by telling you a little more about ourselves.'

'You listen to me,' Mega snarled, cutting short the stream of patter. 'Have the human liberators just struck at your colony?'

'Colony?' MI asked, looking puzzled and turning to his brother. 'What's a colony, 2?'

'Pass on that one, I,' the other replied jauntily. 'Unless we're in one now. Because one thing's for sure – this is no laboratory.'

Now it was Mega's turn.

'What's a laboratory?' he asked furiously. Something about this pair got right under his skin!

'Well, it's not like this shed place of yours,' the first mink replied, sniffing, like Pussles, in the general direction of the latrine pit. 'It's, how can I put it, a shade more advanced, more civilised.'

'A little more high-class all round,' the other said, wrinkling his nose disdainfully.

'But what is it?' Mega screamed, beside himself.

Mata and Psycho exchanged alarmed glances. Their leader wasn't handling this at all well.

'Let me talk to them, Mega,' Mata intervened gently.

She turned to the pair, who had now gone into a pained huff.

'I'm Mata,' she introduced herself, 'and this is Mega, our leader, and Psycho. And you're absolutely right — we are in charge of the bodies here.'

This polite formal introduction appeared to mollify the duo.

'We're MI and M2, and we're twins,' the first one repeated his introduction, adding a piece of information that was essentially gratuitous. They were so similar it was virtually impossible to tell them apart. 'And as I was about to tell you, before I was so rudely interrupted, we have been living in a laboratory, doing highly specialised work alongside the humans.'

He gave Mega a superior smile, whilst his twin looked aloof.

'It was such mind-bending stuff that I'm afraid, living in this shed of yours, you wouldn't understand a word,' he went on. 'You see, we were part of a special research project testing the limits of mink intelligence. It was a major exercise carried out over many moons, with stiff competition from all kinds of animals — and birds.

'Needless to say though, being mink, we came top of the class in every subject.'

As the three colony mink stared at him blankly, his twin seamlessly took up the running.

'What you need to know, in a nutshell, is that we've been gifted with massive intelligence,' M2 announced glibly. 'And don't think for a moment it's just us saying that. The humans' tests showed we were somewhat off the map IQ-wise. In other words — and we don't mind at all you knowing this — we're bright. Very bright. So bright that quite honestly we don't expect to stay very long in this low-class establishment — with all due respect to your good selves, of course!'

Mega spluttered. But Mata gave him such a black look he went quiet.

'How absolutely fascinating,' she replied enthusiastically. 'You'll have to tell me all about it before you go. But first, if you're so bright, why are you here?'

'We're not quite sure actually,' MI conceded, revealing the first crack in the know-it-all fasçade. 'Our programme was nearly finished anyhow. Then there were all sorts of rumours about trouble with the smoking dogs, and in the end we were just moved out. You know what the humans are like when they decide to do something – everything happens very quickly. They really are extraordinary creatures, aren't they? I'm sure you've found the same dealing with your Keeper guy. Something else, eh? Wow!'

He sucked his breath in sharply through his teeth and shook his head in wondering admiration.

'Totally amazing, aren't they?' M2 exclaimed rapturously. 'You see, our speciality was studying them in depth while they were studying us. It was an extremely productive interface for both sides, I can tell you. We both really got to like them – and the things we got to know! We're not saying we covered all the available ground but we did come up with some very exciting stuff, very exciting indeed.

'I think we can rightfully claim that we know humans backwards, forwards, sideways – any way you like. But the thing that's dynamite as far you're concerned is that we got heavily into an area we're now very keen to develop in conjunction with your good selves.

'Gentlemales and gentlefemale, allow me to make a presenta- tion of our initial material.'

The torrent of spiel switched to the other newcomer, M2 – or was it MI?

'We know you're just going to love this,' he grinned fervently. 'First we're going to talk critical paths and where we're coming from. Then I'll be leading a group discussion to plan our campaign. First, though, let's take a snapshot of exactly where we're at.

'You all live in this cage complex, right?'

'Shut up!' Mega shouted in his most authoritarian voice, thumping the floor.

He'd had quite enough of this bollo, whatever it was. As he'd listened to their odious stream of self-advertisement, he'd had to concede these mink were exceedingly clever. But their arrogance was quite astounding. Meanwhile, their remarkable smoothness was making him feel horribly inadequate. Their silvery-backed fur had a rich, glowing patina that made all the rest of them look rough, even Mata. Whatever they ate was obviously better than shed fodder. But what really set them apart was the feeling that they obviously regarded themselves as something the colony had never come across before: sophisticated mink. 'Dapper' was undoubtedly how they liked to think of the way they presented themselves, in both appearance and manner. But Mega had already decided 'oily' was more appropriate. He didn't like them. They were like Psycho, but worse — if that was possible. Too clever by half and even more garrulous. The way they talked! He had never heard anything like it, in either quantity or content.

The twins meanwhile shrugged their shoulders helplessly as they looked at each other in pained surprise. What had they done wrong so to upset their client? It was all straightforward stuff, wasn't it? This temporary glitch must be due to these colony mink being unused to marketing — which was fair enough if all they knew was this shed place. They needed to be introduced to the kind of concepts and parameters marketing revolved round. Once put on the correct learning curve, they would straighten out.

MI frowned at his twin to stay quiet.

'Perhaps we've been going a little too fast for you, gentlemales and gentlefemale?' he inquired sympathetically. 'Maybe you'd like to throw a few questions our way instead? Don't worry — we can field anything.'

He'd like to throw more than a few questions, Mega thought. He looked across and saw Psycho's weird eyes gleaming with excitement. As they caught his leader's his spin-doctor flicked his pointed head to indicate they should go outside.

Not a bad idea, thought Mega. This was one occasion

when he definitely needed Psycho to tell him what was
going on.

'In a word, what do you think?' Mega demanded as soon as he,
Psycho and Mata had got into his cage after pushing through
the rowdy crowd of youngsters outside. She had invited herself
along unasked.

His spin-doctor used three.

'Overall, good news,' he replied instantly.

'Mata?'

'A change, and welcome for that reason alone, Mega,' she
replied slowly. 'I often find one change presages an even bigger
one to come.'

Mega stared at her, feeling frustrated. She spoke so many
times in riddles, which didn't mean anything to him. What he
needed was something more definite, something he could latch
on to. He was sure they could use this extraordinary duo who
had landed in their laps. But not, his first and disappointing
impression had been, to help with an actual escape. These new
mink might come from another world, but they could hardly
be described as physical. They probably had no idea how to
break out. But whatever marketing was, it could presumably
be immensely beneficial in other ways. The main point was that
he could relax about them mounting any challenge. Plainly they
were eager to serve.

'What shall we do with them?' he demanded of Psycho.

His spin-doctor battled with his mixed feelings. These
were just the type of mink he had been yearning for. They
had brains, like him. They were sharp. They were quick.
Once he learnt their arcane language matters would lift
on to a completely new plane. The scams they could cook
up together. Yet at the same time a large potential rock
loomed – with their blend of sophistication and inside information, the newcomers could quickly come to overshadow
him.

'We can use them, Mega, but not yet,' he replied carefully.
'The danger as I see it is they're taking things too far too fast.
Right now we should slap them down – give them a kick in

the goolies, so to speak. Then they'll adjust to us and we'll all be in business.'

Mega was pleased by this confirmation of his own thoughts.

'How shall we sideline them, then?'

'Why not ostracise them, Mega?' Psycho said with a sly grin. 'Better still, ban them from contact with anyone except with me. Then I'll get inside their heads for you.'

Psycho's grin faded as Mega continued to hold his gaze. For once it was his turn to shudder. His own eyes might be able to hide his thoughts, but his leader's were making him feel totally transparent. Mega had sussed that it was his personal crown that was now under threat.

'That would suit you very well, wouldn't it?' he asked with a smile half cruel and half affectionate. 'Well, you're in luck — it suits me too. Mata?'

She nodded, but said nothing.

'They're all yours for the moment, Psycho,' Mega informed him, his smile slipping into a friendlier grin. 'Report to me when you've completed your strategy appraisal, or whatever bollo that pair would call it.

'Meanwhile, let's show them to the others before the moon comes up and things get too out of hand.'

30

Out

As human footsteps crunched on the hoar-frost outside, Mega sat bolt upright. It had been a weird enough night already. First there had been his speech, then the arrival of the two new mink, and finally the appearance over the rooflight of a moon so huge and powerful that the colony had erupted in an unprecedented orgy of madness. The youngsters had temporarily regained the wild enthusiasm they had shown at the take-over after Mega, as energised as the rest, had curtly instructed the protesting Maxi to let it rip. Now, in the darkest hour before dawn, they had retired to their cages and crashed out, drained emotionally and physically.

Mega, however, had stayed awake to fulfil his vow to himself to remember Sheba. Yet while he had been mentally conversing with her, something had been making him tingle with anticipation. Now, as he heard the noises outside, he knew instinctively that his moment had come. It wasn't just that it was night, or that the footsteps were unfamiliar – that didn't add up to their liberators. But he still knew, without thinking, that it was them. Silently he thanked Sheba, while chiding her gently for making him wait so long.

He heard his fellow mink stirring as they, too, pricked up their ears. Someone was fiddling with the shed door. There was the soft muttering of human voices and a series of dull knocks before it opened and two humans stepped into the gloom. Mega, remembering Solomon's story about the liberators running off, remained frozen. The others might know it was not the hated figure of their Keeper, but how many instinctively understood that these were their liberators was a different matter. One noise and their saviours could be gone.

Without warning, a searing beam of light suddenly pierced the darkness. Mega was temporarily blinded as it swept down the cages, shining directly into his eyes, before it was gone, dancing down to the end of the line. The excitement level in the shed went up another notch. A sharp rattling echoed off the rafters as individual mink began running up and down their cage floors. As the humans meanwhile moved stealthily forwards Mega's certainty increased. His heart started pounding, while everything around him seemed to move into sharper focus. He felt so fantastically aware he could sense, even from this distance, that the humans were hardly daring to breathe. Everything about their furtive movements screamed that they knew they should not be there.

He recalled Mata's earlier enigmatic remark. Had she guessed that the two new mink were the sign he had been looking for? He hadn't seen it himself at the time, but with hindsight the clue was the superior human, with whom the Keeper had so carefully checked all the locks. The liberators must have followed the laboratory mink. One change had indeed presaged another.

'Right, Mata,' he hissed towards her cage.

'Right, Mega,' came a hiss back.

He heard a sharp snicking noise and craned his head to look up the line, just as the human huddled over the first cage stepped backwards. The wire peeled away and fell to the floor and Mega was gripped by a wave of elation. The barriers were coming down! It was really happening! The freedom he had promised was just a snip away! Feeling a throb of energy surge along the line as the rest of the colony also began to realise, he moved to take up position in the middle of his cage. He would give his saviour a special welcome.

He waited, trembling, until the liberator reached his cage and started work on the wire. Then, as he examined him carefully, he felt a terrible sense of let-down. His rescuer should be exciting and glamorous. Yet he looked much the same as their Keeper — except that, like some other humans they had seen in the shed, he had face-fur. He was as white as the rest though, when somehow Mega had imagined he would be dark brown, like a mink. He knew there were humans of different colours because of the black one who occasionally came into the shed. He seemed to have a low status, merely carrying the heavy boxes that contained their food, meanwhile working harder than they had ever seen the Keeper do. That must have been the key to his expectation, Mega now thought. As an oppressed underdog, a brown human would have more in common with them.

He sniffed as he realised his white liberator stank as badly as other humans. All mink found their foul odour particularly repulsive and this one's was stronger than normal, because he was sweating so copiously despite the cold. Mega's black nose wrinkled in disgust as the peculiar sharp smell cut through the all-pervading stench of the overflowing latrine pit. But what he found most odd was that his rescuer didn't seem to want to look at him. He was keeping his gaze studiously averted as he snipped away. I'm not having that, Mega thought. We should at least be exchanging mutual looks of respect. He focused his stare on the top of the bent head, willing the human to raise his eyes. To his amazement he felt a flash of fear in response. The liberator was afraid! But of what? Surely not of him! He increased the intensity of his stare, watching the head slowly drag itself upwards. Then they made eye contact and he locked on and pulled the human in. It felt different to being eye to eye with the Keeper. Despite everything, the mink still deferred to him. But here was a sense of knowing, a feeling of inevitability applying to both sides. It must be like this when you had a hot spurts victim in your sights. As he gazed even deeper into his liberator's eyes Mega knew who was possessing whom. He, Mega, was the master. He, Mega, was dictating the situation. He knew the human, but the human did not know him.

Thrilling to his power, he continued to hold the human's gaze ruthlessly. Then, slowly, he broke into his most wolfish smile. You're just a tool, he beamed. You don't know what you're doing, or why you're doing it. It is I who have summoned you, I who understand, I who am in command. The fear in the human's eyes deepened and they flickered sideways as he made desperate attempts to break away. But they always slid back while Mega held him, trapped. Thank you for being the cipher, he signalled. Thank you for coming to release what you do not know. For if you had known what we were really like, you would never have come near us.

Then he let his victim go. He had made his point, established his domination. Now he knew he had been correct about mink's place in the world. No wonder the humans had caged them. Liberators or not, they were afraid.

He watched dispassionately as his liberator hurried to finish his work on the wire, before pulling it away and moving on to the next cage, all the time keeping his eyes firmly fixed downwards. Then came the first magic moment when Mega could see without the criss-cross lines that had hampered his vision from the moment he had first opened his eyes. It was like removing a veil from the faces his imagination told him he could see on the wall.

He waited silently while the liberator worked to the end of the line and tiptoed back to the shed door, skirting the cut wire lying in untidy festoons on the floor. As his confederate joined him, the pair were briefly framed again in the doorway. They switched off their moonbeam lights, gave a little wave of farewell and vanished into the night, leaving the shed door ajar.

A wave of fresh air surged in, whipping away the sour stench of the latrine pit, while an unnatural calm settled over the shed. It felt as though time was standing still.

Mega remained frozen along with the others. Next came the moment of truth, the moment when, according to the Elders' shibboleth, if any one of them took a step on to the table edge, the sky would fall in. As yet they had done no wrong. They were poised on the cusp, their salvation still in their own paws. The liberators might have provided the opportunity, but the mink's crime would be capitalising on it. They could still avoid the Elders' predicted doom by all remaining meekly in their cages. In the morning the Keeper would presumably replace the wire and restore their old world. Far from punishing them, he would then probably reward them for staying loyal.

The mesmerising silence was broken by a furtive whisper that it might be a trap, followed by scattered squeaks of assent. Mega was suddenly spurred into action. He must move before the colony, losing its collective nerve, faltered. Yet still he hesitated. Without those familiar criss-cross lines the cage-front gaped at him like an enormous mouth. It seemed to be luring him to step through, bringing about his and everyone else's destruction. Then he was then struck by the reverse doubt. Intellectually he might know there was no longer an obstacle, but his heart still found it hard to believe. What if an invisible barrier held him back, rendering him powerless?

Then he heard his mother's muffled last words from inside the sack: 'Be ready, my son! Be ready!' He was ready, he thought, bracing himself. Always had been. He had kept Sheba's faith for so long, he would not fail her now.

One slow step at a time he walked towards the front of the cage.

'Bollo! Bollo! Bollo! The Keeper's a load of bollo!' he sang loudly.

He was rewarded by a few giggles as he tucked up his haunches. The atmosphere was electric. Everyone knew that the next small step for him would represent a giant step for them all.

Without further ado, he stepped over the forbidden threshold.

As his front foot descended on to the hard table-top, he paused to sniff the air, recalling Psycho's advice to appear as nonchalant as if he was going for a casual stroll. The other mink, peering out of the sides of their cages, held their breath, their nervous giggles cut short. Their leader was radiating an aura of supreme confidence, looking as if he hadn't a care in the world. Yet underneath the blithe exterior his heart was pounding as he waited for the terminal blow. Mind the gap! his brain kept saying. Mind the gap! The Elders had always repeated it as part of their predictions of doom. Cross the gap and the sky will fall in! The sky will fall in! Mind the gap! Stay inside! Never escape! The sky will fall in! Stay inside! Mind the gap! – it raced though his head in a constant litany.

He walked forward out on to the table top and cautiously raised his head to look round. The silence just dragged on. The sky hadn't fallen in. Everything was just the same. The greatest threat of the Elders had been scotched, finally exposing them as the charlatans they had always been. The human liberators might have vanished as if they had been a dream, but the yawning cages and rolls of cut wire bore mute witness to their reality. Meanwhile the shed door remained enticingly ajar.

He saw Mata emerge from her cage and gave her a huge grin of relief. But she only glanced at him briefly before turning her back, ignoring him. She was acting as if she had arranged the whole thing. Mega took refuge in jauntily waving his paw towards the farmhouse in a rude gesture which was so natural and cheekily rude the watching mink burst into renewed giggles. He hammed the gesture up even further, this time hearing genuine laughter. It wasn't that funny, he knew, but it was serving its purpose in puncturing the tension that had held them in suspended animation.

There was no problem. There was also no time to lose.

'Maxi, come here,' he shouted.

Much of the credit for preparing for this moment went to his military adviser. With no way to simulate the reality of freedom, Maxi's training sessions had had their difficulties. As he had complained to Mega, the young mink had varying degrees of belief, and many were unable to treat his preparations as anything more than a game. Now, as his leader instructed him to give the command 'Out', he was about to find out how well his hard work had paid off.

Some mink obeyed instantly, without question, stepping over their individual thresholds as if sleep-walking. As the reality hit them they broke into a squeaky babble, while Maxi ran up and down, barking fiercely to try to silence them. But many remained huddled at the back of their cages, not budging even when he shouted at them directly.

He rushed back to report to Mega.

'Some of them won't obey, boss. Do you want me to have them dragged out?'

Mega was not surprised by this news. He had always known that not everyone would be with him. He personally had the faith his mother had instilled in him. But even his closest supporters were not necessarily true disciples, as the incident when Psycho had laughed about freedom had illustrated. He didn't want all of them anyway. He had already marked down the ostracised Elders, for a start, to be left behind. If any of those pathetic has-beens tried to leave their cages he'd have Maxi shove them back in again. In fact he didn't want any of their generation. They had all been lukewarm, if not actively hostile. He could do without the timid and subservient in his own as well. All he wanted were red-blooded mink, raring for adventure, not wimps who couldn't make a commitment.

'Tell them it's now or never,' he instructed Maxi. 'If they still won't come out, leave them be, except for those two new mink. Whatever you have to do, make sure they come with us.'

He looked down the table-top to where Mata had been gathering a small coterie of her female 'warriors' and gave a nod. They jumped down to the floor as one, beckoning their supporters to follow. In a rush some did, tumbling over each other in their haste and momentarily entangling themselves in the discarded wire. Others, however – including, to Mata's dismay, some of her esteemed warriors – stayed hovering on the brink.

'Jump, my mink! Jump!' they both hissed upwards, while Maxi ran along the table-top issuing the 'now or never' ultima-tum.

A few more followed. But the rest remained dithering on the edge. Peering up from below, Mega couldn't determine whether it was deliberate insubordination or they were just funking it. But in practical terms it made no difference. There were to be no passengers on this trip.

'Leave the buggers and get down here,' he hissed up to Maxi.

The instruction was overdue. While he and Mata had been

concentrating their attentions upwards, more idiot minions had already forgotten the drill Maxi had tried to instil into them. Chittering excitedy, they were fanning out to explore their new surroundings, while a chorus of 'Here we go! Here we go! Here we go!' started up.

All in all the escape was falling apart.

Maxi landed heavily on the floor.

'Line up!' he bawled as loudly as he dared, signalling his low-browed muscle-minks to aid the process with a few well-placed cuffs.

Mega stood to one side as the ranks were shuffled into some semblance of order. The column was ragged and a lot shorter than it should have been. But it would have to do. Placing himself at its head, he gave a last glare upwards at the ones still refusing to jump.

'Traitors!' he hissed, striding towards the shed door with Mata at his shoulder.

His followers, now officially emancipated from their slavery, followed obediently. Few had yet comprehended the full turn of events and most moved as if in a daze. Some, still fearing the Elders' predicted apocalypse, balked as they reached the new threshold to the outside, until a combination of shoves from the muscle-mink and pressure from behind pushed them through.

Then the mood changed as they thrust their muzzles up and gazed in awe at the full glory of the clear night sky. And not just any old sky. The full moon still bathed the land in its soft light, while a rime of frost made everything sparkle. A communal sigh floated upwards alongside their clouds of steaming breath and they instantly forgot their former companions inside.

'It's beautiful, Mega,' Mata exclaimed.

'It's amazing,' Mega breathed, overwhelmed by the vast scope of their surroundings. He felt unutterably humbled. 'The space, Mata — how can there possibly be so much space?'

All the time he had promised freedom, he had never imagined he would deliver anything as grand as this. Never had he seen such splendour. Everything that had previously enclosed them had gone. There was no wire, no shed walls, nothing above them, nothing surrounding them. The ground underfoot even felt firm in a way that it never had on the cage floors. They were standing on the edge of the world. Suddenly the mood switched. It was not only amazing – it was terrifying. Freaking, several mink turned to run back inside their familiar sanctuary. But Maxi's planning had anticipated them and they found their way blocked by his pair of glowering muscle-mink. Pausing uncertainly like sheep, they rushed back to burrow into the comforting huddle of their fellows.

Mega and Mata stood together watching in a detached fashion. Mata, at her leader's elbow as if his natural consort, allowed her warriors to be swallowed up into the general herd while they both felt the affinity between them. Although they had had no more idea what to expect than anyone else, their attitude had been different. Separately and together, they both now truly believed that this wide world was their natural home. Made for mink to rule, it held no terrors for them. They were both simply thrilling to the promise that it held out. They grinned at each other, stiff with pride, as they felt the constrictions of the cages falling away like a sloughed skin.

'Onwards and upwards,' Mata grinned.

Mega grinned back warmly, then switched his attention to Maxi. With relief, he saw his military adviser was keeping his head, whilst once again his planning had anticipated what was now happening.

'We must keep the ranks moving when we break out, my leader,' he had continually emphasised. 'If we give them time to think their imaginations'll get the better of them. Then they'll panic.'

That was a problem that wouldn't face you personally, Mega had thought affectionately as he listened with grave attention.

But he could see now how right Maxi had been about the others. Eyes screwed up to shut out reality, they were pushing into a confused ball like blind kits against their mothers' teat's.

'Right, you lot, you're not here to admire the view,' Maxi – who had only glanced at it – whispered ferociously. 'Form up. We're moving out.'

So far the escape had gone according to Maxi's meticulously

arranged Plan A. This now stated the next objective was to be to make a stealthy exit from the farm, while specifying that above all it was imperative the pack be kept together. Mega had always taken a positive view when Psycho had sneered at the more aggressive minions boasting about how they were ready to tackle the real world. He admired their spirit, while at the same time never labouring under the same illusion himself. After spending their entire lives in captivity they all had to be woefully ill-equipped, both mentally and physically. But he had instinctively agreed with Psycho's endless emphasis on the importance of their always having lived in a group. When – or, as his spin-doctor silently thought – if they were outside, group mentality would bind them together more than anything else. However independent each individual might think themselves, none was used to thinking on their own. Once separated, like the mink Solomon had described, they would be lost, ripe to be picked off one by one. The Elders' sky-falling-in thing might have been exposed as a load of bollo, yet the hazards and pitfalls out here must be real enough. Even for all-conquering mink the only way to face them would be together.

Where was Psycho anyway? Mega suddenly thought, finally locating him in the middle of the defensive huddle.

'What are you doing?' he hissed, noticing how different his voice sounded outside the shed.

'I'm all right, Mega – at least I think I am,' came a quavering reply.

Mega snorted with laughter. All right indeed! He'd never seen a mink looking so petrified. That would teach the little runt not to have faith.

But there was no time to gloat. Leaving Maxi and Mata in charge, he crept along the edge of the shed to reconnoitre the next hurdle of the breakout, the exposed journey across the yard to the gate.

But as he peeped round the corner, a factor outside Maxi's Plan A unexpectedly intervened. There, right out in the open, prancing across the farmyard in her poncey fashion, was Pussles.

'Kill! Kill! Kill!' all Mega's instincts started screaming.

PART III

31

Hereby Hangs a Tail

Mega pulled his head back slowly and carefully. They might all rightfully despise Pussles for her cold-blooded aloofness and the way she had lorded it over them, but she was still not to be underestimated as an opponent. What was she doing, though? Then he saw the limp mouse dangling from her mouth. Preoccupied with hunting inside the barn, she must have missed what had been happening and was now making her leisurely way back to the farmhouse. The legendary luck she always boasted about had just run out.

Mega already knew what she would do next. As she had wickedly informed them previously, she delighted in taking her victims into the house, which she entered through the personal catflap she always pointed to as yet another sign of feline superiority. She would then consume her prey, she explained, leaving the unwanted bits lying around as a supposed 'present' for her humans. In reality, she smiled archly, these gruesome offcuts disgusted and horrified them. Yet she was immune from punishment, on the grounds that she was only doing the job she was there for.

As Mega reversed quickly to collar Maxi, he had already

decided he could not resist the temptation. Bollo to Plan A — how could they possibly pass up such an opportunity for their first hot spurt? And what a massive one Pussles would be — never mind settling such an old score. She would find out first that she was now living in minkland, then immediately that she wasn't going to any longer.

Maxi, coming forward with him, poked his head out and gave a low whistle of surprise as they together sized up the situation. Yet, when they pulled back to consult, to Mega's amazement he instantly advocated caution.

'We have to stick to Plan A, boss,' he whispered urgently, smoothing his whiskers. 'If we go for her it'll introduce all sorts of complications. The others haven't seen her yet and if we let her go they'll be none the wiser.'

'But the element of surprise is totally on our side, Maxi,' Mega burst out, taken aback. 'Even the wind's in our favour. And she's so heavily outnumbered that even ninety-nine lives couldn't save her now.'

Maxi brushed his whiskers vigorously. He knew full well why he had never challenged Mega, despite his physical strength. If he won and became leader he would have to confront all manner of baffling problems. What he craved instead was what he had got — a boss who looked after the big picture, leaving him free to get on with his forte of organisation. The reason he had drawn up Plan A so meticulously was precisely in order to avoid the ghastly spectre that was now looming — an unstable situation, when he might be required to make instant decisions on the spot.

'Stage 2 of Plan A lays down that we must leave as quietly as possible,' he reminded his leader agitatedly. 'If we kill Pussles it's bound to be a noisy business and will only raise the alarm.'

'It will indeed be a noisy business, Maxi,' Mega grinned evilly, licking his lips in anticipation. 'And what a glorious noise that's going to be.'

Turning his back, he peered round the end of the shed. Pussles had now stopped in the middle of the yard and was playing with her victim, encouraging its feeble attempts to escape, then zapping it with her paw every time it threatened to drag itself out of reach. Preoccupied and stationary, she was even more wide open.

He overrode Maxi's continuing stream of objections.

'Get them ready. And quickly,' he ordered.

There was a chorus of excited squeaks as Maxi went back down the side of the shed.

Mega cursed. Pussles had at last sensed something was wrong. Pinning the mouse down with her paw, she had turned and was staring in their direction. Mega froze, instinctively knowing the slightest movement would give him away, until the squeaking stopped. Then he saw her relax and resume her one-sided game.

He waited on tenterhooks while the others crept up behind him

'All ready for action, saah,' Maxi finally whispered.

'Charge!' Mega cried, placing himself in the vanguard as the pack hurtled across the yard in a brown blur.

Pussles saw them almost instantly. But then, torn between bolting for the house or back into the barn, she hesitated for a fatal second. Finally plumping for the latter, she turned tail and fled, with the pack veering round in hot pursuit. But in her desperate haste, and with her fur standing on end in fright, she found the tiny gap in the bottom of the door such a tight fit that her bum and black and orange tail were still sticking out as mink thudded into the woodwork round her.

Rows of needle-sharp teeth latched on to her rear and a grisly tug-of-war began, with neither side seeming able to gain an advantage.

'She's stuck, Mega,' Maxi yelled from the front of the action. 'She must have hooked her claws into something. 'We can't shift her.'

As the sea of mink flailed about, Mega realised the disorganised pushing and shoving was being largely counter-productive. The vile animal was obviously so securely wedged that, short of actually pulling her arse off, it looked as though they would never get her out. Worse still, her fur was becoming so lubricated with mink spittle that she threatened to slither out of their grasp completely. In theory the pack could follow her through the gap and kill her inside the barn. But there was no longer time for that. Maxi had been entirely correct about the noise coefficient. She was now howling loudly enough to wake the dead and an upstairs light had already gone on in the farmhouse.

For a second Mega regretted his impetuosity. If they lost her now it would be a crushing blow to morale. Then he stiffened his resolve. He had to find a way. Yelling at Maxi to help clear his path, he barged up to the front, where he shoved aside a couple of mink and sized up the bristling rear. Then, from nowhere, Mata was suddenly crouched opposite him, teeth bared, lips drawn back in snarling aggression. As their eyes locked he knew they had the same idea. They were to repeat their combination over the bird in the cages.

Mata nodded at him to go first. He took careful aim and bit down as hard as he could into the base of the writhing tail. His teeth sank into gristle and bone and he pulled his head back to spit out a mouthful of fur. Mata followed, biting down into the same place. Then they set to work, turn and turn about, while the blood flowed as they pulled out more fur to expose the tender pink skin underneath. As Mega bit yet again his jaws were aching, while his head had begun to ring with the jarring blows. Suddenly he felt a crunch. Mata put everything she had into her next bite and this time everyone heard the sickening crack as something gave. All the time the other mink had been pulling ferociously at the end of the tail and now, with a soft tearing noise, it slowly came away. As Pussles' bloody rump shot out of sight the mink hurtled backwards, landing in an untidy heap, the detached member twitching violently in their mouths. As a heart-rending caterwauling came from inside the barn, Mega and Mata grinned at each other exultantly.

Just then an upstairs window shot up in the house.

'Pussles! Oh my poor Pussles! What is it? We're coming,' came a distraught female cry.

Mega looked round and saw more lights come on, while the howling rose to a hideous crescendo that set all their teeth on edge. Maxi's prediction that the attack would destroy Stage 2 of his Plan A was being amply fulfilled. They had to move fast.

Mega ran over to the still-floundering mink and seized the detached tail in his mouth.

'Onwards, my brave mink,' he shouted, his voice muffled, while the tail jerked up and down in ghastly parody of its just-ended life. He bounded towards the gate, adjusting it to get the balance as its ends drooped down like an obscene furry moustache. There was a ragged cheer and the pack closed in behind him just as their former Keeper burst out of the farmhouse. But, preoccupied with pulling on his jacket, he failed to spot them as he ran across the yard and began wrestling with the barn door.

Speedily Mega led the pack under the gate and out on to the rollway. He turned left, as dictated by Custard, and struck out at a brisk trot, the ends of the cat-tail swishing on the hard surface either side of him. Beside him Mata was at his elbow, while the pack had instinctively arranged itself into a tight V-formation. Overwhelmed by pride, he glanced first at her and then over his shoulder. The eager, questing faces behind him were those of his mink — the true mink who had loved freedom enough to put their lives on the line for it. And as ordained, he, Mega, was leading them to the Promised Land. The open rollway was ahead, while above there were only the moon and the stars. They had done it!

Casting aside Maxi's strict rule of silence, he let out a wild whoop of joy. As it echoed round the ranks the pack members broke formation and ran to embrace each other, punching the air with their forepaws. He turned to Mata and they hugged fiercely, their lips writhing together round the cat-tail as they rolled around and shook their heads in joint exultation. They were cementing their partnership, Mega thought as he felt the tautness of her body against him. He, the proven king, was accepting her as his queen. But then, as her eyes bored commandingly into his, he realized it was she who was assuming the mantle. She was taking the lead just as she had done before. She was subjugating him.

Then, abruptly, she broke the spell by disentangling herself.

'Do it to Psycho,' she cried as she stepped back, her black eyes now dancing with merriment.

Mega burst out laughing.

'There's no other creature in the world I'd do that for,' he shouted, dropping the cat-tail and running over to the little runt.

Seizing him from behind, he lifted him off the ground and squeezed him in a bone-cracking bearhug. As Psycho let out high-pitched squeals of terror and excitement, the rest of the pack ran madly about, screaming their heads off.

They were holding an impromptu party in the middle of the rollway, Mega suddenly realised. But why not? Who cared if anyone heard them now?

Dropping Psycho, he ran back and picked up the cat-tail again, motioning them all forward to get a taste of their trophy. Ecstatically they passed it from mouth to mouth, growling and worrying at it, until everyone had felt the black and orange fur wet on their tongues. Then he placed the tail on the rollway and, Mata at his side, led off a triumphal dance round its curled length.

'Here we go! Here we go! Here we go!' the pack thundered, cock-a-hoop with triumph. 'Here we go! Here we go! Here we go!'

They had done it. They were free. And, as Mega was very well aware, for the first time in their lives they were on their own.

32

Clean Break

'Vole-are!' Owl sang in his head as he sent himself gliding silently along, 'Vole-are, oh oh! Vole-are, oh oh oh oh!'

But although in a good mood outwardly, underneath he was worried. He had been making a determined effort to steer well clear of Burdock, Dandelion and the other CWGs who had got into his life. He had largely succeeded physically, but their spirit had remained with him. What was afflicting Owl was not the Venerable Buck's 'big trouble warning', or even the old sage's thoughts on the bigger picture, but what Dandelion had said. Ever since her exhortations to 'be nice' he had begun making silly mistakes when out hunting. His killing efficiency, which he had been so proud of until then, had deteriorated and several of his intended victims had slipped through his talons. It wasn't yet so serious that he didn't have plenty to fill his stomach, but his uncharacteristic clumsiness was making him more and more annoyed, while he suspected Ula might be becoming aware of it. That in turn was making it more pronounced.

He had a shrewd idea what the trouble was about. His father had always stressed, as he made his first blundering descents on living prey, that to be an effective hunter he must live entirely in the present.

'Concentrate solely on what you're doing, son. It's the only way to release your full energy. If any of your mind is blocked up by thinking about either the future or the past, you'll lose that vital edge. You've got to learn to wipe your mind of everything else. That's what I do. It's nothing personal, son, but if you tried to halt me in mid-strike I wouldn't even recognise you.'

Owl now knew that Dandelion had caused him to lose the edge he needed. Not that she had succeeded in making him feel guilty, but what she had said had come to preoccupy him, putting him off his stroke. The only way out, he had concluded, was to try her CWG 'niceness' and see where it got him. If it only succeeded in clearing his head, that would be enough.

His latest turn was taking him along the river, the home of various furry little creatures he approved of from an eating point of view. His eye was caught by a ripple at the edge of the water, and he thought he might have found a bank vole. But when he swerved silently over he found it was only a warty toad, hanging about after laying its string of slimy spawn. Owl was sick of their croaking. They had been blundering clumsily about attempting to find mates for a whole moon.

Rejecting it as his next meal, he swerved back on to line. The full moon did not help his cause, as with his night-sight he did not need its illumination to detect little movements on the ground. Meanwhile, however, its brilliance was going against him, as it made him much more visible. Idly he recalled one of his father's favourite sayings:

> Bright at night,
> Vole's delight,
> Dark in the morning,
> Owl's warning.

Owl was still glorying in the moon's beauty, though, even if it was not in his favour. It was so clearly visible he could see the faces which he and his father had always imagined whenever they gazed at its full splendour. Below, the wood was a kaleidoscope of blacks and greys shading almost to white, the trees and clearings were so brightly lit. At the moment he was just cruising contentedly, waiting for the moon to set, after which he would have his window of opportunity before the sun rose. As he looked down, considering the Dandelion problem, he thought how much he enjoyed swooping on voles, and how much he appreciated his good fortune in there being different kinds to swoop on — not just bank voles, but field voles, water voles, short-tailed voles . . . There were the different kinds of mice as well — harvest, wood, field — all part of the wood's rich pattern that he had been appreciating more and more, until the reality of CWG affairs had largely closed down that line of thinking.

Suddenly spotting a different movement near the edge of the water he saw immediately he had not been wasting his time. He liked this aspect of hunting. You might be in a slack period, when you were unlikely to get any action, yet as long as you kept on looking there was always the prospect of a reward. For this time there was no doubt — an innocent vole was questing feather-footed through the splashy marsh down by the alder tree. There was no need to hurry. His potential prey had neither seen nor heard him, while Owl himself was not so hungry that he had to kill. But he would appreciate another meal and anyhow, by appearing so unexpectedly, the vole had inadvertently put itself into the frame for his Dandelion experiment. Why not carry it out now, and in a big way?

His mind made up, Owl dropped and braked hard with his wings. Then, rather than reaching down to grip the vole in his normal steely embrace, he crashed down in front of it in a flurry of spray.

'Good evening,' he said, furling his wings and glaring down at the motionless creature. 'I trust you will forgive this intrusion. I am also aware that we have not been formally introduced. Allow me, therefore, to do the honours. My name is Owl, and I am most pleased to make your aquaintance.

'And you, if you don't mind me asking, are . . . ?'

The vole remained rigid. Making no sound, it stared at him with its beady eyes.

Ten points to me, Owl thought with great satisfaction.

In CWGland it was extremely impolite not to reply when spoken to.

'Well, vole — if you don't mind me calling you that in the interim — I'm sorry to have to tell you I'm about to eat you,' he continued, discovering he felt rather jovial about this nonsense. 'However, I would like to take this opportunity to stress that it is nothing personal. Rather it is merely that, as a predatory carnivore, I have no choice.

'By way of consolation, however, I can offer you the strongest possible assurance that your killing will be merciful. I am an expert executioner and therefore in a position to promise you most sincerely that you won't feel a thing.

'Before I dispatch you it is also both my pleasure and privilege to grant you one last wish. What shall it be? An acorn perhaps? Maybe a berry of some sort? Anything you fancy.'

The vole stayed silently rigid.

'How about any last words?' Owl suggested helpfully. 'A message to your loving mate or adorable young ones, for example? Or maybe something more selfless, such as a pearl of wisdom we can all treasure and remember you by?'

The vole continued to stare fixedly at him. Then, its body caught by a sudden gust of wind, it abruptly fell on its side.

Surprised, Owl walked up and poked at it with his talon. There was no movement. It was then he realised: it had died of fright, almost certainly at the moment he had dropped out of the sky in front of it. All that time he had been addressing a corpse. Suddenly ashamed of his game, he felt a fierce flare of anger against Dandelion. This stuff wasn't even funny, it was just plain sick — and he was equally angry with himself for even listening to her, never mind taking what she had said the least bit seriously.

He hit the vole with a killer blow to the back of its neck to make doubly certain it was out of its misery before pulling it apart with his beak and munching his way steadily through it. As he did so he thought how, if that was being nice, he would much rather be nasty. Being nice was just another meaningless muddle, like 'Concerned' and 'Guardian' themselves. Never mind his promise to the Venerable Buck, he had had enough. He would revert to being a full-blooded predator, with no apologies to anyone. He might even take Ula for a fly to make up for the lack of nest repairs. The mating season was now just round the corner and suddenly the thought of her company, compared to the Dandelions of the wood, was unexpectedly appealing.

But he would do one more thing before he finally left the CWGs behind for ever. The previous evening Burdock had bearded him, pleading that he make a final appearance as Executive Chaircreature. The crucial meeting – planned to be the biggest ever – to pass the Woodland Code and Bill of Creatures' Rights was scheduled for that afternoon, he had explained. Owl must help. He had never been needed more.

All night Owl had been watching the head rabbit and his supporters scour the wood in a desperate last-minute frenzy to make sure every possible creature was present. Even the despised insects were being roped back in for the occasion and Owl felt obliged to attend, if only for his own sake. Having come this far, he must go to the end of the line to satisfy his sense of honour.

Niceness deleted and his headspace clear again, he took off and banked over to cruise the Ridge, confident he would have no further difficulty in dispatching – what was it Dandelion had called them? – his 'ill-fated victims'. Behind him he had taken great care to scatter about the unwanted bits of vole as messily as possible.

With the end of his CWG involvement in sight, the least he could do was give her clean-up party something to really grumble about.

33

Shafted

As the pack padded along the deserted rollway Mega had expected the mink to rush off and explore every sight and sound. But the thrill of the Pussles incident and the euphoria of the impromptu party had already evaporated. There was too much to take in at once, while the rollway itself didn't help. Its acrid, tangy smell ticked nostrils previously accustomed only to blandness, while its brutal surface rapidly abraded pads softened by cage life. The bonus for Mega was being relieved of any worry that the pack might split up. On the contrary, the mink were huddling so much they were almost tripping over each other in their anxiety to feel the reassuring touch of a fellow warm body. Many were also now puffing so hard from the unaccustomed exertion that Mega risked slowing the pace. Master species mink might be, but at this precise moment you wouldn't know it.

'So far, so good,' he remarked quietly, looking at Mata.

'Indeed, Mega.'

They knew equally though that wasn't strictly true. The number of mink who had remained in the shed had shaken them both. Mega, sensing Mata had been particularly devastated by so many of her warriors letting her down, let the fiction lie.

He knew they shared a nagging feeling that the cowards had spoilt the cleanness of the break. There was something deeply unsatisfactory about the way they had voluntarily stayed in their prison. It made the whole escape feel like unfinished business, rather than a triumph.

Mega was just chewing on this, along with the cat-tail, when bright lights suddenly lit up the rollway behind them. As they heard the harsh note of an approaching volver, Maxi yelled for them to dive into the ditch. While they lay there, shaken by the machine's roaring passage, Mega recognised its note as the particular one they had constantly heard in the yard. He could have sworn he glimpsed the strained face of Pussles' mistress, with Custard staring out of the back window as she bounced along. Pussles was no doubt being rushed for treatment. There wouldn't be much anyone could do for her though, Mega grinned, readjusting the wet fur in his mouth. An essential part of her was destined to stay with the mink pack for ever.

Eventually Mega acknowledged he must bow to his senses and admit they were lost. They had taken the first two turnings as Custard had directed but never reached the bendy bit, where Master shouted at other volvers. Then the rollway had begun climbing sharply upwards, which didn't fit at all, and now, just when Mega estimated they should be near the wood, they had emerged on to the wilderness of a bleak moor.

He looked at Mata and Maxi and received grim nods of confirmation before dropping back to consult Psycho. So far the little creep appeared to have been useless. Mega had not seen what part – if any – he had played in the Pussles attack, but since then he had remained at the back, staying uncharacteristically silent as he desperately tried not to draw attention to himself.

'All right?' he asked, pulling him to one side, although he could see the answer written in the bony narrow face. Psycho was clearly spraint-scared.

'Sorry not to be up front, Mega,' he apologised, the quavering edge to his high-pitched voice betraying him further. 'To be honest, I wasn't really expecting any of this to happen and it's taking me a bit of time to adjust. I'll be better soon.'

'You'd better pull yourself together right now, you lit-tle bastard,' Mega hissed, dropping his voice to a whisper. 'We're lost.'

Psycho, sensing too that they were going wrong, had been trying to pretend it wasn't happening. But being put on the spot now jolted his brain back into action.

'Why not call a rest halt, Mega?' he whispered furtively. 'Then we can think what to do.'

Mega saw immediately that that made sense. After marching up towards the crest of the moor most of the mink were completely winded and Maxi was having to chivvy them continually to keep them moving.

When he ordered them to stop they were pathetically grateful to be parked behind some wispy gorse bushes, while the leadership gathered on a large hummock. Mega had briefly debated whether to include the laboratory newcomers, MI and M2. The pair had been eager escapees and seemed quite cheerful about their adventure, especially after Mega had lifted their ostracision at the impromptu rollway party. It would have been good to have their thoughts, but in the end he had reluctantly decided to dispense with them. They might have inadvertently been their deliverers, but they were an unknown quantity and there was always the danger they would come up with something disastrous. For the moment he would rely on his more trusted assistants.

'The only way to sort this out is by going back,' he announced bluntly. 'Quite apart from the effect on morale, though, we can't do that. The Keeper is bound to come looking for us as soon as it's light.'

They all looked gloomily at the lightening flush in the distance.

'And I don't need to tell you he's going to be after our blood, not just for escaping, but for this,' Mega went on, indicating the black and orange length of Pussles' tail beside him. 'We'd probably walk straight into a lynch mob. Meanwhile volvers are bound to come along the rollway, so we need to be well away from that.

'Our only course, therefore, is to strike off across the moor.

But I don't mind telling you I'm reluctant to do that. It's the only feature we can recognise on this landscape. So, any suggestions?'

Maxi's contribution only increased the general gloom.

'I have to report, my leader, that, even if that is our decision, I do not consider the ranks to be in a fit state to go anywhere,' he announced. 'They're all pretty well bushed and if we push them much more I fear some will collapse. May I take this opportunity to remind you, my leader, that an army marches at the pace of the slowest.'

Very true, Mega thought, looking at him gratefully. He had forgiven Maxi for his caution over the Pussles incident, recognising that in many ways he had been correct. Now his thinking was right again. Out here they all had to bear in mind how dependent they were on each other. Yet at the same time that didn't solve anything.

'Thank you for the reminder, Maxi,' he replied. 'But we can't stay here. So what are we going to do? Hide behind a bush?'

Seeing how distressingly visible the rest of the pack was through the thin branches, they stared moodily round the bleak landscape, devoid of any other cover. Mega's irony, however, seemed lost on his military adviser, who was obviously highly upset by this unplanned turn of events and smoothing his whiskers continually.

'If you wish, boss, I could organise some camouflage,' he said lamely.

Mega grunted and turned to Psycho, who was looking even more rat-like than ever in this wide-open space. But at least he was now just looking exceedingly nervous, rather than completely terrified.

'I've got an idea, Mega,' he piped up. 'The last place that the humans'll expect to find us is on the rollway, isn't it? They'll think we'll be well off it by now.'

'Correct,' Mega growled back. His spin-doctor must have recovered some of his poise to be talking in this pedantic fashion. He had used it before to dress up some of his best ideas.

'But there is a place where the humans'll be even less likely to expect us, isn't there?' he cackled feebly, revealing his latest twist. 'And that,' he giggled, 'is not on the rollway, but underneath it!'

Which was how, in the absence of any other suggestions, they ended up in the culvert.

If this was what the outside world was like, Mega thought as he stared out at the damp curtain of mist, it was no wonder his followers weren't impressed. The culvert was horrible – dank, depressing, and littered with ugly human rubbish – while its unnatural rough surface gave no relief to bleeding pads. Meanwhile the mink had become preoccupied with their stomachs. Where was their breakfast? they were whining. At least back in the cages, they'd been fed properly and, more to the point, on time.

Maxi and his muscle-mink were having their work cut out preventing them from going out to forage. Their frame of mind had not been improved by Psycho going too far as usual and adding an unhelpful spin by impressing on them that there was nothing outside worth foraging for. The most un-Psycho-like truth of this statement had been emphasised by the cloud that had decended at dawn like a blanket, reducing natural activity on the frozen turf to virtually zero. Even the proud trophy of the cat-tail, laid reverently to one side of the thin trickle of water, avoiding the twin avenues of green slime, could no longer cheer them with its reminder of recent glory.

Was it bad luck, or bad judgement, that they had got off to such a disastrous start? Mega wondered. As expected, volvers had been passing regularly overhead since first light. That and the nil visibility in the mist, which was further complicating matters by dampening all sound, made it impossible to plan the next move. As Maxi had just pointed out, the escape was losing all its momentum. If individuals wandered off, inevitably they would scatter, thereby negating Plan A. Even worse, if morale sank too low, they would lose all commitment to the enterprise and drift back to rejoin the yellow-bellies in what now seemed the comfort of the shed. Mega couldn't blame everyone for feeling disappointed. He was as disappointed himself. But, for the present, they had no choice except to sit it out.

Eventually, towards sunhigh – or what should have been sunhigh – Maxi peered out of the round end of the culvert and reported the cloud was lifting. Mega, deciding to take a chance with a passing volver, ordered him outside, and along with Mata they climbed a nearby knoll, from whose commanding position they could see the landscape spread out below them. Mega's heart lifted with a new sensation. They were on top of the world, masters of all they surveyed! They might have seen far-off lights in the darkness, but nothing to match this vast panorama. The immensity of it – stretching in every direction, with no apparent limit, until finally swallowed up in the grey haze. It was covered in lines surrounding different shapes and colours, all of which beckoned with the promise of delights to come. Everything – human habitations, rollways, trees, the few birds in the sky – was all theirs to take. Yet at the same time he recalled Solomon telling Sheba how the released mink had just wandered aimlessly about. No wonder, with so much to go at. It was impossible to know where to start. More than ever he was aware of the urgency to provide the anchor they needed by reaching Custard's wood. But where was it?

Then, as they had identified the farm which had been their former prison and traced the network of rollways, Mega gasped as he saw how simple the answer was.

'The stupid bitch can't tell her left from her right,' he exclaimed bitterly.

Mata, who seemed strangely subdued, nodded in silent confirmation, while Maxi, obviously delighted at someone being rightly castigated for being even dumber than him, yelled: 'Absolutely correct, boss!

'We should have realised all along she was thick as a post,' he added unhelpfully. 'However, may I point out that the position may not be as bad as it initially appears. Look over there.'

Following the direction of his pointing paw, Mega saw in the distance a wood which superficially resembled the one that Custard had described. He quickly reversed her directions along the rollway network, making allowance for her left-right errors, and found it all fitted. But Maxi was right: things could be worse. The rollway they had been wrongly following curled round, which meant they had made some progress, albeit in a crab-like fashion. To reach the wood, they only had to cut down the hillside, cross a couple of shallow valleys, and then go over a low ridge.

'Well, Maxi, you saw it first. Is it the right place or not?'

'I am afraid I am unable to answer that for definite, boss,' Maxi replied, smoothing his whiskers. 'However, may I point out that it is definitely a wood, and therefore would be a substantial improvement on our present position.'

Mega silently thanked him again for his down-to-earth approach. As he grimly reflected, the only real way to tell would be by going. That was where the job of being leader came in. It was your responsibility to make a decision on the information available. Whether it was right would only become apparent later.

'We'll leave as soon as it's dark,' he instructed. 'I'm looking to you to plot the route.'

'Very good, boss,' Maxi bawled back, grateful that life was simple again now he had been told what to do.

They started to made their way back to the culvert only, to their horror, to come across stray mink bounding about in the heather.

'What do you think you're doing, you insubordinate bastards?' Maxi shouted, beside himself with rage. 'Get back in there immediately!'

He ran on ahead, to find the muscle-mink trying to push back a heaving mass of mink determined to get out of the culvert. Psycho, almost in tears, was vainly imploring them to stay where they were. Maxi had just pushed him aside and was wading in, paws flying, when they heard a volver approaching. They waited, frozen in a mid-action tableau, as it came closer. Their hearts stopped as its noise faltered and it slowed, before it passed, resuming its steady beat as it picked up speed. Looking at each other in shock, they all began breathing again. That had been too close for comfort!

The interruption had, however, taken the steam out of the revolt and as the main body of the pack retreated surlily into the middle of the culvert, the few who were still out slunk back, looking guilty.

Psycho, already the recipient of a withering look from Maxi, quivered as his leader approached.

'There was nothing I could do, Mega,' he gabbled, looking terrified again. 'As soon as you'd gone they said they'd had enough and were getting out. We've really got trouble on our paws. Some are still with us, but most just want to go "home", as they put it. A few have even decided they'd be better off on their own.'

The fainthearts, Mega thought for a moment before checking himself. He mustn't blame them. It wasn't their fault they had never known anything except the cages. None the less, with this kind of dissent simmering, it was too dangerous to hang round here any longer. The ranks might have been temporarily suppressed by shock, but they would soon rebel again. And in a way they would be right – they couldn't stay in the culvert for ever. Recalling Maxi's advice about it being imperative to keep the pack moving, he decided to resume the march immediately. It would be risky out there in daylight, but the miserable weather must cut down the chances of there being many humans out and about. If they kept well off any rollway they might be all right.

He made the announcement, his voice echoing uncannily in the confined space, to find the pack still showing little sign of cheer.

'When are we getting something to eat?' came a mutinous cry.

'Yeh, where's our food? It'll be teatime soon, never mind breakfast!'

'You'll soon have everything you want, and more,' Psycho cut in reassuringly. 'Trust your great leader.'

He was about to continue when he saw Mega glaring at him and went quiet. For once, he privately conceded, his leader was right. It was pointless to pretend that any amount of honeyed words could make up for the rumbling in their bellies. With the exercise and fresh air, he was just as famished himself.

'Form up!' Maxi shouted after the next volver had passed

overhead, and the pack sullenly obeyed, following its leaders across the wet grass until they were well off the rollway.

There Maxi shuffled them into a group for Mega to address them.

It was Psycho who had insisted he say something.

'You've got to pull them together, Mega. But keep it short and snappy – there'll no point in going on with them in this mood.'

'Here's the line. It's all been a conspiracy by Custard, working in conjunction with the Keeper to lead us astray. Follow through with the "good news" that you've overcome the disinformation, then come out with a few lines about "consolidating our position" and "resuming the triumphant march forward". That should shut them up.'

'Sounds a bit thin to me,' Mega had replied unenthusiastically. It was all limp excuses, when what they needed was something to charge the pack up and get it going again. 'Why can't I show them the wood?'

'No, Mega, we mustn't get them too excited,' Psycho had squeaked, shaking his pointed head in vehement refusal. 'What if it doesn't turn out to be the right place after all?'

Mega, seeing the point, had reluctantly acceded. As Sheba had kept reminding him so long ago, there would be no point in his having advisers if he didn't listen to what they said.

'My noble fellow mink, I have some grave news,' he now announced from the top of a small hummock. 'It will not come as a surprise if you recall the deviousness of our former Keeper, the human oppressor from whom I so recently liberated you.'

He paused, hoping for at least a smattering of applause. When none came he ploughed on: 'A conspiracy has been mounted against us, my mink, a conspiracy I am happy to say I have now overcome. Let me tell you how carefully the dastardly plot was hatched to mislead us . . .'

As he spoke a crack opened in the grey clouds and in the distance a shaft of white sunlight poured down, so bright and clear-cut it was like a solid bar connecting the sky and the land. This sudden apparition so diverted his audience's attention that Mega himself broke off to join in gazing at it, only to see it was falling on the very wood across the valley which they had identified, for good or ill, as their destination.

Psycho was the first to react.

'See the sign!' he cried, instantly forgetting his recent advice about not identifying the wood in favour of this opportunistic new scam. 'Behold the sign our great leader Mega has brought us!' He gestured towards the illuminating rays. 'It is the sign putting us back on course by marking the whereabouts of the Promised Land, the fabulous wood where happiness and hot spurts await us all.'

His dramatic intervention extracted the first faint cheers from more credulous minions, on the strength of which Mega instantly decided to can the rest of his speech. It had been going nowhere anyhow. Instead he let Psycho take the lead in ramming home their new advantage, incidentally noting that the two new mink, MI and M2, were grinning in happy approval.

'Follow me, fellow mink,' Psycho squeaked, skipping persuasively in front of them. 'Follow me to the sign our great leader Mega has brought us.'

There was a moment's hesitation as the pack looked to their leader. Mega played his part by giving an authoritative nod and got a leery grin back as Psycho struck out over the scrubby heather. Yet, although the stunted figure danced in front, eagerly beckoning them on, the sunbeam he was still waxing lyrical about had already vanished as quickly as it had appeared. The vista in front of them reverted to its previous uniform grey and as Mega negotiated the awkward tufts of lumpy grass and dripping heather, wet fur plastered to his back, he thought how badly they were cocking it up. MI and M2 might have applauded Psycho's cynical sign bollo, but personally he had no faith in it whatsoever. The truth was that they had experienced a series of shocks, starting with him and Mata not carrying as many with them as they had expected. Psycho had since tried to put a positive interpretation on this by arguing they had cut out the dead wood of the uncommitted, confining their band to the truly dedicated. But with all the moaning going on, if these were the dedicated where would they be with the rest on board? Probably back in the cages by now, Mega thought gloomily.

He chewed on the cat-tail for comfort, trying to suppress a feeling that the whole thing was sliding away from him. It wasn't just his followers, but he himself, who had a lot to learn, – Mata, too, judging from the way she had gone so quiet. It had been so foolhardy thinking that they could swan straight out of the shed to dreamland on the word of an idiot like Custard. Now it was very much a question of confidence, and for the first time his was deteriorating. The only thing holding the pack together at this moment was fear, which was bad. What had an Elder once said to him: 'The only thing to fear more than fear is fear itself'?

The real world had already manitested itself as very different from their previous safety net of the cages. The Keeper's system had given way to freefall and they all urgently needed an edge to cling to, a refuge where they could harden up.

It was now his opinion that they had only one more shot. It would take more than any Psycho sign bollo to save him and the other leaders if they cocked it up once more.

34

The Pursuit of Others

Perched for the last time on Mighty Oak's solid branch, Owl stifled a yawn. As the massed ranks of CWGs agonised beneath him, he found to his huge delight that they were no longer getting under his skin. Chatter, chatter, chatter, he mouthed silently to himself. And all hot air, as Boris had rightly said. For finally – or hopefully finally, as a CWG would put it – Owl knew why it all added up to nothing. He had identified the quality that distinguished him, the one he possessed but they all lacked. It was common sense – which he personally rated higher than wisdom, gravitas, bottom or anything else that bloody rabbits approved of. Congratulating himself again on reaching this conclusion, he found the temptation to swoop down and give Burdock's fat bum a mighty kick almost irresistible. At this precise moment it was writhing odiously away as its owner nodded in approval of the current speaker, a shrill wren. Words like 'reasonable', 'consensus' and 'fair' impinged vaguely on Owl's consciousness, as he thought how the wren's brain matched its featherweight body, while his head gradually drooped down on to his breast.

'. . . naturally we wish to take into account the feelings of every creature, thereby ensuring all viewpoints are adequately represented,' the wren prattled away. 'I therefore appeal to you, comrades, not to do anything too hasty but defer the matter for further consultation. Could I suggest, in accordance with our time-honoured practices, that we set up a committee?'

Owl snapped awake as this conclusion — if you could call such a load of verbal diarrhoea a speech, or indeed the conclusion a conclusion — was greeted by applause and further bottom-waggling. He selected a male dunnock as the next speaker, sneering at it contemptuously as it fluttered on to the Stump.

'Fellow Concerned Guardians,' the dunnock piped up, casting aside the wren's obsession in favour of his own, 'the last thing I wish to do is to cast a pall over today's proceedings. However, on behalf of all dunnocks, I do feel most strongly that it is my unfortunate duty to have to draw attention to the inconsistency apparent in sub-clause B of the Woodland Code, which, in our humble opinion, contradicts the penultimate paragraph in sub-section E of the equally important Bill of Creatures' Rights.

'This, while stating in no uncertain terms . . .'

Owl nodded off again.

The Woodland Code and Bill of Creatures' Rights meeting had been in progress since mid-afternoon, and a gloomy afternoon it had been at that. After the frost accompanying the clear full moon, the sky had clouded over. The crisp air had been replaced by a cold drizzle, that now immersed them in its grey mass. While heavy plops of water dripped from Mighty Oak's bare branches, providing a monotonous undertone to the dunnock's tinny warbling, Owl thought how glad he was that both Code and Bill were something he would never have to hear about again.

Burdock had been merciless in his instructions before the meeting started, lecturing Owl as if he was not only a junior rabbit, but dumb to boot. Even Dandelion had acquired a temporary harder edge, refusing to apologise for him.

'It's not his fault Burdie's so wound up,' she had impressed on Owl with unaccustomed forcefulness. 'You can't realise just how important this is for him. It's the culmination of his life's work and he's been working himself absolutely to the bone to ensure everything goes all right at the meeting.

'Not that we're expecting any problems,' she had added hastily. 'I'm sure Burdie's tied everything up beautifully. But you must still be at your most alert. After all, he does have enemies, and you never know what might happen, do you?'

Not if you're a rabbit, Owl had thought. How could you ever know anything if you tried to control things as they did? Life was bound to be a succession of constant surprises.

'Voles never know when I'm coming, nicely or not nicely,' he had remarked, making an oblique reference to their previous conversation.

He had smiled in satisfaction when Dandelion had hurriedly excused herself to avoid grasping that particular nettle. He wondered if the leaf-litter party had yet dealt with the carnal rubbish he had left for it. Nice! He'd give them nice, he thought, coming out of his daydream and looking round at the rapt audience. Burdock's recruitment drive had gone well, he had to admit. Owl had never seen such a turn-out. A huge circle round Mighty Oak was packed with creatures and insects of all shapes and sizes. Practically every veggie in the wood must be there and, judging by the vast number of rabbits, every one from the surrounding fields as well. He had never seen so many in one place in his life – never mind what looked like ten moons' supply of voles.

It was a shame it was all for such a lost cause, but none the less it gave him a chance to show them a thing or two before he left. Mischievously, he began glaring at the dunnock, knowing it was to be the last speaker before Burdock moved the meeting to the vote. Under his steely gaze it began shifting on its spindly legs, before drawing to a faltering close, the inconsistency it had been pointing out still unresolved. As it flew forlornly back, its fellows proffered timorous sympathy, meanwhile staring at Owl in a hurt and accusing manner.

Entirely unexpectedly, he responded by shooting his head forward, hissing, and then flapping his wings violently as if to take off. The dunnocks rose off the ground in a panic and circled, twittering with alarm, while a nervous tremor ran through the rest of the packed audience.

Burdock, who had just risen to his feet prior to sauntering over to the Stump, froze in mid-step and turned to look up at Owl in horror.

'Sorry! Something bit me,' he called down in cheerful apology before recycling Freddie's joke. 'Free the Flea must be back.'

There was a stony silence from the audience, while Burdock glared at him, uncertain whether to make an issue of it.

'Just a bit of fun,' Owl beamed placatingly. 'Do carry on!'

He was getting demob-happy, he thought to himself. Maybe he should calm down a bit and let Burdock get on with his business. That was the essential trouble with the meetings though, wasn't it? They were so heavy it got to the stage where you welcomed absolutely anything that lightened them up.

Burdock allowed the pregnant silence to continue while the shocked dunnocks gradually fluttered back to earth. Only when they were entirely settled did he resume his journey to the Stump, Owl's intervention now put behind him. This was the moment he would always savour, the moment when reason replaced anarchy, providing a blueprint that would in future spread out from Old Wood across the whole world. He intended to make a personal meal out of it, but then why shouldn't he? Making the Code and Bill official would be a personal triumph, leading to his being forever celebrated as the architect of everything great and good. Thanks to endless pre-meetings, lobbyings and plain coercion, coupled with Owl's authority as his back-up, he was now supremely confident there would not even be any abstentions. Both would be endorsed unanimously. His assured immortality was only a show of wings and paws away.

Slowly he mounted the Stump and cleared his throat.

'Fellow Concerned Woodland Guardians, this is indeed an auspicious moment in the long and distinguished history of Old Wood, a moment to be treasured as marking the climax of our ceaseless struggle for fair rights for all. Today, brothers and sisters, we come to the fruition of our endless quest for natural justice. No more, dear comrades, will the paw of one creature be raised against another. No more will the doctrine "might is right" hold sway, here in our wood and its surrounding fields.

'For let me remind you how our great Bill begins: "We hold these truths to be self-evident, that all creatures are created equal, that they are endowed with certain unalienable rights, that among these are life, liberty and the pursuit of happiness—"'

'Happiness' was what Burdock actually mouthed. But nobody heard him. Instead his voice was drowned out by a loud shout of 'others' from Raka who, unnoticed by Owl, had perched herself on a branch of Mighty Oak above him. He was momentarily as startled as everyone else. He had thought Raka had wiped CWG affairs off her map. All the time though, she must have been clandestinely watching and her timing was so perfect that Owl burst out laughing. Feeling a rush of warmth towards his old friend for having taken her opportunity so brilliantly, he looked up and gave a huge congratulatory grin. She gave a gratifying squawk back, while Burdock went stiff and silent with fury.

Marcus Mole promptly jumped into the gap.

'What Comrade Burdock was saying before he was so rudely interrupted,' he declared, glaring blindly in Raka's general direction 'was that what the Code is actually about is how we must show respect and concern for each other, no matter how humble, creepy or thick.'

This pronouncement, gabbled in his normal speedy fashion, contained a typical Marcus blunder of the type that had already caused his popularity to nosedive. Now it sparked off a noisy protest.

'You're not allowed to say "thick" any more,' came angry cries. 'You've got to say "mentally disadvantaged".'

Owl sighed. He had hoped they had got rid of all that pellets when the insects had been canned.

'Mentally disadvantaged, then,' Marcus hastily conceded, popping a worm as he struggled to get back into his stride. 'And what the Code says is that we're all the same because we're all equally important so we've got to be nice to each other because we're all separate parts of the whole, if you smell what I mean . . .'

Bother, he thought as he felt it slipping away. This was what always happened. He'd just get going, then he'd lose the thread.

He popped another worm.

'There we have it,' he squeaked. 'That's what it's all about. And it's about time you thicker creatures understood that.'

As the meeting erupted in another chorus of angry squawks and grunts at the repetition of the forbidden 'thicker', Burdock signalled furiously at Owl to take control. He gave a weary hoot, as he had to due to Marcus's blindness, which he in turn used as his excuse for speaking from the grass, on the grounds that he could not see the Stump. Forgetting Marcus was another very good reason for leaving the CWG scene.

Everyone dutifully fell silent, while Raka, having had her fun, flapped off towards the rookery with her fellows, cawing victoriously.

'Goodbye, tossers, goodbye!' Her voice faded into the distance.

'Forget that asinine and common bird,' Burdock resumed, stuggling to get his temper under control. It was quite scandalous of Owl to allow such a piece of heckling to slip past his Chaircreatureship on such an auspicious occasion. He would have a strong word with him later.

'Fellow Guardians, we are now at the moment in our history,' he began again.

Owl, up on his branch, studiously avoided a shocked glare from Dandelion. He could see from the way Burdock's big arse was writhing that he was going to spin this out as long as he could. Ludicrous though both Code and Bill might be, Owl didn't really blame him. Nearly through the daymare, he could relax. As he listened to Burdock's eulogy to himself he still could not decide whether he liked Big Arse. One thing he certainly did not thank him for, though, was introducing him to politics. This had been a new word in Owl's vocabulary, and one he had instantly decided he didn't want to know about. What was there to know anyway? he had asked himself. He might now understand more of the rabbits' earnest concerns and in an odd sort of way − perish the thought − even admire them, especially the bits from the Venerable Buck. But with no sign of his predicted 'big trouble', Owl's conclusion had to be that CWGs did not live in the real wood, as the cumbersome edifices of the Code and Bill were ultimately confirming. Why were there two of them anyway? he asked himself. Why were CWGs so long-winded they couldn't wrap both into one, thereby saving everybody a great deal of trouble? For a start there were shortly going to have to be two separate votes.

But he was determined not to be upset by all the nonsenses any more. The CWGs had been a virus, polluting his life. However they were about to be eradicated — especially, he smiled to himself, now he could apply his own reverse logic. If the Code and Bill were taken at their word — or rather their very many words — they solved all the wood's problems — or at least problems as perceived by the CWGs. In the future, therefore, everyone was going to be so nice to each other that his authority would be rendered redundant. Whatever, he was bored with following the crazy loops of it all. Meanwhile Burdock was giving him an opportunity for a long doze before the grand vote. He shut his eyes and his head went down.

The woodland creatures sat stoically in the steady drizzle, occasionally lifting a paw to wipe the water out of their eyes, as Burdock droned on. He had been speaking for so long that the rapt attention greeting his initial pronouncements had since been replaced by soporific lethargy. Owl, up on his branch of Mighty Oak, was plainly fast asleep, as were the showy pheasants perched round him who had been drummed up from the surrounding fields to contribute towards the record turn-out. They had such silly brains and miniscule attention spans that this did not surprise the vast multitude of rabbits who had come from valleys all over to grace this historic occasion. But even they were beginning to shuffle their feet as they wondered when, if ever, Burdock would draw to a close. He seemed in a trance, in which his audience had ceased to exist. Some creatures, to disapproving glances, were even giving up and creeping away, including Marcus who, having exhausted his stockpile of worms, had no choice.

As he disappeared into the undergrowth a goldfinch, who had been surreptiously tiptoeing away beside him, launched himself into the air. He rose upwards, only to see the mink pack emerging out of the treeline. Automatically he let out the loudest alarm call of his life, its tone so shocking and urgent it snapped the meeting into instant alertness. But it was still too late. Nobody had a chance to move before the pack of brown predators was amongst them. The carnivorous horde seemed to have just dropped out of the sky. Snarling and biting in a frenzy of bloodlust, the invaders were everywhere, the ferocity of their joint attack sending a wave of terror surging through the woodland creatures. As the predators began tearing their victims limb from limb the meeting erupted in panic, while from the ground arose a communal wail of horror, distress and pain. The first gurgling death throes mingled with high-pitched chittering as the attackers dug their teeth into helpless necks, sending glistening red arcs up towards the sky, now black with the birds that had risen as one.

The woodland creatures had been right in thinking that until that point Burdock had been in a world of his own. He was aware the weather was rotten and he was going on for too long, but as he spoke there seemed such a multitude of threads and angles that needed pulling together to encompass the full breadth of the many, many matters contained in his beloved Code and Bill. Carried away and preoccupied with the sound of his own voice — or, as he interpreted it, his vitally important speech — he was the last to react. He whipped round to see the lead invader coming at him, but had no time to do anything before, with a furious snarl, he was enveloped by a wave of rank, meat-eater's breath. His attacker crashed into him, knocking him sideways off the Stump and he thumped to the ground, his shoulder stabbing with pain where a bite had been taken out. He could feel the blood already coursing down his fur. Swaying on his feet, he reeled with the shock of being confronted by a creature the like of which he had never clapped eyes on before. It was like a weasel, but considerably bigger and bluey-brown, while its most fearsome aspect — and the only one that concerned him at this point — was the naked aggression he could feel quivering from its every hair. The predator had landed on its side and was spitting anger and hatred as it thrashed about, trying to regain its footing. Burdock knew he had only moments. This was death staring him in the face.

Instinctively he turned and whacked out with his hind legs, feeling a harsh jar as he contacted bone. He had been lucky enough to catch his attacker – whatever it was – square on the head, sending it slithering across the wet grass. But he wasn't going to look back to see how effective he had been. Code and Bill already a distant memory, he grabbed his chance and shot across the clearing into the undergrowth, fighting his way past his fellow CWGs as he joined in their panic-stricken flight for secure hiding places.

Behind him he left air already tainted with the heavy smell of fresh blood.

35

The Big Clearing Massacre

Mega could hardly believe his eyes when he first saw the woodland gathering spread out below them. It was a gigantic living feast, the entire menu for the hunters of the free world. A hot spurts banquet – and just in the nick of time!

The journey towards Psycho's disappeared shaft of sunlight had gone badly. It had been nerve-racking being so exposed, and such hard going over the rough terrain that the pack's tight V-formation had soon disintegrated into a straggling line. Mega, tiring of the surly grumbling and general lack of enthusiasm, had ignored pleas from Psycho to try to boost morale with more speeches. Instead he had put on the squeeze, as recommended by Maxi.

'The only thing that'll drive them forward now is fear,' his military adviser had stressed. 'Let me give them the works, boss. If they're frightened anyway, they might as well be frightened of me.'

'I suppose you're right, Maxi,' Mega had replied, feeling depressed. What a way to march into the glorious future!

'Allright, you horrible lot, you're all in it now,' Maxi had bawled as the mink stood dripping, heads hung low. 'You can't go back to the cages even if you want to. For your former human oppressor, the Keeper, will be waiting.

'And what will he be thinking? I'll tell you what he'll be thinking, he'll be thinking you're even more horrible than I do. Above all he'll be thinking about what you all did to Pussles, his dearly beloved pet. And as a result, I can tell you, he will be merciless. So, if you want to die horribly, go back.'

He had noted with satisfaction the pack becoming even more despondent as the message sank in.

'Down there is the past,' he had gone on, gesturing at the valley. 'But your leader has informed me he is prepared to be generous. On this, our great enterprise, he has told me, there is no room for shirkers. So, any who wish to leave, step forward.'

The pack had frozen, while the muscle-mink prowled round the edges, until Mega stepped forward and wordlessly resumed the march. But the imposed unity had been only superficial and the renewed silence indicated how the mood had soured. As on the rollway, the minions should have been quivering with the joy of being free, overwhelmed by the sights, sounds and smells that assailed their senses. But they had hardly lifted their eyes. Only the indefatigable Maxi had retained his jaunty stride as he bustled up and down, urging them on.

Although the journey had not been that far, it had seemed to take an age, and the light had already been fading as they approached the wood. Even then spirits had failed to lift. A strange lethargy had settled into the mink's movements and as Mega watched them morosely putting one paw in front of another he could see they were dead-beat. They were as all as weak as cubs, he thought with a renewed flare of anger against the Keeper. Only now that they were out of the cages was he beginning to perceive the full extent of their deprivation. How dare the humans have subjugated them for so many generations! How dare they have reduced once-proud mink to such a pitiful state!

But what Mega could now see had changed all that in an instant. Thanks to the muddle caused by Custard's directions, the pack had not entered the wood from the bottom of the valley but had climbed up to the ridge, enabling them to look down on the place as a whole. From the first glance it was obvious this was Custard's special place. There was the rollway, the long marshy field separating the wood from the river, the hump-backed bridge and presumably the five-barred gate, although that was hidden by the trees.

But it was the extraordinary sight in the largest clearing that sent the adrenalin surging through every vein. Mega had expected the wood to be closed down when they arrived. As the pack made its way down the barren hillside on to the lusher green fields he sensed that it was clearing the ground of life, as if it was pushing a bow-wave in front of it. As he and Maxi had previously agreed, the only way to arrive surreptitiously would be by waiting until sunset, or rather, in the miserable conditions, darkness. With the curtain of drizzle so set, it was obvious there would be no more sun that day. But Maxi had warned ominously that if they stopped they might never get going again, while Mega had appreciated it made little practical difference in the end. They were going to make their presence in the wood felt soon enough. Yet now it appeared that, rather than going to ground, virtually all the creatures who lived there had gathered out in the open, apparently heedless of the danger they were in. They were sitting ducks – some of them literally, as he could hear from the occasional quack.

Mega ordered Maxi to pull the ranks back below the skyline as he tried to fathom it out. Why hadn't the alarm been raised? It was almost as if the woodland creatures had known the mink were coming and decided to put themselves on offer. It appeared some sort of meeting was in progress, and the only explanation had to be that the creatures were totally preoccupied with some crucial business. But what could that possibly be, when their lives were in such dire peril? There was something so odd about their blithe disregard that Mega was faintly suspicious. Yet, when Maxi voiced the suggestion that it could be a set-up, he instantly dismissed the idea as too far-fetched.

Anyhow, nothing was to be gained by speculating as to why the creatures were there. The point was the result, a wide-open target infinitely more mouth-watering than the hated Pussles.

An unscheduled attack would of course be yet another departure from Maxi's Plan A, which specified the first job on arrival to be establishing a secure base. But, like Pussles, it was too good an opportunity to miss and anyway an attack fitted with correct thinking. Any mink worth his or her blood should pride themselves on being opportunist to the core.

'We're going in,' he said bluntly, noting with pleasure that Maxi did not argue but immediately immersed himself in practical details, reporting that with the rain and light breeze in their faces their scent would not give them away.

'Although we're going for it, Maxi, it's still vital we keep everything under control,' Mega informed him 'The ranks must not be allowed to scatter. We're after a run and hit — one flying sweep. Wham! Bang! Then reassemble. Got that?'

'Yes, saah,' Maxi bawled back, black eyes glittering cruelly. Despite his reservations, he was determined to enjoy the attack as much as doing in Ramses!

'Operation Meeting Storm,' he informed the pack, was to be a lightning raid, as he had taught them in his training sessions.

'Guerrilla tactics,' his troops nodded knowledgeably to each other before he gave them the crucial rider.

'Now get this, you lot. You can each choose your own target, but your great leader, Mega, wants you to understand absolutely that the big bastard in the middle who's doing the talking is his, and his alone. No-one else is to touch it, do you hear me?'

The prevailing breeze and drizzle meant they could not hear what was being said down below. But Mega presumed that the creature standing on the tree stump, lecturing the others, must be the woodland leader. Even at that distance, from its body language he could make out it was preaching some sort of pompous bollo. As a sudden vision of the old Elders floated into his mind he found himself already hating the bloody thing. And the hot spurt that would fountain out of that rounded bulk, with such a gigantic arse! He was already slavering so much that the cat-tail dripped with saliva as he parked it under a convenient bush.

After Maxi had drawn up the pack just below the skyline Mega gave the command to attack. As they hurtled down the slope, his tiredness and despondency vanished as if they had never been, he felt at his most powerful. Pussles' dry tail had been no substitute for the succulent, fat-arsed bundle of bunny now firmly in his sights. The wind of his passage rushed past him as, still in the lead, he cleared the last trees and burst into the clearing. He strained his leg muscles in a final burst of acceleration to close on his selected victim, bracing himself for the spring which would send him flying upwards at its throat. But as he launched himself he skidded on the wet grass and, thrown, only managed to catch the rabbit on the shoulder, tearing out a lump of flesh and fur, before they were both sent bowling sideways by the force of the impact.

To Mega's misfortune he fell awkwardly on his side, whilst the rabbit, luckier, landed on its feet. As the mink leader scrabbled about, trying to regain his footing, his intended victim was astonishingly quick to react. Lashing out with its powerful hind legs, it administered such a thump on his head that Mega saw stars. By the time he had staggered back upright, his head ringing, it had vanished into the undergrowth along with the other creatures scattering in the frenzy of panic. With its intimate knowledge of the terrain, and presumably a handy hiding place nearby, there was no point in even thinking of pursuing it.

Mega shook himself. He was not yet very good at this. But now he could see he had more urgent responsibilities. The cornerstone of Plan A — keeping the pack together at all costs — had already been dislodged. The minions, carried away by the heat of the moment, had completely disregarded their strict instructions to reassemble after one sweep. Half of them were still in the clearing, mostly tearing triumphantly at various corpses. But the others had vanished, and into the furthest recesses of the wood, judging by the sounds of furious pursuit coming from all directions.

For a moment Mega was disgusted. The idiots had already let him down. Then, instantly, he forgave them. Who could blame them for losing their heads when the clearing was splattered with the red splashes that marked so many hot spurts? And the pride that was being restored by these successful kills! Next to him a female was mewing with joy as she tore the wings off a small bird, while beyond her a pair rolled ecstatically in the blood of their victim. Others were worrying at lifeless heads as they worked on smashing the skulls to suck out the brains while one, with an enterprise Mega instantly admired, was holding its mouse-like victim by its tail and pounding its head against a stone.

Nearby, in a comradely way he also approved of, two males were pulling in a joint endeavour to break the jaw of a furry grey creature with a bushy tail in order to prise out the prime delicacy of its tongue. Judging by the gaping hole in its head the brains had already gone. All over the clearing there echoed a chorus of ecstatic chittering, mingled with the crunch and snap of breaking bones, while from the undergrowth came the angry boom of Maxi's voice trying to restore order.

Putting aside his envy at the successful kills and hoping that in the mêlée no-one had witnessed his personal balls-up, Mega charged into the bushes to add his weight to the round-up. Beyond the first tree trunks, he almost ran straight into another rabbit, which was sitting frozen motionless with fear. Without thinking he launched himself at the stationary target, this time hitting it fair and square on the side of the neck, just above the throat. As he felt the pumping between his teeth he unlocked his jaws and pulled his head back to release the fountaining hot spurt he had been seeking. The taste of that thick red liquid! Then, as he ripped the skin back, the equally hot flesh! He tore at it, cramming more and more into his mouth until he thought he would choke. Still he stuffed in more, the blood running down his chin as meat, muscle and sinew welded themselves together in his mouth until they stuck in a solid lump. He gave a gigantic gulp, gagged for an instant, and his throat bulged as he swallowed the package in one. He was ingesting pure energy, which was now whacking into his veins and flowing round his body until he was tingling from ears to toe.

'Yahoo!' he cried, seizing the limp head and spearing an eyeball with his teeth. He gave a bite as massive as he had to Pussles' tail and felt a gritty crunch as the skullbone collapsed.

Then his tongue was in there, sucking out the sweet liquid brain slurry. He slurped down the steaming skull contents in bubbling, choking ecstasy. The hit! The hit! He was seeing red! He was soaking in red! Drowning in red! The world was red! Red for him! Red for them! Red for all mink!

His initial euphoria spent, he then settled down and began to appease his still-gnawing hunger in a more leisurely and controlled way.

It took until well into the night to get the pack back together, by which time Maxi, who seemed take it as a personal affront, was virtually hoarse. The most stupid mink, who had simply lost all control, were easily apprehended rushing wildly from one potential target to another. But some had been so excited they had pursued their victims right out of the wood into the fields beyond, then been unable to find their way back, while the last few were tracked down, doggedly sitting it out in secure hiding places from which their quarry could obviously never be dislodged. But there was one great advantage in all the running about required. When all their various information was pooled the wood had effectively been reconnoitred. And all the reports, both individually and together, showed that although Custard might have messed up her directions, she hadn't been exaggerating about what a wonderful wood it was. The thrill of the chase and reality of hot spurts had transcended their wildest dreams and the negative atmosphere vanished.

'The attitude towards you personally has changed just as radically,' Psycho reported, delighted and still slightly amazed at having creamed a small bird which had been slow off the mark. 'Your popularity rating's zoomed, Mega. The minions aren't grumbling any more about you leading them into the wilderness. Now you're the heroic leader, who's fulfilled his promise and transported them to the Promised Land.'

'Well, so I have,' Mega replied frigidly. Psycho was making his blood run cold. Didn't he ever stop analysing things? Then he grimaced as the runt added slyly: 'Shame you weren't so lucky, Mega. Never mind, we all make mistakes.'

The patronising little sod! Psycho was the last mink he needed to have witnessed his embarrassing blunder.

'Don't worry, Mega. I'll keep it to myself,' he now grinned, giving a conspiratorial wink.

Mega fought back an impulse to seize him by the thoat and throttle the life out of him. Mata, who now came towards them, had suggested he go easy so as to get the best out of him, and Mega knew she was right, even though it went so much against the grain. He was beginning to discover there were more aspects to leadership than he had ever imagined, and compromising his feelings was one. He had to remember Psycho was the one who found it hardest to adapt. Instead, when Mata suggested they return to the ridge to retrieve the stashed cat-tail, he simply cut him out by leaving him in charge alongside Maxi. He could afford to be benevolent, he thought, as he and Mata bounded along side by side, smiling at the rustles and crashes in the undergrowth as every form of life hurried to get out of their way. Mink already ruled. They had turned the corner. From now on things would settle down.

'We've done well, Mega,' Mata commented as he pulled the tail out from under the bush. 'You and I together.'

We have indeed, Mega thought. It would be easy for each of them to criticise the other for their failures, but there was no point. If Mata wanted to claim equal credit, he didn't mind. She had done her best, they were here, and that was all that mattered.

'You're my mate, aren't you?' he said softly.

Mata smiled knowingly, turned her back and set off down the hillside. He followed more slowly, the cat-tail tickling his mouth and making him grin. How proud Sheba would have been to witness him now. And he was about to remain true to her trust by successfully re-establishing the bloody ways of their ancestors.

Mata was waiting patiently where the trees ran out and they entered the clearing side by side, to be greeted by the pack squeaking increasingly tall stories of their individual prowess, while Maxi gazed on proudly. The sight of their trophy sparked off fresh excitement.

'Mega! Mega! Mega!' the pack chanted ecstatically, rushing towards him.

Smiling proudly, he jumped up, placed the tail on the tree stump and gave a big grin as they gathered admiringly around.

'Let's gather all the bits of creatures together,' someone shouted excitedly.

'Yeh, heap them all up.'

'In a big pile dripping with blood!'

'Good idea,' Mega beamed magnanimously as he stepped down off the stump. That would keep them busy while the leadership reverted to Plan A. Now they had to decide where to establish their base.

36

Plateauing Out

'I cannot emphasise too strongly that security must come first in our thinking,' Maxi urged. 'If the humans find us, we can kiss our arses good-bye.'

'Yes, Maxi,' Mega replied soothingly. 'But you must realise there are other matters we must take into account.'

He looked carefully at his military adviser, who was agitatedly smoothing his whiskers. This was the third time Maxi had surprised him by his caution and his security obsession now smacked of paranoia. More importantly, it was deadlocking the conference over the positioning of their base, which they all had no doubt would be the key to the success or failure of their venture. As it was so critical, Mega had been trusting the decision would be unanimous. But thanks to Maxi a serious dispute had arisen.

Now they were safely in the wood, Mega had pulled in the two new mink, MI and M2, who had already stated their opinion – the minions might be ecstatic about their surroundings in general, but, although they didn't know it, their base was going to be immensely more significant to them.

'They need the security they had in the cages, but somewhere much better, a glittering alternative they can be proud and happy to call home,' they had pronounced at the beginning of the discussion, which had started well. The large clearing they were in was obviously the focal point of the wood, but they had all agreed that from a mink point of view it was too open for comfort, which left two choices. The first – or 'Site One', as Maxi called it – was a deep hollow in the hillside under the ridge where they had entered. Its sharp sides and flat floor showed it to be unnatural, and they were presuming the humans had gouged it out in the distant past, although its neglected appearance ruled out any current danger they would return. Maxi was now insisting on it at all costs.

'It gives us the high ground,' he stressed on an inspection visit. 'It's not overlooked and its commanding aspect means we'll have full control in any potential situation. And who knows what's going to happen next? In my view it's imperative we prepare for any eventuality.'

Very true and a point – if not two – to Maxi, Mega thought as he watched him demonstrate how easy it was to run up to the ridge.

'If we post look-outs up here,' he bawled, graphically outlined against the horizon, 'we will be able to observe the whole landscape, including the direction of the most likely source of pursuit, the farm we came from.'

Mega, running up himself, could see Maxi was right. But although the view might be excellent, it only raised the deeper question of how much they needed to bother about the humans any more.

Mata had given him her private opinion before the conference started.

'My gut feeling is that after the initial pursuit's died down we'll be left alone,' she had explained. 'Even if our presence is discovered, the only human with a vested interest in us is our former oppressor. And I doubt whether he'll want us back after what's happened.

'Other humans, I think, will be content to leave us to our own devices. The only possible exception is the one whose territory we must be on. But whoever he is, he obviously takes no interest

in it. All the signs confirm Custard's description of it being devoid
of human activity. All in all, Mega, I know that the humans
won't be coming for us.'

'How do you know?' Mega asked, intrigued.

'I just know, that's all.'

She might well be right, Mega thought, although she still
hadn't convinced him. How could it be that simple?

Then he remembered something.

'I outstared the liberator back at the farm, Mata,' he
confided.

'So did I, Mega,' she smiled back conspiratorially.

'We're right not to be afraid of them, but rather to see them
as afraid of us, aren't we?' he asked.

'I think we are, Mega. And that confirms that even if they
find us, they won't want to know.'

She was right, Mega had since decided and on that basis they
could do what they liked, which meant choosing Site Two. This
had already unimaginatively been dubbed the Plateau and was
diametrically opposed to the lofty Site One in being set down
by the river. It was a smallish, flat area, past the end of the
field that ran between the wood and the water, where the
river curved and narrowed as it entered a gorge, changing from
shallows to a deep pool. On the far bank the rollway curved
away behind a vertical rock face, while on the woodland side
the ground rose to form a low hill. The Plateau was halfway
up this, directly overlooking the water.

Mega didn't need to be informed this was where the pack
really wanted to be. It was the river that made it. On what
MI and M2 had already labelled the 'Long March', as they
set to work composing the official history of the escape, the
pack had crossed several streams. These had briefly energised
the mink as they luxuriated in squashing themselves flat on
their bellies and ducking their heads under to come up sleek
and dripping. They had been nothing, however, compared to
the river, which carried a good head of water. The pool below
the Plateau could have been designed specifically for swimming,
it was so satisfyingly wide, long and deep. During the round-up
Mega himself had shared in the joy of its discovery, plunging

into the icy water to frolic alongside others. All the pack members had since rushed to visit it, going equally wild with enthusiasm.

However, as they now stood looking down into the black depths, Maxi attacked the location bitterly.

'We must tuck ourselves away, where the chances of human detection are lowest,' he reiterated. 'It's asking for trouble being so near the rollway, even though it's on the other side of the river. And being so low down will make us wide open to surprise attack from above.'

To a large extent Maxi was right. The cliff-face opposite loomed upwards, while on the other sides trees largely obscured the view.

'But there is a security defence, Mega,' Psycho fired back. 'The rollway might be near, but it's tucked round the corner out of sight and, though the view's limited, we'll also be virtually invisible.'

Maxi, unhappy at being challenged on the ground of his own speciality, was already frothing before Psycho went too far. 'Anybody would think you were afraid of the humans,' he taunted.

Mega had to intervene as Maxi snapped furiously at him.

'That's enough,' he reprimanded him. 'Psycho's only doing his job.'

Maxi then raised his fallback, which was admittedly a secondary factor to take into account.

'Site One is spacious, my leader. But while Site Two may seem enormous after the shed, it can only be described as cramped. Look at those steep sides – there's absolutely no room to expand. I can see it causing huge problems, especially when the next generation of cubs arrives. There's no future in it.'

But Maxi had no answer to the Plateau's unexpected bonus. A large ash tree, previously eking out a precarious existence on the edge of the river, had crashed down and wedged itself against the opposite cliff. Its sloping trunk now made a natural slide into the water, which the minions had already tried out to hoots of glee, excitedly chittering about its endless potential for fun and games.

'Site One's so dry and bare, Mega. Even Maxi can't guarantee the minions won't mutiny if we try to force them to stay there,' Psycho insisted. 'It'll be useless telling them it's safer in the long run even if it's true. They'll just vote with their feet and spend their time here regardless.

'We all have to go with the flow, Mega,' he concluded, grinning smugly at the watery pun.

Mega overrode Maxi's final attempt at a compromise by suggesting they begin at Site One and move to Site Two later.

'We can't spend our whole time thinking about security,' he explained shortly. 'We've come here to live in freedom, not fear.'

'I hope you're not suggesting I can't do my job, my leader,' Maxi glowered back. 'As far as I'm concerned, the price of freedom is eternal vigilance.'

'But it's this endless talk about the possibilities that induces fear,' Mega said impatiently. 'How can we be free if we spend all our time guarding against things which will never happen? How can we feel secure looking over our shoulders all the time?'

'Well, when it all goes wrong, don't tell me I didn't warn you,' Maxi muttered.

'Don't worry,' Mega replied, suddenly feeling weary. Now they were in this new environment he had to make allowances, but Maxi was none the less so far proving a major disappointment.

'Anyhow,' he added, trying to cheer him up, 'It does mean there is one job that I'm sure you'll enjoy.'

The leaders returned to the big clearing to find the pack still gathered admiringly round the pile of corpses they had heaped at the base of the cat totem and which Mega now clambered over to reach the stump.

'We're moving to the Plateau,' he announced to huge cheers. 'Who wants to help?'

'We all do.'

'Good,' their leader smiled cruelly. 'Because there are some creatures already there who seem to believe that it's their home, not ours. Shall we put them right about that?'

'Yeh! Let's show them who's boss, Mega,' the mink cried, charging about and snapping at each other in parody of the promised action.

'That's my boys,' Mega smiled proudly. 'And girls as well,' he added as a sop to Mata's warriors. She rewarded him with a warm smile. 'Now listen to Maxi.'

Maxi had indeed brightened up at the vision of leading a raiding party to swoop on the Plateau. It would be just like the meeting massacre! But as the pack made its way towards the target, some individuals, still on a high, were far too excited to maintain the discipline he had demanded. The crashing, banging and squeaking as they barged through the undergrowth were excruciating to his ears.

'It's not working, my leader,' he complained despairingly. 'They seem to have forgotten all I told them about keeping quiet.'

'There's nothing to do, Maxi, can't you see?' Mega snapped back, losing his patience with him again. 'These aren't automatons you're dealing with, they're your fellow living creatures.'

It had been all very well surprising the woodland creatures when they were preoccupied with their meeting, but now they were forewarned. Anyhow, dawn was already lightening the sky and the pack's progress had shattered the silence of the night. Not at all surprisingly, they descended on the Plateau to find it deserted.

'It's all your fault for not obeying my orders,' Maxi shouted at everyone furiously, but nobody was listening. The initial anti-climax already forgotten, the mink were now careering about exploring the abandoned burrows complex, still redolent with the heady smell of rabbit. Of course they should have evicted their floppy-eared inhabitants and then, by way of a bonus, eaten them. But the furry creatures had left behind such superb tailor-made housing that the minions were now delirious with fresh joy.

'They've only just left,' one shouted to Mega excitedly. 'You can feel where they've been sleeping.'

'We won't need a house-warming then, will we?' Mega

shouted back and they all creased up with laughter. 'Now, who's going to be first down the slide?'

They charged off to the fallen ash and the still black water of the pool began boiling as they hurtled in one after another, all except for Maxi, who continued to stand woodenly above. Mega, surfacing in a cloud of exhilarating bubbles, couldn't stop himself calling up: 'Still want Site One, eh?'

'Leave him be, Mega,' Mata scolded him as he received a murderous scowl in reply. 'You can't make him enjoy himself.'

She swiped the surface with her paw, sending a shower of spray into his face.

'Why, you . . .' Mega laughed, setting off in pursuit.

To put the area in full working order they still needed to clear the scrub and brambles that had crept in round the edges, despite the efforts of the resident rabbits. But that could wait. Life here was already as sweet as Mega had dreamed it would be.

He took a deep breath and went under, determined to be the first to reach the bottom.

37

Pop Go the Weasels

'We don't care what anyone says, they're not one of us,' the weasel squeaked defiantly. 'Or stoats either,' he added, to nods from his group of fellows. 'And we also want to stress that nobody's more surprised to see them than we are.'

Boris, shelving the differences created by Owl's CWG Chaircreatureship, had taken responsibility for reconstituting the Dead Vole Society to investigate the invaders, for which Ollie was grateful. He felt an urgent need to discuss the invasion with other predators, rather than useless rabbits. The badger had also decided the first task must be interrogating the stoats and weasels, who had come under immediate suspicion as having something to do with the unwelcome arrivals. They were anyhow convenient scapegoats, universally disliked for their conniving, slinky ways and nasty habits like sucking out other creatures' eggs.

'They look like both of you,' Owl said, staring accusingly at the narrow, pointed faces with their bristling whiskers and shifty eyes.

'A crow looks like Raka to the ignorant,' the weasel replied scathingly. 'But we don't think she's one, do we?' he asked 'What are you, stupid or something?' he sneered.

Raka frowned at this mention of her name, while Owl and Boris both struggled to keep their tempers. It was hard being even-pawed with such vicious creatures, who seemed so determined to put everyone's backs up. The least they could do in the circumstances was show some respect.

'Are you all blind to boot?' the weasel squeaked, putting Boris's blood pressure up another notch. 'Can't you see they're a different colour as well?'

The stoats, currently turning from ermine as they shed their winter coats, nodded emphatically.

'And so unobservant you can't see they're bigger?' the weasel added spitefully, causing Boris's stripy head to weave angrily up and down. Knowingly or unknowingly, the weasel had hit a nerve. Boris's eyesight was so bad he probably had little idea what the invaders looked like, although what he did say was that they stank. Owl, who had seen them more clearly, agreed with Raka that they weren't either stoats or weasels. But he still backed Boris's interrogation proposal, suspecting there was some knowledge to be gained.

'Well who are they then?' he demanded.

The weasel's eyes flickered.

'We think they're our notorious cousins, who normally live a long way away,' he admitted uneasily. 'We have heard rumours the humans have been keeping some near here in cages, like chickens.'

'Come across anything?' Owl asked Freddie. Chicken-house raves were one of his prime satisfactions in life.

'Not me, Ollie,' Freddie replied airily, looking at the weasels and stoats with interest. 'Whereabouts?' he asked.

'You must be as stupid as the rest of your friends,' the weasel said. 'Didn't I just say it was only a rumour? We never investigated it because we didn't want to know.'

'Why not?' Boris growled.

'We just didn't,' the weasel muttered, looking at the ground. There was silence.

'If you don't tell us all you know right now,' Boris suddenly harumphed, 'I personally will break every bone in your body, one by one!'

The weasel's composure slipped.

'Are you sure?' he asked pleadingly. 'It's not good news – for us or anyone else in the wood.'

'Absolutely certain,' Boris growled.

The weasel looked directly at him.

'We don't want you getting this wrong,' he said, tight-lipped, 'but we admit they're fellow members of our *mustelidae* family. That's where any similarity ends though.'

'What's their name?'

'Mink.'

'Mink?'

'Yes, mean, nasty, vicious, mother-copulating mink.'

'Meaner than you lot?'

'Much.'

'More vicious?'

'Much.'

'More aggressive?'

'Much.'

'Anything in their favour?'

'Nothing. Their reputation is for being absolute bastards through and through.'

Boris scratched his head in a cloud of dust. He was running out of questions.

'Tell us what you saw,' he instructed Owl weakly.

Owl had been asleep when the creatures burst into the clearing. As he sprang awake, their appearance so surprised him he almost fell off his perch. He had taken off automatically, despite his mind telling him that, up on his Chaircreature branch, he was not in any immediate danger. Looking down, he had watched with professional interest as the invaders ripped into the fleeing CWGs.

'I've never seen anything like them,' he explained. 'They were running as a pack, yet operating as individuals. They caused absolute chaos – what Freddie would call a headless-chicken situation.'

The fox licked his lips.

'Where did they come from?' Boris asked.

'Nowhere I could see.'

'And what was different about them?'

That wasn't an easy question, Owl thought as he bent his mind to answering it as best he could.

'Well, from the first moment I saw them it was obvious they were extremely serious predators,' he said slowly. 'They're very quick, very focused, and very well equipped. But what I think impressed me most was the alacrity with which they dispatched their victims. All of us kill, of course, but this lot seemed to me so ultimately feral — brutal, uncompromising. Savage, you might call it.' He fished around in his head, but the right word still refused to come. 'So hard and sustained, absolutely no messing about. No playing, no hesitation. Just straight for the jugular.'

He still couldn't wrap his head around it, he thought as he saw them all looking at him blankly. There was another aspect he had had confirmed since, however, and which was something new in his experience.

'I know that might sound like any other predator,' he admitted. 'But what puzzles me particularly is how they've been operating since. They're going on killing, but I don't know why. Their main interest seems to be breaking open their victims' skulls to eat the brains. They do eat some other parts as well, but the thing I find oddest of all is that in most cases they just leave the bodies lying about. It's almost as if they were more interested in the killing than in eating their prey afterwards.'

'Exactly right,' the weasel's thin voice cut across trium-phantly.

'What do you mean, "exactly right"?' Boris demanded.

But the weasel had gone surly again.

'Never mind,' he muttered. 'Either you get it or you don't. But what I can tell you is that we weasels and stoats do, and as a result we're leaving.'

'You can't do that!' Owl screeched, shocked.

'You just watch us.'

'But you say they're your relations. Haven't you talked to them?'

'There's no dialogue to be had,' the weasel replied grimly. 'We've got three dead already to our certain knowledge. And as we're the ones in most direct competition for their food resources, you must see we're the most affected.'

That did shake Owl. So it wasn't only CWG creatures who were suffering. Predators were under attack as well. Yet he still couldn't believe the weasels and stoats were crumbling so easily.

'You're saying you're ceding your individual territories – never mind your place in the woodland hierarchy – without even a fight?' he asked, wanting to make sure he had heard correctly.

'Yes,' the weasel replied without a trace of hesitation.

'But the mink are only predators like us,' Owl protested.

'Only like us, are they?' the weasel replied with a thin laugh. 'You'll soon see how they'll change things.'

'So this is how your world ends – not with a bang, but with a whimper?' Owl sneered, trying to provoke a retaliation.

But the weasel remained unashamed.

'Absolutely. And if you weren't all so stupid you'd follow our example and get out before it's too late.'

'Stop calling us stupid,' Boris roared, thumping the ground with a great digging paw. 'As far as I'm concerned you can all leave now. You're worse than the tossers – and that's saying something!'

Owl knew the weasels and stoats were so unpopular most other creatures would be glad to see the back of them, whatever the reason. But the look Raka gave him indicated that she had grasped the same point – mean and conniving they might be, but no-one had ever accused them of being cowards. Rather, they were aggressive predators to the core. Things must be very serious indeed if they weren't brave, or foolish, enough to stay.

'We have to talk about this,' he announced to the others as the last *mustelidae* member slunk off into the darkness without a backward glance.

'We can't just stand by and watch them rip the place apart,' Owl protested.

'Are they really that bad, Ollie?' Freddie asked laconically. 'I, for one, have never taken a weasel's or a stoat's word for anything. What difference do the mink make to us? We're getting along all right. Anyhow, have you thought there are some creatures here who actually welcome them?'

'What do you mean?' Owl asked suspiciously, knowing how Freddie could twist a viewpoint round.

'Just that carrion-eaters like the crows, or scavengers like beetles — they aren't complaining, are they?' Freddie asked, innocently looking up at the sky. 'There are more bodies lying around than they can cope with. And think how ecstatic the bluebottles'll be with so much rotting meat to lay eggs on. The wood's going to be maggot city.'

'Are you saying that because some particular species have their own axe to grind, they don't care about the rest?' Owl inquired caustically.

'You know as well as I do that's the way the wood goes round, Ollie,' Freddie smiled, unabashed. 'There's always someone in the chain to profit from someone else's misfortune.'

Ollie frowned. The Venerable Buck had said they were all part of the same whole, but somehow he had meant it as a good, rather than a bad, thing.

'I know one creature who's profiting more than any other,' Raka suddenly interjected, staring at Freddie accusingly.

The fox curled his top lip back in a sneer.

'Freddie's right,' Boris then chipped in. 'Your trouble, Ollie, is that you haven't recovered from hanging around with the tossers. This is a free wood, where different creatures live according to their own rules. And who are we to criticise them for that?'

'You're all right,' Owl retorted angrily. 'You're big enough to look after yourself. But what about those who can't?'

'They just can't, Ollie,' Boris replied dismissively. 'That's the way it is.'

'So what are they supposed to do?' Owl asked.

'Adapt, Ollie, adapt.'

'As some of us are already doing,' Raka interjected, staring at Freddie again.

'Maybe we are, Raka,' Freddie replied with a smooth grin. 'Maybe we are.'

Ollie got much the same message back at the nest.

'Have you forgotten we've got an egg to hatch?' Ula screeched angrily. 'It's time you got on with your own life instead of trying to live everyone else's.'

'But that's the whole point the Venerable Buck was making,' Owl shouted excitedly. 'That's what I've been trying to explain – that everyone's lives control ours because we're all in it together. Can't you see that?'

'What I can see is that you're becoming more like a rabbit than a rabbit,' Ula shouted back. 'And what I definitely can't see is my supper, which is what I need right now, not this constant talk, talk, talk which gets us all nowhere.'

You mean you can't see further than the end of your own beak, Owl thought bitterly.

'The stoats and weasels have already left,' he said, expecting the information to jolt her.

But it was like water off a duck's back.

'Good riddance,' she snapped. 'I never had any time for them. The only shame is that the rabbits haven't followed their example. Now, where's that food?'

Owl flew off to get it. Whatever his opinion of Ula, he enjoyed his responsibilities as the father of the little image of himself at present forming within the egg.

Passing over the Plateau, he could see it was the seething hive of activity, it had been ever since the invaders arrived. He had never come across anyone as active as these mink, as he now knew them to be, not even the constantly bustling shrews, or worm-popping Marcus. Didn't they ever sleep, rest or just take it easy? One thing they had already abolished was the notion of peace and quiet, which predators and non-predators alike had previously enjoyed. For Owl, with his sensitive ears, the noise rising up towards him was quite deafening. What would the Venerable Buck have made of his big trouble now it had arrived? he wondered. More than Boris, that was for sure. For there was a huge irony in the weasel's 'seeing' remark which had so got under Boris's skin. He was too short-sighted to see beyond his own selfish interests. To understand the mink's overall impact Owl knew he would have to take on board some CWG thinking, which meant talking to Burdock. Big Arse might be a pale substitute for the VB, but he must have some knowledge that would be relevant.

That was, if he was still with them and Owl could actually find him. Since the mink arrived rabbits had been scarcer on the ground than magpie's teeth.

38

Enterprise Zone

MI and M2 instantly became the driving force behind a ceremony to mark the pack's successful arrival in the wood.

'We must build it round a concept which everyone can base their consequent thinking on, great leader,' MI explained, dancing alongside Mega as he went for an early evening prowl. 'Something that binds the pack irrevocably together and unites it. Something that encapsulates, in a word, the essence of minkishness.'

'We've already got that – it's called hot spurts, if you didn't know,' Mega growled. One of the most irritating things about this pair was the way they seemed to have no idea of personal privacy. Couldn't he even go for a walk round his new domain without them pursuing him?

'That's two words, great leader, not one,' MI replied playfully, running ahead with his twin before stopping to block the path.

As Mega drew to a halt he cocked his head and looked at him persuasively.

'Seriously though, great leader, hot spurts are only what the pack does. Our vocation is to look beyond the prosaic "what" to the more esoteric "why".

'We therefore recommend a naming ceremony to make occupation of the wood official, but what we're really going for is a "whyness" name, rather than a "whatness" name.'

'The only whyness I'm interested in is not being able to tell one of you from the other,' Mega growled, trying to wrap his head round their baffling phraseology as the pair set off again, flitting in and out of the lengthening shadows. Their similar appearances, which continuously baffled him, were somehow part of their being so oily and hard to pin down.

'Why not treat us as one, great leader?' they squeaked in unison. 'You could call us the Marketing Mink. After all, that's what we're here for – to make sure your message achieves maximum market penetration.'

Mega winced. This new talk of the mink as a 'market' was as bad as Psycho and his 'minions'. Only that morning the pair had been fussing around, 'marketingwise', as they put it, and recommending that he brush the fur on the top of his head upwards to make himself look taller, while at the same time pricking up his ears so as to appear more alert and aggressive.

'These days, if you want to play a part, first and foremost you've got to look the part,' they had emphasised cheerily. 'And to be the great leader you need to be dead butch.'

Since then Mega had secretly tried their suggestion when he was sure they weren't looking, and been rather pleased on inspecting the result in a pool of water. Publicly, though, he had torn them off a strip.

'My job is to lead, not spend my time faffing around with a pair of fur-stylists,' he had roared. 'Get lost, will you?'

Now, as he angrily repeated the same demand, they retired, looking hurt, and he continued his solo perambulation until he ran into Maxi returning from inspecting the sentries he had posted on the ridge above Site One.

'All present and correct, saah!' he bawled, sending a startled pair of pigeons clacking out of a nearby tree. 'And I've just had a blackbird for breakfast, my leader, if you don't mind me informing you.'

Mega could see the bloody evidence plastered over his face and breast. Maxi's appearance was going downhill fast. Maybe the Marketing Mink should advise him next.

'Well done, Maxi,' he replied offhandedly. 'Now, about this celebration.'

His military adviser fell into step beside him, his face screwed up in an expression of distaste.

'I don't see any need for that kind of malarkey, my leader,' he barked. 'The ranks have got plenty to keep them happy. The last thing we need to do is spoil them. They'll only start demanding more and more treats.'

'There's no harm in a bit of fun, is there, Maxi?' Mega chided him gently. 'Don't you think they deserve a reward?'

'Well, yes, my leader,' Maxi admitted grudgingly. 'But we must keep them in their place — strapped down to basics, as it were. Otherwise, who knows what type of fancy notions will get into their heads?'

Mega glanced thoughtfully at the ramrod-stiff figure beside him. Personally he might be sceptical about the Marketing Mink's 'whyness' bollo, but the prospect of a ceremony was appealing.

'Should life be all blood and no circuses then, Maxi?' he asked, smiling.

'Why not?' Maxi yelled, a murderous flare of anger making him temporarily abandon his customary deference. 'As far as I'm concerned what we're here for is blood, blood and more blood! Hot spurts and smashing skulls to lick out the brains — that's what you told us. And if that's good enough for me, it's good enough for them.'

What was the matter with his leader? he thought anxiously. First he hadn't got the point about security, and now he was going soft on the ranks.

'After all, my leader, what else is there to life?' he asked, sounding puzzled.

'Just a few other things, Maxi,' Mega replied with a sigh.

There was no point in discussing it with him any further.

*   *   *

'I'm calling it Freedom Wood,' Mega told M1 and M2 firmly. 'That's what I promised and that's what I've delivered.'

Although he hadn't informed them of the fact, he wasn't putting forward a new idea. Before they had arrived in the cages there had been various discussions, with sycophantic minions fawningly making suggestions like 'Mega Wood', which their leader, while appearing suitably flattered, had smilingly declined.

Psycho had endorsed his decision.

'I'm building up your personality cult, Mega, but my soundings indicate a need for a title that they can empathise with more,' his spin-doctor had explained, making the same basic point as the Marketing Mink.

Various unoriginal suggestions had then followed, with 'Mink Wood', 'Minkland' and the 'Freedom Wood' he had chosen emerging as the most popular.

'Sorry to have to differ, great leader,' one of the Marketing Mink now replied, sounding not the least bit sorry. 'But that simply doesn't take our concept far enough up the line. Naturally, we'll choose a name that endorses our glorious freedom. But our market research identifies an overriding need to stress the quality that got us here, the "whyness" of being a mink.

'I am pleased to be able to announce that our preferred concept suggestion is . . .'

As the spiel poured out Mega wondered where in the real world this pair fitted. They appeared quite unfazed by their rapid transition from laboratory to cage to wood, and had immediately got busy compiling what they called 'in-depth market surveys'. The earth walls of their holt were now covered with a spidery network of graphs and charts, interspersed with crude drawings of woodland creatures, which were the source of the strings of figures they constantly bombarded him with. Not only did these make his head spin, but their relevance escaped him. What use was bandying figures about, when deeds spoke so much louder than words? Their trouble, he had concluded, was that they had no soul. Did they even know what a hot spurt was?

But this time, as they yattered on, he had to admit they might have hit on something. He had never considered the 'whyness', as opposed to the 'whatness', of being a mink before.

Maybe it was time he did.

'Why are mink mink, Mata?'

'Why are there stars in the sky, Mega?'

'Because there are.'

'Precisely.'

Mega hadn't got much out of Mata since they entered the wood. Now, relaxing in their holt as he snacked on some crunchy black beetles, he was hoping that she would open up at last and give him some guidance. If only she'd stop speaking in her infuriating riddles, though.

'The Marketing Mink want to hold a celebration.'

'I know,' she replied promptly. 'I've endorsed their concept suggestion and told them to go ahead. They've got the "whyness" we've been looking for.'

Mega spluttered and spat out a carapace.

'You've done what?'

Mata spat out her carapace in turn.

'Mega, why not relax and leave it to me?' she said coolly. 'It's my end of things. You need to be a female to understand "whyness" fully.'

'Or a pair of fur-stylists,' Mega replied bitterly. He shouldn't be cut out in this way — these were supposed to be his decisions.

'Anyhow, all this stuff is just talk,' he added. 'Life's not what you say, Mata, it's what you do.'

'I know that, Mega. But it still does no harm to say things occasionally. First, though, you need to fully understand yourself.

'Let me explain it to you . . .'

By the time she had finished putting his jumbled thoughts in order Mega was halfway convinced. The Marketing Mink were proving their worth. Hot spurts were still the essence of being a mink, but now they had been joined by something else.

*   *   *

The Plateau had its own version of the woodland creatures' Mighty Oak in a misshapen beech. It had previously struggled in the shade of the ash, but since that had fallen it had been branching out in its heady new freedom, symbolically as it seemed to Mega. As the Plateau's natural focus it had automatically become the meeting point – although, as Psycho had rushed to reassure everyone, in the new climate of freedom meetings would be few and far between. Maxi, meanwhile, insisted on referring to it as the 'parade point'.

To launch the naming ceremony Mega took up position underneath it, with Mata next to him and Pussles' tail on the ground between them. At first Mega had feared their totem might rot and fall apart, but being composed almost entirely of gristle and bone, it was drying out into a dessicated state that was rendering it as hard and stiff as a board. The evening was still, with black clouds darkening the sky in line with the warmer and wetter weather they were now experiencing. And did they all love the rain!

'Well, my mink, what do you think of it so far?' he roared.

'Brilliant!'

'Amazing!'

'Ace!'

'Mega Mink! Mega Mink! He's the mink! He's the mink!' The pack broke into a delirious chant. They had been looking forward to this special do; there was so much to celebrate! The moor glitch had receded into the dim and distant past and the escape was now universally adjudged a rip-roaring success.

'And what do you like best?' Mega shouted.

'Hot spurts!'

'Smashing skulls to lick out the brains!'

Mega grinned, then immediately looked grave.

'I won't seek to sadden you by harking back to the past, my mink. None the less, let us spare a moment to remember our wasted generations, who suffered the ignominy of cage life. Let us honour their selfless sacrifice.'

He allowed a suitable pause to elapse.

'Those were the Dark Ages,' he went on quietly. 'The days of the spineless Elders and the cowed subservience to their system.'

He allowed another pause to sink in. Then his voice rose.

'Today, however, we are burying that past to celebrate our present. For here in this wonderful wood we can pursue that excellence which has always distinguished us mink and set us apart from other, inferior creatures. Here we are — and here we rule.'

The gathering erupted in a storm of ecstatic squeaking and chittering.

'Mega Mink! Mega Mink! He's the mink! He's the mink!'

Their leader waited modestly for the chanting to subside.

'I led you here, my brave mink,' he continued. 'But it is not just I who have been responsible for our glorious success. For we also have a thank a quality which has enabled us to win through when all others would have failed. Remember how we were led astray through the vile conspiracy mounted by our enemy, Custard?'

There were growls at the now-hated name.

'Remember the night in the culvert?' Mega continued softly. 'Remember the Long March? The aching bones? The bleeding pads? Remember how, on occasion, your spirit may have faltered?'

Some of the pack looked distinctly guilty.

'Those were early days, my mink, the days of the past. But now the past is, officially, a foreign country.'

He could see the expressions of relief. Psycho had told him they were all worried, especially about the mutiny in the culvert.

'Each of you has played your part magnificently,' he smiled reassuringly. 'On this, our celebration night, I am proud to be among you, proud of being a mink.'

He swept his eyes across them.

'But, my mink, above all this brave new world is a triumph of the quality that binds us together, the quality of enterprise. Let me remind you what that means, my mink. It means boldness; it means daring; it means, more than anything, not being afraid to take risks.

'By coming out of your cages, where everything was handed to you on a plate, each and every one of you has demonstrated that quality of enterprise to a supreme degree. As a result you have become the victors. And to the victors – as you already know – go the spoils.'

He stepped towards the cat-tail and the pack pressed into a tighter circle, its members jostling for the best view.

'Remember Pussles?'

They thundered their agreement.

'She paid the price, didn't she?' Mega yelled, throwing his head back.

'Well, let the whole wood now see the price paid by those who stand in our way,' he bellowed.

At a signal from Maxi a muscle-mink hauled on a length of ivy that had been looped over one of the beech branches. The cat-tail rose jerkily off the ground until it hung down, swaying fluffily. Assiduous combing by Mata's warriors had restored it from its bedraggled state to its original black and orange magnificence.

'Let everyone look on this and tremble at the power of mighty mink,' Mega solemnly intoned. 'For by this, our emblem, I hereby name this wood "Enterprise Wood". Let it always be a symbol of our great enterprise. For, as it will remind all other creatures, hereby hangs a tail.'

Mega had previously complained that this line, dreamt up by the Marketing Mink, was silly, if not plain cheap. But they had pleaded with him to include it above all others, assuring him nothing was too corny for the minions. They'd love it, he'd see.

The oily duo now smirked gleefully as the pack doubled up with laughter. Hereby hangs a tail! What a joker their leader was!

Flushed with triumph, the marketeers now stepped forward in unison. Earlier in the day they had taught the minions the song they had jointly composed, and which had instantly become so popular it was all they could do to stop them singing it continually.

> Rule Minkmania! [the pack thundered]
> Minkmania rules the wood,
> Creatures ever, ever, ever,
> Shall be food!
>
> Rule Minkmania!
> Give us our hot spurt,
> Creatures ever, ever, ever,
> Shall be hurt!
>
> Rule Minkmania!
> From mornings until nights,
> We shall ever, ever, ever
> Give you frights!
>
> Rule Minkmania!
> Rabbits, birds and voles,
> We shall ever, ever, ever
> Scream down your holes!

MI had fussed that the last line of verse four didn't scan, but it had had to stand because neither could think of a rhyming substitute. Song-writing was not normally part of a marketing brief, they had reassured each other, and anyway the mink in general were so uncultured they wouldn't notice – as was now proving the case.

'Enterprise Wood is yours, along with everything in it,' Mega yelled. 'Yours by right! Yours by conquest! Yours by being what you are, red-blooded mink! So take it, my brave ones! Take it gladly! Take it proudly!'

Swelling with pride, he glanced at Mata as the minions broke into their rhythmic chant: 'Mega Mink! Mega Mink! He's the mink! He's the mink!'

What magnificent beasts they were, with their glowing coats, their strong limbs, their bright, alert faces, and their shining white teeth. How could anyone deny their natural superiority? How could anyone deny their destiny was to dominate all other creatures? The shame of their past had been buried for ever, and thanks to their enterprise and human liberators – whose part he had been careful not to mention – they were back to being true free spirits, in the wild where they belonged. Whatever bollo its inhabitants might previously have called it by, the wood was now a mink enterprise zone — and that was official.

Mega, finally alone with Mata after they had gone down to the river for a swim, lay on his back gazing contentedly up at the lightening sky as he felt a huge wave of contentment sweep over him. All was well with the wood, as the steady roar of happy activity coming from the Plateau testified. What could be better than being here with his mate under the stars, the undisputed leader of such a happy band?

He pushed up against her, tickling her lazily and sexily. He wasn't the only one feeling the change in the atmosphere. Even before they had left the cages the males had been eyeing up the females as the build-up to the mating season began. Since they had got to the wood they had been scrapping, the fighting made fiercer as they simultaneously established their new hierarchy. The fact that more males had joined the escape than females only increased the rivalries and jealousies.

The leaders, following their laissez-faire attitude, had left them to sort it out among themselves — not that there was much they could do anyway, with Maxi and the muscle-mink just as involved in shouldering rivals aside. While the males were sniffing round, the females, becoming excited as they felt themselves preparing to come on heat, paraded up and down the Plateau, flaunting themselves and proffering their swaying rears. Mega, too, felt the stirring in his loins. Yet he noticed that, in contrast to the other females, Mata seemed to be withdrawing even further into herself.

'In case you're wondering, Mega, the answer is no,' she said suddenly, breaking away from his embrace.

Mega sat up, taken aback. Until that moment he had taken their mating for granted.

'It's not that I don't love you, Mega,' she went on, gently but firmly. 'But never in that way. I'm not having any kits from anyone, including you.'

'What do you mean?' Mega asked, aghast. 'What about the dynasty? Continuing the line? Little Megas?'

'And little Matas,' she replied sharply. 'I've told you, no! I'm not joining the female ghetto – all those gooey mothers with their fat bellies and swollen teats.'

'But Mata, that's entirely natural,' he protested.

'Oh, I know, and so is what comes before it,' she replied bitterly. 'It's a shame my father isn't here, then you could ask him what he thinks is natural. The bastard raped me, Mega – forced me against my will – when I was only a tiny cub. Not just once, but over and over again. You wouldn't understand, being a male, but it was horrible. It killed something inside me. And it hurt so much.

'I've tried and tried to erase the memory but I just can't. I couldn't stand for you, or anyone else, to do it to me again. I'm not asking you to feel sorry for me, Mega, I'm just telling you the way it is.'

Mega recalled the ugly sounds that had continually come from within their family cage – Mugger's angry shouts, Mata's sobbing and crying, mingled with her mother's, the thud of heavy blows, the squealing. How different from the description Sheba had given of her mating with Solomon. As she had described it that had been true romance – joy, wonder, passion.

'It was a long time ago, Mata,' he said quietly. 'Can't you put it behind you?'

'I wish I could, Mega,' she replied sadly. 'But it's not possible. He's scarred me for life.'

'What if I decided to have you, whether you liked it or not?' Mega said slowly, aware he was treading on delicate ground. It wasn't an empty threat. An the males were naturally so much bigger and stronger than the females that they always got their way if they wanted it. Yet even as he spoke he knew his heart would not really be in such base behaviour. He was looking for something that went further than that, something higher, as well as deeper.

'I'm not sure you could even if you tried,' she replied sharply. 'I'd fight you all the way and I do have my friends, you know. But if you succeeded, against my express wish, I could never forgive you. It would be the end of everything.

'We're a good partnership, you and I, Mega. I want to keep it that way. Please show respect for me by holding back. I'll repay you, I promise you. It would be the truest test of our relationship, that we could keep it pure. Really, Mega, if I felt I could allow anyone, it would be you. I just can't. It really is nothing personal.'

That was precisely the trouble, Mega thought. No wonder he found Mata such a cold fish.

'Why not have all the other females, Mega, each and every one of them?' she asked. 'It's your right as leader. You can't stop the other males having them as well, but all the children would be yours, in a way.'

'We'll see, Mata,' he replied resignedly.

He sat there, saddened by what she had said, yet already knowing he would accede to her suggestion. He did not want to lose her — could not lose her — needing both her friendship and her guidance. They were a good partnership, that was true and there was no other particular female he wanted to replace her with. The alternative would certainly fully satisfy his sexual desires, yet he felt at the same time that it had introduced some sort of endstop to their relationship.

39

Decoded

Burdock looked so dreadful that Owl knew immediately something terrible must have happened. After the Big Clearing massacre the rabbit leader had gone underground, constantly being passed from one burrow to another. Owl had needed to send four separate messages through the CWG network before he had succeeded in arranging this meeting. He had chosen the copse on top of the low hill out in the surrounding fields, which he was virtually certain the mink had visited only cursorily. Within it he had located the well-hidden site of a sunken bowl, thinking absent-mindedly at the time it was big enough for a creatures' meeting. Just in case any mink did unexpectedly decide to visit, he had further selected a perch on the low branch of an elm that gave him an adequate view through the trees across the dun fields to the edge of Old Wood.

He waited there patiently until he saw Burdock, alone, hopping nervously towards him. Then, beset by a sudden doubt as to why he had called the meeting in the first place, he waited in silence for the rabbit to speak.

'Dandelion's dead,' Burdock eventually said in a broken voice.

'The mink caught her and interrogated her. I can still hear her screams. The thing I feel most terrible about, Ollie, is that I didn't do anything to help.

'But then what could I do?' he pleaded.

'Not a lot,' Owl replied softly. 'You're not alone. There doesn't seem to be a lot any of us can do.'

Or some of us want to do, he thought, remembering the gathering of the Dead Vole Society.

'But what have we done to deserve this horror?'

Tears were streaming down Burdock's face. He looked haggard and drawn, the wound on his shoulder had still not healed, and even his bum seemed to have got smaller. Overall he had aged so shockingly he now reminded Owl of his great-grandfather.

'The Woodland Code and Bill of Creatures' Rights were to have ushered in a new world,' he sobbed. 'A world of peace and love, where creatures like mink were simply not allowed to exist. Now, just as I was making it official, it's gone, and my beloved Dandelion with it!'

He looked up at Owl pathetically from inside the sunken bowl.

'All our efforts, hers and mine. All our work – for this! Is there no justice?' he asked in a cracked voice, sinking his head into his paws.

Owl couldn't help finding that a bit rich. Justice was one of the lines the CWGs had always so assiduously peddled. He was sad about Burdock's loss, for he had seen how close he and Dandelion had been. But nothing would bring her back and it was useless simply wallowing in emotion. Anyhow, he couldn't let a remark like that pass.

'Remember your lucky escape,' he reminded the distraught rabbit. 'Wasn't that justice? And what about the natural justice you were always going on about?'

'There's nothing natural about mink,' Burdock spat back, hatred lighting up his eyes. 'They're the most unnatural creatures I've ever come across.'

'Aren't they just being themselves?' Owl asked, pleased to have at least provoked a reaction.

'Being bloody predators, you mean,' Burdock replied bitterly. 'No herbivore could possibly have such a blatant disregard for other creatures' rights, especially the basic right to exist. Don't you realise what they're doing to the wood?'

'I've some idea,' Owl replied non-committally. 'But I expect you know more.'

'In a nutshell, as a squirrel remarked to me the other day, the wood as we know it has already been destroyed,' Burdock pronounced dramatically.

'Surely it's not as bad as all that,' Owl protested. 'There are still plenty of us left.'

'Plenty of predators, you mean!' Burdock replied quickly. 'But we rabbits have lost dozens and dozens already. Not just Dandelion. Groundsel's gone, Blackberry . . .' He rattled off a string of various other plant names that meant nothing to Owl. 'You saw the weasels and stoats leave yourself and you know only too well what sudden death sounds like – the nasty thump, the squeal, the choking death rattle, the noise of something being dragged through the leaves, the horrid scrunching and slurping.'

Burdock shuddered, wincing at the sudden shooting pain in his shoulder. 'Don't deny it Ollie, you've been hearing a lot more of that recently, haven't you?'

Owl, recalling his conversation with the now-late Dandelion, could not help feeling that somehow he was being got at.

'What you don't realise is that that's only part of it,' Burdock continued. 'Whatever it's like on the surface, underneath it's all over. Nobody's safe, for a start. These mink eat anything that moves, right down to woodlice, earwigs, beetles, worms, grubs, ants, bugs – even slugs.'

That did surprise Owl. Nobody he knew ate slugs.

'Nobody's living any more, Ollie,' Burdock went on urgently. 'They're just existing. That's what my Bill and Code were about – the right really to live. But now the entire wood's developed a siege mentality.

'Comprehension differs of course,' he said, a trace of his old sneer back. 'For the lowlife it's just more confusing and baffling activity at grass level. But we more intelligent creatures, who have the capacity to care, appreciate only too well how life has changed so drastically.

'It's the not knowing as well as the knowing. Nobody can predict when these murderers are going to strike, or how — as lone assassins, small killer groups, a pack. Then the Leaf-Litter Louts are continually roaming about, killing any creature unlucky enough to cross their path.

'Do you know, Ollie, some creatures like mice are already starving because they simply daren't go out to feed? Others are so nervous they're having heart attacks just because they hear a sudden noise. You can't understand how bad life has become for us earth creatures. Imagine if you had no wings — how would you feel?'

The remark took Owl back to his childhood, when his father was teaching him how to fly. On one of his first flights he had stalled, bounced off a branch and then, for the first time, failed to recover. With a crashing jar he had landed head-first on the ground and found himself scrabbling for a firm footing on the wet grass, so disconcertingly soft and slippery after the hard bark that was all he had previously known under his talons.

Flapping madly, he had finally hauled himself upright, only to see his father had disappeared. He felt peculiarly destabilised. The wood was no longer a place he looked down on. Instead it now reared up around him. The trees, and even the bushes, looked enormously tall and seemed to tower over him. As they swayed in a gust of wind, he experienced the dreadful feeling that they were about to crash down, crushing him. Robbed of his natural third dimension, he felt hugely vulnerable and had a gut-wrenching sense of being trapped. What if he couldn't take off again, he thought in panic?

The horrible moment passed as he made a clumsy take-off, then felt a wave of relief as his father flew back into sight.

'You should have seen yourself,' he laughed. 'Come over to a branch, son, and tell me all about it.'

'It was awful, Dad,' Owl said, quite unable to accept the comical side. 'Instead of being free, I felt sort of tied down — you know what I mean — as if I was rooted and couldn't move.' Still shaking, he shook his head, ringing with the blow of his fall. 'Is that what it's like for earth creatures all the time, Dad?' he asked wonderingly. 'How can they stand it?'

'Don't ask me, son,' his father replied kindly. 'We've all had that feeling once, which is why I left you to experience it fully on your own. Now you'll realise how fortunate you are to be a bird, never mind an owl. For the one thing we never have to think about is how to fly. Come on, it's time for your next lesson.'

That had turned out to be leaf-touching and the hardest of all. His father had constructed a vicious slalom circuit through the treetops, and young Owl had no sooner learnt to master it than it was updated to make it harder. He floundered in his father's wake, his juvenile wings aching as he tried to keep up with the flickering shape in front of him – turning, braking, stalling, accelerating, swooping, diving and, with each rapid change of movement, touching a leaf with a wingtip. Owl grew to hate the sight of that smoothly tapered rear, but when he fell so far behind that only a trail of trembling leaves marked his mentor's passage it became even worse. From nowhere, Dad would suddenly be hard up behind him.

'Touch the leaf! Shake it!' he would shout, harrying him on.

Whenever Owl complained about the merciless training, his father looked at him fondly, but was unsympathetic.

'It's my job to push you to the edge,' he explained. 'That way you'll never end up grounded again. There's nothing for you in the middle, my son. The edge, Ollie, always strive for the edge. Just don't go over it.'

Being grounded, as Owl had known ever since, was the worst thing of all. And if in addition a mink was liable to pounce on you at any moment . . .

'Are you listening, Ollie?'

Owl snapped out of his dream.

'At least we birds are safe,' he remarked.

'In general they haven't had such a hard time,' Burdock admitted. 'But they're far from immune. You're a carnivore, Ollie, so you wouldn't appreciate just how long it takes us herbivores to get our nutrients. Many birds, like the dunnocks, have no choice but to spend much of their time on the ground, eating. The mink climb trees as well, so the roosters are exhausted simply by staying awake. Then everyone's laid their eggs. How many of those are they going to leave to hatch?

'It's just as bad on the river. FARF's reporting the mink have now learnt to swim so well they're catching the trout. The longer they stay, the better they get at hunting. Now they're mounting undergrowth ambushes everywhere. Even where there's no cover it's just as dangerous, they're so quick. Both the Big and Small Clearings have been abandoned, and you know about the Ride? That was always the most pleasant place in the wood for a saunter. Now it's called "Murder Alley" and no creature dares set foot on it.'

Owl was silent. He hadn't appreciated quite how long and melancholy the list was.

'But we woodland creatures aren't daft, or without resource,' he protested. 'We've survived for hundreds and thousands of seasons. Anyhow, aren't replacements making up the numbers?'

'They were,' Big Arse replied grimly. 'As soon as any creature was killed an outsider would ignore our warnings and move into the vacated territory. But now that word's spreading the flow of new tenants is drying up.'

'So what's everybody planning to do?' Owl asked. 'Leave?'

'To go where? The mink range over such a wide area small creatures can't get far enough away. Even if they do their fellows aren't prepared to move over and share, however sympathetic they may be. How can they, when each only has a territory big enough to support themselves?'

Burdock was too negative, Owl thought. There must be a ray of hope somewhere.

'The stoats and weasels left successfully,' he pointed out.

'I wanted to ask you about that. Why did they go, when they were always so capable? Too capable, most of us would think,' Burdock added acidly. 'What did they say was so awful about the mink that they were giving up so easily?'

'Just that they were known as absolute bastards through and through,' Owl replied, trying to think back.

'Nothing more particular?' Burdock persisted. 'Nothing about killing for the sake of it?'

'No,' said Owl, surprised.

Burdock was surprised in turn. Owl might not be as bright as the CWGs had buttered him up to be, but surely he wasn't that dim?

'Don't you realise that's what they do, Ollie?' he asked. 'That that's precisely why it's the end of the wood if they continue to stay? Imagine if you and your fellow predators all set out to kill as many creatures as you could, regardless of whether you needed to eat them? How many voles could you dispatch every night for example?'

An awful lot, Owl thought, although he had never tried since the childhood nights when he used his victims for experiments, rather than meals.

He motioned with his wing for Burdock to stop talking.

'Let me get this right,' he said slowly, almost talking to himself. 'You're saying that unlike the rest of us predators, these invaders don't know when to stop?' Even as he spoke he realised that Burdock had spelt out the different thing about the mink that he had been trying to put his talon on. 'They're mean, they're vicious, they're intelligent, they're brilliant hunters. I thought the wood could take all that,' he continued wonderingly. 'But you're saying the weasels and stoats left because they knew mink just kill and kill and go on killing? What — until there's nothing left?'

As the rabbit nodded back gravely all the stuff from the Venerable Buck slotted into place: the balance, the interdependence, the food chain . . .

'But, Burdock, no-one can carry on like that without destroying the whole wood,' he burst out.

'Precisely, Ollie,' Big Arse replied, looking sadly down at the ground.

He raised his head and looked Owl straight in the eye.

'Now do you see why we've got to do something before it's too late?'

40

Calling a Holt

'That's a chaffinch, Mega. Hot-spurt rating two.'

Mega stared at the small bird on the branch above him. It looked vaguely similar to the one he and Mata had killed in the cages so long ago.

Psycho's paw pointed at another tree. 'That's a great tit over there. Hot-spurt rating three.'

Mega yawned and Psycho felt disappointed. He was proud of his ratings idea, which he considered infinitely preferable to the Marketing Mink's ponderous 'eating popularity league'. He had been hoping his leader would share his enthusiasm.

'How do you know all this stuff, Psycho?' he asked in a bored fashion.

'Much of it came from a female rabbit whom Maxi pulled,' his spin-doctor replied eagerly. 'Under treatment she identified virtually everything. It's a long list, Mega, and an impressive one.'

'I'm sure.'

Although many of the pack were excitedly zooming about trying to kill as many different creatures as possible, personally Mega couldn't see any point in ticking off a list.

'Did you learn anything more useful?' he growled.

'As a matter of fact, Mega, I did,' Psycho replied, eyes gleaming. 'Remember that rabbit with the big arse which got away from you?'

Mega scowled. The little rat was pushing his luck bringing that up.

'Well, he isn't the woodland leader, as we first thought,' Psycho explained knowingly. 'He's only head of some committee like our Elders. As far as I can tell, it just peddles hot air rather like they did. And we can trust the doe I interrogated to be correct,' he added with a ghastly smile. 'She was his mate.'

Mega smiled. That was a spin he could appreciate.

'What committee?' he asked, now curious.

'It's called the Concerned Woodland Guardians or some such bollo, and seems to be mostly made up of rabbits. It doesn't approve of normal predators – never mind us. It was one of their meetings that was in progress when we arrived.'

'Well, there won't be any more now,' Mega commented, his interest evaporating. He waited until it was obvious Psycho was going to make him take the initiative.

'Who is the real woodland leader then?' he asked grudgingly.

'He's a bird, Mega, a male owl called Ollie. You've seen him.'

Mega pictured the bird with huge black eyes and cruel talons that he had seen several times swooping silently over the Plateau, observing them.

'But what does he lead if there's only a committee of rabbits?'

'I'm not quite sure of that myself, Mega. There is some sort of connection but I'm still trying to get to the bottom of it. I thought you'd like me to size up the opposition for you.'

'The whole point is that there is no opposition, Psycho,' his leader replied crossly.

'Yes, Mega,' Psycho replied dutifully, trying to keep the scepticism out of his voice. It was courting danger to be complacent in such early days. Mink, and especially himself, might be clever, but it was always wrong to think you were too clever. His researches into the woodland creatures were turning up angles on life that he'd never imagined.

'What do you make of this place, Mata? It's quite amazing, isn't it? Yet Mega doesn't seem interested in any of it.'

Psycho still found Mata an enigma. But then, he supposed, they all did. There had been less of her feminist line since they got to the wood, for which he was grateful, although she still referred proudly to her 'warriors'. What was so unnerving was the way she was so quiet and kept her thoughts so much to herself. When she did open her mouth, though, she usually seemed to say something that he found perspicacious. And she was always there when it mattered, even if only in the background. How much did she reveal to Mega? he often thought. And what influence did it have on his thinking?

'Why do you wonder so much about everything, Psycho?' she asked calmly.

'So I can see what's in it for me,' Psycho grinned, knowing, as she did, that it was only half a joke. 'But seriously, look at the astonishing variety of life here and the way it all interconnects. Where does it all come from?'

The pair were indulging in a leisurely stroll down the broad avenue that Psycho had already informed her was called 'the Ride' by the woodland creatures — or 'woodies', as the minions now referred to them in a crude pun about their thickness. Psycho found the way most of the pack pretended to be knowledgeable about everything, when their talk was mostly blind ignorance, alternately amusing and infuriating.

'You know, Mata, I had to inform them that many of the creatures here — including their favourite hot-spurters, the rabbits — are called herbivores and eat vegetation rather than flesh. But like Mega they didn't seem interested. Some idiot just said, "That's why they're called the woodies, because they eat wood!" and they all collapsed in hoots of laughter.'

'Why should they be interested, Psycho?' Mata asked, suddenly bounding to one side and pouncing on a black beetle that had blundered clumsily into their path.

'Tasty snacks, these,' she remarked, crunching it up.

'They're all right,' Psycho replied, miffed at not being offered a share. He tried to soldier on with his main subject. 'The minions should be interested, Mata, if only for their own sakes. Many of them — and that includes your warriors — have been given some nasty shocks, especially by insects.

'Instead of using the intelligent approach, they've had to find out the hard way about stings, jaws, claws and poison, let alone brilliant camouflage and shells they can't crack. You know the trouble they got themselves into with that hedgehog? They could have avoided all that.'

'I know more about it than you do,' Mata replied. She had personally removed the wicked spines from bleeding pads and sensitive noses, and was currently worried about a couple of wounds that had gone septic.

'They still haven't unrolled it despite all their efforts,' Psycho persevered. 'It's sheer arrogance, isn't it, believing you can rip into a creature like that without even thinking?'

'But why aren't they entitled to be arrogant, Psycho?' Mata said impatiently. 'Don't you share their feeling that we mink are ahead of everything else in the wood?'

'Maybe. But that shouldn't stop the variety of life making them feel sort of — you know — humble.' For once Psycho wasn't sure he'd chosen the correct word. 'Take the trees alone,' he said, gesturing vaguely at the branches on either side of them. 'I've discovered there are all sorts, deciduous and evergreen, oak, beech, sycamore, ash, elm, holly. Never mind ivy. And all with different characteristics.

'Think of the creatures — voles, mice, shrews, rabbits, all those peculiar things down by the river, the eels. You know the minions have found out that if you eat them from the head down they're still alive when you get to their tail. They say the thrill in feeling the life force drain away as you munch down a writhing slippery body is as good as a hot spurt any day. But they never stop to consider how extraordinary it is that a creature can have such a tenacious hold on life. What about worms? You bite them in two and you've then got two live creatures!

'And the birds are a story in themselves. Imagine being born from an egg, for a start.'

Suddenly there was a commotion further down the broad
open expanse in front of them and a gang of Leaf-Litter Louts
charged out of the undergrowth. They were giving clumsy chase
to a small bird, which seemed to have a broken wing and was
alternately hopping and flying in a desperate fashion. The noisy
calvacade crashed out of sight, the hooting and jeering gradually
fading into the distance.

'They're so crude, it makes me ashamed,' Psycho complained.
'Haven't they ever heard of stealth, stalking, something requir-
ing a modicum of subtlety and intelligence?'

Mata stopped and turned over a stone to reveal the prize
delicacy of a centipede in the wet earth underneath. As she put
her head down to pop it into her mouth, Psycho found himself
becoming irrationally annoyed. How did she do it? He had yet to
find anything worth eating. Worse still, she then pushed aside
a dead branch to uncover a whole family of tasty snails.

'On the subject of intelligence, haven't you found out yet,
Psycho, that you can eat excellently by gathering as well as by
hunting?' she smiled as she crunched them up one after another.
'You have to know where to look, mind you. Maybe you haven't
mastered the art yet.

'What I'm saying is that you don't have a monopoly on how
to do things. So why not let the others develop in their own
way, rather than judging them and finding them lacking all
the time?'

What is your way, Psycho was about to ask when she
suddenly cut the conversation short.

'I've got to get back,' she announced. 'The Marketing
Mink asked me to judge the best holt competition. Come on
– race you!'

She streaked away, leaving him floundering in her wake.

When the pack moved in, the multiple chambers of the rabbit
warren on the Plateau had provided instant housing. Mega had
taken the best for what the minions grumblingly referred to
as his 'palace', with four different chambers, one of which
was reserved for Mata's exclusive use. Psycho had moved in
next door, taking three for himself, while M1 and M2 had

opted for a burrow set apart from the rest and containing a vast central chamber which they had now designated 'market research HQ'. Maxi and the muscle-mink were also set slightly apart, in a burrow at the back that he proudly referred to as the 'barracks'.

Psycho had strongly advised Mega not to allow the minions just to grab their own places, as that would lead to uncontrollable and ongoing arguments. Maxi had therefore doled out individuals' homes, the muscle-mink quashing disputes and evicting the few brave souls already squatting superior locations. Fortunately the Plateau rabbits had been rampant enough for everyone to be able to have a place ranged round the central area. It was tight, though, and further accommodation was now being developed by excavating the loose and crumbly soil of the cliff-face overlooking the river.

The Marketing Mink had then come up with the wheeze that had really got things going.

'Back at the farm everyone had identical cages, so they thought in terms of communal housing, rather than their own "homes" *per se*,' they had earnestly explained to Mega. 'In reality many of the holts here are just as uniform. However our accommodation research has revealed that if we ran a campaign bulling up the idea of holt ownership, each mink would regard theirs as their personal territory. Then, if we load in the concept that their condition and appearance make a statement about them as individuals, you'll see them really get interested.'

Mega had been mystified by this, although Mata had nodded in full agreement. He had since had to admit, though, that the ruse had worked, tapping a pent-up desire that had spawned a whole industry of do-it-yourself holt improvements. Extensions and conversions were multiplying daily, and with the warmer weather now coming, the current craze was for elaborate entrance porches constructed out of gnawed-off branches. Meanwhile females had set themselves up as interior designers, sparking off huge competition for the best-decorated holt. The first fashion had been for plastering walls with starry white blackthorn blossom, but trendies had now thrown that out in favour of 'hint of pink' hawthorn, with floors carpeted with contrasting bluebells, interspersed with delicate white wood anemones.

Mega and Psycho himself had left their own homes simple and spartan, neither being very interested, and as he now toured the dwellings with Mata, Psycho winced at the clashing colours and crudely executed interior features that various proud owners had installed. Meanwhile, he grudgingly wiped his feet before entering, as required by a succession of over-holtproud females.

'Doesn't it make you want to throw up, Mata?' he whispered, staring contemptuously at a particularly inept false ceiling, wildly inappropriately decorated with garish and prickly holly leaves. It was already sagging dangerously. 'Have you ever seen anything as naff in your life?' he giggled.

But when she just glared silently back at him he could see he was getting nowhere. In her book taste was apparently as much up to the individual as everything else. Cutting his losses, he walked outside and went to inspect the activity by the river.

Again under the careful tutelage of the Marketing Mink, a myriad of sporting activities had sprung up, the most popular soon proving to be acornball. Matches had taken over the Plateau to such an extent that they had been moved to a special pitch marked out further up the hill. This was now the venue for a series of league and knock-out competitions whose permutations baffled all those except the most closely involved. Towering above even this in the minions' estimation, however, was the Waterama complex. This had taken off beyond the Marketing Mink's wildest dreams and constantly resounded with shrieks of excitement and delight. It had begun by formalising the natural slide over the river created by the fallen ash, whose smooth trunk lay at a convenient angle for launching into the deep water. Two main branches, sloping down more steeply, now formed fast slides, while the one branch sticking upright had been designated as the high diving board. Plans were now advancing for a complicated 'Tumbletower' attraction, designed to bounce participants through the smaller branches.

Maxi was currently bawling at a group of minions working on the latest embellishment, a swing being manufactured from a length of baling twine found out in the fields. He was obviously having difficulty with the logistics of the construction work.

'No, no, no!' he was yelling in exasperation at the minion who was trying to secure one end to the top ash branch. 'Don't push, pull, you idiot!'

Spotting Psycho, he broke off.

'Come to watch some proper males, eh?' he taunted. 'Mind you don't get your feet wet.'

Psycho ignored him. If he was the only mink who didn't welcome going into the water, that was his affair.

'How about some real work for a change?' Maxi jeered. 'Or are you working like you normally do, by sitting on your arse?'

Psycho still ignored him. Their relationship had deteriorated since he had acidly pointed out that any moron could do physical work, but if they did it left them no time to think – or to listen, he suddenly realised.

'Quiet!' he yelled with such an unaccustomed edge of authority that Maxi froze.

Psycho strained his ears. It was faint, but unmistakable.

'Custard! Custard!' a human voice was shouting.

41

Runny Custard

So far Mata's contention that the humans wouldn't want to know about them had been borne out. Various humans could be seen active in the surrounding fields, riding the special volvers that ran without rollways, but they were obviously content with their own territory, always sheering off at the shiny human wires marking the wood's boundaries. But although most minions were too dim or unthinking to make the Custard connection, Mata had appreciated that one particular human would eventually come into the wood, simply because of how the pack had learnt of it in the first place. Maxi, put in charge of preparing for this, or any other invasion, had shown each minion his or her own hiding place, with strict instructions on how to disappear if they heard the alarm call. At Psycho's suggestion, and earning more of Maxi's wrath, his earnest training exercises had then been turned into a game of hide and seek, making them so immensely popular that in the end Mega, worried more would mean a real emergency not being taken seriously, had stepped in and banned them.

As soon as Psycho raised the alarm Maxi sprang into action. Both the construction work and the best-kept-holt competition were hurriedly abandoned as the minions scattered. Maxi's planning paid off and by the time the idiot labrador had lolloped up the slope the Plateau was deserted except for Mata, who had insisted beforehand that she be the one to deal with her.

'You found it then,' Custard barked, tail wagging. She had been missing the mink and hoping she would find them. After the escape she had felt guilty about not hearing the intruders, but when she had tried to make amends by pursuing the pack up the rollway, Master had unceremoniously ordered her back into the house. She had then kept a low profile until, as the dust settled, she noticed Master didn't seem that upset. A new and shiny volver had appeared, which was much more comfortable and smelt so wonderfully fresh! Then, instead of new mink arriving, the remaining ones had been taken away, along with their cages, and Master had filled the shed with smelly stuff in which he now grew mushrooms. Custard was a bit sad about that, though. You couldn't have much of a conversation with a mushroom. A mournful, truncated figure now moped permanently about the farm as a reminder of the Pussles incident, of course. Again, though, Custard wasn't too upset. Pussles had asked for it by winding up the mink, whereas she had been their true friend. And now that they were in the wood this female mink, whom she recognised as the one she had talked to before, was going to play as promised.

The labrador bounded happily towards the waiting figure, anticipating it would run off so she could follow in playful pursuit. Too late, she realised the mink was standing her ground, and as she skidded to a halt in front of her she was rewarded not by thanks but by a vicious swipe across her nose. Yelping with pain, she sat down to rub the wound with her paw, only to hear the mink hiss venomously: 'Piss off, you cur, and never come back.'

By now Master's cry of 'Custard! Where are you, you dratted animal?' was dangerously close.

'You saw what happened to Pussles,' the mink growled ominously. 'Breathe a word to her, or anyone else, about us being here and we'll be back to give you the same treatment.'

Custard's tail went down as she felt a sudden imaginary pain between her legs and she backed off, only for her rump to come into contact with something solid. Jumping with fright, she whipped round to find herself face to face with the fetid cat totem. Its black and orange length swayed menacingly as the bluebottles that had taken up permanent residence on it rose in a cloud and Custard's bowel control went. Howling with fear, the wet running down her legs, she ran for it.

Maxi lifted the security alert after Mata had watched her and their former Master roll away in the new volver. The cat-tail story provoked huge merriment, while Maxi strutted about, delighted at the success of this first test of his security arrangements.

There was nothing he, or anyone, could do however to prevent the next incident. And by any standards that was a disaster.

At first it had seemed to all the mink that there were no creatures in the wood they had real reason to fear, although the minions soon showed healthy respect for the large and lumbering badger, who simply brushed them out of the way as if they weren't even there. Many, it was true – principally birds – were proving difficult to catch, and the attempts to trap the flashy kingfisher that dipped over the river had now developed into an ongoing saga. They had made no attempt to build a rapport with other predators, simply tearing to pieces a couple of their *mustelidae* relations, the weasels and stoats, after which they had all hastily decamped. There was a range of winged predators who could obviously inflict at least a nasty wound, but when the Marketing Mink assembled the natural pecking order of woodland society it was clear that the pack, both together and individually, came out top. And, as Mega had emphasised at the naming ceremony, that was precisely how it should be.

Then the otter arrived, and suddenly it was a different story.

The mink did not know it, but Owl had been responsible for activating Orwella. After his depressing conversation with Burdock he had racked his brain for someone who could take on the mink, even briefly considering having a go himself. Then, deciding there was little he could do on his own, he had thought of the otter. As he flew down-river beyond the gorge where the mink lived, following its winding course through gently sloping farmland, he couldn't help noticing how birds like moorhens and ducks were now notably absent. Only when the wood was far behind him did activity return to its normal level.

He had found Orwella friendly enough. She had heard on the network about the fearsome killing machines laying siege to Old Wood, but found it hard to separate fact from rumour. The only thing clear was the position of their base, which happened to be next to the rock on which she left her spraint to mark the end of her long riverbank territory. She had never tried to continue further upstream. That would involve exposing herself to humans using the rollway and her attitude to them was as wary as that of the woodland creatures. Her holt being so far downstream, she had since decided to relax about the incomers to Old Wood. She had never seen the place as much to do with her, and sometimes did not visit for over a moon. She did, however, respect Owl from her occasional visitations and although his anguish about the wood's problems soon bored her, she did get his point that the mink might be peripheral, but they were now wandering down the riverbank, invading deeper and deeper into her territory.

'Why not teach them a lesson?' Owl had asked, on the strength of which she had decided at least to find out exactly what she was up against. Apart from humans, there was nothing she was afraid of, and as she alternately bounded and swam towards the cliff pool she did not doubt her power. She might be only one, while these mink were apparently many, but she was bigger and stronger. As long as she stayed in the water, where she was at her most adept, she was confident she could maintain her edge. Anyhow, whatever Owl might have suggested, she was not planning her expedition to end in confrontation. A mutual stand-off, with both sides agreeing to respect each other's space, would be much more agreeable.

In retrospect none of the pack leaders accepted blame for what happened. Nobody had told the sentries posted at the end of the gorge to have a go — quite the reverse. According to Maxi's strict orders, their job if threatened was to abandon their posts and run back to raise the alarm. A party could then be got together to deal with the intruder. But overconfidence about mink's natural superiority went to the sentries' heads and they decided to take on the interloper. Whether they merely intended to drive Orwella off, or wanted the kudos of killing her, was never known. The only definite information came from the one sentry who, horribly mangled, dragged herself back to the Plateau to gasp a few garbled details before she too expired. From what could be pieced together from her words and an inspection of the scene, the trio had slipped into the water to mount a concerted attack. At that point Orwella, seeing there was to be no negotiation, had obviously decided to teach these aggressive upstarts the lesson that Owl had requested. Coming silently up from the murky depths, she had cut two out and pulled them down by their rudders to drown them by entangling them in the dense thicket of ash branches on the river bed. The third, finally appreciating the danger, had scrambled out of the water, but not before the otter had pursued her to the shore, inflicting a series of what proved to be mortal bites. Wisely, Orwella had not continued her pursuit overland but, according to the dying sentry, set off back the way she had come.

Maxi sent a team of minions into the water to dive down and extricate the corpses, which were pulled down into the shallows, water pouring from their gaping mouths. Mega went down to inspect them, while the colony erupted in outrage. As he sadly surveyed their faces, lips drawn back in a last defiant snarl, he thought how much smaller and more harmless they looked in death. His emotions were mixed — pity for their bravery, but cold anger that they had so blatantly ignored the instructions that would have saved them.

Round him an immediate cry was going up for revenge, with individuals already rushing about getting up a lynching party. Mega vetoed the idea on the spot. He might feel just as much hatred for the creature that had done this, but as leader he could not let blind emotion cloud his judgement. It might help salve the pack's wounded pride, but nothing would be gained by allowing a disorganised mob to go charging off in pursuit.

'I'm not at all sure what we could do even if we caught up with a creature like that,' Maxi whispered, still in deep shock at the hole that had been blown in his security operation. 'And the last thing we need at this point is more deaths.'

As tempers cooled vague promises were made and the matter officially closed, with Maxi requesting, and obtaining, permission to double the sentries on duty.

'I do have to point out, my leader,' he added, 'that neither this nor the Custard incident would have happened if we had based ourselves at Site One.'

'Thank you, Maxi,' Mega replied stiffly.

'And I said it might be wrong to think there was no opposition, Mega,' Psycho weighed in.

'Thank you for that as well,' Mega replied even more stiffly. He was trying not to show it, but the very fact that there was a creature out there more deadly than a mink — apart from the humans — had shaken him to his very roots. Of course they had never known what they would be facing, but even under his leadership, apparently, they were not invincible. He was not sure where that left them — or him. The knock-on effect of the Custard incident had already been insidious, dragging distant memories back into all their thinking and sending the rumour machine into overdrive. Psycho had helpfully pointed out that the double shock to Custard of her hostile reception and the cat-tail horror undoubtedly meant they had seen the last of her, but it had been poor consolation, especially as Mata now made the most chilling remark of all.

'One thing I've noticed, Mega,' she announced coolly, 'is that bad things always come in threes.'

'Thank you for that most of all, Mata,' Mega replied, now stiff as a board.

42

Coneycide

In the end Mega had decided to put up with the Marketing Mink's endless figures as long as they kept the oily duo happy. In the heady first days their 'woodland projections', 'availability to eat charts' and 'expotential growth curves' – along with a mass of other jargon he didn't try to understand – had all been hugely optimistic, especially when widened to include the surrounding fields the pack was increasingly roaming. All indicated there was sufficient life to keep the pack going for ever and when they were revised downwards Mega didn't at first take it very seriously, especially after Psycho had acidly commented that statistics could be made to prove anything.

There had been a slight relief when the colony diverted into its brief mating season. Following Mata's suggestion, Mega had had all the females brought to his holt, where he had mechanically processed them one after another. All had showed great enthusiasm, and some pleased him more than others, but he had to admit to himself afterwards that, highly enjoyable though the physical process had been, it had left him feeling empty inside.

Recently, though, he and everyone else's personal experiences had forced them to take more notice of the endless stream of marketing factoids, and the current leadership conference had been kicked off with the bleakest statistics yet. Mega stared balefully at the Marketing Mink as they seamlessly double-handed their presentation, thinking that it was almost as if they delighted in making such gloomy predictions.

'Put simply, the pack is running through the woodland creatures at an unprecedented rate,' MI concluded. 'We therefore most strongly recommend the immediate implementation of a structured eating programme, so as to allow organic resource renewal.'

He sat back to await the expected explosion.

Underneath their smooth exteriors, he and his twin were equally nervous. The philosophy driving the mink equation defined the wood as a free market. The last thing the leadership should ever consider was putting a brake on minion activity. That had been, and always would be, the most vile heresy. Yet, they had decided, they could not avoid their responsibility to present marketing truths, however unpalatable.

Sure enough, Mega's jaw had dropped.

'You're not suggesting I step in to stop my boys doing what comes naturally, are you?' he growled, lip curling in contempt. What sort of place was a laboratory to produce these wimps, seemingly incapable of grasping the most basic fundamentals? They might show bags of enterprise in what they called their 'packaging', but underneath he deeply suspected their personal dedication to being true mink. MI's shallow laugh and shake of his head only confirmed their overall impression of insincerity.

'Not exactly, great leader,' he replied, looking towards Mega's blackened brow whilst studiously avoiding eye contact. He would have been even more upset to know his leader was just thinking he'd send his twin back to the cages if he considered it in his own interest. 'But we must all bow to market forces, great leader, even yourself, I'm afraid. And they dictate absolutely that we have no choice but to make adjustments in the light of the current situation.'

'Nothing too radical, of course,' M2 chipped in breezily.

'Merely an element of slight restraint in view of the ongoing supply and demand situation . . .'

As Mega's eyes narrowed he faltered and looked towards his brother. The presentation was going as badly as they had both feared. But if they were on a loser anyway, they might as well get it over.

'To recap, my leader, all our forward eating projections prove that the victim market is overheating and therefore certain to crash,' MI stated firmly, feeling he was taking his life in his hands. 'We are already in danger of exhausting some species, while total food resources will be reduced to a non-renewable base factor within three moons at the outside. Current indiscriminate killing activity must therefore be drastically reduced immediately.'

Mega's brow was positively thunderous.

'You're saying that if my mink carry on being true mink, there's going to be nothing left to kill?' he growled, eyes mere slits.

'Not quite as bad as that, great leader,' MI rushed to reassure him. 'But none the less it is true that we are moving towards that situation in the fullness of time.'

Mega stared suspiciously at their petrified figures. Why had they used that particular phrase? The fullness of time was when Sheba had promised the freedom of endless hot spurts, not voluntarily curbing the pack's killing.

'You must listen, Mega,' Mata muttered to him in a quiet aside. 'I know they're right.'

Ignoring her, Mega turned to Psycho.

'More doom and gloom, I suppose,' he sneered.

'It is true that a hot-spurt problem is developing, Mega,' his spin-doctor confirmed, visibly trembling. 'Of course in many ways that's a tribute to the minions for becoming so much more effective and already cleaning up much of the easier prey.'

He cackled ingratiatingly.

'The problem is being contained to a certain extent by encouraging them to go further afield, my leader,' Maxi chipped in. 'You should hear them boast about the distances they're covering.'

Psycho, grateful for the momentary diversion, licked his thin lips nervously. His leader definitely wasn't going to like the next bit.

'I'm afraid a new factor has now come into the equation, Mega,' he ploughed on. 'The minions are getting bored with simply counting kills. There'll never be anything to equal hot spurts, but the novelty's wearing off. They're complaining they've done that.'

'Be more specific,' came a growl.

'Well, take robins for example,' Psycho continued reluctantly. 'The minions used to be excited by them — sweet little song, plump red breast, friendly. Not the greatest hot spurt, admittedly, but still a satisfying hit. I gave them a hot-spurt rating of four. But these days news that one's been killed makes everyone yawn. "Not worth getting out of bed for," they say.'

The Marketing Mink, hugely relieved at being backed up by this new angle, nodded vigorously.

'Our woodwide robin survey already reveals a severe ongoing supply deficiency in this area, great leader,' M2 interrupted helpfully, before a fearful glare reduced him to silence again.

'No-one's blaming you of course, Mega,' Psycho grovelled. 'On the contrary, you're more popular than ever. It's just that random serial killing seems no longer to be enough.'

'What about smashing the skull?' Mega inquired.

'They're saying they've done that too,' Psycho replied unhappily.

MI, having already decided to risk all, intervened again.

'Resource conservationwise, great leader, we must agree. I'm afraid, you see, that your emphasis on hot spurts and skull-smashing has been a little too successful for its own good.'

His fawning chuckle died away as Mega said in a terrible voice, 'No more hot spurts? No more being a true mink? No more essence?'

'Of course not entirely, my leader,' Psycho cackled madly. 'There's no question of us standing in the way of all that.

'But what if we were to reorganise the minions?' he went on, eyes flashing. 'What if we set them the target of killing the most difficult species in the wood? That would keep them busy, wouldn't it? You know, Mega, they'd tire themselves out so much they wouldn't have the energy to kill everything else.'

Mega was overwhelmed by a sick feeling as he saw the Marketing Mink brighten up.

'We're not here for that kind of devious bollo,' he shouted. 'We promised them freedom to kill whatever they liked, whenever they liked.'

'No, Mega,' Psycho interrupted, quite forgetting his normal restraint in the heat of the moment. 'We only promised them freedom. You've got to remember, Mega, that what they're really looking for is freedom from, not freedom to. That's the whole beauty of the word — it's what we define it to be. And we can change that any time we want. So it's we leaders, not the minions, who have the real freedom.'

'Yes, great leader, freedom's only an attitude of mind,' MI jumped in, equally excited. 'If you think you're free, then you are. And if you think you're not, then you aren't.

'It's a concept, great leader, and you know what do with concepts,' he added with a meaningful chuckle.

'Well you can stuff your concept up your arse,' Mega said coldly and deliberately. 'Your brother as well, you pair of spraintbags. And you, Psycho. You should be ashamed of yourself.'

With that he stalked out.

'Really,' MI remarked, looking round shocked. 'There was no need to be personal about it.'

That was the trouble with marketing, he thought, exchanging a worried look with his twin. Those not in the know regarded it as some type of dark art that suborned creatures from being their true selves, when in reality its purpose was to channel them into the way best for them. The difficulty, of course, was them not understanding that.

Mata's soft voice came unexpectedly from the corner.

'Tell me more,' she said.

Under Mata's direction the session to determine the most difficult creature to kill started in the air. There were various suggestions: the heavy and intimidating buzzards; the wary heron on the river, too canny to allow itself to be dragged down by its stick-like legs; the still-elusive kingfisher; the owl who lived in the beech. In the end, though, it came down to the bats. Scaly, fleshless, with reptilian leathery wings – everyone agreed they were horrible. They lived just down the gorge, in a cave that all the mink avoided. It was a gloomy place, entered through a dark and dank cleft dripping with green slime, and within it the bats, hanging asleep from the ceiling, were totally inaccessible. And while their high-pitched signalling might be audible to everyone when they were on the move, their jinking radar-controlled flight made them impossible to intercept.

However the bats proved an unpopular conclusion.

'The ranks could spend the next ten moons without getting near one,' Maxi protested. 'I can't see them treating that as a challenge. It might keep them occupied for a bit, but when they saw they weren't going to get their teeth into anything they'd soon lose interest.

'Who wants a bat anyway?' he inquired, making a rare stab at a joke. 'In my view they're more correctly described as a cold chew, rather than a hot spurt.'

'I had occasion to sample a toad down by the river,' MI chimed in. 'The legs were all right, but the rest!' He shuddered with distaste. 'A bat must be even more loathsome, as is borne out by them being bottom of the eating popularity league, even though no-one's tried one.'

'The only nil hot-spurt rating I've awarded in the whole wood.' Psycho stuck his oar in.

After having switched tracks via the toads, the discussion then turned to creatures on the ground. Squirrels always proved a tough nut to crack, as Plateau wits put it, but not tough enough. The mad hares were more promising, and the Plateau still resounded with the story of the one that had escaped its pursuers by turning and leaping clean over them. The hedgehog had still not been unrolled. None, though, really hit the button. It was such a delicate balance they sought – a species to kill occasionally, but not too occasionally; one that wouldn't kill them in return, as the otter had done . . .

'Or, just as importantly, be wiped out,' Maxi pointed out.

'I'm sure we all appreciate that that would defeat the object of the entire exercise.'

'Which leads us to a species with a high regeneration rate,' M2 interrupted. 'Now, if we look at the problem from the self-renewing angle . . .'

'The coneys,' Psycho suddenly burst out at the top of his high-pitched voice. From nowhere an explosion had taken place in his head, like the sun leaping over the horizon at a hundred times its normal speed.

'The coneys,' he squeaked wildly. 'That's what we need, everyone. A coneycide campaign!'

He hung on in there while his brain went spinning through the permutations. He'd never had a scam like this before; it was checking out so fast. In the round its circles were as complete and endless as the spreading rings on a pool of water. When, wth a mind-bending wrench, his system switched mode, he saw a lateral line that stretched for ever. His pointed face screwed up in agony as he struggled to get out. His overheating cells were welding themselves together, sending him into terminal meltdown.

The others stared in amazement as his features went into a frozen rictus of ecstasy, whilst his body juddered with racking spasms. The enormity of it! The perfection of it! The sheer, rounded beauty of it! He couldn't take any more, he thought as his brain went shooting round another perfect loop. It was too much! He was going to crash!

Then everything went black.

Psycho looked up to see a ring of concerned faces bent over him. Where was he? he thought before the scam hit him again. He gulped for air and, with a supreme effort, managed to regain control. Gradually he quietened down and a huge, rapturous grin spread over his rat-like features. Topsy-turvy, that was it! Not the most difficult creature to kill, but almost the easiest. Not the rarest, but nearly the commonest. Not the most unpopular, but the most popular. Eat your hearts out, MI and M2!

'Fantastic. Fan-bloody-tastic,' he exclaimed, shivering with fresh delight as the unintended pun tripped effortlessly off his lips. 'Mata, I may have had some scams in the past, but this one you're not going to believe.'

'I don't like it, Mata,' Mega said gruffly.

'Well, you should, Mega, and you should be grateful to Psycho for solving the problem for us.'

Mega sat nonplussed. He had come back into the meeting, feeling slightly ashamed of his walk-out, only to be hit by his still fired-up spin-doctor.

'I give rabbits a rating of ten, Mega,' Psycho gabbled. 'They're so satisfyingly large and those powerful hind legs make them great to chase. And the hot spurt they let out, while they've got big enough brains for a really good suck. The minions love them, as you know.

'The main point though as far as we're concerned, Mega, is that they're so many of them and they're so fertile,' he continued ecstatically, studiously avoiding referring to Mega's massacre failure. 'As soon as we cream one lot another springs up in its place, not only inside the wood, but out in the fields as far as you can see.'

MI made to intervene, but Psycho cut him short. This was his scam and he didn't need a marketing data bank to prove his point.

'What we do, Mega, is declare the entire rabbit race Public Enemy Number One,' he went on, nearly urinating in his excitement. 'We tell the minions they're trying to take over not just the wood, but the world. Then we give the pack the impossible job of exterminating them, right down to the very last bunny.

'That's the real spin, Mega, making them believe they're on a continuous crusade. It'll give them something to believe in that will keep them busy for ever. The heat'll come off the other woodland creatures and hey presto! we'll be in business.'

Thinking all this over, Mega shuddered.

'What Psycho said about the rabbits taking over the world isn't true, Mata,' he protested.

'Who are you to say what's true?' she shot back.

'I'm the leader,' he was about to reply, when he remembered

the remarks Psycho and the Marketing Mink had made about freedom. He faltered and then stayed silent. Maybe, he suddenly thought, he didn't have a monopoly on truth either? Just the thought was horribly destabilising after having always been so clear about things.

'There is no universal truth, just truths,' Mata said, smiling sympathetically, 'and as leader the first you have to recognise is that MI and M2 are entirely correct. It's not easy to face, but you know as well as I do how fast we're running out of creatures.

'Your next truth is recognising you have to do something about it. What difference does it make if Psycho's coneycide justification is "true" or "not true", so long as it answers to that greater truth?'

Mega didn't reply immediately. Mata's statement was too riddle-like for him to grasp all the subtleties. But he could see the only other alternative was moving out. But to where? They had nowhere better to go and, he suspected, they never would. With all Enterprise Wood had going for it, and the huge success of the Plateau and the Waterama complex, there would be a riot if he even mentioned the idea.

'There's still something that feels all wrong about it, Mata,' he protested feebly.

'I know, Mega,' she replied comfortingly. 'But it can't feel right all the time.'

43

Snared

The day began with a soft dawn, heralding a pretty morning that sparkled with fresh dew. But that did nothing for Mega's foul mood. Everyone studiously avoided him as he stomped round the Plateau, angry breath rising in steaming clouds. It was not only their leader who was exceptionally grumpy, the minions soon discovered. Maxi barked ferociously at them during the compulsory reveille round the cat totem, then the Marketing Mink subjected them to a battery of aggressive questioning and finally Psycho crept around, glaring so weirdly that he sent shivers running down every spine. Finally, as the leaders disappeared into Mega's holt, word flashed round. There was a crisis. Everyone instantly had a shrewd idea what it was about. Two nights ago a young female had unaccountably gone missing. No trace of her had yet been found.

Unknown to the rest of the pack, however, in the middle of the night another female had rushed back to the Plateau to blurt out to Maxi that she had discovered the body out in the fields. Maxi, threatening her with the same fate if she breathed a word to anyone, had informed his leader and together they had gone out and found she had been caught in a trap that had been set by the humans in a hedge. Her frantic efforts to escape had tightened the wire noose round her neck so she had gradually throttled herself. The gruesome and depressing sight sparked pity and rage in them both.

'We can keep it quiet for a day or so, my leader, but it's bound to leak out in the end,' Maxi had stated. 'I think we should get it over with by telling the ranks straight away.'

Now, back in his holt, Mega posed the only question on the agenda.

'What shall we say?'

The leaders looked at the floor.

'What had the humans set the snare to catch?' Psycho finally asked.

'Rabbits,' Mega growled. 'We all know that.'

'But maybe we don't all know how we can use it, Mega,' Psycho replied, undeterred. 'We were about to launch the coneycide campaign, so why not put the two together?'

'What do you mean?' Mega growled, suspicious.

'It's quite simple, Mega.' Psycho warmed to his theme. 'Why not tell the minions the rabbits killed our sister, then take them on a pilgrimage to see her?'

'I've never heard anything so entirely dishonourable,' Maxi burst out, unable to contain himself. 'Denigrating her like that, when it isn't even true. It's sheer exploitation!

'Please don't get me wrong, Mega,' he appealed anxiously to his leader. 'I'm completely behind the coneycide campaign, and Psycho's right – I've finished the preparations and it's ready to go. We're just waiting for a hook to hang it from. But not this, my leader. Anyhow, it's much too far-fetched. It has no logic. The ranks'll never wear it, mark my words.'

He twiddled his whiskers furiously.

'There is a logic, though, Mega,' Psycho persisted infuriatingly. 'If there weren't any rabbits there wouldn't be a snare. So who is responsible, if they aren't? Anyway, once you whip the minions up you know they'll lose all sense of reason.'

That is, if they have any in the first place, he added silently to himself.

'I don't care. It's still out of the question,' Maxi fired back.

Mega let them continue arguing. He was feeling lost and torn. What were things coming to? He might eventually have sanctioned the coneycide campaign, and to a certain extent, like everyone else, even come to believe it himself in a way. He still felt it was a retrograde step, though, despite what Mata had said about 'the truth'. But Psycho's latest cold-blooded cynicism crossed a line he had never imagined they would reach. Now he could see the so-called 'truth' being extended into anything that the pack could be persuaded to swallow. Yet, while he could understand Maxi's rigid mind not being able to make the jump, he could see how he could make the pilgrimage idea work. It would be a personal challenge, but he could manage it.

'It's one of my warriors who's died, Mega,' Mata quietly intervened. 'We've got to explain her death away somehow. If we can use it to get the coneycide campaign off the ground, why not?'

'But Mata, that would be using one dishonesty to promote another,' Mega protested, while Maxi looked on, appalled.

'Maybe, Mega,' she replied frankly. 'But who are you to deny her her contribution?'

Mega felt completely lost. All the important things – freedom, the truth, death – had seemed so clear until recently. Now this shifting, amorphous mass of double-think was clouding them over, obscuring his view of them. What was it with his advisers, that they had to make everything so complicated?

'Our overall responsibility, Mega, is to make this show run,' Mata reminded him.

'But at what sacrifice, Mata?' he asked despairingly.

'Whatever it takes, Mega.'

Mega stared at her, stumped.

Then suddenly he was grimly determined. If he had to do it he would make a first-class job of it.

After two days of heavy downpours the river below the Plateau was running in brown and choppy spate, swollen by the input of a hundred streams and darkened by the soil it had leached off the fields. But its steady roar was now overriden by the gale that had sprung up, thrashing the trees and sending the cat-tail swaying wildly backwards and forwards. The pack members, huddled below it, had to strain to hear their leader.

'My mink, you may have thought I brought you here just so you could be free,' he shouted. 'Yet, as befits the woodland master species, there was always more to it than that. For, I can now reveal to you, we are here on a mission, a mission to save not just the wood, but the world.

'Let me tell you, my mink, that we, your leaders, have uncovered a new and ruthless enemy, an enemy it is both our destiny and our duty to destroy.'

There was a flurry and the ranks parted to let through two muscle-mink dragging a dead rabbit behind them. They dumped the corpse at Mega's feet and he briefly inspected it amidst relieved sniggers. Whatever horror was to be revealed, which presumably was worse than the otter, it couldn't possibly be a copulating coney!

'As you can see, this is a rabbit,' Mega shouted, seeming to read their minds just as Gabbla once had. 'A dead rabbit, and therefore no more threat. Yet its many, many fellows still alive are exactly that.

'Why, my mink? Because they are breeding. They are breeding and breeding and breeding again. They never stop breeding — and they never will.'

The minions' sniggers had died away and they nodded at each other knowingly. The coneys' capability to multiply did indeed amaze them.

'You know the woodland creatures paint us as the destroyers,' their leader continued. 'But who says that most? It is the rabbits. Yet all the time their dastardly plan is to destroy the whole wood as we know it.'

Now the minions were puzzled. Rabbits were so pathetic they couldn't destroy anything, except maybe blades of grass. Had their leader gone mad?

'We all know rabbits are an inferior species!' Mega thundered in confirmation. 'Picture one in your mind. What do you see — silly buck teeth, receding chin, stupid floppy ears, huge fat bum . . . ?' He poked at the corpse with his front paw. 'Hopeless, eh? And harmless, you think, don't you?'

'Right, Mega,' a bold minion cried. 'Just victims, aren't they?'

He shrivelled as Mega roared: 'Wrong! Wrong! Wrong!

'It's not your fault for not knowing this,' he went on more gently, 'but underneath that foolish exterior lies a ruthless determination to conquer. Rabbits may look stupid, but that has been their cunning – in deluding us into thinking they are nothing. Yet all the time they are working towards taking over the world through sheer weight of numbers.

'Still enjoying your hot spurts?' he asked, suddenly switching tracks.

There were loud cheers of agreement.

'And smashing skulls,' someone shouted.

'I'm glad,' Mega thundered. 'But now we are here for an even greater purpose. For it is we mink who have been sent to lead the fight back that will prevent the wood, and the world, being over-run by the rabbit horde.'

Amidst stunned silence he gave up the stage to MI and M2, who deluged the pack with statistics 'scientifically proving' that if rabbits continued at their present breeding rate they would not only eat all the vegetation, but leave no room for anybody else. The pack members began growling in assent. They might not fully understand 'scientifical proof', but they could still get the point.

'We have been making a terrible mistake, fellow mink.' Psycho now weighed in, glorying in his moment. 'Naturally we have been presuming that the fiercer creatures here are our real enemies. Yet all that time these seemingly timid creatures have been the canker in our midst.

'Look at their burrows that you live in. Do these reveal them to be stupid, ineffectual creatures? No, they do not. They are real works of art, skilfully excavated as part of the rabbit master plan. Rabbits are the hidden worm, fellow mink, the worm inside, eating away at the life chain that supports us all.'

'Yes, my mink, rabbits are the true vermin,' Mega shouted, resuming centre stage. 'Rabbits are the rubbish, the filth, the scum. They pollute the earth, even as they destroy it. For they also bring the killer plague we have heard about. You would expect that to wipe out any species. But not rabbits. Because they breed, my mink. They breed. The only way to stop them is to make them die. And that is what we mink are here for – to kill them and kill them until we have taken them out for ever.'

Despite the roar of the gale that periodically whipped his words away the minions remained gripped. Rough weather always sparked them up anyway and Psycho noted with glee that they were now beginning to share their leader's rage. One male had already bounded forward and was worrying at the rabbit carcass.

As the muscle-mink stepped forward and gently prised him off, Mega gestured for calm.

'We must all keep our heads,' he said, a sad note entering his voice. 'For now we have uncovered their plot, the evil rabbits have already struck back.

'My mink, we must make a sorrowful journey, a journey that will bring home to you that rabbits are also killers. Not bold, honourable killers like us, but cold-blooded, calculating murderers. Murderers of mink.'

The minions looked at each other in horror.

Mega regarded Maxi affectionately as he mustered the pack into line, no easy task in such wild conditions and with everyone on such tenterhooks. But however much Maxi disagreed with Psycho's pilgrimage scam, he at least had the good grace to work with his customary gusto and efficiency.

When the pack was in order Mega led the way up to the Ridge, where the full force of the gale hit them head-on as they emerged into the open fields. He looked back, seeing how the wind flattened the fur on their faces to expose their gleaming eyes. How lean and mean they looked, while their gait was so purposeful compared to the plodding footsteps that had characterised the Long March. No wonder it was mink, rather than the rabbits, that were eating everything *en masse*. Since they had been in the wood they had grown in strength and confidence, sloughing off the excess fat they had carried in the cages as they attained true fitness for the first time. Now they were wilder, their eyes beadier, their limbs more supple, their efficiency as killing machines more finely honed. On any scale of predatoriness they must command huge respect. Yet at the same time, moving again as a group under the vast sky, with its scudding black clouds, was reuniting them as a pack and bringing back vivid memories. Unconsciously they rubbed against each other for companionship, fearful of what they were being led to.

When he reached the second hedge, Mega stepped into its lee and turned to address them.

'Even I, your leader, could not prevent the tragedy you are about to witness,' he said sadly. 'And for that I most humbly apologise.'

The mink exchanged worried glances. It wasn't like Mega to apologise for anything.

'Before you gaze on this pitiful sight, let me tell you that our new enemy, the rabbits, were responsible for this terrible deed,' Mega shouted. 'They knew the snare was there, laid for them. They lured our hapless sister into it and then stood by and watched her die – and die most horribly. Here is the proof of how evil they are. Here is the proof of the danger they pose, not just to the world, but to us.

'Behold, my mink, and mourn with me.'

Without further ado he led the way briskly along the bumpy hedge-bottom to where the dead female was lying on a well-worn path between two gnarled hawthorns that was an obvious rabbit-run. The shiny metal of the snare had sunk deep into the thick fur round her throat, while her tongue stuck out and her eyes bulged grotesquely. The blood on her pads and the way the earth was torn up round her showed how prolonged and terrible her death throes must have been.

Many of the mink appeared in deep shock as they filed silently past. They had seen the bodies of the sentries that the otter had drowned, but this sight was infinitely more pitiful. They all winced as they imagined the agonies she must have suffered before death mercifully released her.

'What could be more horrible than being trapped like that?' Mega asked as Maxi herded them gently back together. 'It's vile, it's ignoble, it's the worst thing of all. Using the humans to murder for you is, my fellow mink, typically rabbit.

'So let us all now work — work to ensure that our dear sister's death has not been in vain. Let us work to destroy the rabbit conspiracy, before it destroys any more of us.'

Psycho smiled as the minions filed past again to pay their last homage. Not for a moment had any of them stopped to question the logic. And neither did any notice now as he slipped away.

As Mega led the subdued pack back across the fields he wished he had said no to the further scam his spin-doctor was now engaged in. He had nearly balked, but in the end had wearily submitted after Psycho had worn him down with endless persuasion and justification. Now he was so far down the line and had already lost his bearings, what difference did it make? Addressing the pack on the Plateau he had been fired by his own rhetoric and pumping adrenalin, but seeing the dead female again had induced a deep melancholy. Suddenly he wanted to have no more truck with the whole sorry business. Was he getting too soft to be the leader? he thought. Too affected, too emotionally involved? All the others — even, or especially, Mata — seemed to have this cut-off ability, enabling them to view events dispassionately. Psycho had even lectured him about the dangers of becoming too personally involved as he was laying out the current scam. Yet shouldn't all true mink have fire in their belly, burning convictions, a sense of involvement with their fellows that bound them irrevocably together, sharing each other's sadnesses as well as joys? That wasn't being soft, it was being truly caring. Instead he had sanctioned Psycho's sick scheme as if he was as big an arch-cynic. He could imagine the twisted runt back at the Plateau at this very moment, cackling with glee as he put what he called his 'top spin' into practice.

It was too late to stop him now, though, and Mega had no choice but to play his part. He led the pack along as slowly as he dared, to give his spin-doctor maximum time to prepare, while reflecting how the funereal pace matched the mink's mood. With the wind now comfortably on their backs, they were huddling again, just as they had on the Long March.

Psycho ran up as planned as they drew near the Plateau, appearing highly agitated.

'Come and see what the rabbits have done,' he shouted, rushing off into the trees.

After a moment's hesitation the pack broke into a run, catching up with him as he stood breathlessly on the edge of the Plateau. He pointed with a quivering paw at the cat-tail, still attached to the beech branch and waving wildly in the wind. It was no longer proudly and stiffly erect, but had been remodelled into a rounded shape that hung down in a passing resemblance to a pair of floppy ears.

'Look how the rabbits struck the moment we turned our backs,' Psycho screamed as the minions stared in awe-struck horror.

Psycho was right. It was the first time they had ever left their base unguarded.

He ran across the grass, scampered up the beech and bit through the ivy rope. As the tail fell to earth, its new rounded shape caused it to roll, and it was blown along by fierce gusts of wind until it stopped where the rabbit corpse had lain. The minions gasped again as their attention was drawn to a fresh horror. The body had gone!

As Psycho ran over to snuffle at their vandalised symbol they chittered in alarm while he raised his rat-like muzzle towards the roaring heavens.

'Rabbit,' he pronounced in as terrible a voice as he could muster. 'I smell rabbit everywhere.'

'Me too,' individuals began shouting, running about in agitated circles.

Psycho was exultant. Any minion who stopped for a moment would have realised the gale was so strong it would have whisked away even the rank scent of a fox. But, as he had been banking on, their reason had entirely deserted them. Now they were convinced they had a real enemy, an enemy so wicked and cunning it could first murder, then take advantage of their grief to violate their most sacred symbol and then – on top of all that – even cause its dead to disappear! How had the rabbits come and gone so clandestinely? Where were they now? And what would they do next?

Psycho waited confidently.

'There's one,' he suddenly shouted, gesturing at the wildly swaying bushes.

As a crowd ran across cries started coming.

'There's another!'

'There's one over there!'

Soon everyone was dashing about in confusion, imagining eyes and shadowy figures all around them.

'Attention all mink!' Maxi's voice cut across the hubbub. 'Volunteers for the coneycide campaign, with its mission to eliminate all rabbits, over here!'

The entire pack ran to him as one.

'Who wants to go on the first raid?'

'We all do!' the fierce cry came back.

44

Peace in our Wood

Although spring was always beautiful in Old Wood, this time round it seemed to Owl to have a richer patina than ever. First the glowingly white blackthorn blossom had brought with it the traditional cold snap, before sharp showers and buffeting winds washed everything down, while the river carried away the winter debris. Now, with the rosier but duller hawthorn in full flower, growth had commenced in earnest. All the creatures agreed that the greens of the unfurling leaves appeared more translucent than they had ever seen, the crab apple blossom more pinkly delicate, the primroses more creamy, the mist of bluebells carpeting the ground so much deeper it shaded almost to indigo. Of all the seasons, this was normally the woodland creatures' favourite. The miseries of the Big Cold were forgotten as the earth and air warmed up and the rising sap sent energy surging through a community busying itself with mating and home-building.

This spring, however, despite all the usual vigour all around, the shadow of the mink interlopers hung in a hideous pall over everyone. While there was not complete silence, the normal joyous birdsong was thin and hushed, reflecting how many of its inhabitants had been removed, while the remaining ones, feeling there was nothing joyous to celebrate, had been plunged into deep gloom. It didn't help that the Big Cold had been a particularly lean one. Hard frosts had accompanied piercing winds, which moaned eerily through the bare branches and chilled to the bone. Snow had descended like a white blanket, hushing the normal woodland sounds and lying for more than half a moon to reduce the wood's resources to their lowest ebb. Digging creatures had scratched forlornly at the rock-hard earth, while plant and seed-eaters roamed further and further afield in their desperate search for nourishment, putting themselves more and more at risk from the equally deprived predators. At times such as these, however hard you worked, death by freezing or starvation was a very real possibility. Then, no sooner had the majority struggled through that than the mink had arrived to turn life into a day- or nightmare, depending on which way you clocked it.

It was, thought Owl, infinitely depressing to see the wood waking up so wonderfully, while things within it were going so badly. Burdock's latest report had only brought the contrast into starker relief. But it was the proposal he made on the back of it that Owl found hardest to cope with.

'I'm going to call as large a meeting as I can,' the rabbit with the white blaze announced defiantly.

'What will that achieve?' Owl asked, flabbergasted. He knew the chattering creatures had been holding furtive unofficial meetings, but nothing official or above ground. As far as he was concerned that had been the only wholly positive result springing from the mink invasion.

'It isn't a question of achievement, Ollie,' Big Arse replied vehemently. 'Nor, in case you're thinking that, is it anything personal. I've lost my mate, whom I held most dear, as you know, but this is something bigger than that. Can't you see that we mustn't abandon our procedure? That our protocol must remain paramount, whatever? That if we allow the mink to intimidate us into dismantling meetings, we're as good as admitting they've won? Anyhow, have you any better suggestion?'

'Not if the mink are as bad as you say they are,' Owl

admitted reluctantly. He had thought long and hard since he and Burdock had last talked, but nothing had sprung to mind. 'A meeting would be awfully risky, though. Where could we hold it?'

Burdock looked round the copse approvingly. 'Here's as good as anywhere. You made a good choice, Ollie — it's away from the wood and we're well hidden. Look, there's even a stump!'

As the rabbit pointed approvingly towards a jagged tree trunk in the centre of the sunken hollow, Owl felt flattered. Not that Burdock wasn't right — the site had proved to be as good as was available, which was why he had chosen it again for them to compare notes.

'You'll want me to be Chaircreature, I suppose?' he asked, already knowing the reply.

'More importantly, Ollie, I also want you to persuade as many other creatures as possible to come,' Burdock said animatedly. 'Not just CWGs, but predators, carnivores, omnivores — everybody. They've got to understand we're all in this together.'

'I appreciate that myself,' Owl replied not unkindly, wondering how many others did. He could understand the reasoning. As they were all in it together, presumably they could only get themselves out of it together.

He saw Burdock suddenly flag and thought how defeated he looked. It was as if all the cares of the wood were on his shoulders and he appeared even older and sadder than when Owl had last seen him.

'Don't worry too much,' he said, trying to introduce some cheer into that gloomy face. 'Something's bound to turn up.'

'Maybe, but I doubt it,' said Burdock, hopping off and wincing at the shooting pain that still afflicted his shoulder.

Owl, watching his halting progress, couldn't help but silently agree. There was no way out that he could see.

'At least it's a start, Raka,' Owl pleaded.

'Start and finish, more like,' the rook squawked disdainfully. 'When did a meeting of CWGs ever achieve anything?'

Owl sighed. It was a hard question to answer.

'There's got to be a first time,' he said feebly. 'Anyway, their meetings are the only forum that the wood's got. You must agree that the more non-Guardians who attend, the more chance there is of getting something done.'

'Getting what done?' Raka demanded annoyingly.

'We don't know yet,' Owl admitted.

He thought for a moment of repeating the Venerable Buck's warning about the 'big trouble' that was coming. At least that showed in retrospect the rabbits had been aware something was going to happen. But he decided against it. He was growing weary of his attempts to persuade fellow predators and had just returned from a visit to Orwella that had only increased his despair.

'The problem's solved as far as I'm concerned,' the otter had announced tartly. 'I now keep out of their way and they keep out of mine. I'm afraid all of you in the wood will have to sink or swim on your own.'

Owl had since tried the alternative line that predators, even if they didn't take part in the meeting as such, could at least attend and help with the security operation in case of a mink attack. But even that had met with a mixed response.

'I can understand that some creatures are scornful about my having been Chaircreature in the past,' he complained to Raka. 'That's fair enough, I suppose. But what Boris and others have been saying is that I'm only trying to recruit them because I've become a meetings creature, and that simply isn't true. It's just that I feel that I've recognised what they seem to be unable to grasp and that they're being totally selfish.'

'I wouldn't dispute that, Ollie,' Raka replied with an unexpected grin. 'And I wouldn't worry too much either. They're just giving you a hard time. I think you'll find they'll be there. I certainly shall.'

Owl relaxed. Maybe he had been taking the various remarks too seriously, and at least he still had one firm friend. He still hadn't dared ask Ula though.

As he settled on his new Chaircreature's perch on the elm branch, Owl could see Raka had been right. His fellow members of the Dead Vole Society were there – Boris on the sidelines, already giving snorts of disgust, whilst Freddie popped up round the edges, as elusive as ever. The buzzards, as he had expected, had refused to come down to ground level, but he was pleased to see them fulfilling their promise to sail overhead as watchdogs and deterrents, incidentally creating huge nervousness amongst the assorted voles, mice and shrews gathered in their shadows.

Burdock, also looking round, was disappointed to see fewer than he had hoped but then he supposed that just demonstrated how far ranks had been devastated. The rabbits, though, had not let him down, coming from great distances to show solidarity with their besieged comrades. They motive was not entirely unseflish, mind you, he thought. As the mink pack widened its range of activity, more and more of them were finding themselves under threat. Numbers had also been swelled by swarms of dragooned insects, attending in their revised capacity of non-voting observers. In the small bowl in the copse, rather than the vast space of the Big Clearing, superficially the attendance looked respectable, especially when you took into account the potentially dangerous journey many had had to make.

They had been starved of a proper meeting for so long that Owl would not have been surprised to find the various factions back at each other's throats. But to his relief in the new atmosphere of realism all talk of Superslug, Ant Rule and the previous nonsense had vanished. Even the odious Cowslip had abandoned her bleating about Worms' Lib. For once the chattering creatures really had something to chatter about — and chatter they did.

Eventually, after a series of long grumbles and much paw-wringing about the wood's plight, a dunnock fluttered on to the improvised Stump.

'I propose that we send a petition to the mink,' he piped reedily.

Owl groaned out loud at this lurch back on to familiar CWG territory. Petitions had been commonplace in the past, protesting about this, calling for a ban on that, expressing concern about the other. Owl saw them as a ploy to give an impression of dynamic action and they were certainly universally ignored by those they were aimed at. The same fate had overtaken Burdock's beloved Woodland Code and Bill of Creatures' Rights, although both since been formally passed at a hurried meeting, with only a few rabbits present.

'The mink's woodland crimes and atrocities are too legion for me to list,' the dunnock went on. 'They have violated every principle and ethic that we Guardians stand for. Yet, being birds of reason, we are confident that once we communicate our views to them, old-fashioned common decency will dictate they either acknowledge their errors and mend their ways, or depart from here.

'Our dunnock working party has therefore drawn up a proposal according with our underlying ethos. We have more-over borne in mind that, although we are required by the circumstances to be firm, it would still be politic to be as nice as possible to the mink, so as not to upset them too much.'

What did all that mean? thought Owl, baffled. If the dunnocks were being nice to the mink, surely they would let them stay? He nearly burst out laughing as he tried to conjure up a vision of a dunnock being nasty. Boris, he could see, was having much the same thought, but not seeing the funny side at all. His head was now weaving up and down in a way that Owl recognised presaged an explosion.

The dunnock self-importantly cleared his throat with a high-pitched cheep.

'This is our preferred wording: "We, the animals, birds, FARF (Fish and Allied Riverside Folk) and MOCS (Myriad Other Creatures) of Old Wood, together comprising the Concerned Woodland Guardians, in view of your repeated and flagrant violations of our Woodland Code and Bill of Creatures' Rights, hereby request and require that you mink either entirely cease your activities, or depart to another place, as your unseemly presence here is ravaging our community, upsetting its balance and destroying its ecology."'

The silence as the meeting digested this mouthful was broken by a loud and disgusted snort from Boris.

'We, the tossers, do hereby propose we do bugger all except

faff about as uselessly as we always do,' he harumphed, in a parody of the dunnock's piping, before lumbering off into the falling darkness.

The silence was broken by a loud clamour of competing creatures, all wishing to change the original wording. Owl groaned again as he looked round at the multiple arguments breaking out as everyone charged off on this sideshow. He was about to hoot for silence when Burdock sprang up from the audience and delegated the obviously hugely lengthy task to a sub-committee.

'A petition's all very well,' Owl observed loudly, unable to stop himself butting in. 'But the real question is: who's going to deliver it?'

That shut them up, he thought triumphantly as they all suddenly looked shifty. Then his beak dropped open as Burdock broke the silence.

'I am,' he announced quietly, before embarking on such an impassioned speech about the power of reason that Owl, concluding he was listening to the longest suicide note in history, gave up. With attitudes like that these creatures deserved to die. Yet the rest of the audience heard their leader out in respectful silence and the trouble only started when a dove followed Burdock on to the makeshift Stump.

'I shall go as well, bearing an olive branch,' she cooed.

'A what?' shrieked Raka from the middle of the crowd of her fellow rooks who had perched themselves on the branch above Owl. Proud of having done her bit by persuading so many to attend, Raka was now appalled and embarrassed at the surfacing of the very nonsense she had feared. She should never have given in to Owl's blandishments.

'An olive branch,' the dove repeated softly.

'But there aren't any olives in the wood, you stupid bird.'

The dove's soft eyes regarded her innocently.

'A sprig of hazel will suffice — or oak, ash, sycamore — it doesn't really matter', she said, quite unperturbed. 'The point is that the branch, carried by myself, represents a universal symbol which automatically stops killing by restoring peace and harmony.'

Raka's fury increased as the dunnocks twittered in support of this ridiculous statement. She knew she should be treating it with the contempt it deserved by just ignoring it, but she was now too outraged.

'And how, precisely, will peace come?' she asked rhetorically, answering with heavy sarcasm, 'Don't tell me – you'll fly along to the Plateau, branch in beak, and the mink will immediately see the error of their ways.

'Maybe you'll coo for good measure?' she squawked, mimicking the dove's soft tones. ' "Coo-coo, nasty mink! Coo-coo! Be nice, nasty mink! Coo-coo! Please go away, nasty mink! Coo-coo!" '

' "Oh dear," the mink will say, "we have been nasty, haven't we? Gosh, look at that branch – it's the universal symbol come to show us where we've gone wrong. Aren't we ashamed of ourselves, eh? Golly, we must leave straight away, so all the nice woodland creatures can live happily ever afterwards. Bye-bye everybody. Sorry we caused you a bit of trouble, but you needn't worry any more. We're gone." '

'Have I missed anything out?' Raka demanded as her fellow rooks grinned in appreciation.

'In a way,' the dove replied, glistening white feathers entirely unruffled. 'I'm afraid, though, that we doves don't know that much about the universal symbol. You see, our job is merely to be its harbinger.'

'Carrier, you mean,' Raka yelled, now quite beside herself. 'Why do you bloody Guardians always use a complicated word when a simple one will do? Harbinger or not, you tell us how your universal symbol can possibly do any good whatsoever.'

'By appealing to the mink's better natures,' the dove promptly replied, looking slightly puzzled. 'How else?'

'Haven't you grasped yet that mink don't have better natures?' Raka cawed disbelievingly. 'Don't you know that the only language they understand is kill or be killed? That if you give them a stick, as you're planning to, they'll only beat you with it – or worse?'

Owl, listening to this interchange, couldn't help being moved by the plump beauty of the gentle snow-white creature. The contrast between her and the raucous black rook couldn't be greater. Why couldn't the rook accept that the dove was just a dumb blonde, and not take her so seriously? As the forest of waving paws and wings correctly indicated, Raka was well out of order.

He swivelled to look upwards and glared at her to be quiet, only to see he had no need. She had now reduced herself to such incoherent rage that all she could utter was strangled squawks.

'Next item on the agenda,' he hooted imperiously.

But of course there wasn't one. Immensely satisfied, now that at last something was being done, the chattering creatures were already nervously dispersing to set off on their perilous individual journeys home.

'Meeting closed,' Owl hooted.

There was at least one consolation. It had been the shortest he could ever remember.

45

Run Rabbit, Run Rabbit

'The teams are ready for you to make the selection', Maxi announced, knocking deferentially at the entrance to Mega's holt.

'I'll be out in a moment.'

Mega brushed the hair on the top of his head upwards, as he had found himself unconsciously doing ever since the Marketing Mink had suggested it. His qualms about the fundamental dishonesty of the coneycide campaign had gradually faded as he saw how effective it was becoming. Maxi had built up a structure of activities that now spread way beyond the wood and even back as far as the moor, where they had spent that first dreadful night in the culvert. And now that the minions' bloodthirsty antics had been given a framework, the colony was acquiring the central focus it had previously lacked. Only the previous night the Marketing Mink had proudly invited him to their holt to receive their latest report.

'It's all working, great leader,' they had announced smugly. 'While we cannot yet say the heat has come off the other woodland creatures entirely, our statistics show their slaughter is now carried out almost exclusively for genuine eating purposes. Just look at these.'

They ran up and down beside their multiple graphs and charts on the wall, indicating how the latest lines all pointed encouragingly upwards.

'We can now say beyond any shadow of contradiction, great leader, that the woodland market has bottomed out. Availability to eat is already up five per cent and still increasing.'

Mega had decided not to upset them by telling them he did not need figures to confirm his own gut feeling. Everyone could see that the mass killing of rabbits was exactly the kind of sheer bloody murder the minions loved. He could sense the anticipation in the air as he stepped out on to the Plateau to resounding cheers. The selection he was now being called on to make was one of the series of interlocking events Maxi had carefully designed round the climax of 'red rampages' that had rapidly become the cornerstone of mink society. He had split the pack into different teams, which had just returned from days and nights of scouting for the juiciest warren they could find.

Mega's task now was to listen gravely as they noisily debated the respective merits of their different choices, and then to announce which of them would be the next formal target. In reality Maxi always informed him beforehand, but Psycho, beside himself with glee at the way his scheme was working, insisted on the charade.

'What we're after, Mega, is anything that will help channel the minions' aggression. So, if we encourage the different teams to compete with each other, they'll do half the job for us by taking it out on each other.'

Or maybe on you, one day, if they ever realise what you've been up to, Mega thought. The most insidious thing about the coneycide campaign was that it had a kind of insane logic. The longer it went on, the easier its invented justification was to accept, until even he was beginning to believe in it implicitly. He had even decided that was the way he preferred it to be, rather than dwelling on its base origins.

He could see Psycho sniggering away as the argument rose to fever pitch, before he called for silence and pronounced Maxi's predetermined judgement: 'Tonight's winners are the Gladiators, with Warren B.'

To cheers from the winners and groans from the losers, Maxi plunged them into the detailed preparations.

The ritualistic ceremony to lead off the evening's carnage always took place round the cat-tail, now back hanging vertically from its branch. There had been a sharp debate about whether it should be straightened out. Psycho, bursting with self-importance at the success of his ploy, wanted it left as it was in order to provide a constant reminder to the credulous minions. That had, however, made Maxi doubly furious. He had not been let in on the ear-bending scam and fallen for it completely, giving himself an unwelcome reminder of the tricks that had been played on him in his youth.

But his anger had also been righteous.

'It is our sacred emblem and I insist it be kept sacrosanct, my leader,' he had protested vehemently. 'You should never have allowed Psycho to use it in the first place.'

It was unusual for him to criticise Mega so directly, but his leader had let it pass. Privately he agreed. By now he had lost patience with his spin-doctor's clever tricks. Psycho always pushed it too far. He never seemed to know when he had achieved his objective and it was time to leave well alone.

Mega had resolved the issue by simply picking up the tail and straightening it out himself. It had then been hauled back up to hang as before and a substitute object of outrage since been provided by the building of the larger-than-life replica rabbit which now reared up beside it. This masterpiece of construction, supervised by Maxi and upholstered by Mata's warriors, had a frame of branches covered with the skins of real victims. Its grotesquely realistic glowing eyes were manufactured from white stones picked off the river bed, while pale holly wood had been carefully gnawed into shape to provide the huge claws and inanely grinning buck teeth.

According to custom, the victorious Gladiator team now had the honour of leading the ceremonial dance round this totem,

singing the immensely popular rabbit song the Marketing Mink
were as proud of as 'Rule Minkmania', despite sour grapes from
Psycho that it was too lightweight.

> Run, rabbit, run rabbit, run, run, run!
> Giving the nasty mink their fun, fun, fun!
> You can't get by, for you must die!
> So run, rabbit, run rabbit, run, run, run!

Individual minions began making darting runs towards the
replica rabbit, swiping it with their paws as they bared their
teeth and let out blood-curdling growls.

The chant began: 'Kill the coneys! Kill the coneys! Kill!
Kill! Kill!', until finally Mega gave the signal and the snarling
pack was off and running. It was always a journey, as Mega
had now laid down that rabbits within the wood itself were
off limits. It was the Marketing Mink who had pointed out
how comprehensively they had already been reduced there. A
concerted drive against them would soon wipe them out entirely,
they smugly pointed out, thereby completely negating Psycho's
breeding thesis.

Psycho had protested volubly at this intrusion into his
territory.

'The minions will never wear that,' he had squeaked. 'On
the contrary, we should instruct them to clean out the wood
and make it a rabbit-free zone.'

'No, Psycho,' Mega had replied firmly. 'You said it yourself
– the whole campaign is aimed at getting them out and killing
elsewhere.'

But Psycho had found himself unable to agree with his
leader. Not a great one for getting out and about himself,
he wanted visible evidence to please him as he strutted about
the wood.

'Doesn't free-market philosophy dictate that you hit every
potential victim regardless, Mega?' he had asked spitefully.

'Don't talk to me about this market nonsense,' his leader had
roared back angrily.

Psycho had skulked off, later finding unlikely allies in the

Marketing Mink, who had agreed that he was correct. Mata was dismissive, but he had found an even more unlikely potential ally in Maxi, who had already voiced different doubts to his leader.

'I'm not at all sure I can enforce that, boss,' he had said worriedly. 'The minions have taken so many out already it'll be hard stopping them now.'

'I thought you were a believer in discipline, Maxi,' Mega had replied sharply. 'Just do it.'

But when it came down to it, Psycho had found none of his theoretical supporters prepared to go to the wall.

'It's like I always say, Psycho,' Maxi had tediously repeated. 'Mega's the boss and you have to do what the boss says. And so we should. He knows more than we'll ever know in our entire lives. That's why he's the boss.'

And that's why you've never have an original thought in your head, Psycho had muttered under his breath. Didn't Maxi realise that without him and his constant flow of scams, Mega would never even have become leader, let alone have stayed securely at the top of the tree?

The sun was setting in a fiery red ball as the pack broke out of the wood and charged across the fields. The longer evenings made the rampages better and better. Not only were the rabbits breeding even more prolifically, but they rejoiced in being outside in the warmer air. Nibbly shoots sprouted everywhere, while the tender new grass exploded on taste buds dulled by the tough residue of the Big Cold. At the end of every day it was a sheer delight to gambol with new offspring, play happy games, admire the view or simply enjoy the luxury of contentedly grazing. Although aware of the rampages, the different warrens still could not resist going outside, trusting to statistical luck not to have been marked out.

The pack's movements changed as they neared the Gladiators' 'B' warren, which was five fields beyond the Ridge. As Maxi had taught them, they squirmed along the hedge-bottom on their bellies, using every dip and fold in the ground, while carefully testing the wind. It didn't always work, and an aberrant gust would sometimes give them away. Many warrens were also hard to approach surreptitiously, even though accessibility was a criterion in determining the choice.

This evening, however, there was not the slightest breeze and the pack managed to creep undetected to within half a field, before Mega gave the prearranged double mew.

The Gladiator team raced ahead to cover as many entrances and exits as possible, cutting off any rabbits too slow or far away. Then the real fun began as pack members piled inside and raced through the network of living chambers and connecting passages, killing every rabbit they came across. Meanwhile, others waited above to pick off any emerging above the ground. As usual they encircled them and the fun began as the mink deliberately opened enticing-looking gaps, encouraging their cowering prey to make a break for it. When they did the gap was promptly closed, before the more disappointing victims, who just sat rooted by fear, were homed in on and contemptuously dispatched.

The real mayhem, however, was underground. Maxi, supervising the operation from above, grinned with satisfaction as he heard the succession of squeals and thumps while more and more mink faces, spattered with blood, popped up from the exits until finally the pogrom was over.

'Get them up,' Maxi bawled, and the slow process began of hauling out the bodies to be laid in line according to size, from the biggest adults to litters of babies. Dismembered bits were shoved into separate piles roughly corresponding to one complete creature.

By now it was dark and time for the next stage – the eating competition.

Grouped opposite the line, the pack waited, slavering.

'On your marks! Get set! Eat!' Maxi bellowed, and they rushed forward to begin their feast. Maxi stalked up and down behind the crouched figures, ensuring none of them ate grass to make themselves sick, a ruse that Mega had just officially disallowed. While the competition was ostensibly a team one, even more status was attached to the parallel individual one and all the mink were cramming more and more coney into their bellies in an attempt to beat the record, currently standing at one complete creature and two legs.

As the pack, farting and belching, staggered on its bloated way back to the Plateau, Mega knew all the mink, high on fulfilled bloodlust, would be sated for days. The level of aggro in the community would drop until, as it rose again, Maxi started the cycle again and defused it by scheduling the next rampage.

As he had feared, the ranks had grumbled mightily about the ban on killing the rabbits in the wood, and it had required some heavy work by the muscle-mink to make them respect it. The rabbits, however, had responded magnificently. They multiplied not only within the wood, but also in the warrens that had been hit by previous rampages. Their systems were invariably so confusing and disorientating that the pack missed various nooks and crannies, while a few of their inhabitants were inevitably out or succeeded in fleeing. One way or another, there were always survivors. The mink teams were soon reporting blitzed warrens to have been re-occupied and producing a stream of new little victims. Periodically MI and M2 weighed in with more 'scientific proof' of the continuing rabbit threat, but there was no longer any real need. Given their head, the minions had done the rest, and their ranks now contained a number of self-appointed 'experts', always ready to air their blind prejudices.

Arriving back at the Plateau the pack settled itself down for the last act of the night's drama. This was yet another Psycho spin, it's origins harking back to the days of the Elders in the cages. Not all the rabbits in the targeted warren were killed. Some were taken prisoner and marched back to be ritually 'tried' in a ghastly parody of their Concerned Woodland Guardians' quest for justice.

The show trials were held in front of the replica rabbit. Psycho, bedecked in a white wig made from the tail of a previous victim, alternated between playing judge and prosecutor, with the minions forming the jury. The hapless rabbits were then tried for a selection of various 'crimes' he had dreamt up, ranging from eating grass and having a white tail, to living in a warren and possessing buck teeth, floppy ears, a big bum or all three.

To maintain the parody Psycho had ruled out the jury's distressing tendency to shout 'Guilty as charged!' before the trial had even begun, and as tonight's victims were lined up he solemnly intoned: 'You, the Warren "B" Five, stand accused of being rabbits and thereby displaying bunny-like tendencies. For, as the evidence will clearly demonstrate, being of some sort of mind, you did each knowingly, and with malice aforethought, consume multiple blades of grass, an offence contrary to the Keep Off the Grass Act.

'Call the blades of grass,' came a cry.

Psycho promptly tore up a pawful and placed it on the ground in front of him, provoking more hilarity as he questioned it in a deadpan fashion, before supplying its answer in a quavering squeak.

'It was terrible, your honour. There we all were, minding our own business, just growing, when, for no reason, we were viciously attacked. With those teeth, my lord, my colleagues didn't stand a chance . . .'

Abruptly cutting this short Psycho moved on to his favourite role of judge.

'Members of the jury,' he solemnly intoned, 'you may think those ranged before you are kind and harmless creatures, whose intentions are entirely honourable. On the other paw, you may already have concluded that they are nothing but odious pieces of spraint. That, of course, is a matter which I leave entirely up to you.'

'Guilty as charged!' came a cry, earning a minion a heavy frown of disapproval.

'Silence or I will have the court cleared,' Psycho shouted, triggering off another round of giggling.

'Suffice it to say, esteemed members of the jury,' he continued, attempting a deep, authoritarian voice, 'that on the clearest evidence I have ever heard, the correct verdict on the accused could not be more obvious.

'It is clear to me that these five dangerous and devious subversives, whose individual wickedness is without parallel in my experience, have been indulging in a vile conspiracy of the gravest nature. However that, of course, is yet another matter which I leave entirely up to you.'

The verdict, as usual, was instantaneous and unanimous and the minions waited on tenterhooks as Psycho took off his white wig. Slowly he replaced it with a black moleskin cap made from a different kind of victim. As he did so he recalled the interrogation of the creature that had provided it, which still puzzled him. The mole had promptly confessed his name was Marcus and seemed only too eager to give all the information he possessed. Yet, as he babbled on, Psycho had been unable to understand a word of what he was talking about and in the end had had to execute him without having learnt anything.

Psycho knew his next move was not going to go down well. He had devised a number of punishments, which he varied according to his whim. Always popular was 'Kiss my arse', in which minions took it in turns to sit on the guilty parties' faces, farting copiously as they ground their loins into quivering noses. Not so popular, but universally acknowledged to be more useful, was 'colony service', through which the convicted were employed for mundane tasks like keeping down the grass.

Tonight, however, he was going to disappoint them. What the minions liked best to round off the night's events was for the guilty to be made to run the gauntlet to the end of the Plateau, where they were thrown to the howling mob waiting in the river below and simultaneously drowned and dismembered. However, Psycho had now become preoccupied with a new interest of animal experiments, for which he wanted all five. He was carrying these out strictly in private, with genuine curiosity about what he could discover. So far he had only proved elementary conclusions, such as rabbits being unable to hop with broken legs, or see without eyes, but he had high hopes for more sophisticated programmes in the near future.

'You have all been found guilty, and rightly so in my opinion,' he pronounced, eyes gleaming. 'I therefore sentence you to be remanded for tests.'

He waited for the expected angry cries.

'Except for you,' he added quickly, pointing at the biggest of the five.

Mollified, the excited minions ran to set up the gauntlet, while the muscle-mink marched the remaining four off to the prison Maxi had constructed in his barracks.

46

Survival of the Noblest

'Although I didn't take it as seriously as she did, I was as appalled as Raka,' Owl told Burdock. 'You know as well as I do that this olive branch business is all a load of pellets.'

'I'm afraid it is in real terms,' Burdock sighed heavily. 'How wonderful if life was as simple as that. But I have to admit you're right.'

'So the dove's no use?' Owl sought confirmation, pleased to have secured such ready agreement.

'Not in the kind of practical way you would understand,' Burdock replied. 'But she will still be playing a vital part in symbolising our CWG beliefs.'

'I can't see how,' Owl said.

Then he saw the potential side morass looming and quickly switched to Big Arse's personal situation.

'The dunnock petition is just as much pellets, isn't it?' he inquired.

'I do quibble with the precise wording as it stands,' Burdock replied calmly. 'But that's an easy enough matter to clear up. What it will do is provide a focus for reasoning with the mink.'

'So let a dunnock go and do it,' Owl burst out, his anger already overtaking him. 'Why volunteer yourself? You know it'll get none of us anywhere. If you were as stupid as the rest we wouldn't be talking, so why not send some idiot in your place? How about Cowslip?' Owl had taken particularly against this large and ugly doe, with an even bigger bum than Burdock's, who was incongruously named after one of the most beautiful flowers of the meadow. She was younger than Burdock and her unashamedly feminist stance added particular fuel to yet another CWG obsession. Owl felt she had more of a down on him than most, presumably because he was both male and a predator, and had noticed several times that she pushed herself forward to criticise anything vaguely positive. She seemed to be a past master of making grandiose statements that sounded convincing until you examined them, to find no meaning that at least he could understand. The thing that got most under his skin though was her silly grin, which he found unbelievably irritating. She wore it almost continuously, as if her sole intention was to put on a show which used clever words and a superior expression to mask what always translated into a distinct lack of action.

Burdock looked at him as if he was a simpleton.

'I'm not at all sure that she in particular would be all that keen,' he said, smiling as if at a private joke. 'But that's not the point, Ollie. You see, I have a personal responsibility to put my body where my mouth is.'

'But you'll have no body left – you'll die,' Owl exclaimed, aghast.

'If I must, then so be it.'

Behind the scenes was an unspoken subtext Owl could partly guess, even though he and the rabbit had never exchanged deep personal confidences. Burdock's mate was dead, his dreams in ruins. The interminable meetings, the lobbying, the clandestine scheming, the fixing, the machinations – all had come to nought. The arrival of the mink had relegated his Code and Bill to irrelevancies. Far from being a more caring community, Old Wood had been sent back into the dark ages.

The last straw had been the backlash after the mink had selected rabbits for special treatment. There had been whispers among other creatures, brought together through shared relief at not being so singled out, that rabbits brought bad luck. They were fated, it was being said. If it had not been for them the mink would not be in the wood. There had even been a wild suggestion at a fringe meeting that they be expelled, with the consequent nonsequitar that the mink would go with them. Being classed as the main enemy by both sides was more than Burdock could bear.

Ever since he could remember he had been painfully aware there were two sides to his personality. He had been far from his great-grandfather's favourite. That accolade had gone to a gentler brother, who had fallen victim to a sparrow hawk. After that his great-grandfather had been warmer towards him, but Burdock had always known he still considered him too sharp and worldly. He never fully confided in him and was always lukewarm about the meetings, which he had never taken much part in.

'That son of yours is too ambitious by half,' Burdock had once heard him remark to his father, which had hurt. He had gone on desperately trying to seek his great-grandfather's approval, frequently calling on the old buck as he became increasingly weighed down by his cares. In particular, he had questioned him endlessly about how he knew that 'big trouble' was coming, but the Venerable Buck had always merely assured him he would have a part to play in due course.

Burdock had felt keenly that he was somehow being excluded from a whole higher dimension of life. The more successful the meetings had become, the worse the feeling had got until he felt more and more that he had taken the wrong track in life. The parts of the conversation between Owl and his great-grandfather that he had overheard had been the most recent and depressing confirmation that the old buck's fundamental opinion had not changed. Meanwhile learning he was known as 'Big Arse' had done nothing to help his frame of mind.

Now, though, things had changed. With nothing left to lose, he had at last found how to bring about his personal resolution in a way that would earn his mentor's respect, even though he was no longer with them. He would pay due homage to the beliefs his great-grandfather had held, to which in many ways he himself had only paid lip-service. Not only would he put an end to his own misery, but he would turn it into a triumph.

Owl spent half the night trying to talk Burdock out of it, chasing him round so many loops of logic he became dizzy. Eventually it was the rabbit who broke it off by insisting that he must get some sleep, by which time Owl had become exhausted by the endless circles.

'Let me make one last attempt to sum it up for you,' Big Arse said. 'It may be impossible for you as a predator to grasp, but we Concerned Guardians refuse to believe there is a creature in existence who is incapable of listening to reason. Look at yourself. You used to pour scorn on us, but now you've spent the whole night arguing with me.'

That reminded Owl he was ravenous. For once Burdock had got the better of him by hopping around as they talked, chewing on various pieces of vegetation.

'But you must be able to see that Raka was right – mink don't have better natures to appeal to,' he said despairingly for the umpteenth time. 'They won't even listen to you.'

Burdock looked him steadily in the eye, knowing their profound disagreement was increasing their mutual affection and respect, even as it confirmed the gulf between them.

'There is good inside every creature, however misguided they may appear on the surface,' he intoned, almost, it seemed to Owl, as if he was reciting some litany. 'Everything we stand for flows from that principle, and it is my duty now to put it into practice. I can assure you, my friend, that any suffering by an individual such as myself is nothing compared to the greater good that will flow.'

'The only thing that'll flow will be your blood,' Owl said bitterly

He was tired of what sounded more and more like pious muck. Burdock's talk might sometimes contain shades of the Venerable Buck, but this was more like archetypal muddleland.

Meanwhile, although the rabbit might be prepared to sacrifice himself, Owl was no longer prepared to sacrifice his dinner.

'You know something,' he said quietly. 'You're mad.'

'The saddest thing, Ollie,' the rabbit replied, sounding graver than Owl had ever heard him before, 'is that I know I have become saner than I have ever been in my life. And, with all due respect, than you will ever know how to be. I can't really explain it, but somehow I have seen the light. Everything is now clear.'

'Sane creatures know how to stay alive!' Owl snapped back angrily.

'Better like a mink than extinct, eh?' Burdock replied sorrowfully. 'One day, Ollie, you will learn there is more to life than that kind of base predator talk. However hard they try, attackers never win. It is only those with the capacity to suffer and endure who survive in the end.'

'Well don't include me in that victim category,' Owl said in a last retort before opening his wings.

He flew off without another word, to drop immediately, with his normal unerring accuracy on to a vole. This is one sacrifice I do understand, he thought, gulping it down whole. He recalled consuming the Voles Against Violence representative in a similar fashion at his first Chaircreature meeting. He and Burdock had been together then. Now their paths were diverging in a way that left Owl angry and frustrated. He knew he shouldn't be either. Burdock was quite right in saying that it was his life, to live or end as he wished.

And despite Owl's anger, he couldn't help feeling deep admiration for the rabbit's stance. Or maybe that was causing it, he suddenly thought as he took off in search of another furry meal. How wonderful to have such a clear sense of purpose to take you above mere humdrum existence. Burdock had changed, acquiring a nobility Owl was now aware he was envious of – especially as nobility was not something he habitually associated with rabbits.

But then, he supposed, as he had always recognised, Big Arse was no normal rabbit.

47

Petitioned to Death

Psycho had resigned himself to getting nowhere in his attempts to interest Mega in the affairs of the Concerned Woodland Guardians. Whenever he raised the subject his leader was invariably crudely dismissive.

'They're just a bunch of jerks, Psycho! And who cares what a bunch of jerks thinks or does?' he would growl angrily.

Psycho got flickers of interest from Mata, but she still held to her line that it was each individual's choice whether to take an interest in life in the wood, or to remain entirely ignorant. The Marketing Mink, meanwhile, were obsessed with their statistics, while the gulf between him and Maxi just continued to widen.

None the less Psycho soldiered on with his researches on his own. He was routinely interrogating a nondescript field mouse when he found out about the big meeting at the copse. Recovering from his initial anger at not knowing about it beforehand, he quickly extracted the full story of the intended petition. He had struck gold at last.

With a sense of eager anticipation, he rushed along to Mega's holt, only, as he expected, to be hit by the 'bunch of jerks' reaction with a vengeance.

'How many times have I told you not to waste my time with this Concerned Guardians' crap?' Mega shouted. 'Your job is to keep me informed about the minions here, not the morons who live out there. Maxi runs the coneycide campaign, so keep off his grass.

'I've told you — if you're that interested in rabbits you can spy on them in your spare time. Just don't bother me about them ever again, do you hear?'

Psycho sat unperturbed and let it wash over his head. Then he set out to exact his revenge.

'As you wish, Mega,' he replied casually. 'But now I'm here, I just thought you might be interested to know I've discovered the Guardians are coming to see us.'

'Coming to see us!' Mega gasped incredulously. 'See us about what?'

'They're going to bring a petition.'

'What sort of petition?' Mega demanded angrily.

'A petition about us,' Psycho grinned. 'Some bollo about how awful we are, how we're wrecking the place and how we must therefore go away.'

'Well, we're not any of those,' Mega replied ungrammatically, his anger increasing. These jerks seemed to think not only that they owned the place, but that they had the right to tell everyone what to do. 'Are they stupid enough to think we'll take any notice?'

Psycho grinned more broadly. Being a connoisseur of bollo, the petition was dear to his heart and now he had his leader on the hook.

'I'm afraid they are,' he said, shaking his head in mock sorrow. 'Amazing, isn't it?'

He stopped and let a long pause elapse.

His leader breathed heavily as he continued to fume.

'Oh, there is one other thing, Mega,' Psycho eventually smiled, dropping the remark as if a mere afterthought. 'I have reason to believe that the petition bollo will be delivered, here to the Plateau, by the head rabbit personally. You know, the one you missed at the meeting.'

'What?' Mega roared, leaping to his feet. 'I thought you were supposed to be clever, Psycho? Why didn't you tell me that in the first place?'

Because I'm clever enough to enjoy winding you up, Psycho smiled to himself unctuously as he watched his leader striding furiously up and down. He knew full well that he had touched a raw nerve. His leader was still smarting from the way the 'big bastard', as he referred to him, had slipped through his clutches.

'What are they saying, Psycho?' he had regularly asked after the incident.

'I don't want to make too much of it, Mega,' Psycho would reply with malicious satisfaction. 'But I am afraid some are still saying that if you're the almighty leader, how come you couldn't get your act together?'

'The insolent bastards!' Mega would roar.

After the massacre Maxi had issued a strict order to all minions that the big-bummed rabbit with the white blaze was reserved for their leader. The instruction had, however, become an increasing embarrassment when he proved impossible to track down. Mega had soon recovered much of his ground through the spectacular kill of a squirrel, the pack gasping in admiration as he followed it from tree to tree until he finally panicked it into losing its grip and it dropped for him to dispatch it triumphantly.

But Psycho was fully aware that the big rabbit still loomed as a serious piece of unfinished business.

'So he's coming here, is he?' Mega ruminated. 'You've done well to find this out, Psycho, very well indeed.'

Mata had reminded him again recently that to get the best out of the little runt he must praise him more. While knowing she was right, he still found it difficult.

'I shall make sure you get more rabbits for your experiments,' he promised.

Psycho smiled, knowing that privately Mega found these embarrassingly pointless. It was the same with the show trials, which he felt were somehow demeaning and only allowed to continue because of their popularity with the minions.

'Meanwhile, Psycho, you must keep this entirely between

us,' he added. 'If that big-arsed bastard is coming to see me personally, it'll be me who'll give his personal reception.'

'Naturally, Mega,' Psycho smiled. 'And I'm sure you'll get it right this time.'

He gulped as he saw his leader turn apoplectic.

'You can trust me absolutely, Mega,' he said, hurriedly leaving.

Giving Maxi strict orders he was not to be disturbed, Mega closeted himself away with a malicious scowl on his face. The whys and wherefores of the petition bollo didn't interest him. It was just more jerk activity, inexplicable and boring as always. He was concerned with a personal grudge that he was going to deal with on a one-to-one basis.

But how? Suddenly he rubbed his paws together with delight. He could settle his old score by taking the minions right back to Psycho's cat-tail bending at the launch of the coneycide campaign!

I'll show you a double spin, you rat, he thought, cackling in anticipation.

'The big rabbit's on his way, my leader.'

Mega leapt to his feet, pushed past Psycho and hurried to the front of the buzzing group at the edge of the Plateau. The rabbit with the white blaze and the big arse was indeed coming up the slope, just as Psycho had said he would. But what was that white bird doing immediately above him, and the one flying higher, whom he recognised as the owl his spin-doctor had told him was the true woodland leader?

As the minions fell back he could see they were looking to him. They were utterly gobsmacked at the way the rabbit was making his unerring way towards them with no attempt to conceal himself. No-one had ever marched boldy towards them like this — especially not, of all creatures, a coney!

'What is it, some sort of joke?' they asked each other in amazement.

'Here comes breakfast!' a wag suddenly shouted.

'And tea as well!' another cried in reference to the dove.

Maxi hurriedly emerged from his barracks and joined the babbling group.

'I don't understand it, Mega,' he confessed, smoothing his whiskers. 'Maybe it's a trap – or the coney's gone mad? Whatever, allow me to sort him out for you.'

By now, despite his foreknowledge, Mega felt shivers running up and down his spine. As the minions also sensed, there was something eerie about the way his particular personal enemy was moving so dispassionately to what he must know was certain death. Where did he get his nerve from? For a moment Mega regretted he had not allowed Psycho to inform him more about how the Concerned Woodland Guardians' minds worked. Could it be, after all, that they knew something mink did not?

Whatever, it was too late to think about it now.

'Hold them all back, Maxi,' he ordered. 'And get the cat-tail down. I'll deal with this.'

Burdock chose dawn for what he sensed would be his first, and last, pilgrimage. He had returned to his burrow to spend the night alone, sleeping little while he communed with his dead great-grandfather and mourned his lost mate. Since Dandelion had been killed he had welcomed his underground existence, moving from one warren to another to stay a step ahead of the mink pack. There had been solace in the company of others, and much warmth from being with so many comparative strangers.

But all the time he had mourned for his lost mate, only fully recognising now she had gone how much of a companion and a support she had been. He had worked so hard for her, as well as for himself, he now knew. Her implicit trust in him had never wavered and she had uncomplainingly pandered to all his wishes and desires. Lying in their once-comforting burrow reminded him of the amount of happy time they had spent there together. Without her he felt surrounded by an echoing well of loneliness.

He had fortified himself by thinking of the Venerable Buck. His decision to take the petition had been made without any thought of political advantage, which had first surprised him and then become increasingly obvious as he thought back over his life. It was political thinking that had inexorably taken him so far away from the real truths, the truths that mattered. Now he felt he had returned to the track his great-grandfather had always been on. He was almost light-headed, as if a heavy load had been removed from his psyche. Lots of things he had thought important dropped away, and to his further surprise he realised he was not even particularly interested in who would succeed him. In a return to old political-think, he had a shrewd feeling Cowslip would be the front runner. If so she was welcome, even though he found her in many ways quite obnoxious. It no longer concerned him. As with his great-grandfather, the whole meetings thing had become a minor matter compared to the individual and personal reckoning he was embarking on. The fractured and argumentative proceedings, with everyone squabbling for personal advantage, had gone, to be replaced by an all-pervading feeling of serenity. At last he had found his balance and squared his own equation. It was more than just having nothing to lose. As dawn approached he realised he had come through that, to reach a position where he could do nothing except gain.

Knowing he was ready at last, he hopped outside to greet the clutch of anxious CWGs waiting to see him off. His good-byes were curiously unemotional, even to Owl, who pleased him by his offer to fly above and lend support, though both knew there would be nothing he could do. Owl in turn was initially pleased to find Raka also turning up.

But as Burdock set off, the dumb blonde dove fluttering above, Owl soon found the rook was not joining in the assorted cries of good luck. Rather than giving support, Raka had come determined to have the last word.

'Doom! Doom! You're both doomed!' she cawed as she flew above the petition-bearing duo, until eventually Owl dive-bombed her enough to shoo her away. In the silence that followed he circled above, seeing how all other creatures had melted away. He felt a heaviness in the air, as if a thunderstorm was imminent, although the a mackerel sky of high cirrus clouds disputed it.

The portents felt bad and he was appalled at the way Burdock's fellow CWGs, while ostensibly wishing their leader well, were so studiously avoiding putting themselves at risk. It might be understandable for earth creatures, but birds would be in no danger, so long as they stayed airborne. He had expected some – especially the dunnocks who had thought up the petition in the first place – to fly alongside the rabbit leader. But as they trotted out a succession of feeble excuses he realised they had never had the slightest intention of getting themselves more involved.

Burdock, meanwhile, savoured every nuance and gradation of the wood as he hopped steadily along. Even the pain in his shoulder had miraculously vanished. He felt physically, as well as mentally, at ease. Everything – the sounds, the smells, the sights – sprang into extra-sharp focus as he was overwhelmed by a wave of affection for the wood and all its inhabitants. He could already feel that he was leaving it to enter a world of his own – a bubble of peace that nothing, or no-one, would ever disturb.

Then, as he reached the slope at the bottom of the Plateau, he had a sudden fit of nerves. He paused prior to the final ascent. He had taken no heed of danger on the way, knowing instinctively he would be allowed to make his passage unhindered. He began treading methodically up past the holly bush. He had already seen the sentry scurry up to the Plateau and knew he was to be allowed on to it for his moment of truth. He would try to present the petition, which he had reworded himself, although he had no great expectation of its outcome. But whatever happened, he would have held true to his great-grandfather's principles and done his very best, while he still nursed the faint hope that if only he could get a dialogue going something might come of it. Concerned Guardian beliefs must prevail.

Arriving at the top, he stepped gingerly on to the short grass and hopped gradually forward, trying to shut out the ghastly image of the replica rabbit and suppressing a natural instinct to run. He could see the main body of the mink being held to one side, while their leader – the one who had attacked him at the meeting – advanced towards him. In his mouth was the black and orange tail that everyone knew came from some unfortunate creature outside the wood.

When the mink was close enough for him to sniff its rank smell, he extended his paw in greeting.

'I come on behalf of all the woodland creatures to reason with you,' he began.

That was as far as he got.

Quick as a flash, the mink leader whipped behind him, jumped on his back, and inserted the black and orange tail under his throat. Burdock made no attempt to resist as he began pulling ferociously. There was little he could do anyhow to shake the mink leader off, he was clinging so strongly. His head now pulled right back, he could see out of the corner of his eye the fierce face, with its flattened ears and wild stare.

'I've been waiting for this, you bastard,' the mink hissed. 'Now shut up and die!'

Burdock's senses reeled. He was choking!

'I forgive you, for you know not what you do,' he managed to gasp out.

There was a furious roar and the pressure increased.

The watching minions cheered as the rabbit's eyes bulged and his tongue slowly emerged until, with a loud crack, his body went limp. Stepped proudly backwards, their leader brandished the cat-tail, demonstrating how he had bent it into a distinct curve. Then, to a mighty roar of approval, he placed it on the ground and jumped up and down on it until it was straight again.

'Mega Mink! Mega Mink! He's the mink! He's the mink!' the pack chanted deliriously.

All this time the dove had been flying above, branch in beak. Owl had already noted that, in the absence of olive, she had chosen sessile oak.

Now, apparently judging her moment to have come, she fluttered down on to the Plateau.

It happened so fast Owl almost missed it. The head mink swung back the cat-tail, brought it whistling forward and, with one enormous blow, knocked her head clean off. It flew across the clearing, while her truncated corpse jerked briefly and then fell over, red blood welling out bright against the snow-white feathers. The mink leader sauntered over to the head and inspected it with interest. Then he picked it up in his mouth and, with one large gulp, swallowed it whole. To the accompaniment of more delighted roars from the pack, he retrieved the sessile oak branch, walked to the cliff edge and threw it into the river.

Then, giving everyone a broad grin, he disappeared into his holt.

'Rule Minkmania!' the pack thundered out as the cat-tail was hauled back to hang from its branch. 'Minkmania rules the wood, Rabbits ever, ever, ever Shall be food!'

Listening from inside his holt, Mega was delighted at the impact of his dramatic gestures. Yet he also felt unnerved. He had not really expected the rabbit to turn up, and when he did there had been something uncanny about his appearance. Mega had felt an urgent need to defuse him, which was why he had been so determined not to let him say his piece. As it was, he reckoned only he had heard his last words. 'I forgive you, for you know not what you do,' indeed! How dare he say that to him! Forgive what — being a mink? He'd shown him forgiveness!

As far as the pack was concerned the way he'd played it should have done the trick. He hadn't given the rabbit time to mention whatever petition bollo Psycho had been babbling on about. Meanwhile the minions weren't going to waste their time speculating on the motives behind what had looked like an obvious suicide trip. It had only been a stupid coney, after all. Instead their admiration would be reserved for what he had done. From the noise outside he could tell they had already switched their attention to dragging the corpses across the grass, ready to throw over the cliff edge. He would stay inside and let them get on with it.

There was a rustle at the entrance as Mata came in.

'Weird, wasn't it?' she remarked. 'I suppose Psycho told you they were coming?'

'The rabbit, yes. But not the dove,' Mega admitted grudgingly. 'But you're right, Mata, it was weird. Did you understand it?'

'Not completely, Mega. But I've listened to Psycho more than you about what he's been discovering since we got here. It's interesting, I must confess. I never thought about it before, but what he's been explaining to me is that there are all sorts of different creatures here in the wood, with equally different ways of looking at life – and death. Like him, I'm now prepared to recognise there is no constant which every creature has to subscribe to. We've got our way, while other creatures have theirs. And who's to say who's right and who's wrong? It's the same with the truth, Mega – for you, and everyone else, it's whatever you perceive it to be.'

'Well that bastard rabbit didn't perceive anything that got him very far, did he?' Mega said irritably. Mata was back to her riddles. 'What did you think of the way I dealt with him?'

'I think it was right from your – and our – point of view,' she agreed. 'But where it got the rabbit depends entirely on where he was going.'

'Nowhere,' Mega said shortly, deciding not to confide the 'I forgive you' statement. 'Rabbits aren't clear about where they're going, like mink.'

'Aren't they, Mega?' she asked, looking at him thoughtfully. 'Do you really think that rabbit, acting in the way he did, wasn't completely clear? Or do you think he just got here by accident, having not thought it out at all? And what about you? Were you completely clear, or were you just reacting without really knowing why? Maybe it's never occurred to you, but it could be we, not they, who don't really know where we're going.'

'It hasn't occurred to me,' Mega replied, his irritation increasing. Until this moment he had been happy with the result. Now Mata was spoiling it by raising all sorts of doubts in his head. 'And it's not going to start now,' he added defiantly. 'I'm like all creatures with any sense. I just get on with it.'

'Get on with what, Mega?'

'Living, Mata,' he snapped. 'Isn't that what we're here for?'

'Not just living, Mega,' she said scornfully. 'I thought you told everyone we were here to be free.'

'Exactly Mata. And freedom is what they have all been given.'

'Exactly, Mega.' Mata's tail had now bushed up and she was, if anything, more angry than he was. 'But it hasn't occurred to you, has it, that most of the minions weren't looking for freedom to do anything? They only saw freedom as a negative, the freedom not to do things? They wanted to be free of living in the cages, eating their filthy slop, using the latrine pit, having to suck up to the Keeper. All they knew was what they didn't want – not what it was like outside.

'But now they are here don't tell me that they're clear about where they're going. They're not going anywhere that I can see. They're just rushing round mindlessly killing everything.'

'They're being mink!' Mega roared, beside himself. 'And what's wrong with that?'

There were times he thought he was the only one who understood what was going on.

'And the rabbit was being a rabbit, Mega!' she yelled back, her face thrust into his, whiskers bristling.

Mega got up to leave. He wasn't going to put up with any more of this stuff.

'Look, Mata, if some manky old rabbit is quite clear that he wants to get on with dying, he's welcome to it,' he shouted. 'But as far as I'm concerned nothing's changed: live or die – whichever you choose, they're both a simple enough business.'

'Only as simple as you make them, Mega,' she said in a infuriating last word as he stomped out of his holt, to be greeted by a cheerful shout from Maxi.

'Shall we chuck them off now, my leader?'

'Wait for me,' he shouted, running over to the Waterama slide and splashing down into the water to join his jostling fellows.

As the rabbit corpse came tumbling down he shoved the others aside and seized it in his mouth. He pulled it under and stayed down for as long as he could, anchoring himself on a branch near the bottom, his vision increasingly obscured by an inky cloud of blood. Eventually he dragged it to the surface by its head, to find Maxi grinning fiercely beside him as he gasped for breath.

'Tug of war?' he inquired, grinning back.

Maxi promptly latched on to a leg and they began to pull.

As the minions splashed alongside, cheering them both on, Mega felt a tremendous wave of exhilaration. This was real life – doing things, not Mata's interminable faffing about where everyone was going and whether they were clear or not. He was clear enough about this bloody rabbit. There was only one place that was going, and that was under.

He dragged the corpse down again, this time managing to pull Maxi along with it.

As the singing started Owl saw that was to be the end of that. He had swooped down low as Burdock was being strangled and with his acute hearing picked up his final statement, which had been even shorter than he had expected. Now he would never know what the petition had finally been redrafted to say. Not that it made any difference, he thought, as he wheeled round and flew back to the beech.

Ula had just woken.

'What happened to the floppy then?' she greeted him with a yawn.

'He was killed,' Owl replied shortly.

'The dove?'

'Her as well.'

'Told you,' she replied triumphantly. 'It serves both the fools right. Now you won't be bothering with their pellets any more.' She rummaged in the bottom of the nest. 'And about time, too,' she added gratuitously. 'Because it's your turn to sit on the egg. From what I can feel going on inside we're going to have a youngster soon to keep us busy.'

'It was really sad, Ula,' Owl tried to explain. 'The head mink didn't even allow either of them to get a word in edgeways.'

'Which only goes to show he's got more sense than you,' she replied nastily. 'How many times have I told you that talking gets you nowhere? Let's face it, we could all do the same as that ridiculous rabbit if we were as demented.

'Anyway, I'm going out now. I don't want to hear another thing about it – ever.'

She gave him a perfunctory peck on the cheek and flew off, leaving Owl feeling particularly low. She could have been a bit more sympathetic, he thought to himself. For all that the delegation had been a total disaster, it had stirred up a curious mix of emotions, which he needed to share with someone. The roundness of the egg was some comfort in reminding him he would be a father again. Maybe Ula was right in thinking he had got too involved in other creatures' business, but he was still feeling pangs of sadness as he mentally reran Big Arse's pitiful demise.

He was determined not to feel guilty, though. It had been Burdock's clear choice and Owl had done everything he could to stop him. As he would have liked to explain to Ula, you had to admire any creature with the courage to die for what they believed in – and die so horribly at that. It didn't matter how misguided they were. It was the same with the dove, dumb blonde though she had confirmed herself to be.

'I forgive you, for you know not what you do,' he thought. It was a strange statement when the mink leader had obviously known exactly what he was doing. But then, Burdock had demonstrated how he been just as clear – more clear, Owl suddenly realised. Big Arse had created the event. The mink leader had merely reacted to it.

There was a splash on the branch beside him and to his astonishment Owl saw he had unconsciously shed a tear. He must be getting soft in his old age! Either that or he was tired out. For the other thing uppermost in his mind was that the debilitating effect of the mink was filtering through the entire woodland system. Even Ula, for all her attitude that the mink were something they had to live with, complained that hunting for their required intake of voles was taking longer and longer. With a chick to feed it was going to take longer still. It all went back to those conversations with the Venerable Buck: the shaky paw, the interconnecting lines in the dust, the long words – balance, interpendence, symbiotic relationships. Now that Owl understood more of it, he had a sinking feeling that the failure of Burdock's initiative had been the next stage in a process which was eventually going to take all their food away. The mink leader could not have demonstrated more comprehensively how there was to be no negotiation.

Owl had done his bit in fulfilling his pledge to the Venerable Buck. He'd presided over CWG meetings, helped Burdock force through the fur and feather motion, tried to stop the petition being presented, then, when that had failed, had at least had the decency to go along. But what could he do now? Call a special meeting of the Dead Vole Society? He already knew how pointless that would be. Raka would simply be ecstatic at being vindicated, while Boris, Freddie and any others would just toe Ula's line and repeat that they had to live with the mink.

He rearranged himself on the egg, thinking of how the incomers had introduced a new and ongoing element of butchery into the wood. But all predators – including himself – and even omnivores, were just as bad in many ways. He was a killer too and, like the mink, he didn't finish all his meals. He still remembered his mother constantly scolding him for not eating up his claws.

Anyhow, with the rabbit show now over, he at last had the headspace to consider the other matter pressing urgently on his mind. Hardly ever having seen a human in the wood before, over the past couple of days its inhabitants had been watching more and more of them cross the bridge, walk up the Long Field and enter through the five-barred gate. They had brought with them strange devices on shiny legs, along with wooden stakes, which they had then knocked into the ground. They had hung these with brightly coloured tapes, which now flapped and clacked in the wind as a constant reminder of their alien presence.

Owl had not been able to discuss any of this with him, but Burdock was so preoccupied with his own preparations.

A quick chat with Boris had only served to increase his sense of foreboding.

'There's no point in talking to you while you're still messing around with tossers,' Boris had said grumpily. 'But I can tell you that I smell trouble, Ollie. Freddie's looking into it. Why not try him?'

The fox, however, had been strangely elusive and when Owl had asked around, nobody else had professed to know anything. It was like with the mink, he thought – the same 'don't want to know' attitude coupled with trying to pretend they weren't there. However, Owl had been struck by a horrid thought. What if this human invasion, and not the mink, was the big trouble the Venerable Buck had foreseen? If that was the case, with what Owl had seen the humans were capable of doing to the landscape, the animal intruders would pale into insignificance.

His thoughts turned to the contents of the warm egg. He was about to be responsible – along with Ula, of course – for bringing a new creature into the wood. What was he going to tell it – that life, once such a simple and happy business, had become increasingly fraught with difficulties? That the future looked as uncertain as when storm clouds were banking up on the horizon? Or that nothing was wrong and Daddy was just digging his own pit by making life less and less easy for himself?

His ears, which had already caught wafts of shrieking emanating from the Plateau, now picked up the sound of singing. The mink were marching – striding up and down, up and down, an occupying army celebrating its latest success. That was now total, Owl had to admit. But for how long were they here to rule? Were they now about to face their own nemesis, from an enemy greater than any other creature? Were they to join the woodland creatures in being subjugated?

He would have to wait for the answer to reveal itself, he thought, as he stared morosely out at the greening treetops. But not, all his senses warned him, for very long.

PART IV

48

How is the Mighty Fallen

'Stay away – or they'll get you!'

Owl's father had drilled the message into him about the humans from the first moment he could remember. Ula had got the same from her parents, as had Boris and Raka and everyone else Owl knew. For the humans were the most fearsome predators of all, their parents had emphasised. They were so clever that no creature could ever grasp the extent of their terrifying battery of weapons, lures and tricks. Never, ever, must any creature be tempted by the array of goodies they appeared to have on offer. No matter how alluring these might seem, every single one was designed solely to subjugate other creatures to human power.

Shortly after Owl had learnt to fly, to ram the point home his father had taken him out one evening to the outlying fields.

'Look at these animals,' he said, indicating the cud-chewing cows and grazing sheep. 'We call them the "semi-domestics". The humans have led them into a stupefying existence, in which they are given their food in return for being trapped behind fences and wire. See how they've lost their freedom to move as they wish.'

He had pointed out the unnatural sharp lines that enclosed them.

'It may look like a soft life, son,' he said grimly. 'Everything they need is provided. They don't have to do anything. But really their lives have been taken away so completely they don't even realise what happened. Every creature in the wood would rather starve than give up control over their destiny like that.'

The interface with the humans wasn't quite as black and white as a magpie though, he had gone on to explain.

'You'll find birds prepared to flirt with the danger they pose. Some – like those raucous seagulls who flock here during bad weather – are quite blasé about them. It's the same with many of the migratory birds who come here in the summer. Birds, of course, are relatively safe in the air, compared with earth-bound creatures. But as far as you're concerned, son, the message is always the same "stay away or they'll get you".'

He had then taken young Owl to look at the hard stuff beyond the river along which the humans' volvers rolled.

'Stay right away from this as well,' he told him sternly. 'You may hear earth-bound mothers telling their children never, ever, to play on it. Watch, and you'll see what they mean.'

They waited close to the side of the rollway, until a volver came hurtling along at terrifying speed, the valley reverberating to its roar. Like everything to do with humans it had unnatural sharp contours and garish colours. The evening sunlight bounced off it so brightly Owl had to screw his eyes up to prevent himself being blinded. His father repeated the exercise later, when it was fully dark, and young Owl was blinded again, this time by the searingly bright lights the volvers carried. And terrified. How could anything move as fast as that – not even a peregrine falcon?

Finally his father had pointed upwards at the boxes that rumbled from time to time through the sky, leaving white lines behind them higher than any bird could fly.

'We're sure those are the humans as well,' he said. 'They're too straight to be natural. It all fits, anyway, when the humans seem so determined to dominate everywhere and everything. But, my son, always remember that you've been lucky enough to have been born into Old Wood. No-one has ever known why, but apart from one human who visits occasionally with a yellow dog, the others leave us alone.

'That doesn't mean you must ever forget the cardinal rule though. Now, what is it?'

'Stay away or they'll get you,' Owl repeated dutifully, taking the point.

In a way – although he hadn't mentioned it to his father – he hadn't needed it drummed into him. He had already been given the same message by his own instincts. As he began exploring a wider and wider area round the wood he had increasingly come across the humans and always sensed the same thing – that any contact with them would be bad. They frightened him to death, in a way that no other creature did. He didn't know why, as he knew so little about them, yet neither did he want to acquire any greater knowledge of their ways. That would only involve him with them more. Without thinking, he knew they were best avoided at all costs and left as a mystery. All the other creatures in the wood, he found out when he grew up, felt the same.

But by the time a long volver stopped by the bridge one bright morning, the wood as a whole already had a sixth sense that its seclusion from this fearsome predator was to be shattered for ever. In the half a moon since the failure of Burdock's petition more humans had kept on coming. Now, as a smaller, yellow volver was unloaded off the back of the long one, alarm calls echoed through the trees and glades. A pair of wood pigeons, flying over for a closer inspection, rushed back to report that the yellow volver was different from the ones that usually went along the rollway. Looking down through the trees, the creatures felt their foreboding increase. It coughed and grumbled into life, greasy black smoke pouring from its top and as it started to move they saw what the pigeons had meant. This volver had unusual long feet, that squeaked uncannily like the sound of the mink chittering. And it was wheeling round, rumbling across the bridge and coming up the Long Field, followed by a more normal volver carrying humans with shiny white heads.

They were laughing and joking as they got out to approach the five-barred gate, shut for so many seasons that it was quite overgrown with scratchy brambles. The previous humans visiting had all used the stile. But now the gate itself was being dragged back on its hinges.

'The volver's invading the wood,' came startled cries.

As it started up the Ride the cries multiplied.

'It's coming to get us,' came panicky shouts.

'Listen to it roaring – it's angry!'

'It's a monster!'

'It's going to eat us all up!'

'Look, it's tearing up the ground to dig everyone out!'

The panic veered between the general and the particular. No creature could rid itself of the underlying fear the horror was coming to get them personally. Yet their observations told them it was making a more general attack. Either way, the point was that it was here and to many of the woodland inhabitants it was the largest thing they had ever seen. For insects with vantage points only a fraction above the ground, it seemed to tower above even the treetops. Its long feet did not move along harmlessly, like those of the normal volvers on the rollway, but bit into the ground like vicious claws, leaving behind twin lines of raw earth. More awe-inspiring still was the great silver blade on its front, which was now pushing up curls of grass and earth as easily as peeling the bark off a silver birch.

None of the woodland creatures had ever experienced such power so directly. It felt greater than the most violent thunderstorm, while for the trees and plants standing in its way it was proving more devastating than the strongest gale. Unceremoniously the digger was flattening stout saplings, previously flexible enough to bend before the most howling wind. It was even toppling medium-sized trees, scattering insects in profusion, only for its tremendous weight to grind their bodies into the dirt. Underground inhabitants like worms, sensing it coming, were trapped, unable to burrow deep enough to escape being crushed as it compressed the earth above them.

'It's killing everything,' came more cries. 'It's coming to get us next.'

Yet at the same time, after the inital mass panic, a sense of reason returned. More level-headed creatures now began to see that, far from rushing about eating everything, like the mink, the yellow digger seemed to be pursuing a different mission. It was ripping out the vegetation in the Ride, even as it flattened out bumps and undulations. In a sudden lurch in understanding a new frisson of fear ran through the wood. The digger was making the Ride into a rollway!

After driving a rough swathe through the thickets beyond the five-barred gate, the digger backed down amid more mighty roars and pushed the crushed vegetation into an untidy heap. The white-headed humans now brandished things which began to make hideous buzzing noises, cutting through the deeper roar of the digger to set the creatures' teeth on edge. Panic set in again as the buzzers' whirling teeth began slicing through the pile of trunks and branches as easily as caterpillars munching through leaves.

The feared attack on the wood had begun.

Faced with a crisis greater than they had ever known, the creatures naturally gravitated to its centre, Mighty Oak.

Owl, leaving Ula with the egg, flew over to find Cowslip already on the Stump.

'Where have you been?' she shouted furiously as he dropped on to his Chaircreatureship perch. 'Couldn't you see we had to hold a formal meeting immediately?'

Owl grimaced at her. After the death of the only two rabbits he had any time for, he had monitored the power struggle to become Burdock's successor with considerable disgust. As far as he could tell, it was more about personal aggrandisement than about upholding any principles. On that basis, and with his jaundiced view of her, he was surprised to learn that Cowslip had come out on top. Not, he had thought at the time, that it made any difference to him. If it had not been for this emergency, as he had already promised Ula, he would never have had anything to do with the CWGs again.

'Get on with it then,' he scowled at Cowslip, sitting there angrily while she bleated on with her silly grin about how they must all remain calm.

But she didn't get far. All the time assorted birds flew in

to shout that the digger was heading up the Ride, directly for them.

'It's following us!' the cries started.

'We were right! It is coming to get us!'

'It's going to eat us!'

Alarm gradually turned to panic, until even Cowslip abandoned her homily and joined the creatures in running for cover. Meanwhile the digger moved inexorably up the gentle slope, flattening everything in its way, until it burst triumphantly out of the undergrowth. Squeaky feet festooned with brambles, it performed a victory circuit of the deserted clearing before drawing to a shuddering stop under Mighty Oak. With a final roar, it abruptly fell asleep and in the sudden silence they could hear its body making sharp ticking noises, while the air above wavered with the heat it threw off.

A human clambered down from its back and greeted his fellows with the shiny white heads, who seemed more jolly than ever. They all laughed as one held up the body of a rabbit that had died of fright and made eating motions, before casually tossing it into the bushes. Then they settled round the base of Mighty Oak, just like the CWGs at their meetings, with one, to the creatures' horror, even perching on the Stump itself. Extracting food from bundles of shiny stuff they began eating it, meanwhile drinking from containers they burst open. After they had finished, they put white sticks in their mouths. The transfixed creatures froze, gripped by a new and more fundamental terror, as the humans lit the white sticks with flames. A pungent smell of burning drifted across the clearing, tickling sensitive nostrils and triggering everyone's natural instinct to run away. But, even though their hearts were pounding, they stayed glued to their hiding places by horrendous fascination.

The humans woke the digger again and it wheeled round with another plume of black smoke, killing many of the dimwitted insects who had gone to investigate it. Then it set off back down the Ride, felling more saplings as it widened the line it had already drawn. As its roar receded the humans carrying the fearsome buzzers strolled round Mighty Oak's massive girth, pointing up at its branches and drawing white marks on its trunk. Then, without warning, they attacked it. The creatures quaked as they saw the buzzers biting into the bark, sending shards spraying out in huge arcs. A terrible rending noise filled the air while piles of yellow sawdust formed on the grass, turning a darker and more ominous hue as the teeth cut through the sapwood into the tree's heart.

The humans widened the initial narrow wound to a gaping cleft before moving round to the opposite side of the trunk and beginning to cut again, this time more slowly and carefully. At that point many of the watching creatures scurried sur-reptitiously round to get a clearer view, thereby inadvertently saving their lives. For, as they peeped out from their fresh vantage points, they saw Mighty Oak beginning to list.

'It's falling!' they gasped, unable to believe their eyes.

'It can't!'

'It's not possible!'

Mighty Oak was not merely the meeting place for Concerned Guardians. It was the proudest and greatest tree in the wood – its central symbol. It had been there for hundreds and hundreds of seasons, as far back as anyone could remember. As such it represented the continuity that held them all together. More than any one thing, it stood for what they believed in. The humans simply couldn't just walk in and destroy it!

Or could they? The creatures looked at each other in trembling fear.

Just then there was a loud creak and the angle of lean became more pronounced. The humans sprang backwards, while the stunned woodland creatures held their breath. Mighty Oak was toppling. Or was it? For a moment the massive bulk of the great tree tottered in suspended animation, as if making a last effort to regain its balance. Then it crashed irrevocably to the ground, its momentum twisting it sideways and its branches snapping with ear-splitting cracks as they drove into the earth.

With a last shudder, it lay still.

'Oh no!' every creature gasped.

The humans lit more firesticks and strolled over to inspect their handiwork. Then they walked out of the clearing and back down ruined Ride, laughing and joking more loudly than ever.

After the humans had rolled away in their volver, the creatures crept out and gathered round the wreck of their former totem. The shock of the disaster had been so great that everyone – even CWGs – was reduced to silence. Cowslip seemed the most shattered of all and just sat, looking dumbfounded and making little keening noises. Others, devastated, walked the tree's enormous length in huddled little groups, sniffing the redolent and ominous tang of fresh-cut wood. Heavy sap, oozing from the ruptured end of the trunk, broke the awed hush as it dripped on to the ground with heavy plops. Owl even imagined he could hear a communal sigh coming from the freshly opened leaves, already drooping now the life-force was no longer being pumped into them. Of the tree's previous majesty all that remained standing upright was the shattered bole, ending in an ugly mass of jagged splinters. Like other birds, Owl was reminded of the solitary elm in the outlying fields which had been blasted by lightning the previous summer. But this was far worse. There was a gap – not just in the sky, where the light breeze now passed silently without those massive limbs to obstruct it. An emptiness had opened up in all their lives. Something had gone forever, and they all knew it could never be replaced.

Just as dreadful was the portent it had set. Even on its side Mighty Oak was gigantic, its branches towering above them and spreading out for vast areas on either side. All the creatures goggled at the thickness of its trunk as they reverently touched it. Yet the humans had not only destroyed it, but destroyed it so quickly, and with so little effort.

'Well, I for one can manage without it,' Boris eventually broke the silence by announcing bravely, still shaking his great head in dazed wonder. 'At least it'll help to shut the tossers up now they've lost their meeting place for ever.'

'Don't you have any feelings?' Cowslip snapped back, breaking out of her trance. 'Can't you recognise that this tragedy affects us all equally?'

Of course Boris could, Owl thought, recognising how the

crassness of the badger's remark was his way of trying to come to terms with the event. He was just about to intervene when Ula, having temporarily abandoned their egg, landed beside him.

'You should see it from above, Ollie,' she said quietly. 'There's a massive scar. It looks as though the wood's had its heart ripped out.'

Owl could already sense that. Destruction on this scale was hard to comprehend, but it would be for the birds most of all that the wood would never look the same. The gap would always be there, a constant reminder of the power of the humans and the vulnerability of the little woodland world. Mighty Oak had been shattered as surely as a snail dropped by a thrush.

'I'd better get back, Ollie,' Ula said, jerking him back to their primary responsibility.

'Ula's right. We can't stand here all night,' Boris harumphed. 'I've got important things to do as well you know.'

They all had, Owl thought, catching Raka's eye. The rook, he knew, also sensed the speed with which change was about to overwhelm them.

'The humans have put down their marker, haven't they?' she murmured uncharacteristically quietly.

'Just like the mink did,' he remarked, the image of the Big Clearing massacre suddenly flashing into his mind.

By now the creatures were beginning to creep quietly away, still stunned to silence by the enormity of the event. Owl knew most would spend the night quaking in anticipation of what was to come next. He could feel a shiver running up and down his own spine at the very thought.

Now the humans were here, it was not only everybody in the wood who was under threat. It was everything as well.

49

Kitted Out

The next morning everyone was quivering and trembling when the humans arrived. All except for a group of woodlice. Ever curious, they had crawled inside the things the humans had drunk from and sucked up the dregs, only to first double up with hysterical laughter and then abruptly collapse into comas. While everyone else braced themselves for the fresh invasion, all they could think about was their dreadful headaches.

And while no single thing could ever equal the shock of Mighty Oak's destruction, over the next few days the cumulative effect of the buzzers and the yellow digger was even more shattering. Even more worrying was the way the humans worked to a pre-arranged plan the creatures could not fathom. The only thing clear was that they were establishing their base in the Big Clearing. After the buzzers had sliced up Mighty Oak's branches, the digger pushed the trunk to one side to make way for a trail of volvers carrying heaps of stuff up the Ride. Every evening the creatures inspected new unnatural objects with hard sharp edges and bags and packages that contained all manner of funny-smelling substances.

Meanwhile the CWGs had collapsed into nervous indeci-
sion, until Cowslip eventually emerged to fudge the issue by
proclaiming it would be best to wait.

'They might just go away,' she suggested one evening with
a kind of knowing foolishness. 'You never know what's going
to happen, do you?' she added hopefully. 'In the meantime we
must all exercise restraint and be patient. It would be extremely
unwise to do anything that might upset the humans, wouldn't
it? That could make things much worse.'

Owl felt unbelievably irritated. Even Dandelion wouldn't
have been that naive.

'Why don't you send the humans a petition?' he asked nastily.
'Or have you run out of doves?'

Cowslip glared aggressively at him.

'The trouble with you predators – and males in general – is
that you're always talking about doing things, when there's
nothing to be done. Discussing any course of action would be
premature at this point. We Guardians are open-minded enough
to consider all options, which is absolutely the correct thing to
do. It would be in the interests of everyone if you adopted a
similarly responsible attitude.

'There is one other thing,' she added in an irrelevant aside
that had Owl grinding his beak in frustration. 'Have you noticed
that the humans doing the damage are all males? I think that
says a lot, don't you?'

'It says that females like you can't cope,' Owl retorted
sharply.

Yet he was aware that nobody really knew, or had any way
of knowing, what it all meant. He did not pretend to be any
wiser than anyone else, although like them he could see that
the humans were fanning out their activity. Every day, as the
yellow digger roared and squealed about, pushing down more
trees, the Big Clearing became bigger.

Meanwhile, whatever the humans' motives, Owl could
feel the woodland community fracturing. All the creatures –
including to his surprise even Ula and Raka – were withdrawing
into themselves, as if trying to avoid taking any knowledge
on board. Despite his dislike for her, he could sympathise

with how Cowslip took refuge in her mixture of inaction and meaningless platitudes, all hidden behind that silly grin. It would be pointless trying to get her to admit it, but underneath she, like him, was more scared than she had ever been. The mink threat – which continued much as before – was something involving creatures a bit like them. But the all-conquering humans engendered such an awful feeling of powerlessness that the entire wood was just giving up. Owl had to admit to himself he had no more desire to face the developing tragedy than anyone else. Yet something – maybe his conversations with the Venerable Buck – compelled him to dig deeper.

He tried Boris.

'If we could only find out what the humans were up to, then at least we'd have a better idea of where we are,' he pleaded. 'Surely you must want to know?'

'Certainly not,' Boris replied firmly. 'I know what I know and that's all I want to know.'

Owl wasn't really surprised by the reply. He might have expected the stick-in-the-mud badger to be more determined than most to close his eyes to what was going on.

'Anyhow, I do know what they're doing,' Boris grunted unexpectedly. 'Freddie told me. And I'm not thanking him for it either, I can tell you. So before you say anything else, don't ask me, ask him.'

Owl hadn't talked to Freddie since the humans had arrived. In fact, like most other creatures, he had hardly seen him. Even before the human invasion, suspicion had been growing that the fox was in contact with the mink – or 'establishing a bridgehead with the interlopers', as Cowslip had put it. Since then everyone had given him a wide berth.

Owl was still hesitating about contacting him, when the fox resolved his dilemma by appearing below the beech just after the humans finished work for the day – the same time that Burdock and his rabbits had used to call.

Ula was just as scathing about him as she had been about them.

'He's up to something,' she muttered suspiciously, peering

down as if trying to define his motives visually. 'Don't you know by now that you can't trust him?'

'I've got no choice,' Owl replied shortly. 'I need him to tell me what's happening.'

'All you'll find out is what suits him,' Ula said dismissively. 'On your own head be it.'

She gave him a little peck and hopped back inside the nest.

'Be careful, though. I'd hate to lose you,' she called from inside.

Owl flew down feeling touched. It was a long time since he could remember her making such an affectionate remark. Maybe she too at last recognised that something had to be done, no matter how risky? Had her mind been changed by the birth of their scrawny little chick, now huddled, chirping feebly, in the newly repaired corner of the nest? To Owl's disappointment she was a female, when he had wanted so much to have a male that he could teach, as his father had taught him. A female would be much more Ula's responsibility. But the event had turned both their thoughts towards the future. Neither dared think what fate awaited her.

'I knew as soon as I saw the humans stick the white square on the bridge,' Freddie said casually.

'When was that?' Owl asked, already angry.

'A couple of moons ago.'

'I never saw it.'

How could Freddie could have been so lackadaisical?

'You wouldn't have done, Ollie — or most of the others. It's still there, but it's hard to spot. And you know how everyone stays well away from the hard stuff. Anyhow, it wouldn't mean anything to anyone. It doesn't look like much, I can tell you.'

'Do you understand it?' Owl demanded.

'I'm not exactly sure that I do, Ollie,' Freddie admitted. 'But I've been asking around. Plenty of foxes have seen ones like it. They say they're some sort of sign the humans put down to claim territory. Afterwards they either develop habitations for themselves or lay down more hard stuff.'

'Which is it in our case?' Owl asked. He was here to find out the worst.

'I'm not sure, but my guess is the former,' Freddie shrugged. 'After all, we like living here, the mink like it, so why shouldn't the humans?'

How can you be so flip? Owl wondered. Yet at the same time he recognised the fox was probably the most knowledgeable of them all. No wonder Badger didn't want to know. His sett wasn't that far away and what could any of them possibly do if the humans had decided to move in? It was the stuff the worst daymares were made of.

'My further guess is that the actual development is bounded by the fluttery tapes,' Freddie added. 'But human activity is still bound to spread right through the wood. The whole place is stuffed, Ollie.'

Owl, recognising how this chimed with his own instinct, felt sick to his stomach.

'How long do you think we've got?'

'A few moons before they're actually living here. The works are just going to get bigger though, so essentially the wood's already a goner.'

How could he sound so matter-of-fact? Owl wondered. Didn't he care at all?

'Why didn't you mention any of this before?' he demanded angrily.

'Why should I?' Freddie shrugged. 'I'm entitled to my secrets, aren't I? Anyway, we foxes don't share your "stay away" mindset about the humans. These days we're thinking we're actually better off closer to them. There's a lot to be said for having them on your doorstep, you know. You can get an awful lot out of them if you've got the right attitude.'

'But what about the hunt? It exists specifically to kill you,' Owl asked, firing his standard jibe. There was no way Freddie could actually want to live closer to humans, whatever he might say.

'We keep hearing that the humans in the big habitations

are quite different,' Freddie went on, refusing to rise to the old bait. 'You may find this hard to believe, but they actually seem to welcome us. It's almost as if they've developed into two distinct species.'

He hesitated and Owl thought for a moment he was about to confide something. Then he seemed to change his mind and went silent.

'I can't think why any humans would welcome you,' Owl remarked uncharitably.

Freddie scowled.

'What's so awful about rubbing along with your fellows?' he demanded. 'And fellows the humans are, whatever you and the others may choose to pretend.'

'Just like the mink, eh?' Owl could not help remarking. 'You must know what everybody's saying, Freddie. Why don't you admit it?'

'We've been in touch,' Freddie said defensively, looking shifty. 'What's wrong with that?'

Everything, thought Owl, although he refrained from saying so.

'What do the mink think of the human invasion?' he asked instead. 'Are they going to leave?'

'I wouldn't know, Ollie,' Freddie replied airily. 'We're not that close. But if you do want to drive the humans out don't ask me how, ask them. They're the only creatures here who might have any idea.'

'How come?' Owl asked suspiciously.

'Well, they lived with the humans once, so they know how they work,' Freddie replied. 'And if they were clever enough to escape from them, why shouldn't they be able to get the better of them again?'

Owl was suddenly on his guard. As Ula had pointed out, this meeting was too convenient to be just a coincidence. Freddie was leading up to something. Yet at the same time he was raising a point which had also vaguely occurred to Owl. The wood as a whole had long since accepted the weasels' and stoats' explanation of where the mink had come from.

'Why not cut a long story short by levelling with me, Freddie?' he suggested.

'You know that's not my style, Ollie,' Freddie grinned disarmingly.

There was a long pause. Owl felt both frustrated and, for the first time, slightly hopeful.

'Come on, Freddie,' he wheedled.

'OK, Ollie, I'm bringing you a message from Mega, the mink leader,' the fox replied slowly. 'He wants you to go and see him to discuss a plan he's got.'

Owl stared blankly for a moment before he recovered his wits. Of course — if there was to be communication it was bound to be Freddie who was in the middle.

'Either we abandon the wood to the humans, or we meet the mink, Boris. Can't you see that the way things are we need them more than they need us?'

Owl had not expected it to be easy convincing his stubborn old friend. None the less he was still reaching the end of his patience. He had now spent half the night trailing round with the badger after he only agreed to talk on condition his normal routine was not interrupted.

'I'll kill the two-timing bastard if I see him,' was his furious reaction to confirmation that Freddie had definitely been consorting with the mink.

Ula was just as disgusted. Exactly how much the fox was in with them, no-one cared. As Raka acidly remarked, it made little difference. If you wanted to keep your friends, you couldn't run with the wood and hunt with the mink.

'I don't see what they can possibly offer us,' Boris grumbled again as he scraped away great lumps from an earth bank to uncover more worms. 'How many times do I have to tell you, Ollie, they're no good.'

'I know that as well, Boris,' Owl repeated for what seemed the forty-third time. 'But who else is there?'

'And you're saying the buzzards have definitely agreed to go?' the badger went on, his voice now muffled by a mouthful of writhing pink bodies.

'Absolutely, Boris,' Owl said, for what was definitely the forty-third time. He had to admit he himself was slightly surprised, although delighted, by their ready agreement. They would help give the delegation the heavyweight edge that would convince the mink they were nothing to do with Concerned Guardian froth.

'And none of the tossers are involved?' Boris asked yet again, chomping noisily.

'Absolutely not, Boris, I promise you. They know nothing at all about it.'

Burdock had been one thing, but the prospect of Cowslip arrogantly lecturing the mink was one Owl hadn't dared think about. Any meeting with them had to be strictly predator-to-predator, a point the inclusion of Boris would drive home even more strongly. Owl had studiously, and successfully, avoided Cowslip, while experiencing momentary twinges as he thought how pathetically irrelevant Burdock's brave gesture now appeared.

'You must come, Boris,' he begged. 'You must want to hear what the mink have got to say and we're bound to get something out of it.'

'Well, what ever it is, I won't agree with a word of it, I can tell you that now,' Boris grumbled. 'So don't expect me to be polite, that's all.'

'Don't worry, Raka and I will do all the talking,' Owl rushed to reassure him, sighing with relief. It had been a long haul, but worth it. The mink leader's invitation was supposedly one-to-one, but the badger and the buzzards would be the minders he felt he needed.

'All you'll have to do is just look heavy, Boris,' he repeated. 'You know how the mink respect you.'

'And so they bloody well should,' the badger harumphed. 'I didn't get where I am today by allowing scum like them to mess me about.'

The other creature Owl decided to rope in was Raka who, like Boris, took some time to convince. But the rook did help to settle Owl's mind by filling in one piece of the equation that Freddie had not mentioned.

'I can't understand why the mink aren't just moving out,' Ollie complained to her. 'I would if I didn't have any allegiance to the wood.'

'You're a solitary bird though, Ollie – apart from Ula, of course,' Raka cawed back. 'It's easy to make decisions when you're on your own. In a group there are all kinds of things to consider, different viewpoints to be taken into account. That's what half the squabbling in the rookery's about. It may seem chaos to you, but it's how things get done when there's more than one of you.

'And there's one thing that may have escaped you. Like most of us, the mink are either about to have, or have just had, their babies. How's yours, by the way?'

'Fine, thanks. She's a female. We've called her Blinkie,' Owl said, thinking again how her birth had increased his depression about the future. 'But what is it that you're trying to say, Raka?'

'My guess, Ollie, is that the mink can't move, even if they want to. On top of that, I'm not even sure whether they do. The wood's been as good for them as it once was for us. One way or another, I reckon they're as stuck here as we are.'

'Or else Freddie's setting us up,' Owl added bitterly. If the mink leader really wanted to meet him, why had he confused matters by employing such a slippery intermediary?

'Freddie wouldn't do that,' Raka pronounced definitively. 'That would mean him having to take sides.'

Owl laughed as he began to relax. Good old Raka! By now he had forgiven her outrageous performance as Burdock had departed. After all, he had to admit that her prediction had been entirely right. The rook's approach could sometimes be a little too no-nonsense to allow for any of the subtleties, but at times it had a lot to recommend it.

Raka's assessment of the state of play at the Plateau was more accurate than she realised. When the digger first appeared the colony panicked, with the minions rushing about yelling that the Keeper must have run them to earth.

'He's coming to get us!' they shrieked.

'Custard must have given us away!'

'He's going to take us back to the cages!'

'We're done for!'

Once again, Mata was the first to react. Whipping round, she ordered Maxi to send in the muscle-mink. Then she waded in herself alongside them, snapping and snarling as they gardually herded the wild-eyed minions into a group under the cat-tail, where Mega bellowed at them to get a grip on themselves. Finally, when Maxi's scouts ran back to report that the humans had stopped at the Big Clearing, they calmed down.

By then Mega had adjusted. One of the prime reasons for their being in the wood was the absence of their hated enemy, but the humans visiting recently had signalled what might follow. This invasion might the last thing they wanted, but it did not altogether surprise him. The humans were, and always would be, the ultimate enemy — not just of mink, but of all creatures. Every excursion the pack made served only to underline how completely they dominated the rest of the world. That they should now come into the wood was just more of the same. Mink theory dictated the simple answer — the pack should simply move out. Except that it couldn't. The real world had intervened. Amid wild joy, the first litter had been born outside captivity half a moon ago. The celebrations had been muted when it was found to be so premature that only one sickly infant, since named Minimus, had survived. But four healthy litters of between three and six had followed and the rest of the females — bar Mata — were expecting any moment. Staying put for the present was now unavoidable. As all the leaders agreed, the well-being of the mothers and potential mothers was paramount. For if the colony could not successfully reproduce, there would be no future for it anywhere.

A desultory discussion about the possibility of driving the humans out followed.

'Why don't we organise the woodies, my leader?' Maxi suggested. 'They're so terrified by the humans they've no idea what they could do if they tried. I know many are pathetic, but there's the basis for a damn good army there. If I could get my paws on them and lick them into shape, I guarantee the humans wouldn't know what had hit them.'

It was an intriguing prospect, which they had batted about at length. But no-one was able to suggest how they could get the co-operation required before Psycho took great delight in killing the whole idea off.

'Who would you back, the woodies or the humans?' he asked Maxi spitefully, following through before he had a chance to reply. 'I'll grant you the wood might win the first time because of the element of surprise. But the humans would only regroup and rearm. Then they'd be back and everyone would really be in the spraint − including us.

'As it is they don't even know we're here, my leader,' he added, appealing direct to Mega. 'If we stay at this end of the wood and keep our heads down when they're in it, they never will. All we have to do is synchronise our killing time with their working time.'

Mega nodded at the logic of this, while Maxi, scowling, moved on to the urgent need to increase security. Then MI butted in.

'But we can use the woodies, great leader,' he cried, quivering with uncontrollable excitement. 'You see, 2 and I have come up with a marketing proposition which they could help us carry out. And are you just going to love this one! We know you're going to find it as immensely innovative and hugely exciting as we do!

'Will you all please stand aside, while 2 proudly makes what we already know is our most dramatic presentation yet!'

50

Blood and Bones

As Owl looked down at Boris plodding towards the Plateau in Burdock's ill-fated footsteps, the picture floating in his mind was not of that unfortunate rabbit being throttled, but of the way the mink leader had knocked the dove's head clean off. Owl had once witnessed a peregrine falcon, flying at some insane speed, take out a pigeon, and felt the utter finality as he watched the victim dissolve into a cloud of feathers. It had been the same watching the dove's head arc across the Plateau, while its truncated body remained incongruously upright. The falcon, of course, had only been doing what falcons did. But the mink leader had unleashed an extra element of aggression Owl had never come across before. It was different from his swooping on a vole. There had seemed a driving force behind it denoting a hidden dimension – a taste for cruelty so strong and insistent it was almost as if the mink leader had no choice but to assuage it. Owl shook his head to clear it, only for the image of the dove's head to be replaced by the sea of blood at the Big Clearing massacre. At least he wasn't trying to delude himself like Cowslip, but it was not a healthy state of mind for such a vital meeting.

They had chosen dawn as the best time to approach the Plateau. Owl had spent the night mulling over various scenarios, starting with the hope that they would begin by being greeted with the respect due to fellow predators. Now, as a cry of 'Who goes there?' brought Boris up short, Raka moved as agreed to deal with the expected challenge.

'We have come to meet your leader,' she cawed, feeling slightly foolish at speaking into thin air as her eyes searched for the cry's origin.

'Before you can proceed you must give the password,' replied the voice, which she now located as coming from inside a large holly bush.

'As woodland creatures we do not know the password,' she cawed back.

'In that case you cannot proceed,' the voice replied.

Raka cursed, her suspicion that mink could be fundamentally stupid confirmed.

'We have come to meet your leader,' she repeated, indicating Owl, Boris and the buzzards with her wing.

There was silence.

'I don't hold with all this pissing about,' Boris growled.

Owl frowned down in reply. They had all vowed to tread softly during the first delicate interface.

'Do not proceed − on pain of death,' the voice then came again, before a mink broke cover and streaked up the slope.

A particularly fierce mink face, sporting bristling whiskers, now presented itself at the edge of the Plateau.

'Attention!' it barked. 'Our great leader, Mega, has said you may enter. However for security reasons you must each give today's password, which for your further information is "blood and bones". Got that?'

'We accept,' Owl hooted back, muttering it as he swooped down to be the first to land. He watched Boris appear and push past the fierce-looking mink without saying a word, and breathed a sigh of relief when he was allowed through. At least they had arrived in one piece.

It was their first opportunity to examine the mink's power base at close quarters and Owl was particularly curious about the mink emblem Mega had used to throttle Burdock, which obviously had some huge significance. He was stepping forward to examine it closely when the mink with bristling whiskers brought him up short.

'That's not for the likes of you,' he snarled. 'Stay there while you await our great leader.'

Owl decided not to push it. The little group was now surrounded by a circle of excited mink and both sides examined each other with great curiosity. The mink were certainly fierce enough, Owl thought as he saw how eagerly they sniffed the air and how quickly they moved. He gave a warning hiss to make sure they appreciated that they were meeting one of their own kind, while the buzzards hooded their eyes and glared menacingly.

The pack was already retreating slightly when the fierce mink suddenly bellowed to clear a path and an imposing mink stepped into the middle of the circle.

'I am Mega,' he said simply. 'Thank you for coming.'

Owl didn't need to be informed this was their leader. Mega might be no larger than the others, but he had an easy way of carrying himself that denoted both authority and supreme confidence. Yet, as Owl stared into eyes as black and unblinking as his own, he thought he saw a weird spark, a kind of cold craziness that chilled him. His mind filled again with the picture of the dove's head arcing through the air.

He snapped out of it.

'I'm Ollie,' he said, and introduced Raka, Boris and the buzzards in turn. 'And before we start I'd like to make it clear we don't normally like meetings. We think they're boring, they waste time, and they don't get anything done. However, we do recognise that there are times when you have to talk.'

'I'll agree with all that,' the mink leader smiled wryly. 'We've had a lot to talk about recently as well. So why don't we put our differences to one side and have a chat? Can't do any harm, can it?'

The question triggered a horrid cackle from a little mink with an extremely pointed head, who had now taken up station beside his leader. Owl took an instant dislike to him.

Yet that only reinforced his feeling that he and the mink leader both recognised there was a rapport between them. Mega, in turn, warmed to Owl's down-to-earth approach. It was ironic, considering he was a bird, he smiled to himself. But it did at least confirm Psycho's favourable report that he was someone they could do business with. He could see the wisdom of bringing the others along, especially the big badger and the cruel-looking buzzards, although he had a shrewd idea they might have been the idea of this intriguing black rook. Psycho had reported the rooks were clever in the way they lived and worked together so effectively.

'As you must be aware, we've got as big a problem with the humans as you,' he addressed Owl straightforwardly. 'So I'd like you to hear an idea of ours, which might get rid of them.'

'After which you lot can piss off as well,' Boris unexpectedly interjected.

Owl winced, while Mega turned with interest towards this huge black and white animal with its distinctive striped muzzle, whom the minions referred to in awed tones.

'That's not exactly what I have in mind,' he said mildly.

'Well you bloody well should have,' Boris harumphed noisily. 'I'm a plain creature and I didn't get where I am today by beating about the bush. So let me tell you now, we're not your manky rabbit tossers come to see you with some petition bollocks. We're the predators who've always ruled this wood and we're fed up with you wrecking it. We're only here because of the humans. They may be scum like you, but compared to them you're mere chickenfeed.'

The fur on the watching mink bristled and there was a chorus of low growls. Nobody called mink chickenfeed! As for scum!

'Tell him where to get off, Mega,' came a cry as the muscle-mink stepped aggressively forwards. All eyes turned to their leader, while Boris growled back and scratched a deep groove in the ground with his enormous forepaw.

But Mega merely made a placatory gesture, indicating he was letting the insult ride. It was predictable enough after all. Not even the most boneheaded minions believed they were actually popular.

But Boris was not through yet.

'It's you mink tossers who should be getting the whacking, not the humans,' he shouted, lumbering towards the fierce-looking mink who had demanded he say the password. He only stopped when he had shoved his great muzzle right into his face. As they both stood rigid, eyes blazing, the buzzards unfolded their huge wings.

Owl, seeing how ugly things were getting, nodded at Mega to imply they should combine to defuse the situation.

To his gratification, the mink leader took his cue.

'That's enough, Maxi,' he ordered, stepping up to Boris without an apparent trace of anxiety as the fierce-looking mink backed off a couple of paces.

'It might be better if we discussed this in private,' he suggested, turning to Owl and Raka.

'Cool it, Boris,' Owl entreated, playing his part. 'We mustn't fight among ourselves when we're here to face our common enemy.'

He went on imploring until Boris made a snuffling withdrawal, at which he and Mega nodded in mutual respect.

'Why don't we retire to my holt?' the mink leader suggested.

Owl hesitated. He would feel more comfortable staying outside. He wasn't even sure he could cope with an enclosed meeting. Yet the idea was a sensible one if they were to avoid more confrontations, while he didn't want to lose face in front of the mink leader. Anyhow, logic told him that if the mink truly wanted to attack the delegation, with their numbers they could do so just as well outside as in. If Raka came with him he wouldn't feel so claustrophobically isolated.

When Mega countered that in that case he would bring in the pointy-headed mink, whom he now introduced as Psycho, the deal was struck.

'You're not going off with those two pieces of scum, are you?' Boris grunted, incredulous. He and Owl might go back a long way, but this was the last straw!

Owl took him to one side. Would he please stand guard outside, along with the buzzards? he begged. You never knew what might happen, and Boris was so strong and fearsome!

Eventually Boris, unused to such direct flattery, grudgingly agreed, and Raka and Owl went in. They heard the badger growling as he hunched himself up, willing any mink to take him on. Owl could only hope none would be so foolish. That would be the end of everything.

51

We Have a Market!

O wl and Raka were both fascinated by the prospect of entering the mink leader's domain. Disappointingly, though, they found themselves confined to a small ante-room. It was sparse, simple and, with its low headroom, slightly claustrophobic, although Owl countered this by telling himself it was bigger than his nest in the beech.

Mega attempted to put them at their ease by ensuring they stood where the roof was highest, while Raka struggled to decipher the dim shapes in the gloom, though Owl and the two mink had no difficulty in coping with the low light-level. All four were aware of how delicate a bridge they now had to cross. As non-placatory creatures it went very much against the grain for either side to be considering a partnership. However, as they began to level with each other, they began to appreciate more of each other's predicament.

On a personal level, although he would never have admitted it, Owl found the mink leader unexpectedly spellbinding. In spite of his unsettling eyes, he seemed straightforward and easy to talk to and was more reasonable and open than he needed to be. Owl began to feel hopeful that something useful might come of their mission. Raka was right, the mink leader cheerfully acknowledged – the pack did have to stay in the wood because of their babies. If the woodland creatures wanted to know, two more healthy litters had been born that very morning. Yes, they had escaped from a habitation where the humans had held them in cages, as the weasels and stoats had guessed.

'Mega is the mighty leader who freed us,' the pointy-headed mink pitched in at that point, weird eyes flashing.

Owl looked at him critically. However honest Mega might seem, Psycho was obviously more slippery – devious even, Owl thought. He looked almost like a rat rather than a mink, and those unnatural opaque eyes confirmed all Owl's initial impressions that he was deeply untrustworthy. But he was undoubtedly there for a reason – presumably because he was clever. Yet, Owl thought uncharitably, it was in a Freddie-like way that put him on his guard. Glancing at Raka, he could tell she felt the same.

As if sensing this, Mega took up the running again, while his sidekick went temporarily quiet. Yes, they did know all about humans and how they worked. They had, Owl would be interested to hear, studied them in great depth. Then he relayed the story of how the yellow dog had brought them to the wood in the first place, along with why it no longer came, as well as the further story behind the puzzling mink totem. Finally, questioned about the replica rabbit, he confirmed the coneycide campaign. Then he in turn began to ask questions about the wood, with Raka warily saying nothing while Owl tried not to reveal too much.

But when Psycho took over Owl found him a skilled prober. His dislike for the rat-faced creature intensified as he felt more being wheedled out of him than he had intended. But he soon decided it made little difference: there seemed to be so little that the mink didn't know already. Anyway, most of the questions were about precisely what the humans were doing on the ground. That was information Owl was only too happy to give if it would help.

However when he started his own questioning about the humans' motives, Mega stepped in to halt the conversation.

'It's too long and complicated a story for you,' he said firmly. 'Just take it from us – as if you didn't know already – that the humans are like no other creature that exists. They are driven by some notion they call progress. Even we mink don't fully understand it and you woodland creatures never will. Roughly, though, it translates into their never being satisfied with anything as it is. You've already seen some of what they do as a result.'

'Do you hate them?' Raka suddenly croaked.

'Yes,' the mink leader replied without hesitation. 'After what they did to us for so many generations, probably more than you do.'

'Do you hate us as well?' Raka demanded, to Owl's consternation. This wasn't what they were here for!

'We don't hate you, we just prey on you,' Mega replied, looking amused but slightly perplexed as well. 'Why do you ask?'

'I just wondered whose side you were on,' the rook replied enigmatically.

'They're on their own side, just like us, Raka,' Owl jumped in. 'Can we stick to the point, please. What you're telling us is that we have to take what you say about the humans on trust?' he asked Mega.

'Yes,' the mink leader replied, unperturbed. 'That is, apart from any knowledge of your own.'

'Why should we?' Owl countered

'Because we know,' the mink leader said flatly. 'You see, I've a pair of experts in my pack who used to be extremely close to them. They claim to have a device that will beat the humans at their own game. To be absolutely honest, I'm not sure myself whether it will succeed, although they, as you'd expect, are completely convinced. Why I asked you to come here was to consider the offer I'm making – to lend them to you. You'll have to do your bit as well. But if we work together, they say, we can use one lot of humans to drive out the other. I don't pretend to grasp all the details, but why don't you meet them? Then you can draw your own conclusions.'

He dispatched Psycho, who returned with a pair of dapper

figures. They smiled silkily as they proffered Owl their front paws.

'This is MI and M2, the twins jointly known as the Marketing Mink.'

'Delighted to make your acquaintance,' the pair smirked.

Owl felt repulsed. They both seemed more akin to the creepy rat-faced mink than to their leader, who Owl had a curious feeling shared his distaste for them.

'Not only are the Marketing Mink extremely clever, but they have their paw very much on the modern human pulse,' Mega explained, staring at them disdainfully.

'Indeed, we bring to your cause the modern science of marketing,' the mink pair chorused. 'For, we can categorically assure you, we have a market!'

'What's a market?' asked Owl.

The pair tapped knowingly on the sides of their noses.

'A very good question,' one – was it MI? – replied brightly.

'I can already see you have the makings of an ideal client,' his twin added, chuckling.

'What's a client?'

And so it went on.

The pair were so similar, with their unusually smooth fur and matching white bibs, that half the time Owl was struggled to decipher who was who, never mind wrapping his head round what they were on about. Raka's squint indicated that she too was floundering.

'Why not leave all this stuff to us experts?' one eventually asked. 'Don't worry, though, when we start working together there'll be plenty for you to do, gentlemale and gentlefemale. Without your input, you see, our campaign couldn't even get off the ground, so it has to be a partnership.'

Owl, having already decided marketing was more baffling and jargon-laden than CWGland, reverted to the main point, that it involved co-operation with the mink.

'There's no risk, either now or in terms of future comebacks,' the pair kept repeating. 'No violence, we can categorically assure you.'

Owl felt inclined to believe them as he saw them shudder in

a most unmink-like fashion. They certainly didn't look born scrappers.

'All you woodland creatures will have to use is your heads,' they sought further to reassure him. 'Now, that's simple enough, isn't it?'

Not if you know how simple some of those heads are, Owl was thinking, when Mega broke in.

'Anyhow, that's the proposition. And as MI and M2 have emphasised, we can't give it a go without you. On the other paw, what have any of us got to lose?'

As Raka shot Owl a warning glance he knew they could not reach a decision on the spot. They would have to confer, just like the Concerned Guardians, and this was definitely not the place for that. He stretched himself gratefully as he prepared to leave. The session had been as mentally exhausting as meeting the Venerable Buck.

Recalling the gentle old rabbit prompted him to round the conversation off in what seemed a suitable manner.

'I'm glad we've had this talk,' he said to Mega politely. 'You have my word that we'll consider your suggestion and come back to you.'

'It's been a pleasure,' Mega replied equally courteously.

Emerging from the holt to call off the buzzards, Owl saw Boris frowning heavily. The frown deepened into a scowl as the group of mink followed, smiling.

'One of your friends, eh?' said M2, proffering a paw.

'I'm not so sure about that any more,' Boris growled in reply.

The paw dropped back, to be reproffered to the buzzards, who totally ignored it.

'Well, I'm sure we'll be getting to know each other better soon,' MI said with a hollow laugh.

'Speak for yourself — and your new friends,' Boris grunted, glaring at Owl and Raka.

'We'll be in touch,' Owl said hurriedly.

Owl gave in to Cowslip's pressure for a formal meeting to consider the mink's proposal. It was fair enough when they were contemplating such a serious step, he had to admit, and he could understand the high degree of anxiety the rumours about it had already engendered. Anyhow, as Raka quite rightly emphasised, they had no choice. If the Marketing Mink required the whole wood to co-operate in their scheme – whatever that was precisely – not just the predators, but the CWGs, had to assent before it could go ahead. Owl grumblingly agreed, then introduced his own condition – that she, rather than he, did the explaining. That way, he explained, it would not be seen as coming solely from him.

But what he had not anticipated was that the rook would take delight in doing so in a such a brutally uncompromising fashion.

'The mink confirmed our worst fears,' she stated flatly to the apprehensive gathering. 'The humans are definitely coming to live here. There's no reason to disbelieve that, so we can either watch our wood be destroyed, or give this marketing stuff they have proposed a go. I'm not even going to try to explain it. Owl and I still don't understand it ourselves and the mink said we never will. We've no choice, they've told us, but to take it on trust.'

Owl, up on his branch, winced. Raka might be right, but she was laying it down in a way he would never have dared. The audience now looked even more worried, while Cowslip's reaction was predictable.

'Trust the mink!' the long-faced doe exploded incredulously. 'The only thing we can trust them to do is kill us!'

'Would you rather trust the humans?' Raka retorted nastily.

'Well, not exactly,' Cowslip replied, seeing that she was being led into a trap. 'But you're saying the end justifies the means and that's not the point.'

'What is then?' Raka asked, continuing to pin her down mercilessly.

Owl, looking round, saw to his surprise that some of the audience were now nodding affirmatively.

'That we might be better off not doing anything,' Cowslip replied lamely, peering about for support.

Yet, when the gathering just looked shifty, she and everyone else could see that sympathy for this negative CWG mindset was evaporating.

'Typical!' a bold vole shrieked. 'What have you ever done anyhow?'

'Exactly,' tweeted an equally intrepid wren. 'Speaking for myself, comrades, the thought of the mink scares me to death. But what choice do we have, when the humans scare us even more? At least we know the mink can act. So why doesn't Cowslip come up with something positive as an alternative?'

There was a ragged cheer.

'How dare you talk to me like that,' Cowslip retorted, incandescent. 'Do none of you have any respect for your elders and betters? However, since you insist, I will come up with something positive. I hereby propose that we form a sub-committee to investigate further and report back.'

This limp proposal received equally short shrift.

'In how many moons?' a shrew squeaked aggressively, to more cheers.

'What is there to investigate?' came another cry.

Owl, seeing from Raka's disgusted expression that her patience had run out, jumped at the opportunity Cowslip had just presented.

'I think a committee is an excellent idea,' he enthusiastically congratulated the fuming rabbit. 'Just what we want in the long term. And because you're so good at them, who better to organise it than yourself? We'll consider its findings the moment they're reached. In the meantime, though, in view of the fact that we have so little time, I propose we go in with the Marketing Mink.'

As Cowslip screwed her face up and gave him her filthiest look, Owl thought what a shame it was Burdock was no longer present. He would have been proud of the way she had been so neatly sidelined.

'You can't say fairer than that,' cried members of the meeting, nodding at each other emphatically. Meanwhile, as the wind shifted, large pieces of wood ash started raining down in an acrid reminder of the urgency of the situation.

'You sanctimonious creep,' Raka mouthed, although Owl could see that underneath she was smiling.

He smiled back as he shouted 'Those for!' and watched paws and wings gradually being raised, before going for the *coup de grâce*.

'And you, Cowslip?' he inquired politely

Shaking with rage, the doe slowly raised a paw.

52

Mission Impossible

As marketing required a positive approach, MI and M2 refused to see the woodland creatures as a problem. Rather, they were the toughest client brief ever, a magnificent challenge to stretch the imagination and resources of any marketeer!

As soon as Owl returned to the Plateau with the go-ahead they zoomed across to set up shop in the Small Clearing, explaining that the first thing they needed was more specific information to feed into the bulging data banks already built up for the coneycide campaign and forward eating projections.

Owl dutifully flew round drumming up as many creatures as he could for them to bombard with questions.

'What's your favourite time of day?'

'Which food do you enjoy most?'

'Which is your preferred activity?'

'How do you see yourself in relation to others?'

'Apart from yourself, which creature do you most admire?'

'If you could be any creature in the wood, whom would you choose?'

Although nobody could see any rhyme or reason in the multiple interrogation, they all tried to help by answering as best they could. Meanwhile, the mink recorded the results by making marks on sheets of bark, which immediately aroused Cowslip's suspicions. As enthusiasm for the wood's potential saviours receded, she and her remaining coterie of CWGs had clawed back some of the ground they had lost and now she tried to capitalise on this by bombarding the mink with questions in turn.

'What are you planning to do with all this information?' she demanded. 'How do we know you won't use it against us? Are you aware that many of your questions are highly personal, thereby constituting a clear invasion of privacy? What is the exact purpose of your activity? What precisely is marketing, anyhow? We think you owe us an explanation.'

Oh no, we don't, MI and M2 thought to themselves. They had already agreed how to conduct the woodies' interface. With such unsophisticated folk there was no point in trying to define key marketing tools like 'audience profile', 'ad strategy' or 'market penetration'. Equally fruitless would be explaining the loops of human behaviour they planned to exploit. However, recognising questions were bound to be asked, they had hammered out a strategy to deal with them, which MI now put into effect.

'To answer your last question first, marketing is the twin art of identifying the goods targeted consumers want, then presenting them in the most attractive way,' he rattled off.

'What are the goods?' asked Cowslip, mystified.

'In our case, the wood's the goods.'

'I see,' Cowslip replied uncertainly. 'Consumers?' she went on hesitantly, her brow furrowing.

'I'll field that one,' M2 jumped in, smirking to himself about how easily the rabbit was being bamboozled. 'Consumers are customers, that is, the users of the goods and services we provide after we have first targeted them and then identified what they want.'

'Targeted?' Cowslip struggled on with a bemused expression.

'Targeting is the art of narrowing down from the widest possible field available in order to select the appropriate consumer grouping the goods will be marketed to,' M2 barked.

Cowslip at last had the good sense to realise she had met her match.

'Thank you,' she said as brightly as she could manage. 'I'm sure that's cleared up all we wanted to know, hasn't it, everyone?'

The other creatures looked mystified.

There was a long silence until a pigeon reckoned she had got to the bottom of it.

'The wood's the goods,' she cooed enthusiastically.

'The wood's the goods,' the other creatures nodded sagely, taking grateful refuge in this catch phrase.

MI and M2, their faith in their art confirmed, smiled benevolently. These woodies were going to be even more of a push-over than they had imagined.

'That's right. The wood's the goods,' they endorsed to the gathering. 'That's all you need to know.'

Afterwards Cowslip surreptitiously attempted to regroup by organising a non-co-operation campaign. But she found few takers. Apart from odd die-hards like Boris and the buzzards, who didn't want to know her anyway, the woodland creatures were beginning to enjoy themselves. This pair of immaculately groomed creatures seemed much less fearsome than they had expected. To everyone's surprise, they had even turned out to be exceedingly polite. And while their questions might be bizarre, having your view so carefully recorded made you feel enormously important. Fancy mink being interested in what you thought! It was more than their CWG leaders had been, they muttered.

Amid more unctuous smiles, the questioning continued.

'Our new woodland profile is based on the most comprehensive survey ever carried out,' the Marketing Mink proudly informed Mega. 'Furthermore, we can report excellent progress in our efforts to establish a satisfactory bridgehead with the woodland community. They may be thick, but they're malleable enough and we're getting them exactly where we want them. Look at those.'

They pointed to the small army of spiders crawling about the walls of the holt spinning thin silk lines.

'We didn't even have to ask them, Mega. They volunteered.

And they're just what we need to come up with a positive results interpretation.'

'I'm sure,' Mega replied, looking away from the intricate and baffling patterns before his eyes completely crossed. 'So are you now ready to get on with it?'

'Indeed, great leader,' MI replied enthusiastically. 'This very morning we'll be getting into the really exciting stuff by first formulating our mission statement, then going for what we're really after – our UWP.'

'I hope it goes well,' Mega said, hastily making for the exit. The last thing he was going to ask was what that all meant.

He left MI and M2 feeling slightly crestfallen. Their principal regret about having joined the mink colony at such a late stage was that they had missed being in on the ground floor, when the fundamentals that underpinned any successful business were laid down. Their consolation, however, would be in rectifying that omission with the woodies, as MI explained at dawn in the Small Clearing.

'Ladies, gentlemen and hermaphrodites,' he began brightly, 'the correct way to start our marketing campaign is to establish where we're at. So, who can tell me exactly what we are trying to achieve?'

His audience looked blank.

'What are we here for then?'

A few creatures stirred uneasily on the wet grass.

'Let me put it another way. What's our aim?'

'To get rid of first the humans, then you lot!'

In the absence of any other contributions, Raka had volunteered her view.

Owl glared at her. He had already given everyone a lecture about the Marketing Mink being sensitive, due to being creative creatures. Raka pulled a sour face in reply, but at least went quiet.

'I'll put it as simply as I can,' M2 struggled on in the face of the renewed silence. 'What's our mission?'

'Forget it,' MI hissed sotto voce. 'You're going to have to tell them.'

'No-one knows?' M2 went on, accepting the point. 'Well, our

mission is to save this wood, and that is therefore going to form our mission statement. Any questions?'

There were none.

'Now, what do we need to fulfil our mission statement?' MI cut in. 'We need our UWP.'

The silence remained deafening.

'I expect you were just about to ask,' MI went on enthusi-astically. 'Our UWP, ladies, gentlemen and hermaphrodites, is the goods that will save our wood.'

The audience brightened slightly at this familiar phrase.

'In the modern wood jaw-jaw speaks much louder than war-war,' M2 smiled greasily. 'So we're going to win the humans' hearts and minds. Not only are they going to save us, but they're going to love doing so. And in return we're going to love them back, OK?'

The nods were half-hearted.

'How can we love the humans?' the creatures whispered to each other. 'They're the ones causing the problem.'

'All on board?' MI asked, ignoring the huddled conversations as he rubbed his front paws briskly together. 'Now, let's get our teeth into some material.'

There was a start from the rabbits, while the rest of the audience stared at the ground in embarrassment.

'What's a UWP?' Raka eventually demanded.

After hearing Cowslip so comprehensively demolished she had sussed that MI and M2's key was wrapping things in complex jargon. That was how you marketed marketing. After smiling to herself at the way Cowslip had been beaten at her own game of pompous words and phrases to establish supposed superiority, Raka had decided to fight back by not being afraid to ask, as was her natural inclination anyway.

'Our UWP,' MI rapped out, 'is our Unique Woodland Proposition — the thing our wood has that its competitors haven't and which therefore sets it apart, making it more than any old wood.' He smiled in huge delight at his own pun. 'We require our UWP to be exotic, attractive and, above all, vibrant,' he continued, adding extra emphasis by punching the air with his forepaw.

'Vibrant!' M2 burst in. 'Something bursting with the joy of life! Something beautiful! Something wonderful! Something unforgettable!'

The creatures cheered up a little.

'The beauty of the changing seasons?' a wood mouse suggested timidly.

'Good! More suggestions!'

'The dappled panoply of light thrown by scudding clouds?' ventured a trembling vole.

'Yes! Anything else?'

'The luminosity of daybreak,' Owl hooted. He might as well throw in a contribution.

'The glorious autumn colour,' a chaffinch shouted.

'The great trees in all their silent majesty,' a magpie weighed in.

Answers started coming thick and fast.

'The peace of shady glades.'

'Drowsy buzz of bees on the perfect stillness of a summer day.'

'Dew on a spider's web at dawn.'

'Soaring flight of the skylark.'

'Patterns left by the plough on autumn fields,' Raka cawed, determined not to be left out.

The cries tailed away as the creatures heard MI and M2 tut-tutting irritably. Given their head, the idiot woodies had already careered up the wrong track.

'These are all boring,' they complained. 'The humans have seen them a hundred times!'

'We've seen them a lot more than that and we don't think they're boring. We think they're wonderful,' the creatures shouted back, but apparently to no purpose.

'Marketingwise,' MI informed them harshly, 'you lot aren't even in the ballpark.'

He looked at them sadly, while they in turn looked back helplessly.

'Maybe a really heavy brainstorming session would get things moving,' M2 hissed.

MI rolled his eyes heavenwards, but didn't disagree.

'Because humans only possess flickering attention spans, they require constant stimulation,' M2 explained. 'Which means our UWP has to be something new and different, as well as vibrant. Otherwise they just won't be interested. The difficulty is that our woodland profile has thrown up nothing of note. However we have composed a checklist, just in case we've overlooked anyone. Are there, by chance, any natterjack toads amongst you?'

'Just ordinary ones,' came a croak.

'Red squirrels?'

'Only grey,' came a squeak. 'We got rid of the other lot ages ago.'

'Black kites?'

'Certainly not,' squawked the buzzards.

'Great bustards?'

'How dare you!' the buzzards squawked, having misheard.

'Russian nut-crackers? Red-rumped swallows? Short-toed larks? Blue-cheeked bee-eaters? Pine buntings?'

The improbable list continued, with every answer in the negative.

'What have you got then?' MI finally cried, exasperated.

'Volumes of voles,' came a shrill cry.

'Stacks of shrews,' came an even shriller cry.

'Waves of worms.'

'Convoys of caterpillars.'

'Millions of moths.'

'Billions of bees.'

'Armies of ants.'

'Groups of grasshoppers.'

'Swarms of starlings.'

'Droves of dunnocks.'

'Tons of tits.'

'They're all as common as muck,' MI shouted above the din. 'How can they possibly be our UWP?'

Owl, thinking that this was coming to resemble a CWG meeting at its worst, intervened, partly to restore order but also to put forward his own suggestion, of which he was rather proud.

'Fellow creatures,' he hooted, commanding instant silence. 'We have never pretended to be anything other than ordinary creatures living in an ordinary wood, have we? And is there anything wrong with that?'

'Nothing at all – we're happy being ourselves,' came a shout amid assorted cheers.

Owl rounded triumphantly on the mink.

'Then why not make the fact that it is so ordinary the wood's UWP?' he proposed.

For a second MI and M2 were almost deluded into believing this imposing bird cleverer than themselves. They'd never even considered that. Yet it was a fact that unspoilt woods were becoming rarer and rarer, so being ordinary could be a UWP. What a marketing breakthrough!

But the moment passed as quickly as it had come. This Owl might have a reputation for wisdom, but he could only have hit on something so inspired by luck. There might be the odd occasion in marketing when you trusted your gut reaction, but in reality it was a science, which succeeded by following the rules.

'They haven't a sensible thought in their heads,' MI whispered to M2. 'We'd better take a break.'

Leaving Owl in charge, they went into the bushes.

'Tough, eh?' MI wiped his brow with his paw.

'You bet,' his twin agreed. 'But then we always knew they'd be difficult.'

'Maybe, but I can't believe some of them. Talk about bug-eyed, pointy-headed dingbats.'

'Those revolting toads belching away at the back.'

They shook their heads in wonder that such forms of life could exist.

'Talk about cellular,' M2 sniggered. 'Some of them are celluless.'

Really, though, it wasn't the least bit amusing. M2, who considered himself the more level-headed of the pair, had already detected the first twitch in his brother's right eye that indicated he was suffering from stress. Effective marketing was such a delicate exercise. Both sides had to get deeper and deeper into each other's psyche until they reached joint inspiration. If the clients were hopeless the whole exercise got bogged down.

'There's nothing worth bracketing in the entire dump,' MI remarked, morosely chewing a shield bug that had unwisely crawled on to his front foot. 'There's no choice, 2. We're going to have to import the UWP.'

It was the definitive conclusion both had feared, introducing all kinds of complications.

'You're right, I,' M2 sighed reluctantly. 'Let's break the news.'

Cowslip sprang noisily to her feet.

'You're saying you want us to find a creature from outside, bring it into the wood, and then pretend it's always lived here?' she asked, perplexed.

'You've got the general idea,' MI replied urbanely. 'As I've just explained, you're all too ordinary.'

'But that would be downright dishonest,' Cowslip spluttered. 'We Concerned Woodland Guardians could never be party to a deception as monstrous as that.'

As the flock of dunnocks fluttered feeble support, various insects, dimly perceiving they should be doing something, began waving feelers and mandibles, while MI raised his eyes to the sky. Next the stupid big-arse would be wheeling out her Woodland Code bollocks, not to mention the bloody Bill of Creatures' Rights!

Sure enough, Cowslip was broadening her argument.

'As you may, or may not, be aware, our equality principle states that every individual is as valuable and important as every other,' she announced. 'It would be a fundamental breach to bring in someone new on the grounds that they were "better" or "special". I am therefore sorry to have to inform you that we simply can't allow it to happen. Rather, we insist that our appeal to the humans is based on simple truth and, moreover, made to their natural decency.'

The Marketing Mink, who were sitting with their mouths open, recovered some of their equilibrium.

'Natural decency!' they chortled. 'The truth!'

'And what, may I ask, is wrong with those?' Cowslip inquired huffily. 'A little more decency around here wouldn't go amiss, I can tell you. As for the truth, may I remind you that it is all that we have?'

MI's right eye was now twitching uncontrollably.

'Is it indeed?' he yelled. 'In that case, why don't we tell the humans the real truth — that you're such a bunch of tedious tossers you could all be wiped out tomorrow without anybody noticing, never mind caring. That it makes no difference, except to your idiot selves, whether you exist or not. That, to a creature, you're totally dispensable. That there are millions and millions of others like you — and all just as dull, dull, dull!'

Not just Cowslip, but all the creatures, quailed in dismay. They were wrong in thinking the mink were not so bad after all. The mask had slipped, revealing the true natures hidden under those smooth veneers.

M2 looked equally aghast. However low your opinion of your clients, you never let them know. Otherwise you destroyed the mutual confidence the whole marketing exercise was built on.

'Come away,' he whispered urgently to his twin.

'That's all for the moment, folks,' he announced, bundling MI out of the clearing as fast as he could.

Back at the Plateau he pushed him into their holt and reported to Mega, glossing over the difficulties as best he could. His leader, being in a good mood, let him off unscathed. But next time, he warned, it would be different. The humans were stepping up their activity level. He required something now.

M2, after making profuse promises, re-entered their holt, where his still-twitching brother greeted him with a despairing cackle.

'I've just thought of a new mission statement, 2,' he giggled. 'Mission Impossible!'

53

Beaky Bertha

The next morning MI began the meeting in a determined mood, having decided he had no reason to worry. Owl had explained to him beforehand that the creatures had turned against Cowslip for causing them to incur the mink's wrath.

'Everyone's very willing and interested,' he explained. 'It's just that they don't quite understand what you want them to do. There is another thing,' he went on, indicating the grass around them still littered with dead insects. 'With the best will in the world many creatures here don't possess brains big enough to storm. It was all too much for them and they simply overheated and then expired.

'I'm sure they'll be better now they're getting the hang of it,' he added, loading in the dash of the flattery he suspected would go down well. 'Especially with creative geniuses like you in charge.'

Creative geniuses they were indeed, MI thought triumphantly as he held up a piece of bark covered by a curtain of sycamore leaves. Pausing until he was sure he had everyone's full attention, he then whipped the curtain aside to reveal a drawing of a human face. But no normal human. The creatures gasped in astonishment: this was a monster, with mad staring eyes sticking out on huge stalks that had the frogs and toads goggling in disbelief.

'This is a unique species of human known as a "twitcher",' MI explained, delighted at the success of his dramatic presentation. 'Due to mental aberrations, it has developed a maniacal interest in spotting birds. But the twitcher, ladies, gentlemen and hermaphrodites, is not interested in just any old bird. He demands something special, a bird that is rare. If it is endangered, so much the better. But rarity is prized above all else – as well, of course, as being vibrant. So, let's get our thinking caps on and see what we can come up with.'

'The blue blob,' a hen goldfinch yelled immediately.

'Yes, the blue blob,' chorused the other creatures.

The blue blob was an oddity. It had arrived unexpectedly in the wood one summer day, attracting much attention because of its pale blue plumage. It was quite small, remarkably plump and clearly lost. Nobody knew where it had come from, or what it was doing in the wood, but it had proved incapable of managing for itself. After pining mournfully for a few days – no-one knew for what – it had fallen off its perch and died.

'What's a blue blob?' M2 inquired, genuinely puzzled.

As various tits joined the goldfinch in twittering out descriptions the mink's jaw gradually dropped.

'That's a budgie,' he finally burst out. 'The humans know all about budgies. They aren't the slightest bit rare.'

'They are to us,' the chorus came back. 'We've never seen one before – or since.'

Both Marketing Mink ground their teeth at this infuriatingly inescapable logic.

'Stay cool,' M2 whispered, seeing MI's eye twitching again, before taking refuge in addressing the woodies as if they were children. 'We're going to have to do a bit better than that, aren't we?' he said sternly. 'A budgie's silly, isn't it? Shouldn't we come up with something more sensible?'

'A golden eagle,' one of buzzards croaked.

After escorting Owl to the Plateau the buzzards had lost their previous indifference to woodland affairs, and had quickly run through peregrine falcons, harriers, kestrels and other fearsome winged predators before arriving at their joint judgement. A golden eagle had to be the best UWP. It was rare, endangered, vibrant and above all so large and distinctive that no human — never mind a member of the twitcher species — could possibly miss it.

Risking a bold foray into marketing-speak, the buzzard added, 'We believe a golden eagle's visibility potential to be incredibly high.'

The meeting cheered enthusiastically.

To everyone's surprise, however, MI and M2 responded with a bout of hurried coughing. If the buzzards themselves were already too large and daunting to be on the mink hit list, the arrival of a huge aerial killer, capable of picking up a mink in its talons and whisking it away, would blow their woodland superiority to pieces.

M2 moved quickly to defuse the crisis.

'A very good suggestion there,' he beamed. 'The buzzards deserve a round of congratulations.'

There was loud applause before he held up his paw for silence.

'But I'm afraid there's a serious problem they seem to have overlooked. Can any of you tell me what it is?'

The creatures looked puzzled.

'Well, while a golden eagle is undoubtedly a magnificent creature fulfilling many of our requirements, how precisely are we going to attract one here?' M2 inquired smoothly.

The buzzards stared at him balefully. They'd never thought of that. They knew golden eagles had a reputation for being extremely dour, as well as fierce. And while buzzards themselves were hardly the life and soul of the party, golden eagles were even more unsociable. They lived in remote mountain eyries, as far away from humans as possible. None, presumably, would abandon their voluntary seclusion without some irresistible inducement.

Stymied, the buzzards remained silent, while the hunt for the elusive UWP resumed.

*   *   *

As the meeting got back under way, a hen blackbird called Bertha suddenly remembered what her friend in the next valley had once told her. Why hadn't she thought of it before? she tutted to herself. Trust her, with her scatterbrain! She could never recall anything from one day to the next. But now it was all coming back. Her friend's tale had been of a fabulous creature who had visited the previous summer. He had been so absurdly handsome, so resplendent in his exotic plumage, so proud and cocksure, that when her friend first saw him strutting though a glade she thought he must be some sort of vision. However, as she had recounted with great relish, she had soon found him to be not only real, but real enough to start mating vigorously with her. She had surrendered in ecstasy.

Alphonse, this flying Adonis, had stayed in the wood long enough to run through most of the hen population, before finally departing for home, warmly inviting them all to come and visit him. But, despite their longing, it was such a long way no-one had yet dared make the trip.

'Really, we all should go, old hen. It'd be the trip of a lifetime,' her friend had concluded, dewy-eyed. 'I've never met a cock who was better in the bushes.'

Sliding surreptitiously to the back, Bertha now flew out of the meeting. She was going over to have a word . . .

Bertha arrived back to find the meeting in noisy uproar. She had been in luck. Her friend had confirmed the previous details and then repeated the instructions on how to find Alphonse the golden oriole — for that, apparently, was what he was.

'Take your chance, love,' she had urged. 'I wish I could come with you.' She looked ruefully round the untidy chaos of her nest. 'But I've got to stay here. You go though, dear, and when you find him, remember me to him.'

Working her way unobtrusively to the front Bertha waited for a break in the wall of sound. The Marketing Mink, judging by their frazzled appearance, were near the end of their tether and MI was currently rubbishing the latest suggestion, made by a dunnock.

'What bloody use is a pipit?' he shouted. 'It's duller than

you are — and that's saying something! Look at you all sitting there. There are hundreds of you, yet not one can come up with anything worth talking about. You're all useless, useless, useless!'

The dunnock sniffled miserably, while its fellows studiously looked away.

'We're going to be here all night if somebody doesn't think of something soon,' MI barked peremptorily, looking accusingly at Owl.

Owl had thought of various relatives, especially the snowy owl, a huge white fluffy bird, which he had never seen but was certain scored highly on the vibrancy front. But after the way the golden eagle had been thrown out he wasn't going to risk public humiliation by nominating someone he couldn't deliver. He had a shrewd suspicion Freddie might have come up with a good idea, but he wasn't present — like Boris, who had refused to turn up for the session, declaring it 'tosser-like'.

'I'm not storming my brain for anyone, least of all that pair,' he had added angrily.

The silence dragged on while MI glowered at the audience.

'I think I've found what we're looking for,' Bertha piped up. 'It'th a bird called a golden oriole. And I happen to know where one called Alphonthe liveth.'

There were giggles. Beaky Bertha was the last creature anyone expected to come up with anything. Maybe a dumb blonde dove, with some romantic nonsense. But not a hen blackbird, especially not such a dowdy and unattractive specimen, with her crossed bill and consequent lisp!

MI was no surer himself. But if this golden oriole was as dazzling as Bertha was now going on, he could be what they were looking for. However cocks in the audience now voiced widespread scepticism.

'How will you persuade him to come back — sing to him?' a jay cried raucously.

'I have my wayth,' Bertha smiled mysteriously, provoking more merriment and scorn from the chauvinist faction. But both Marketing Mink also noticed several cock blackbirds winking at each other and opening and shutting their yellow beaks.

What was that all about? they frowned at each other They disapproved of private jokes, feeling they undermined their position.

Then Bertha's suggestion took off as support appeared from an unexpected angle. The hen blackbird belonged to one of the woodland species whose cocks were considered to have all the finery and the fun. In the heady days of the Concerned Guardians hens had continually protested at having to live in such a cock-dominated world and now the old obsession surfaced again. Further fuel was poured on by Bertha's lisp, which in CWGland registered her as officially disadvantaged and therefore even more worthy of support.

'Why shouldn't Bertha come up with the best idea?' hens screeched noisily at the cocks. 'It's typically puerile dismissing it out of claw. But then, of course, you're all worried a golden oriole would outshine you and rule your roosts, aren't you?'

Owl could see that Cowslip, far from joining in, was shifting restlessly from one foot to another. He began to grin as he slowly realised her dilemma. After totally disapproving of the whole UWP concept, she was now being asked to abandon that stance to support the feminist lobby. What would she do? he wondered, fascinated. She had to declare herself one way or the other.

The answer came quickly and, he supposed afterwards, predictably enough. Deserting her previous obsession as though she had never mentioned it, Cowslip slid shamelessly and seamlessly on to the latest bandwagon.

'On behalf of the Concerned Woodland Guardians I utterly deplore the sexist comments being made by these ignorant male chauvinists,' she declared. 'I therefore insist our sister be given the fullest possible backing for her proposal.'

The Marketing Mink listened in near despair. Bertha's supporters were clearly only interested in bolstering the hen lobby. They weren't considering Alphonse's merits in the slightest. None the less, the hen blackbird might have something. And even if she couldn't deliver it personally, at least she knew where to find it. The other woodies might be contemptuous, but they plainly had nothing better to suggest, except for the golden eagle, of course. But that had been comprehensively trashed.

Meanwhile, they had to admit they were desperate. If they failed to come up with the goods they were looking at a massive bollocking back at the Plateau.

'Why not go for it?' M2 whispered.

'Because she's a total dumbo,' MI was whispering back when Raka unexpectedly intervened.

'I'll go with Bertha to fetch Alphonse,' she cawed.

That decided the issue, especially when Owl and other more level-headed males weighed in with their support. When Cowslip stood up to demand a vote MI, prompted by urgent whispers from his brother, stifled the snide remarks that rose automatically to his lips and let her have her way. Even though some cocks defiantly abstained, the verdict was conclusive, with only the buzzards, still miffed about their golden eagle, voting against.

As they made their way back to the Plateau, the Marketing Mink consoled each other that at least they had something positive to report. They had dispatched Raka and Bertha immediately, without waiting for clearance from their leader, and were now facing a nerve-racking delay. In the meantime, however, they could always junk Alphonse if the woodies came up with something better.

'Some chance,' MI commented bitterly, right eye still twitching.

'You never know,' M2 said with a hollow laugh that failed to hide his anxiety.

But what they did both know was that their personal fates, not to mention that of the wood as a whole, now hung entirely by the delicate thread of a particularly randy golden oriole.

As Raka flapped solemnly along her smaller, browner companion below, it looked almost as if they were travelling singly, rather than together – which the rook wished was indeed the case. Bertha, she concluded, was as dumb and witless as members of the meeting had made her out.

'Innit . . . !' she kept exclaiming as they followed the ribbon of shiny volvers along the massive rollway. 'Innit grand flying along? Look at that, Raka! Innit amazing?'

It was indeed amazing, Raka had to admit, as were many things that they saw. Until now she had thought her flock of rooks got around as they went out to cull the fields. But nothing had prepared her for the scale she was currently witnessing. The humans seemed to have turned the whole world into a giant ants' nest of activity. Everywhere teemed with both them and their artefacts, while she already had a splitting headache from the noise that poured up to fill the sky. None the less, determined nothing should divert them from their mission, she remained studiously indifferent to the marvels and mysteries unfolding below them. Not Betha, though. She was simply thrilled. In one bound she had broken free of the constraints of the wood, with its sneering, dominating cocks and stifling hen parties, and embarked on a breath-taking adventure. At last she was living life to the full!

'Innit wonderful?' she sang exultantly. 'Innit marvellous? Innit just too grand for words?'

'Shut up!' Raka bellowed. But it was no use. Bertha was in a world of her own.

Apart from the inane commentary, the day was going well and the pair had now reached the Big Water, which Alphonse had warned was the major obstacle. Although they could see land on the other side, Raka decided to call a halt. It was close to sunset and, never having flown so far in her life, her wings felt as though they were about to drop off. Surveying the landscape, she located a convenient copse and they both drank from a stream before taking up their respective stations for the night, Raka jammed in the crook of a stout sycamore, with Bertha below.

As the darkness closed in, the babbling continued, the 'innits' now replaced by 'wannits'. Raka grunted monosyllables in reply. She realised she hadn't been thinking when she volunteered for the trip. Instead she had made an impetuous and foolhardy gesture. Bertha's description of Alphonse had impressed her, as well as chiming with gossip she remembered hearing at the time, while the brain-storming session had been falling apart. If she had not intervened Bertha would have been shouted down. But now, with hindsight, she could see that virtually all her support had come from the bigoted feminist lobby, which Raka definitely was not a member of. How, she wondered, could she possibly have believed a fluffhead like Bertha could persuade any creature to do her bidding – never mind one as reputedly magnificent as Alphonse? He'd just laugh at her. Worse still, she'd simply bore him rigid. Then what was Raka supposed to do, pick the golden oriole up by the scruff of the neck and drag him back? Just at this moment Bertha was in her perfect setting, she thought moodily, a moonless night that rendered her invisible. Maybe when we get there I should put a leaf over her head, she thought despondently. Meanwhile, she should find out what – if anything – was going on in that idiot mind.

'You must be looking forward to meeting him,' she interjected into the flow of chatter.

'Innit going to be grand?' the cheerful reply floated up.

Raka craned her neck over the edge of the sycamore branch, but even in the gloaming there was no improvement. Bertha still looked dull, dowdy – somehow so tremendously nesty.

'Don't take this personally, Bertha,' she went on, tapping into the confiding atmosphere of the falling darkness. 'It's not that you're not beautiful or attractive, or anything like that. But I still can't help wondering how you're going to persuade Alphonse to return with us. Have you got a plan?'

'I'm going to theduthe him,' came the giggly reply.

Raka's patience snapped.

'Don't be so ridiculous,' she burst out. 'Look at yourself – you're nothing but a bag of old feathers. Alphonse is bound to have hundreds of hens to choose from. What's so special about you that'll make him drop them all?'

Even as she spoke Raka was angry with herself. She knew she lost her temper too easily. But it had been a long day and anyway her inquiry was quite legitimate. Then, as she peered down furiously at the dim outline, she was certain she saw Bertha smile.

'Don't you know, Raka?' her voice came back, radiating total confidence. 'The fact of the matter ith, I give the wood'th betht beak job.'

Raka, shocked, fell silent. So that was what that crooked bill was about!

54

Roi du Bois

The next morning Raka felt embarrassed. Due to the worry of being in an unusual place with no proper nest she had slept only lightly. The unaccustomed saltiness in the air had made her desperately thirsty, while all the time the Big Water further upset her by making a continuous roaring noise like a gale going through the wood, even though there was no wind. She had also been kept awake by thoughts about the area Bertha had mentioned. In the noisy chaos of the rookery Raka had always avoided the female circuit involved in endless groupings and couplings of what she thought of as various aberrant practices. Not, she told herself, that she was averse to sex — she just preferred keeping it straightforward.

As they descended to the ground and picked up some early worms, she avoided catching Bertha's eye before they set off to cross the Big Water. Even on this vast surface they could see that human activity was rampant. The huge volver-type things ploughing along were curiously reminiscent of the volvers that ploughed the fields in the way they criss-crossed the calm water with lines and furrows. Was there no surface, Raka wondered with horror, on which the humans did not make their constant mark?

Bertha, however, was as wooden-headedly enthusiastic as ever.

'Innit busy?' she cried between bursts of the 'innit' song. 'Look at that one, Raka. Innit gigantic?'

Wincing, Raka took advantage of a convenient thermal to rise above her and concentrated on their route. Alphonse's instructions, as relayed by her friend, had sounded daunting. But then a pair of swifts had filled in more detail, as well as providing reassurance by informing her they had once seen a golden oriole. It had been just as fabulous-looking as Bertha claimed, they added enthusiastically.

Raka followed the various huge rollways as directed, picking out the vast human habitations Alphonse had said to look for, including the monster one he had apparently said they could not miss.

'Innit ginormous?' Bertha cried as they flew over it for what seemed an age, choking on the fumes that filled the air. How could the humans live crammed together like that? Raka wondered. It was worse than the rookery!

Reaching the far side of the Big Water, she picked up the big rollway and began following it in the direction of the midday sun, seeing that the day was obviously going to be a scorcher. Raka didn't like hot weather at the best of times and the heat rising off the land was sending up bubbles of hot air which made their passage increasingly bumpy. Nevertheless she was determined to press on without stopping, to make Alphonse's wood in one go.

What they would do when they got there she was not so sure. While she had no plan of her own, she couldn't share Bertha's sublime confidence in her distasteful speciality. The only consolation was that it was not she who would be administering it.

Raka knew they had arrived the moment she glimpsed the sickle-shaped wood. It was the distinctive shape they had been told to look for and a cross-reference of all the landmarks tallied. But they had no idea whereabouts within it Alphonse resided.

'Just ask for *moi*,' he had airily told Bertha's friend. 'Everyone, they know Alphonse.'

Seeing nowhere more obvious, Raka landed at the edge of an open space similar to the Big Clearing and they sought the welcome shade of a stand of leafy beech. As they recovered from the long flight, a small, dunnock-like bird settled on a branch nearby.

'Hello,' Raka said by way of introduction. 'We are friends of Alphonse, come from across the Big Water to visit him.'

The dunnock-type, after looking at them nervously, flew off without a word, leaving Raka unsure as to whether they had made the connection. But by then she and Bertha were too sleepy to care and they both nodded off, only to be jerked awake by a soft rustle. With a flurry, what they presumed must be their quarry suddenly took off and flew towards the middle of the clearing. At first glance he didn't look much. Then the rays of the late afternoon sun hit him and they both gasped in astonishment. Was he vibrant? He was spectacular! Bertha's friend hadn't been exaggerating — he did seem more like a vision. He was about the same size as the blackbird, but the similarity ended there. Alphonse's plumage was like that of no other bird they had ever seen. He had a black head, tail, and wing-edges, while the rest of his body had lit up into a dazzling mixture of yellow and orange that instantly reminded Raka of the funny-smelling stuff the humans planted in the fields and which the bees grumbled made their honey peculiar. Or was it ripening corn, just as it turned to a deeper gold? Or the shining kingcups and buttercups that shimmered in the Long Field? Where did you start? Or stop? She was simply amazed.

The effect on Bertha though seemed even more pronounced. Raka felt a stab of alarm as she saw her nearly keel over until she realised the blackbird was swooning! There was to be no pretence about this. Bertha had been well and truly smitten.

On being informed he had visitors Alphonse experienced a moment of panic. After his miraculous return from across the Big Water the aura of romance he exuded had put him at the top of the pecking order, and as he concentrated on the present his travels had quickly receded into the past. But now his mind raced back over a hundred incidents. Fortunately, although he had invited back hens from all over the place, none had so far taken him up on the offer. But it had always been at the back of his mind that one of his many holiday romances would catch up with him eventually. Surely, though, this frowzy and frumpy *merle*, with her twisted beak, couldn't be one of them? Certainly not the *corbeau*. She was much too heavy-looking for his taste.

As Raka introduced them both, explaining where they had come from, he was still none the wiser.

'You mutht remember my friend,' the *merle*, Bertha, insisted. 'The'th ever tho pretty.'

'*Ah oui*,' Alphonse replied guardedly, automatically monitoring the effect of his dulcet tones. 'It was a very fine place she lived, near to your Ald Wood — ees that'ow you say it?'

Really he couldn't recall anything about it, or her friend. It had been just another wood, just another banging session. He must get rid of this pair before they screwed things up for him back here on his own *territoire*.

He moved closer until he was almost nuzzling the blackbird. She blinked to show her willingness, while Raka disgustedly noted the smoothness of his technique. Not, she thought bitterly, that he was having to try very hard. Bertha's ecstatic expression said it all.

'Tell me, *mon petit choux*,' he wheedled as he continued to try to find his bearings, 'why 'ave you come to my *bois*, eh?'

Bertha scratched flirtatiously at the ground with her toe.

'For a thtart, Alphonthe, all your old friendth can't wait to thee you again,' she replied archly. 'Pleath come back, they all thay, they're all waiting.' She smiled crookedly. 'But the real thame, Alphonthe, ith that you never came to vithit Old Wood. You thee, I had thomething thpecial waiting for you . . .'

Lowering her head, she rubbed her bill along the grass, at which Alphonse began breathing heavily.

'*Spéciale*?' he inquired, his legs stiffening as he put his beak down to touch hers.

Their rumps waggled in unison.

'You tell me, eh?'

'If we went thomewhere private, Alphonthe, inthtead of telling you, I could thow you.'

Raka failed to suppress a snort of disgust. Bertha was an outrageous old tart! Until now Raka had rather regarded herself as being *in loco parentis*, or at least chaperone. What she hadn't counted on was feeling as she did now — like a dirty old cock pimping on the blackbird's behalf!

Raka was no voyeur and the last thing she wanted to see was what went on behind the nearby bush. But she could not shut out the deep groans emanating from the greenery. She was just wondering how much longer she must endure this appallingly embarrassing situation when the groans speeded up and peaked in a moaning climax. A long silence was followed by loud crashing as Alphonse staggered out of the undergrowth, his appearance transformed. His vibrant yellow feathers were dishevelled, his legs splayed, and there was an enormous, blissful smile on his face. Behind him came Bertha, smiling demurely and looking the picture of innocence.

'Ooh-la-la,' the golden oriole exclaimed as the rays of the setting sun caught his feathers and lit him up again.

'Ooh-la-la,' he repeated, a stunned look in his eyes. He might have had more than his fair share in his time, but never anything like this Bertha. She was *magnifique*! He lurched past Raka without even apparently seeing her, while Bertha clicked her lop-sided bill conspiratorially. Together they watched the rolling gait of their receding victim, and Raka had to admit that, disgusting though it might be, Bertha's speciality appeared to have scored a direct hit.

'Why should I come to your *bois*, when I 'ave everytheeng a cock needs 'ere?' Alphonse protested.

He had returned at the crack of dawn to be serviced by Bertha, after which Raka had pitched in, laying out Old Wood as a straightforward business proposition.

'It's a tremendous deal we're offering,' she emphasised. 'There's no-one there to touch you. You'll be king of the birds. Furthermore, I can guarantee anything you fancy —

starling, swift, pigeon, a pheasant if you want the run-round. Or how about a buzzard, to give you something you can really wrap your wings round?'

As Alphonse suddenly looked alarmed Raka realised she was overdoing it — which was all to the good. She could envisage the female buzzard's outraged croak of refusal, never mind her mate's reaction. But she was still sticking to plan. She and Owl, without consulting MI and M2, had agreed she could promise Alphonse anything. They'd sort the rest out later.

'They're all yours, old cock,' she urged brightly. 'Some tits to play with? We've got the lot, blue, great, coal, marsh, long-tailed. Something different maybe — a throat warbler?'

Seeing a new light in Alphonse's eye, she hurried to press home her advantage.

'I've already assigned your personal team of dunnock slaves. Their instructions are to carry out your every wish!' Raka smiled, remembering Owl's particular pleasure at dreaming up that incentive. 'Every bird, every creature in the wood, will be your subject. You won't be *Roi* of all you survey — you'll be *Empereur*!'

With a flash of vibrant yellow Alphonse ducked his head to preen his wing. Not just *Roi*, but *Empereur*!

Raka now reconsidered her decision not to mention the human invaders. She and Owl had previously decided that would only alarm Alphonse. But, if she pulled it off, it could now be the clincher.

'How would you like to be famous, Alphonse?' she asked casually.

Instantly she saw she had made a correct decision.

'Already I am famous,' Alphonse retorted sharply. 'Everybody in the *bois* knows who I am.'

'I'm sure,' Raka replied soothingly. 'But I mean seriously famous. I mean being a legend in your own lifetime, forever revered, not just in your own *bois*, but in the entire annals of woodland history.'

''Ow come?' Alphonse asked suspiciously.

Raka explained how the humans had moved in and Alphonse had been chosen as the only bird who could save the wood, while carefully avoiding any reference to the mink. That was the one piece of news she and Owl had agreed she must suppress. Meanwhile, Alphonse was thinking back to how his appearance had considerably excited the humans across the Big Water. They had often pointed at him in an animated fashion and one group had chased him for nearly a day, making him highly alarmed. But instead of bang-bangs the humans had only stared at him with devices that gave them huge eyes and made clicking noises. What this *corbeau* said made it all fit together. Alphonse's normal view of humans was entirely negative. In his land they were ruthless hunters, who pursued even the tiniest and most innocuous birds with anything they could lay their hands on. However, in the land across the Big Water he had not found them so rapacious. Maybe he could become a *cause célèbre*. He could pose in front of rapturous and adoring crowds. He could be an *étoile*. No wonder this pair had come all the way to see him. And what they were offering was *pas ordinaire*, even by his high standards.

There was another side to take into account, which he wasn't going to reveal. His current worry was that his hitherto iridescent plumage was showing hints of grey. Meanwhile his devoted following of groupies were becoming increasingly interested in virile young toy-birds, rather than a distinctly middle-aged male such as himself. Eventually a young cock would challenge him. Even if he fought off the first, there would be a second. In the end he would be toppled. More challenges would follow and then it would be the steady slide down the pecking order. He would have to resign himself to his increasingly humble position or else leave the *bois*. And where could he go, apart from this unexpected possibility of Old Wood? There, as *Empereur*, he would no longer have to rely on the undoubtedly fading charms that stared back each time he examined his reflection in a pool.

There would be drawbacks, of course, he reminded himself. The weather across the Big Water had not been good, and the food dreadful. Such a dreary selection of nuts, seeds and berries! However the promised slave dunnocks would compensate to a large extent. He would get the best available without having to lift a wing. And of course there would be endless time with Bertha, and as many other hens on top as he could cope with. Or rather underneath, he smiled to himself, delighted at his own witticism.

Overall, it was hard to say '*non*'.

'How can you lose?' Raka insisted. 'If you don't like it, you can always come back.'

'*Bon*,' Alphonse said, making a snap decision. 'Maybe I weel come. But first I come 'ere, eh?'

With a flash of his yellow wing he beckoned Bertha, who had been diplomatically waiting out of earshot.

'You like my leetle joke?' he leered at Raka. Bertha led him into the bushes, dutifully put her head down and got to work. Not, she thought as she vigorously applied herself, that it wasn't a positive pleasure.

Raka, left to play gooseberry again, tried to shut out Alphonse's groans. She was not enjoying her stay. The *bois* was far too hot, dry and dusty for her taste and while she could meet plenty of other birds – starting with the contents of the local rookery – the last thing she must get involved in was a diversion of her own. Speculation about her and Bertha's presence must be spreading as it was. But while her self-appointed task was to shepherd Bertha and their quarry back, at this precise moment she felt totally redundant. Bertha was weaving her web round Alphonse as adroitly as any spider.

She gestured the blackbird to one side as Alphonse staggered out with the same dazed and blissful expression, repeating more 'Ooh-la-las'.

'It's time to close the deal,' she whispered.

'Betht to strike while the beak'th hot,' Bertha grinned back.

Raka, shocked by her crudity, just glared at her.

Alphonse had numerous temporary good-byes to say to the flock of adoring hens gathered to see him off. But, as he spun them all the line about saving '*Vieux Bois*', Raka could see from the glares Bertha received that most weren't swallowing it.

The journey back, although punctuated by stops for another 'leetle speciality', was uneventful. To Raka's relief Bertha's new companion so preoccupied her that she abandoned her constant 'innits' and instead Raka couldn't help noticing how closely she and Alphonse flew together. Their brown and yellow colours intermingling, they resembled a giant bee as they soared and wheeled, seemingly just for the sake of it. Bertha was madly in love, Raka was now certain. Whether Alphonse was capable of such a pure emotion after his lifetime of philandering was a different matter. And while she was happy to witness the blackbird's joy, a passionate affair could introduce all kinds of complications. Raka also had a nasty premonition it would end in Bertha being hurt. Cheerful and willing she might be, but she had never played in Alphonse's league.

Raka pushed these dark thoughts to the back of her mind as she bent her will to getting home safely, where she could pass Alphonse over to MI and M2.

Then she could leave them to press the golden oriole into the job he was really being imported for.

55

Grovelling for Gold

Bertha and Raka flew into the Small Clearing to a heroes'
reception. While they had been away even more humans had
arrived in the wood, while an attempt at another brainstorming
session was abandoned amid noisy recriminations. The Marketing Mink had since retired to the Plateau in a sulk, leaving the
golden oriole as the wood's sole hope.

Owl, roused from his daytime slumber by an excited squirrel,
got a favourable first impression as he swooped over the crowd
pushing and shoving for the best view, to land next to Raka.

'Not bad, is he, Ollie?' she beamed at him proudly. 'Mind you,
it's Bertha, not me, whom you should thank for doing such a
good job.' Raka could not bring himself to detail precisely the
job Bertha had excelled at. 'But look at her,' she whispered,
indicating the blackbird gazing simperingly at their quarry.
'She's fallen in love.'

Oh pellets, Owl groaned. Trust Bertha!

'Come and meet him,' Raka urged. 'But first you need to
know I had to make it a condition of his passage that he would
be "Emperor Alphonse I", with everyone swearing allegiance
to him.'

The emperor business had been Raka's own idea, thought up on the spur of the moment. Now she was nervous that Owl might feel he was being upstaged. To her relief, however, he just seemed amused.

'The way things are, I'd lick his toes if required,' he smiled.

During the long wait Owl had had plenty of time to reconsider marketing, together with Ula who, although not wholly supportive, for once had not put him down.

'I don't know what to think, Ollie,' she confessed. 'But I can't see any alternative. At least the mink have got a definite idea, which is more than you can say for rabbits.'

When other creatures expressed similar sentiments, Owl came to the firm conclusion he should throw all his weight behind MI and M2's initiative. In a way the Marketing Mink had put the woodland creatures on their mettle. Now he was determined to show they could deliver.

'He doesn't yet know about the mink, of course,' Raka shouted over her shoulder as they pushed their way through the crowd.

'I'll see to that,' Owl reassured her.

'Welcome to Old Wood, Emperor,' he dutifully greeted the yellow bird, thinking he was not so impressive at close quarters. 'It is indeed a great honour.'

'Our leader, Ollie,' Raka explained. 'As I promised, he's only too happy to acknowledge you as Emperor. There is, however, another matter he wishes to inform you about—'

There was a sudden flurry as MI and M2, obviously furious at not being given the news first, came bounding into the clearing. Alphonse took one look at them and then he was in the air, the early evening sunlight lighting him up in dazzling yellow against the dark green of the trees. The woodland creatures gasped in wonder, and the Marketing Mink, brought up equally short, joined the universal cries of admiration, their irritation vanished.

'Talk about vibrant!' MI shrieked.

'Positively iridescent!' M2 shouted.

'Totally effervescent!' MI yelled.

The twins, hugging each other, began dancing round the clearing, whooping with delight. The woodies might have been nervous, but that was nothing compared to the tenterhooks they had been on back at the Plateau, where Mega had made it plain that his patience was virtually exhausted. Only Alphonse himself did not join in the general celebrations. Perched at the top of a towering beech, he refused to come down, announcing instead that he was going straight home.

Bertha flew up to quell his alarm, her heart in her beak.

'Mais I 'ave 'eard of *ces animaux*, Bertha,' he wailed. '*Ils sont* murderers *par excellence*.'

'It'th different here, Alphonthe dear,' Bertha explained soothingly, distraught at seeing him so upset. 'In thith wood they're on our thide — our friendth helping uth beat the humanth.'

But Alphonse was inconsolable. '*Avec amis* like that, who needs enemies?' he cried.

While Bertha did the pleading Raka, as before, hammered home the advantages of being Emperor.

'I should 'ave known eet all sounded too *facile*,' the golden oriole complained bitterly, trying to come to terms with his dilemma. He couldn't stay here, but how could he go home after so grandly announcing that he was off to save a wood? Admitting failure would be the first step in the downfall he had been anticipating.

Then he began to cheer up as he saw Bertha appeared to be correct about the dreaded mink. *Vraiment*, they were not eating the other creatures, who didn't seem alarmed by their presence but just kept waving upwards in a friendly fashion. Meanwhile a steady stream of birds were flying up to swear their allegiance, while on the branch below the promised slave dunnocks timidly awaited his commands. Maybe it was not so bad after all. The real clincher, however, was Bertha. Alphonse had already cast a beady eye over the promised throat warbler, and hens of all kinds had openly made themselves available to him. Yet he had felt curiously uninterested, which at first had alarmed him. What if being in this strange land was causing him to lose his libido? *Quelle horreur!*

Yet it hadn't been like that when he had last visited, while

every time he so much as glanced at Bertha he was consumed by
fires of lust. It went further than that. He had only to gaze on
her to lose all his bearings. No longer was she the nesty, dowdy
hen she had first appeared. An extraordinary inner beauty had
transcended her frowzy exterior, while she talked so sweetly
and kindly it was obvious she loved him. How different from
the harridans back in his *bois*, smarming up to him and acting
all lubby-dubby before tearing him to pieces behind his back.
With a start Alphonse realised that, for the first time in his life,
he wasn't interested in anyone else. He just wanted to be with
Bertha all the time. And now, being Emperor, he had something
to offer.

He looked into her black eyes, senses reeling.

'*Ma chère* Bertha, *mon amour*, will you consent to be my
Empress *à tout jamais*?'

'Oh Alphonthe,' she breathed ecstatically. 'I will.'

Owl was becoming exhausted flying backwards and forwards.
At the top of the tree he confined himself to nodding vigorously
in confirmation of what Raka and Bertha were saying, before
zooming back to ground level to organise more birds to fly up
and swear allegiance. Meanwhile he tried to make sure all the
ground creatures bowed and scraped suitably deferentially.

He had to cope with a crisis as Boris came barging up,
demanding to know what the fuss was about.

'It's Alphonse,' Owl explained. 'He's so afraid of the mink
he won't come down.'

'Don't blame him,' Boris grunted, waving his stripy head
at the Marketing Mink. 'Tell you what, why don't I give
one of those buggers a clout? Then he'll see there's nothing
to fear.'

For a moment Owl was tempted. MI and M2 did seem
the most wimpish of the mink. He watched them waving
sycophantically upwards, and thought how slimy they were.
But Alphonse was still teetering on the brink. If there was the
slightest hint of violence he would be gone.

'I have to say no, Boris,' he replied reluctantly.

'I don't understand you any more, Ollie,' Boris harumphed.

'Can't you see that working with these buggers is bound to end in trouble sooner or later? Why not now?'

'No, Boris,' Owl repeated more firmly. 'You mustn't upset things. We have to give this a go. Think of all Raka's and Bertha's efforts. What you could do to help is to join everyone in swearing allegiance.'

'You must be joking,' Boris spluttered. 'I'm not bowing down to some poxy bird just because he happens to be yellow and – what is it? – vibrant and then has the gall to style himself Emperor!

'You lot should be ashamed of yourselves,' he shouted, turning on the assorted creatures watching the interchange. 'Bowing down like that! Haven't you any pride left?'

Owl observed the reaction nervously. Some key creatures, such as Freddie and the buzzards, were notably absent and he had already heard Cowslip muttering ominously to her cronies about the slave role unilaterally assigned to the dunnocks. If the CWGs teamed up with Boris things could become tricky. However as the badger's angry gaze swept across them Owl saw their eyes go down. He relaxed. The unlikely alliance was not going to happen.

'Sorry, Boris,' he said, meaning it.

'Well I've had quite enough of this nonsense,' Boris retorted. 'You can count me out from this moment on.'

Owl watched his lumbering rear recede with mixed emotions. He suspected the badger might be correct. The mink fraternisation might well end in trouble. But that didn't change anything. Right now, they were all locked in.

He turned to a huddle of wide-eyed field mice who had just arrived.

'Alphonse is at the top of that tree,' he informed them. 'The others will show you what to do.'

A shrew had already importantly started squeaking the deference procedure as he flew back to the treetop, where he found that Alphonse appeared to have missed the Boris incident and had perked up enormously. The real surprise, however, was seeing Bertha so positively glowing with pride.

'Allow me to present you to *la belle* Bertha, the new Empress

of Old Wood,' Raka greeted him, turning away so the pair
would not see her rolling her eyes upwards.

Owl struggled to keep a straight face. Dowdy old Bertha
an empress – or rather 'empreth'! His next thought was
the problems that was bound to cause with other hens.
But, accepting Raka knew what she was doing, he made
no comment.

'My warmest congratulations, Emperor,' he instead obsequiously
played along. 'You are indeed a lucky cock!'

Alphonse simpered disarmingly.

'*Belle* Empress, I am delighted,' Owl added, turning to
to Bertha and giving a little bow. He was rewarded by a
sweet smile.

'Emperor Alphonse I has laid down his terms and conditions
for staying in our wood,' Raka informed him.

'*Oui*,' the golden oriole interrupted, looking down his beak.
'These meenk must now join the rest of you woodland creatures
in swearing their allegiance. Only then will I believe they are
– 'ow you say – on our side.'

Seeing Raka nod vigorously in affirmation Owl did not stop
to argue. He flew down to inform the Marketing Mink of this
latest development, finding them highly agitated.

'What's the matter with the stupid bird?' MI asked through
clenched teeth as he continued to smile idiotically upwards and
wave a front paw. 'Can't he see that we're being friendly?'

'You may look it,' Owl replied with huge satisfaction. 'But
now he says you've got to prove it.'

He gestured them away from the crowd at the bottom of the
tree with his wing.

'He'll only stay if you bow down and swear allegiance to him
as "Emperor Alphonse I",' he explained in a low voice.

'What!' the mink twins were just chorusing in disbelief when
Raka flew down to join them.

'Owl isn't joking,' she confirmed cheerfully. 'If you don't
comply Alphonse says he's going home immediately, and never
coming back.'

MI and M2 looked at Owl in horror. He shrugged helplessly.

'Well I, for one, refuse,' MI burst out, glaring venomously upwards. 'Who does he think he bloody well think he is?'

'He thinks he's Emperor Alphonse I,' Owl replied crisply. 'And that isn't our fault. Remember you explained we wouldn't be able to persuade a golden eagle? Well, when Alphonse insisted he be made Emperor, Raka and Bertha had no choice.'

He gave Raka a crafty wink, and they both stared at the mink, thoroughly enjoying their discomfiture. It would serve them right to have to kow-tow to the newcomer like everyone else.

'He didn't know about you lot until just now,' Owl explained. 'And as you can see, you've made him very unhappy. There's another thing I'll tell you. If he does leave I personally will ensure your leader knows you are entirely to blame.'

'You wouldn't,' MI gasped.

'I most certainly would,' Owl replied gravely.

MI and M2 went into a quick huddle. Mega had already informed them he would brook no more excuses.

'You tell me you're the clever marketing boys,' he had growled. 'So be clever and make it work — right now.'

As he spoke they saw Psycho eyeing them beadily. There would be no mercy from that direction either.

There was nothing to discuss.

'OK, you win,' MI told Owl resignedly. 'But only if we can do it in private, with absolutely no other creatures watching.'

Owl flew back to the treetop and delivered the message to a somewhat mollified golden oriole.

He chose the Quarry as the site for the Marketing Mink's obeisance, charging Raka with ensuring everyone stayed away or — he added with a grin — at least well hidden. Then he went ahead to clear the ground, finding the area was as deserted as ever. Nowhere was totally private, but in the end he chose a secluded rowan, near where he and Burdock used to meet. If he placed Alphonse on a branch well out of the mink's reach, under the pretext of giving him a suitably elevated position, it would at least help secure his safety. The golden oriole's confidence had obviously been boosted by the many creatures who had already sworn allegiance to him. Yet he had no idea how big a risk he was taking in seeking to impose his arrogance on mink. MI and M2 could easily snap.

When they walked stiffly into the Quarry he showed them the tree before flying to fetch Alphonse. Left on their own they looked round, sharing the awful feeling that various pairs of eyes were on them. Which would be worse, they wondered apprehensively, having their performance monitored by the woodies or by their fellow mink? Yet though they inspected the neighbouring bushes closely, they had still not detected anyone when Owl flew back and directed Alphonse to the branch he had selected.

The Emperor settled, Bertha by his side.

'We said no other creatures to be present,' MI immediately protested.

Alphonse stared angrily down.

'This ees is not any other creature, this ees my Empress,' he rebuked them sternly. '*Maintenant*, shall we, 'ow you say? Proceed?

'*Premièrement*, grovel!'

Seeing Owl was not going to intervene on their behalf, the Marketing Mink, teeth clenched in ghastly smiles, lowered their hind legs infinitesimally.

'*Plus bas!*'

The legs sank slightly more.

'Did you not 'ear *moi*? *Encore plus bas!*'

The pair's plump bellies sank until they were resting on the quarry's sharp stones.

'*Bon! Maintenant*, swear your allegiance,' Alphonse commanded.

'We, MI and M2, do hereby humbly acknowledge you as Emperor Alphonse I and therefore ruler of the wood and all you survey,' the mink mumbled in miserable unison.

Alphonse stamped his foot on the branch.

'You 'ave forgotten *ma belle* Empress,' he screamed.

The Marketing Mink looked at Owl pleadingly.

He stared back, stony-faced. This was for Alphonse, not him, to decide.

'We, MI and M2, do hereby humbly acknowledge you as

Emperor Alphonse I, along with *la belle* Empress Bertha, and therefore ruler of the wood and all you survey,' they repeated shamefacedly.

'I cannot 'ear you,' Alphonse shouted, cocking his head. '*Plus fort!*'

By now both mink were convinced they could hear stifled giggling in the bushes. Raising their voices as little as they dared, they repeated the oath for the third time.

'*Bon,*' Alphonse pronounced, regarding their squirming figures with lordly contempt. 'I 'ereby accept your obeisance and confirm your new status as my most 'umble subjects. You may now depart *mon présence!*'

Owl blinked. Did this extraordinary bird really believe he was an emperor? Bertha, knowing much more about mink, was looking distinctly queasy.

Yet still Alphonse had not finished.

''Alt!' he commanded, causing the mink to freeze in their tracks. 'When dismeessed from the presence of an Emperor it ees necessary to marche backwards, so as not to present your *derrière* to 'is visage!'

If looks could kill, Owl thought as he watched the unhappy pair shuffle awkwardly backwards, bellies scraping the stones, until they finally reached the sanctuary of the shrubbery and disappeared from sight.

'What you've got to do to keep your clients happy!' MI exploded as they bounded along the path to the Plateau. 'Honestly, 2, have you ever come across such a vain creature in your life?'

'The trouble is, he's serious,' M2 shouted back. 'He must think he's cleverer than Psycho.'

But although they were still smarting from their humiliation, their grumbles were light-hearted. Even white grovelling they had been unable to suppress their enthusiasm for Alphonse's visibility potential. Their report to Mega was going to be as glowing as the wood's new UWP.

'Stars are always temperamental,' M2 consoled his brother, before daring to voice the horrible thought at the back of both their minds. 'But what if he insists Mega grovels as well?'

'Don't even think about it,' MI replied hurriedly. 'We must make sure they never meet. We'll tell Mega Alphonse is already petrified of us and that he, being so much more dominant and powerful, therefore must stay away. He'll wear that, surely?'

'Maybe,' M2 replied uncertainly.

But he was already cheering up. Tomorrow, Emperor or not, they were going to strap the golden oriole down, meanwhile getting the woodies behind them. Even the most dense would see that if Alphonse didn't subject himself to their marketing dictates, there would be no point in grovelling any further to him, or taking any notice of him whatsoever. For all the difference it would make, he could go back his bloody *bois*!

'Unless we save him the trip by having him for breakfast,' MI grinned.

'Number one in the eating popularity league, eh?' his brother grinned back.

'Absolutely,' MI smiled, licking his lips. Marketeers might be sensitive, but they enjoyed their hot spurts as much as anyone.

56

Gotcha!

Next morning the succession of sunny days had unexpectedly broken. The sky was blanketed with cloud when MI and M2 turned up at the Small Clearing, to find Alphonse already up and about.

'*Non*!' he was screeching at his slave dunnocks as he surveyed the selection of titbits laid out in front of him. '*J'ai* already *dit* that *pour mon petit déjeuner* I 'ave *toujours les* snails et *les* frogs' legs.'

The dunnocks, faced with a demand so contrary to CWG ethics, shuffled miserably.

'*Bonjour*, Emperor,' MI cried, bowing in ludicrously exaggerated fashion as he set out to calm ruffled yellow feathers. 'How is His Magnificence this morning — not forgetting, of course, *la belle* Empress Bertha?'

The twins, their confidence boosted by lavish praise from Mega the previous evening, were in high spirits. All their requirements had been set in motion. Maxi had issued strict instructions to the minions not to alarm the golden oriole in any way whatsoever, while Mega had agreed to stay away after they pitched him as planned. But best of all they had come to terms personally with their position. They would play up their flattery for all it was worth, turning it into a game. How far would they be able to go before Alphonse realised they were just taking the mickey?

'Greatest Eminence, we have come to launch you on the path to mega-stardom and eternal fame,' MI fawned, kicking the process off. 'Pray permit us, your most humble and dutiful subjects, to demonstrate the programme we have exclusively prepared to enable you to display your full glory.'

From behind his back he produced a piece of bark, on which he and his twin had scratched a 'show flight routine'. They had based it on two key factors — keeping Alphonse's human audience well away from the Plateau end of the wood, while also ensuring he did not cross the river. Not only did they consider that too risky, but the water provided a natural barrier which would hold back the expected crowds. At the top of the bark they had drawn a target twitcher, next to the outline of a bird, while below an oblong route ran along the edge of the Long Field before wheeling round to the tatty alder tree by the reedbed.

'This will be your main stage, Your Most Colourfulness,' MI explained. 'We ask that you stop here to pose for the human click machines, with which we presume you are already familiar.'

Alphonse nodded condescendingly.

'After that, Your Most Exceeding Yellowness,' MI continued, keeping a straight face despite his twin's snorts of suppressed laughter, 'we humbly request you fly back along the river, as shown here, before completing your circuit by returning over the five-barred gate, here, and coming back up the Ride.'

Alphonse, the clutch of dunnocks hovering at his heels, studied the diagram critically.

'That weel suffice,' he finally pronounced. 'But I only fly on condition *ma belle* Bertha is by my side.'

'We're not having that old bag of feathers messing it up,' MI snapped, temporarily forgetting he was in full grovel mode.

'Pardon?' Alphonse inquired, looking down his beak. 'You do not understand. *Je suis* Emperor Alphonse I *et je* decree: "*Pas de* Bertha, *pas de* show". That is eet.'

Both Marketing Mink looked in appeal towards Owl.

'I'm not sure that's wise, Emperor,' Owl said slowly as he searched for a way not to upset the golden oriole too much. He had to agree with the mink. Sweet though she was, nobody wanted Bertha getting in the way. 'With all due respect to *la belle* Empress, it is the Emperor the humans will be coming to see.'

Alphonse stamped his foot.

'You are correct I am Emperor. And that means what *je dit* goes. Otherwise I leave – *maintenant.*'

Owl was secretly warming to Alphonse. He had no idea how closely he was sailing to the wind, but it was hugely satisfying listening to him lay down the law to the mink.

'Careful, or he'll make you reswear allegiance in front of everyone,' he stage-whispered to MI and M2.

There was a burst of sniggers from the watching creatures. The mink had been quite right in suspecting several various pairs of eyes were on them the previous evening. Graphic accounts of their grovelling had since provoked huge merriment throughout the wood.

'OK, Most Esteemed Emperor,' MI acceded, cutting their losses. '*La belle* Empress can fly by your side. She is, after all, so extraordinarily beautiful it would be awful if the twitchers missed her.'

Smiling with hideous insincerity, he pointedly scratched the outline of another bird on the bark mapping out the show flight routine. As Alphonse flashed Bertha a triumphant smile Owl's heart sank at seeing how adoringly she gazed back. He had already tried to warn her off, agreeing with Raka the relationship was a potential disaster.

'Don't get in too deep,' he had pleaded.

But it was obvious Bertha wasn't listening. Raka was right. She had been well and truly smitten.

Alphonse's first attempts to attract the target twitchers did not go as smoothly as the Marketing Mink had anticipated. Rather than a mega-star, Alphonse was a mega-flop, jealous cock pheasants were soon remarking in a loud voice. Previously regarding themselves as the most glorious birds in the wood, the cock pheasants had had their beaks put out of joint by this new rival. But cocks of other species – especially equally miffed male blackbirds – quickly joined in the sneers as Alphonse and Bertha went round and round the show flight route to indifference from the volvers on the rollway. Finally, to huge jeering, the Emperor, after casting increasingly pained glances back at the wood, flapped back to announce sullenly: '*Je suis fatigué.*'

MI and M2 looked at him worriedly as the slave dunnocks attempted to revive his flagging spirits with titbits and a beak massage. As he grew increasingly weary, Alphonse had already become less and less vibrant, while the sun still refused to shine and light him up. When he announced he was suspending flights until further notice, the mink did not stay to argue. Instead they rushed back to the Plateau, where they were already late in delivering the progress report Mega had ordered. By now they were bitterly regretting their over-optimistic predictions of an instantaneous result.

'It's not our fault, great leader,' they pleaded in whining voices. 'The humans are so locked in their volvers they're oblivious of the rest of the world.'

'Get him to fly directly in front of them then,' Mega barked unsympathetically.

'Great leader, that would be too risky,' MI explained. 'Not that we care about Alphonse,' he hurriedly added, 'but we can't afford his total loss. Our only hope is to make the volvers stop in some other way.'

'Your only hope, you mean,' Mega growled, baring his teeth. 'You should have thought of this before. What are you going to do?'

'We could try a brainstorming session,' MI said weakly, looking at his twin in near despair.

Mega stared at him disgustedly, and ordered Maxi and Psycho to be summoned.

Grumpily he explained the position.

'Psycho's got a whole load of rabbits waiting for his experiments, my leader,' Maxi suggested, eager to get in on the action. 'Why don't I get the muscle-mink to make them lie down on the rollway? If they're strung across in a line, the volvers'll have to stop or run them over. I believe they'll halt, achieving our objective. But even if they don't the rabbits are totally dispensable. It would make no difference if they were squashed as flat as a leaf.'

Mega shot MI and M2 a withering glance.

'An excellent proposal,' he congratualated Maxi, who stiff-ened with pride. 'Any thoughts, Psycho?'

His spin-doctor had been planning a mass experiment that very evening, but instantly saw he would have to concede.

'Squashed rabbits would certainly add interesting information to my files, Mega. Can I further suggest we entice them by offering freedom in return for success? That way they'll see they've everything to gain. Of course we'd recapture them afterwards,' he continued, his voice rising to an eerie cackle. 'Then I'd ceremonially try them for a new crime I've just thought up — deliberately, and with malice aforethought, trespassing on the rollway.'

Mega stared at him with a mixture of admiration and distaste. Where did he get these perverted ideas from? His court dramas might amuse the minions, but personally Mega didn't like them. Hadn't the nasty runt ever heard of death with honour? Yet, covering all eventualities as it did, he had to admit it was a clever suggestion. He gave a curt nod of approval.

'We ought to inform the woodies beforehand,' MI faltered.

'Forget it,' Mega cut across flatly. 'Just remember that if Alphonse doesn't do the business it's not the rabbits who're in for the high jump — it's you two.'

The first the woodland creatures knew of Maxi's 'Operation Coneyline' was when they saw the miserable group of prisoners shuffling across the Long Field, muscle-mink snapping at their heels. Owl had to deal with the uproar as they were herded over the bridge and on to the rollway, to be laid out in a line blocking it from side to side, while their mink escort hid behind below the riverbank. Feeling slightly ashamed of himself, he resorted to his hissing and feather-fluffing display to silence Cowslip and other aghast CWGs, before he set off, furious, to the Plateau. He had to have it out with the mink leader. Just seeing the rabbit prisoners had been enough of a shock. It was no consolation that the Concerned Guardians were effectively history. Using any woodland creature in such a callous fashion was an attack on them all.

Then he saw the Marketing Mink running towards him waving and swooped down.

'We're sorry, Ollie, but Mega said we've got to stop the volvers somehow, otherwise we're all for it,' MI pleaded inaccurately.

'We've negotiated their freedom when it works,' M2 chipped in.

'And if it doesn't?' Owl demanded.

But MI wasn't listening. 'We haven't got time to hang around talking,' he reminded Owl urgently. 'A volver could come along at any moment. If Alphonse isn't ready the coneys will have had it anyway.'

Owl, knowing he was right, saw he would have to postpone the clash until later. He flew back to the Small Clearing, only to discover that in the meantime Cowslip had been at work: Alphonse was now declaring solidarity with the rollway rabbits.

'*Vraiment*, you are right – these *pauvres lapins*, they too are my 'umble subjects,' he said, while the slave dunnocks piped timid approval. 'I weel not fly until the meenk release them.'

'Why can't you keep your nose out?' Owl was just demanding of the smug-looking CWG leader, when the Marketing Mink came running up, their previous smarmy manner abandoned. They listened to Alphonse's pompous refusal for only an instant before MI rushed over and seized Bertha from his side. When Alphonse made to follow, the mink clamped his teeth round her neck and emitted a low growl. Now Owl could see it was the Marketing Mink's turn to be driven by fear. Their leader must have put them on the line as squarely as they had placed the rabbits on the rollway.

Alphonse was looking uncertain.

'If you want your Empress to survive, prepare to fly,' M2 commanded.

'*Vous etes fous*,' Alphonse gasped disbelievingly as Bertha emitted a terrified squawk. But he had already buckled. For a moment the arrogance instilled by being Emperor had been stripped away, revealing him as just another medium-sized bird, underneath as frightened of the mink as all the others.

Then he rallied. 'Bertha, *ma chérie*, I will show these meenk the stuff we Emperors are made of,' he cried. 'I will fly – *seulement pour toi*.'

At that moment there was a cry came from a chaffinch in the treetops: 'A volver's coming!'

It was more a tribute to the fear Maxi had instilled than Psycho's freedom inducement that the coneyline held. The woodland creatures were already covering their eyes when, at the last second, the volver screeched to a halt. The row of rabbits, now beyond caring, remained prone even when the stinking monster looming over their heads emitted an ear-splitting blare of rage. However, instead of moving forwards to put them out of their misery, it remained stationary, while the next one, coming along shortly afterwards, stopped behind it.

The Marketing Mink waited tensely as a pair of humans got out, walked up to the line, and prodded the rabbits with their toes.

'Go for it, golden oriole,' MI shouted.

Alphonse shot out of the wood just as the sun came out for the first time to highlight him in all his glory. He swooped over the Long Field in a dazzling yellow blur, already determined to junk the cautious show flight routine. Taking heart from the sudden warmth and brightness, he zoomed across the river and swept directly over the humans' heads.

'*Courage, mon brave!*' he shouted as he banked steeply and committed himself to a low jinking run that turned him into a succession of iridescent flashes. Amid excited cries from below the humans raised their pale faces skywards as he turned again, feathering his wings to pass over them more slowly. Only then did he recross the river to the safety of his posing alder tree. The thudding in his chest died down as he tried to gauge the reaction. One human had run to the riverbank and was pointing at him in high excitement, while the other had dived back inside his volver. As he re-emerged, holding something up to his face,

Alphonse gasped with relief and delight. He had the mad staring eyes the Marketing Mink had drawn on the piece of bark. It was a twitcher! He had saved Bertha's life!

Heart swelling with pride, he opened his wings to give his full display, watching the great twin eyes remain glued onto him. There was no mistake. He had done it! Satisfied, he took off, rejoined his prepared route, and flew back over the five-barred gate.

Owl watched with bated breath alongside the other wood-land creatures. He had decided not to intervene, judging that Alphonse had taken the heat out of the situation by caving in so promptly. But he had still been highly nervous about the fate of the rabbit-line. Not as nervous as the Marketing Mink, though, he thought as he scrutinised their apprehensive faces and saw how rapidly MI's eyelid was jerking. It speeded up when Alphonse ignored instructions and crossed the river, only to slow down as the twitcher appeared.

'Gotcha!' he yelled in delight and the two mink hugged each other in triumph and relief, while the woodland creatures cheered to the echo. The cheers intensified as Alphonse landed but he had eyes only for Bertha, whom MI now released. She ran towards him, her expression indicating how she had never doubted him for a second. Meanwhile both Marketing Mink, hard-line attitude abandoned, rushed to clap him on the back. MI ostentatiously brandished the show flight routine bark then scratched a huge tick next to the drawing of a twitcher.

'Bullseye!' he shouted, while for once Alphonse displayed a modicum of modesty by bowing his head to acknowledge the plaudits coming from all sides.

As Owl's hoots mingled with the whoops and whistles he saw Raka close her eyes in relief. He knew exactly how she felt. It had been a closer call than any of the others realised, especially for Bertha.

57

Digging for Victory

After his first success there was no stopping Alphonse, and no more need to use rabbits to stop the volvers. The prisoners had anyhow seized their opportunity and legged it over the far hill while the humans were concentrating their attention on the golden oriole. The cheering from the wood became even louder when everyone saw that Maxi and his muscle-mink were now trapped, not daring to move as more and more volvers stopped and their human occupants crowded onto the riverbank.

The Marketing Mink, back in deferential mode, pleaded with the Emperor not to take any further risks by crossing the river, to which Alphonse was only too glad to consent. Both sides, meanwhile, quietly forgot the Bertha incident.

'The news will reach the hard-core twitchers next,' MI announced happily at the end of the day. 'That will usher in Stage Two, when we predict a substantial rise in audience ratings.'

He was proved correct sooner than even he had expected. The rollway was already littered with volvers as the sky lightened the next morning to usher in a classic sunrise. Once started off so gloriously, the day stayed that way and all the creatures could sense the wood had settled into a period of clement weather. Almost as if in compensation for their other miseries, the late spring and summer had been the best they had known and for many this was now the nearest time to perfection. Like the others, Owl felt a slight tinge of melancholy in knowing they were about to pass the longest day. Yet that only gave a further reason for enjoying the period before the wood slid into heavy sultriness. Every morning would begin with ecstatic skylarks pouring out their joy as they ascended into the purest blue and end, late at night, with a sunset of unsurpassing glory, while in between puffy white clouds would sail serenely overhead, occasionally dispensing their necessary sustenance of soft showers.

The wood had already responded to this climate for growth. As the greening over of the tree canopy blocked out much of the light, the spring flowers had run to seed. Now it was the turn of grasses and more mature plants to expand in lush tangles of new vegetation and carpet the clearings and glades. Sturdy shoots turned into strong plants, fighting each other for the light, while those equipped with writhing tendrils clambered cheerfully over them. The plants grew in a more steady and assured way, their energy different from the fierceness with which they had initially established themselves. Now they relaxed into reaping the alternating cycles of sun and rain while a confident feeling filled the wood as it sensed how it was successfully reproducing itself as an entity. It was settled, in the powerhouse of its regular cycle when nothing or no-one was held back from developing.

And it was so pretty, especially where the dancing leaves provided a filter that dispensed dappled sunlight, in stark contrast to the deep shadows and blinding light in the clearings. Prettiest of all, most creatures thought, when the fat raindrops had finished pattering down and the following sun picked them out as glittering highlights on the refreshed leaves, while steam rose gently from the dripping grass.

The wood and surrounding fields buzzed, hummed, squeaked, chirped and rustled with new life, much of it by now well advanced. Most young birds, grown from scrawny bare chicks into fully feathered miniatures of their parents, had already left the nest, while the rest were nearly ready. To Owl's regret his daughter, Blinkie, left home before he had hardly got to know her. Yet he had always understood that Ula, as a fellow female, would be the one to bond with her most strongly. Owl complained of feeling shut out, feeling she was taking over more responsibility than was right, but was never to answer when she countered that he was entirely preoccupied by events in the wood. Not that she was rejecting him out of hand, she emphasised in a more kindly way than Owl was used to.

'The point, apart from anything else, is that you have more important things to do,' she insisted gently. 'Trust me to enable her properly, Ollie, then you can relax and get on with your bit.'

After that Owl, recognising the inevitability of what she was saying, largely did so.

But it was not just in his nest, and those of the other birds, that development was taking place. Down on the ground litters of naked pink babies grew just as fast to become fully furred adolescents taking their first faltering steps towards lives of their own. Exhausted parents were now relaxing. For them it was the time of consolidation, when they could at last turn their attention to themselves and repair the ravages to their health caused by the strain of rearing young.

The summer visitors were well settled in. Swallows darted over the sparkling river, where the first run of sea trout and salmon splashed heavily to knock off the sealice, their grip weakened ever since their hosts removed them from their native salt water. The fish, coursing with energy imparted by their rich life in the ocean, did not linger. Before even the mink could get them, they cut effortlessly through the current to pass quickly upstream on their driving mission to gain the headwaters.

Everywhere newly hatched insects pitched eagerly into their short life spans. Monstrous-looking larvae crawled out from previous existences, either deep in the earth or under stones both on land and under water, before metamorphosing into unnaturally bright beauties like trembling dragon flies. Meanwhile burst-open chrysalides marked the hatching places of the butterflies that fluttered gaily through the glades. Ladybirds, flies, wasps, bees, moths and bugs of all sizes, shapes and colours filled the air, their dancing hordes recalling the heady CWG days of organisations like Gnat Attack.

The profusion of insect life now munching its way through the succulent vegetation provided natural feasts for other creatures, although not all the traffic was one-way. Larger creatures scratched and cursed as they endured the bites of a multitude of mainlining bloodsuckers from fleas to ticks. But nobody really minded. It might be a pretty time, when everyone in the wood was at their best, but more importantly it was a period of grace and plenty, when everyone could afford to share – a time to revive faded hopes that, despite the mink, the wood would go on for ever, just as it always had.

As always though, it was not all good news. The early-morning sun might delight by quickly replacing the chill of the coldest time before dawn, but as it rose high in the sky its rays became harsh and searing. Few creatures enjoyed basking in it by the middle of the day, when it had become almost an enemy that drove most of them into the welcoming shade, where it was simply a matter of keeping comfortable while they lazily indulged in the luxury of doing nothing. But for those with wet skins, avoiding shrivelling over-exposure was a matter of life and death and the hard, dessicated carcasses of creatures like worms and slugs were a constant reminder of those who had paid the ultimate penalty for failure. By late afternoon, though, the sun's power had waned sufficiently for everyone to enjoy the balmy evenings, invariably tempered by the light breeze that sprang up as the shadows lengthened and turned the woodland mantle a darker shade of green. Then, as the wind died away, slowly and almost imperceptibly the first stars would replace the last flush of sunset, while the light lingered on in the sky. All night the temperature remained pleasantly warm.

It was a liberating atmosphere, and one filling Owl with renewed faith that maybe everything was going to turn out all right after all. Surely an entity so settled and confident in itself could not possibly be destroyed? Certainly Alphonse and Bertha had responded to it that morning by going to greet their audience as if to the manner born.

Elation surged through the wood as the happy couple soared in loops and whirls, just as on their return from Alphonse's *bois*. Flushed with triumph, they returned periodically to the Small Clearing to be refuelled by the dunnocks whilst the creatures cheered them on. Everyone could now see how strongly they were locked together and their joy in each other's company gave such a fillip to their display that other birds forgot their jealousy. Instead they could not resist joining in and the sky became alive as they rose exultantly above the treetops, while the crowd of gesticulating twitchers grew ever larger and the click machines fired constantly.

The only sour note was that the humans destroying the wood turned up for work as usual. Alphonse was initially alarmed as the yellow digger began roaring away, especially when the Marketing Mink emphasised that he must stay away from it at all costs. However they soon found the Emperor, apparently oblivious of the danger it posed, changing his mind.

'I 'ave just noticed 'ow perfectly it matches *mon* plumage,' he announced during one of his breaks. 'I think it ees 'ere to be my, 'ow do you say?, throne.'

'Hardly, Most Eminenceful!' MI replied in horror.

''Ow dare you contradict me,' Alphonse reprimanded. 'Already we are so famous, Bertha and I, another deeger 'as come to provide us with 'is and 'er ones.'

The Marketing Mink, peering down, saw to their surprise that he was right. A long volver, carrying a new yellow digger on its back, had indeed stopped by the bridge. The humans unloading it had now been surrounded by a group of twitchers and the two sides were bumping into each other as they milled around. Then, with a puff of black smoke, the digger broke free and set off up the Long Field. But far from letting it go, the twitchers were in pursuit, waving their arms and shaking their fists.

'A confrontational situation!' MI screamed in huge excitement. 'We've moved to Stage Three!'

Then, before they could stop him, Alphonse suddenly got up and flew out of the wood. The mink's hearts were in their mouths as they saw him swoop down to land on the digger, only for the twitchers to start waving as if to shoo him away. Obviously thinking better of it, the golden oriole backed off and remained circling, while the mink's glee increased as the group of twitchers pursued the digger up right up the Ride into the Big Clearing. There they accosted the working humans, all the time pointing upwards. There was a fierce altercation, before one of the working humans raised his arm, pointed it at Alphonse and made a noise like a bang-bang. A pair of twitchers promptly lay down in front of the digger, just as the rabbits had lain on the rollway, halting its progress in a similar fashion. Finally, after much shouting and arm-waving, all the humans left the wood together and the workers returned to their volvers and rolled away.

The creatures pestered the Marketing Mink to explain what this was all about, but to no avail.

'Too deep for your little woodie brains, I'm afraid,' MI smiled patronisingly.

Finally, after they had gone on and on M2 took pity on them and agreed to answer one question.

'Is Alphonse now famous enough to save the wood?' Owl asked simply, on behalf of them all.

'Put it like this,' M2 beamed. 'He's now flavour of the moon. We're looking for a very significant development shortly. Meanwhile it's essential he keeps flying.'

There wouldn't be any trouble with that, Owl thought. It would be hard keeping Emperor Alphonse away. He was having the time of his life.

58

Neenaw!

'How's it going, you two?' Mega grunted.

'Brilliant,' MI grinned confidently. 'The working humans
– twitcher interface is becoming increasingly confrontational,
while Alphonse and Bertha's audience profile rises daily. Our
latest move has been to slim down the show flight routine to
a leisurely start, various morning breaks, a long lunch and an
early wrap.'

'Wrap?' Mega asked, irritated.

'Shut-down,' M2 quickly interjected.

'Why?'

'Always starve the customers when they're eating out of the
palm of your hand,' MI smiled mysteriously, tapping the side
of his nose with his paw. 'It's when they're hungry that they
really want the goods!'

Mega continued to look irritated, while M2 thought to
himself, 'The wood's the goods!' Maybe they should teach
the idiot phrase to their leader. It might stop this insistent
questioning.

'What happens now?' Psycho chipped in.

'We wait.'

'How long?' Mega demanded. 'A moon?'

'No, no, great leader,' MI rushed to reassure him. 'Please be patient. It's all working.'

'Is it?' Mega growled. 'Well, it's not working for me. Everyone's getting restless. I want a result soon.'

'Soonest,' Psycho added spitefully.

The Marketing Mink could not help letting out deep sighs.

'Did you say something?' Mega asked sharply.

'No, great leader,' MI replied hurriedly.

'Well you'd better have something to say this evening,' Mega growled, stalking off.

'Mega's right in a way,' M2 remarked, rather disloyally, his twin thought, as the pair walked the familiar path to the Small Clearing. 'Something should be happening by now.'

'What precisely?' MI inquired angrily.

'I don't know,' M2 confessed. 'Anything would do.'

'Like that?' MI asked casually, stopping to look down through a gap in the trees at the valley floor.

M2 followed his gaze. A long black volver had drawn up and the door was being opened to a glittering human. As he strolled to the riverbank he was immediately surrounded by bowing and scraping twitchers, who pointed deferentially to the alder tree.

'It's the first VIH!' he yelled.

'Right, 2! We've cracked it! Quick!'

The mink duo, trembling with anticipation, raced to the clearing.

'The VIH has come,' MI shouted, dancing up and down. 'Straight to your posing tree, Most Magnificent Emperor – as *vite* as you can!'

Alphonse, relaxing with one the dunnock massages he was becoming addicted to, regarded them superciliously.

'Tell me, what is this, 'ow you say, VIH?' he inquired, idly motioning to the dunnocks to continue.

'A Very Important Human, Your Exceeding Wonderfulness,' MI gabbled. 'The one who has the power to save the wood. Please, please, Your Most Majesticfulness – and Your Most Divinely Beautiful – go and fly your hearts out for him!'

He was almost on his knees.

Alphonse waved away the dunnocks, stretched his perfectly preened wings and inspected them critically.

'*Bon*! Bertha and I were of course expecting this Very Important 'Uman,' he announced with imperial coolness. 'You will therefore be glad to 'ear we 'ave prepared something a leetle special for this occasion. Come, *ma chérie*.'

In line with MI's plea, the loving couple flew staight to the alder tree. At first it seemed they were just going to do their normal side by side display. Then they started to sing.

As the undisputed ruler of all he surveyed, Alphonse had never joined the dawn or evening choruses by which his subjects carried out the mundane task of reinforcing their territory. But now a melodious stream poured from his beak and as Bertha joined him in perfect harmony the pair began a joyful duet to their love. On the rollway the VIH stood stock-still, as if mesmerised, while various twitchers rushed to switch off the engines of their volvers. Within the wood every creature, enchanted, fell silent. Even the river seemed to mute its chuckling passage over the shallows, allowing the liquid tones to float unhindered across the valley. As an envious nightingale remarked afterwards, it was so quiet you could hear a leaf drop.

Finally, drawing to a glorious crescendo, Alphonse and Bertha dipped their heads brietly to their spellbound audience and flew back into the wood. Back on the rollway all the humans, including the VIH, burst into ecstatic applause.

It was all over the next afternoon. Another long black volver arrived, this time disgorging a pair of grim-looking humans clad in matching grey. Not pausing to linger on the rollway, they marched straight across the bridge and set off across the Long Field towards the five-barred gate.

'Stage Five!' MI shrieked.

'Don't count your chickens!' M2 shouted back. 'But it sure looks good.'

The pair of humans stopped at the gate and produced a small white square, which they attached to the top bar. Then they started up the churned-up expanse of the Ride, picking their way delicately through the mud and making fussy diversions to avoid the worst patches. Reaching the Big Clearing, they briskly handed another white square to each of the working humans before walking over and sticking one on each digger. When a worker tried to stop them there was a brief argument before they broke away and walked back down the Ride. They emerged into the Long Field to loud cheers from the twitchers, got straight back into their black volver and rolled away.

Back in the wood the working humans had stopped in their tracks. Both diggers were shut down as they gathered in a huddled group, examining the white squares and talking in subdued tones. Eventually, looking reluctant, they packed up early and walked back down the Ride. Meanwhile the twitchers had abandoned their normal watching position and gathered in a group by the bridge. As the workers crossed it, they surrounded them, dancing round in glee.

MI and M2 were beside themselves with fresh excitement as the sound of angry voices drifted up from the Long Field, and the two sides began making threatening gestures at each other. The woodland creatures watched spellbound as one pair raised their fists and squared up to each other, while the angry shouting swelled. The rest gathered round and the first scuffles started, soon erupting into various small pitched battles. The humans were fighting, the creatures yelled in delight as they spilled out onto the rollway. Just then a volver making a fearsome noise roared up and screeched to a halt, a blue light flashing eerily from its top.

'It's a neenaw!' the Marketing Mink cried, dancing up and down in alloyed triumph. 'We've pulled a neenaw! Stage Six reached as planned! Campaign one thousand per cent successful! The show's over! Bring the curtain down! We've done it!'

'Done what?' the creatures asked, dumbfounded.

'Saved the wood, you morons,' MI shouted. 'Can't you see that's what the humans are fighting about?'

'But how?' the creatures clamoured.

'The twitchers have delivered the goods, you fools,' MI

shouted. 'The white squares, you dimwits — they make it official!'

The creatures stared at him, gobsmacked. Were they seriously supposed to believe something as insignificant as a white square had saved them? Nothing much had happened, bar the unusual sight of seeing humans fighting. But all species fought, one way or another, and in the still-struggling mass there was no indication either side had won.

Suddenly a cock pheasant, cogitating on these baffling events, piped up: 'The wood's the goods!'

'That's right! The wood's the goods!' the creatures chorused, taking comfort in the familiar phrase.

Meanwhile the Marketing Mink ran back to Alphonse, who had remained behind, being ministered to by his posse of dunnocks.

'Out you go!' they screamed at the golden oriole

Alphonse looked at them bewildered.

'You've done it! Go and celebrate your success, Your Most Arrogantly Pompous, Incredibly Vain, Insufferably Foolish and Exceedingly Jaune Nincompoopishness,' M2 yelled, bursting with laughter. He rounded on Bertha. 'You too, Your Most Dismally Dimwitted, Turgidly Dull and Horribly Frowzy Crossed-beakiness!'

Alphonse's jaw dropped, while the slave dunnocks stood equally open-mouthed.

M2 creased up even more. 'Oh get on with it, you stupid birds, before you kill me,' he shouted, cackling insanely as he held his sides and rolled about on the ground,.

'I surrender,' his brother howled, similarly jack-knifed. 'You win, 2! I'll never think of anything better than that.'

But when Alphonse and Bertha still failed to move the mink's mood switched.

'Fly now, you bastards! Both of you!' they snarled, running towards the startled pair.

Alphonse and Bertha, looking completely lost, both rose hurriedly from the ground and flew uncertainly out of the wood towards the rollway, where more neenaw volvers had drawn up, bringing droves of identical humans who were now wading in to stop the fighting. As the pair came into view, twitchers, neenaw humans and workers gradually stopped struggling with each other and looked upwards, the twitchers cheering and punching the air with elation. The message sank in and Alphonse and Bertha began a series of victory rolls over the remains of the fracas to even greater jubilation. Finishing their display with a grand flourish, they flew to the posing tree, where they sat, grinning from ear to ear, as they basked in the glow of appreciation from their supporters.

That evening, when the last of the twitchers had left, a few of the creatures crept down to the five-barred gate. Although nobody commented on it, there was a whiff of euphoria in the dry air, a feeling that, at last, they might have made the breakthrough. The sky sparkled with brilliant stars, while the early crescent moon cast a watery light, enabling them to see close up that the seemingly white square in fact had black marks all over it. Smaller, more agile creatures scrambled up the gate to sniff at it, with one brave vole even nibbling at a corner, yet they could find no clues to the central mystery it posed. How could a powerless object like this have brought their salvation in such a curiously undramatic way?

Eventually it was Cowslip, emerging from a huddle of her CWG rabbits, who claimed to know the definitive answer.

'It's a petition,' she announced smugly, giving a her silly superior grin in pity for the others' ignorance. 'You see, you should have listened to us Concerned Guardians. We always maintained that a petition was the correct instrument for getting things done.'

'It's bloody gobbledy-gook, if you ask me,' Boris — whom nobody had — harumphed noisily before turning viciously on Cowslip. 'Trying to don your late fellow's mantle, are you, you ugly tosser?' he barked nastily. 'Well just remember — you've only the mink's word that your so-called petition works!'

That was true, the other creatures thought, suddenly looking sombre, while Owl, aware he knew more than they did, kept his thoughts to himself. He wasn't going to get into an argument with Boris. Yet Freddie had already told him that the white square originally stuck to the bridge indicated that the work was to start. That this one signifying it was now ending was therefore a bit of a puzzle, but it did confirm the power of white squares. The Marketing Mink, Owl had a shrewd idea, were telling the truth. Alphonse really had done it.

He soon found out how right he was, as the crowd of twitchers on the rollway grew ever larger while the working humans stopped coming altogether. The wood stayed deserted for days until one morning a convoy of volvers drew up on the rollway and disgorged a small army of workers, which marched up the Ride and woke up the two yellow diggers, causing consternation. However, instead of resuming their destruction, these now ignominiously retreated down the Ride, white squares still attached to their sides. The volver convoy then ground up and down all day, loading up the workers' stuff and taking it away. Finally, as dusk was falling, the last departed, its humans sealing the five-barred gate behind them.

'That's it,' MI announced smugly as he prepared to go back to the Plateau and give Mega their definitive last report. 'We won't be seeing them again in a hurry – as long as you keep up your flights,' he added sternly, turning to Alphonse.

'*Mais certainement*,' Alphonse replied aloofly. 'As my 'umble subjects, you should know it is not the 'abit of Emperors to deesappoint their audience. You may trust my Empress and me to fly without you.'

The other creatures applauded with relief as the Marketing Mink left. There was still much they did not understand, but now they had seen the result of Alphonse's work they had lost interest in any further questioning. All they knew was that they were safe. They could start forgetting about the humans all over again.

59

Youngies will be Youngies

The wood was well into the heaviness of late summer. After starting clear and blue in the morning, by midday the sky now usually clouded over to a steely grey, dispensing a flat light which glared and flared, making everyone screw their eyes up. The pattern of hot weather, with baking days and stiflingly warm nights, had been set for nearly a moon, making the wood dryly and grittily uncomfortable. There had been occasional showers, but no proper downpour, while the morning dew had been so light as to be almost non-existent. Everything, and everyone, was gasping for rain. The plants on thin stony ground, such as the Quarry, had turned brown and brittle, frizzled by the searing heat, while the leaves of the other bushes and trees had become darker and more leathery in their maturity. Some were now drooping permanently, while on the ground every movement caused dried-out sticks and leaves to rustle and crackle. In some places the earth had become so parched that it had split, opening up mini-chasms which hapless insects tumbled into. The Ride and the Big Clearing were ruined. The ruts and mud left by the human workers had set into an ugly mess of lumps and grooves that were as hard as rock. In the middle of the wood the stream had stopped running, its pools reduced to skins of sticky mud, imprinted with the tracks of creatures vainly searching for water. Damp and mossy places had dried to shrivelled patches, and the river, reduced to its lowest ebb, streamed with weed and algae.

Yet even without rain it often felt sultry, the heavy and musky scent of the hogsweed and elderberry flowers adding to the stifling atmosphere. The last pink bells of the foxgloves, exposed on their tall stems, hardly stirred, and barely a ripple disturbed the grass of the Long Field. The sweltering heat sapped so much energy that throughout much of the day few creatures stirred. These were the days of the dog-roses, the days the wood-land inhabitants were meant to enjoy, but this time round felt more they were having to endure. Some were actually suffering, with digging creatures in particular scratching forlornly at the hard earth, while the worms within it drove ever deeper as they tracked the receding moisture. Meanwhile everyone was noticing how the evenings were becoming shorter as the wood began its long slide towards the Big Cold.

It was a jangly time, when they were often tired and irritable for no particular reason they could put their paw on — apart from the twin problems of the mink and Alphonse. The mink activity seemed to have increased, rather than abating with the departure of the humans, while Alphonse was simply more and more of a problem.

To begin with, loving his work, he had found no difficulty in fulfilling his promise to the Marketing Mink.

'Mes crowds await me,' he announced every morning as the clutch of dunnocks fussed over him. His snails and frog's legs breakfast forgotten, he now fed greedily on the more conventional titbits they slavishly presented to him, while his personal dressers arranged and re-arranged his plumage until every feather was in perfect place.

But as he flew ostentatiously about, strutting and posing in a manner he deemed worthy of an Emperor, his high profile promoted vast dissension. Jealous cock birds of different species, fed up with constantly having to defer to him, had their ire increased by seeing their hens openly swooning. He was

completely over the top, the cocks grumbled, only to find hens
rushing to defend him. Why couldn't they be as sexy and
glamorous? they demanded. The cocks' normal answer would
have been to gang up on such an upsetting interloper and driven
him out. But, stymied by the Marketing Mink's insistence he
must be kept entirely happy, they had to hold back, meanwhile
catering for his every wish and foible catered for as assiduously
as if the white squares had never appeared.

'We've done our job,' MI snickered in response to the
grumbles. 'Now it's up to you to do yours. And if you don't
like Alphonse don't blame us. Who chose him?'

However the mink's attempts to distance themselves from the
daily running of the show flights soon rebounded. After a happy
period when he and Bertha gloried in flying totally unsupervised,
just for the joy of it, Alphonse began to tire of the continuous
routine. His love affair with Bertha was as strong as ever and
he was enjoying the hot weather, so similar to what he was
used to in his *bois*. Otherwise, though, he was beginning to
wonder why he was still there. His flights were becoming a
daily grind which he increasingly sought to escape from. He
became erratic and unpredictable. As his schedule degenerated
he began imposing conditions — he would fly only when the sun
was shining brightly enough; he must have a long siesta during
the heat of the day, with all other creatures, under Imperial
Decree, ordered to remain quiet so as not to disturb him; he
would perform only if he judged the crowd of twitchers large
enough . . .

The Marketing Mink grovelled and cajoled. How could his
Exceeding Eminence disappoint his multitude of fans by not
demonstrating his full magnificence? How could they possibly
live without the uplifting sight of His Most Vibrantly Handsome
to cheer their hearts and fulfil their dreams? But they soon found
the flattery had worn thin.

When Alphonse failed to respond however fancy the phrases
they thought up, they moved to a harder tone. It was his
responsibility to carry on, whether he liked it or not — otherwise
the yellow diggers would be back! The new approach was
effective for a short period, but when it wore off MI and M2

descended to the bottom line. If they couldn't persuade him to fly they would make him. In consultation with Maxi, a rota was drawn up by which a mink stayed with him constantly, silencing his protests and forcing him and Bertha to fly by growling and baring their teeth.

Under this pressure Alphonse surlily returned to carrying out his duties in a lacklustre way, only to hit the next problem. His novelty value had diminished and his human audience was shrinking. On occasions it was well into the morning before the first twitcher arrived to take up station by the river, while on one particularly embarrassing afternoon there was no-one at all and the golden oriole's bleats of protest reached a new peak when his mink minder forced him to play to an empty house.

'He's peaked,' MI concluded mournfully, staring at the audience rating graph which now resembled a drawing of a mountain in profile.

'Over the hill,' M2 agreed sadly. 'He's dropping out of the charts and becoming just another bird.'

And an extremely odious one at that, the woodland creatures continued to mutter.

Meanwhile the Marketing Mink's attempts to keep both Alphonse in the air and interest in him from flagging were being hampered by the growing crisis back at the Plateau. As the leaders were well aware, summer was not the best time for mink. Even though their heavy coats moulted, they still found it desperately hot and spent much of their time panting in their holts or cooling off in the river. It was now that the chance of dissent in the colony was at its greatest. With tempers on such short fuses, there was always a danger the most petty squabbles would flare up into a full-blown riot.

The real problem, though, was the youngies. The birth of the colony's infants had been the high point. After the arrival of the lone Minimus, the females had produced litters of bouncing babies, with one even managing the magic seven. The rejoicing at the time had been spontaneous and genuine, but everyone could also see that the newcomers so vastly outnumbered their parents they were causing a population explosion. Maxi's original warning, when he pushed for the Quarry site, had come home to roost.

Neighbourly relations had now reached a new low. The holt-improvement mania had spawned such a plethora of extensions and conversions that they had run into each other, sparking a series of bitter territorial disputes. Desperate for space, neighbours quarrelled unceasingly, the problems exacerbated daily as the kits grew quickly into vigorous cubs. As an interim measure a few extra holts were dug out at the bottom of the riverbank, but everyone knew they were only temporary and would flood as soon as the river rose. There was desultory talk about developing a subsidiary colony on the acornball pitch further up the slope. But, as the Marketing Mink kept impressing on Mega, that would only fudge the overall problem. It wasn't just on the Plateau that the vastly enlarged pack needed more room, they emphasised. All the forward eating projections demonstrated conclusively that, with so many mouths to feed, the pack needed more space to hunt in.

The Marketing Mink's initial answer had been setting up 'Project X', a series of inducements and rallying speeches by Mega to encourage the youngies to go out and conquer fresh woods of their own. However this flopped immediately, as the youngies made it clear they regarded the wood, Plateau and Waterama complex as their birthright. Not only did they have the normal boundless energy and confidence of youth but, unlike their parents, no past memories of cage life either held them back or bound them together. Born straight into this place of glorious freedom, they simply took for granted that it was their property.

Mega found himself torn by the conflict. The colony had established itself so successfully he wished nothing more than that it go on expanding for ever. Yet at the same time, because of that very success he had to accept that it was heading inexorably for the crunch. With both generations determined to drive each other out, the only question now was who would win. Mega knew it was one that the older mink did not want to address. Like him, they did not see the result as a foregone conclusion in their favour. He sympathised with their attitude as facing up to things meant abandoning the dream of a united colony. But there was still no choice.

'We'll have to hold a leadership conference to hammer out our strategy,' he informed Maxi. 'It needs to be in secret, well away from the Plateau.'

'Why not use the Quarry, my leader?' his military adviser suggested, vastly relieved. His faith in Mega had never wavered, and now, once again, his leader was proving to have the courage to square up to the issue which they all knew they had been avoiding.

Sitting on the hard stones of the Quarry, the Marketing Mink stared mournfully up at the tree under which the leadership had gathered and which, by the unhappiest of coincidences, was the very one Alphonse had humiliated them from. As far as they knew, no report of their grovelling had ever reached the Plateau, but being reminded of the grisly incident did not help to improve their frame of mind. Neither did Psycho.

'We have to face the fact that Project X has failed,' he said with malicious satisfaction. 'My intelligence sources report the youngies hatching all sorts of plots to try to force us out.

'Of course, Mega, they're entirely juvenile,' he added with a sycophantic laugh. 'Nothing you couldn't quash with a mere flick of your paw. However, they do indicate the way things are going. So what we have to decide now, I'm afraid, is whether the showdown is to be on our terms or theirs.'

'Ours,' Mega growled, brushing aside his spin-doctor's grovelling agreement.

'We should treat the little bleeders like coneys,' Maxi barked. 'Take them out. Then we'd have no more trouble.'

Maxi had been more affected than anyone by the youngies' insubordination, finding himself taken back to his childhood as they subjected him to cheeky taunts and jibes about missing brain power.

'It's not just that they're rude and insolent, my leader,' he whined. 'They seem determined to break the rules just for the sake of it. I don't know what to do with the buggers. I've stepped up the official rampages, but the coneycide campaign doesn't work very well with them. Unlike us and our generation, they don't really seem to believe in the rabbit threat. The little bastards won't stop killing anything that moves — even rabbits inside the wood, directly against your specific orders.

'I've even seen them making rude gestures at our emblem,' he concluded in a voice of deepest outrage, brushing his whiskers reverentially. He personally saluted the rigid cat-tail every night and morning, without fail.

'That is bad, Maxi,' Mega sympathised, though he felt curiously unemotional about this aspect himself. Maybe he was just becoming jaded under the strain of being the leader. Yet he doubted it. He had never attached the same significance to the cat-tail after mistakenly permitting Psycho to use it for his cynical rabbit ploy. It now seemed a relic of a time so long ago he had difficulty in recalling it. They could hardly expect the youngies, who had nothing to relate it to, to appreciate what it stood for.

'What have you got to say for yourselves?' he asked MI and M2.

'Difficult one this, Mega,' MI replied with a failed attempt at heartiness. 'As we all know, the availability-to-eat graphs show us heading towards a permanent deficit situation with a consquent market collapse. We still haven't given up on Project X, though. More brilliant speeches about the glories of conquering fresh woods may well win us through in the end. Meanwhile we've come up with something new, which we think very exciting — a Minions' Charter.'

'A what?' Mega's voice was cold.

'A Minion's Charter,' M2 repeated, taking up the running. 'It's a concept we're particularly proud of, great leader. What we do is give a pledge to the youngies that they have all sorts of rights. Then we guarantee that if we fail to deliver these as promised, they have the further right of redress.'

Mega shuddered. The success of the golden oriole campaign had obviously gone to this pair's heads. Pledges, rights, redress — what was this? They were supposed to be discussing mink leadership style.

'Of course we won't actually give redress,' M2 added

enthusiastically. 'But the Charter will still work for the youngies by reconceptualising their existence.'

'By doing what?' Mega growled in horrified fascination.

'Making them see their position differently,' MI made a desperate attempt to explain. 'At present the youngies are claiming we leaders take no heed of their wishes. But once a Minions' Charter has made us accountable, they'll believe that they're in charge. Brilliant, isn't it? A real breakthrough, we both think.'

Mega suppressed his automatic reply. He still needed this pair, however tiresome and out of touch they might have become.

'Very interesting, I'm sure,' he replied coolly.

He turned from the crestfallen twins to Psycho, who had been monitoring this exchange with ill-contained glee.

'Tell me more about the youngie plots,' he ordered.

'Well, Mega, if you really want to know, there has been some wild talk about bumping you off,' Psycho replied nervously. 'None of them has the nerve to take you on in a straight fight of course,' he added quickly. 'Instead they've been discussing ambushes — but security is so good I can't see much danger from that direction.'

He simpered at Maxi, who ignored him.

'There's also been loose talk about undermining you in some way by making you look ridiculous,' he cackled. 'The latest nonsense is some herb they've extracted the name of from a coneycide rabbit. I've heard them speculating that if they can get you to eat it, your hair'll drop out. It's all total bollo, of course . . .'

Even discounting Psycho's normal weird eyes, Mega was sure he detected a new shiftiness in his manner. How reliant he had become on him to keep informed, he thought. Maybe he should find out more things for himself. But then this sounded like kids' stuff, rather than anything putting his leadership in imminent danger. Didn't Psycho, or any of the others, recognise that youngies would always be youngies? That it was entirely natural for them to challenge their elders and tilt at his crown? They should be proud of rearing mink with such spirit. On the other paw, maybe he should consider this

Minions' Charter bollo. It might at least help keep them in check for a time.

'They're only teething troubles at the moment, Mega,' Mata added quietly, unasked. 'I'm organising the mothers to do what they can. There is one youngie we must watch very carefully though – Minimus. He's the real troublemaker.'

As Psycho nodded in confirmation Mega suddenly thought how the two resembled each other. Both were small and now, apparently, nasty and devious. Yet he had never seen Minimus like that. The little youngie was certainly clever, but he seemed very friendly, as well as cheerful and willing.

'Every generation has to have one and they're not always apparent,' Mata added, echoing his thoughts and causing Psycho to wince.

Did he suddenly look guilty as well? Mega wondered, before finding himself asking Mata something he would normally only have put to her privately.

'What's your prognosis then?'

'Little cubs get bigger every day,' she replied coolly. 'And little teeth get sharper.'

Mega grimaced. What help was that? He still sought Mata's advice and respected her judgement, but his attitude towards her was changing. They continued to share their holt amicably enough – incidentally causing huge youngie grumbles about the space they had to themselves – but recently a burning resentment had been growing inside him. Since the kits had been born he had felt keenly deprived of being a specific father, rather than just theoretical father of them all. Although he had not yet voiced his feelings to Mata, he sensed she knew about them. Did she now regret her decision not to become a mother? he wondered. Was she, after all, not such a cold fish? He had spotted her, several times, looking longingly at mothers as they suckled their infants. She had worn the same look later when watching the playful antics of the young cubs as they chased butterflies, insects, dead leaves – anything that moved. How could she not feel the same as him in the face of such vitality, such exuberance, such eager joy in just living? The youngies might spell trouble, but at least they were at the opposite end of the spectrum from the cold-hearted analysis their leaders were at present indulging in. Youngies didn't calculate life, they just lived it.

It was all so confusing, especially as the other leaders seemed unwilling, or unable, to face up to things. The conference was just fudging the issue – as maybe he was. What he needed was more time to think. He could start by giving himself a breathing space. He would go back to the Plateau on his own, without for once being trailed by one of the thick muscle-mink who now guarded him constantly and were at present waiting discreetly out of earshot.

'I insist, Maxi,' he cut across his security adviser's stentorian protests.

60

All that Glisters

Mega trod the path through the trees with a light step. 'Rule Minkmania, Minkmania rules the wood!' he sang contentedly, crushing up a violet ground beetle and absent-mindedly spitting out the carapace. As he had hoped, his gloom lifted the moment he left the Quarry and he savoured the wonderful feeling of sauntering through his own domain. Even better, he could sense a heavier feeling than usual in the air. That could mean a thunderstorm was on its way, which was just what they needed to help disperse the tension in the atmosphere.

But as he drew nearer to the Plateau his benign mood was interrupted by an urgent warning from his senses. Something was wrong. He stopped to sniff the air, but it was so redolent of wild garlic everything else was drowned out. It was only when he concentrated on listening that he realised what was odd. All he could hear was an occasional birdcall. None of the normal happy noise was coming from the Waterama complex. It almost sounded as though mink headquarters was deserted – which couldn't possibly be the case.

He dropped down and hugged the ground as he approached

the holly bush, waiting for the challenge from the duty sentry. As part of Maxi's security obsession, even he as leader had to give the password and he was ready with that moon's code of 'wet slippery fur'. But although he got closer and closer the challenge still did not come and finally, when he looked inside, he saw the post was empty.

His alarm bells rang immediately. Abandoning sentry duty was a crime so heinous it had never happened before. As thoughts of the ambush mentioned by Psycho floated into his mind, caution dictated that he now go back, or at least adopt a roundabout route and approach more circumspectly. Best of all, he should wait until his advisers caught up with him. Then he felt a sudden surge of anger. Why should he wait? He was the leader of the pack. Surely he hadn't reached the day when he was afraid to walk openly into his own powerbase?

He continued to climb slowly up the dry crumbly earth, knowing he was giving his presence away but unable to avoid stepping on dry debris and twigs that snapped under his feet. He could still hear no noise from above, and his senses were screaming stronger and stronger warnings. At the top, for once he did not bound confidently onto the grass but instead slowly raised his head to peer over the edge. His first glance confirmed his suspicions. There were no minions to be seen, although the replica rabbit grinned inanely at him, the cat-tail hanging stiffly by its side as usual. But what was now underneath it made him jerk with shock. As if to emphasise how its constant exposure to the elements had faded the orange in the tail's fur, the green grass had become a sea of vibrant yellow. He could pick out the two wings, the ripped-open body and one foot standing absurdly upright, attached to nothing. Nearer him, lying forlornly on its side, was the golden oriole's detached head. One lifeless eye stared vacantly at him, while the hole in the top showed where the brains had been sucked out. What had been going on? None of the possible scenarios Psycho had put forward for the youngie challenge had included anything as dire as this. How could the juvenile idiots have been so selfish? Surely they must have known that for their own petty ends they were killing the one creature who was saving them all from the humans?

They weren't that stupid though, he realised with a further jolt. They had been clever enough to do it while their leaders were absent at the secret conference. Maxi's brief had been to ensure nobody knew where they were, which would explain why nobody loyal had run to warn them. It wasn't just clever though — it was too clever. There must have been a leak, or else someone had given them a tip-off. But who would have done that? And even then, how had they acted so quickly? They must have planned it in advance. In which case, why hadn't Psycho's intelligence network uncovered their scheme?

Mega looked back down the slope and saw that the others had still not emerged from the trees. He was on his own, wide open. If the youngies were going to attack, they would do so now. He braced himself as he thought he heard a noise in the bushes opposite, while his mind went on racing through the permutations. Just because the entire pack was missing didn't necessarily mean all the mink were involved. He was certain his generation was still on his side. Where were his loyal supporters, though? Had they fled, fearful he would deem them to have been involved? Or had the youngsters used some pretext to lure them away? Maybe they were simply hiding in their holts, lost without their leader?

His head snapped up as he distinctly heard a dry stick break in the bushes, followed by a stifled snort. So that was where the bastards were skulking. That was how they were mounting their challenge — by attacking a defenceless bird when his back was turned, then hiding. In that case he would deal with them here and now.

All his positive thoughts about them forgotten, he raised his pointed muzzle and gave a bay of defiance.

'I know you're in there!' he shouted through bared teeth. 'And if you're true mink you'll come out and fight. Otherwise be forever branded as the craven cowards you are.'

There was a rustle, but no reply.

'Come on out, you yellow bastards!' he shouted, wincing as he realised the unconscious pun. 'I, Mega, am waiting for you!'

The rustling got louder.

'In that case I'm coming in to get you!' he shouted, setting off stiff-legged across the grass, fur bristling and tail bushed up. Never in his life had he felt so angry. It didn't matter how many of them there were. The entire pack could come at him – he was ready.

Ignoring the yellow feathers under his feet, he walked to the beech tree and jumped up to wrench down the cat-tail with one huge tug. Picking it up, he began to whirl it round his head faster and faster, all the time screaming with rage and frustration, until finally he let go and hurled it into the bushes. As it smashed into the greenery his opponents' nerve broke. Pandemonium shook the bushes, making them quiver as if they were alive, and he heard the sound of bodies crashing away through the trees.

'Come back, you scum!' he bellowed, jumping up and down in his fury. 'You're not fit to be called mink – you're worse than bloody coneys!'

But he made no attempt to chase them. Through turning tail like that they had placed themselves even further beneath his contempt. If the culprits didn't identify themselves by simply not coming back he'd give the job of fingering them to Psycho – which might in turn put a whole new spin on the equation. Someone, somewhere, must have sold him out. Meanwhile he needed to concentrate on the present and, the best way to start was to eradicate all traces of the slaughtered bird. Expunging it visibly would be the first step towards wiping the incident from the colony's consciousness.

Leaving the cat-tail, he strode back across the Plateau and looked over the edge. The rest of the leadership was halfway up the slope, Maxi puffing hard at the front, MI and M2 behind him and Psycho trailing at the rear. Mata was nowhere to be seen.

'Where's the sentry, my leader?' Maxi shouted up anxiously. 'Are you all right?'

'Of course I'm all right,' Mega shouted back. 'All of you, stop right where you are.'

His voice was so dreadful they froze like statues, while he turned to address the deserted Plateau.

'Attention all mink!' he shouted. 'If any of you are in your holts I order you not to move under any circumstances. I will not repeat this warning.'

'Has there been a security breach, Mega?' Maxi's worried voice floated up from below.

'You lot listen to me as well,' Mega shouted down. 'Then do exactly what I say.'

He waved them up on to the Plateau and allowed them one gasp of shock.

'We'll sort the rest out later,' he growled as they stared open-mouthed. The Marketing Mink, not surprisingly, looked the most deeply affected. MI's eye twitched violently, whilst M2 just stood looking pole-axed.

'I want everything assembled into one heap,' he ordered. 'And by that I mean every single, solitary feather.'

As they scurried to obey they pointedly avoided catching his eye, while he crouched down and began eating the body of the golden oriole. None of them had ever felt such a strong aura of brooding rage as the one he was giving off. The air of menace about him was utterly chilling.

When they had finished he ordered them to remove the pile to a deep hole further up the slope, which he helped Maxi fill in. Then they all quartered the Plateau until he was entirely satisfied every trace had been obliterated

All, that was, except for one large and glowing yellow wing feather, which he had stored in his holt when none of them was looking. He would have a use for it soon.

61

Hitting the Rocks

Rumours of Alphonse's death flashed round the woodland community almost instantaneously. Owl, rudely awoken from a deep sleep by an excited companion of Bertha's, flew straight to the Plateau. What the pellets had the mink been up to now?

He arrived to be greeted by a curious sight. The area was deserted except for the mink leaders, who were running round collecting what were clearly the late Alphonse's scattered feathers. The unfortunate golden oriole had obviously been not just killed but torn into pieces, and the sight of that yellow heap, speckled with red, made Owl's heart sink. Worse still was the spectacle of Mega crouched down, finishing off the main part of the carcass.

Owl made no attempt to communicate but flew straight to the Small Clearing. He found Bertha sobbing her heart out.

'Why?' she was repeating, while Raka tried to comfort her.

'She's taking it badly,' the rook whispered, folding Bertha's head under her wing and rocking her gently. All round stood a subdued ring of silent creatures.

Owl ushered the stunned slave dunnocks to one side and

interrogated them as sympathetically as he could. But the story he pieced together did not make much sense. Alphonse's mink minder had apparently taken a break, just before the appearance of a young mink whom the dunnocks hadn't seen before. The youngster had then fawningly informed the Emperor that his presence was required at the Plateau. Mega wished not only to meet him for the first time, but to give him a special reward. The dim-witted dunnocks had welcomed this initiative, assuming the small and slightly sickly-looking youngster just the kind of junior to be sent on such an errand. They knew only too well, from the way he treated them like dirt, that the Alphonse show had soured. Plaudits from the mink leader should not only cheer him up, but put some pep back into his performances and take the pressure off them.

Although treating the mink emissary in his normal supercilious fashion, Alphonse had obviously been flattered.

'It is about time your leader kow-towed personally to his Emperor,' he announced loftily. 'I weel therefore deign to come, accompanied, of course, by *ma belle* Empress.'

But Bertha pleaded she was exhausted. Aware that the mink regarded her as a sideshow at best, and a positive hindrance at worst, she had seen that her presence would only complicate matters. Alphonse informed the mink messenger he would be at the Plateau shortly, before fussing over her solicitously and instructing the dunnocks to find her some reviving berries. After a quick coiffure, he had finally flown off alone. That was the last they had seen of him.

Owl cursed. In retrospect Alphonse's behaviour had been unbelievably reckless. If only some more effective woodland creatures had been present. But that had to be down to the golden oriole. He had become so insufferable it was not surprising everyone avoided him whenever they could.

Bertha, however, didn't see it like that. 'It'th all thankth to me,' she sobbed. 'If I'd only gone, I could have thacrifithed mythelf. Now my poor Alphonthe ith gone, gone, gone . . .'

Owl and Raka looked on helplessly as she beat her head on the ground.

'I'm going back to the Plateau,' Owl whispered.

But Bertha had overheard. 'I'm coming too,' she wailed. 'I mutht thee him.'

Knowing the grisly sight that would confront her, Owl sternly refused, provoking a fresh outburst of grief.

'Ollie's going to do a job,' Raka tried to console her, signalling with her eyes for him to leave.

With a last pitying look at Bertha, Owl flew off in a cold fury. Until now he had had no reason to disbelieve Mega's solemn promise that Alphonse would not be harmed under any circumstances. There must be some rational explanation for what had happened.

But when he arrived back over mink headquarters his anger and puzzlement increased. The pathetic pile of Alphonse's remains had entirely disappeared. There was now not a single yellow feather in sight. Instead the pack was back, gathered in a group, with Mega addressing them, while Maxi and the muscle-mink prowled round the edges. This was getting odder and odder. Yet Owl wasn't going to involve himself in any meeting. He had to have this out with the mink leader one to one.

He flew down to the holly bush.

'Tell Mega to meet me at the Quarry — now!' he hooted imperiously at the sentry.

'What's the password?' came the wooden-headed reply.

'If you don't get a move on, for you personally it's death,' Owl shouted, pointing to Boris, who was lumbering towards them.

The sentry took one look and scampered upwards, while Owl departed for the Quarry leaving Boris to his own devices. If the badger wanted to have a go, good luck to him. There was no point in holding him back any longer.

Owl was so blinded by righteous anger it never occurred to him Mega might not make the meeting. All he could feel was renewed rage when the mink leader came not alone, as required, but with Maxi.

'Get that moron out of here,' he screeched.

Mega, swallowing hard, instructed Maxi to withdraw.

'It could be a trap, my leader,' his military adviser hissed, looking worried.

'That's an order,' Mega snapped back.

Surlily Maxi retreated, all the time keeping them both in sight. When Owl was satisfied he was out of earshot he posed Bertha's blunt question. 'Why?'

'I'm sorry. It wasn't intended,' Mega replied, looking contrite.

Owl felt startled. He hadn't been expecting an instant apology. Yet the reply still wasn't good enough.

'But I saw you myself eating Alphonse's body,' he exploded.

'I had no choice. We had to get rid of it,' Mega sighed, sucking his teeth. 'It wasn't us leaders who killed him though – it was the youngies.'

As he paused and looked reflective something told Owl to be patient and give him some space.

'You won't like what I'm going to say, but you have to believe it,' the mink leader eventually continued. 'I'm afraid the young ones in the colony have been causing a few problems lately. It's been nothing too serious up to now, which is why we never thought it would come to anything like this. I'm as sorry about it as you undoubtedly are.'

Owl paused. Suddenly a lot of things were falling into place. With the humans gone, he had thought the mink were simply reverting to type. But now, if he hadn't got it wrong, basically Mega was confessing he had lost control. So that was why the coneycide campaign seemed so much more vicious. That was why rabbits were how being killed inside the wood as well as outside. That was why the mink tyranny didn't just seem worse, but actually was.

'I'm dealing with things,' Mega added, breaking into his chain of thought. He looked grim. 'There'll be no more trouble in the future, I can assure you.'

'It's a bit late for that now,' Owl retorted, trying to keep his temper in check.

Yet he still felt he had to give the mink leader a chance. And if he was sincere in wanting to punish the guilty parties there was some information Owl could usefully add.

'For what it's worth, Alphonse was set up by a young mink who brought him the message that you wanted to see him at the Plateau. The dunnocks said he was small and slightly sickly-looking. Of course Alphonse fell straight for it—'

'Thank you,' Mega replied. 'That's just the kind of lead I need. I'll deal with it, don't worry.'

Yet, as he spoke, Owl thought his voice sounded slightly hesitant, lacking its normal firmness and conviction. Come to think of it, he had never seen the mink leader looking so down. Pellets! he suddenly thought as full realisation sank in. He's blown it. He's lost his touch. Until now Owl had been conducting negotiations in full confidence the mink leader would deliver. That was the entire basis of their alliance. But if Mega no longer ruled with an iron grip his promises would be worthless. Anything could happen. For all Owl knew, what Mega had called 'a few problems' could be a euphemism for the mink colony teetering on the brink of civil war.

Feeling almost sorry for his opposite number, he half-sincerely tried a friendly leader-to-leader approach, whilst also reckoning it his best route to further information.

'I know what it's like,' he said sympathetically. 'There've been times when I've felt I was losing control myself.'

But he had crossed the line.

'I've not lost control,' Mega flared, suddenly back to his old dominant self. 'I didn't have to come here to tell you anything and I'm not having you interfering. Stay right out of it, do you hear? This is mink business.'

Angrily he waved Maxi over and the pair swept out of the Quarry, leaving Owl feeling slightly floored. Not only was his collaboration with the mink leader apparently over, but he had failed to ascertain why Alphonse's remains had disappeared, or where they had gone. The mink leader might have eaten the carcass, but there had been feathers all over the place. All Owl knew was that the golden oriole had disappeared as completely as if he had never been in the wood.

Owl stayed on in the peaceful seclusion of the Quarry for a think, quickly concluding he had to believe Mega's explanation. It had the ring of truth and it also ushered in another truth Owl could no longer deny. Until now he had stifled his regrets about working with the mink against the common human enemy, justifying it to himself by taking Ula's line that at least they should be given credit for effectiveness. Now, though, he couldn't think of one creature who would have any more time for them — least of all, of course, the human twitchers, still waiting patiently on the rollway in what was now a vain quest to spot their prize.

Owl jumped, suddenly so mortified he wanted to kick his own smoothly tapered bottom. He'd been so close he hadn't been able to see the wood for the trees. Talk about dim! And not just him — they'd all been so mesmerised they'd overlooked what was staring them in the face. What they must do now was reveal both the mink's presence and Alphonse's murder to the twitchers. They would do the creatures' job for them by taking their revenge, but how to alert their potential saviours? He could have dropped some of Alphonse's feathers in front of them as an indication, but with the golden oriole's body entirely vanished that was impossible. How else then?

Wearily, Owl realised he was just raising another question he couldn't answer. The Marketing Mink would probably come up with something, he thought with grim humour, but he could hardly consult them. Who else could he ask, bearing in mind how careful he had to be? He could certainly trust Boris, but they had fallen out so badly over the golden oriole they had stopped speaking. Owl wasn't at all sure he could repair the damage. Anyhow, a combination of the badger's 'don't want to know' attitude and general lack of imagination meant there was scant chance of his coming up with a worthwhile suggestion. Consulting anyone else would be very tricky. Owl gave a sharp intake of breath as he thought what would happen if he confided in Cowslip and her CWGs. She would be worse than useless, giving the game away by holding a meeting. And if the mink were to discover what he was contemplating, then the pellets would really hit the gale. They would never forgive a wholesale betrayal like that. Their reply was bound to be all-out war and then everybody in the wood would pay the penalty — himself especially, as the perpetrator of the idea. Owl was under no illusions. If the mink pack targetted him, it would probably get him, and Ula as well.

Once again there rose in front of his eyes the vision of the carpet of red at the Big Clearing massacre. It faded, to be replaced by the mink leader knocking the dove's head off. Owl had tried and tried to wipe both from his mind, but they still came back to haunt him. Every moment would be like that. The mink wouldn't rest until they had slaughtered everything. The alternative, if the young mink really were out of control, was them simply bleeding the woodland community to death more slowly. The problem was as knotty as an oak branch, yet he would gain nothing by sitting here in a futile attempt to solve it. At least he could tell Raka and Bertha why Alphonse had died.

But when he returned to the Small Clearing the hen blackbird had disappeared.

'She said she needed some time on her own, so I decided to respect her wish,' Raka explained. 'She promised to be back soon.'

'Where's everybody else gone?'

'Cowslip took the dunnocks away and the others followed. She also told me to inform you she was convening an emergency meeting and that you were to chair it.'

'She can forget that for a start,' Owl said shortly, dismissing the stupid rabbit from his mind. He didn't have time to waste on that pellets any more.

'Meetings are what she does,' Raka replied offhandedly.

Owl stared at her, thinking how darkly brooding she looked.

'What's wrong?' he asked.

'I'm worried about Bertha, Ollie,' she confessed. 'She should have been back by now.'

'She'll be all right. She's a big hen,' Owl said absent-mindedly.

He was preoccupied with putting his scheme into operation before the twitchers cottoned on that Alphonse was no longer present. With no reason to suspect anything was amiss, they would presumably think he had just flown off and would melt away. He must confide in someone soon and Raka was the one creature he should be able to trust. She was a fellow bird, had never let him down, and had a particular interest, besides which Owl felt sorry for her present predicament. She might have volunteered to go with Bertha in the first place, but she shouldn't be lumbered with being her keeper. Something new would be a welcome distraction for her.

He took a deep breath. 'I want you to listen carefully, Raka . . .'

'There's only the Marketing Mink,' Raka mused.

The rook had instantly agreed with Owl's thesis, but like him had since failed to come up with anyone to help. As she also depressingly commented, the Alphonse disaster couldn't have come at a worse time. Everybody was preparing for the Big Cold and from now on even rabbits wouldn't be able to breed fast enough to make up for further erosion of their numbers.

'And there's Freddie, of course,' she added, as though thinking out loud.

'That devious bastard!' Owl burst out angrily.

Yet at the same time he instantly knew she was right. With his skill at playing both ends against the middle, Freddie was undoubtedly the creature they needed. However, as Owl volubly protested, his mink connection meant he was also the most likely to betray them, which was why Owl had previously ruled him out.

Raka waited paitently until he had finished his tirade.

'I know all that, Ollie,' she said quietly. 'But who else is there?'

'It's too risky,' Owl protested. 'We must be able to think of something ourselves.'

Raka was about to reply when a pair of distraught blackbirds flew up with a whirr of wings.

'It's Bertha,' they cried. 'Come quickly.'

Bertha's body had been found in the Quarry, her neck broken. The sole witness, a shocked wren, explained she had flown into the rock face at full speed, as if she simply hadn't seen it. As he bent over the sadly twisted body, Owl could see Raka was close to tears. She had grown inordinately fond of Bertha. Despite her elevation to Empress, the blackbird had kept up surreptitious little meetings between them. Raka had admired the way she was keeping her feet on the ground, while still fearing for her, as she had from the beginning. Now those fears had come true.

'Poor Bertha,' she said sorrowfully. 'You know, there was one thing that struck me about Alphonse, which I never mentioned to you – or to her. I wonder if she knew?'

'What's that?' Owl asked, not really listening.

'Yellow is the colour of learning,' Raka replied.

Owl was puzzled by the remark. He didn't know that. Nor could he think of anything that Bertha – or Alphonse, come to think of it – could have learnt during their tragically short love affair.

'The learning's not for them, Ollie,' the rook added softly. 'It's for us.'

Owl looked at her in astonishment. For all her rough and raucous edges, Raka could go remarkably deep. What she said suddenly made everything spring into sharp focus, as if a gust of wind had blown the last mist off the Long Field. There might have been no alternative at the time, but now he could comprehend fully what a terrible mistake it had been to throw their lot in with the mink. Boris had been right all along. It wasn't just a question of the youngsters getting out of control, as Mega had claimed. The entire situation had now hit the rocks just as surely as sad Bertha. Owl could already sense the despair that would spread throughout the wood as this latest blow became public knowledge. He must act now.

'I've changed my mind,' he announced. 'I will go and see Freddie after all.'

'I'm glad about that, Ollie,' Raka replied gratefully. 'Remember, he's always been a true woodland creature at heart.'

'I'll try,' Owl promised. 'But it'll be hard.'

62

The Brush-off

Owl circled in the half-light of evening, watching Freddie emerge warily from his den. The fox lived at the edge of the wood, furthest away from the mink and near the top of the Ridge, where he had a good view over the surrounding fields but could duck into the trees if required. Typically Freddie, Owl thought, neither in nor out.

The fox allowed the rest of the family to follow him and began rolling and playing with his cubs. As Owl saw how patiently he endured their childish nips and fur-pulling, he was amazed at what a family animal Freddie obviously was at heart. It was a side of him Owl had never seen before and as he lovingly finished off the game it was clear he had adored it. Then, bidding the cubs and his vixen a tender goodnight, he slunk off on his familiar route that ran parallel with the Ridge crest. If he had noticed Owl above him, he gave no indication.

As he padded along, Owl admired the easy grace with which he moved his long body, his gorgeous red coat echoing the first hues of autumn and contrasting splendidly with the cool green of the grass. How magnificent his old friend looked, and, knowing his ways so well, how easy it was to read his passage.

Swooping surreptitiously down, Owl took up station on the branch of a small ash, where he knew Freddie would be unable to avoid him as he came out from behind a clump of bushes.

The fox emerged, stopped in his tracks and then stood nonplussed, one forepaw in the air.

'How goes it, Freddie?' Owl called cheerily.

'Fine, Ollie,' the fox replied guardedly. 'And you? It's been a long time.'

He didn't sound as though he had been missing him much, Owl thought – which was fair enough. Freddie had every reason to be suspicious of this obviously contrived meeting.

'I'm all right – apart from the mink,' Owl said non-committally. 'How are they affecting you?'

'I manage.'

I bet you do, you old dog, Owl thought. If you were more honest you'd confess you were doing very nicely out of them, thank you very much.

'Mind you, they are back with a vengeance, aren't they?' Freddie added unexpectedly. 'I've never seen them so fired up. These youngsters really are something else.'

'Aren't they just,' Owl agreed, taking advantage of the opening. 'Getting rid of the humans doesn't seem to have done much good, does it? We just seem to have swopped one tyranny for another.'

As if in confirmation a sudden burst of shrieks came from the direction of the Plateau and they both stiffened as they strained to determine whether they were pain or pleasure. Pleasure, they concluded simultaneously, nodding at each other.

'That bloody Waterama complex again,' Owl sighed. 'Try getting a good day's sleep with that going on.'

Freddie nodded sympathetically. The hideous shrieking stopped, to be replaced by the last notes of the birds who were bedding down for the night. As the convoy of rooks flapped heavily overhead Owl looked up but could not spot Raka. The silence dragged on, with Owl aware that it was up to him to break it. Freddie always made the other party take the lead.

'Not keeping you from anything?' he inquired casually.

'If you must know, I heard there was a rabbit rampage last night,' Freddie replied, looking directly up at him for the first time. 'I was going to see if there were any pickings. But it can wait.'

He sat down, scratched his ear and grinned in a not unfriendly fashion.

'You've heard about Alphonse?' Owl asked.

Freddie could hardly deny it. The wood had been talking about nothing else for days.

'I've heard.'

'What do you think?'

'I'm not surprised.'

'Well, I for one was disgusted,' Owl exclaimed, angered by the fox's cool dismissal. 'After all he'd done for us, he deserved a better fate than that.'

'That's mink for you.'

You should know, Owl thought savagely. He tried to suppress his anger by recalling Raka's remark about Freddie being a woodland creature at heart, while he sidled round the subject.

'You're very chummy with them, aren't you?'

'Maybe at one stage,' Freddie replied defensively. 'We all have to live. Not any more though, Ollie. These days they're too over the top even for me.'

Owl was surprised. It wasn't like Freddie to condemn any situation that benefited him.

'They're not like us woodland creatures, are they?' he agreed warmly. 'They don't have any respect.' He struggled for the right phrase. 'They don't understand live and let live, do they?'

'Live and let die, more like,' Freddie commented before reflecting for a moment. 'When they arrived, Ollie, I thought: here's something new, something that could be good for us — or at least for me.' He gave a self-deprecating grin. 'I couldn't see any harm in the wood having a shake-up. It might give a new edge to things.'

What was the old rascal up to? Owl thought. He sounded almost honest!

'I realise it now though, Ollie. You're right. The mink don't belong here and they never will. They're aliens.'

That was the word Owl had been racking his brain for!

'You've put your paw on it, Freddie,' he cried excitedly. 'They are aliens.'

Now was the moment to commit himself.

'The humans recognised that before by keeping them in cages, didn't they? And now they've killed Alphonse, the twitchers will hate them as much as we do, won't they? What I'm trying to say, Freddie,' he stumbled on, 'is that maybe, if they knew the mink were here and what they'd done, they'd get rid of them for us.'

There! He'd done it by putting himself in Freddie's paws. If the fox now reported back to the mink it would be — a CWG phrase popped into his mind — the end of the wood as they knew it.

Freddie's nose twitched.

'I've had similar thoughts myself, Ollie, but it doesn't really concern me any more,' he replied slowly, before seeming to make up his mind. 'I was going to tell you something for old times' sake, so I might as well now. Me and the family, we're leaving.'

Owl was stunned by the bald announcement. Despite his ways, Freddie lived there just like everybody else. Why would he now want to go? Surely it couldn't be because of the mink? Why, at this very moment the fox was unashamedly on his way to capitalise on their massacre of some of his fellow creatures.

'I know what you're thinking, but it's nothing to do with them,' Freddie continued, defiantly raising his head before looking down and moving a small stone about with his forepaw.

Owl felt lost.

'Why then?'

As they talked the dusk had deepened and now, with the moon still not over the horizon, it was almost pitch black.

'Come and see me tomorrow and I'll explain. You'll find it easier to understand once you've met the rest of the family.'

Owl saw he would get no further at this point. He was anyway quite satisfied with this initial re-exploration of their old friendship. However devious and untrustworthy Freddie might be, it was a relief to talk to someone so sharp. He was also flattered by the invitation. Even in the heyday of the Dead Vole Society they had all conducted their relationship away from their homes.

'Delighted,' he replied, adding by way of a thank you, 'You're right about a rabbit rampage last night. The mink hit a warren down-river, near where the heron used to stand. The crows will have been, but it'll still be worth the trip.'

'Thanks, Ollie,' Freddie replied with a friendly smile. 'Maybe we woodland creatures should stick together more, eh?'

Owl spent a pleasant interlude the next evening being introduced to Freddie's vixen and watching him play with their cubs. Although she was quiet and seemed shy, she obviously adored him as much as he did her. The relaxed family atmosphere made Owl slightly jealous and he felt well-disposed towards Freddie as they made their way in the gathering gloom to the Quarry, which they had agreed was the best place for a chat. But he still shivered slightly, knowing it was not because of the damp chill in the air. If Freddie had betrayed him, this was when he was likely to find out. But there was no ambush, and he came off guard as Freddie amiably thanked him for the rampage tip-off.

'Not that I've got anything against rabbits in particular, Ollie,' he added by way of justification. 'It just seems a waste not to take advantage.'

Owl steered him away from this tricky subject.

'Why are you leaving, though?'

'What's the worst thing in your life, Ollie?' Freddie retorted unexpectedly.

Owl was unprepared for the question. He didn't think about that sort of thing much. The mink, he supposed, or Ula's grumps.

'The worst thing in mine is the hunt,' Freddie went on, not waiting for his reply. 'It's the same for all us foxes. There you are, minding your own business, keeping the line going, providing for the family, making sure the den's secure – never mind taking a few moments off to enjoy yourself. Then suddenly, over the brow, comes a pack of maddened hounds and a load of humans. And they're after you, and you alone.'

Owl looked at him, startled. He had never seen him so animated.

'Of course, in your heart of hearts you know it's not that bad,' he went on. 'You can shake them off one way or another, even outrun them if you're cool enough. One slip, though, one wrong turning, and you're a goner. And the older you get the more the odds become stacked against you.'

He looked at Owl with uncharacteristic directness.

'It's the uncertainty that's the worst thing, Ollie — never knowing whether everything you've worked for will be ended tomorrow. Forget the human twitchers coming to our rescue. They may have stopped the diggers, but have they done anything to stop the hunt?'

Owl had been thinking the humans had plenty of reason to hunt the Freddies of this world, chicken-house raves for a start. Foxes crossed too many lines for any creature's comfort — and that presumably included the humans.

'Not easy, eh?' he said, taking refuge in a neutral phrase.

'It's bloody hard, I can tell you,' Freddie replied grimly. 'That's why, like most fox families, we've decided that these days we're safer living closer to humans, rather than trying to stay away from them. And the way to do that is to move into one of their big habitations.

'Do you know, Ollie, the humans that live in towns and cities throw away food as a matter of course. And what food. Exotic meats, fiery sauces, some delicious stuff called cheese, crunchy bones — you've no idea what delights. They even collect it in bins for you, which suits us foxes fine, as you'd imagine.

'We may be perfectly able to kill for ourselves, but we still prefer someone to do it for us,' he added self-deprecatingly.

Like mink, Owl thought uncharitably, being careful not to say anything that would interrupt the flow. He had never heard Freddie open up like this before and he was putting a fascinating counterpoint to the wood's over-riding ethos.

'Such riches, Ollie, you wouldn't believe!'

'Sounds fantastic,' Owl replied, meaning it literally. He had always thought the big human habitations were the ultimate daymare. 'But you know what the CWGs say about the grass always being greener? Anyway, surely you're too set in your ways to start again?'

'It'll be a wrench for me personally,' Freddie admitted. 'But I have to think of the kids, Ollie. They keep going on about the bright lights, the street life, the bin hunting. What really swings the balance, though, is that the big human habitations may contain millions of volvers, but the one thing they don't have is hunts. That's why all foxes are now saying: "We can't beat them, so we might as well join them."

'The world's changing, Ollie, and the wood with it. It's not just the mink. Everything's faster now. There's much more pressure. It's going to be harder and harder for everyone to stay true to the old ways — you know that.'

He paused and looked pensive, while Owl, fascinated, stayed mum.

'I'm going to tell you something, Ollie, something I've never told anyone except one or two other foxes. It's my last memory of my mother. One day, when I was very small, we heard the hunt. It's funny, isn't it, how you remember some things so clearly?

'"Mummy's going out to do something very important, dears," she said to us cubs. "You must all promise to stay completely still while I'm away and make no noise whatsoever. And whatever happens, remember Mummy loves you."

'I can still see her, silhouetted against the light, looking as though her heart was breaking. I'd never seen real fear on her face before, but I saw it then and somehow I knew I was never going to see her again.

'We all huddled together as the earth round us shook, and then waited and waited, but she never returned. I know now, of course, that she was drawing off the hunt. But all I could think then was that she had abandoned us. My father did his best to make up for her, but he couldn't supply the motherly love we needed. Life was tough for a long time.'

'That's awful, Freddie,' Owl said, genuinely moved.

He felt a sudden need to confide his own experience.

'I lost my parents too, you know. My father disappeared last Big Cold – just vanished one night, after giving my mother the usual peck on the cheek. She quartered the wood and a wider and wider area of the fields but she couldn't find any trace of him. Then she disappeared just as mysteriously.

'I searched for them both for a long time but never found anything. She might still be out there looking for all I know. In a way though, Freddie, I have to say her disappearance was a relief. I've never seen anyone decline so quickly. It was horrible. She was wasting away in front of my eyes . . .'

He stopped, not wanting to think about it any more.

'Yours sounds worse, though,' he said reflectively. 'What a shame the hunt doesn't go after mink instead of foxes.'

'Indeed,' Freddie replied with an evil grin.

He had thought long and hard before deciding to sell the mink out. But the killing of the golden oriole continued to appall him. It was such stupid, mindless violence. He would never go as far as that – unless he was in chicken-house-rave mode. He'd had enough of them, he'd realised, not that he was apologising for his collaboration. It had seemed fair enough at the time. Anyhow it hadn't been as serious as the rest of the wood seemed to think. He'd merely given a few snippets of information in return for a truce. But now he could see how to make amends. Furthermore, hopefully he would even kill three lots of hated creatures – humans, hounds and mink – with one stone. For if the mink ran true to form they would stand their ground. It would be one pack against another, with the humans sandwiched in the middle.

He dropped his bombshell. 'What if it was the hunt, rather than your twitchers, who discovered the mink?'

Owl sat gobsmacked. Merely thinking about the confrontation was mind-boggling enough.

'How though?' he asked, trying to recover his wits.

'I'll lead it on to the Plateau,' Freddie replied casually, running his tongue along his chops and grinning from ear to ear.

'You can't do that,' Owl gasped disbelievingly.

'Why not? Once I've put myself up the hunt will chase me everywhere I go.'

'But the risk!'

'It'll be tricky, Ollie, I'll grant you. But you know me. I'm not one to put myself too much on the line. I wouldn't suggest it if I didn't think I could pull it off.'

That was true, Owl thought as he struggled to take in the full import. If Freddie was being serious — and you never really knew with him — Owl liked it instantly. It was very Freddie, sly, but with an inspired type of slyness. And if it worked how neatly it would solve everything. The biters would be bit, the hunters hunted, the circle closed! Of course it was so brave as to be almost foolhardy. But if Freddie was prepared to do it, who was Owl to stand in his way?

'You're on,' he replied, not thinking any further. 'What can I do to help?'

'Just keep your beak shut,' Freddie laughed. 'Leave it to me to give the mink the brush-off!'

Laughing back, Owl spread his wing and clapped him on the shoulder. When Freddie was on your side he could be quite something.

63

We're All Victims Now

After disposing of the Alphonse evidence, Mega's next move was to send word out through Maxi that those mink return‑ing voluntarily would be treated with clemency. Gradually the members of the pack drifted back in small, guilty groups and were ordered to go to their holts and stay there. When everyone had been accounted for, the inquest started. It didn't take long to establish blame. To a mink they all instantly confessed, the older ones ones saying they were as ashamed of running away as the youngies were of carrying out the deed. They hadn't meant it, they pleaded. It had been a game that had gone too far.

'It was MI and M2 who really triggered it off,' Minimus squeaked. 'We overheard them one day asking who would rid them of this querulous bird? So we thought we'd help. It was just a bit of fun to start with, then it sort of got out of control. We're all very sorry.'

'I'm sure,' Mata interposed caustically. 'You most of all, I suppose?'

Minimus just looked contrite, while Mega, who had listened to this piece of justification with particular interest – as well as grave suspicion – tucked it away for later. He had kept Owl's information about how Alphonse had been lured to the Plateau to himself and planned to confront the little mink on his own. With the questioning completed, a picture of the sequence of events had been built up, except that everyone claimed it was a mystery to them exactly why Alphonse had fluttered so innocently down on to the Plateau. After that they were all in complete agreement. The sudden appearance of the golden oriole had sent the youngies mad. He had only strutted about for a few brief moments, pompously announcing he had come to collect his reward, before a screaming gang had jumped him.

No-one responsible had had time to react before the mob, bloodlust up, had killed him and then rampaged round tearing his corpse to shreds. Only when they finally ran out of steam did the full realisation of what they had done hit them. The first few – as Mega had correctly guessed – had fled. Others, fearful of being blamed when their leaders returned, followed and the process rapidly became self-perpetuating until the last few had finally decamped. Meanwhile, the older ones explained, there was nothing they could do to summon their leaders as they did not know where they were.

Mega, satisfied he had got at least part of the picture right, then moved on to question in greater depth the only individual who was specifically in the frame, Alphonse's minder. She was an unexceptional female, not particularly bright but, according to Psycho, with no track record for causing trouble. She was also plainly genuinely distraught.

'I know I did wrong,' she sobbed. 'But Alphonse was annoying me so much I felt I had to have a break before my temper snapped. Everything seemed to be all right and I only went off for a moment or two. I'm not the first who's done it,' she pleaded. 'Ask the others. You've no idea, my leader, what hard work he was and what we've had to put up with.'

'You're saying you were so wound up you'd have killed him yourself if you'd stayed?' Mega demanded, cruelly catching her on her own hook.

'Not exactly, my leader,' she mumbled wretchedly.

'What did you do then?' he demanded.

'When I saw he'd gone I ran straight back to the Plateau.

But it was already over and I couldn't find Maxi, or any of you, anywhere. Then I got scared and ran like all the rest.'

Mega contemptuously let her go. As everyone agreed later, her excuse might sound limp, but it did exonerate her from complicity in a plot. Meanwhile everyone who had done a turn of Alphonse duty empathised with her completely.

The discussion turned to the more immediate question of how to deal with the – in many cases – snivelling youngies.

'After so specifically countermanding your orders they should be executed like coneys, my leader,' Maxi barked emphatically. 'May I request that I personally be allowed to lead the gauntlet squad?'

'We can't kill off a whole generation,' Mega replied, appalled. No wonder the youngies made jokes about him!

'But this is our chance to get rid of them and resolve our dilemma, my leader,' Maxi protested. 'They've made the challenge. We can't just allow them to get away with it. We must punish somebody in the interests of discipline and security. Why not at least execute the ringleaders?'

'And who exactly are they, Maxi?' Mega asked, voice as cold as ice.

'Well, I'll admit we don't rightly know that yet, my leader. But if you allow me to put the screws on I'll soon find out.'

'That's my job!' Psycho protested.

Mega stared at them both, thinking Maxi was right in a way. This was their chance to deal with the youngies. But not by the method he was suggesting. The main reason the issue had been fudged at the secret leadership conference was that the older mink, for all their parental authority, were so heavily-outnumbered they might well lose a head-to-head confrontation. A witch-hunt – particularly of the brutal kind he could imagine Maxi conducting – could well start, or at least sow the seeds of, what would become civil war. It might expose the ringleaders, but only at the cost of alienating the rest of the youngies for ever.

And there was another specific problem.

'As we've heard it, all the youngies were involved,' he pointed out. 'Meanwhile no-one from our generation seems to have done anything to stop them. That makes everyone guilty, one way or another. Punish one and we have to punish them all. And do you seriously believe we can do that? We'd lose all sympathy.'

'Exactly, Mega. I couldn't have put it better myself,' Psycho jumped in, quickly switching horses to rubbish his rival. 'Now we've got a chance not to lose, but actually to increase, sympathy. All we have to do is play the "magnanimous Mega" card again. Remember using it with the old Elders after Ramses had been murdered by we know who?' he plunged the knife into Maxi again. 'Give them all a general bollocking, Mega, the whole works. Make them feel like worms. But don't do anything. Then they'll think of you as "merciful Mega" and stay with us. We'll let the dust settle, and I'll get to work behind the scenes. That's when I'll bring you the names of the really guilty.'

You will, will you? Mega thought. And will you be starting with yourself, by any chance? Or perhaps with Mata? He had thought long and hard after the shock of discovering that someone in the leadership must have tipped the youngsters off. Maxi, he was still certain, was loyal, for all his faults. Indeed, because of them – he didn't have the imagination for a scheme like this. MI and M2 didn't possess the nerve, and anyhow had more of a vested interest than anyone in keeping the Alphonse show going. Mega found it hard to assess precisely what the traitor had been planning to gain. At first he had thought the youngies had intended to carry out an ambush, then lost their nerve. But he'd soon realised that couldn't possibly be the case. His decision to go back to the Plateau on his own had been a snap one, that even he had not foreseen. What then? Putting the leaders in a position where they appeared the aggressors by acting in the way Maxi had suggested? Then Psycho or Mata, or both, siding with them and leading a revolt to overthrow him? It was impossible to know. But whatever, it was obvious which direction the plot had been heading in – or rather beheading in. And could still be at this moment for all he knew, which was why he had already decided what to do before any of the others put forward their suggestions.

First, though, he had wanted to hear what both suspects had to say.

Mata's contribution, as always, was briefer, but pithily incisive in contrast to her normal riddles.

'Alphonse was played out,' she said coolly and dismissively. 'We'd all watched his audiences shrinking and knew how fed up he was. He probably would have left shortly anyway — he'd been threatening to. He's just another victim. These things happen to us all.'

'Do they indeed?' Mega replied equally coolly.

'Yes, Mega, they do,' she said firmly. 'It's only you males who think you control everything to the extent you do. Surely you must realise by now — however superior we mink undoubtedly may be, in the end we're as much victims as anyone. What's different about us? We have to react to circumstances as they arise just like every other creature. What are we doing right now?'

'Maybe some of us are realising we're more victims than others,' Mega growled back, watching her face carefully for clues. If she had been involved, she certainly had a nerve wrapping the matter up in such a generality. And what a generality! Was she right — did he really think he controlled the world? Maybe once, but not any more. Yet that didn't mean accepting that mink were as much victims as any other creatures. They were the ones who always made the running. If they were victims at all, it was solely of their own actions, not circumstances that were thrust upon them. Not that he personally held a torch for Alphonse. Rather, he had pointedly avoided ever meeting him face to face, knowing he would probably loathe him more than anyone else.

He didn't bother to round off his canvassing of opinions by asking the Marketing Mink, who quite rightly regarded themselves as in disgrace. Minimus's explanation had put them squarely on the spot. No youngie could possibly have dreamt up 'querulous'.

'We didn't mean it, great leader,' MI had resorted to pleading like everyone else. 'The last thing we wanted was anyone killing the bird that's laid the golden egg for us all — our one and only

UWP. We might have said something like that, I'll admit, but we didn't mean it literally. Why couldn't the youngies see it was just a figure of speech?'

'Everything you do is just a figure of speech, never mind what you say!' Mega replied scathingly.

Now he moved to lay down the law as he had previously decided.

'I am going to take no action at all,' he pronounced. 'No bollocking, nothing. I'm burying the whole thing, just like we buried Alphonse himself. None of you is ever to mention him again. We're starting with a completely clean sheet.'

'We can't just pretend it didn't happen, my leader,' Maxi burst out.

'Just remember that nothing would have happened if your minder hadn't let us down,' Mega snapped back.

Maxi went quiet, not daring to say another word. The tone of Mega's voice had the same finality and authority as when they had first got back to the Plateau and discovered the golden oriole's corpse. Maxi recognised it as brooking no denial, and as such warmed to it. After feeling somehow that Mega was letting things slide, it was good to have his leader back to his true self.

As he waited patiently in the Quarry, Mega looked around, recalling his past encounters there. The last one had been with Owl, which in turn had led to him being here now. What had happened to the woodland leader since? he wondered. Although he had lost his temper at the end of their last meeting, he still thought of him as a bird he could do business with. On the other paw, what business was there now left to do between them?

He looked at the brown, withered plants around him before his eyes followed the bare rock-face up to the top of the Ridge. How inhospitable this place was, and how deserted. It was as if all other creatures pointedly avoided it. Yet its very bleakness was somehow hugely attractive. It was the only place in the wood, or the surrounding fields, where he felt truly solitary. He wondered if any woodland creatures ever came here to give themselves a little quiet time to commune inwardly. Just being here soothed him and he was totally relaxed as to whether Minimus would make the meeting. The little youngie was already late, but there could be plenty of valid reasons. Mega had impressed on him that the meeting must be entirely secret and he could well be experiencing difficulty in giving his fellows the slip.

Mega let his ruminations continue. The speed at which he had recovered from the shock of Alphonse's killing amazed him. The feeling had started almost immediately on the Plateau. As he swung the cat-tail round, roaring his defiance, he had been aware of an immense wave of relief washing over him. Suddenly he was on his own again, without minders or assistants to help him see off his opponents – or to tell him what to do afterwards. When he had received Owl's message from the sentry, it was his decision – against Psycho's protests – to go and see the woodland leader alone. Maxi had then sorted out the problem of the badger lumbering towards the Plateau by getting him to back off through an overwhelming show of force, before pleading to be allowed to come along as a precaution. Mega had given in to him, but then acceded to Owl's demand that he be kept right out of it. Once again his instinct had been correct. By doing that, he alone had received the specific information about Alphonse's abduction that he had thought he might glean.

Since then he had pondered Mata's remark that they were all victims. The more he thought the less apposite it seemed, unless it was in the sense that he had been a victim of his so-called fellow leaders. He had let the reins of power slip from his hands. The situation was largely his fault for allowing – if not even specifically relying on – the others to do his job for him. True leadership was not the team job he had let it become, a committee with everyone allowed to have their say. It was a solo affair, as when he had first flung down the gauntlet to the Elders. No wonder, with or without the complicity of his betrayer, that the youngies had moved against him. What sort of example was he? He was disgusted, not with them but with himself. The youngies were looking for a firm, but fair, father figure, someone to respect and gladly defer to. Not just to keep them in their place, which was all Maxi could think about, but to inspire them by setting an example they could follow. Each, after all, knew he was in a way their individual father, as well as their leader. Yet he must seem like some dithering old fart, always being bashed from pillar to post by his clutch of over-eager, self-serving advisers. Worse still — at least recently — some, if not all, must have known one of those advisers was betraying him. No wonder they felt free to run amok. He must have looked a pushover!

A vision floated in front of his eyes of the bloated Massam back in the cages, the almost equally rotund Gabbla at his elbow. Then he saw himself, hair brushed upwards in the poncefied way the Marketing Mink had taught him, Psycho, the skinny Gabbla substitute, whispering in his ear. So deeply involved in politicking, he must appear as bad to the youngies as the Elders had to him. Without realising, he had allowed his advisers to degrade him. What had happened to his spirit since the moment Sheba informed him of his destiny and he grasped it so firmly? He had been so crystal clear then, so utterly determined to sacrifice his life for what he believed in.

He had seen the same conviction in Burdock before strangling him with the cat-tail. He might have been only a rabbit, but he too, in his own way, had understood life was not just about putting yourself first. It might be selfish in being what you wanted to do, but you still elevated your principles and beliefs to become your life's primary purpose. They became the only yardstick by which you judged yourself, a neutral standard. You constantly tested yourself against it. That was where real power lay, not, as Maxi or Psycho thought, in exercising negative control over others. It was something quite apart from any other creature, something giving you unassailable strength. That was why he had moved so quickly to kill Burdock before he could communicate with the rest of the pack. It wasn't a question of what the rabbit would have said, but the way he would have said it. All the mink would have recognised instinctively that he had the inner power. As it was 'I forgive you, for you know not what you do' was a message that had burned its way into Mega's consciousness. He had just put into practice with the youngies.

Thinking of whom, where was Minimus?

Mega broke off from his reverie and rose from the uncomfortably stony ground to stretch his legs, just as the little youngie bounded up.

'Sorry to be so late, my leader,' he said cheerfully, sounding not the least bit guilty. 'I just had a feeling that Psycho might be following me. I wanted to make doubly sure I'd shaken him off.'

'That's all right,' Mega said amiably, noting the Psycho point. 'How are you?'

'Fine, thank you, my leader,' Minimus replied politely. 'And yourself?'

'Fine,' Mega said equally politely, before walking across to the tree under which the leadership had gathered. On the stony ground he had placed the yellow wing feather that he had previously secreted away in his holt.

He waited until Minimus had seen it.

'Any message? Am I wanted at the Plateau, for example?' he asked.

'There once was a message like that for someone else,' the youngie replied, looking deadly serious but at the same time quite unperturbed. 'However I hope that my being here means it has been received by the one it was really aimed at – and that is yourself, my leader.'

64

Minimisation

M ega stared critically at the young cub in front of him. He could see he had been a sickly infant. He might have grown fast and filled out, but even though he was the first-born of the new generation, he was still the smallest. Small, maybe, but perfectly enough formed, Mega thought, not runtish or ratlike, like Psycho, and without his pointy features or weird eyes. Rather, his face was friendly and open and his frank demeanour belied Mata's scathing assessment of him. But what interested Mega most was the way he was now acting. He had responded to the sight of the yellow feather completely coolly, as if he had nothing to hide or be ashamed of.

'How did you know we leaders would be away?' Mega asked him bluntly.

The youngie hesitated, before looking at him fair and square.

'It was simple enough. We overheard Maxi instructing the muscle-mink about the arrangements.'

'How did you manage that?' Mega asked, open-mouthed. Surely Maxi couldn't have been that stupid!

'We didn't hear if from him directly,' Minimus explained.

'You know he keeps the rabbit prisoners in his barracks while they're waiting for Psycho's experiments? Well, a few of us started doing deals with them some time ago. We offered them freedom in return for reporting anything interesting they heard.

'We never had any intention of freeing them, of course, and they probably didn't believe we would. But they were so desperate they helped us. It was easy enough to go in and see them from time to time — we just told Maxi or the muscle-mink we wanted to study them so as to be better at the coneycide campaign.'

Mega's jaw dropped almost to the ground. All this time he had been condemning his advisers unjustly. He had let his imagination get the better of him and drawn quite the wrong conclusion. The other leaders hadn't betrayed him after all. He was quite wrong to lose trust in them. The fact that Maxi, with his tedious security obsession, had inadvertently given the game away raised a different question — not trust, but competence. Yet once the seed of doubt had been sown, it had grown so fast he had moved to a position from which he could not go back. Unless what Minimus said was part of an elaborate cover-up. But that only led into the shadowy world of Pyscho-think, where nothing, or nobody, was treated as it appeared to be. It wasn't Mega's world, no matter how much he might have been temporarily sucked into it. Neither, by the sound of it, was it the world of this candid and likeable youngie, who seemed only too willing to answer questions openly.

'So none of the other leaders — Psycho, Mata, Maxi, MI and M2 — had anything to do with it?' he asked to make doubly sure.

'No. It was all our idea — that is myself and some other youngies, not all of them.'

'But I still don't understand. Why did you want to kill him?'

'We all thought he was the pits,' Minimus replied. 'When we were on minder duty he treated us as if we were vermin. None of us had ever felt so degraded. It cut so much across what we were being taught — and felt — about being proud to be mink. We simply couldn't understand why we had to put up with it. As a result he became the ultimate woodland challenge. Everyone was daring everyone else to have a go at him. Then, as I told you, we overheard the Marketing Mink and that put a top on it.'

'But the whole point was that he was saving the wood.'

Minimus paused. 'We knew that. Just the same, myself and some friends thought that an even better reason for getting rid of him.'

'What good did you think it would do?' Mega asked, puzzled.

He felt strangely apprehensive about what this obviously bright youngie might reply. He spoke almost like – if not more maturely than – an adult.

'Well, my leader, being so young I can only put it from my point of view. You don't mind if I say anything I like, do you?'

'Quite the contrary. I want you to,' Mega replied, meaning it.

'Well, speaking for myself and some of other youngies – not all of them mind you – we feel hemmed in here,' Minimus explained. 'We do appreciate we've got the Plateau and the Waterama complex. But the overcrowding, the concentration on holt improvements, the endless acornball competitions, MI and M2 asking questions, Maxi pushing us into line, Psycho creeping around – it doesn't strike us as what we mink are here for.

'We know we've got the wood and the surrounding fields, but it doesn't help having rules about where we can kill and where we can't. Then there's the coneycide campaign and the structured rabbit rampages, with the eating competitions and Psycho's trials. The older ones might believe it, but we can't see how the rabbits are taking over the world. They don't seem dangerous to us. We just see them as hot spurts.

'How can I best put it, my leader? It seems as if everything's been organised to stop us doing what comes naturally. We think there must be more to life than this, yet you leaders seem determined to keep us down and not allow any change.

'Am I making myself clear?' he asked anxiously.

'I hear what you say,' Mega replied, suppressing a strange stirring of excitement. 'But still, why kill Alphonse?'

'Because we thought it would bust things up,' the youngie replied candidly. 'If it was right that he was saving the wood and thereby keeping us here, once he'd gone everyone would have to move out.'

'But you could have moved anyhow,' Mega shouted, suddenly angry. There was a limit to what he was prepared to hear. He had been wrong about MI and M2 – their Project X had been hitting the right button after all. So why hadn't the youngies responded?

'Weren't you listening?' he asked. 'Didn't I tell you again and again about the glories of going out to find fresh woods to conquer?'

'You did, my leader,' Minimus replied, looking slightly scared for the first time, yet still standing his ground. 'That's what upset us most. You sounded as though you were trying to get rid of us, when that was the last thing we wanted – or at least some of us. We do want to go out and conquer fresh woods! We think that's what mink were born to do. But not on our own, feeling rejected. Quite the opposite. We want you to, to lead us out. We want to follow you.'

A wave of tenderness swept over Mega and he looked at the little cub with fond longing. All the time, if he had but known it, the eager youngsters had wanted to be his pack, his family! And just as strongly, he now realised, he dearly wanted them to be. Out of the mouths of babes and sucklings, he thought. Minimus was right. Hang the Plateau, the Waterama complex, the artificial coneycide campaign – hang Enterprise Wood itself! He should never have allowed the Marketing Mink to involve him in the sideshow of saving the place. A good temporary expedient leading them up a blind alley. Hang collaborating with the hopeless woodies! Hang the UWP bollo! And, he now saw through this clear-sighted youngie, that meant hang Alphonse! It was the woodies, not the mink, who were stuck in the wood, whether they liked it or not. The golden oriole had only been benefiting them. From a true mink point of view,

Alphonse had been not a liberating force but a millstone that had weighed them down by tying them there.

At first the wood was bound to have seemed the ultimate freedom. None of them would ever forget the trembling excitement of those first hot spurts and smashing skulls to lick out the brains. Neither should they! But what they had since forgotten was that it had been intended only as a starting place. To the youngsters, who had never known anything else, it must appear a prison, trapping them just as the cages had once trapped their elders. True mink knew instinctively that they didn't lock themselves into the narrow concerns of one particular area, no matter how wonderful. They didn't want the security of familiar territory where everything was always the same. Their nature was to be bundles of raw, tough, driven energy – marauders, vandals, avengers, who tore into an area and ripped its arse out. Then they were out and gone, back on the trail, free spirits answering to no-one and nowhere.

Mega broke off from his thoughts as he saw Minimus looking at him with a pleading expression.

'Will you do it, father?' the youngster asked softly, looking deep into Mega's eyes with ones equally black. 'Take us out – me and the others who want to go?'

Father, Mega thought with a sudden thrill. This was his child talking. All the youngies were his sons – and his daughters!

'I will, my son,' he promised.

His mind raced ahead. He would dump his advisers, whether they liked it or not. They were entirely welcome to Enterprise Wood if they wanted it. But he was leaving. Of course there were fresh woods to conquer – always had been, always would be. He would be starting all over again, rerunning that glorious moment when he had first led the pack down the rollway in the moonlight, the eager, questing faces behind him and nothing above but the sky and stars. And by his side would be this unabashed youngster, maybe physically small, but with such a mature head on his shoulders.

Mega thought back to the time he had impregnated Minimus's mother, Mo. She had been good fun rather than inhibited and overawed like some of the others. The absolute opposite to Mata, he had thought then, an uncomplicated, natural creature who knew how to enjoy herself. Like his own mother, Sheba, she had cheerfully endured the taunts of other females for having only produced one. He gulped as it sank in. Why had he never thought of it before? Minimus was like him. As an only child he too must know the feeling of being an outsider. He would adopt Minimus as his own, so he came to know his father in the way he himself had never known Solomon. Sheba would have wanted it that way. It had always been her keenest regret that her son had been so deprived. As for Mo, she had not taken up with any other particular male, but kept herself fiercely independent. Mega had observed with approval how she had dedicated herself to giving her only son a good start in life. So, if she wanted to come along, why not? She would be a good friend and companion and they would become a family, building a future. Minimus would be not just his son, but his adviser, someone he could trust absolutely and groom to take his place one day. Not an aide, but an heir, bound to him by ties of blood. All his new pack would be bound to him like that. With a new sense of united purpose, he would lead them on their mission, not the Marketing Mink's mission statement bollo, but the only mission worth talking about – the freedom mission.

He held his front paws open wide.

'My son!' he smiled.

'Father!' the cub replied, running to him and surrendering to his embrace.

They both remained silent for a long time, revelling in the warm, close contact as they hugged each other.

As he padded back on to the Plateau in the early-morning light, Minimus at his side and the rest of the pack round him, Mega felt a deeper contentment than he had ever known. The killing of Alphonse had proved to be the catharsis that not just he, but everyone, had needed. The new spirit it had engendered in the colony had manifested itself in an upsurge of rabbit rampages, like the one they were returning from now, which everyone happily and wearily agreed had been the most successful ever. Everything had worked, from the first glorious hit to the equally glorious eating competition. Maxi was glowing with pride at having gained the personal kudos of raising the individual record to a new height of two complete rabbits, one head and two legs, while Pyscho was rubbing his paws in anticipation of experimenting on the positive herd of prisoners they were bringing back.

It hadn't all been easy though and Mega had faced a personal crisis when Mata had rounded on him in their holt after his seminal meeting with his newly adopted son.

'I know what you're up to,' she had spat. 'And I'm absolutely disgusted to see you demonstrating what a fool you are. Never mind me — if you've thought about me at all, which I doubt. You know Minimus is the youngie I specifically warned you against.

'Can't you see he's winding you round his little paw? I can just imagine the sort of clever stuff the little runt's been pouring out, all about being an only one like you. All about being different, being an outsider. But you're such a mug you can't recognise a show, can you? You've fallen for it, Mega. And mark my words — you'll live to regret it! As for his mother, you can have her for all I care.'

Mega had been shocked, both by her venom and by how quickly she had picked up on what was happening. He had been to see Minimus's mother, receiving a welcome which warmed his heart. But he hadn't seen that as meaning he was replacing Mata. On the contrary, he had been reconsidering his decision to dump all the leaders and thinking of inviting her to come and share his brave new world. Had she known that? he wondered. If she did, she showed no sign, concluding by announcing that she was moving out into her own quarters.

He had not tried to dispute what she said, feeling almost pity for her. Within himself he felt it wasn't just Minimus personally she was so bitter about. After her determination not to have cubs of her own, any youngie might have produced the same reaction, if not to the same degree. Yet their views of Minimus could not be more opposed. So had she seen the bond between him and the youngie before he had, then tried to subvert it? Under that cold-fish exterior, was she really as warm-hearted as Minimus's mother, but simply unable to let it out? He didn't know and there was no point in dwelling on it, sad though it might be. He had made up his mind and if she had done so just as firmly he must respect that.

He and Minimus had been busy selecting the youngies they would take with them. Mega was delighted by his son's quick-wittedness. His character assessments were shrewd, while invariably fair and positive, and the youngies in general, although unaware of the plans being made for them, were at their best. Realising Mega was giving them a second chance, they responded positively to their leader's leniency, their new compliance and eagerness to please immensely cheering Maxi. Mega had not mentioned the rabbit prisoners' security breach to him, but partly solved the problem by encouraging Psycho to speed up his animal experiments, in turn pleasing him. As for MI and M2, he allowed them to push the button on their Minions' Charter bollo, making them feel they were being welcomed back into the fold. There was no cynicism in these actions, even though he was preparing to leave behind their backs. No longer feeling directly involved, he found himself able to view matters dispassionately. He wanted to depart in a spirit of goodwill, without rancour and wishing them the best for themselves. What they then made of it would be up to them, but at least he would ensure they had a flying start.

The rampage had gone on so long it was broad daylight when they got back to the Plateau and it was agreed Psycho's show trial should be postponed until the evening. As bloated and fulfilled as the rest, Mega headed for his holt to sleep it off. After closely watching several youngies he had finally decided whom he, Mo and Minimus would take with them. Now there was nothing to hold them back any longer. It was time to go. No-one would be doing much today, that was for sure, but tonight they would be refreshed. There was also a particular reason for choosing then to depart. All through the rampage, the yellow disc of the rising harvest moon had lit up the countryside. Tonight it would be full. When it rose they would steal away.

Mega drifted off into a half-sleep, his mind full of the moon madness of the old cage days.

'Out! Out! We're getting out!' he whispered to himself, picturing the mink he took with him hurling themselves one after another against the wire, until it shuddered and trembled with the succession of impacts.

'Go! Go! Go for it!'

'Mega mink! Mega mink! He's the mink! He's the mink!'

He was the mink, he thought, falling into a deep and satisfied sleep. And tonight he was going to prove that beyond any doubt.

Totally comatose, neither he nor anyone heard the first toot of the hunting horn. Only the duty sentry pricked up her ears, but at first she was reluctant to disturb her leaders. It was only when the sound came closer and closer that she eventually decided she had no choice and left her post in the holly bush. Slowly padding up the slope, she swept the horizon. Although it was a sparklingly clear day, she could still see nothing through the trees. But now she could now identify the sounds as emanating from the Long Field. And, without doubt, coming their way fast.

Gripped by sudden panic, she ran to the barracks to rouse Maxi.

65

The Last Hunt

Although the woodland creatures were fully aware of the hunt, its activity had never touched them directly. Occasionally it would hurtle across the outlying fields in a terrifying blur of noise and colour, but as far as anyone knew it had never come into the wood. All the creatures had learnt long ago that its sole interest was in pursuing foxes and as long as they stayed out of its way they would be safe. Owl had fudged matters with Raka, merely reporting that Freddie was trying to think of something, so only he understood the full significance when he was jerked awake a few days later by the bray of a far-off horn. Electrified, he shot out on to the beech branch to hear the strident toot repeated, more loudly. Swivelling his head, he identified it as coming from upstream on the river.

'What is it now?' Ula demanded grumpily from inside the nest. 'Don't you ever sleep?'

'The hunt's on its way,' Owl whispered dramatically.

'So what?' came the sleepy reply. 'It never comes into the wood. I just hope it gets Freddie.'

Ula might have been caustic about the CWGs, but her

condemnation of the fox's reported fraternisation with the mink had been vitriolic.

'Some company you keep!' she had screeched. She agreed with Raka that the correct neutral standpoint was to accept the mink were in the wood, even join forces with them if necessary – as the wood had – but never, ever, cross to their side.

'The hunt *will* get Freddie if his plan doesn't work,' Owl retorted enigmatically, launching himself through the branches.

He rose to see the fox just crossing the bridge into the Long Field. His red coat was streaked with mud and he looked as though he had had a hard run, but he still managed a reassuring wave of his front paw to demonstrate he was far from beat. As the fox hot-footed it across the Long Field, Owl shivered at the awesome sight behind him. Until now he hadn't appreciated quite what an extraordinary risk Freddie was taking. The hounds, in full cry, let out a hideous cacophony of baying and yapping. There were so many of them, and they were so huge, while such a multitude of humans on horseback streamed in their wake.

Freddie reached the far side of the field and slipped safely through the fence into the wood, producing a hiatus amongst hounds and horses that put him safely out of their reach. Making his way niftily through the trees and up the slope to the Plateau, he paused enticingly on the skyline, waited until the lead hound was almost snapping at his brush, then disappeared over the edge.

Throwing caution to the wind, the hunt charged after him. There was a brief silence. Then mayhem broke out.

Freddie might be an opportunist, but he preferred to plan his moves carefully, rather than acting on impulse. From the start, though, he had known he would have only limited control over this event. He had reconnoitred the different approaches to the Plateau, carrying out a series of dummy runs, but his heart hadn't really been in the preparations. He couldn't dictate where he could pick the hunt up. Anyhow, however much he calculated distances, the biggest unknown would be the state of the mink colony at the moment he, and hopefully his pursuers, plunged into its midst. Freddie was relying on speed to fulfil his number one priority of saving his own skin. He would shoot cross the Plateau before the mink could react and dive into the river, as he would naturally do to cover his scent. What incidental satisfaction he would gain from using the horrible Waterama complex as his getaway route, he thought with a grin. He was counting on the mink to stand and fight, but even if they ran he was confident they would at least divert some of the hounds, while the humans on horseback would be unable to follow him down the precipitous bank.

After long thought he had decided not to worry his vixen by revealing his scheme to her. She always left woodland affairs very much to him. When the mink arrived they had agreed that only he should communicate with them. With little idea of what he had been up to since, she was simply thrilled by his announcement that the family was finally departing to town. Ever since their cubs had been born she, more than he, had been certain it was the future.

Freddie had been staking out the hounds' kennels until this bright morning, when the amount of activity had convinced him the hunt was preparing to ride. He ran back to the den and dispatched his excited family to wait for him in a safe spot many fields away, making the excuse that he had to stay for his last good-byes. Then, adrenalin pumping, he set off to make himself the object of the chase. His opportunity came almost immediately when the hunt flushed out one of his fellows and began pursuing him in the general direction of the wood. Cutting rapidly across the fields, Freddie suddenly manifested himself next to the intended victim, indicating he was voluntarily putting himself in the frame. His fellow, not stopping to ask his motives, gave a grateful but uncomprehending smile before scarpering to let him take up the running.

Freddie's original game plan had been to conserve his energy by leading the hunt along at a light trot but now, with its blood already up, he was straight into full-scale flight. Yet he had the advantage of being much closer to Old Wood than he had anticipated. With the distance so compressed the chase was going to be short and sharp.

You can do it, he told himself as the hounds battened on to his scent. He accelerated to full speed, already breathing hard, as much through nervous excitement as anything. For the first couple of fields he wanted very much to be somewhere else. You can do it, he repeated to himself as he slipped through the second hedge, carefully selecting a spot with a deep ditch that would cause the horses the maximum difficulty. You can do it, he said with more confidence as he settled down into a steady lope which ate up the ground. You can do it. You're a fox and much brighter than these stupid hounds — as they are about to discover. You are doing it, he changed his tune as he emerged onto the rollway just up from the wood. You've almost done it, he exulted as he crossed the bridge into the Long Field and saw Ollie fly out of the wood. He gave him a wave and glanced across the river, where he could see the twitchers erupting in consternation. He was causing a bigger sensation than Alphonse! You're nearly there, he finally told himself as he shot into the wood.

All the time, though, he could see his mother's frightened face as she set out to play the same dangerous game and had to steel himself not to panic. Don't count your chickens, he told himself as he tore up the slope to the Plateau, suddenly fearful of what might be awaiting him. He stopped at the crest of the slope and his heart leapt with joy as the unknown factor in his equation was filled in. He was in luck. The mink were not only there, but milling around in confusion. A few had formed a nucleus round their leader, but the rest were running chaotically about, with Maxi bellowing at them. It was headless chicken land — precisely what he had hoped for. He took a quick snapshot and worked out his best route through the mêlée before looking back, only for his heart to leap to his mouth again, this time with fear. He had cut it almost too fine. The jaws of the lead hound were so nearly on him he imagined he could smell its rancid breath.

He catapulted himself on to the short grass and streaked towards the cliff-edge. A pair of quick-witted mink lunged at him, but he jinked past them with ease, while the rest just stood frozen in astonishment. Then he was through, out on to the Waterama's tree-slide and letting go to plunge down into the welcoming deep water. Immediately he struck out downstream, crossed to the far bank and leapt out. He worked his way steadily downstream, crossing and recrossing, until he was sure he had covered his tracks. Only then did he pause, shake himself vigorously and prick up his ears to listen. Judging by the dreadful shrieks and cries coming from the Plateau, his plan had worked. But he wasn't going back to confirm. Whatever the result, he had done his bit and said his honourable farewell to Old Wood. Now it was time to head for his new life in town while the going was still good.

Chest heaving, red fur dripping, he padded off on a round-about route to retrieve the family.

The hunt was nothing new for the mink, either. Freddie had informed them about it, but emphasised that it never came into the wood, a statement that Psycho had checked out at various interrogations. After that Maxi decided this human phenomenon only merited an amber security alert, it was so extremely unlikely it would ever come close to the Plateau. What would possibly cause a fox to run in their direction? he had said to Mega.

The plodding footsteps of the sentry going to raise the alarm reflected the same attitude. By the time she had cottoned on and succeeded in shaking Maxi out of his deep slumber, the hunt was already crashing about in the bottom of the wood, rousing lighter sleepers.

Maxi rushed over to Mega's holt.

'It's coming our way!' he yelled. 'What are we going to do?'

Mega ran outside, furiously trying to clear his befuddled head. But the second he emerged he could see it was already too late. The ranks, tumbling out of their holts, were in a flat panic, rushing about out of control. He ran over to the cat-tail and shouted to everyone to form up round him, while Maxi shot over to the Plateau edge, still desperately hoping there was time for the emergency-dispersal routine they had used with Custard. But when he saw Freddie halfway up the slope he bowed to the inevitability of what was about to occur.

Mega, who had already recognised there was no contingency plan they could draw on, was still attempting to marshal a coherent group, but to little effect. The pack remained a disorganised rabble.

'Every mink for themself!' he cried in desperation, turning to face the enemy as Freddie outlined himself on the skyline.

'You bastard!' was all he had time to shout before the fox streaked agilely through them, followed by the first of the hounds.

But disorganised though they might be, his ranks did not let either him − or Freddie − down. To a mink, they united to stand their ground.

The hounds, pounding full-tilt up the steep slope, were initially caught off balance as they burst on to the flat surface. Braking hard on splayed feet, they saw a mass of new and unexpected quarries barring their way, while their fox disappeared over the far edge. They stopped, confused. They had never had to face a situation like this, and their humans had not yet arrived to guide them. As they milled around, not knowing whether to attack, the mink took the initiative by running towards them and hurling themselves at their throats. The hounds squealed with pain and astonishment as they vainly attempted to shake off their attackers. Foxes never fought back! In the face of so many determined enemies, pack discipline broke down. Each hound was suddenly on its own, and on the defensive.

Owl, looking down from above, was fascinated to see how correct Freddie's thinking had been. No-one seeing this could doubt the mink's bravery. The yelps and cries of the maddened hounds changed from triumph to terror. Some were now down, streaming blood as mink clung to them with vice-like grips. Others, their control gone and unable to focus, chased round in circles, snapping at thin air, while a few were already running away, tails between their legs. One, to Owl's astonishment, was not pursuing, but being pursued by, a mink!

But the battle wasn't all one-sided. In the far corner a group of hounds had surrounded a mink and were tossing it into the air, to catch it in wide-open jaws. Owl shuddered as he heard the shrill, yet still defiant, screams of agony. That would have been Freddie's fate if he had got his timing wrong. The hounds' powerful jaws clamped down on to the stretched limbs and pulled until, to the accompaniment of a final ghastly scream, the mink's body split down the middle and the two halves flew apart.

By now the humans on their horses were catching up, crashing on to the Plateau. The previous tight group had degenerated into a straggle as the riders battled to get into the wood over the fence, and, watching their blundering progress through the trees, Owl could now understand why they had never come into the wood before. The horses were much too tall to follow any of the tracks or paths of smaller creatures and he could hear their riders cursing as they struggled to push aside the tree branches threatening to unsaddle them. Once out on to the comparatively open slope up to the Plateau, however, they recovered their momentum and their curses were replaced by guttural cries as they urged their steeds into a final charge. Sods flying, they thundered up the slope and leapt forward, only to surge helplessly into the mêlée.

The mink now turned their attention to the horses' legs. The terrified animals, whinnying with fear and eyes rolling, bucked and kicked, while their riders leant over, trying to thrash these unexpected adversaries with their whips. But the mink were far too quick and easily avoided the wild swipes as they darted in and out. Meanwhile, more and more horses were cresting the rise and cramming themselves into the small space. As it got hopelessly crowded the horses began bumping into each other, becoming more and more panic-stricken as they felt themselves increasingly hemmed in, until finally a collection of them went down in a wild sprawl.

As the humans were pitched off their backs the mink moved to attack their real enemy directly. Owl watched one scrabbling desperately with his hands to pull off a mink who had flown for his throat. Other humans ran up to help and grabbed the creature from behind, pulling with all their might. Yet it would still not let go. The human it had attached itself to staggered about, bellowing with pain and fear, until finally his companions prised it off, hurled it to the ground and stamped up and down on it until it went still. All over the Plateau, amid the rolling tide of horses and hounds, the humans were desperately engaged in individual battles, as they tried to get to, or stay on, their feet and saddles, while simultaneously warding off enemies coming at them from all sides. For a moment Owl thought they might even break ranks and flee. Then he heard the blare of the hunting horn and saw the other humans running towards it to form a tight circle. Back to back, they at last began combining to drive the mink off.

As if recognising this new show of force, the mink retreated, enticing them forwards. Then, as they advanced, a group of the creatures suddenly ran at three still-mounted riders who had allowed themselves to become slightly separated. Either by luck or by judgement, the mink began to push them backwards by darting at the horses' hooves, opening up a widening wedge between them and their fellows. Owl, appreciating from his aerial viewpoint what they were trying to achieve, watched transfixed. The horses, wild with terror and bucking and plunging madly, their riders powerless, were being inexorably reversed towards the cliff. Only when their back hooves reached the edge did they become aware of the even greater danger they were now in. The mink, with perfect timing, made a concerted charge, causing them to rear up in renewed fright. All three teetered side by side on the brink, hooves clinging desperately to the crumbling earth, before sliding irrevocably over the edge.

The first bounced awkwardly off the fallen ash trunk, threw its rider and landed with a sickening thump, half in the water and half on the mudbank. It instantly went still, its head at an unnatural angle. The other two pitched into the deeper water, also jettisoning their riders. As they felt the sinister touch of the slimy branches under the surface they began thrashing frantically about, heads rising vertically and eyes rolling as they scrabbled for a firm footing and found none. Their thrashing became more despairing and the water boiled and foamed round them, while Owl could see one had its reins firmly entangled. The other, meanwhile, managed to break free and began swimming steadily towards the shallows. This only seemed to increase its fellow's panic, almost as if it saw itself being abandoned to its fate. The more it heaved about in the water, the more firmly it seemed to get enmeshed. Owl saw its body sinking until only its head still appeared above the surface. Teeth bared, eyes by now all whites, it leered up at him in a final appeal, before disappearing beneath the surface with a despairing whinny, as if dragged down by a giant talon.

Even though the fighting raged on the Plateau, Owl could detect the moment of silence as the human riders, now safely on the mudbank, looked at each other in horror, waiting for it to re-emerge. When it failed to do so, they began shouting at the tops of their voices to their fellows above, who abandoned their attempts to push the mink back and ran across to gaze down, equally impotent.

At that moment Owl heard a shrill series of chitters. The remaining mink scattered, a few of them running directly into the wood. Most, though, in a last gesture of defiance, simply hurtled through the human group and took to the tree-slide, just like Freddie. As they splashed into the water on top of the string of bubbles coming up from below, Owl was staggered by the nerve and the presence of mind that caused them to choose the correct exit. The mink might have been dwarfed and outnumbered by their canine opponents alone, but a combination of bravery and strategy had enabled them to acquite themselves better than he had ever imagined. Or Freddie, he guessed. If only the fox could have been present to witness his creation!

But the mink had paid a price. A number of their corpses now lay outstretched, along with the bodies of at least three hounds who, if not dead, were certainly not moving. Meanwhile their fellows, thirsting for revenge, had set off in shrieking pursuit, promoting renewed panic amongst the riderless horses crashing aimlessly about in the trees.

There was a lull as the stunned humans walked about, assessing the carnage and examining each others' injuries.

Then the twitchers arrived.

The twitchers had kept coming to stand on the rollway, even though nobody in the wood had done anything to make up for the loss of Alphonse. The creatures had waited to see if the Marketing Mink would reappear, possibly to revive the buzzards' golden eagle suggestion. But when they failed to do so not even Cowslip had any ideas. Bereft of their mink leadership, the woodland creatures had to accept they were lost.

Although the twitcher numbers had shrunk from the large crowds of Alphonse's heyday, that morning, attracted by the bright sunshine, there was a particularly good turn-out. They were sitting on the riverbank, gazing earnestly at the wood with their mad staring eyes, when Freddie ran along the rollway towards them. As he crossed the bridge and set off across the Long Field past Alphonse's posing tree, they stood up, open-mouthed. Their consternation increased as the hunt poured after him and they began shaking their fists at their human enemies. But they only really reacted when bedlam broke out on the Plateau.

Some ran back to follow in Freddie's footsteps and cross the river by the bridge, while others simply jumped into the gravelly shallows regardless and waded across. On the other side they formed up into a determined group that followed the tracks of the hunt through the now-broken fence. Like an avenging army, they charged up the slope to the Plateau, picking up sticks as they went. When they arrived at the top they appeared not even to pause to consider the situation, but simply set about their fellow humans. It seemed to Owl that the hunt humans responded even more angrily than they had to the mink attack. As he looked down on the mass of rolling bodies, hearing the clash of whips and sticks, he thought there was no dispute more bitter than a falling out between creatures of the same kind. He also felt vindicated about the twitchers. They seemed just as effective as their hunting counterparts, if not more so. Maybe they were just fresher, but they were acquitting themselves splendidly.

Yet at the same time the fighting, like the fracas with the working humans on the rollway, seemed curiously tame compared to the ferocity and determination of the mink attack. Maybe the humans, despite their battery of devices, lacked the killer instinct — at least when in dispute with each other? Their fighting was certainly degenerating into a series of futile struggles.

Then Owl heard the first neenaw noise and looked across to see a white volver with a blue flashing light hurtling along the rollway. With a screeching noise it turned, flew over the hump-backed bridge, and began bouncing across the Long Field before suddenly stopping as it became bogged down in the marshy place. A posse of identical humans leapt out and began running towards the wood, while more neenaw noises sounded in the distance. That, Owl knew, meant the end of that. Exultant at Freddie's triumph, he turned for home. It would take some time for the full import to sink in but, superficially at least, the mink tyranny seemed to be over.

Unless, as he already had a peculiar feeling, they were not out of the wood yet.

66

Homeward Bound

The creatures had little taste for closely inspecting the clear-up operation which inundated the wood with humans for the rest of the day. Saviours or not, the old adage to stay away still stood. Everyone hid as humans crashed around, combing the wood for lost horses and hounds. The twitchers and hunting humans in their red coats were joined by so many others a wild rumour shot round that the workers were back, while so many volvers lined the rollway they eclipsed even Alphonse's heyday. The different humans all looked grim as they stalked about the Plateau, talking quietly to each other while some made marks on white squares similar to the one that had saved the wood. Among them, looking lost, there briefly wandered the human with the yellow dog, who was kept on a tight lead, cowering and whimpering and only perking up when she was finally led away. Meanwhile females stood on the top of the bank crying, while humans wearing black skins descended into the deep pool, eventually to surface with the body of the horse that had drowned. Together with the one that had broken its neck, it was dragged with ropes into the shallows before being loaded on to the back of a volver and rolled off across the Long Field.

The humans then began a systematic and ruthless destruction of the Plateau and the creatures quailed and trembled as they saw that their revenge was far worse than anything they had previously brought to bear. First they dug out and stamped in the whole of the old rabbit warren, before moving in with buzz-machines to fell the remains of the beech and effortlessly slice up the fallen ash that had formed the Waterama complex. The larger pieces were tipped into the river, to be floated down and taken away on more volvers, while the smaller ones, with the chopped-up beech and the carcass of the replica rabbit, were gathered into a heap in the middle of the Plateau. Then came the worst horror of all. A new machine, unlike any the creatures had seen before, was painstakingly dragged up though the wood, while other humans followed with containers, from which they poured an acrid-smelling liquid over the entire area.

A horde of humans fiddled with the machine on the edge of the Plateau, before suddenly jumping backwards as it sprang into life. A huge tongue of flame poured from its mouth, red and angry and making a tremendous roaring noise, while the other humans ran for the trees, as if terrified of it themselves. The one controlling it directed the fire tongue up into the air before bringing it downwards and sending it whooshing along the ground in fierce bursts. A searing ball of fire that seemed to have a life of its own burst from the surface of the Plateau, instantly igniting the remaining grass and the remnants of the two trees. It shot upwards, sending showers of sparks soaring into the sky while yellow flames, darting and flickering, ran eagerly outwards, feeding voraciously on the liquid soaking the ground. Urged on by more whooshing blasts from the red tongue, the flames reached the edge of the Plateau before stopping, The leaves of the surrounding trees shivered in the sudden wind the firestorm was creating, before almost simultaneously drooping and shrivelling as the intense heat burnt them to a crisp. The roaring grew louder as the fire centred itself on the pile of cut-down branches, which fizzed and popped and crackled as they were consumed, while round the edge the humans contained the damage by stamping on smouldering tussocks of turf.

All the time, in the middle, the fire still grew, its yellow flames gradually blacked out by the thick pall of smoke that rolled upwards, becoming denser and denser, until it blotted out the sun. The distinct shapes of the humans turned to misty figures, glimpsed in the half-light as they flitted through the billowing clouds, shouting and cheering in wild exultation. Meanwhile a rain of ash pattered down steadily to layer the surrounding area with a universal film of grey, interspersed with darker, wispy particles and ominous-looking black lumps. A greasy scum formed on the dark surface of the Big Pool as the smoke billowed higher and the acrid fall-out spread, until ashes from the funeral pyre drifted to taint every corner of the wood.

As the flames died down the humans began to disperse, walking back down through the wood in satisfied little groups, carrying their equipment and nodding to each other as if saluting a job well done. There was an air of finality about their departure which all the creatures recognised and encouraged them to come quickly out of their hiding places. They're gone, they whispered to each other. They're gone.

But although some creatures were prepared to creep near, few wished actually to tread the ground they had been barred from for so many moons, particularly as the cataclysmic events had been additionally shocking because so unexpected. One or two gingerly took steps on to the fragile mounds of ash, only to draw back quickly as these collapsed in clouds of grey dust. Feeling the heat still radiated by glowing embers and the scorched earth, they confined themselves instead to gazing round in awe. Did the humans know how to do a comprehensive job! The mink colony had simply ceased to exist. It and its inhabitants — dead or alive — had vanished as though they had never been. In their place was a stinking, sombre circle of death and destruction that chilled the creatures' hearts. Within it nothing stirred, giving an air of brooding melancholy, while the smoke-blackened trunks stood around it in silent mourning. How quiet and empty the place seemed, now its driving force had been removed. It was impossible to imagine it had been the powerhouse of such a reign of terror. Except that it retained an aura, a presence which, like that of the Quarry, made everyone sense something had been imprinted for ever. Like the Quarry, it was something evil, something that made the creatures shudder. Such was its power nobody, not even the rabbits, spoke a word.

Owl did not linger long. Leaving the gobsmacked circle of creatures to stare, he flew to check out Freddie's den, only to find it deserted, as he had expected. If only the brave fox could have stayed to receive the grateful thanks of his fellow woodland creatures. By now, though, presumably he was well on his way to his destination. Owl would miss him. Maybe one day he would even go and visit him, although he doubted it, he had been so appalled when Freddie informed him which human habitation he was heading for.

'The big one, Ollie,' he said with a sly grin.

'You can't go there, Freddie!' Owl replied, aghast. He had flown over the place during his search for his parents and its size, never mind the amount of human activity within it, had made him feel dazed and ill for days.

'If I'm going I might as well go in a big way,' Freddie smiled. 'There's life in the old dog yet, Ollie. Anyway, it'll be just as busy here when the workers come back.'

The remark had touched on a point Owl was now fully aware of. With nothing any longer extraordinary Old Wood was back to where it had been, wide open once again. So would the working humans come back? Yes, Freddie said emphatically. I don't know, Owl still admitted. No, Cowslip now pronounced.

The CWG leader, absent during the human activity, surfaced, already primed by furtive underground discussions. When Owl refused to chair an all-creatures' meeting, she began arguing with him on the spot and as other creatures gathered round he realised she was holding her meeting by default. But he decided to let it run. There was something he wanted to say.

'You can all thank Freddie,' he informed everyone. 'It was his idea, and he carried it out with conspicuous gallantry. I'm afraid, though, that he is no longer here for you to thank personally. A key element of his plan was that he was leaving for ever to move to the big human city. Some of you birds will know the one I mean, across the five valleys.

'All I can say is that I know we wish him good luck,' he concluded, deliberately keeping it as short as he could. The last thing he needed was to get into the complication of Freddie's double spin against the hunt, never mind the fundamental dichotomy of using the human enemy to defeat the mink enemy.

He was rewarded by a thin smattering of applause. Most creatures by now had a fair grasp of what had happened, but wheeling their mindset round to hail the fox as a hero still involved a serious mental adjustment.

'Freddie was acting entirely out of self-interest,' Cowslip announced smugly. 'His object was purely to get revenge on the hunt. We Guardians, on the other paw, have been acting selflessly, for the benefit of all.'

'Won't you even acknowledge the wood owes him a debt?' Owl asked increduously, at the same time angry that the long-faced rabbit had put her paw so accurately on Freddie's ulterior motive.

'Debt?' Cowslip replied haughtily. 'There is no debt. The mink were going anyway. It was only a matter of time. You see, no creature can carry on as they did without eventually seeing the error of their ways. The working humans will do the same, if they haven't already have done so.'

'How can you be sure of that?' Owl asked, furious.

'I don't know exactly!' Cowslip replied, becoming angry in her turn. 'Maybe they've already lost interest, or just gone elsewhere. Anything could have happened. Why be so negative, when you could be thinking positively?'

'Because your kind of positive thinking is pure pellets!' Owl screeched, fed up beyond belief. 'It's just stupid hopeful statements, based on nothing but hot air. Go elsewhere, lose interest, see the error of their ways – you haven't one single fact to back any of it!'

To his anger, Owl realised he was launching himself into a diatribe, which was the last thing he had intended. Yet he couldn't stop himself.

'You're setting yourself up so you can't lose, aren't you?' he accused. 'Justifying the futre, so in retrospect you can claim it was all your doing. If the humans don't return, it'll all be thanks to you. And if they do you'll just walk away, saying it isn't your fault and there's nothing you can do. "At least we tried," you'll whine before blaming creatures like me for bringing it on everyone by not adopting what you call a "positive attitude".

'Well, at least the mink had a truly positive attitude. They took responsibility for their actions. When's it going to be the turn of you and your Guardian cronies to be like everyone else and see the error of your ways? Your life is such a sham — such a show — it's no wonder you mask your incomprehension with that silly grin!'

By now Owl was beside himself, as much for falling into the trap of letting himself become angry in the first place. Cowslip had also divined this, and the result was the silliest grin he had ever seen.

'We don't make errors, do we?' she smiled patronisingly, turning to her fellow rabbits and the dunnocks for dutiful support. 'We have right on our side. You're like all predators — so impatient. You'll never understand, will you, that all things come to those who wait.'

'No I bloody well won't!' Owl screeched. 'And we shouldn't be waiting now either. We should be out there, tracking down the mink.'

The other creatures looked down at the ground. Many were now wondering at Freddie's imagination and daring, while some quietly expressed their regrets for what they had said about him in the past. But, once bitten, they were now twice shy. They didn't want to be involved in anything that would risk provoking the mink's further wrath. Owl sympathised to some extent. The remains of the pack would now be desperate, and therefore doubly dangerous. But he was still certain it had to be done.

Cowslip was about to reply when Boris came puffing up.

'Did I just hear you say we should be out finding the mink?' he bellowed. 'Wrong, Ollie! Wrong, wrong, wrong! We should be forgetting all about them. Good riddance — that's the only thing we should be saying.'

'But this could be your chance to have a go, Boris,' Ollie

protested, remembering how the badger had backed down from attacking the Plateau. 'They'll be so down we might even be able to finish them off ourselves. Or maybe we could reveal them to the humans again.'

The other creatures swung towards him a little at that point. Knowing that there was no chance of the mink ever returning would set everyone's mind at rest.

'We know they weren't all killed,' Owl urged. 'I saw many escaping myself. We must find out where they are, and how many are left, before we can ever feel free of them.'

Boris curled his lip and bared his teeth contemptuously.

'The way you talk, Ollie, I'm beginning to wonder whose side you're on,' he growled.

Owl swallowed hard. That was going too far. And, even though Cowslip smiled with satisfaction, the others recognised it.

'Take that back!' came cries.

'Shame!'

When Boris just snarled his refusal Owl made a last effort.

'I don't know about anyone else, but I intend to run them to earth,' he announced.

'You're obsessed, Ollie,' Boris harumphed angrily. 'They've gone, but you can't let them go, can you? "Stay away or they'll get you" — you never even realised that applied as much to the mink as the humans, did you? That was your problem, Ollie, you never knew how to stay away. And you still don't.'

Knowing how near to the bone this cut, the other creatures stayed silent, except for Cowslip.

'You tell him, Boris,' she cried triumphantly, grinning in unconcealed delight at this further falling-out. 'You see, Ollie, even he knows reason always prevails in the end.'

But the badger wasn't having that.

'Don't you reason me, you tosser!' he bellowed, lumbering towards her. 'Never mind Ollie. Now the mink are gone it's time to get rid of you as well.'

Owl looked on, fascinated. Couldn't Cowslip see that Boris was so terminally upset by the series of events he had to take it out on somebody?

Too late, the rabbit recognised that she had turned the badger's ire against herself. She began backing off, looking uncertain, while the dunnocks and the rest of the rabbits distanced themselves from her by staying where they were.

'Really, there's no need for anything like this,' she pleaded, grinning more falsely and sillily than ever. 'Boris, please be reasonable.'

But it was too late. With a sudden darting run that belied his huge bulk the badger had already shot behind her and clamped his jaws on to that enormous bum. As he worried and shook it, making her whole body jerk around, Cowslip out high-pitched screams. Owl could tell that at first they were mainly hurt pride, but when Boris still did not let go she suddenly realised he was going to show no mercy.

'Help me, fellow Guardians,' she begged the horrified-looking rabbits and dunnocks as she tried to drag herself free.

When no-one came to her aid, the tenor of her cries changed.

'Cowards,' she screamed. 'You'd watch me die rather than do anything, wouldn't you?'

Yet still none moved. Owl was just wondering whether he should step in when Boris abruptly released her.

'Now do the only thing you're good at, you wordy old, turdy old tosser,' he snarled. 'Run for it and never come back or I'll bite your bum clean off.'

Taking one horrified look round, Cowslip hurtled for the bushes without another word. An enormous grin spread over Boris's stripy features as he watched the two huge red weals already swelling up on her prominent posterior.

'I should have done that ages ago,' he sighed in satisfaction, running his tongue round his chops to collect assorted bits of fur, which he spat out on to the ground.

'There'll be no mistaking her in the future,' he nodded to himself. 'She'll have those marks for life!'

Owl beamed at him. In getting it out of his system he had so shredded the rabbit's dignity Owl doubted she would ever recover.

'Any of you want to see her again?' Boris demanded fiercely, rounding on the quivering collection of vegetarians.

They shook their heads in miserable denial.

'Well do us all a favour and piss off as well then,' the badger shouted.

As they disappeared in a frightened flurry he came over to Owl.

'Sorry if I said anything to upset you, Ollie,' he apologised. 'You know how much I've hated all this stuff. I just want things to get back to normal.'

Owl was embarrassed. He already had a horrid feeling there might be some truth in what the badger had said about his being obsessed. He hadn't thought about it before, but he could already feel that the mink's departure had left a gaping hole in his life. A whole side of it had disappeared – a dark side, which he knew he should not dwell on.

Yet he could not pull himself away.

'I'm still going to find them, Boris,' he said as gently as he could.

'Go then!' the badger shouted, losing his patience again. 'Go to please yourself! But make sure they know it's only you who's interested. None of us has an argument with them any more.'

'Just as long as they're not near your sett, eh?' Owl could not stop himself replying as his mind flashed back to Orwella the otter.

'Absolutely right – for once,' the badger shouted back. 'And what applies to them applies to you. Good riddance, Ollie!'

Left alone with Raka, Owl sat for a few moments reflecting sadly. Then he rallied himself. Surely, after volunteering so heroically to fetch Alphonse, at least the rook would help?

But it was Raka, who had cawed with noisy pleasure at seeing Cowslip get her come-uppance, who spoke first.

'I'm like Boris, I'm afraid, Ollie,' she said uncharacteristically quietly. 'I just want it to be over. Bertha finished it for me. I've had no real stomach for things since she died. Freddie did wonderfully for us, so why not leave it on that high note?'

'We have to find them, Raka, can't you see?' Owl replied, bitterly disappointed. 'Otherwise they could make a surprise attack without our having any idea what was coming.'

'Precisely, Ollie,' Raka cawed back, getting angry. 'Just like we didn't the first time. Meanwhile at least we'd be living, as we were then, rather than eternally worrying what was going to happen. Life's too short, Ollie. You'll burn yourself out if you go on like this.'

Owl was about to make an equally angry reply when he checked himself. Why was everyone quarrelling at the moment when they had won?

'What's wrong, Raka?' he asked despairingly. 'Everything seems to be falling apart.'

'I don't know, Ollie,' the rook replied morosely, now more calm. 'I noticed it in the rookery when I came back with Alphonse. I can't put my claw on it precisely, but ever since the mink arrived – and then the humans, of course – everybody seems to have become nastier to each other, or at least more uncaring.

'Not in a rabbit way,' she added, gazing into the middle distance as she collected her thoughts, 'not just stupid words. More in what everyone's doing. I've felt there hasn't been the same give and take. Do you know what I mean, Ollie? Take us rooks. We've always squabbled and argued, but underneath there was once a camaraderie, an acceptance of each other, with all our individual faults. Tolerance, I suppose you'd call it. It may just be me, but I feel it's gone to a large extent. There seems to be less of a community than there was. It's as if everybody was suddenly in it just for themselves. The whole place has a harder edge.

'Have you ever thought that the same thing's happened to you personally, Ollie? Ula certainly thinks it has.'

Owl had been with the rook until that point. Now he bridled.

'That's the trouble with you females, you want everything soft and mushy, don't you?' he screeched. 'Remember Dandelion and her "being nice" pellets? The world isn't like that these days, Raka. You have to be tough to deal with it. Surely the mink taught you that?'

She looked at him sadly, not saying anything.

'Well, are you coming or what?' he finally yelled

She continued to regard him mournfully.

'You've gone quite beyond everything, haven't you?' she finally asked.

'Well, beyond everything or not, I'm going,' Owl shouted defiantly, taking off in a furious flurry of wingbeats.

He cut a driving swathe through the air to rid himself of some of his aggression before flying aimlessly about, waiting for the full moon, so big and bright the night before, to come to his aid. But before it could rise black clouds rolled up, the skies opened and driving rain cut visibility to nil. Owl cursed. He should have started his search earlier. Now it was almost as though the elements were siding with his fellow creatures, signalling him to stop. Knowing telltale mink footprints were being washed out by the moment, he flew moodily back to the beech, reflecting on the difficulty of his self-imposed task. He had seen the mink scatter but which direction had they taken? And how far had they got? The biggest unknown factor was how badly injured any of them were. They could have dumped their wounded, or even split up and gone their separate ways, but Owl was certain they had stayed together.

'No luck, I suppose?' Ula asked sympathetically as he crawled dripping into the nest, nearly slipping on the slimy bark of the drenched beech branch.

'What do you think?' he replied defensively, shaking himself to rid his feathers of the rain. 'I'm not giving up, though,' he added, looking her straight in the eye.

'Neither should you, Ollie,' she said softly. 'You need to get them out of your system before you can come back to me.'

'Have I been away then, Ula?' he asked, surprised and at the same time not quite clear what she meant. Yet he felt she had struck some deep chord.

'Further than you'll ever know, Ollie,' she replied quietly. 'For these past few moons you've been somewhere else.'

Owl stared out at the solid sheet of rain. Ula sounded so sympathetic it was almost like a different bird talking. No, not a different bird, but her old self, as she had once been, caring, supportive, understanding. Yet he still had to unravel a fundamental knot.

'So why didn't you come with me, Ula?' he asked gently.

'Because you left me behind, Ollie. I wanted to come, but then I found you going somewhere I couldn't follow. Nobody could. You had to be on your own to get there.'

Owl continued to stare at the rain. It was drumming on the leaves and beat on the ground so loudly he had experienced some difficulty in catching her words.

'So where am I now?' he asked above the roar, suddenly feeling an urgent desire for her guidance.

'You're on your way back, Ollie – to me and everyone else.'

Owl felt a rush of warmth at the thought.

'Are you welcoming me, though, Ula?' he inquired gently.

'Of course I am,' she smiled. 'You know I still love you, always have. And there's something else I should tell you, my dear – whatever I may have said, I never really thought you were a pillock. Come here and let me give you a cuddle, Ollie. It's been hard for you, I know. But now it's nearly over.'

Owl smiled fondly back and hopped across the floor of the nest towards her. She must have cleaned it up recently without his noticing. It felt cosy and inviting, but not as much as her affectionate and cheering embrace. Had he missed her company, he suddenly realised! He must have shut her out without knowing it while he concentrated all his energies elsewhere.

'We've got the whole place to ourselves again, Ollie,' she reminded him, grinning conspiratorially. 'Let's get back to the old days, shall we?'

Suddenly, like everyone else, Owl desperately wanted things to be normal. Yet the mink were still out there. Whether or not he was obsessed, he had to find them to lay them to rest.

'Are you letting me go first, dear?' he asked, feeling the hotness of her body against him as he held her tightly.

'Absolutely, my love,' she whispered back. 'I've always let you do what you need to do. When you come back then we'll be free to concentrate on what you want to do.'

Owl gave her a grateful hug. What he very much wanted to do, all of a sudden, was stay at home. Yet, heedless of the elements, first he must launch himself into the teeth of the storm.

67

We'll Rule Again

Owl turned for home on the fifth night, entirely frustrated at how effectively the mink had hidden themselves. Meanwhile, although Ula still gave him huge encouragement, every time he returned to the wood it was to stick from Boris, infuriated by his refusal to give up.

'Still obsessed, Ollie?' he shouted up from the bottom of the beech. 'Not learnt to let go yet?'

Partly goaded by the badger, Owl had just made a renewed effort, extending his search way beyond the balance of probability by going out across the five valleys to the edge of the big human habitation where Freddie had gone to live. But the exercise had proved as fruitless as his other searches and as he flew back over the bleak moor he paid little attention to the lifeless area underneath him. Then, out of the corner of his eye, he caught the flash of a creature bounding across the heather. He swerved to fall in behind as it disappeared into a tangle of gorse, maintaining station until it emerged on to a patch of open ground and gave him his first decent look. With a thrill of excitement he saw instantly that it was a mink. There was no mistaking the quick and purposeful way it flowed across the ground, almost as sinuously as if it was in water. To his further excitement, it was carrying something in its mouth. If he was in luck, it had been out hunting and was returning to its base.

He waited for the creature to reach the rollway which bisected its path, when he would get his clearest view. But instead it slithered down on to the bed of the stream it had been following and vanished into the culvert. Owl remembered investigating one of those when he was a youngster, thinking it would be a good place to find a water vole. But he had found it chill and lifeless, like so many human artefacts, with an eerie atmosphere he had not liked.

Giving a couple of wing beats, he moved across and waited for the creature to emerge from the other side. When nothing happened, he felt perplexed. It appeared to be remaining in there, which would have made him doubt his vision and hearing if he had not been so confident in them. This couldn't possibly be the mink hideout. It would be madness staying right by the rollway with the humans still after them, especially in an expanse of nothing like this, with nowhere to run. Then he thought with a start that it might not be such madness after all. To begin with, it would explain why he hadn't found them in the thousand more likely places he had already scoured. He would never have thought of looking in there in a hundred seasons, and the humans presumably even less so. If the creature inside was a mink it would be very bold − typical mink-think.

Yet an element of doubt still gnawed at his mind. He couldn't be certain the creature wasn't a weasel or a stoat, maybe even one who had fled from Old Wood so long ago. And his doubt was compounded by a fresh uncertainty. Now he was potentially so close, did he really want it to be a mink? Or would he prefer not to find them after all? Was he really like the others, not wanting to know? But it was too late. As woodland leader it was now his duty to investigate.

He landed on the low stream bank just above where the crea-ture had disappeared and cocked his sensitive ears. Murmurings above the noise of the running water told him there was more than one creature in there, although not how many. But there was no indication that they had detected his presence and he wondered for a moment if he should just creep away. Then he realised he couldn't. The round end of the culvert drew him in irresistibly. He had to check it out. He stepped on to the stream bed, careful to tread only on dry stones that gave his talons a secure footing, steadied himself and peered into the depths.

The first thing that caught his eye, instantly banishing his lingering doubts, was the black and orange cat-tail, propped haphazardly against the wall near the entrance. Next to it was slumped a mink whom he thought he recognised as MI — or was it M2? Whichever, he wasn't moving. Beyond, in the greater darkness, a small group of mink was clustered round a boulder in the middle of the shallow watercourse, tearing ravenously at the corpse that had been brought back. A mink hobbled slowly towards them, trailing one of his back legs; Owl identified him beyond doubt as the fierce-faced Maxi. A few others, clearly hurt, were lying on the green slime that bordered the thin trickle of water. One licked desultorily at its torn-open stomach, while another lay prone, eyes closed. Owl, catching a whiff of putrefaction, recognised the scent of death.

Maxi was the first to spot him. He stopped in his halting tracks and hissed a warning, causing the others to jump round. Owl involuntarily jerked upright, only to relax slightly. The image of sleek power had gone, replaced by a sorry-looking collection of bedraggled creatures plastered in mud and, in most cases, blood as well. As they backed towards the culvert walls, hissing their defiance, Mega was revealed at the front. His appearance was so dreadful Owl could not stay a momentary pang of pity. The mink leader's head was encrusted with dried blood, while a gaping wound on one side gave his whole visage a ghastly lopsided appearance. One eye was so hidden under matted fur Owl thought he might even have lost it.

'You!' he spat, a loose flap of flesh next to his mouth jerking obscenely up and down. 'I might have known it'd be you. It's not you we're after, though. We want that bastard fox, Freddie. We should have known he'd double-cross us.'

Though the words were slurred, the venom was still there.

'When you see the bastard inform him he's officially dead,' Mega continued, almost as if he had been preparing for this moment. 'We've vowed to track him down, even if it takes the rest of our lives. And we're not like the human hunt, either. There's no escape from us. When we get to him it'll be like one of his chicken-house raves — except he'll be the chicken. You tell him this from me — nobody, but nobody, betrays mink like that and lives to tell the tale.'

'The bugger'll wish he'd never been born!' Maxi boomed in confirmation, amid fierce squeaks of assent.

Owl stood dumbly taking this in, thinking that the aggression only sounded a shadow of the old days. He hadn't seen mink on the defensive before and it wasn't a pretty sight. For all Mega's bluster the remains of the pack looked almost as if it was cowering in its refuge. None seemed to have any intention of coming out to attack him. He was still keeping a wary eye out behind him though, just in case any other, or others, returned and tried to jump him. He couldn't be too careful, however pathetic they might look, and their threat to the fox was probably real enough.

'Freddie's gone,' he couldn't stop himself replying. 'But it's not him who's finished, it's you. You'll never find him in a thousand moons.'

'We know where he is,' what sounded like Psycho's voice suddenly squeaked from the back.

Owl, shocked, craned his head but couldn't identify where the voice had come from.

'You tell me then,' he said defiantly into the darkness.

'He's gone to the big human city across the five valleys,' Psycho declared confidently, at the same time revealing himself by stepping out from behind Maxi. He looked quite unhurt.

'How do you know that?' Owl asked, trying to hide his mixture of amazement and horror.

'We've been back to the wood, you dumbo,' Psycho sneered. 'You don't think you get rid of us that easily, do you?'

Mega smiled cruelly as he saw Owl could no longer hide his consternation. He had seen no harm in revealing Freddie's destination and everyone in the wood had been talking about it ever since. It would have been simple enough for a mink raiding party to trap some hapless rabbit or vole and extract the relevant information. How could he have been so thoughtless as inadvertently to betray the very creature who had saved them all! Rather than being safe with the humans, thanks to him Freddie now had a real problem. And he didn't even know.

'You always thought you were so bloody clever, didn't you,' Mega spat, the culvert walls giving his voice a hollow ring, while a spark of hatred flared in his one visible eye. 'You bastard woodies, bringing in the humans like that! We mink would never stoop so low. You know better than I do how despicable it was. And then to go round claiming the credit for being the almighty leader who had fixed it all.'

Owl didn't reply as he played for time. After his initial shock, the inaccuracy of the last statement helped him recover his bearings. That had to be guesswork, and inaccurate guesswork at that. Owl had deliberately dropped out, leaving the absent Freddie to collect the plaudits, partly because it was all the fox's idea, but also because he felt there was something fundamentally dishonourable about the whole episode. He didn't want to think about it any further. .

'You asked for it,' he replied shortly, suddenly feeling indifferent.

The mink might still be fearsome adversaries, but much of their spell had been broken. Now they were out of the wood he could see them as they truly were, alien vermin. For the first time, if he was not mistaken, he felt almost bored by them.

'We asked for it, did we?' Mega growled, the spark of hatred in his leering eye now replaced by a colder gleam. 'You and your thick woodie friends thought you'd banished us for ever, didn't you? Well, you dim bastard, you couldn't be more wrong.'

'Mega's right,' Psycho added in his high-pitched squeak, scampering to stand at his leader's shoulder. 'We'll be back. But even if we didn't bother, there's no need. Now we've introduced mink-think into your pathetic old wood it's changed for ever. Once anyone's experienced us, and the way we live, they can never forget, no matter how much they may want to. Don't think for a moment that you can pretend we were never there. We've moved your wood on. It can never go back.'

Owl could not stop himself lifting a foot in his anxiety.

Something about Psycho got straight under his skin. And what he said chimed so accurately with the disquiet that Raka had voiced. For a moment Owl regretted that he had ever set off to find the mink. He should leave now, before he got too sucked in.

Yet still he stayed, driven by his desire to hear them out.

'You wait,' Mega snarled, loose flap of flesh jerking up and down. 'You'll find out how different your wood is now – if you don't know already. And one day we'll be back to rule it again.'

'Yeh, we'll rule again,' came a feeble chorus.

Owl recovered his composure. He didn't know whether to laugh or cry. In their present state this lot couldn't rule a meeting of the Concerned Guardians.

'You're out and you're staying out,' he replied sharply. 'And you've only yourselves to blame for that. You never belonged – Freddie recognised that. You were a group of aliens, tearing the arse out of the place. That's why he did what he did. He knew it was either us or you.'

He shook his head. He was wasting his breath. Maybe, though, there was one way of putting it that would get through.

'As for this pellets about ruling again,' he pronounced with great relish. 'It's bollo, nothing but pure, unadulterated bollo!'

He felt a thrill of satisfaction as he was rewarded by series of angry snarls. He had accomplished his mission and it was time to go. He launched himself off his stone and flew a short distance up the bank. Then he landed again, still unable to tear himself away. Somehow it wasn't enough, leaving them like that. He needed a sign, something to establish clearly in his mind that they were done for. Something that would mark the end of them.

As he remained rooted to the spot he heard scratching noises on the hard inside surface of the culvert. Maxi's gruff voice rapped out a series of urgent commands and there was a succession of soft bumps. Then the noises abruptly ceased. What were they up to? It had sounded as if they were all shuffling about. But why? And why had they now gone so still?

He waited until he could resist no longer. Then he fluttered back down to the stream bed and, still keeping a cautious distance, peered again into the end of the tunnel. As before, the first thing that met his eye was the cat-tail. But it was no longer propped forlornly against the wall. Now, jammed into a crack in the floor, it stood proudly and stiffly erect. But it was the sight beyond it which really made the feathers rise on the back of Owl's neck. The mink had retreated further into the pitch darkness and grouped together. Now they appeared as a solid wall of glowing eyes, with the huge solitary one in the middle gleaming wildest and maddest of all.

Owl felt a wave of malevolence surge towards him and, spooked, automatically went into his fearful feather-fluffing and hissing display. But the wall of eyes stared back, unflinching. Opening his black orbs to their fullest extent, Owl hissed with all his might. Still the eyes did not falter. The stalemate dragged on and on until, with a snort of disgust, he broke eye contact.

He retreated up the bank, shaken and furious. How dare they outface him like that! Then the feathers on the back of his neck rose again. A thin sound was drifting out of the culvert end:

> Rule Minkmania,
> Minkmania rules the wood . . .

Spooked once more, he could not prevent himself rising into the air. He hovered over the middle of the stream, legs and talons at full stretch, defying them to emerge. If one dared so much as to stick its snout out he would pounce. But the round end of the culvert only stared blankly back at him, while the singing continued. It had started quietly, but now it was building, the culvert walls lending it a curiously booming amplification.

> Creatures ever, ever, ever,
> Shall be food!
> Rule Minkmania,
> Mornings until nights . . .

As the volume swelled the mink voices changed. No longer so reedy and thin as to be almost dunnock-like, they grew

firmer and more confident with every word. To his horror
Owl detected the old note of triumphalism creeping back in.
Suddenly he was back in the wood, hearing the anthem drifting
across from the Plateau as it had used to during the arrogant old
marching days.

> . . . We shall ever, ever, ever,
> Give you frights!

The dreadful words, made even louder by the culvert amplification, were now being positively thundered out. Once again
into Owl's head floated the twin visions of the sea of blood at
the Big Clearing massacre and the dove's head arcing across the
Plateau. He shook himself disbelievingly. He must be dreaming!
It was impossible, with their ranks so devastated and after all
that they had been through, that the remnants of the pack could
sound so powerful. Yet they did — and they were spooking him
for a third time.

Unable to bear listening any longer and close to panic, he took
off, beating his wings frantically to gain height and distance. He
closed his ears as he pushed himself harder and harder. Only
when he was finally approaching Old Wood did he slow and
dare to listen.

To his immense relief, the ghastly strains had faded entirely
into the distance.

68

Back to the Edge

The horizon was already bright as Owl came in over the Long Field, the mink anthem superceded by the first optimistic notes of the dawn chorus. Soft light illuminated the ghostly mist that blotted out the grass and still rose in curls from the limpid river. The mist was thicker these days, now the sun rose later. Throughout the night its wraithlike tentacles had been snaking out, like living things, before blindly linking up with each other to fill the folds and hollows and coalesce into the present solid blanket. Almost as if floating on the mist, the panorama of the wood reared up, as beautiful, rounded and whole as ever. Owl looked down on his entire world, frozen for a second in his vision, yet all the time on the turn. On the turn in every way — night to day, summer to winter, past to future, mink to no mink, humans to no humans. There were no volvers on the rollway, and there would be few later. Only a few desultory twitchers now visited, following a burst of activity after the hunt drama. There was no hint of excitement in their movements, as if they knew that Alphonse was no more. The lower number of volvers fitted the season anyway. Alphonse or no Alphonse, lessening rollway activity was always a sign summer was ending. The dampness in the air and the ceasing of the rising sap already carried a hint of the Big Cold that was on its way. With growth stopped and the verdant vegetation on the retreat, the wood's summer party was ending as untidily as it always did. Like an old creature gradually losing its faculties one by one, it was slowly collapsing.

'Change and decay in all around I see,' Owl found himself saying as he circled over the river.

The last swallows were already up and about, jinking and swerving to snap up insects and flies anyway approaching the end of their natural lives. Many were already torpid and would soon be carried off by the first frost. The swallows, in turn, were flocking as they prepared to fly to their warm wintering places, fair-weather sailors bound for a sunnier shore. Owl gave them a cheery wave of his wing, and they flicked back in salute. Much of what had happened in the wood had passed them by. They would leave with no regrets, and without even properly saying farewell. The wood was not the same for them as it was for its permanent residents, with nowhere else to go. That was the main reason Owl loved this time so much. Visitors would always be just visitors. The feeling of really belonging – that this was truly your home – came from being here day in, day out, enduring the hard times as well as the easy.

Seeing a squirrel in frantic gathering mode, he swooped down to the treetops to say hello. She chirruped back in a friendly fashion, but was so obviously busy Owl did not linger. How fortunate he was not to have to depend on disappearing insects or stored nuts for his existence, he thought as he did a circuit over the empty rollway. The falling leaves and dying back of the long summer grass only exposed his victims more, while the longer nights gave him more darkness to hunt in. All in all, had it not been for the mink, Owl would have been entirely happy. Yet instead an immense despondency had come over him. Old Wood might appear unchanged on the surface, but he had to recognise that underneath, as he remembered Burdock telling him so long ago, it was now different.

He had hoped – even presumed – that with the mink gone the wood would revert to what it had been before they polluted it. But now he, and all the creatures, had to face the reality that Raka had put her claw on: it had changed. Everyone might try to ignore it, some might not even be aware of it, but Owl now had to recognise, with a terrible sinking feeling, that Psycho might well be right. The mink had left a permanent mark. Mink-think had seeped into every pore and crevice of woodland society, infecting it like a virus. The realisation made him feel tired beyond belief. At last he fully understood what the Venerable Buck — and Burdock — had been talking about! It had been a long journey, leading to a comprehension so deep it shook him to his very roots. All that effort, all that struggle — Freddie's brave and selfless gesture, Bertha's suicide, the killing of the hapless Alphonse, the slaughter of Burdock and the dumb blonde dove — had it all been for nothing? He shuddered as he again pictured the wall of eyes, Mega's crazy one gleaming in the middle, while his head filled with the sound of the supremely arrogant mink anthem thundering out of the culvert.

He wasn't to blame, though. He had dedicated himself to trying to lead the others through the daymare of events, even though his motives might on occasion have been selfish. Gravitas and bottom, he suddenly remembered with a wry smile. What nonsense it seemed now. Most of the time he had been more like a rabbit than a predator, reacting to events rather than creating them, and no wiser than anyone else. Except know-it-all Cowslip, of course. But, as events had so graphically proved, she and her Guardian cronies had no more control over events — never mind their own lives — than the members of Worms' Lib she had once so boringly represented. All they could do was sit, frozen in action, until they were overwhelmed by disaster, almost as if they were deliberately courting it.

Owl shook himself vigorously. His next job was to report back that he had succeeded in locating the remnants of the mink. What would he tell everyone, though? The only thing they wanted to hear was that the mink were beaten, washed up, finished, gone for ever. He could tell the brazen lie that he had found them all dead. That might even be the reality before long. Apart from their injuries, they must be further weakened by the meagre diet in their cruelly bleak location, while the humans were presumably still after them. They couldn't stay in the culvert for ever. Once they surfaced, could the wood trust the humans to finish them off?

But he already knew, without stopping to consider, the answer had to be no. Rather, if he felt like it, he could reveal to everyone that the mink had already been back on a raiding party. With mink, while there was life there was more than hope, there was certainty. The only valid question was not whether they would survive, but where.

Owl peeled off from his favourite Ridge beat, which he had been unconsciously following. He felt a sudden need to check the Plateau to be absolutely certain it was devoid of life. As he soared over it in the growing daylight, he stiffened as a bright streak moved on the scorched black earth. But when he focused and scrutinised it more closely, he saw it was only a solitary yellow feather. The last remnant of Alphonse was stirring, gently wafted by the morning breeze.

Then he spotted another movement. A vole, late getting home, was nervously stumbling across the desolate wasteland of chewed-up bumps and humps. Owl had fed well before his close encounter with the mink and wasn't the slightest bit hungry. Nevertheless he suddenly experienced an irrational and overwhelming desire to kill. Without thinking, he swooped, seized the vole in a talon and rose back up, giving a casual flex to silence its shrill shrieks. He was as satisfied as always by the efficiency of the kill, that efficiency which was his security, and which Dandelion's misguided thoughts had once caused him temporarily to lose. But he also felt something else, something which took him back to his days as an owlet, when he had carried out his first clumsy experiments on living creatures. At that stage of his life, still being fed by his parents, he hadn't needed to kill his own food. Yet he had experienced a tremendous thrill in treating other creatures as living toys, to play with, torture, swallow whole – or even let go – as he wished. The revelation of the shattering power in being able to kill and kill and go on killing had excited him beyond belief. He was a creature who could end lives willy-nilly, simply on a whim. Shaken by the strength of his recall, he realised he had not experienced that feeling since. Having felt the power, he had soon laid it back, using it only to acquire the food he needed.

The old feeling, after permeating his whole being so strongly, had now vanished as instantly as it had arrived. With it, too, had gone any further desire for the corpse he was carrying about. He flew around, wondering what to do with it, until, in the absence of any other ideas, he returned to the Plateau where he had just ended its life. Opening his talon, he looked down, watching the body as it hit the ground, did 'the dead vole bounce' in a puff of grey dust and then lay still. Another pointless victim, he thought, disgusted with himself, as pointless as any of the mink's multiple discarded carcasses. He could try to justify his action by arguing that the vole had only itself to blame for making itself so conspicuous. But it wasn't true. It was he who had been hit — hit by a burst of mink-think!

Shocked, Owl turned to fly to the Big Clearing. He would try to take his mind off it by giving the other creatures the news about mink, although only sketching in the briefest details. If asked, he would add his personal opinion that the mink would never come back to live in the wood. Then he would announce that he was relinquishing his post as woodland leader. As far as he was concerned there would be no more meetings. As he would explain, first the mink and then the humans had brought the creatures together. But with both these oppressors removed what was the further point?

Even if the humans did come back — and Owl decided he would gain nothing by thinking about that side of things — meetings would be useless. Bereft of the mink, the woodland creatures would be as powerless as they had always been. Maybe Freddie was right to move in alongside the humans — he was certainly correct in seeing how they had blown away the wood's security. But then it had experienced other changes in the past, as the deserted Quarry bore mute testimony. Yet Owl still felt the current change was not only different, but infinitely greater. Raka had given him a graphic picture of the extent to which the humans had taken over the rest of the world. If Old Wood was no longer an immune and isolated unit, that should come as no surprise. Looking back, it was precisely because they had sensed the way things were going that the creatures had all closed their eyes to the humans for so long. These days how could anyone reasonably expect to live in a sanctuary?

For, as he would emphasise to everyone, the change was not just greater, but faster as well, which made it infinitely more destabilising. It was not just in Old Wood, but in the whole world, that everything was speeding up as it became more crowded. Everyone everywhere was bumping into each other, receiving more input from outside. That alone meant the old order was finished. New thoughts, new ideas, things the creatures had never dreamt of – all these would come flooding in to banish the constants everyone had relied on. Yet had they been constants in the first place – or just a determined face set against reality? Just a mindset, that nobody had allowed anything they saw to alter?

For it wasn't only the mink, or the humans in the wood. Something had changed in what the Venerable Buck would have called 'the bigger picture'. Everything had gone into a state of flux. The very weather itself said it all, it was so unsettled. No longer could they even rely on the seasons delivering regularly. Any thought encouraged by rabbits of there being reason and order to events had now to be treated as dead. Increasingly it was chaos, making all predictions based on the past more and more useless. Owl didn't know why. Maybe it was the humans, with their ceaseless activity. Or maybe they were as caught up as the woodland creatures in violent changes over which they had no control. Whatever, the real rub was that both the mink's and the humans' input into the wood had been superimposed on a backdrop which was now shifting violently and erratically in itself. Which came first, therefore, the chick or the egg? How ironic that it had been the harvest full moon the night after the mink ejection, and what a bittersweet harvest the wood had reaped!

For now, with the mink and humans gone, everyone had to face up to the choice that they had posed. But Owl was no longer convinced by Psycho's contention that once infected by the mink virus the wood would automatically maintain a harder edge. Once introduced to it, it was now the prerogative of everyone in Old Wood to live the mink way, that was true. But as he would tell everyone, from Raka and Boris through to Cowslip and the dunnocks, it was more than just a prerogative – it was something they had to take on board in order to deal with it. Each, whether they liked it or not, had to attend to their own life by deciding which side of the equation they fell on. The real casualties would be those who dithered on the fence, taking refuge in vague concern for others, or by pretending that pellets like the Code and Bill could come to their rescue. They had to take responsibility for themselves. It was no use pretending that was easy, either. You could only do it if you accepted that life was difficult, and used that as your starting point. The real victims would be those refusing to face that. But if they did they also had to accept that it was their own choice – after all, being a victim was the easy way out. But for those facing up to it, the mark left on each by the mink would be as eradicable as they decided to make it. And as each, individually, drew their own conclusion, they would then collectively determine whether the future was to be good or bad.

And what about himself? His choice was one of the most open of all. As his parents had quite rightly taught him, he was a top predator. The wood and the world were his oysters, to do with as he wished. Even though, to his shock and regret, he had just experienced a dose of mink-think himself, his initial depression about the mink had vanished. He had been closer to them than had many other creatures, so maybe more of it had rubbed off on him. Meanwhile, and more importantly, he thought back to the rabbits' endless moaning about 'the good old days'. Even if that was true, he wasn't going to waste his time with that pellets! He, like them, was in the here and now and why should he allow the mink to degrade his life? Just because they had lived beside him, introducing him to a new kind of thinking, didn't mean he had to act like them. The art, the one piece of mink-think they all needed to retain, lay in seizing the moment. He must live for the night! *Carpe* noctem!

But that didn't mean following the mink's example by turning into a serial killer. Aggression, Owl realised, shouldn't be confused with action. Now he could see that mink-think wasn't the solution, it was the problem! Slaughter for its own sake — killing more than you needed or could ever cope with — was just striking out. It wasn't clever, daring, bold, risky, enterprising — any of the things that were claimed for it. Rather its fault was precisely that it never changed. Its proponents, once started, could never stop. They were trapped by their dull, rigid thinking, which always added up to a negative, forcing them to push the margin further and further in never-ending lust for satisfaction. For his own sake, he must now delete that negative from his life. He had seen that those who practised mink-think might have a rapid rise, but afterwards came an equally rapid fall. It was nothing but a degrading, coarsening, brutalising loop, which simply dumped you back where you'd started — or worse.

If not just the wood, but the whole world, was becoming more unsettled, and therefore more confusing, he must become settled by finding true happiness within himself. That was where his only real security lay, in being entirely unafraid to be himself. It couldn't be based on any place, or anyone, no matter how much he might love each and every aspect of them. He must do what he did, honestly and without fear or favour. Not perfectly — how could anyone be perfect? — yet all the time doing his best to ensure he left space for others, rather than trying to eliminate them for his own selfish purposes. He must be happy to take, yet equally happy to give. Yet he, like anyone else, could be at one with himself only when he was also at peace with everyone the wood contained. Anger was the most fearful thing, while the key was tolerance. He was an owl, while a vole was a vole. He should love it for it. Yet still, of course, be quite happy to eat it. Hopefully everyone would become like that. In love with the whole, the whole brilliant series of circles, where nothing was constant, everything changed, and the only thing that counted was being there!

He wished the Venerable Buck could be present. What would the old sage say about the consequences of the 'big trouble' he had foreseen? His greatest emphasis had been on how everyone was equal, equal in what they did and equal in what they said. The mink, the humans, Cowslip, himself — all part and parcel of the same rich pattern, no less than the trees that made up the wood or the stars that shone down on it.

And what stars there had been recently! So bright they had made him want to reach up and touch them, while odd ones periodically hurtled across the sky as though they were flying like himself. So fast did they shoot that they burnt themselves out, unable to maintain their suicidal velocity. Like the mink, he suddenly thought. But never mind the stars — or the bloody mink! Was Old Wood something to be in love with! For all that its dreams had been shattered, its Ride destroyed, its Mighty Oak felled, it was still a beautiful place. The very sight of it, as its myriad inhabitants rejoiced in this bright morning, soothed him by the moment. How could anybody in their right mind not hold their breath in wonder that so many different forms of life could coexist? How could anyone not want to share the magic of such mysteries and marvels? How could anyone experience anything but pure joy at such a kaleidoscope of shapes and colours, darkness and light, calm and storm? And here he was, above it, part of it, and with wings to fly. He must fly. He must soar and wheel and dive and drop — simply to celebrate the wonder of it. He must delight in it, squeeze it, milk it to the last drop!

The first rays of the morning sun touched the tops of the elms near the Ridge, sparking off a chorus of raucous caws as the inhabitants of the rookery took to the air. Owl saw Raka rise with the others, black as night against the flawless eggshell blue.

She gave a cheery wave as she spotted him.

'Back to work, Raka?' he shouted in a friendly fashion.

'Absolutely, Ollie,' she cawed back happily. 'You know there's nothing else I'd rather do. How's Ula?'

'Never better,' he hooted back, meaning it with all his heart.

Since his mate had endorsed his mink hunt with such affectionate understanding, Owl had felt a weight lifted off his shoulders. Only now did he realise how lonely he had been without her. But equally, he was going home to share his life with her, going home having dealt with the mink virus and re-equipped himself for the future. Whatever it might bring, nothing could spoil it for him now. He was himself, living for the moment. And he revelled in it. Never, ever, had he felt so hugely alive!

He stared affectionately after the receding black shapes of the rook convoy until they were mere specks. Good old Raka, so loyal and constant when it counted, yet so happy to revert to her simple life. He felt almost jealous of the comfort she derived from being part of such a settled community, with such a regular and steady routine.

But he was himself again. Involuntarily he jack-knifed forward, committing himself to a screaming dive. The air rushed past his face and the wind buffeted his body as he zoomed down towards the treetops. They reared up to meet him and then he was in among them, levelling out, wings straining, turning, braking, stalling, accelerating, swooping, diving. He touched one, then another, and another, until only a succession of trembling leaves marked the impact of his hurtling passage.

And all the time the face of his long-lost father floated in front of him, while his voice rang in his ears.

'The edge, Ollie, always strive for the edge. Just don't go over it!'

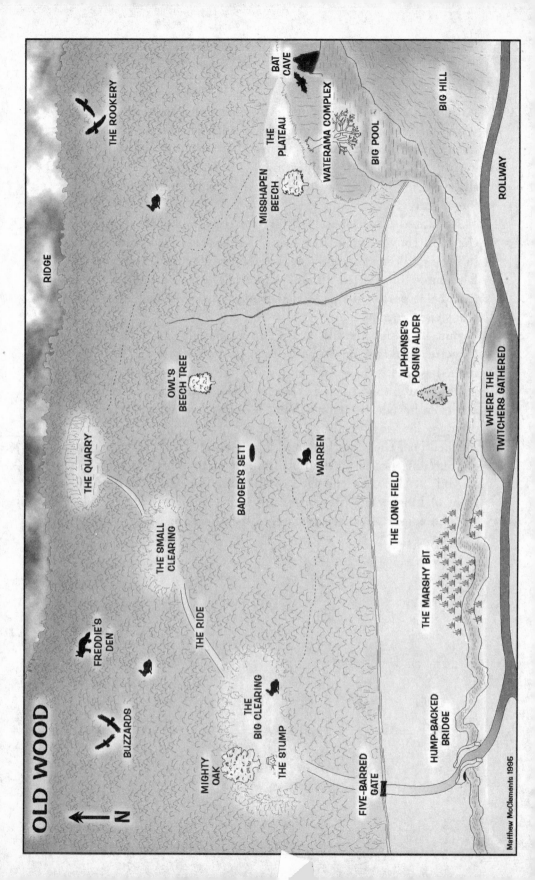

OLD WOOD

Matthew McClements 1995